AQUA TERRA IGNIS AER

ZODIAC ACADEMY
SHADOW PRINCESS

CAROLINE
PECKHAM

SUSANNE
VALENTI

Place
Terra House
Hall
Mars Laboratory
King's Hollow
The Howling Meadow
The Wailing Wood
The Orb
Earth Observatory
Venus Library
ercury
mbers
Aer House
Air
Cov
Fire Arena

WELCOME TO ZODIAC ACADEMY

Note to all students: Vampire bites, loss of limbs or getting lost in The Wailing Wood will not count as a valid excuse for being late to class.

DARIUS

CHAPTER ONE

I brought us back to King's Hollow, riding on the energy of the stars as the stardust swept us away from the cliff and my father and the horrors that had happened there.

The Vega Twins appeared in front of me as my feet hit the wooden floor in the central room of the huge treehouse that the other Heirs and I had claimed for our own personal sanctuary. I'd never thought I'd bring Roxy here, but I'd needed somewhere safe to bring them and this was the only place in the world where I'd ever felt entirely out of my father's reach.

Lance looked at me as he appeared at my side, his forehead furrowed with concern and so many questions that he didn't seem to have the energy to voice any of them.

Roxy pushed herself to her feet, the blue robe I'd wrapped around her slipping off of her bare shoulder.

"Where have you brought us now?" she asked, her voice strong but her eyes darting around nervously. She thought I'd taken her somewhere to hurt her again and the idea of that carved a fissure right through the centre of me.

"We're back at the academy," I said quickly. "You're safe. You're both safe now..." I trailed off, unsure what they even thought had happened to them after my father had forced that Dark Coercion on them. He'd made them forget what he'd done, so maybe they were just confused or-

"Your father is a goddamn psychopath," Gwendalina hissed, glaring at me as she shifted closer to her sister, taking her hand.

"I know," I said, my voice hollow because that was the truth I'd lived with my whole life and it didn't even matter.

Power was everything in Solaria and Father was one of the four most powerful Fae currently alive. At least until I completed my training and was able to challenge him. But that day seemed further and further away with each passing moon and now that he'd harnessed the shadows...

He'll be more powerful than the other Councillors. He could claim the crown for himself alone.

"Fuck," I spat, turning and stalking to the far side of the room as I pushed my hands through my hair.

I started pacing, the blue robe I wore swishing around my legs in an irritating as hell way until I tore the damn thing off of me and headed for the chest in the corner of the room where we kept the spare clothes. If I had an aura for every outfit I'd destroyed when shifting into my Dragon form, I'd probably be twice as rich as I was now. I threw the chest open and grabbed a pair of black sweatpants before pulling them on.

I flinched in surprise as Roxy appeared beside me, but she didn't even look at me as she dropped her robe too, revealing her body like it made no difference to her at all before she yanked a red T-shirt on. It was mine so it swamped her, hanging to her mid-thigh like a dress. I opened my mouth to say something, but I wasn't even sure where to start. Before I could say anything, Lance beat me to it.

"Do you remember anything, Blue?" he asked slowly, his voice gentler than I thought I'd ever heard it.

I turned to look his way in surprise and found him reaching towards Gwendalina like he wasn't sure if he should touch her or not.

"Like what?" she asked, her voice trembling slightly. "The part where we were kidnapped or how we were forced into that pit? The bit where the shadows tried to drag us down or how we managed to pull each other back away from them? Maybe the part where we finally emerged into our Order forms? Or are you referring to the way Lionel tried to Coerce us to forget all of it?"

"You remember?" I asked, my eyes widening as I looked to Roxy beside me, wondering if she did too. She gave a sharp nod, her gaze not turning towards me but staying fixed on her sister across the room. "How?"

Father had used Dark Coercion on me more than once and I couldn't fight it off. He used dark magic to strengthen the power of his words. It was why I couldn't tell the other Heirs the details of what he did to me. He'd used it to make me stay still while he was beating me before. Even the pain of my bones breaking wasn't enough to motivate me to tear through it. I thought it was impossible.

"It was our Order," Roxy said grimly. "Apparently our fire can burn right through bullshit."

A laugh spilled from my lips before I could stop it. My father had just fed her to the shadows, her Order had Emerged and her body had been turned into a conduit for the dark power he'd stolen from the Shadow Realm and yet she was still biting at me.

I caught hold of her without thinking about it and dragged her into my arms, crushing her against my chest. My heart leapt as she pressed her cold hands to my skin and I kissed the top of her head as relief spilled through me. She should have died. What my father had just done to them should have been more than they could take but here she was, wrapped in my arms and-

Power slammed into me with the force of a battering ram and I was thrown backwards across the room before crashing into the wall so hard that the whole treehouse trembled.

Pain echoed through my spine and I shoved myself upright, a snarl leaving my lips as shadows danced across my vision for a moment. My lip curled back and a low growl escaped me as the dark power beneath my flesh ached to be set loose. Shadows licked their way between my fingers as they sprang free of my flesh, awaiting my desires with a hungry craving which set me alight from the inside out.

"Don't give in to them, Darius!" Lance shouted and the call of his voice was enough to pull me back from the darkness.

I blinked the shadows away and felt the power of them slipping from my grasp.

"What the fuck was that for?" I demanded of Roxy as she glared at me,

her hands still raised as power coiled around her.

"Don't you fucking touch me," she growled, her eyes filled with more venom than her words.

"I...you have to know I didn't set you up," I said, shaking my head as I realised she was blaming me for what my father had just done to them. "I fought against him! I tried to get you away from him. I-"

"Yeah, you did," she agreed. "Until you didn't and you just let him have us."

"He had Xavier," I replied desperately, my heart pounding unevenly as I took in the rage in her. She had to know that it had broken me to watch my father push her into that pit. It had felt like carving into my own heart with a rusty knife and offering up a piece of my soul for him. But the alternative had been Xavier's life. It was no choice. But I knew she was strong; I'd known she could survive anything and even though it had killed me to watch him do that to her, I hadn't had any other option that I could choose.

"I know," she replied, her gaze softening for a moment and I could tell she really did understand that much. She'd do anything for her sister too. "That's the only reason I haven't burned you alive." Red and blue flames flickered between her fingers and Lance moved to stand between us.

The fight went out of Roxy and she hooked another T-shirt and a pair of sweatpants out of the trunk for her sister, moving across the room to hand them to her.

Gwendalina turned her back on us before dropping the blue robe and I looked away so that she could get dressed in privacy.

Lance shifted closer to me and as I looked into his eyes, a shadow slid across them before fading away again.

I swallowed thickly, feeling the shadows beneath my skin too. They were a part of me now and the most terrifying thing about that was how easily they sat there. Like I'd always had space for such darkness in me and they were just coming to claim their place.

I chewed on the inside of my cheek and strode away from them, crossing the wide living room before opening a drawer in the kitchen and pulling out the Atlas I kept here. I sent a message to Xavier, asking if he was alright, what had happened to Mother, all of it. It wasn't enough but I knew Father wouldn't hurt him now. He might have been willing to kill him to force my cooperation in his quest for the shadows but killing his own son wasn't something he could easily get away with. He wouldn't do it for no reason. I could only hope that Mother was okay and that he'd be able to call me soon.

"You got very lucky when Lionel mistook your Order forms," Lance said to the girls and I looked over at them with a frown.

"What do you mean he got it wrong?" I asked before either of them could respond. When the girls had reared out of the shadows and sprouted wings of flame before leaping into the sky, my heart had almost beat a path right out of my chest.

They were so bright against the black canvas of stars that it had been hard to make out the details of their forms, but I'd seen those red and blue flames and huge wings like they were two angels set alight by their power. Fire Harpies: rare but not unheard of, even more powerful than their more common cousins but not strong enough to challenge a Dragon.

My relief at their survival had been compounded by the fact that they weren't Dragons. I was sure that Father would have killed them if their forms had been something powerful enough to rival him.

"Lionel said they were Fire Harpies," Lance said slowly, his gaze fixed on Gwendalina like she fascinated him. "But he was mistaken. He saw the flames and the wings and made an assumption. Their mother, the Queen, was a Harpy so that had always been a likely outcome for them. They were only in their Order forms for such a brief moment that it was an easy mistake to make."

"So what are they?" I demanded as the twins shared a look that let me know they already knew.

"Phoenixes," Lance breathed, the awe in his voice pulling a frown to my brow.

"Not possible," I replied with a shake of my head. "There hasn't been a record of someone having the Phoenix Order in…"

"Over a thousand years," Lance murmured, still staring at Gwen like the world began and ended with her.

My eyes fell on Roxy and my heart thumped to a different tune. It wasn't true, it couldn't be. Phoenixes were practically a myth. No one was

11

even sure they really *had* existed. They were supposed to have been the most powerful Order of all, their flames capable of all kinds of insane things. Some people even claimed they'd been immortal but if that was the case then where were they? How did a species die off if they couldn't die?

"They can't be," I said.

"We are," both girls replied at the same time, an amused glance passing between them as they spoke in unison.

"We have to keep this a secret," Lance said, looking at me.

"Why?" Roxy demanded.

"Because if the things I've read about Phoenixes are true - even *half* true - then the two of you could be more powerful than any Fae who has walked the earth in the last millennia. You're like the Fae of old, legendary... I don't even know what your limits would be, but I do know that you pose an even greater threat to Lionel now. If he finds out about this before you've learned to harness these powers-"

"He'd kill you," I finished for him, because I knew it was true. I'd learned more than enough about my father to realise this about him. He would do whatever it took to claim his position as the most powerful Fae in Solaria. And if he realised that the girls were Phoenixes then he'd eliminate them before they could lay claim to that power. I could barely even grasp the idea of something so impossible. It was no wonder Father hadn't realised; he was distracted by the shadows he'd just harnessed and who would ever suspect something so insane anyway?

"So we should hide what we are?" Gwendalina asked, sharing a worried look with her sister.

"Until you have a better grasp on your gifts and can defend yourselves, I think it should stay between the four of us," Lance agreed.

Roxy glanced at me and my gut lurched as I realised that the look in her eyes was mistrust. She didn't think I'd keep their secret.

"I won't tell anyone," I growled. "You have my word."

She scoffed beneath her breath then stalked towards me. I stilled as she drew closer, but her gaze slid beyond me to the kitchen sink. She took a glass from a shelf and poured herself some water before draining it in one go.

I watched her silently, wondering if there was something else I should say to her but not even knowing where to begin.

We were like magnets, destined to gravitate towards each other or repel each other, but nothing in between. And I didn't know how to flip it back to how it had been just before my father had shown up. It should have been the last thing on my mind, but in that moment all I wanted to do was take hold of her and pull her into my arms. My heart was still beating out of rhythm with the shock of what had nearly happened to her and I just wished that I could fix it somehow. I wanted her close even though the moon was gone now, the Eclipse over and its effects waning. But it didn't seem like she felt remotely the same way anymore.

"Do you both feel alright?" Lance asked, though his question seemed to be aimed at Gwen who was lingering close to him. "Lionel used your bodies as vessels for the shadows. That amount of dark power passing through you could leave its mark, a scar on your soul…"

"I feel okay," Gwen replied slowly. "Though I don't know how I'm supposed to inspect my soul for scars." She gave him a ghost of a smile.

Lance reached for her for a moment then dropped his arm again. I guessed he was feeling his own bout of guilt over our part in this mess. We'd spent the last four years training together to try and stop this from ever happening and we'd failed abysmally. His sister had died the last time and now all our fears had come to pass. Not only had Father gotten what he wanted but the twins had nearly died and we'd been cursed with the shadows too.

"At least you don't have to bear the burden of harnessing the shadows," Lance said gently. "They only passed through you, they didn't take root."

His gaze found mine and I knew he was worrying about us having to deal with it. I agreed with him. But we were also prepared in a way. We'd been dancing with the shadows for years when we practiced black magic and if they might give us an advantage in a fight, then I'd accept the weight of carrying them. I had no choice now anyway. Father hadn't bestowed this gift on us for any altruistic reasons like wanting us to have more power too; he'd made us into accomplices. By holding the power of the shadows, we were just as guilty as him. He'd bound us to him with them, made sure we couldn't go to the authorities unless we wanted to end up imprisoned too.

Roxy placed her glass down on the counter and pursed her lips like she had something to say, but she stayed quiet. Her eyes were locked with her sister's and I was sure they were communicating something to each other but I had no idea what. Roxy shook her head a little and Gwen sighed but agreed with a nod of her head.

"You wanna share that little exchange with the group?" I asked, scrubbing a hand over my face.

"Obviously not, dipshit," Roxy snarled. "Contrary to what you may think, we've never wanted anything at all to do with you or your bullshit throne. But one way or another we keep getting dragged into this drama. So if there's something I choose not to say to you then that's up to me."

I bristled at her tone, a growl rattling through my chest as I looked down at her and she just stared right back into my fucking eyes. Why was she always baiting me? And why did some fucked up part of me like it so much?

"All of this is a lot to take in," Lance said loudly. "Perhaps it would be best if we all got some sleep and discussed this more later."

"Fine by me," Roxy said, striding away from me, her legs bare beneath my T-shirt and her give-no-shits attitude right back in place. "The further away I am from Dragons the better."

"I think it might be a good idea for the four of us to remain here until the sun comes up. The moon's influence will still be potent until then and we've all been through a lot," Lance said.

Roxy scowled at him, looking like she was about to tell him to fuck off, but Gwen caught her arm.

"He's probably right, Tor. Let's just get some rest here."

I blinked in surprise as the fight went straight out of her and she bowed to her sister's suggestion. I'd begun to think that girl didn't know how to do anything other than argue. It seemed like that was just how she was with me. At least most of the time. For a moment I remembered laughing with her after racing on my bikes and wondered if there was any chance she'd ever look at me like that again.

"There are bedrooms here, I can show you to two of them," Lance said, moving forward to show them the way.

"We'll stay together," Gwen said and he nodded like he'd expected that.

Before they could leave the room, I stepped forward and caught Roxy's arm. I needed to say something to her, apologise, try to explain myself, I wasn't quite sure what yet. But I wanted to do something to combat the hate that was rearing up in her as she looked at me.

"Can I have a word alone, Roxy?" I asked as she pulled against my grip on her arm.

The other two headed down the corridor before she could respond and I shifted a little closer to her.

"I don't know what it is you want from me," she said quietly. "But I don't care either. You think because you've decided you want to talk to me then that means I must want to too? Well I don't. And I don't know what makes you think you can keep laying your hands on me either. Fire doesn't burn me, Darius, my Order is more powerful than a Dragon. I don't have any reason to fear you anymore and I don't have to do anything you say."

She snatched her arm out of my grip and stalked away after her sister and Lance. I felt like we were on a merry go round that wouldn't stop turning. We kept coming back to this point and maybe I should have just accepted it. Because I couldn't keep trying with her and having it thrown back in my face. So if she wanted us to hate each other then I'd just have to play my part in it. Because I couldn't keep away from her, that much was becoming abundantly clear. So I'd just have to keep being her villain.

DARCY

CHAPTER TWO

Orion led Tory and I upstairs along a wooden corridor and into a room with a king-sized bed sitting at the heart of it. The back wall was painted with a mural of the sea and a water feature in the shape of two fish curling around each other made a soothing splashing noise in one corner. It was pretty obvious which Heir this room belonged to.

Tory headed across the space, marching straight through a door I guessed was a bathroom and slamming it behind her.

Orion caught my hand, tugging me close for half a second and crushed his lips against mine. Emotion welled inside me and I clutched onto his robe, a tear spilling from my eye.

"Fuck, Blue. I'm so sorry," he whispered, squeezing my hand.

"It's okay." I breathed, desperate to fall into the comfort of his arms for a moment, but the sound of the toilet flushing made me pull away.

"I'll cast a silencing bubble for you so you can have some privacy," Orion said in a louder tone, raising a hand to do it.

"Thanks…bye."

His eyes remained on mine until the door shut between us and I moved toward the bed just as Tory returned to the room. My heart was thumping wildly and I rested a hand to it as I willed it to slow down. I was so exhausted, but wide awake at the same time. This night was the longest one I'd ever endured and as I checked a clock on the wall, I realised it wasn't too far from dawn.

I slid under the covers and Tory did the same, the two of us shifting close together like we had back in our shitty apartment in Chicago. That sofa-bed had forced us together, now we did it voluntarily, needing to draw on the comfort of our bond. We faced each other, propping our heads up on the pillows while our free hands clutched together.

"Orion cast a silencing bubble," I told her. "We can say what we like."

"I'd say what I like anyway," Tory said with a hard look.

"Do you really blame Darius for what happened?" I asked with a tug in my gut. I understood why she was angry at him, but I couldn't blame him for the choice he'd made for the sake of his brother.

"Not for what happened, but I blame him for being too much like his father. And for not trying hard enough to help us."

My throat constricted at the memory of being in that pit with Orion's hand locked around mine, his apologies falling over me like rain. I'd never seen him look so helpless. I'd never felt so helpless either. He and Darius had tried to help us but they'd just…failed.

"I think he wanted to help," I said gently.

"It wasn't enough," Tory snarled and for a second darkness seemed to curtain her eyes.

I frowned, a rush of powerful energy spilling into my body as if it came directly from where our hands met. A deep well of darkness seemed to open up inside me and as I pictured Darius's face, I hated him too. I hated him so much I could feel it burning a path right through to my soul. And I wanted to drown in this dark feeling until it consumed me.

"Darcy, your eyes," Tory breathed in alarm, sitting up and dropping my hand.

The darkness still swirled in my chest, seeming to call to me. I blinked hard, looking to Tory, focusing on her and forcing that frightening feeling to recede.

I moved to kneel and gaze into Tory's eyes, checking there was no sign of that lingering shadow.

"What's wrong with us?" I whispered, my voice abandoning me as anxiety stroked my heart.

Tory swallowed, shaking her head. "Maybe it's just an after effect of what Lionel did. We were in the shadows, they passed right through us."

I nodded slowly, pressing a hand to my chest as that dark pit stirred inside me again and fear crept into my bones. "What if they didn't pass on? What if they're still here? Don't you feel it?"

Tory pressed a hand to her own chest, worry entering her gaze. Her lips parted in horror. "Oh fuck. I think you're right."

"We have to tell Orion." I moved to get up but Tory snatched my wrist.

"No! We can't tell him. He'll tell Darius."

"So?" I shook my head at her and the shadows swirled in her gaze again.

She blinked quickly, releasing my arm. "Please," her tone softened. "I don't trust him, and what can Orion do anyway? We'll figure this out on our own, like we do everything else."

I frowned, biting into my lip. "Orion will know what to do. He's been teaching Darius dark magic, he must know about the shadows too."

"Yeah and look what happened the last time we hung around him and his dark magic bullshit."

My heart pinched sharply at the memory of Tory with that draining dagger, bleeding out on the ground. Then the way Darius had reacted…

"Alright," I whispered, slipping back under the duvet and trying to chase away the chill in my body. "But if it gets out of hand, I'm telling him. We don't know what this means and we can't exactly look it up in any old textbook."

"I know…but just for now, okay?" She slid back under the covers with me and my heart began to slow.

"Okay."

"At least one good thing came out of this. We've got our Order forms," Tory said with a half-hearted smile.

I returned it, trying to draw on the positives, though it was hard after everything we'd witnessed. "Yeah and now we have to hide it." I rolled my eyes and Tory snorted a laugh.

"I know, right? When are we ever gonna get a break around here? I wanna go flying and knock Darius out of the clouds."

I broke a small laugh, my eyes aching from how tired I was. It felt like the world had flipped on its axis since midnight. Like we'd stepped into an alternate reality where we were stronger than the Heirs and Lionel Acrux. We still had to harness that power and maybe in the meantime, these shadows would pass out of our bodies and we wouldn't have to live with the oppressive weight of them I could feel growing in my chest. But I had the horrible feeling, it wouldn't be that simple.

I woke early to the smell of coffee and groaned longingly, dropping out of bed and squinting at the clock. It was just after eight am but it didn't look like Tory was going to wake up any time soon. She was spooning a pillow overly sexually, her ass hanging out from beneath Darius's T-shirt.

I couldn't help a smile as I headed to the door, tiptoeing outside and wondering what kind of welcome party I was going to get from Darius this morning. But his anger never seemed as strongly aimed at me as it was at Tory. And sometimes the look in his eyes seemed so much more impassioned, like it wasn't just fury he felt toward her.

I crept downstairs, the heat of a fire washing over me as I moved into the lounge/kitchen where Orion was making coffee. I did a sweep of the room, but there was no sign of Darius. And though I longed to walk straight over to Orion and wind my arms around his waist, I didn't think it was worth the risk.

"White, black, sugar, none? It just occurred to me I don't know nearly enough about you, Blue." Orion turned to me with a slanted smile. He was shirtless which was impossible not to notice, but all I could think was *what if someone heard you say that?*

"Darius has gone for a fly," he answered my panicked look. "And I can hear your sister snoring a mile off."

"She doesn't snore," I laughed and he smirked.

"Alright, wheezing then."

"She'll kill you if she hears you say that," I teased, but my heart felt weighted with lead like I couldn't quite let the joke distract me from everything that had happened yesterday.

"So? Coffee?" Orion raised a brow.

"White, one sugar," I said and he turned to finish it. "Thanks."

I moved toward him, my arm brushing his as he passed me my coffee and I took a sip of the life-giving nectar. I sighed, finding Orion watching me and blushed under his intense gaze. I nudged his knee with mine, figuring that was safe territory.

"What?" I whispered and his expression hardened.

"I just didn't picture this being the first time we woke up in the same house together."

My brows knitted as he reached out to brush his fingers along my jaw.

"Lionel won't ever get near you again," he swore and I shook my head.

"You can't promise that, Lance. And I don't want you to. I'm not your responsibility."

He opened his mouth to argue then jerked his head back to look at the ceiling. A second later a loud thump signalled a huge beast landing on top of the treehouse.

"That woke Tory up," Orion murmured and I nodded, moving away and sitting down on the couch.

Darius dropped through a hatch in the roof butt naked and strode toward the chest at the back of the room, yanking on some clothes.

"Flying didn't burn off any of that anger then?" Orion asked and Darius turned to him with a dark look. His eyes slipped to the coffee and he moved forward to fill a cup, but by the time he made it there, Orion had already done it for him with his Vampire speed.

"Thanks," Darius muttered, taking a long swig. "And it did burn some of it off, actually. This is me happy by comparison."

"Well at least I got an extra hour of sleep while you were gone," Orion said with a yawn.

"Dude you totally starfished the second I got out of bed," Darius said with a low laugh.

"Wait, did you two share a bed?" I balked and the two of them turned to me like they'd just remembered I was there.

"We fell asleep talking," Orion said in an extra stern voice like I was suddenly his student again.

I cocked a brow; that bullshit was not working on me one bit.

Tory appeared on the stairs with a grin on her face. "You fell asleep talking like little girls at a sleepover?"

"Pfft." Darius pointed between the two of us. "You two did the exact same thing."

"We're twins!" we said at the same time.

Tory moved down the steps, heading to the chest of clothes and pulling on some pants which were much too big for her. "Whatever. You guys can go back to canoodling. We're leaving."

I folded my arms. "I think we should talk about last night."

"What else is there to talk about?" Tory asked, shooting a glare at Darius. "And I'm certainly not talking about things with *him* anyway."

Darius scowled at her and Orion shot me a weary look.

Tory looked around the lounge with a frown. "How do we get out of here?"

Darius pointed at a door in the tree trunk which parted this room from another.

"Great. See ya." Tory flipped Darius the finger then strode toward it and slipped through the door.

I finished my coffee, looking to Orion and releasing a sigh.

"I'll find out more about Phoenixes and message you all later," he said. "There's no classes today. I imagine most of the students and the faculty will be hungover as fuck."

"Especially Washer." Darius grimaced.

"Ew," I breathed, setting my coffee cup down on the table. "See you later then." I headed out of the door, feeling both of their eyes burning into me as I left and I imagined they were about to talk about us the second I was gone.

I caught Tory at the bottom of the stairs and we headed out into The Wailing Wood with no shoes on – which was especially crappy as it happened to be a frosty morning. I shivered as we hurried along the path, sending a wave of fire into my veins to warm me up.

"What else do you think our Order can do?" Tory wondered aloud.

A smile pulled at my mouth. "Let's hope it fights off shadows."

She nodded seriously. "Shadows and big fat iguanas."

"Yeah," I laughed, thinking of Lionel Acrux until my mirth burned up and died because we really were screwed if he ever found out what we truly were. And the fact that the shadows hadn't passed through us at all, but had stayed right here with us. "I really goddamn hope so, Tor."

MAX

CHAPTER THREE

I woke with the most satisfying ache lingering in my body. Flashes of last night rode through my mind over and over again, pulling a smile to my lips and making me hard for another round.

I peeled my eyes open and looked up at the glass dome which made up my room. Above my head, light was just beginning to spill into the lake and I watched the water moving in a gentle current.

I reached across the bed and ran my hand down Geraldine's side, a groan of longing escaping me at the feeling of her exposed skin beneath my fingertips.

She had rolled away from me in the night, her bare back and just-fucked hair all I could see of her. I wanted more, I fucking needed it. I'd never experienced anything like I had last night. I was used to controlling and boosting the emotions of other Fae while we screwed; girls went wild for the extra shot of lust I fed them. But Grus wasn't like that. She was fucking immune to me. Strong enough to block me out and make me work my ass off to satisfy her.

Which I absolutely had. The sound of her screaming my name was the most arousing and rewarding thing I'd ever heard. And I was going to hear it again in about five minutes.

I leaned forward and pressed a kiss to her shoulder blade, trailing a line of kisses down her spine and smirking as a sleepy moan escaped her. A trickle of lust came to me as she stirred and I moved lower, turning her gently so that she rolled onto her back and I could gain access to all of her again.

For a moment I just looked down at her as I braced my hands on either side of her hips, my muscles bunching as I held myself up. *Fuck,* why hadn't I ever looked at her properly before last night? I'd been so blinded by the royalist bullshit she spouted all the time that I'd missed the perfection of her curves. I'd never seen such perfect, round tits before and when she'd ridden me I'd had to fight the whole fucking time not to explode before I'd given her what she needed. I'd never had sex like it. And I wasn't going to let her go any time soon.

I pressed a kiss right beneath her navel and started working my way lower. I'd wake her up screaming and be eight inches deep in her before she'd caught her breath again.

My mouth made it lower and she twisted beneath me as she came to a little more.

"Oh holy manoli, I'm sleeping in a fish bowl," she gasped as she opened her eyes. Those exclamations got a whole lot filthier last night and I was looking forward to earning some more from her.

I dipped my head between her thighs, running my tongue straight up the centre of her and groaning with desire as I prepared to devour her.

"Sweet noodle balls, Max, don't start all that hoo-ha again now," she said, reaching down to grip my hair and pull me off of her.

"What?" I asked with a frown.

"I need to get to The Orb for breakfast before the buttery bagels are all snaffled up!" she shoved me aside like she had zero interest in what I'd just been about to do to her and I frowned as I reached out to read her emotions, not understanding what the fuck was happening.

I caught a whiff of lust but it was fading. More prominent were frustration and concern.

"I'll get someone to bring some bagels here," I said, sitting up so she could get a clear view of my abs. "Wouldn't you rather come back to bed?"

Geraldine turned to look at me with a laugh falling from her lips. "Why ever would I want to roll in your haystack again, Max Rigel? I can add a notch to my bedpost when I get back to my own room and go right on back to the important things in life."

"Important things?" *What the fuck is happening right now?*

"Shall we keep this little noodle blip to ourselves?" she asked as she pulled on her panties.

"What the fuck is a noodle blip?"

She giggled at me and I had to watch as she covered up those perfect tits. "You know, silly bear. When your noodle gets scrambled by the moon and you get the hormone hotties for someone ridunkulous. It's just a little embarrassing, don't you think?"

"I...are you worried I'd be embarrassed to tell people about us?" I asked as she drew her dress over her head and stole my last hope for morning sex.

"Why in Solaria would you be embarrassed?" she asked, widening those big blue eyes at me and capturing me in them. *"I'm* the one who's got to play the shame game. Whatever would anyone think if they realised I'd bumped bottoms with an *Heir?"* She said the word like it was dirty.

I stared at her as she actually fucking shuddered, trying to understand what she was saying.

"What? Just...wait. Are you saying you're *embarrassed* about last night? Didn't you feel what I felt? That sex was fucking mind blowing."

"Yes, yes, you were perfectly adequate," she said as she moved to look in the mirror, standing by my closet and fixing her goddamn hair.

"Adequate??"

"Well, I cant stand around here gossiping with you all day, I need to check in with the A.S.S. and see who else fell for the moon crazies. I doubt anyone else had quite such a slip of sanity as me though." She chuckled again.

"Wait. Slip of sanity? Are you saying this isn't going to happen again?" I got to my feet and followed her as she headed for the door, not really knowing what the fuck was happening. She'd been there last night, I'd given her the time of her life. That was more than just sex, it was like riding a high. Why wasn't she still in my bed begging for more? And how the hell was I losing out to buttery bagels?

"Of course it isn't, silly sausage." She laughed as she pulled the door open, not even bothering to check me out as I stood naked before her. "See you later, baked potata!"

The door shut with a harsh click and I was left with a sinking hard-on and no idea what had just fucking happened. Hurricane Geraldine had torn through my bedroom and I was left reeling in the wake of her departure.

I gritted my teeth as I headed away to take a shower. This was not going to stand. There was no way she didn't feel this connection between us. No way in hell. So I was just going to have to work on her until she'd admit it.

Because now I'd had a taste of Grus, I wasn't going back. That girl was going to be mine.

ORION

CHAPTER FOUR

Darius was in a foul mood as he slumped down in a chair and nursed his coffee with a scowl.

I moved to sit on the arm of his seat and clapped a hand on his shoulder. "She'll come around."

"She won't." He shrugged me off. "She's always hated me, and why wouldn't she?"

I sighed but I bit my tongue on saying anything else.

"What?" he growled, giving me a prompting look.

"You're not just Tory's enemy, Darius, you're your own. It's like every time you punish her, you're trying to punish yourself too."

"Thanks for the pep talk, *Dad*," Darius said scathingly, clearly not in the mood to have a rational discussion about the subject.

A low growl rumbled through my chest and my fangs were on the verge of sliding out. I needed blood. I was utterly drained after last night but I'd refused to take it from Blue after all she'd been through. Darius had offered but as we'd been sharing a bed at the time, I'd figured that was a bad idea. The Guardian bond always made me feel weird shit when I fed from him.

"Drink," he demanded, rising to his feet and tilting his head to one side. "You look like you're about to lose control and do it anyway."

I stood, my throat tight and the well of my power so hollow that I was on the verge of desperation. I lunged forward, digging my fangs into his throat and his arm wrapped around me immediately. The bond between us flared and as his blood spilled onto my tongue, a low groan of need escaped me. His grip became firmer and his hand slid into my hair as I took what I needed, devouring every drop as my heart pounded and I clutched his shoulders in an iron hold.

I broke away at last and we lingered too close to each other, his forehead knocking against mine. He pushed me back with a grunt of determination and I regained control of my emotions, detesting Lionel for the twisted bond he'd cast on us. I didn't even know which feelings were my own when it came to Darius anymore and I hated to think that some of the love and trust we had with each other might not even be real.

I dropped down into the chair he'd vacated and he moved to sit across from me on the couch, healing the mark on his neck with a taut frown. "My fucking father has so much to answer for."

"And he will," I swore. "But in the meantime, it's imperative we look out for the Vegas. Now more than ever before."

Darius shook his head at me. "You sound like you're on their side."

"You know things are different now. And I'm not fucking blind, if you think I don't see beneath this asshole bullshit you throw at Tory Vega, you're wrong. I know you care for her. And we have to protect her and her sister from your father. From the Nymphs too." I lowered my tone to a whisper despite the silencing bubble I'd cast. "You realise how big of a threat they are to you now? To your throne?"

He nodded firmly, his eyes swirling with darkness and making my chest tighten. "Yes."

"But you'll still protect them because you're a good man, Darius. And there is more to the world than power, no matter what society teaches us."

He swallowed, looking away. "I'm not a good man," he said thickly. He glanced at me as shadows curtained his eyes and he blinked to draw them back. "And you're not either. We're just two fuck-ups who keep fucking up."

I bit down on the inside of my cheek, the truthful sting in his words quieting my argument. "Well maybe it's time we stop fucking up." I stood, heading toward the door and glancing back at him. "We'll have to train harder now that we have this dark power. Your father is gifted with the shadows too, but it will take him longer to harness them. My mother will no doubt help him, but even my family has never had access to this shadow Element before. I don't know what to expect."

"You'll figure it out," he said, his confidence in me bringing half a smile to my lips.

I nodded in goodbye and walked out the door. I needed to be alone with my thoughts for a while before I started my studies. It was my nature to sit in solitude on occasion; my Order form required it.

I headed outside where the morning sun was spilling through the branches above, making the frost on the ground glitter like broken glass.

I put on a burst of speed and ran along the path as a coil of mist swirled through the trees around me. I let my Vampire abilities carry me back to Asteroid Place, halting outside the fence just as a few snowflakes began to fall. I headed to the gate and it opened at my touch, recognising the signal of my magic as I walked inside.

The faculty pool looked like a bomb site. Towels, bottles and rubber rings were strewn across the place and a pair of speedos circled slowly at the heart of the water.

I moved toward my chalet, halting with a grimace as I found a sun lounger pulled across the alley that led to my door. Washer was laying face up on it with no fucking clothes on, his legs wide and hanging off either side of the seat.

"Fucking hell," I muttered, trying to avoid the sight of his tanned junk but it just kept staring at me. For the sake of every man, woman and goddamn tree in the vicinity, I scooped up a discarded towel and tossed it over his lap.

I used a gust of air magic to carry me over the lounger and headed into my house, closing the door with a breath of relief. Silence hit my ears like the sweetest kind of music. I needed the quiet and the still to process everything that had happened.

I headed into the shower to wake myself up more fully. I'd barely had any sleep, but I was anxious to read up on Phoenixes as soon as possible. I needed to offer something useful to Blue. I felt like I'd failed her so completely last night that I didn't know how I was going to ever make it up to her.

As I stood under the heavy flow of hot water in the walk-in shower unit, my hands curled into fists and I started to shake as I relived the entire night again. I squeezed my eyes shut and pressed my forehead to the tiled wall as the memories found me. The way Darcy had bravely knelt and faced the shadows with her sister, the way fear had occupied every inch of my being. I could still feel her hand bound to mine by Lionel's magic, still feel the suffocating powerlessness that had consumed me and made me realise how fucking precious she was to me. I'd lost my sister because of my mother and Lionel, and I'd nearly lost the only girl who'd filled the void Clara had left in her absence too. I didn't care if Stella was my flesh and blood, I'd fucking kill her and Darius's father for this.

With a shuddering breath, I turned the shower off and headed back to my room to get dressed. It wasn't long before I was heading out of Asteroid Place again in the direction of Venus Library. There was only one section of the library I needed and it resided in the archives beneath the building. I let myself in with magic and headed through the quiet space. We'd locked most of the buildings on campus last night to ensure the students didn't start screwing in every damn classroom and damage valuable school possessions like these books.

In the far right corner of the library was a long oriental carpet between two shelves. I rolled it back, pressing my hand to the hatch concealed beneath it and a click sounded as I was admitted. I opened it, heading down the wooden staircase into the dark chamber below, using air magic to close the hatch and draw the carpet back over it as I went.

It was icily cold beneath the building but as I passed through a barrier of magic and arrived in the enormous archives, the air became more bearable. The power humming through the chamber was put in place to preserve the texts of old. The towering shelves were built from stone, wielded by earth magic to house thousands of scrolls and leather bound books.

Pillars intersected the echoing space and I moved through it, eyeing the alphabetical markers as I searched for the texts on rare Order forms. Part of my job was to know all about each Order, and though I didn't know a whole lot about Phoenixes, I recalled taking an interest in them back in my early days of working at Zodiac. They'd stuck out in my mind, fascinating me because of the mystery surrounding them. I'd poured over artists' sketches of them many times and I'd recognised them instantly when Darcy and Tory had emerged.

The twins would pass as Fire Harpies long enough. They were reasonably rare; there were no students in this school with that Order, but my concern was them attending Order Enhancement classes. I'd needed to find a way to avoid that happening, because if they shifted regularly in front of Professor Avem, she would soon figure out they weren't Harpies.

I located a section on Orders and began thumbing through the scrolls and books, hunting for something that could give me what I needed. It might take me all day, but I was going to stay here until I knew everything there was to know about Phoenixes to prepare Blue and Tory. Because there wasn't a soul on earth who could help them right now, but me.

I sat in my office later that evening with my Atlas in front of me. I now had an album full of pictures I'd taken of every page in a book I'd discovered that detailed the gifts of Phoenixes. Typically, half of the book had been burned away in some long forgotten fire and I was furious because it had clearly once housed all the information about Phoenixes and their abilities we could have wished for. At least I had some answers to give the twins though. I'd invited Darius here too because I knew it was best to keep the four of us up to date.

As I waited for them to arrive, a heavy pressure built in my chest. Whispers filled my ears and darkness curtained my vision, making my breathing ragged. I felt the call of the shadows like I never had before, like I couldn't escape it because it lived beneath my flesh now. There was nowhere to run from it, no way to pull back. And its allure was so inviting, I wanted to give into the encouragement of the whispers despite all the reasons I knew I shouldn't.

My eyes drifted shut and a deep thrum of power flowed through my veins. I drew in a breath as ecstasy accompanied the sensation, urging me on, letting that well of dark magic pour into my blood.

I opened my eyes and found a coil of shadow wrapped around my hand and my lips parted in awe. I knew what it was. The Fifth Element. And I'd somehow wielded it, though I feared what it was capable of.

A knock came at the door and I forced the shadows away, pushing them back as I used my years of training to rip myself free of their seductive call.

"Come in," I called as the magic vanished and relief rushed through me.

Darius entered first followed closely by Tory and my eyes moved instinctively beyond her to Blue. Her hair was pulled into a ponytail and loose coils of shining cobalt tickled her neck. She gave me a small smile and I fought the urge to return it.

"Sit down," I commanded.

I'd brought another couple of chairs into the room so the three of them moved toward the desk to sit, Darius to the left and Tory firmly taking the right chair so Darcy was left with the middle opposite me. Her knees brushed mine under the desk and I hooked my foot around hers on instinct.

"So…" I started, bringing up a screenshot on my Atlas, sensing tension building in the air. "I've found some information on Phoenixes." I waved a hand to cast a silencing bubble around us, though I doubted it was necessary. I'd been on campus all day and the only place anyone was heading was to The Orb to get supplies of food and water to nurse their hangovers. I'd had to heal several headaches myself today, but that wasn't due to alcohol. It was fucking stress and lack of sleep.

"What did you find?" Darcy asked, her brows raising with intrigue while her sister tried to peer at the picture on my Atlas.

"The text was damaged but I've been able to discern some of the gifts you'll have," I started.

Tory shot Darius a glare. "I'm voting the Dragon steps out of the room. Maybe I don't want him knowing my gifts."

"Tough shit, Roxy. I'm staying." Darius leaned back in his chair, dominating it and I gritted my jaw, looking to Tory.

"He's staying. I'll discuss it with him either way, so there's really no point in even starting the argument, Miss Vega."

Tory rolled her eyes at me, looking like she was about to argue further.

"Just drop it, Tor. I wanna hear this," Darcy urged and her sister gave in with a shrug.

I leaned forward in my chair, zooming in on the highlighted text at the top of the page. "Phoenixes are endowed with the capacity to exhibit high levels of resilience pertaining to the Divisus Orders and the subliminal

Cardinal Magics."

"What the shit does that mean?" Tory asked.

"It means, you're easily able to fight off psychological magic. Like Coercion." I gave Darius a pointed look and he sat up straighter.

"That's why Lionel's power didn't work on us," Darcy said, looking fascinated and I nodded, rubbing my knee against hers under the table. She was always such an enthusiastic student and fuck if that didn't get me so hard for her. She shared my love of learning and I'd often enjoyed the way her eyes lit up in awe in my classes.

Focus, asshole.

I cleared my throat. "Now your Order has emerged, it seems it will be almost impossible for any psychological magic to be used on you. That includes a Siren's emotional persuasion, I'm sure you'll be glad to hear. Plus the memory probing of the Cyclops Order and the more subtle manipulation of trust by Vulpeculan Foxes."

Both Tory and Darcy smiled at that and I looked to Darius to see his reaction. His face was impassive but a concerned look flashed through his eyes. He was going to have to fight against his natural instincts to squash the threat of the Vegas when it came to protecting them from his father, but I had no doubt he would be calculating a way to ensure he kept his claim on the throne. It was Fae nature. And I couldn't really fault him for it. It was still my intention to ensure he claimed it too and unseat Lionel Acrux. But a small, niggling voice in the back of my mind was starting to suggest another way to resolve that issue. One which was a dangerous idea to even consider putting forward when it came to the Heirs.

I turned back to the text, reading the line which explained this particular gift in more detail. "The magical block against such powers is described as a fiery blaze, coursing under the skin like a barrier."

"Yes," Darcy said excitedly. "I felt it when Lionel cast the Coercion."

Tory nodded, her eyes brightening. "So no one can ever get in our heads again?" she asked, hope burning in her gaze.

"So it would seem," I confirmed and she gave me a triumphant grin.

Darius rapped his knuckles against the desk impatiently. "What else does it say?"

A shadow in my periphery preceded a knock on the window and everyone jolted in surprise as my heart lurched.

"Who the fuck is that?" Darius balked and I rose from my seat in shock as I found Gabriel goddamn Nox perched outside on the windowsill staring in at us. His huge black, feathered wings were folded behind him, revealing the artwork of tattoos covering his broad chest.

"By the stars." I jogged around the desk, wrenching the window open and Gabriel jumped inside gracefully. He was only half shifted into his Harpy form, his jeans still in place instead of the silver armour that would normally cover most of his body when he was fully transformed. "Noxy! I thought you weren't arriving until tomorrow?"

Gabriel embraced me with a bark of laughter. "Thought I'd drop in on this conversation, Orio. The stars told me to come." He pulled away and we turned to the others who were all staring at Gabriel like he had two fucking heads.

"This is Gabriel Nox, your new Tarot teacher," I explained then frowned as his words registered with me. "What did you see?"

Gabriel's brows knitted together. He had the gift of The Sight and our friendship stretched back far enough for me to trust him implicitly. And more than that, he was my Nebular Ally. If he was here now, it was for a reason. And I wondered if our circle of four was about to become five. We'd met years ago when a bunch of students from his school had done an exchange with a group from Zodiac. It had coincided with a Pitball match between our academies too and we'd bonded after I'd given hell to a couple of guys he didn't get along with.

"Last night I woke to one of the most powerful visions I've ever experienced." His gaze fell on the Vegas and my heart beat harder at his expression. He moved toward them, bowing his head slightly.

"Phoenixes," he breathed. "I saw you both as Phoenixes."

"Well that's just fucking great," Darius huffed, rising from his seat and receiving a slap of feathers in the face as Gabriel moved to embrace Darcy and Tory in turn. Darius scowled as he stepped firmly away from him, looking to me. "We don't need this secret reaching any more ears."

"You can trust Gabriel," I said firmly. "He's my Nebular Ally."

38

"It's nice to meet you," Darcy said with a wide smile and Tory gave him one too, the two of them already seeming enthralled with him. He tended to have that effect on people, but something about the way they looked at him made me wonder if there was more to it than that. Something intangible. They didn't seem remotely disturbed by the company of a stranger despite the subject we were discussing.

Darius stalked toward me and gritted his jaw. "I don't think we should be letting random Fae in on all of this."

"He's not random. You've met him before," I growled. "And besides, he's my Ally. The stars chose him as my soul friend so he won't betray my trust."

Darius frowned at that, glancing between us with his scowl intensifying.

"How do you only shift so your wings are out?" Tory asked, her eyes sparkling like she wanted to learn that very thing.

"I can teach you," Gabriel said and the two of them smiled.

"We have to keep their Order a secret," I told him and he turned to me with a serious nod.

"How did it happen? How did they emerge?" he asked and I could feel Darius's eyes boring a hole into my head. I decided it was best to keep the shadows a secret and everything else that had occurred last night. And though I hated lying to my Nebula Ally, I had a firm loyalty to Darius which I wouldn't break.

"I guess the Lunar Eclipse brought it on," I said with a shrug.

Gabriel smiled darkly. "What a night, huh? Trust me, I did *not* want to leave my bed this morning."

"How are things with-" I started but Darius cut over me.

"*Fun* as this reunion is, could we get on with learning about Phoenixes?" he growled irritably.

Gabriel's gaze narrowed on him. "How's your father, kid? You have that same tight-arsed expression he's always sporting. Are you growing into his shoes well?" he asked coldly and I pursed my lips as Tory snorted a laugh and Darcy elbowed her.

"He's not like him," I said but Gabriel didn't look convinced. He knew about my Guardian bond with Darius, but he'd never accepted that I was truly friends with Lionel's son. He hated the Acruxes and I couldn't exactly blame him for that, but Darius was different.

"I'm just as powerful though," Darius snarled, not helping the situation.

Gabriel's eyes swept over him, then he pushed a hand into his ebony hair with a yawn, turning away from him toward the girls.

"I'd love some time to get to know you both," he said. "The stars have sent me to help you, I felt it in every part of my being."

"I'd like that," Darcy said with a keen look.

"If you take us flying, you'll be my new best friend, dude," Tory said with a grin.

"Why don't you teach them?" I suggested suddenly. "I need a reason to get them out of Harpy Order Enhancement classes. We're going to pretend they're Fire Harpies so Lionel doesn't get wind of what they are. You know what he'd do if he found out what a threat they are. Do you know how powerful Phoenixes are rumoured to be?"

Gabriel nodded slowly. "I don't know much, but I felt their power through The Sight. It was like nothing I've ever experienced."

"I'll forward you the texts I found today," I said. "Will you tutor them? I'll tell Elaine they need time to adapt to their new powers."

"Of course," Gabriel said. "I'd be honoured."

At least that was one problem solved. I moved back behind my desk, dropping into my seat while the others returned to their chairs and Gabriel stood behind Darius.

There was a natural aura flowing from Gabriel and I could tell the girls trusted him already. I half wondered if he might be Allies with them too, though it seemed like quite a coincidence if he was. Nebular Allies were common enough, but it would still be pretty unlikely. Though the way they were taking to each other made me think it was a real possibility.

Darius was a whole different matter. As a Scorpio and a Leo they were capable of forming a strong friendship, but only if the Leo could let go of their superiority complex and if the Scorpio saw past their own pride. But fuck if I saw either of them managing that.

I forwarded the texts to Gabriel before proceeding to explain the notes I'd made on their Order form. "I guess most importantly for now, you should know that your magic regenerates via fire. You need to be close enough to feel the warmth of the flames and you will be able to draw magic from it. Which explains why you had a hard time figuring out exactly what it was that regenerated you as there are fires constantly burning all around the academy. Not to mention the fact that as fire Elementals you can self-replenish whenever you need."

"So what you're saying is, our power is endless?" Tory asked, grinning in a way that was only going to piss Darius off. "As in, so long as I can cast fire, I'll never run out of magic. Unlike big fat lizard shifters who have to pop off for a snooze on a heap of gold whenever they're running low?"

Darcy tried to hide her laugh as Darius growled and I shot him a look, begging him to keep the peace so that we could get through this meeting amicably.

"What else?" Darcy asked eagerly, clearly realising the same thing I had and helping me out to distract the pair of them before they could start bickering or worse.

"Phoenix fire is born of the sun itself. It's capable of destroying all matter and is able to sever many magical spells. In both Order and Fae form, Phoenixes are impervious to all types of fire, including that produced Elementally or through other Order forms. It is also capable of harming Orders which are resistant to fire like Manticores, Hydras and... Dragons."

Darius stilled, his hands tightening on the arms of his chair while Gabriel chuckled under his breath. The twins shared a look, their eyes wide and full of excitement.

"So you're saying that this big ass lizard can't burn me at all, but I can totally cook his ass if I want to?" Tory asked with a smirk as she pointed at Darius.

"Why would you want to?" I asked, not really wanting to say yes and piss Darius off any more than he already was but I could see that her comment alone had been enough to do that.

"It's just nice for all of us to know our capabilities," Tory replied with a shrug. "And our *limitations,*" she tossed at Darius.

I chewed on the inside of my cheek as I surveyed Darius, wondering if he might come around to the idea that was circling in my mind. If he did, it would benefit every Fae in Solaria. Because Darius Acrux might not ever rescind his claim to the throne and I didn't want him to. But *maybe* I could convince him to share it with two more candidates. I just had to ride out the fucking hurricane it would take to persuade him.

TORY

CHAPTER FIVE

I woke up in a cold sweat with my heart pounding and darkness coiling around me. Someone had been calling to me in my sleep. Her voice echoed in my memory like she'd really been there with me instead of a figment of my imagination.

I chewed my lip as I sat up and scrambled for my Atlas to check the time. Classes were resuming today and now that we'd passed The Reckoning, things were due to get a lot harder. The gaps in our timetables had been filled with new lessons and we were expected to really pick up the pace in our other classes too.

It was five to six and I cursed my luck. I hated waking up earlier than necessary, but with the fear that nightmare had roused in me, I knew I'd never get back to sleep now.

My horoscope arrived just as I was about to put my Atlas down and I read over it quickly.

Good morning Gemini.
The stars have spoken about your day!
Beware the wrath of the scorned. Today could be a tipping point for you in a far greater journey. Think carefully about where your anger is directed. Some things can be cast in stone without you even realising when it happened.

Another day, another confusing as fuck prediction. One day I'd open up my Atlas and the horoscope would say: *avoid the eggs today or you'll get the shits and* I'd know exactly where I stood for once.

Until that day, I was going to do as I always did and spend zero time trying to work out the ridiculously convoluted message from the stars and focus on what was important. Namely running until I burned this nagging fear out of my limbs and eating until I soaked up the last dregs of the alcohol I consumed before I went to bed last night. Because, *fuck* my life had flipped on its axis fast and the only way I'd managed to sleep at all was by chasing oblivion with a bottle of tequila. *Bad call Tory.* But better that than me ending up knocking on the door of the Dragon upstairs and admitting that Darcy and I had the shadows too and it fucking terrified me. Because in the cold light of day it was much easier to remember that said Dragon could not be trusted. Which meant I was fucked, because I had no one else to turn to aside from Orion whose head was so far up the Dragon's asshole that I was sure he could taste his meals for him from a distance.

I sighed. Why did everything always have to be so complicated? There was an itch trailing along my shoulder blades and I just knew it was my Order form begging to be set loose. And yet I couldn't risk anyone seeing me while I was transformed yet because Lionel Acrux couldn't find out what we were. So even after all this waiting, I still couldn't explore the part of me that had been hidden for so many years. I couldn't find out any more about my powers or test my hand at flying. Nothing. Not until we got permission from Darius's pet teacher anyway.

I huffed my irritation and shoved the blankets off of me before heading for a quick shower.

By the time I'd run a circuit of the academy grounds and the fire in my muscles was sharp enough to burn out the stress of the shadows that had haunted my dreams, it was nearly half seven.

I jogged to The Orb, cooling down slowly as I used my water magic to clean the sweat and mud from my body.

I paused outside the doors, resting a hand against the curving golden wall of the building as I stretched my calves out and caught my breath.

"Did you miss me during the Eclipse, sweetheart?" Caleb breathed in my ear and I flinched away from him in surprise.

"Fuck, Caleb don't do that sneaky Vampire shit to me, how many fucking times?" I snapped, my frayed nerves surfacing again as he pouted at me mockingly.

"Jeez, Tory, who shit on your shoes this morning?" he joked.

Anger bubbled beneath my skin and for a moment darkness pushed across my vision. I blinked furiously to clear the shadows from my mind and managed to force them back through pure strength of will. *Where did that come from?*

"What the hell was that?" Caleb asked, tipping his head as he peered into my eyes.

"What?" I asked innocently, although it was obvious he'd seen the shadows.

"For a second your eyes went all dark..."

I cast about for an explanation, landing on the only one that made sense at all. "My Order Emerged on the Eclipse," I admitted.

"Oh?" he asked curiously though it wasn't very convincing. Darius obviously would have filled him in already, and I guessed he must have thought I was a Fire Harpy.

"Yeah so, sorry but in answer to your first question, the answer is no. I was not thinking about you during the Eclipse. I was busy."

"So the moon didn't drive you towards anyone else?" he pressed, pinning me in his gaze.

I shrugged, brushing past him as I headed into The Orb and he fell into step beside me. "I didn't hook up with anyone else if that's what you're getting at."

"That wasn't what I asked though," he pushed. "I asked if you were drawn towards anyone?"

I took a deep breath as I turned to look up at him. "Yeah. If you wanna know, it pushed me towards Darius."

A bit of irritation and jealously flashed through his expression, but then Caleb actually smirked. "But you didn't act on it? You resisted the full weight of the moon driving you together?"

"Not exactly," I said, but I couldn't tell him about Lionel and all the other shit that went down. "Like I said, mine and Darcy's Orders Emerged and my mind wasn't really on hooking up with anyone after that."

He thought on that for a second and I headed inside for the coffee machine with purposeful strides.

Caleb caught up to me again as I stuffed a cup into the machine and he leaned against the table so that he could look at me.

"So hypothetically, if your Order hadn't Emerged and nothing like that had gotten in your way. Do you think you would have ended up with Darius that night?" he asked.

I watched the coffee trickle into my cup with an ache in my chest which spoke far too strongly about my caffeine addiction.

"Honestly?" I hesitated, not really wanting to admit the answer to myself, but if I was going to have insane urges about Darius then the least I could do was own it. I took a deep breath. "I imagine so, yeah. I don't know what it is with me and him, but we just keep ending up in these situations where it's like the tension between us is unbearable. So yeah I'm drawn to him but I can only think I'm insane for feeling that way because all he ever does is piss me off or hurt me."

Caleb looked at me for a long moment. "You know, you could have just lied to me," he pointed out, pushing his tongue into his cheek like he was trying to stop himself from saying something else.

I snorted a laugh. "Yeah. Seems like a bit of an asshole move though and I think you and Darius have that covered so I thought I'd just go with honesty."

"Okay…"

I raised an eyebrow at him as I waited for him to think about that and he frowned.

"So. Basically you think Darius is hot?"

I smirked at him tauntingly and nodded because the guy was fucking irritating as all hell, but he was also practically a demigod and trying to deny it was ridiculous.

"But you think I'm hot too…?"

I made a show of running my eyes over him, taking in the way his muscles pressed against his shirt and the perfectly mussed up way his curly hair sat.

"Yeah, I guess so," I agreed casually.

Caleb smirked.

"And you think I'm funny?" he pushed, shifting closer to me so that he could pin me against the table, forming a cage with his arms.

"Sometimes," I hedged.

"Is Darius funny?"

I rolled my eyes. "He hasn't graced me with much opportunity to find out. He's usually more concerned with shoving me in the mud or trying to drown me…"

"Both things I haven't done."

"You stood and watched which is arguably just as bad."

Caleb huffed before carrying on. "You and me have other things in common too."

"Like what?" I asked.

"We had fun at the Fairy Fair."

"I could have had fun at that with anyone."

"We both…like…"

I waited for him to figure out an end to that sentence and he grinned as he thought of something.

"We both like it when I hunt you."

I laughed. "Nice save dude, but that's more about sex than having things in common."

"Well you don't have anything in common with Darius either," he pointed out.

I shrugged because that wasn't true, but I didn't really want to start listing reasons why I was compatible with Darius Acrux. It was something I tried not to think about much on account of him being a total dickwad.

"What's that look for?" Caleb asked, realising I was holding back.

"It's just not strictly true. We have the same hobbies and we both grew up having to deal with shitty parental figures…"

His jaw tightened and I decided not to add anything else.

"Fine. But you know the sex with me is fucking amazing," he said triumphantly.

"Sure," I said, shrugging like I wasn't really sure and drawing a growl of frustration from him as he pressed even closer to me, my heart beating faster at his proximity.

"Darius could be awful in bed for all you know," he breathed against my ear.

"He could," I agreed.

"And when you had the chance to test that theory during the Eclipse, you passed on it," Caleb pressed.

"Well, lucky for me I went poof at midnight and turned into a pumpkin like Cinderella before I could make that lapse in judgment," I agreed because it *was* damn lucky. Moon Tory absolutely wouldn't have said no to Darius if we'd spent even another moment alone down on the beach.

"That's...not how that story goes. Cinderella isn't the pumpkin. How can you even get it that wrong?" Caleb asked, frowning at me. I tiptoed up to speak in his ear and he stilled to listen to my answer.

"I'm not really a Princess kind of girl," I whispered.

Caleb's eyes lit at the double meaning to my words and I offered him a teasing smile before slipping out of the cage he'd created with his arms.

I pulled my coffee out of the machine and started adding sugar and he moved close behind me again.

"Okay, so what's your Order?" he asked.

"I don't believe for one second that your little buddy hasn't already sent you all the information you could ever want on my Order," I deadpanned.

Caleb laugh. "Alright, you caught me. I know you're a Fire Harpy. That's pretty cool, right? You know Harpies can fly almost as fast as I can run?"

"Maybe I'll race you one day then," I taunted, though as the words left my lips I instantly wondered if they shouldn't have. I wasn't actually a Harpy and I had no fucking idea how fast a Phoenix could fly.

"I'd win, sweetheart," he assured me. "I always do."

"So why did you ask me all those questions about Darius if you aren't going to react to my answers?" I asked, switching the subject back off of my Order because I didn't even know what lies to tell yet.

"I'm deciding how to feel about it," he said, his jaw ticking and giving away his irritation over the issue even if he was trying to hide it.

"That's not how feelings tend to go," I pointed out. "You usually just get lumped with whatever emotion your subconscious wants to kick you in the teeth with on any given day. Look at me for example, every day I go to bed deciding to wake up perky and peppy, making friends with everyone and anyone I meet. And yet when the morning swings around, I'm still the same mean bitch I was last night."

Caleb laughed like I was joking and maybe I fucking was. I didn't even know.

"Alright then. It pisses me off," he admitted in a low tone.

"What are you gonna do about it then?" I asked, the look in his eyes making my heart beat a little harder.

Caleb reached out and took my coffee from my hands, placing it down on the table beside us before moving so close to me that our bodies were pressed flush together.

"I'm gonna prove to you that I'm the better choice. You'll fall for me so hard you'll break bones."

I scoffed lightly but he caught my chin and pressed a kiss to my lips to make his point. My stomach flipped over and I caught his blazer in my grip, tugging him closer as he pressed his tongue into my mouth.

Caleb might not have been the best choice for me, but he made a lot of damn good points. Besides, if he succeeded in making me forget about Darius I was all for it because that asshole had hurt me too many times for me to be looking at him the way I did sometimes.

He pulled away and I smirked at him before pushing him back a step. We were in the corner of the room but it was fast filling up with students who had come for their breakfast and I didn't really want a photo of us making out splashed all over FaeBook.

I retrieved my coffee from the table beside us and started walking towards the *Ass* Club on the far side of the room.

"Aren't you interested in who the moon pushed *me* towards?" Caleb asked as he hounded after me.

"Not really. But I'm getting the feeling this conversation won't end until you've told me. So…"

Caleb smiled knowingly but didn't say anything.

"Oh so this is one of those situations where you insinuate something then leave me hanging, desperate for the answer, right?" I asked, taking a sip of coffee which tasted like heaven and made me groan beneath my breath.

"Right," Caleb agreed, baiting me. The problem was, I wasn't going to bite.

I turned away from him and weaved through the crowd towards the *Ass* Club and felt him following a second later.

I got half way through the crowd before Caleb shot around me using his speed and came to a halt, blocking my way.

"Fine. The moon was just making me think about you all night. And the idea of you hooking up with someone else drives me a little bit insane," he said. "Especially Darius."

"Why especially him? Because he's your friend?" I asked.

"He's more like my brother than my friend and that's not what the issue is. The issue is that all of our lives, people have tried to pit us against each other because we're equals. They're always trying to figure out if one of us is stronger even though they know we're evenly matched. So when they can't differentiate us because of our power, they try to divide us because of our other strengths or weaknesses. And nothing anyone has ever tried, said or suggested has ever even come close to dividing us. So there's no chance in hell I'm going to fall out with him over a girl."

"Okay." I shrugged, trying to step around him but he still barred my way. "Am I missing the point of your whole speech here or something?" I asked. "Because it kinda feels like you're trying to break up with me even though we aren't together. If you wanna stop screwing me then just stop, you don't owe me some elaborate explanation. It's fine."

Caleb groaned like I was the one confusing *him* even though I really didn't know what was wrong with him.

He stepped forward with intent, catching my cheek in his grasp and looking into my eyes.

"What if I asked you to be mine. Just mine?" he offered and I laughed.

"And what would your mom think of that?" I asked.

"I'm not inviting you to meet my family any time soon," he countered.

"But that's where this path leads, isn't it? If you expect me to commit to you then you're making your own kind of promise. You're saying you see this becoming something that might last and if you're saying that, then there's no expiry date on it. Assuming everything goes well, you're saying you'd want to be with me long term. So is that what you're asking me or not?"

Caleb frowned. "You know I'm not," he said slowly. "No matter how I might feel or not feel about you, I obviously couldn't ever marry you and put you in a position of power like that. The combination of our genes would create a child more powerful than the other Heirs' children because we inherit our most powerful parent's power. It would disrupt the balance of the Celestial Council and-"

"See?" I interrupted. "That wasn't that hard, was it? You don't want me long term, so why would I commit to you short term? We have fun Caleb but I'm not your girl. If you can't handle the idea of me meeting other people, maybe even hooking up with them, then we can just call time on this thing between us. Because I'm not ever going to put my life on hold for a man. Especially one who doesn't think I'm good enough to make the cut long term."

I stepped around him but he caught my arm, whirling me back and almost sloshing coffee all over me. I managed to stop the liquid from hitting me at the last minute with my water magic and I directed it back into the cup with a scowl aimed at him.

"I never said I didn't think you were good enough," he growled. "But my situation is complicated. Being in a position of power means taking on certain responsibilities and-"

"And that's exactly why I never wanted the stupid throne in the first place! Who wants to be shackled to some chair when you could be free? Fuck that." I rolled my eyes at him and he almost smiled.

"So you're telling me you're not willing to be exclusive?" he confirmed, his lips twitching with amusement like he'd expected that anyway.

"No, idiot. Now can I go get my breakfast?"

"Do you wanna hang out later?" he asked, still blocking my way.

"If I say maybe, will you let me leave?"

"You're busy later, Roxy," Darius said from right behind me and I jerked around, scowling up at him and wondering how much of our conversation he'd been eavesdropping on.

"No I'm not," I replied, wondering what he was going on about.

"Well as you just found out your Order bursts into flames when you coax it to break free of your flesh and heightened emotional experiences can cause inexperienced Fae to lose control of their Order form, it seems like a bad idea for you to be hooking up with anyone for a while," he pointed out.

"That's obviously not the real reason you don't want her hooking up with me," Caleb scoffed and Darius's gaze darkened.

"I'm just looking out for you, Cal. I wouldn't want to risk her setting *my* dick alight," Darius replied tauntingly.

"Good thing I'm not offering then," I snapped.

Caleb bit down on a smile and Darius looked between me and him for a moment then shrugged. "Well don't come crying to me when she melts it." He laughed tauntingly and strolled away from us to join Seth and Max on their couch. The three of them looked our way as we continued to loiter. He was talking shit anyway. At least I hoped he was...

I glanced down at Caleb's fly for a moment and shuddered at the thought of bursting into flames while we were in the middle of something... *Dammit.*

Caleb looked like he had something else to say, but the protests of my stomach wouldn't be silenced any longer and I took off towards my sister and our friends again, refusing to think about melting his junk off by accident.

"Wait," Caleb caught my arm, his gaze shifting to the other Heirs and back to me again. "You haven't given me a proper goodbye."

"Don't," I warned as he shifted towards me, his eyes on my mouth. "I'm not a lamppost to be pissed on. If you try and kiss me here in front of all these people I'll launch you across the room."

"That's a bit dramatic, sweetheart," he complained.

"Yeah, well you're the one asking me about the Eclipse then trying to stamp your mouth all over me the second Darius shows up. I suggest you go and talk to him if you've got some issue going on between you two because I'm not playing piggy in the middle with your insecurities. I just want to eat my breakfast."

This time I finally managed to escape him and I made it to the *Ass Club* with a sigh of relief. Angelica greeted me warmly, waving a hand at the mounds of food that had been gathered on the tables the group dominated and I snagged myself a few slices of toast before piling scrambled eggs on top. I dropped down opposite Darcy and Sofia with a word of greeting and fell on my food like a savage.

"Is Caleb back in the running then?" Darcy asked teasingly.

I tsked around a mouthful of food, swallowing before I replied. "Maybe I should swear off the Heirs altogether and find myself a nice, normal bad boy. You know, the kind who hangs out in biker bars and beats people up for fun. Your run of the mill psycho like I usually go for. There would be so much less drama involved."

Darcy smirked into her coffee and Sofia laughed.

"I've just been reading an article in the Celestial Times about Aurora Academy which is down in Alestria," Sofia piped up. "They're saying if any more students die there, they're going to have to think about closing it. Perhaps you could find a nice, normal psycho there? We have a Pitball match against them coming up."

"Perfect," I agreed. "I'll be sure to get a seat on their side of the stands for the match."

Sofia grinned but Darcy didn't, her lips pursing as she looked across the room at something over my shoulder.

I raised an eyebrow at her, following her gaze until I spotted Diego taking a seat at a table in the corner on his own.

He looked our way and I caught his eye, pursing my lips slightly as he tugged his beanie hat a little lower over his ears.

"I still can't believe he called you both whores," Sofia whispered as if he might hear her from across the room.

"I know," Darcy agreed. "I thought he was our friend…"

My gaze darkened at the hint of hurt in her voice and for a moment the shadows rose to dance across my vision.

Diego straightened in his chair, his gaze sharpening as he stared at me, his lips parting like he'd noticed the dark magic which came alive with my anger.

I blinked, turning away from him and looking down at my food as I fought them back beneath my skin. A little ache rose in my chest as they faded away and a part of me longed to call them back. I was afraid of what might happen if I gave in to their call though. The shadows weren't like the rest of my magic. They were an invading force, part of me and separate at the same time. Where I was sure my magic would never hurt me, I could only feel mistrust of the shadows. They weren't mine. But they lived in me now all the same.

"Well slap my toosh and call me Molly, I've had a most frustrating morning!" Geraldine exclaimed as she arrived and fell into the seat beside me.

I snorted a laugh and looked up at her in surprise.

"What happened?" Darcy asked.

"*Well.* I've been working on some T-shirts for the A.S.S. which we've all been most excited to receive-" She reached into her satchel and pulled out a royal blue T-shirt, offering it up for us to look at.

The words *Princess Power* were emblazoned across the front of it in shimmering pink glitter. Geraldine gave it a shake and the words blurred together for a moment before reforming to say *Vegas for the Throne.* I raised an eyebrow at Darcy and she bit down on a laugh.

"So what's the problem?" Darcy asked kindly.

"Aside from the fact that we don't want the throne," I muttered.

"Pish posh, Tory Vega!" Geraldine scalded. "One day when you're ruling over Solaria, I will remind you of this day and you shall have to eat your words!"

"Well I'll concentrate on eating my breakfast for now and see how we get on," I offered. I'd basically come to an unofficial agreement with Geraldine that I wouldn't shout too loudly about my lack of interest in the throne, so long as she didn't push too hard for me to sit my ass on it. We both let the subject drop as the attention returned to her T-shirt.

"The back is supposed to say A.S.S. Forever!" Geraldine lamented.

"Well do you really want to wear something that says *ass forever* on it?" Max Rigel's voice made us all look up in surprise and I lay down my knife and fork as I finished eating, wondering what the hell he wanted.

His attention wasn't on me or my sister though, it was firmly planted on Geraldine.

"It doesn't say *ass* forever," she replied, giving him a flat look. "It's

56

A – S – S."

"Hmm. Well if I was walking behind you and your shirt said *ass forever* I'd be thinking that's where you'd like me to stick my-"

"Is there a reason you've come to ruin a perfectly adequate breakfast or are you just looking to take some more of my buttery bagels?" Geraldine demanded.

Max pursed his lips and I caught a hint of lust coiling from him as if he was trying to push it at us. Or more accurately, push it at Geraldine.

"Your breakfast looks pretty fucking earth shattering to me. But I guess you like to call things adequate even when they blow your mind, right? And if you're offering me your buttery bagels I won't say no to having a taste of them again."

Geraldine laughed and scooped up a couple of bagels from the pile beside Justin Masters. She tossed them at him and Max caught them with a frown as she smiled sweetly.

"Actually, my breakfast is rather unsatisfying now I come to think of it. But feel free to gorge yourself on it, it seems you've got a taste for things that have been taken off the menu anyway."

Max bit his tongue and looked between all of us for a long second like he was trying to figure out how to respond to that.

He placed the bagels back down on the end of the table and brushed crumbs from his shirt. "Well, maybe...I'll just see you in Water Elemental later."

"It's highly likely as we will both be there," Geraldine agreed dismissively, reaching out to snag a muffin and picking a cherry out of it before placing it in her mouth. Her eyes were on her food and Max lingered for another long second before turning and strolling away. The taste of lust spilling from him increased as he walked and heads turned in his direction as girls all around The Orb got caught in the sway of his gifts. By the time he sat back down on the Heirs' couch, a swarm of hopeful girls were surrounding him.

Geraldine didn't even glance his way as she continued to pick at her muffin and a slow smile pulled at my lips as I watched her.

"Geraldine..." I said slowly. "Did you get lucky during the Eclipse?"

Darcy inhaled excitedly, her eyes widening as she looked to Geraldine too and Sofia sat up straighter in her chair.

Geraldine's cheeks pinked as she looked between all of us. Her lips parted and for a moment I thought she wasn't going to admit to anything then she fell back in her chair dramatically, laying her hand over her brow.

"I'm afraid to admit I did," she groaned. "My Lady Petunia set her gaze on a rather virile Siren and he fell prey to her amorous adventures."

Angelica spat out a mouthful of coffee as a bark of laughter fell from my lips.

"Did you just call your vagina Lady Petunia?" I choked.

Darcy covered her mouth to hold back her laughter and Sofia was actually crying real tears.

"Alas I did. And she's a real predator when she sets her gaze on a tempting piece of banana drama," Geraldine admitted.

"Holy shit," I gasped as my laughter made it hard for me to breathe.

Darcy was laughing so loud that people were starting to look our way and Angelica was gaping at Geraldine like she was looking at a stranger.

"An *Heir*?" she asked, a little bit horrified, a little bit impressed.

"He is pretty hot," Sofia added in Geraldine's defence.

"You have to tell us how it was," I pushed, my smile widening as I managed to calm my laughter.

Geraldine cracked a smile too, lowering her voice as we leaned together conspiratorially.

"Well…I will admit he knows how to water the lawn," she said.

"Fuck me, how is that a description?" I asked.

"Okay, he was very thorough," Geraldine added. "He pulled out the old buckaroo and whirl."

"What the hell is that?" Darcy demanded.

Geraldine smirked and I could tell that whatever the fuck it was had been pretty damn good.

"Are you going to see him again?" Sofia asked with a grin.

For a moment, Geraldine's gaze darkened with the memory of the banana drama she'd shared with the Water Heir, but she shook her head dismissively.

"I wrangled that cheeky chappy," she said slowly. "And I've put Lady Petunia back in her cage. She doesn't need another bite of that apple."

"So that's it?" Angelica asked.

"Yes. I'm afraid the scallywag will just have to accept I hit it and quit it. No need to go riding the same horse again, there are plenty more fillies to break in."

"Fuck yes, Geraldine!" I exclaimed, offering her a high five.

She slapped my hand with a shit eating grin on her face and my love for that girl grew tenfold. She was a goddamn savage and she'd caught Max Rigel in her net before tossing him aside like last week's trash.

I got to my feet with laughter still brimming in my throat. I was still wearing my running gear and I needed to get changed before class started.

"I'll see you in Tarot class," I said to Darcy and Sofia and my friends waved goodbye as I jogged away.

I was five minutes late by the time I made it back to Mercury Chambers and I ran down to the basement room before throwing the door open and spilling inside.

Professor Nox was perched on the desk at the back of the room, his long legs crossed as he looked around at the class. His black hair was messed up like he'd been running his hands through it or maybe like he'd been flying now I came to think of it. He wore a pair of black trousers and a white shirt, though he hadn't bothered with a tie like a lot of the staff did and the few open buttons revealed tattoos marking his chest. Even more ink peeked out beneath the cuffs around his wrists, the words *We Fall Together* catching my attention for a moment. He didn't really look like a teacher, he was too young and too cool to be spending his days in stuffy classrooms. But then again here he was, so what did I know?

I muttered an apology for my late arrival which he ignored and slipped around the room to join my sister and Sofia in their usual spots. Diego was still sitting on Sofia's other side too, but he'd inched his chair away from her and was looking straight ahead.

"Um, sir? Professor Nox?" Kylie called out as he paused whatever he'd been saying to wait while I sat down.

"Yes, Miss…"

"Major," she supplied for him with a bright smile, leaning forward to offer a view down her shirt which was unbuttoned enough for me to see her red bra from across the room. "It's just that tardiness usually results in lost House Points," she said, giving me a pointed look as I dropped into my seat.

"Uhuh. Five points from Aer," he said casually.

"That's Tory actually," Kylie put in as I scowled at her. "Darcy has the obnoxiously coloured hair."

"I happen to like obnoxiously coloured hair," Nox replied dryly. "And I'm aware which Vega arrived late. I was taking five points from Aer because I can't stand a snitch."

"But *sir!*" Kylie whined indignantly.

"Five more because I can't stand a moaner," he added with a cold smirk. "Oh and ten more for what you were just about to say about me to your little friend beside you."

"*What*? I wasn't going to say-"

"You were about to say that I might be just as hot as Professor Orion, but I'm obviously just as big of a dick too. And thanks for the compliment but you're not my type and I'm taken." He pointed to his eyes and my lips parted as I noticed the silver band ringing his dark irises. I didn't know how I'd managed to miss it before but now that I'd seen it, I couldn't look away. I'd begun to think the Elysian Mate thing was bullshit, but now I was looking at the evidence of its existence for myself. He'd met his one true love and had been gifted a life with them. My lips twitched at the thought of it, a small, hidden, romantic part of me secretly loving that idea. Not that I'd ever admit to it. But who wouldn't like the idea of knowing you'd found your perfect match in every way?

"I didn't…I wasn't…are you a psychic Order or something?" Kylie spluttered.

"Nope. But I do have The Sight so I get flashes of the future. Some of which are more important than others. So if you'd all like to start dealing your cards, I'll come around and see if anyone else here does too."

I exchanged a grin with my sister and we started shuffling our cards.

Before we'd cut the deck, Professor Nox came to stand in front of us. His strong features were set into a serious expression and he leaned forward slowly, pushing a card across the desk to sit between us.

He lifted a hand and cast a silencing bubble around us and I looked up in surprise as I felt it close around us.

"I've actually had a few strange readings recently," he said in a low voice. "Which is the reason I've joined the staff here at Zodiac. And I believe you might be able to help me find some of the answers I'm searching for."

"Us?" Darcy asked curiously.

"Why?" I added.

He withdrew his hand from the card he'd pushed towards us and my heart leapt as I felt the familiar taste of magic flowing from it. The image on it was of a naked woman leaning over a pool and pouring water from a jar. Several white stars and one large, yellow star hung in the sky above her.

"Is that…" Darcy began.

"Where did you get it?" I asked at the same time.

"I received this card a few weeks ago from someone known as Falling Star. The message attached to it led me to you." Professor Nox flipped the card over and my eyes widened as I read the message.

The Vega twins will lead you to the answers you've always sought.

He flipped the card over again and looked between us. "The Star card is a sign of peace and hope, of coming together and reunion, joy after heartache… For some reason, Falling Star wants to bring us together. And I'm hoping you'll want to figure out why with me?"

My heart started beating a little faster as I looked up at him. I didn't know where the hell he'd come from or why on Earth I wanted to trust him so badly, but I did. It felt like Falling Star was finally sending us something useful, someone who might really be able to help us figure out what all of these cards meant. Gabriel Nox could see the future, he was strong and capable and even better than that, determination shone in his gaze. For some reason he wanted these answers as much as we did. And I was pretty sure that with his help we'd be able to get them.

I looked at Darcy and she grinned as we both turned to accept Gabriel's help.

"We've been getting these cards too," Darcy said.

"But we never know what they mean until it's too late," I added. "Astrum really left us with a mind fuck when he up and died."

"Astrum? The Professor I've replaced as Tarot teacher?" he asked. "What's he got to do with this?"

"I thought you said you knew Falling Star?" Darcy asked hesitantly.

"I do. Well, I don't. I've been receiving messages and money from them for all of my life. Or at least for as long as I can remember anyway. But I don't know their real identity."

I pursed my lips and exchanged another look with Darcy. "Okay well, don't go getting your hopes up about meeting him then," I said.

"Why?" Gabriel asked, the intensity in his gaze making me wonder how he'd react to the answer.

"Because Astrum *was* Falling Star. He was trying to help us. Warning us about someone who was trying to hurt us and they killed him for it."

"What?" Gabriel gasped, his gaze travelling away from us and I was seized with the knowledge that he was having a vision. After a few minutes he shook his head to clear it and a deep frown creased his brow.

"Is everything okay?" Darcy asked him tentatively.

"Yes," he said dismissively. "It was nothing important. Just a possibility too far away to be certain. I'm sure that by being here The Sight will give me more answers in time. I think that the stars have brought us together so that we can figure this out. And I have the greatest sense that this is something truly important. We need to make sure the information we discover is kept between us until we know what to do with it."

"Sure," I replied, his intensity rattling me a bit as Darcy nodded her head in agreement too.

"I'll consult the stars about the details and let you know if I discover anything," Nox said.

"Okay," we agreed.

He gave us a tight smile and dropped the silencing bubble before striding away to talk to some of the other students about their cards.

"So what do you think?" Darcy asked me in a whisper as he moved away.

"That we might just be about to get some goddamn answers," I replied. And the look in her eyes told me she was hoping that was true just as fiercely as I was.

DARCY

CHAPTER SIX

I queued outside Cardinal Magic between Sofia and Tory, eyeing Diego who was close to the front of the line in his uniform and black beanie hat, staring at his Atlas.

"Is he ever going to drop the shit?" Tory said under her breath.

"He hardly even talks to me anymore either," Sofia said with a sad frown.

"I don't get why he doesn't just apologise," I said.

Part of me still felt bad for hitting him after he'd said he wished Orion had died when the Nymphs attacked. But even though I knew Diego had reasons to dislike Orion, I still felt fiercely protective of him and the mere suggestion of him being hurt had sent me to a dark place.

The door flew open and Orion stepped out of the classroom with a stern look. "Are you all loitering out here on purpose today?"

Everyone stared at him in surprise.

"Since when is he *ever* on time?" Tory whispered and I stifled a laugh.

"Today obviously. Miss Vega. Now get inside!" he barked, turning and striding back into the room as everyone hurried to follow.

I headed to my seat, finding Diego's desk vacated beside mine and spotting him walking towards the back of the room, dropping into an empty seat. I pursed my lips, trying to catch his eye but he determinedly looked at his Atlas.

The white-blond boy, Elijah Indus, moved to his desk, his chair still missing since the last time he'd pissed Orion off so he had to remain standing, looking tired already as he laid out his books.

I faced the board, curious as Orion wrote his quote of the day on the board.

YOU ALL PASSED THE RECKONING.

I arched a brow, glancing at Tory. "That's almost a compliment," I breathed and she laughed, but our amusement died away as Orion added more to the board.

THE STARS MUST BE FUCKING WITH ME.

He turned to us with a wide grin and a few nervous laughs rang out. When he didn't rebuke them, several more people laughed and a smile tugged at the corner of my mouth.

"Right, Corbin." He pointed at Tyler in the front row. "Give me one good reason why you're still sitting in my classroom."

"I er, passed The Reckoning, sir?" Tyler tried.

"That's a mindlessly fucking stupid answer," Orion said, his smile withering. "Try again."

"Umm…I got an A on my Tarot paper the other week?" he suggested with a shrug.

"You got a B minus," Orion corrected, arching a brow.

"How did you-" Tyler started, but Orion cut over him.

"You're still here, Tyler, because as much as you irritate the stars right out of the night sky, you also challenge me every damn lesson." He seemed both angry and pleased about that. He rounded on the rest of the class as Tyler seemed slightly dazed by the backhanded compliment. "About ten percent of this class test me on a weekly basis. They question my knowledge, they act out, they talk back to me, they write me endless emails about why they can't do their assignments, or about why it was covered in Dragon shit when they did - *Mr Indus*." His gaze swivelled onto me and Tory as he moved to lean back against his desk. "That ten percent will most likely make it to the second semester of their freshman year. The other ninety…" He shrugged. "Maybe you're wasting everyone's time."

A dark haired girl - who I was fairly sure was called Nicole - raised her hand near the front of the class.

"Miss Metivier?" Orion asked and she cleared her throat.

"Are you saying you *want* us to break the rules, sir?" She frowned, glancing around at the rest of the class.

I sensed an impending storm as Orion drifted closer to her. "I'm saying, Fae don't take shit lying down. So how about you stand up and get the hell out of my classroom if that lesson hasn't sunk into your head yet."

She rose from her seat and Orion smiled manically as she took a step toward the door, then halted.

"No," she breathed and my heart skittered as Orion's jaw clenched.

"No?" he purred.

"No, sir. I'm going to stay." She hesitantly moved back to her seat and dropped into it, her face paling, but her posture full of determination.

An endless pause filled the air between them.

"Good," he said with a dark glint in his gaze. "Detention Thursday."

"*What?*" she gasped.

"You heard me!" he roared and she shrank away from him, nodding quickly. He moved back to the board and tapped the screen to bring up a list of clubs and societies at the school.

Pitball – *try outs will be held each semester. Competition to get onto the official school team is fierce, but substitute positions are always available.*

Cheerleading – *The squad are always looking for guys and gals with upbeat personalities, who love to dance and chant!*

Star Charting – *midnight sessions are required and Orders with enhanced night vision are always welcomed with enthusiasm!*

Tarot Club – *members with an affinity for foresight are encouraged to flex their predictive muscles in our club.*

Elemental Combat – *students will learn how to fight against those who have harnessed other Elements to them. (Please be aware that this is a highly hazardous club).*

Order Mixers – *each term we will arrange opportunities for the different Orders to come together and offer their abilities out to each other. So if you like the idea of riding on a Pegasus or having your stress drained by a Siren then this is the place for you!*

Fate Dodging – *a group dedicated to trying to thwart our horoscopes. If you like the idea of trying to change your fate then why not come and spend time with a bunch of like-minded individuals?*

Blood Donation – *want to earn extra credit by donating blood/power to the vampire students? Or maybe you just enjoy the feeling of fangs in your neck? Whatever your motivation, come and join us at our bi-weekly sessions with the Vampire Order!*

Extreme Hunt – *fancy your chances at evading the hunters? Or would you prefer to join the pack? Then our weekly hunts might be for you! We give the 'prey' two hours to try and escape 'hunters' in their Order forms in a bloodthirsty race which is followed up by a celebration back at The Orb. (Vampires are encouraged not to join due to their dangerous hunting instincts and the guidelines in the Vampire Code).*

Study Club – *a group of serious, like-minded students who prefer the company of books to socialising. We meet in the Venus Library most days and study at separate desks in utter silence – bliss! Sphinxes will find this club particularly favourable.*

Almighty Sovereign Society – *Come and join ranks with the rootenist*

"Now that you have officially enrolled at the academy, you are required to sign up to at least one club or society for extra credit. You should all have sent your choices to me already. The deadline was this morning," Orion said, hooking his Atlas off the desk as my heart sank like a stone.

"What?" I whispered to Tory. "Did you know about that?"

She shook her head. "No idea."

"He sent the email last Thursday," Sofia hissed, her eyes wide with alarm.

Oh shit.

I checked my Atlas emails, scanning through them and locating the one from Orion. I'd been so busy with the Trials and the Reckoning, I hadn't been checking them at all and it looked like Tory hadn't either.

"If you haven't sent in your decision, please stand up now," Orion commanded and Tory and I rose from our seats.

I cursed under my breath as I realised we were the only ones in the whole damn class to have missed this email. I could hear Kylie and Jillian sniggering and heat rose along the back of my neck.

Orion looked between us like we were two rare steaks he was about to devour. "Do either of you have an explanation for not choosing a club? Or shall I just put it down to a lack of intelligence?" He smirked and I rolled my eyes at his crap, making his gaze sharpen on me.

"Something you want to share with the class, Miss Vega?"

"Well is it really that big of a deal? We'll just pick one now," I said.

"Yeah, let's join the Ass Club," Tory said easily, dropping back down into her seat.

"Oh no, Miss Vega, the time for choosing has passed. *Now stand back up!*"

Tory got to her feet again with a huff and Orion smiled cruelly at her, sending a flicker of anxiety through me. He glanced over his shoulder at the list of clubs then turned back to her with his gaze glittering. "I think the cheer squad will suit your jovial nature, Tory. They practice two nights a week on Tuesdays and Thursdays at the Pitball Stadium. I'm sure your Cheer Captain,

Marguerite Helebor, will be most welcoming." He dismissed Tory with a wave of his hand but she didn't move, looking like she was about to spit venom.

I stared at Orion in fury on her behalf. My sister was about as far from a cheerleader as you could get, especially on a team full of Marguerite Helebors.

"No thanks," Tory said with a tsk. "I wanna join the Ass Club."

Orion bared his fangs and my pulse quickened. "You're officially assigned to the Cheer Squad, now sit the fuck down or I'll give you detention."

"Just try not screw every guy on the Pitball team, yeah Tory?" Kylie said in a sweet voice and we both spun around in rage.

"Shut up!" Orion bellowed, throwing out a hand and a blast of air knocked Kylie off of her chair onto her ass.

A laugh tumbled from my throat and I turned back to face the front, finding Orion fixing his gaze on me.

He ran his tongue across his fangs, seeming to consider something. "Pitball team. Tryouts are next Thursday." A few people sucked in breaths as he turned away from me and my ears rang with those words as he tapped the board to start the lesson. I was still on my feet, my heart thrashing in my chest. Not only was Pitball the most brutal sport I'd ever witnessed in my entire life, but all of the Heirs were on the damn team. Why the hell would he assign me to that?

"Excuse me, *sir*?" I questioned icily.

"Sit down, Miss Vega," he growled and I gritted my teeth.

"Do you really think Pitball is a good fit for me?" I demanded.

"Yes. I think it's the perfect fit. Any more pointless questions you'd like to waste my time with?" He glanced over his shoulder, raising a brow and I could see the mischief sparkling under all that assholeness. Whatever reason he had, I'd damn well get it from him outside of class.

I dropped back into my seat and Sofia gave both of us anxious looks. "Maybe he'll let you swap after a week or so," she offered weakly, but I had the feeling there wasn't much chance of that.

"Today we'll be conducting our first official practical lesson of the semester."

Low chatter sounded around the room, but Orion didn't bother to acknowledge it as he tapped the board and the lesson title appeared.

Silencing Bubbles.

My mood picked up at that and I attempted to push all worrying thoughts of Pitball tryouts from my head as I prepared to learn a new spell – which was pretty damn impossible as I kept picturing myself on that Pitch being squashed by the four Heirs like a mouse under a steamroller. It was all very well Emerging as a fiercely powerful Phoenix, but I was pretty sure no Order powers were allowed to be used in the game.

Damn you, Lance. I'm gonna get you back for this.

"Miss Major, can you please tell me about something you got up to this weekend?" Orion asked out of the blue and everyone turned to Kylie in surprise.

"Um…really? Okay. Well I went to the mall on Saturday and my friend Sinead was all like *oh my stars, Kylie, did you notice that freakishly hot Minotaur checking you out?* And I was like-" she continued on but suddenly I couldn't hear a word coming out of her mouth. Everyone started laughing and she became more animated in her story, apparently thinking we were all totally engaged by it.

"Silencing spells can be used to stop sound escaping a certain area or to silence someone or something you would rather not hear," Orion explained. "For example, Miss Major's dull weekend adventures with her vapid friends."

A snort of laughter escaped me as Kylie's mouth stopped moving as she clearly heard him and Orion waved his hand to release her from the silencing bubble.

"*I'm* not vapid," Jillian complained from beside her with a sulky expression.

"Miss Minor, what is the definition of vapid?" Orion stared her down and she froze, glancing to Kylie for help, but she only looked skyward in annoyance.

"Well- er- it means – er – egg-like?"

Laughter poured through the air and Tyler cheered, waving his Atlas. "I totally caught that entire moment on camera, Jillian. Hashtag black hole for a brain."

"Screw you, Tyler!" Jillian shouted, turning bright red.

He started tapping away as he uploaded the post to FaeBook and Orion did nothing to stop him as a low rumble of laughter escaped him too.

Orion tapped the board and everyone fell quiet. "You all need to practice this hand movement." A diagram of a hand appeared which moved to show the twisting flourish I'd seen him cast plenty of times. Most recently to stop anyone overhear us making out or tearing each other's clothes off.

My mind drifted onto those memories and I chewed on my lip as I let my gaze travel down his chest. He was still talking but I couldn't hear a word as my eyes reached his waistband and I fell prey to a seriously dirty fantasy. *I wonder if he keeps a ruler in his drawer he could teach me a lesson with…*

"Are you concentrating, Miss Vega?" Orion barked suddenly and I sat up straight, finding everyone around me waving one hand in the air as they practised the movement. "Would you like to share your little daydream with the rest of the class?" He smirked, telling me he knew exactly what I'd just been thinking about and I cleared my throat.

"No sir," I said firmly.

"Then focus or I'll make you share it," he said and his tone sent a quake through me that set my pulse racing.

I nodded, hiding a grin and he moved swiftly on to start correcting people's hand movements.

I raised my right palm, following the diagram and twisting it through the air in a sort of scooping fashion. Twisting to the right silenced a sound or person and to the left cast a bubble of silence around yourself. I was always worried about people listening in around this school, especially as I had so many damn secrets to carry these days, so this spell was a godsend.

When Orion was satisfied we all had it, he finally taught us the spell.

"Practise by casting a bubble around yourself first. Let your magic flow without Elemental form and use its energy to create a shield surrounding your body. Make sure you feel out any gaps in its surface where sound might slip through."

I shut my eyes to concentrate, moving my hand in the correct motion as I let magic float to the surface of my skin, gently pushing it away from me to encase my body. My ears popped and it felt like pressured air was closing in on me.

I blinked, looking to Tory as she cast her own spell. The world around me was still loud and I spoke to get Tory's attention, the word echoing back to me like a drum. I winced against the noise as it continued to ping off of the solid bubble I'd formed around myself. On the one hand, I'd clearly blocked sounds from escaping it but I'd planted myself inside a goddamn megaphone too.

I dissolved the magic with a breath of relief and my ears popped again just as Tory tried to catch my attention inside her own silencing bubble. I couldn't hear anything and I gave her a thumbs up, realising a second later she could hear me and I released a laugh.

I spent the next twenty minutes practising and finally managed to get the hang of it, allowing just enough magic into the cast so that no one could hear me and I didn't feel suffocated at the same time.

"Good." Orion pressed a hand to my shoulder, making me jump. "Now try reversing it so you block out the sound around you." He walked on and a smile spread across my face as I tried what he'd said, flicking my hand in the opposite direction and forcing my magic out from my body. The world fell utterly silent, except for a very faint noise on the edge of my hearing.

I shut my eyes to try and locate the source of it, pushing my magic toward the edges of the room to try and quiet it. It sounded like someone whispering, but I couldn't quite hear what they were saying. A heaviness seeped over me and the whispers grew a little louder.

"Almost...closer."

A deep thrumming started up in my chest like the dull beat of a drum, the rhythm tantalising, drawing me into a state of utter calm. My body relaxed so much I almost felt detached from it, floating in the endless dark expanse of my mind.

"Into...falling...help."

The voice sounded broken, louder and quieter intermittently and I couldn't grasp any of the words in between the few I caught. But something made me long to reach out to whoever it was as bliss washed through me, asking me to give in to its call.

I hit the floor, blinking hard as pain flared along the back of my head. I found my sister leaning over me, shouting something I couldn't hear. Someone pushed her aside, the world still entirely quiet as Orion came into view, taking my hand so his magic came flooding into my body. I inhaled in shock as his power blended with mine and he dispelled the wall of silence I'd cast around myself so the sound of the class rushed back into my ears.

"-the hell happened?" Orion demanded, his hand still firmly locked around mine and his eyes alight with worry.

My mouth was overly dry and my head hurt where I must have smacked it on the floor. I sat upright, rubbing it and Orion knocked my hand aside, healing the bump in an instant.

I knew what had happened. The shadows had lured me into them and that strange voice...it was the same one I'd heard when Lionel had sent us into the darkness. Fear gripped my bones, but I didn't even know what I was afraid of. Just that I should be terrified.

Tory pushed past Orion and he released me as she pulled me upright. "Are you okay?" she looked between my eyes like she knew exactly what had happened, but I couldn't say anything right then.

"Yeah, I'm okay. I think I cut my air supply off by accident." I forced out a laugh, my eyes catching on Diego who was standing beyond Sofia with a wide-eyed look. As he met my gaze, he dipped his head and hurried back to his seat.

I glanced at Orion who didn't look convinced by what I'd said and I dropped back into my seat, looking away from him until he left.

I shared an anxious look with Tory that told her I'd explain after class and she nodded, chewing on her lip.

By the time the bell rang, I'd shaken off the strange feeling which had lingered with me after I'd come out of the shadows, but I couldn't forget that faraway voice.

As I headed out of the classroom, Orion called to me, "Your Liaison's been moved to tonight, Miss Vega, as there wasn't one on Monday."

I nodded to him, slipping out of the room, certain he was going to grill me on what had really happened today. I wasn't sure why he didn't believe me, but I could tell he didn't. And I wished I could just be honest about it because he was one of the only people in the world who could probably help.

I caught Tory's elbow, drawing her out of the crowd as we exited Jupiter

Hall into the frosty air. Sofia gave us a curious look and I hated the fact I had to lie to her too as I said, "We'll catch you up, we've got to pick up some packages from Pluto Offices."

"Is it another mountain of clothes to feed Tory's habit?" Sofia laughed.

"Yep, she's got issues," I said and Tory shrugged innocently before we hurried away. She immediately cast a silencing bubble around us with a triumphant grin, then tugged me closer.

"So? Was it the shadows?" Her smile fell away as concern took its place.

"Yeah," I said on a breath. "But not just them...I heard that voice again, you know the one we heard when-"

"I heard her again too!" she gasped, her eyes glinting with darkness. "In my dreams, but I couldn't hear what she was saying, it was just distant whispers."

"Same," I said, a chill running through me. "Who do you think it is?"

"God only knows. And I'm not sure I want to find out anyway."

I fell silent for a moment and Tory nudged me to make me spill my thoughts. I sighed heavily, pulling her to a halt. "I think we should tell Orion."

"No," she said instantly.

"*Tory*," I impressed and she pursed her lips, glancing away. I reached out and touched her arm until she looked back at me. "I know you don't trust him, but I do."

"You don't trust anyone," she balked and I realised my mistake, cursing myself internally.

"I mean, I trust him about this. He knows about the shadows and all kinds of dark magic. And it's not like he can tell anyone what we say." I hoped I'd covered my tracks and relaxed a bit when Tory didn't question me further.

"Ugh, *fine*. But I swear to god if he starts lecturing us-"

"He won't," I promised.

"Why have you got so much faith in him, Darcy?" Tory frowned and I wanted to answer her so badly it hurt. My eyes drifted to my shoes and I tried to come up with an answer that wasn't a lie.

"Because I know he can be an asshole, but he's helped us too. And I know he wanted to save us from this happening."

A beat of silence passed between us as Tory considered that. When I glanced up, I found her looking at the sky as a group of Griffins flew overhead. "Wanting to save someone isn't the same as doing it."

"He tried. They both tried," I said, tipping my head back to watch the beautiful beasts soar away toward The Wailing Wood. I didn't exactly like to defend Darius Acrux, but I'd seen what he did that night, seen the position he'd been in. And Tory had too. It wasn't like I was excusing anything else he'd done. For all the other shit, he could rot in hell.

"I guess," she said noncommittally. "Doesn't change who they are though."

"No…they're the only ones who can choose to change."

She nodded and on that, it seemed we agreed.

I brought Tory to my Liaison with Orion at seven o'clock, not bothering to hurry as I was sure he'd be late anyway. As we headed up the marble staircase past a few students loitering in the hallways, I began to grow nervous.

What the hell was he going to think when he found out we had this dark power in us too? Was he going to flip out? Start drinking?

Yep, most likely both of those things.

I was just gonna have to roll with the punches.

Tory stared at her Atlas, mindlessly flipping through the FaeBook feed and she snorted a laugh as she held it out for me to read one of the posts.

Sandeep Athwal:
D.A.A meeting tonight in The Orb. (Dump Addicts Anonymous) Come and drop a load on us for some much needed relief. No judgement. It's okay to crave a brown shower. #everyonelovesasuperpooper #ploptilyoudrop #whyflushit #poosmorefunwithtwo #powerfulsirenswelcome

Comments:
Nicole Neethling:
These rumours about Max aren't true!!
Ashleigh Logan:

The Water Heir don't care, he rubs shit in his hair. #drinkthestink

Barry Gurra:

Anyone spreading these lies will answer to me!

Christine Wortman:

It's never okay to crave a brown shower! #yellowonly

Tyler Corbin:

Max puts the real poo in his shampoo. #tastetheturd
#icandoapooandboxitforyou

I choked on a laugh as Tory continued to scroll, then knocked on Orion's door out of habit even though I didn't think he'd actually be there yet.

"Come in," he called, surprising me and I headed into the room.

He stood, pressing the front of his shirt down with a slanted smile. On the desk was a bottle of red wine and a small box wrapped with a ribbon. With a sharp inhale, he snatched the box, stuffing it in his pocket half a second before Tory looked up from her Atlas beside me. Her gaze fell on the wine and two glasses and her brow furrowed.

"Dude, you are half a percent cooler to me now." She moved to his desk, opening the wine and filling the glasses, picking one up and handing the other one to me. "You'll need an extra glass though tonight."

"I can see that," he said in a low growl, dropping down into his chair and not making a move to get another glass.

I mouthed an apology behind Tory's back, figuring I probably should have given him a heads up about bringing her along. But I hadn't exactly expected him to have wine and a damn gift. But also, *ooh what kind of gift??*

I pulled up a chair and Orion looked between us, stacking his hands on his stomach as he leaned back in his seat. "So why am I getting the treat of double vision right now?"

"Because we have something real fun to tell you," Tory said dryly, sipping her wine.

I took a mouthful of my own to steady my pulse as Orion sat up straighter with a frown. "Like?"

"Well…" I started, biting into my lip. "We kind of lied to you about the shadows."

77

"What do you mean?" A dangerous tone sharpened his voice as he leaned forward and laid his palms on the desk.

"They didn't pass through us," Tory supplied.

"They stayed with us," I finished.

Orion remained icily still, his gaze darkening as he searched our faces for a lie. "Impossible. They can't have." He rose from his seat suddenly, knocking his chair back and clawing a hand through his hair.

"Yeah so...I'm gonna go get dinner now." Tory got up.

"SIT DOWN!" Orion bellowed and she dropped back into her seat like a falling stone.

Tory looked to me with a scowl. "I told you we can't trust this asshole."

"Miss Vega if you think you can talk to me like that and get away with-"

"We need you to help us manage them," I spoke over him. "No one else can."

His eyes whipped to me, an ache building in them like this news was breaking his heart.

He shook his head, starting to pace and I shared a glance with Tory as we waited for him to say something. My insides twisted up as he continued to move anxiously back and forth.

Finally, he slammed his hands down on the desk, glaring at us across it. "This is so much fucking worse than you think. You can already feel its draw, can't you?"

"Yes," I breathed.

His eyes flared with realisation. "That's what happened to you in class," he snarled, but not like he was angry at me, like he was angry at the whole world *besides* me.

I nodded and Tory reached out to rest a hand on my arm.

Orion's brows pulled together. "Do you know what will happen if you give into it? Do you know how many years it takes to master the ability to pull away from them?"

"No, but you can help. Teach us?" I asked desperately and he shut his eyes for a long second.

"Told you he couldn't help us," Tory muttered to me and Orion's eyes flew open, shooting a hard stare at her that could have crumbled the Great

Wall of China.

"I damn well *can* help you. And I will when I get over the shock of this. But here's a quick pop quiz first: are you two conspiring to give me a fucking heart attack?"

A small smile pulled at my lips and his expression softened a fraction. He sighed heavily and sank back down into his seat. "So long as there's nothing else-"

"There is just *one* other thing," I cut across him before he could fall into the hope that that sentence was clearly bringing him.

"What?" he ground out through his teeth and I swallowed the lump pushing at my throat, knowing this was going to sound entirely insane. But at least my sister could back me up on it.

"There's this voice. A woman's voice, I think. But it's so distant, it's hard to tell. Do you hear that too?" I asked, sitting forward in my chair.

"The whispers are souls trapped in the shadows," he said darkly and my heart thumped an uneven beat. "They're Fae who have lost themselves to its power. It uses them to trick you, to lure you into its claws. But if you go, you'll become lost, joining them forever in an endless void."

"Nice, remind me not to book my next vacation there then. But the thing is, Professor, it's a specific voice we're hearing, is that normal?" Tory frowned.

Orion released a hollow laugh. "Nothing is normal about any of this. But...no I can't say I've ever heard a specific voice. I don't know why that would be the case."

"I thought you knew about dark magic and the shadows," Tory said in frustration.

"I do." He thought for a long moment and I shifted in my seat. "Maybe now we're attached to the shadows, the souls can connect to us directly." He shrugged one shoulder. "I don't have a better answer than that right now, it's just speculation. But I'll look into it."

"In your little book of black magic?" Tory taunted and he pursed his lips.

"Yeah I keep it with my Ouija board and voodoo dolls," Orion deadpanned.

I leaned forward, speaking before this could descend into an argument. "So what do we do now?"

He drew in a long breath. "Fuck, well…Darius won't like it, but you need to learn to wield this power. You'll have to join him for our classes in dark magic."

Tory tossed her head back with a groan. "Can't you just teach us separately? I do not wanna hang out with that douchebag."

"It's risky enough as it is. We have to keep the lessons to a minimum, this is not a fucking extra curricular activity, Miss Vega."

She huffed, giving in and rising to her feet. "Fine, let us know when and where. Right now I'm starving, have a *great* Liaison, Darcy." She gave me a sorrowful look like leaving me here was bordering on cruel and I frowned as she slipped out of the door.

Orion got up, heading across the room to lock it with physical and magical locks before knocking his head back against the door.

"I was an idiot to bring the wine," he said, shaking his head at himself.

"No, it was sweet," I said, standing and he glanced at me with shadows swirling in his gaze.

"It was moronic." He kicked off of the door, striding toward me and dragging me against him, pressing his mouth to mine. The blinds were drawn across the windows but I still felt that electric buzz of fear as we did this right here in the middle of campus.

I trailed my hands down his sides, our kiss slow and torturous as we enjoyed the stolen moment of bliss. A deep pit of fiery power seemed to open up in my chest, blazing through my veins and rushing to meet the magic in him. I suddenly felt like I was standing on a precipice, about to tumble into its embrace as ecstasy rippled on the edges of my mind. I moaned and Orion growled, dragging me closer as our power blended and the flow of his energy twisted through me like a tornado.

"Shit," he breathed as he pulled away. "You taste like fire."

"How would you know? Do you often eat fire?" I teased, winding my fingers into his hair as I tip-toed up to brush my mouth over his again, breathing in the scent of cinnamon that clung to him.

"Not every day," he murmured against my lips. "It gives me indigestion."

I laughed and his deep chuckle came in response.

"So…I think I recall you snatching a pretty little box off of the table when my sister walked in." I raised my brows, grinning up at him and I could have freaking sworn his cheeks touched with colour. "Are you *blushing*?" I gasped excitedly and he chewed the inside of his cheek.

"No," he grunted. "I'm just starting to think the present was a stupid idea."

"Maybe I should be the judge of that." I slipped my hands beneath his jacket, hunting for the box and he raised his arms like I was a cop, smirking as I searched him. I tugged it out as I found it and he dropped his hands, sucking on his lower lip as he waited for me to open it.

I untied the ribbon, flipping off the lid and my breath snagged in my lungs as I found a pale pink crystal inside which glimmered like starlight.

"Wow," I breathed, taking it from the nest of silk.

Orion cleared his throat, running a hand down the back of his neck. "It's rose quartz."

"It's beautiful." I turned the silken stone over in my palm, a warm energy seeming to emit from it that felt like a piece of everything good in the world.

He caught my hand, wrapping his around it so the crystal was contained within my fist. I glanced up at him and his eyes flickered with some fierce emotion. "In Solaria we have a tradition of giving rose quartz to someone we want to be exclusive with."

"You do?" I whispered, my heart pounding madly.

"Yeah." He squeezed my hand. "Look, I don't know what this thing is between us or where it's going, Blue, but after everything that's happened, the one thing that's clear to me is that I don't want anyone else. So this crystal is a promise from me that I'm yours. For now. Forever. Or till it all goes to shit, I don't know which yet." He smiled hopefully and my heart could have burst with how much this meant to me.

I reached up to touch my lips to his. "Thank you."

He released my hand and I tucked the quartz into my blazer pocket with a shy smile.

"You're making it really hard to stay mad at you," I said, pulling away from him.

"Why are you mad at me?" He frowned.

"Pitball, Lance? Are you screwing with me?" I placed my hands on my hips and he grinned devilishly, hounding forward as I backed away beyond his desk.

"You're powerful. Once you're trained, you could be a fucking legend on the pitch." He continued to stalk me as I placed his chair between us, smiling cheekily.

His fangs lengthened and his eyes sparkled as he pushed it aside. I leapt toward the cupboard door at the back of the office, wrenching it open and slipping inside. I forgot the game as I found myself in a small room with books stacked neatly on shelves lining the walls. I reached out to brush the spine of a huge leather bound journal which was etched with silver stars. Orion slid an arm around my waist, dropping his mouth to my neck and grazing his fangs across my skin.

"Do you like my tiny library?" he asked in a playful voice and I smiled.

"You're a total geek," I said, loving that about him as he laughed against the crook of my neck. He placed a soft kiss there which sent a deep shudder through to my core.

I turned my head, a glint catching my eye and I pulled away from Orion as I moved toward a line of shelves which weren't stacked with books. Pitball trophies filled every spare space and my heart beat harder as I brushed my fingers over them, all branded with Orion's name. He'd won *Fae of the Match* countless times and there were several tournament trophies in a dusty corner which looked liked they'd gone untouched for years. I located a framed photograph amongst them, glancing over my shoulder as I picked it up, finding Orion watching me from the doorway with a nervous sort of expression.

I gazed at the picture of his team. Orion stood at the heart of it in a pristine Pitball kit in the navy and silver colours of Zodiac Academy. He had a Captain badge pinned to his chest and a Pitball tucked under his arm. He must have been a year or so older than I was now and wore the most carefree smile in the world. I brushed my fingers over the picture, wondering what had gone so wrong for him that he'd lost that hopeful glimmer in his eyes which said he had the whole world at his feet.

"I was an Airsentry," Orion spoke at last. "Best damn one in Solaria for a while."

"You look happy," I said, my voice unexpectedly sad, because deep down, I knew Orion wasn't truly happy anymore. Something had broken in him since this picture had been taken and it hurt me to know it, knotting up my chest like tangled wire.

"I was," he said in a low tone, then cleared his throat. "Maybe we should get back to the lesson now, huh?"

I placed the picture down, painting on a bright smile as I turned to him and took his outstretched hand. The wall in his eyes said he didn't want to talk about it right then, and I would respect that. But I hoped one day he'd tell me. Because then maybe I could try to find a way to reignite the fire that no longer burned in his heart.

TORY

CHAPTER SEVEN

I headed down to Air Cove with Darcy by my side and an uncomfortable feeling in the pit of my stomach. The last time we'd come down here at night and gotten close to dark magic, I'd ended up half bleeding to death and having Darius nearly choke me.

So walking back down to the same spot to meet the same asshole in the dark did not appeal to me on any level.

If it wasn't for the fact that the shadows within me most definitely needed wrangling under control, I wouldn't have been going at all.

But the fact was that the dreams were getting worse. I woke up with a pounding heart and sweat slicked skin several times a night and each time the shadows rose in me, I was finding it a little harder to fight off their lure.

There was something about the darkness in them that coaxed me closer despite the danger I knew they possessed.

I couldn't put my finger on what it was, but even though they inspired terror in me, they whispered sweet promises too. They offered me power and euphoria, the removal of all of my pain. And I knew their call would only continue to grow stronger until they lured me to them unless I learned how to fight them off more effectively.

As we walked across the sand, two dark figures came into view ahead of us and I chewed on my bottom lip as I recognised Darius's huge frame.

Orion stood beside him and I looked between the two of them in the faint silvery glow of moonlight which made it through the clouds.

"You're late," Orion muttered as he spotted us and I scoffed lightly.

"You're a fine one to talk about being late. Besides, *sir,* as this lesson doesn't make it onto the official syllabus I'm not inclined to give a shit," I said.

Darcy snorted a laugh and nudged me with her elbow to tell me off. To my surprise, Orion smirked too.

"You're gonna need that attitude in place if you want to fight off the shadows, Tory. But I'll be happy to give you detention if you keep mouthing off at me," he replied.

"If you give me a detention for something I do or say while we're working on this then I won't be coming back. I've never needed anybody to fix my problems for me before and I'll happily figure this out without the two of you if I have to," I said in return. Because fuck it, there were a hundred places I'd rather be spending my evening than in the company of the two of them and if it became any more torturous than I could tolerate then I was fully willing to bail. I'd figure the shadows out myself if I had to.

"Don't be an idiot, Roxy. You need to learn how to keep control of the shadows or they'll end up destroying you," Darius snarled.

"Well at least then I'd make you happy for once," I threw back.

His gaze darkened as he looked at me. "You can't seriously think that?"

I shrugged and looked away from him because I didn't even know anymore. All I did know was that every time I let him get close to me I got hurt, so it wouldn't be happening again.

"Shall we just get started?" Darcy suggested.

"Good idea," Orion agreed, turning and scoring a mark into the cliff wall beside us using his draining dagger to open the cave entrance. He started guiding it in a familiar pattern and I recalled how I'd opened this place before.

He strode inside with Darius beside him and Darcy caught my arm before we followed.

"I know he's a total dick, Tory, but Darius is a part of this mess. We don't have anyone else we can ask for help with this, so do you think you can at least *try* to be civil? Your temper is only going to make this whole thing harder otherwise." She looked at me sternly and that in itself was enough to make me back off. Darcy hardly ever called me out on my shit, so if she was doing it now then I really must have been acting like an asshat.

I let out a heavy breath. "Yeah, okay," I agreed.

"We just need to figure this out. The shadows make it so much easier to see the worst in things. Once we know how to fight them off better, hopefully you won't still feel so angry..."

I bit my tongue on replying because although I was showing anger to the world, that wasn't really what I was feeling. The overriding emotions I felt whenever Darius got close to me was betrayal. And I couldn't for the life of me figure out why. But for some reason I felt so strongly about it that I couldn't stand to be around him and face those feelings at all.

"Fine. I'll make peace," I promised, reaching out to grip her fingers. Because if there was one thing strong enough to make me swallow my pride, it was my love for my sister. And she needed to learn to protect herself from the shadows too.

We headed into the cave and Darius watched us as he took up position leaning against the back wall.

I took a deep breath, trying to figure out some way to do what I'd said and call time on the arguing with him. Saying sorry was probably my best bet, but the words were sticking in my throat hard enough to choke me.

Darcy gave me an encouraging look and I ground my teeth for a moment before forcing myself to speak.

"Look," I began slowly. "I know that the two of you are trying to help us and me having an attitude like a cat with a knitting needle up it's ass isn't helpful."

Orion and Darius were both looking at me like they couldn't quite believe the words coming out of my mouth, but I pressed on for the sake of peacekeeping and more importantly, making sure that Darcy's progress against the shadows wouldn't be hindered by me.

"So I'm...sorry. For being a bitch," I clarified because I wasn't sorry for any of the things I felt. "And I'm not going to keep causing arguments."

Orion raised an eyebrow at me, cutting a glance to Darcy for a moment before smiling. "Good," he said finally before looking at Darius expectantly.

"It's cute that you think you can just switch off your attitude problem," Darius taunted. "But if you really can play nice then I can too." Of course he didn't apologise to me for any of the shit he'd put me through because why the hell would he? He was an arrogant, entitled, selfish prick and expecting him to take ownership of any of his bullshit was like expecting the moon not to rise because it had offended the sun.

A thousand insults sprang to my lips and I had to bite my tongue so hard I drew blood. But fuck him. I didn't have an attitude problem; I had a Dragon problem. And if I couldn't avoid it then there was one thing I sure as shit *could* do. I'd ignore it.

I smiled sweetly and walked towards Orion like Darius hadn't even spoken. Like he didn't exist. It would be as if there was a Dragon shaped fart in the room and I just had to avoid getting too close to sniff it. Aside from that, I didn't need to acknowledge his presence. If he didn't exist, then I had nothing to get worked up about.

"So what do we need to do about the shadows?" I asked Orion, turning so my back was to Darius.

He glanced between me and the fart then indicated the floor before moving to take a seat on it. Darcy sat opposite him and I dropped down beside her. Darius sat in front of me but I kept my eyes on Orion.

The rocky ground beneath my ass was stupidly uncomfortable and I pressed my palm to the stone, pushing earth magic from my fingers as I willed the hard lumps to even out. With a bit more effort, I even managed to make the hard ground softer so it was kinda like sitting on a cushion.

I smirked at my achievement and pressed my magic out to do the same to the ground beneath Darcy and Orion.

Orion looked at me in surprise as he settled back into his now comfortable spot. "You're gaining better control of your earth magic," he commented and I smirked.

"Geraldine's been helping us practice," I replied.

"She's a really good teacher," Darcy agreed. She touched her own fingers to the floor between us and I could feel her magic dancing in the air for a moment before silver lines appeared all over the surface of the stone as she drew minerals together within the rocks until they formed the image of a rose.

"I should give you both extra house points," Orion said with a smile.

"Why, what did Roxy do?" Darius asked in confusion from his uncomfortable rocky patch of ground. I was half tempted to make his spot even lumpier, but that would involve me acknowledging him.

Orion glanced at me but I didn't react. His gaze shifted to the ground beneath Darius and I could see him trying to figure out whether or not to call me out. I hadn't done anything to Darius so he couldn't really accuse me of anything though.

"So the first thing you need to work on is drawing yourselves back from the shadows," Orion said eventually, clearly deciding not to broach the subject of uncomfortable asses. "You will need to listen to the call of them and let them draw you closer before pulling yourself back again. It's easiest to find your way back with someone else to anchor you initially. It's what the two of you did for each other in the crater when Lionel fed you to the shadows. A part of you stayed latched to each other so you were able to break free of the dark hold of the Shadow Realm."

"So do we need to hold hands then?" Darcy asked, leaning forward a little like learning about this was fascinating instead of terrifying.

"It makes it easier to have a physical connection," Orion agreed. "And that connection is even stronger if you blend your power with your anchor. So if we start off by holding hands then we can work up to using a connection without physical aids."

Orion offered his hand to Darcy and she took it. I shifted back before Darius could claim mine.

"It sounds like the best person to use as an anchor is someone you'd walk through hell to stay with, right?" I asked.

"Well obviously the stronger the bond you feel to the person grounding you, the more you'll want to stay with them," Orion agreed.

"Sounds good." I took Darcy's other hand from her lap and she glanced between me and Orion for a moment like she was unsure before releasing him.

"Tory's right, we broke free of the shadows when they were trying to divide us because of our bond to each other. She's not going to feel that strongly about..." Her eyes drifted to Darius for a moment before she cleared her throat. "Obviously neither of us feel strongly about either of you so we should just do this together."

Orion looked mildly irritated by our decision as he looked between us but he shrugged finally.

"Obviously not," he said, though it kinda sounded like he didn't agree at all. "So the first thing you need to do is reach for the shadows. Close your eyes and let them pull you closer. When you accept them into you, the feeling will be somewhat euphoric which is why they're so dangerous. It feels so good that you just want more and more of it. And if you give in to that temptation then you *will* fall prey to them. I can't impress upon you enough just how dangerous they are. Even after years of working with them, that desire never fades, the danger never lessens. My own father wielded dark magic for years but still fell prey to it one day. This is the most dangerous kind of magic there is. There are good reasons for it to be outlawed. If the shadows hadn't taken root in you, I never would have taught you any of this."

I nodded seriously as I took that in. This darkness in me was dangerous. I knew it in my soul, I could feel it in the unnatural swirling I got in my gut each time they were awoken within me. They wanted to consume me. And we had to make sure they never did. Because they were here to stay so we were going to have to learn how to master them.

"Okay. So where do we begin?" Darcy asked.

"Take it in turns. Does one of you want to go first?"

"I will," I said quickly. Darcy frowned at me but I held her gaze, not backing down. "If this is dangerous then I'm not risking you doing it first," I said simply. "You're the only thing I've got that matters to me in this world. If I lost you, I might as well be dead anyway so I'm not arguing."

"Tory…" Darcy replied with a frown. "Don't say things like that."

"It's true." I shrugged. "And it's not up for debate."

I looked back at Orion expectantly and he hesitated as he looked between the two of us.

"I can't promise you that this isn't dangerous," he said, his eyes on Darcy. "But the two of you are the strongest Fae I've ever met. Hell you're the strongest Fae there is. I believe you can do this. And I swear that if you get into any difficulty with it, I'll do everything in my power to help you."

"So will I," Darius added and my skin tingled at the intensity of that vow.

I lifted my eyes to his for a moment, my heart thumping out of rhythm as I looked into his dark gaze. Whatever the hell else had happened between us, he meant that, I could feel it in every piece of my soul.

I cleared my throat and looked away from him, not wanting to see whatever he was feeling. He was too confusing and if I was being totally honest with myself, it hurt too much.

"What do I need to do then?" I asked, my grip tightening on Darcy's hand.

"Close your eyes, call on the shadows and drop into them for a moment. If the pull of them doesn't overwhelm you then see if you can call some of them into your palm. Once you've done that much, banish them again, call on your connection to your sister to pull you back."

"Easy," I deadpanned.

Darcy squeezed my fingers nervously and I gave her a reassuring grin which felt false even to me before I let my eyes fall shut.

I blew out a breath and relaxed as I let my power merge with my sister's. The feeling was so natural, like we'd always been meant to be one creature instead of two. At least in so far as our magic went. It wasn't like when I'd power shared with Darius and the foreign feeling of his magic had skittered through me like some dark temptation. Darcy's magic felt like an extension of my own. It only made my power burn fiercer, stronger, brighter.

Once I'd adjusted to the feeling of our combined power, I drew my attention to the whispers which lingered in the corner of my mind.

The shadows reared up to greet me as I opened myself to them and with a rush, the dark power of them flooded through my body.

The feeling of ecstasy which accompanied them made me arch my back and a moan escaped me as every inch of my body came alive with their dark power.

"Fuck," I breathed as the shadows kept going, racing through my veins, coiling around my magic and begging me to follow their desires.

"Try to maintain control over them," Orion's voice came from afar. There was a tinny quality to it and a slight echo like he was calling to me from the end of a long tunnel.

I took a deep breath and my lungs expanded with the flood of oxygen, words twisting their way around my tongue and begging me to speak them. Words I didn't understand in a language I didn't speak, the power of them so rich and potent I wasn't wholly sure what they might be capable of if I set them free or if they'd even have any limits at all.

I fought against the desire to speak them, focusing on the sensation of Darcy's hand in mine to centre me.

Once I felt confident that I wasn't going to dive any deeper into this power without making the decision for myself, I pushed my will into it.

I focused on what Orion had said, calling the shadows to settle between the fingers of my free hand and holding it up as I felt them gathering there.

Darcy inhaled in surprise somewhere near and far away at once and I opened my eyes.

Darkness danced before my vision but it didn't stop me from seeing anything.

A smile twisted my lips as I spotted the shadows coiling in my outstretched palm, their potent power waiting for me to bend it to my will.

"Good," Orion said steadily. "Now banish them again."

I looked at him for a long moment, my mind fixing on the various ways he'd humiliated me in his classes, the things he'd said and done which proved his unwavering loyalty to the Heirs and his disapproval of us just because of what we were born to be.

My lip curled back as the shadows danced closer to my soul.

"*Roxy,*" Darius growled in warning and as my gaze slid to him, the anger in me sharpened. "You need to control yourself."

A hiss slid from my lips and the shadows in my palm spread up my arm, kissing my flesh with unspeakable pleasure which grew in intensity the further they went.

"Pull her back, Blue," Orion commanded and I could feel Darcy's magic tugging on mine insistently like a toddler pulling on the hand of their parent. But it wasn't enough to stop me.

The shadows slid across my chest, moving over my body until I was coated in them and the raw power of them sang in my veins like my own personal brand of heroin.

I tipped my head back as I bathed in the sensation, the whispers growing louder in the darkness which surrounded me.

"Come to me..."

A part of me was starting to think that wouldn't be the worst thing in the world.

I got to my feet and the shadows grew thicker still, curling around my limbs and shrouding me in darkness, those foreign words pressing against my lips.

Darcy scrambled upright too, maintaining her hold on my hand, her grip tightening.

My gaze was trained on Darius and I was falling into the swimming pool again, the ice forming above me as I started to drown. I was on the beach again with his hand locked around my throat and a look in his eyes that said he hated me and he might just kill me.

Maybe I should kill him before he gets the chance.

"Stop!" Orion shouted but I barely even heard him.

The shadows didn't own me, I owned *them* and with them I could be unstoppable. Who could possibly stand in my way? Who would I ever have to fear again? I was stronger than Lionel Acrux and now I had the darkness on my side too. Why shouldn't I just destroy him and anyone else who sought to hurt me?

I took a step towards Darius, power coiling in my palm, aching to be set free.

"Come back, Tory!" Darcy's voice broke through the fog surrounding my mind and I stopped as I heard her voice like the first clap of thunder before a storm broke free.

What the hell am I doing?

I gritted my teeth, focusing on my sister's power and presence beside me as I turned to her and she pulled me back out of the dark.

The shadows slipped away, the pleasure sliding out of my flesh and leaving me raw and bruised in its wake.

I sagged in on myself as I banished the last of the shadows, locking them back into the cage I'd created for them as the rest of my magic took precedent again.

Darcy's arms were around me as I crumpled down onto my knees, panting as I tried to recover from the rush and burn of the dark magic which had passed through me.

"Are you okay?" Darcy asked shakily as she pushed me back to get a better look at me.

"Yeah," I choked out, the trembling in my limbs slowly subsiding.

Darius and Orion were murmuring to each other in low voices, but I couldn't focus on their words just yet.

Darcy pulled back and I managed a weak smile as she surveyed me with concern.

I flinched as a warm hand landed on my shoulder and looked around to find Darius way too close to me.

"Have they gone now?" he asked seriously.

A flash of pain burned through my chest as I realised I'd almost hurt him. Worse than that, a part of me had hungered for his blood in a way I couldn't quite understand. But the idea of me doing something like that to him scored a line right through my heart. It felt like the shadows had cut me open, their will pushing against mine and twisting my emotions into something far darker than I felt without their presence.

They'd taken my anger and hurt over Darius and shifted it into something too close to bloodlust for my liking.

I reached out before I could stop myself, brushing my fingers along his jaw.

His gaze flickered uncertainly as I looked at him.

"They wanted me to kill you," I breathed.

His lips parted but he didn't speak for a long moment. "But you didn't," he said eventually.

"No," I agreed.

My gaze fell on my fingers where they still lingered on his jaw, his stubble biting at my flesh. I pulled my hand back and hardened my gaze, fighting off the temptation to stay there and remembering all the reasons I had to hate him.

"Now you understand the pull of them," Orion said darkly as I looked away from Darius. "You did well to find your way back. I've only ever been able to move amongst the shadows before. Now that we can wield them I can only imagine their call will be louder, their pull more demanding. But we will figure it out together. The four of us."

I nodded slowly as he gestured for all of us to take our positions on the cave floor again so that Darcy could take her turn at wielding the darkness.

As my heart finally started to slow and the lingering sensation of ecstasy faded from my limbs, I couldn't help but think about the way it had felt to wield the dark power I'd been gifted.

The worst thing of all wasn't the way the shadows had made me feel or what they'd wanted me to do.

It was how much a twisted part of me had liked it.

And the aching temptation I felt to wield them again.

XAVIER

CHAPTER EIGHT

"Do your job correctly or I'll get a new butler!" Father's voice made me flinch and I turned up the volume on my Xbox to try and drown him out. The stomping of his footfalls made my jaw clench and I frantically turned the sound down again as I feared I'd lured him this way.

"Glitterdragon is AFK," I hissed into my headset before tossing it onto the floor and switching off the sixty inch TV on the wall. I sat upright in my gamer chair just as Father pushed the door open. His eyes swept across the room as if hunting for something to punish me for. I hadn't done anything wrong so far as I could remember, but if Father wanted me punished, he'd find a reason.

A tremor ran through me as he took a step into my domain and my eyes flipped to the door. If he closed it, that was it. I was getting a beating. But all the while it remained open, there was hope.

His bright blonde hair was carefully styled and he wore one of his finest suits. That meant we had visitors. Or we would do soon.

"Is there something I can help you with, Father?" I asked, working hard to keep my voice from shaking. I hated being afraid of him. And I hated myself for not being stronger. For being unable to fight back.

"Your Aunt Stella will be coming for dinner tonight," he said. "Have you practised what she taught you?"

I nodded quickly, lifting a palm and urging the shadows to the surface of my skin. With fear running wild in my body, the darkness quickly latched onto it, multiplying it tenfold and dragging me down into the depths of terror. I sucked in a breath, trying to focus on what Aunt Stella had taught me but suddenly the world was suffocating. My father's eyes were drilling into my head, full of judgement and worst of all, disappointment.

He grunted his irritation as I failed to wield the Fifth Element and my heart stuttered as he stepped even closer. With a flick of his hand, he cast a gust of air to shut the door and my throat thickened.

"I'll try harder," I said, my voice surprisingly even despite the fact my shoulders were beginning to shake.

"You waste your life on that piece of trash." He jerked his chin at the Xbox which was my only companion, my only contact to the rest of the world. Even if I was anonymous and the online friends I'd gathered could never step into my life for real. Father hooked it off of the unit beneath the TV so it hit the floor with a thud.

"Father-" I squirmed, my mouth bone dry, my heart squeezing like it was in a vice.

He stomped his foot right through the centre of it and the strength went out of my body.

Looks like I'm gonna be AFK for eternity now. Fuck my life.

Father lifted his chin, a low growl resounding through his chest. My Order form rose to the edges of my flesh on instinct and I clenched my jaw, determinedly fighting it back.

If I shift, he won't stop until he's broken bones.

When I was younger, Darius had taken the brunt of the beatings. More than his fair share. He'd stepped between us a hundred times. I loved him for it and I hated that he'd had to endure it. But now he was at Zodiac Academy, there was no one to get in Father's way. No one to save me, but me. And still, I didn't try. I knew it was pointless. Fighting back only challenged Father to break my will. But equally, cowering drove him to madness. He'd call me unFae with every strike until I started to believe it myself. So I lifted my chin, balled my hands into fists and waited. Because I *was* Fae, dammit.

"You're glittering," he spat, sneering at me in disgust and I let my eyes drop to my hands which shimmered like starlight.

By the sun, he's going to kill me.

His fist swung at my jaw so fast I hit the floor before the pain found me, ricocheting through my cheekbone. His boot slammed into my gut next. I was pinned between him and the end of my bed, every kick driving me into the wooden panel behind me. I protected my head with my hands, curling in on myself instinctively while I waited for it to stop and endured every spike of pain he delivered me.

"You worthless – pointless - *embarrassment* to our family," he snarled a word with every kick until I coughed blood onto his expensive shoes.

He wiped them off on my jeans with a tut of irritation before striding toward the door. "Dinner's at six. Don't be late." He slammed the door so hard, the sound bounced back and forth through my skull like an endless echo.

I mentally checked myself over as a low groan escaped my lips. Bruised, but nothing was broken, which was a damn miracle. Mother would come to heal me within the hour. Like always. She'd float in, humming softly, brushing her fingers through my hair while tending to my wounds. Like it was totally normal.

I knew she wanted to save me from this life, but like me, she was too much of a coward to do it. She'd tried though. For the first time in her life, she'd been brave. She'd blackmailed Father, ensuring that if he ever killed either of us, the story of my Order would be released to the press. Then she followed Darius's request to take me to the human world on the Lunar Eclipse to save me from Father's ritual. But it had all been for nothing. Stella had caught us before we left the house, stealing the air from my mother's lungs until she'd nearly passed out. But *Aunt* Stella hadn't left it at that. She'd bound Mother's arms with vines and sewn her mouth shut with another, leaving her there to bleed onto her own tongue before taking me to that clifftop by stardust.

Guilt clawed through my chest at the thought of that night. I was the leash that bound my brother to Father and kept him in check.

Without me, Darius would be free.

By the time Mother arrived in my room, I'd managed to get myself into bed. She lay down beside me in her usual way, the comforting scent of lavender sailing from her skin. She pulled my shirt off and healed my wounds, her eyes the only one of her features which betrayed the pain she felt at seeing me this way.

Her dark hair was pulled into a bun, wrapped with a white ribbon and she wore a soft pink shift dress which hugged her figure. I caught her hand as the soothing magic ran through my body, healing away the marks he'd left on me.

"We could run," I breathed. "Fetch Darius and go."

She cupped my cheek, leaning in to press a kiss to my forehead. She lingered there, a slight shake of her hand the only sign of her inner terror. "Don't be silly, my love. Dress nicely for dinner, won't you? The family are coming."

She slipped away, taking her floral scent with her. *The family.* That meant Stella and Father's band of loyal followers. We'd be practising using the shadows again tonight and I wished I didn't have to go. The only thing worthwhile about it was that I could keep Darius up to date with how well Father was handling the Fifth Element. So far, he was still struggling to get a grasp on the darkness. The worst thing about that was they seemed to feed on everyone's deepest emotions. So Father was in a rage even more regularly than before. If he was home, there was a ninety percent chance of a beating these days. Whereas before it had been more like fifty.

My phone pinged and I slid across my bed to pick it up from my nightstand.

Darius:

I'm coming home tonight. I've been invited to funsville. See you soon.

Relief swept through me in torrents. The only thing that made anything better in this house was Darius coming home. Though even better than that was if he was bringing his 'friend' Tory Vega with him. Bullshit was he not obsessed with her. I knew my brother better than anyone. And though I got why him dating one of the Vega Twins was waaaay off limits in this family, I still hoped he plucked up the nerve to rebel against Father. Because he deserved a bit of happiness, even if it couldn't last forever.

Xavier:

Yes! Bringing anyone with you………?

Darius:

Yes...

Xavier:

Are they hot? ;)

Darius:

Dark hair, legs that look great in short shorts and a smile to die for.

Xavier:

Drool. If you don't date her, I will.

Darius:

Great. I'll let Lance know you're interested. The stars only know he needs some action.

I huffed, rolling my eyes as I shot him a reply.

Xavier:

Jerkface.

Darius:

Vamp humper.

I snorted a laugh, dropping my phone into my lap before slowly picking it up again. I supposed it had been pretty stupid of me to think he'd actually bring a Vega home uninvited. But at least I'd have my brother for tonight. And I liked hanging out with Lance too when Father allowed it.

There was one thing circling in my mind as I lay there. Darius was no doubt gonna ask me whether I'd texted the Pegasus girl. He'd given me her number ages ago but I hadn't plucked up the nerve to message her yet. What was I supposed to say anyway? And did Darius really trust this girl? What if she figured out who I was and told the press?

Even though my brother had given her a fake name, could I really risk the wrath of my father if he found out that I'd told someone what I was?

But then again, I was so damn lonely in this house. And now I didn't even have my Xbox to distract me from that. If I didn't make contact with the outside world, I'd go mad.

I tossed the phone back and forth between my hands before finally figuring *fuck it* and tapping out a message to Sofia Cygnet under my fake name.

Phillip:

Hi Sofia, this is Darius's cousin, Phillip. Just wanted to say hey.
How's it going?

I wonder if she's hot...

I brought up FaeBook on my phone and searched for Sofia, using Zodiac Academy as a filter and tapping on her profile. My heart beat harder as I took in the snapshot of her life. At the top of the page was her star sign – Sagittarius – which meant she was a Fire Element like my brother. I scrolled down to the photos she'd uploaded and the first row showed images of a Pegasus herd with the caption *Had a quick fly through the clouds before breakfast – there's no greater way to start the day!*

My heart hammered as I drank in the sight of her herd, something deeply ingrained in me longing to unite with them. I simply sat there staring until it was difficult to breathe. I needed this. My Order was meant to have companions. We were one of the most sociable Orders next to Werewolves and it wasn't just a desire, it was a damn necessity.

I groaned, scrolling away from those images and finding a picture of Sofia in her Fae form. A smile tugged at the corner of my mouth at the selfie she'd taken as she sat between the two Vega Twins. They all had brightly coloured ice creams in their hands and Sofia was sparkling with her joy, her eyes seeming to drink me in right through the screen. Her hair was softest hazel and her lips palest pink. Six freckles dotted each of her cheeks – I counted them twice to check.

My phone pinged and I nearly dropped it as a message flashed up from the girl herself. My tongue felt heavy as I tapped on it, a grin tugging up one corner of my mouth.

Sofia:

Hey Phillip. I thought you weren't ever going to text me – I'm glad you did though :)
How are things since your Order emerged?

I took a measured breath. Darius had told her about my situation and she was clearly dancing around the truth. But she didn't know all of the details. Like the fact that I could only go outside when supervised, that I couldn't leave the grounds at all, that even leaving my room for a piss felt like taking my life into my own hands sometimes.

Phillip:

Honestly, Sofia? Things suck. But I'm glad you replied.
It makes things a little less shitty already.

I laid back against my pillows and the time slipped away as we messaged back and forth. She answered all of my burning questions about my Order and it felt so incredibly good to talk to someone about it who didn't judge me for it. She invited me out with her but I had to decline, vaguely explaining that leaving the house wasn't an option for me. Not unless I stole some stardust from Father's office. And as that idea occurred to me, the thought was so tantalising I almost got up to try my luck. But fear still kept me in place. If he beat me for sparkling, he might just kill me for stealing from him.

Better plan: Darius has his own supply of stardust. So maybe he'll give me some.

I'd just have to wait until Father was at work in the city then slip away to Zodiac Academy for a few hours. *Yeah and show your face to Sofia and give the game away.*

Shit. I was all out of possibilities. The stars rarely shone on me these days. Sometimes I wondered if they'd forgotten about me altogether. My daily horoscopes were almost identical day in, day out. Nothing changed. And I was terrified that they never would.

At quarter to six I headed downstairs in smart trousers and a shirt, my dark, curly hair swept back and my phone tucked in my pocket on silent. If Sofia texted again I would feel it buzz and could slip away to the bathroom to read it. It was something to make this night more bearable anyway.

I headed down the large staircase into the entrance hall and made my way to the kitchen to grab a glass of lemonade before dinner. Father only ever served water or wine at the table and I hated both. When he was away at work, I could guzzle lemonade all day long and I was hankering for my fix before I had to endure the dinner from hell.

As I reached the door, voices caught my ear and I paused. Stella was talking to father's colleague, Alejandro, in a low tone that suggested they didn't want to be overheard.

"-have any more insight than I do, Alejandro?" Stella whispered. "All I can gauge is that this *Shadow Princess* is drawing closer."

"We have received the same message," Alejandro said in his soft accent. "I don't know anything more than you do."

"Liar," Stella hissed and a strange rattle filled the air. "Ah! Don't you *dare*."

"The shadows only provide the information they want to give," Alejandro said in a calm tone which somehow carried a dangerous edge at the same time. "But she is coming."

"And who is *she*?" Stella demanded, her voice rising an octave.

A hand suddenly slid over my mouth and I lurched in surprise as I was half carried across the entrance hall and planted on the stairs. Lance Orion released me and half a second later my father strode into the hall.

Shitballs, I'd have been caught if it wasn't for his bat ears.

Darius appeared behind Orion and we turned to Father as one, tension pooling in the air between us.

"Uncle Lionel," Lance said in a flat tone.

"Lance," Father said curtly before turning to Darius and pressing his lips together.

Mother appeared behind him, seeming to float across the hallway before embracing my brother. "We missed you," she said in an empty voice.

"I missed you too, Mother," Darius said in an equally hollow tone.

"Walk with me, won't you Lance?" Mom's eyes became hooded as she stepped forward, holding out her arm for him to take. Lance's jaw was ticking as he hooked his arm around hers and she guided him away towards the dining room.

I stood on the stairs, nervously shifting from foot to foot as Father looked between the two of us, his gaze fixing on Darius at last.

"How are your Fifth Element lessons progressing with your Guardian?" he asked and Darius pressed his tongue into his cheek.

"I can't wield the shadows yet. But we're getting there."

"You'll demonstrate what you've learned tonight in front of us all. I want to see you every two weeks to determine how you are developing. If I see no improvement I will ensure both you and Lance regret not working harder."

"Yes Father," Darius said and Father nodded stiffly before walking away toward the dining room.

I blew out a long breath as the pressure of his company eased from the air. Darius clapped me on the shoulder before pulling me in to a tight embrace.

"How's Tory Vega?" I whispered in his ear, serving me a thump on the shoulder.

When I stepped away, his expression was taut in a way that said things weren't good at all, but before I could ask him, Jenkins appeared, ushering us into the dining room. "Dinner is served, Master Darius, Master Xavier."

I sat through dinner in silence, eating the pretentiously small portions on my plate, trying to ignore Stella's animated conversation about an advancing magic called Order Selection.

"It's a fantasy, Stella," my uncle Cyril waved a hand, his double chin wobbling as he sipped another large mouthful of red wine. "How can they predict Orders which are chosen by the stars? Not even the best diviners in Solaria are capable of that."

"They're getting closer to achieving it," Stella pressed, receiving a few hopeful nods from around the table. "Imagine if you could pick and choose the offspring you brought to term? There would never be any room for mishaps again. It's fabulous!" Her eyes lit up and I clenched my fork so hard it hurt.

"Yes wonderful, it's a shame the magic hasn't been available for years. I'm sure it would have saved many couples the disappointment of unwanted Orders," my father said dryly, not looking at me, though his words were intended to burn. And they did, all the way through to my core and back out again.

"Maybe your mouth would be better served eating, Stella," Lance said lightly, fixing her with a sharp stare. He never called her Mom anymore. I hadn't been there when his sister Clara had died, but Darius had told me about it. Ever since that day, Lance didn't refer to his own mother like she was related to him. I wished I could get away with that with Father, but if I called him Lionel he'd probably knock me through a wall.

"Oh don't molly coddle me, baby boy. Go on, give us your opinion on Order Selection, we're *dying* to hear it." Stella looked slightly tipsy, though she was always on the crazy spectrum. She just tended to be even more dangerous after a few glasses of wine.

"I think it's barbaric," Lance said firmly, his eyes remaining on her.

"It's no different to mating at certain times of the year to achieve Elemental star signs," Stella countered and Mother nodded her agreement.

"We only tried on the months that would ensure our boys had Fire Elements when they were born," Mom said and I shared a look with Darius, wanting to crawl under the table and disappear.

"As did my husband and I," Stella said, her eyes glittering.

Cyril rested a hand on her arm as she released a sob and Lance groaned almost inaudibly.

"We wanted Lance to be an air sign, but we never considered how difficult Libras can be to raise," she said with a dramatic sniff.

"How disappointed you must be," Lance deadpanned like he gave no shits in the world and Lionel shot him a dangerous glare. He turned his head, scraping his fork across his plate as Darius shifted closer in the chair beside him.

"My second born was a Libra," Aunt Fiona supplied, her nose upturned, giving her the appearance that she always had something rotten beneath it. "Terrible demeanour. Once they've decided what's right or wrong, there's no shifting them. We had to send her to a Star Sign Correctional Centre in the end."

Lance growled and I caught Darius sliding his hand onto his arm under the table. As Father's eyes flipped onto my brother with a warning in his gaze, Lance fell quiet.

"Did it work?" Cyril asked curiously.

"Absolutely," Fiona answered brightly. "She identifies as an Aquarius now."

By the stars, my family are insane.

I barely made it through the final courses without wanting to puncture my eardrums just so I didn't have to listen to the Orderist bullshit spewing from all of their mouths.

We were soon corralled into the ballroom and Father had Jenkins lock all the doors, then he cast a silencing bubble before speaking a word.

"Stella has graciously offered us all a lesson in wielding the Fifth Element. I'm sure you have all experienced the deep power that now lives within your veins."

Everyone nodded their agreement and Darius shot me a frown that made my insides churn. I hadn't had a chance to apologise about what had happened on the Lunar Eclipse. I didn't want to say it in a text message. I needed to talk to him one on one. Brother to brother.

"Come here, my boy," Stella beckoned her son.

Lance moved toward her, his shoulders stiff. She brushed her knuckles across his cheek with a sad frown. "The shadows are going to bring you back to me, do you feel the call of their dark power, cherub?"

"I haven't gone anywhere," he muttered.

"Oh but you have. I don't recognise this boy who stands before me." She turned away sharply as if Lance was too painful to look at and he rolled his eyes.

Stella breathed in deeply, collecting herself. "You must all give in to the shadows just the right amount." She turned, sweeping her gaze across the room. "Let their divine power flood your veins and rush from you like your Elements do." She opened her palm and obsidian smoke coiled in her hand, a shadow in magic form dancing around her skin.

Fear licked its way up my spine at the sight of that dark power. The air seemed to get thicker and the lights above us flickered. Everyone began to practice and I opened my palm, recalling Stella's lessons to try and draw that magic to the surface of my skin. But deep down, I knew I was fighting it.

I'd dreamed about being Awakened my whole life, but everything about this power felt wrong. Twisted. I'd never even experienced Elemental magic pouring from me so I had nothing to compare it to, but I knew in the depths of my bones that this wasn't natural. It felt like living with a demon wrapped around my soul and I was one slip away from it devouring me.

"Are you alright?" Darius asked in a low tone as chatter broke out around the room.

"Yeah," I breathed. "Are you?"

He nodded, then frowned sharply as a ball of pure shadow built in my palm. I inhaled at the intoxicating sensation flooding through me, begging me to fall deeper into it.

Darius wrapped his hand around my wrist and I blinked back the pull of its power with a sigh.

Stella clapped her hands to get everyone's attention. "Are you ready for the demonstration, Lionel?" she asked hopefully and Father smiled one of his eeriest fucking smiles.

"Stella has achieved something quite remarkable with her new power," he explained to the room. "Xavier has volunteered to succumb to it for you all to witness it."

"I have?" I murmured.

"*Father*," Darius said sternly but he ignored him.

"How very brave," Uncle Cyril said, giving me a look of approval.

Father lifted his chin with something that resembled pride and I might have been a fool, but that made me feel too good to ignore. I stepped forward willingly despite Darius's eyes burning into the side of my head.

"Try to fight it off, Xavier," Father said and I nodded, swallowing the lump in my throat. He nodded to Aunt Stella and she stepped forward with darkness swirling in her eyes.

Stella raised her hands and a tunnel of shadow collided with me, seeming to pour through the walls of my skin and bind to every nerve ending in my body. Where it touched, it burned. And it wasn't just any fire, it was propane washing through every cell in my body and bursting into flame. I was half aware that I was screaming, but all I could hear were whispers pressing in on my ears in a language I didn't know.

"Help!" I called to them in my mind as the fire intensified. But no one was coming to save me. Not here. Not ever. I was a slave to my family's new power. And all it meant was that Father had a new toy to hurt me with. Another way to break me.

But somewhere between the pain and the darkness, I found something to hold onto. A pretty girl with bright eyes and skin that sparkled like rhinestones. And as the image of a Pegasus rode through my mind amongst a tumbling sea of clouds, I swore on everything that I was, that I'd join her in the sky one day. The shadows receded and I gasped, finding myself on my knees, panting and slick with sweat.

"He did it," Stella said appraisingly. "He fought them off. And quickly too."

"Well whatever helped you fight them, hold onto it," Father said firmly.

I nodded, having no problem with that at all. I smiled because it felt like I was quietly rebelling against my father. My anchor was a Pegasus like me. So suck on that, *Dad.*

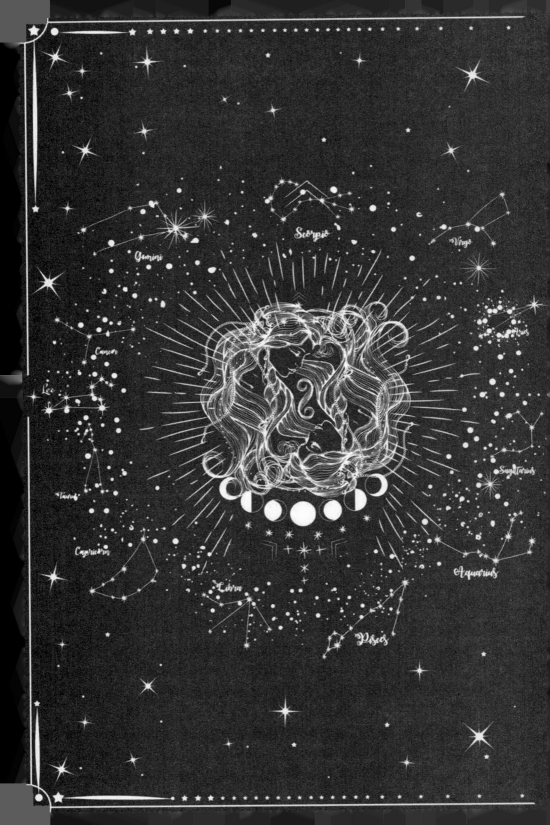

DARCY

CHAPTER NINE

I lay on my bed, bobbing my head to Camila Cabello's Real Friends while I wrote my Tarot assignment, finishing up the final sentence.

As Tarot decks vary from pack to pack and often contain Elemental and Astrological symbols hidden within the pictures, predictions will be more or less viable depending on the Element and star sign of the interpreter. As such, Tarot is one of the more complex of the Arcane Arts but when the study is proficient, it is one of the most accurate.

I chewed on my lip as I read that over and mentally added another sentence. *Which is why Astrum's cards are confusing as hell but make total sense by the time they come to light.*

What was the point in having a glimpse of the future if it wasn't clear until it was too late to do anything about it?

I reached into the drawer of my nightstand, taking out the last one we'd discovered. The Empress.

In the Palace of Souls, rests a secret untold.
Find the light who burned on after the fire...

The Palace of Souls belonged to the King and Queen. I wondered what the Council had done with it now, or if it just sat empty. Would Tory and I really be able to lay claim to it? The idea of inheriting something like that made me nervous. I certainly wasn't ready to be a Princess, but I *was* ready to find out more about my past. And though Tory seemed reluctant to learn more, that need wasn't going to die out for me.

How could she not want to learn about where we'd come from? It fascinated me as much as it scared me.

A knock on the window sent my heart rate rocketing through the ceiling. *What the hell??*

I jumped up, heading across the room and raising a palm defensively as I pulled the curtain aside, fearing the Heirs had come to fulfil their promise of destroying us.

Orion stood on the window ledge one hundred and fifty feet above the ground as if he was totally safe. My breathing became unsteady and my heart turned to hot dough. I unlocked the full-length window, pulling it open so he could step into my room. It was past eleven and the dark was thick outside. I was sure he'd been cautious coming here, but my stomach still fluttered with nerves at the idea of him being seen. This thing between us was all-consuming; I'd fallen down the rabbit hole and I didn't want to ever leave Wonderland, but it wouldn't be my choice if we were ever caught.

I took his hand, finding it cold to the touch from the frosty air. He circled an arm around my waist, lifting a hand to cast a silencing bubble before he uttered a word.

I stopped him with a grin, using my free hand to cast the spell instead, letting it expand around us until it touched every wall in the room.

Orion smiled broadly, but there was a heaviness in his gaze, darkness ringing his eyes.

"What's wrong?" I asked on instinct.

"I'm alright," he said soothingly, leaning down to press a soft kiss to my lips that sent a chain of butterflies diving into my stomach. "I've just been at Lionel's house tonight with my mother and the rest of the asylum. Stella gave us a lesson in the shadows…she hurt Xavier."

I inhaled sharply, my brow creasing. "Is he okay?" He was the only decent Acrux from what Tory had told me about him and it saddened me to know he was being kept prisoner in his own home.

"Yeah," he sighed wearily. "I just wish there was more I could do to help."

I cupped his cheek. "I'm sure you're doing everything you can."

He stepped past me, dropping down onto my bed with a sigh. "I've been training Darius to wield dark magic for years in the hope that it would give him an edge in a fight against his father. We've plotted to get rid of him for so long, I can hardly remember a time before that. But now Lionel has made himself ten times more powerful with the Fifth Element. Not to mention all of his damn friends."

"Us too though," I urged. "And you haven't wasted that time. Lionel might have the Fifth Element but he doesn't know how to cast dark magic as well as you, does he?"

Orion lifted his chin, meeting my gaze with a smile pulling at his lips. "No, you're right, Blue. He doesn't." He patted his thigh and I grinned as I moved to sit in his lap, wrapping my arms around his neck. He placed a kiss on my jaw that sent a rush of tingles along my skin.

"Do you want to know a secret?" he whispered into my ear and a delicious shiver ran through me as I nodded. He brushed his fangs against my throat and his hold on me tightened, his need to drink suddenly so obvious I didn't know why I hadn't realised it the second he'd stepped into the room. "You're what I latch onto to bring me back from the shadows." His fangs drove into my neck and I gasped, shifting in his lap to wrap my legs around him while he fed.

I combed my fingers through his hair, clenching my thighs around his waist as a deep heat built at the base of my spine.

Orion stood, cupping my ass to keep me in place before turning and dropping me down onto the pages of notes scattered across my bed. I smiled, holding onto him as he laid his weight on me, his hand sliding up my top and growling as he found no bra there to slow him down.

He grew hard against my thigh and I arched my back, needing to get closer. I tugged at his shirt and he pulled it over his head before dropping his mouth back to meet mine. His kisses became fierce, lighting a fire in me that sent me tumbling into a pit of desire.

"Lance." I scraped my nails up his back and he groaned into my mouth. He lifted his weight off of me, his hand sliding down to my waistband, dipping his fingers beneath it and –

His head suddenly jerked up and a knock came at the door a second later.

"Who the fuck is that?" he growled.

I pushed his chest, shaking my head in answer as my heart beat a mile a minute. "I don't know. *Go*."

"Don't answer it," he begged but I gave him a firm look.

"It could be Tory," I said.

"Whoever it is, get rid of them." He pecked my lips then grabbed his shirt and shot into the bathroom, shutting the door behind him.

I tried to steady my racing heart and tame my wild hair as I stood and moved to the door, turning the handle and pulling it open.

Diego stood there in jeans and a shirt, his hat in place and a taut expression on his face. He was about the last person in the world I'd expected to find standing there - barring the Queen of England herself.

"Hey Darcy." Diego cleared his throat, then did it again when I remained quiet, unsure what the hell to say.

"Hi," I forced out eventually.

"I know it's late," he said with a frown, tugging at one side of his hat. "But look I, er…can I come in?"

I glanced over my shoulder, my eyes falling on the bathroom door before I looked back at him. I folded my arms, resting my shoulder against the doorway. "I'm not sure that's a good idea."

"I just want to talk," he said, pulling at the collar of his shirt as if he was too hot. "To apologise." He dipped his head. "I'm sorry for what I said to you. And I'd like to explain…" He shot a look over his shoulder as if he was nervous and I frowned.

"Explain what?" I asked.

"Please, Darcy. Not out here."

I sighed, giving in as I stepped away from the door to allow him in. Orion was going to be privy to whatever he said, but there wasn't much I could do about that.

I shut the door and Diego's eyes darted around the room. "Can you cast a silencing bubble? I'm not great at it yet."

"I've done it already," I said as Diego pulled out my desk chair and dropped onto it, wringing his hands together.

I lowered onto my bed, folding my legs beneath me and waiting for him to start talking.

"Okay well...firstly I want to say that I didn't mean what I said about you and your sister. I mean, I do still hate Orion, that's just something I can't change, but the rest of it was horseshit. And I really am sorry for the rest of it."

"I know Orion can be a dick to you," I sighed, not bothering to lower my voice. It was the damn truth and his Vampire ears would pick it up anyway. "And I shouldn't have hit you. That was awful of me. I just had a knee-jerk reaction. I'm sorry too." It felt so good to be talking it out at last. Diego had been one of the first friends I'd made at the academy and I didn't want to lose him. I knew I'd been out of line to hit him for talking shit about Orion, but I just got so damn protective when it came to him.

"I'll say all of this to Tory too, chica," Diego went on. "But there's something I need to get off my chest. I've been debating it for days since..." He cleared his throat, looking to me with a pinched expression. "Don't freak out, okay?"

"Er...okay," I said cautiously, magic rising to the surface of my skin.

"I know you have the shadows," Diego said and I gaped at him, feeling like I'd just been punched in the gut.

"You – *what?*" I spluttered in alarm, sure Orion was having a similar reaction in my bathroom right about now. "How can you know? Did you hear something? Who told you?"

"It's okay," he said quickly, raising a hand in innocence. "No one told me. But I can sense them. I have no idea where you got them. Or your sister... or Darius Acrux...or Professor Orion."

My mouth was literally hanging open like a cartoon character as I stared at him, waiting for some explanation to this that made any sense. "How?"

Diego leaned forward in his chair, his eyes wild with anxiety. "You have no idea what trouble I'd be in if my family found out I told you this."

"Told me what?" I breathed, my heartbeat thrumming in my chest like the wings of a hummingbird.

Diego frowned heavily. "My family use magia oscura – dark magic."

My lips parted and I nodded slowly, waiting for him to go on.

"They've been using it ever since I can remember. My mother, my father, Uncle Alejandro. My father fights it, but the other two..." He shook his head. "They're ruled by the darkness. They gave into its clutches a long time ago and who they were before just desapareció – disappeared."

"Diego..." I breathed as questions cascaded through my mind. "Do you use it too?"

"Not now that I'm at the academy," he said firmly. "I wanted to come here to make a new life. I wanted to escape my family...that house." He shuddered. "Mi casa es donde vive el diablo. I don't want to ever go back. But the shadows..."

"What about them?" I whispered as a prickle ran up my spine.

"I can't escape them. I never wanted to be connected to them but mi abuela said it would help us all, that they'd help us hear dark predictions of the future. So she found a way to connect us to the Shadow Realm permanently. I refused, but Mamá insisted."

"What did your grandmother do?" I asked, fear sliding into my veins.

"She..." Diego looked down at his feet, his cheeks reddening as he struggled to speak the words. He took a long breath. "Darcy, do you know what the shadows are made of?"

My throat constricted as I searched for the answer, but I realised Orion had already given it to me.

"Souls?" I breathed, the hairs rising along the back of my neck.

Diego nodded, his eyes dark. "Si...so mi abuela did something unspeakable." He lifted a hand to tug at the corner of his hat and I swear a cold wind swirled through the room. Either that or I'd seen one too many horror movies. He lowered his voice to barely above a whisper, but I knew Orion's Vampire hearing would pick up every word even though I had to lean forward to do so. "She used the darkest magic of all to bind her soul to objects in the Fae realm. To keep her spirit grounded here before she gave herself to the shadows."

"What objects?" I whispered, my mouth desperately dry.

Diego reached up, pulling the hat from his head and knotting his fingers in it. "This is one of them." He held it out to me, but I recoiled, unsure what I was even discovering right now. *That his grandmother's soul is knitted into that freaking hat???*

"I don't understand," I said, withdrawing from him.

He swallowed, putting the hat back on and tugging it low over his ears. "I can hear the shadows when I'm wearing it."

My jaw went slack and I half expected Orion to burst into the room and start laughing over this elaborate prank he and Diego had concocted together. But silence rang out and the truth weighed heavily on my shoulders.

"Mi abuela speaks to me through it too," Diego said. "She gave every part of her soul to ensure each member of my family would be bonded together through the garments she made."

I nodded mutely, shocked into total silence.

"And the dark magic threaded into it allows me to hear them clearly... to translate the ancient tongues they speak. Also it..." He bowed his head, seeming ashamed. "It helps me control them. When I'm not wearing it, I fall prey to the darkness that lives in my veins. The shadows reside there since mi abuela did this terrible magic. I am bonded to them, but I can't wield them. And I can see them too, like I do in you and the others." Diego reached for me and I tentatively took his hand, squeezing gently. "Don't hate me for this next part."

"I'll try," I said uncertainly.

"Uncle Alejandro works for Lionel Acrux," he whispered. "He asked me to get close to you and your sister. He wants information, but I've never given him anything of any importance. I didn't expect to like you both and I...I never thought of you as anything more than a friend. Alejandro was pressuring me to get information and I thought kissing you was a good way to get near you, but-"

"You're spying on us," I gasped in alarm, my eyes whipping to the bathroom door and back to him. Orion made no appearance, not that I really expected him to, but this news must have been driving him into a frenzy.

"Not anymore," he promised, truth shining from his eyes.

"But if you're all connected to the shadows, can't your grandma listen in?" I asked, anxiety clinging to me.

"No," he said. "They only hear what I let them hear. Look, I don't want to go against you and Tory. You're my friends. You've become more like family to me than mine ever were. I'm loyal to you and her, I swear it." He slipped from his chair, dropping to his knees and bowing his head. "You're my Queens and I'll do whatever it takes to make this up to you. *Anything*."

I stared at him, trying to process all of this and work out what was true. Diego had been spying on us for Lionel Acrux? Though the look on his face now made me want to believe he hadn't wanted to do it, but how could I accept that?

"This is a lot to take in," I said on a shaky breath, pushing a hand into my hair.

Diego looked up at me with a deep frown. "I know, I know. It's all so crazy. I wish I'd told you sooner, but I was afraid. And look, I know this isn't an excuse, but on the day of the Fairy Fair I wasn't wearing my hat. Sometimes it's suffocating. Sometimes the voices drive me crazy. So when I went with you...I wasn't myself. I fell into the darkness in me and it stole away everything else." A tear fell from his eye and my heart twisted sharply. I knew how powerful the shadows could be, I fought them every day.

I dropped to my knees before him, squeezing his arm. "It's okay. I believe you, Diego. It's just a lot to take in."

"I know," he croaked, swallowing back more tears. "I don't want to be a coward, but you don't know what my family are capable of. Betraying them is the most terrifying thing I've ever done. And they can't know." He clutched my hand, squeezing so hard it almost hurt. "*They can't know*," he begged of me and I nodded quickly.

"They won't. How could they find out?"

"I have to keep giving them information," he said, sounding panicked.

"Are you going to tell them about this? That we have the shadows?" I asked, my heart drumming wildly.

"No, I promise I won't." Diego swore then his brows lifted. "What happened to you anyway? How did it happen?"

I pressed my lips together. "I can't talk about it."

"You don't trust me," Diego said, hanging his head.

"I don't trust anyone right now," I sighed.

"I understand," he said gently, rising to his feet and I went with him. He moved toward the door, his fingers resting on the handle. "Will you tell Tory?"

"Yes," I said and he nodded.

"Good. I think she'd rather hear it from you. I don't think she'll forgive me. In fact, I don't know if she ever really liked me."

"Don't say that, it's not true," I said firmly and he nodded sadly, opening the door and slipping into the corridor.

"Maybe I can sit with you at breakfast tomorrow?" he asked hopefully.

"Sure," I said, conjuring a small smile as he headed away and stepped into his room.

I pushed the door closed, sagging against it as I tried to work through everything I'd just heard. Orion was at my side in a flash, tugging me down onto the bed and forcing me to face him. He tilted my chin up so I met his eyes and I found the strength of a warrior gazing back at me.

"You are not to spend time with him ever again," he commanded and I blinked in surprise at his words.

"What?" I blurted. "He just said-"

"I heard what he said!" Orion barked and I flinched. His eyes flickered with darkness for a second before he went on. "That boy is dangerous. I don't trust a word that comes out of his mouth."

"Why would he lie about all of that? Dark magic, the shadows? He's putting himself at risk by telling me."

"His uncle is working with Lionel Acrux," Orion snarled, his fangs bared.

"I know and he admitted it," I pressed. "Diego already knew we had the shadows, he could have told his uncle already if he wanted to betray us, but he didn't. He came and told *me*, what other reason would he have for doing that?"

"I don't know." Orion caught my hands, leaning forward to fix me with one of his fiercest Professor stares. "But you will not be friends with him."

I tsked, dragging my hands free of him. "You can't tell me what to do. I'll make my own mind up about this, Lance. If you think I'm going to be bossed around by you-"

"I'm not trying to control you, Blue, I'm trying to protect you!"

I stilled at the passion in his tone, seeing that this was coming from a good place. "Why don't you trust what he said?"

Orion clenched his jaw. "It's not about him. He's connected to every member of his family through the shadows. Besides, soul magic is the most fucked up magic I know of and it corrupts everything it touches. I don't want you near it."

"He was fighting it," I insisted and Orion dragged me toward him so we were nose to nose.

"I don't care," he growled deeply. "Him and his family are bad news. What's to say this isn't just some ploy to get close to you again? He fucked up and now he's trying to cover his ass and get more information."

"What information?" I laughed hollowly. "I don't have any information to give him. I hardly know anything about my heritage or the way Solaria works. I'm not exactly a fountain of knowledge."

Orion's grip on me eased and a frown pinched his brows. "I just want you to be careful."

"I'm always careful," I said gently.

"And yet you and your sister still end up in more trouble than anyone I know," he said with mock accusation.

I let my hand drift down to his bare chest, the anxiety easing from my body. "Well I think that has a lot more to do with the Heirs and Lionel Acrux than it does to do with me looking for trouble." My fingers drifted to his waistband and I glanced up under my lashes as he gave me a heated look.

"And what about us?" he asked in a rumbling tone which sent sparks darting through to my core.

"What *about* us?" I asked with a playful smile, rising onto his lap and pressing him down onto the bed. His hands landed on my hips and I pushed them away with a smirk.

He groaned, cupping them behind his head to keep them away from me and I tracked my fingers up the hardened ovals of his abs. "Is this my fault, Professor?" I teased, circling my finger around his naval and feeling him harden between my thighs.

"Yes," he breathed, sucking on his lower lip as I rocked my hips.

"No Lance…" I leaned over him, my hair spilling around us in a veil of glittering blue. I dropped my mouth to his chest, trailing lower until he groaned with need. "I think this is all your fault and it's time you learned your lesson."

TORY

CHAPTER TEN

My evening run had taken me out towards the edge of Air Territory and I pounded the track along the cliff above Air Cove with the heavy bass of my music thumping through my headphones and my focus on banishing my thoughts. Thoughts of Dragons and secrets, lies and heartache, Orders and shadows. Most of all shadows.

The whispers were growing louder. They found me in the quiet spaces of my mind, urging my attention to them even when I fought to ignore them.

We were meeting with Orion and Darius again in a few days to work on our control over them. But last night, when they'd woken me and their voices were echoing through my skull, promising me things I knew I shouldn't want, I'd done something which was probably more than a little foolish. I'd given in to their call.

Alone in my room with no one there to pull me back if I fell too far, I'd let myself sink into the darkness.

The rush of dark magic had bled through my veins, the whispers had grown louder, begging, pleading, demanding – and then I'd silenced them. I'd taken the darkness into my grasp and forced it to bend to my will. And it had felt *good.* Worse than that, I'd gone further still, calling the shadows to me the way I had the other night, letting them coat my flesh and imbue my skin with power.

I stopped at the top of the cliff, looking out over the sea as I caught my breath and 99 Problems by Jay Z rang in my ears. *Wasn't that the truth?* In fact, ninety nine problems would barely touch the tip of the iceberg for me right now.

I hadn't told Darcy about my time with the shadows last night and the worst part about that was the reason for it. I was ashamed. Not because I'd broken Orion's rules about risking the shadows without his supervision. But because I liked the way they felt beneath my skin. I wasn't an idiot, I hadn't suddenly started to believe that they weren't all kinds of fucked up. I was just starting to wonder if accepting their magic might not be so bad after all.

I glanced around, making sure I was alone up here before dipping into their dark power yet again. The rush of ecstasy I got from them spilled through me and the whispers got louder for a moment before I commanded them into silence. My heart beat faster as they bowed to my command and a heady sense of satisfaction filled me.

I directed them to gather in my palm, smiling as they circled between my fingers before getting the ball of darkness to rise up and hang in the space before me for a long moment. I ached to go further, do more, but with a force of will, I banished the shadows again and they dispersed.

A dark smile gripped my features as the shadows bowed to my commands and I released a slow breath as the touch of that tainted power slid from my veins. I drew on my water magic instead, sighing at the gentle embrace of my true power and using it to cool me down and clean my skin after my run.

I pulled my Atlas from my pocket, checking the time. I was meeting Darcy and Professor Nox back at The Orb at seven so that we could have our first official Order Enhancement class and to say I was excited about that was an understatement. The Phoenix beneath my skin was aching to be set free and I wanted to learn how to fly more than I thought I'd ever wanted anything in my life before now.

It was a quarter to six so I still had over an hour to burn, but I decided to make the time to tell Darcy about my experiments with the shadows before we set off. I sent her a quick message asking her to meet me fifteen minutes before we were due to meet Nox so that I could tell her. We didn't do secrets and I wasn't about to start keeping them over something this important. I would be honest about my trials with them, but I was also pretty sure I wasn't going to stop. Darius and Orion were teaching us how to use them but they were learning at the same time. So was Lionel. It was a race to find out which of us could claim dominance over them the fastest and I sure as shit wasn't going to let Daddy Acrux beat me to it. The next time I came across that asshole I'd be powerful enough to keep him away from me. Which meant I'd be working as hard as I could to harness *all* of my magic. My Order, water, earth, fire, air *and* the shadows. The combination of our strengths would make us unstoppable once we'd learned how to use them, so that was exactly what I would do.

My Atlas pinged and I looked down at it, expecting a message from Darcy confirming our meet but finding one from Caleb instead.

Caleb:

I've been watching you, sweetheart. Want to try a new game?

My heart leapt and I looked around at the open plain behind me which ran the length of the cliff. The long grass which covered it swayed lazily in the breeze but I couldn't spot a sneaky Vampire anywhere. *Shit, did he see me wielding the shadows?*

Tory:

What do you mean, you've been watching me?

Caleb:

Have I ever mentioned how hot you look in your running stuff?

Tory:

Oh yeah, sweaty chic is my go to look just for you. Why don't you come out if you're here?

Caleb:

Is that a yes to my new game?

I narrowed my eyes at the long grass around me, wondering what the hell kind of game I was letting myself in for as I typed out a single word answer.

Tory:

Yes.

A blur of motion shot towards me from the long grass and I shrieked in fright half a second before Caleb collided with me.

He swept me into his arms and leapt straight over the cliff edge.

My stomach lurched, my heart flipped over and I screamed as we began to free fall straight down towards the sandy beach far below.

"You gonna save us, sweetheart?" Caleb yelled as we plummeted towards the ground and panic bled into me as I realised what he meant. Caleb had earth and fire magic, he couldn't slow our fall and he was relying on me to do it for us.

I threw my hands out in desperation as the beach sped ever closer and air magic burst from me in a torrent, wrapping us up in it and flipping us around as I formed a whirlwind in my panic.

Caleb's laughter found me amid the chaos as my hair whirled around us and I fought to wrangle the magic so that we were deposited on the beach.

We fell back into the sand with a thump, the grains welcoming us in a soft embrace that almost felt like falling into water before pushing us back up again and leaving us panting on the surface.

Caleb's laughter burned through my terror and I stared up at him as he pinned me into the sand.

"What the hell?" I gasped. "You're insane!"

"Don't worry, sweetheart, I had control over the sand, we were never in any real danger."

I gaped at him as my thundering heart tried to adjust to the fact that I hadn't just gone splat. Before I could think of anything to say in response to his insanity, Caleb leaned forward and pressed his lips to mine.

Adrenaline coursed through me in an unstoppable wave and at the touch of his mouth, I melted, needing some way to expel the energy he'd awoken beneath my skin.

I yanked my headphones off of my head, tossing them beside us with my Atlas which I'd somehow managed to keep hold of in our fall.

Caleb growled against my lips, his hand sliding down the side of my body and heat pooling between my thighs at his touch.

His fingers made it to my waistband and I caught his wrist to halt him.

"We're out in the open," I complained breathlessly.

Caleb groaned, taking his hand off of me and pressing it to the sand beside us instead. A deep rumble shuddered through the ground as he wielded his earth magic and rocks burst free of the sand, rising up to create a wall to our right. Once they'd made it a few meters out of the ground, Moss and vines sprung to life all over them, taking root in the stone before reaching out above us, forming a roof then spilling down to the ground until we were encased in a cave created solely for us.

"Better?" Caleb asked as I stared at the incredible magic he'd just created.

"Yes," I breathed, unable to come up with anything more eloquent.

It seemed to be the only answer Caleb wanted though as his mouth instantly found mine again and his hand returned to my waistband.

This time I didn't complain as he tugged my leggings off of my body, removing my socks and sneakers in the same move.

He reared over me again, claiming my mouth and pressing his tongue against mine.

I groaned hungrily, wanting more of him, needing to take the pleasure his body could give me and banish some of the darkness which was hanging over me far too much since the horror that had taken place on the Lunar Eclipse.

I caught the back of his shirt in my grip and tugged, yanking it over his head and tossing it aside as my fingers skimmed the tight lines of his body.

The sand shifted beneath me as he pressed me down into it and I gave in to the demands of his flesh.

Caleb's hand shifted to my sports bra and he tugged it up, drawing it over my head. Cold air spilled across my flesh and a gasp escaped me as my nipples hardened in response. His mouth trailed down my body, sending shivers through my skin. He kept going until he drew my nipple between his lips and a sigh spilled from me at the gentle torment.

His tongue moved over me and his fangs lengthened with desire, scraping against my nipple and making me gasp.

His mouth continued to suck and tease at my breast as his hand made it to the top of my panties and he slowly pushed his fingers beneath them.

Caleb groaned as he lowered his hand, his fingers grazing through the centre of me and finding me ready for him. I panted with need as he stroked up and down, teasing exactly where I wanted him and making me roll my head back in the sand as I begged him for more.

He finally gave me what I wanted, pushing two fingers inside me and growling with satisfaction as I bucked against him.

He started up a torturous rhythm with his hand, pushing his fingers in and out while rotating his thumb in the perfect spot to drive me insane.

I gripped his broad shoulders, my nails biting into his flesh as he pushed my body on, his mouth still worshiping my breasts and his hand making me groan with desire.

Tension was coiling through me, aching for a release as my flesh bowed to his commands and he pulled me apart piece by piece.

Just as I was sure the world was about to come crashing down, Caleb released me, withdrawing his hand from my underwear and pulling it off of me instead.

"Wait," I gasped but he only laughed knowingly, pushing his pants down and releasing the smooth, hard length of him.

I bit my lip as he moved over me, pushing myself up onto my elbows and placing a hand on his chest to move him back.

Caleb growled but I wasn't just going to bow to his desire. I pushed him hard enough to make him roll onto his back and he yanked me over too so that he was pinned beneath me.

The ache between my thighs was demanding satisfaction and I lowered myself onto him with a moan, rolling my head back as I bathed in the feeling of him inside me.

Caleb pushed himself up so that he was sitting with me in his lap, his hands moving to grip my hips as he pressed his mouth to mine.

I melted against him and let him guide my movements as I slowly began to ride him, the ache in my body sharpening as he gave me what I craved.

We found a rhythm which sent pleasure spilling into my body and we started moving faster, his thrusts getting harder and my moans breaking free between our kisses.

Caleb cursed as I moved even quicker, his grip on my hips punishing, demanding, driving me down firmly as he gave me more and more.

I was climbing, my body tightening and my back arching as I danced the edge of ecstasy, building towards it with each passing second.

Caleb kissed me again, pulling back as my name tore from his lips and he spilled himself inside me, breaking the dam on my own pleasure as I followed him into oblivion.

I cried out as he gripped me tightly and I fell forwards, pressing my forehead to his shoulder as my muscles shook. My hands fisted in his hair and I rode out the wave with my chest heaving and our breaths coming fast and heavy.

Caleb's grip on my hips slowly loosened and he pressed a kiss to my neck, his fangs grazing my skin.

I turned to look at him, his navy eyes lighting with a different kind of hunger and I brushed my fingers along his jaw.

"What do you want most?" I breathed. "My body or my blood?"

He looked at me for a long moment, his eyes trailing down to take in our naked bodies still pressed together.

"Both?" he teased.

"What if you had to pick one?" I pushed.

"I've never tasted blood like yours before, it's like a drug in its own right. You're so powerful, so…it's just so fucking addictive, Tory. Even the other Heirs don't taste as good."

"So my blood then?" I asked, my fingers trailing down his chest and over the hard curves of his abs.

"No. I just want you to know what I'd be giving up if you made me pick," he said. "But I'm a selfish creature so I want both. If you forced a decision on me though I'd have to take your body. And I'd have the rest of you too if you're offering it?"

I scoffed lightly and he pressed a gentle kiss to my lips.

"Besides," he breathed. "I could always just challenge Orion and take your sister's blood instead."

I laughed. "Good to know you've got a back-up plan."

"Every good politician always does," he admitted.

His mouth caught mine again but this kiss wasn't as hurried as the last, the strength of his lust burning low for a while. His fingers trailed through my hair as his other hand drew a line down the length of my spine, causing me to arch into him, my chest brushing against his.

His tongue moved against mine and I felt as far from the shadows as I'd been since coming back to campus after the Eclipse. There was something about him that just made me feel calm and kept a smile dancing around my lips. He was unpredictable, funny, sometimes annoying as all hell and a total jackass too but most of all, what we had was simple. And I had far too many complications in my life most of the time.

A low growl escaped him as our kiss deepened, his mind clearly lingering on the desire he'd yet to act on with me. His teeth caught my bottom lip, his fangs almost breaking the skin as he dragged them across my tender flesh.

His grip on my hair tightened as he pulled it into his fist.

"Ask for it," he breathed against my mouth, his other hand splayed at the base of my spine. I still sat firmly in his lap, my legs wound around his waist and nothing dividing our bodies.

"Why?" I asked, drawing back just enough to look into his navy blue eyes.

"Because," he said, winding the length of my hair around his fist at an achingly slow pace. "Your blood gives me more pleasure than I can easily put into words. And the one thing that could make it even better, would be knowing that you want to give me that pleasure just as much as I want to take it."

The heat in his eyes was enough to make my heart beat harder, my pulse spiking and drawing his gaze to my throat. He swallowed thickly, his Adam's apple bobbing as he watched the hammering beat in my neck.

I'd never thought of his bites as something that I could enjoy. They were just a part of the package, a little painful, a touch humiliating, a dash annoying. But maybe that wasn't the only way to look at it. Maybe I should have thought a bit more about the fact that one of the most powerful Vampires in the whole of Solaria wanted my blood above all others. He could have his pick, there were plenty of Fae who would literally give anything to be his Source. And all I'd ever done was complain about it. If I was being honest, the bites didn't even hurt that much. They damaged my pride more than my body. But that was only because I wasn't giving him permission to do it. If I asked him to bite me then he wasn't doing anything against my will. It wasn't humiliating. It was my choice.

Besides, as his gaze stayed fixed on my thumping pulse, the darkness in it called to a primal part of me. He was a monster. And sometimes I was too.

"Caleb," I breathed, drawing his eyes back up to meet mine. I leaned forward, pressing my lips to his once more, my hands sliding over his broad shoulders. *"Bite me."*

Caleb groaned, his grip on my hair tightening as he yanked my head aside and drove his fangs into my neck.

My nails bit into his shoulders as he pierced the barrier of my flesh and my magic simultaneously and instead of waiting for it to be over, I let myself appreciate the moment of this strange connection between us and I dragged him closer.

Power slid from my veins alongside my blood but I didn't look at it as a theft for once. I looked at it as a gift. Just another form of pleasure I was willing to offer him. And as his muscles tensed beneath me, his grip on me tightening even further, I had to wonder which one of us was really at the other's mercy.

He drew back and I couldn't help but smile at the heated look he gave me.

"Fuck, Tory," he groaned. "I'm never going to figure you out, am I?"

"Hopefully not."

I smirked at him and pushed myself out of his lap, standing as I started hunting down my clothes.

I dressed myself and tried to shake the sand from my hair as Caleb pulled his clothes back on too.

I found my Atlas and checked the time, biting my lip as I realised I was going to be late to meet Darcy.

"Any chance you're feeling generous and want to run me back to The Orb so that I'm not late for Professor Nox?" I asked.

"You've got a class with Gabriel now?" Caleb asked in surprise. "What for?"

"Order Enhancement," I replied. "He's a Harpy so he said he'd give us private lessons for a bit to help us adjust more quickly. How come you call him Gabriel?"

"Oh, he's family," Caleb explained with a shrug. "And he's also half transformed into his Order form at practically every opportunity so you'll be in good hands with him teaching you."

He waved a hand, dispelling the earth magic he'd summoned into being around us so that the vines fell apart and the rocks crumbled back into sand like our temporary hiding place had never existed at all.

The sound of crashing waves filled the air and the briny tang of the sea filled my nostrils.

"Hop on then little monkey, we can't have me making you late," Caleb offered.

I grinned as I moved towards him and jumped up onto his back. Caleb caught my thighs as I locked my ankles around his waist and he took off towards The Orb.

The world blurred around us and I squealed as the wind tore through my hair and we shot down pathways, between buildings and around students.

We came to a halt outside The Orb and I slipped from Caleb's back with a shaky laugh.

He turned to face me, grinning as he ran a hand into his blonde curls and I backed up with a smile.

"Thanks for the ride," I said.

"Which one?" he teased and I couldn't help but laugh again.

I turned away from him and headed inside to find Darcy, straightening out my hair as I went.

I spotted her by the drinks chiller and headed over before she could make it to our usual spot with the *Ass* Club so that I could talk to her alone.

"Hey," she said brightly as she spotted me. "Did you have a good run?"

"Oh…yeah. Well I kinda got jumped by Caleb half way through it but I guess exercise is exercise right?"

"So he's back on the menu then, is he?" Darcy laughed and I grabbed a bottle of pink lemonade with a shrug.

"For now," I agreed before leading the way to a small table at the back of the room. "I actually wanted to talk to you about something before we head off."

"Oh?"

"Yeah." I paused to cast a silencing bubble around us and Darcy raised an eyebrow as that got her attention. "So it's...I mean it's no big deal but I thought I should tell you that I've been practicing with the shadows a little. On my own."

"What?" Darcy gasped, leaning towards me as she lowered her voice even though my spell made it unnecessary. "But Orion said it's too dangerous for us to-"

"I know what Orion said," I agreed. "But he's Darius's little buddy, isn't he? He doesn't want us to realise our full strength, he doesn't want us to pose a threat to Darius's precious throne."

"I think he's just trying to help."

"I know he is," I agreed. "But I also think he's probably helping Darius *more*. Making sure he learns how to wield the shadows better than us so that he can be sure he's still the strongest. And I'm sick of always being on the back foot with him and the other Heirs. We're more powerful than them, Darcy. And I'm ready to start proving it."

She pursed her lips like she was unsure but I knew the truth of my words had hit her. "I'm sure Orion really is trying to help...but maybe you have a point," she conceded. "Though I still think it's dangerous to mess around with the shadows alone."

"The shadows are *inside* us, Darcy. We're always messing around with them now whether we want to or not. I'm going to be careful about it but I'm not going to hide from them. I want to master this darkness in me before it has the chance to take the lead."

Darcy opened her mouth to reply but her gaze slid over my shoulder and she shot me a meaningful look. I glanced around too, spotting Professor Nox as he strode towards us through the thin crowd. His shirt was off, revealing a myriad of tattoos all over his flesh and his giant, black wings were tucked tight to his back. He was drawing a lot of stares but he didn't seem to have noticed.

I dropped the silencing bubble as he approached, a small smile pulling at his lips. "All ready to go?" he asked and we got to our feet, excitement dancing between us.

"Yes," Darcy said enthusiastically and he led the way outside as we hurried to follow.

I eyed his huge, feathered black wings as we walked, remembering the weight of my own wings on my back as a line of heat shivered along my shoulder blades like they were aching to be set free.

As soon as we made it outside, he stopped and turned to face us, pulling a small, silk pouch from the bag he held.

"We're going to take these lessons off campus," Nox explained as he held the stardust out between us. "Away from prying eyes."

We didn't get a chance to object before he'd tossed the glimmering black stardust over us and the academy disappeared as the stars tugged us away to our new destination.

Darcy caught my arm as we landed, almost sending us both flying and I laughed as I fought to right her.

I looked around at our new surroundings, taking in the lush greenery of a huge jungle to our left and the massive ravine carved into the ground to our right.

My gut spiralled with vertigo as I looked down into the enormous fissure which tore the jungle in half beside us. Thick, humid heat sat in the air and the calls of strange birds and animals reached us from the trees.

"Where are we?" Darcy gasped.

"The Baruvian Ravine in south Solaria. No Fae live anywhere near here and we're thousands of miles from the academy. No one will see us here and as an added bonus the updrafts here are insane. This is my favourite place to fly in the whole world," Professor Nox said with a dark smile.

"So we're just going to start flying, sir?" I asked, having half expected a really slow introduction to our gifts.

"Can you guys just call me Gabriel?" he asked with the hint of a smile. "I've already seen enough of our relationships in my visions to know we're Nebula Allies and if we're going to be friends for life I'd rather just cut the shit."

I barked a laugh and Darcy rose her eyebrows in surprise. "Are we allowed to just be friends with a Professor?" she asked sceptically.

"Allowed? Well, there aren't any specific rules against it. In fact the two of you should come and hang out with me and my friends this weekend. We've got the VIP room at Celest and there's an open bar."

I'd heard people talking about the exclusive bar in central Tucana, but as far as I knew it was practically impossible to get on the guest list, let alone into the VIP room.

"How did you manage to get tickets like that?" I asked suspiciously.

"Do you seriously think being Heirs to the Solarian throne doesn't make you VIPs?" Gabriel joked. "You could get in anywhere you wanted just by flashing them a smile."

My eyebrows rose at that, I'd never really considered things like that coming with our royal titles.

"I don't really think it would be acceptable for us to go clubbing with a teacher," Darcy added.

"Oh come on, Darcy, people do inappropriate things with teachers all the time," he teased.

"What's that supposed to mean?" Darcy gasped, blinking way too many times as if he'd just propositioned her or something and I snorted a laugh.

Gabriel carried on as if he hadn't even noticed her reaction. "Besides, I've found my Elysian Mate, so you're safe with me. My eyes never stray from my love and they certainly wouldn't settle on either of you."

I laughed, wondering if I should be offended by that statement but not feeling remotely inclined to be. Gabriel was intense and intriguing, there was something about him that drew me in and made me want to spend more time in his company, but there was zero sexual attraction there, even though in a purely analytical sense he was pretty much my type on paper – tall, dark, covered in tattoos and with a glint in his eye that promised trouble. I wondered if it was the mate bond turning me off and looked at the silver ring around his irises with interest.

"What's it like?" I asked curiously. "Finding your one true love?"

Gabriel's gaze softened as he thought about the girl who owned his heart and he smiled as he answered. "Like, getting hit with a truck and having it back over you several times while you lay bleeding in the dirt."

"What?" Darcy laughed.

"Yeah. It takes you by surprise, eats you up, spits you out and keeps you begging for more every single day. And once the bond was sealed between us…I feel like my whole fucking world begins and ends with her. I'll never get enough, the ache in me will never be satisfied. It's the best feeling in the world."

The grin on my face was way too wide to belong to me, but I couldn't help it. He was totally in love and it was too damn cute not to smile over.

"*Anyway,*" he interjected. "I've got a weird gift for you. And I want you to know that I had no involvement in the purchase of these – you can thank Professor Prestos for that. But I thought this would be preferable to the alternative."

Gabriel took two small parcels from his bag and tossed them to us. I unwrapped mine quickly and raised an eyebrow as I found a black bikini top inside it.

"You're going to need your backs bare if you want to set your wings free," he explained. "And this way you won't actually have to be topless. So if you wanna change into those, I'll wait."

I smirked at that and moved away as Gabriel turned his back to us. I quickly switched out my sports bra for the bikini top, tying it behind my neck and low on my back, leaving my shoulder blades free for my wings.

My heart was pounding faster and I turned back to Gabriel with a wide smile as I waited to find out what was next, finding Darcy waiting eagerly too.

"Okay, so I also brought spare sweatpants in case you accidentally set your whole Order free and burn yours off, but what I'm hoping to do is teach you both how to coax your wings out alone. If you can master that then no one will be able to tell you aren't Fire Harpies. Flaming wings are flaming wings after all."

My smile widened at that thought, I loved that we were pulling the wool over Daddy Acrux's eyes. And if we could do this then we could hide our true nature for as long as we needed while still holding the power of the Phoenixes beneath our flesh.

"How do we do it?" Darcy asked excitedly.

"Focus on the sensation in your shoulder blades and only that. Imagine your wings unfurling slowly, setting them free. Don't allow the rest of your

Order form to take any of your attention. Try to focus on the way they felt when you unleashed them before, the weight of them, the heat…"

I closed my eyes and did as he said, the fire in my back burning hotter as I focused on it.

I gasped as a flare of heat tore along my back and suddenly burst free.

My eyes flipped open as a heavy weight settled on my back and found myself looking at Darcy as her own flaming wings spread out behind her.

"Wow," I breathed. The only other time we'd been in our Order forms, it had been impossible to process everything properly. But now, in the blazing sunshine, I could really look at the huge, flaming wings which burned in a mixture of red and blue flames across golden feathers. The flames rippled like water, licking along the length of them and trailing behind the movements lazily.

"Are we going to start setting things alight whenever we touch something with them?" Darcy asked.

"Other Orders who wield a living flame are usually able to choose whether or not the flames hurt anything or anyone," Gabriel explained. "So assuming you maintain control and don't *want* to burn anything, you shouldn't."

He bent down and hooked a dry branch from the ground, holding it out to touch Darcy's wing. She flexed her muscles in response to the touch, her wings spreading a little but the stick remained unharmed.

Gabriel smiled triumphantly and looked towards me, tossing the stick aside. He reached out with his bare hand and my heart skittered in response.

"Do you mind?" he asked and I shook my head warily. "Don't worry, I have seen several snippets of my future, none of which involved me having a burned off hand."

A breath of laughter escaped me and he stepped forward. His fingers brushed down the centre of my wing and I shivered, the feeling almost like someone running their hands through my hair and yet entirely different at the same time.

"I think it's safe to say you won't be burning down any more dorm rooms any time soon. At least not accidentally."

"Any more?" I asked, my heart leaping. Gabriel might have seemed cool, but he was still a damn teacher and what I'd done to Darius's room could get me in a lot of trouble if it came out.

His only response was a knowing smirk before he turned and strode towards the canyon beside us.

"Flying is easy once you get a feel for it," he said. "But the easiest way to begin is by gliding. The updrafts above the ravine will keep you aloft all the time you have your wings spread wide. So the first challenge is to jump. After that you can get a feel for the way tilting and turning your body moves you through the air and try flapping your wings. It's a bit like learning to ride a bike; once you've got a feeling for the motions it's just natural."

He didn't wait for us to respond before leaping off of the cliff and I gasped as he free fell for a moment before snapping his wings out wide and gliding away from us in a graceful arc.

"Holy shit," Darcy breathed and a terrified yet excited laugh bubbled from my lips.

"Together?" I asked, holding my hand out to her.

She smiled as she took my hand. "Shall we just run for it?"

"On three?"

Darcy nodded and I steeled myself to do this insane thing.

"One, two, three-"

We sprinted for the edge of the cliff, releasing each other's hands as we dove over the edge.

A scream escaped me as I began to fall and I threw my arms out, urging the unfamiliar muscles of my wings to follow suit.

They snapped out and the wind instantly caught in them, the feeling of the air pressing into the folds of my feathers making adrenaline crash through my body as the updraft caught me and pushed me higher.

Darcy whooped her excitement and I looked up to see her soaring overhead, flaming wings burning brighter than the sun which was heading for the horizon in the distance.

I tilted my weight to the right and instantly turned that way, sweeping over the canyon and following the line of it for a few minutes as I got the feel for directing my movements. Once I felt more confident, I concentrated on flapping my wings. The first powerful beat of the flaming appendages on my back shot me forward at an alarming speed and I shrieked in excitement and surprise.

There was a lightness in my chest and a huge smile on my face as I beat them again, soaring, higher, faster, further. I'd never felt a rush like it, every inch of my skin was alight with power and energy, exhilaration and *fire*.

I whooped with joy as I spun through the sky, my wings beating hard as I moved faster and faster with my sister beside me.

I was flying, really, truly *flying*. And I'd never felt so alive or so free in all my life.

DARIUS

CHAPTER ELEVEN

I strolled towards Asteroid Place, smoothing down the non-existent creases in my black shirt and expelling a long breath.

With everything that had been going on recently, we hadn't had much chance for any down time and I was determined to make this night a stress free experience. It was Lance's twenty sixth birthday and we were going out partying. We would drink and dance and talk shit about things that didn't matter one fucking bit. Hell, we might even find some hot girls to keep us company and help us forget about our problems. Though as soon as that thought crossed my mind, an image of Roxy Vega came to me.

I growled, forcing the thought aside. It was getting fucking pathetic. I felt like a thirteen year old with a crush. All I ever did was think about her and fantasise about her, wonder what she was doing or if she was thinking about me too. Only to remember that even if by some miracle her thoughts fell on me from time to time, I'd done a bang up job of making sure that every single one of them would be filled with hate. So as far as hopeless crushes went, I was pretty much fucked. She didn't want me. And that should have been the end of it but of course it fucking wasn't. I'd fallen back on my old role of tormentor and I couldn't fucking stop myself from keeping it up. I didn't even know why half the time. Only that the only thing worse than her hating me was her ignoring me. Because then I knew she didn't care about me at all.

I clenched my fist tightly then released it again, forcing Roxy Vega out of my head. For tonight at least, I was going to forget about her. And my father. And my throne, the shadows, my responsibilities, the other Heirs, my school work, my betrothal and every other little fucking thing that caused me stress or grief in my life. Hell, I couldn't even remember the last night out I'd had that hadn't been tainted by something bad. I was probably in need of this as much as Lance was. So I was determined to make this birthday the best fucking birthday he'd ever had. It was going to be epic. Just the two of us without a care in the fucking world for one single night.

I approached Asteroid Place from the east, keeping away from the main path so that I could be sure no other teachers would see me. I was fairly sure a few of them had noticed my visits here from time to time, but so long as we all maintained the ruse of pretending it didn't happen I was pretty confident they wouldn't reprimand me for it. Being a Celestial Heir had some perks after all.

I reached the wrought iron fence that ringed the complex and took hold of two of the bars, exuding heat until I was able to bend them apart. Once I was able to, I squeezed through and fixed the bars back into position again from the other side.

I skirted between alleyways until I made it to Lance's bedroom window where I knocked lightly.

A moment later, he pushed the window wide and I hopped in. He was wearing baggy sweatpants and no shirt and didn't look in the least bit prepared for any kind of celebration.

"Hey," Lance said with a confused frown. "What are you-"

"Happy birthday," I interrupted, pulling him into a tight embrace. "We're going out."

"No," he said, shaking his head as he stepped out of my arms. "I don't celebrate my birthday. Not since Clara, you know I-"

"Oh come on, Lance," I urged. "We need a night out. We need to get out of this place and out of our heads and just forget about all the shit here for one night of freedom."

He groaned, turning away from me and padding back through to his front room where he snagged a glass of bourbon from the counter.

"I'm already having a party for one right here," he said, settling back into his seat on the couch.

"Fuck that. This is the most pathetic birthday I've ever seen. Those pants are stained for fuck's sake. What the hell has happened to you, man? You used to be cool!"

Lance looked down at the orange stain on his grey sweatpants and a smirk pulled at his lips.

"I had spaghetti," he said defensively.

"Please tell me it was at least made from scratch by the kitchen staff and you didn't just microwave it," I said.

"Well it was fresh yesterday…"

"Fuck no. You're not spending your birthday in stained sweatpants eating reheated leftovers. We're going out. No excuses."

"Yeah, okay," he agreed finally, shooting away into his room to get changed.

I crossed into the kitchen and poured myself a measure of bourbon, knocking it back so the strong taste of it rolled down my throat. I poured another and emptied that too. I didn't want to waste a moment of the night I had planned. I'd gotten us a table in the VIP room in Celest so we could do whatever the fuck we wanted without having to worry about the press catching sight of us and I was planning on getting wasted.

Lance returned in a grey shirt and jeans, his dark hair styled and a grin on his face that said he was ready to party with me.

"Fuck yes," I said, enthusiastically, reaching into my back pocket and holding out the envelope for him.

He indulged me with a smirk as he accepted it and pulled out the birthday card, flipping it open to discover his gift inside.

"Pit side seats for the entire Solarian Pitball League Cup?" he said, letting out a low whistle.

Yeah, they'd cost a small fortune but if I wasn't going to spend money on my friend for his birthday then what the hell did I even have so much of it for?

"Thanks, man, these are-"

A loud knock came from the front door and Lance looked around in surprise before motioning for me to hide.

I sighed irritably as I slipped into his room. Though I imagined he'd be in even more trouble if someone found me in his bedroom than he would if they'd found me out there. I was a student out of bounds though, so I guessed I just had to suck up the hiding bullshit.

"Noxy!" Lance cried enthusiastically from the front room and I scowled as the Harpy yelled out his little nickname in return. I hadn't gotten that kind of a welcome and I was his best fucking friend. The two of them acted so fucking weird together, like they were both these cheery, jokey little buddies who giggled all the damn time but when they weren't together, neither of them acted like that at all. Gabriel hardly even spoke unless he had to and certainly not to me. And Lance's reputation as an asshole was well earned. But together they were like Bert and fucking Ernie. *Nebular Allies my ass.* The other Heirs were all my Nebular Allies but I didn't start jumping up and down like a little girl at a princess party every time I hung out with them.

"Orio! Happy birthday! I almost missed the vision about this, but it looks like I just made it. What time are we heading out?" Gabriel's voice came and my scowl deepened.

What the hell? This is supposed to be our *night!*

Great, now I was sounding like a fucking jealous girlfriend even inside my own head.

I folded my arms and waited for Lance to get rid of him so that I could come out again and we could get the fuck out of here, far, far away from third wheels.

"Oh," Lance said, stalling as he came up with an excuse to get rid of the Harpy. "Well I was just going to-"

"It's alright, I know Darius is here and he's coming out with us. I saw it. I also saw myself not being an asshole and ruining the night by turning him in to campus security so we're all cool."

Lance laughed at that and the sound of it was way too loud and went on way too long to be genuine. It wasn't even fucking funny. He was just stating facts about his visions. I could state facts about things that were happening and they wouldn't be funny. *The air is cool. That bed looks comfortable. The door is ajar. Not fucking funny. Dammit.*

"Come out Goldilocks!" Gabriel called. "The bears are promising not to bite tonight."

I ground my teeth and strode out of the bedroom to find Lance pouring him a drink just as Gabriel took a small, square package from his pocket wrapped in red paper.

"Hi," I said to Gabriel and he gave me a vague nod without even looking my way properly.

Lance smirked as he accepted the gift, tearing it open with a swipe of his thumb and flipping the lid on the jewellery box inside.

They both started laughing instantly and Lance cooed. "No fucking way! This is just like the one I-"

"I know! I saw it and I just *knew.*"

"Too right!" Lance could barely get his words out around his laughter and I frowned as he slid a tacky, plastic signet ring onto his middle finger.

"Oooooooooo!" They both started saying together waving their hands like they'd lost control of them.

"Am I missing something here?" I asked as Lance tossed the Pitball tickets I'd bought him down on the coffee table without even looking to check where they'd landed. His gaze was locked on that tacky piece of plastic like it was a goddamn rainbow stone.

"Oh yeah, a few years ago when we-"

"We got lost along the Pontus Bay walk. And do you remember when we-"

"Ohhhh shit yeah! I'd almost forgotten all about that!" Lance fell into laughter again, waving me off as I frowned, looking for the rest of the joke which apparently they weren't sharing.

"You kinda had to be there," Gabriel said with a shrug.

"Yeah," Lance agreed. "It's hard to explain. Don't worry about it. Let's all get going."

"All?" I asked, my gaze fixing on Gabriel. "I only made reservations for the two of us and it's pretty exclusive-"

"It's fine, I already added to the reservation," Gabriel said dismissively, not even looking at me.

My lips parted on another protest, thoughts swirling in my mind as I tried to think of anything I could say that wouldn't come off like I was being a brat, stamping my foot and demanding time alone with *my* friend. But I came up blank.

Lance was grinning like this was a great fucking addition to the night's plans even though until about ten minutes ago his only intended birthday celebration had been reheated goddamn spaghetti and getting drunk alone.

I sighed, reaching into my pocket and pulling out the pouch of stardust I'd brought to get us into the club. Arriving this way meant no press would catch onto us and realise I was there so we could have a night of freedom. Plus, it got rid of the need for designated drivers as we could just reappear back home in the blink of an eye.

I tossed a handful of stardust over us and Orion's house swirled out of sight as we were transported through the stars to Celest.

The heavy bass of the music reached me a moment before the air swirled and the club's arrival hall materialised around us.

A pink lip-glossed serving girl walked forward with a wide smile as she spotted us, holding out a tray with three glimmering glasses of Fae champagne.

I accepted mine with a nod of thanks, emptying the glass and setting it back down on the tray.

The magic infused in the drink bubbled through my veins and I felt myself relax as it got to work stealing my worries and helping me to focus on happy thoughts.

"Good evening, gentlemen, I'm Alissa and I'll be your personal chaperone this evening," the serving girl said with a bright smile. "I hear we have a birthday boy amongst us?"

Lance groaned as Gabriel threw an arm around his shoulders and pressed him forward. "Here he is!"

"The staff at Celest would like to send our warmest congratulations!" the girl said. "Here we think that a birthday boy should be treated like royalty so-" She took a golden crown from the table behind her and placed it on his head. Lance looked like he was caught between amusement and the desire to take it off. "Happy birthday, your majesty." She bowed low and Lance barked a laugh. "If you'd like to follow me, I'll take you on up to the royal table. Your other guests have already arrived."

"Other guests?" I asked with a frown, but she'd already turned away and headed up the silver staircase at the back of the room without hearing me.

"That was my idea," Gabriel said with a knowing smile. "I had a vision about it and inviting them will make your night exponentially more enjoyable, Orio."

Who says exponentially? And who the hell gave him permission to bulldoze our fucking night? If it wasn't for the fact that this whole thing had been my idea and that I wanted to celebrate Lance's birthday with him, I'd have been sorely tempted to bail. I could only hope that whoever the hell else he'd invited wasn't as irritating as him.

Alissa led the way into the VIP room which was located on the third floor of the club. The room was really a balcony which had a magical wall to the right of it where we could look down over the rest of the people enjoying the club. If they looked back our way, all they could see was a sea of sparkling silver stars to maintain our privacy.

Everything in the room was black, inlaid with swirling silver patterns from the floors to the walls, tables and chairs.

Alissa led us through the small crowd gathered around the bar and over to a booth with a padded bench curved like a horseshoe ringing a low table. A curtain of glimmering silver lights hung around it, creating a cocoon of dimly lit space inside. There were two half empty glasses abandoned on the table, one pale pink cocktail with a cocktail stick full of cherries sitting in it and a tumbler which was almost empty and had red lipstick marking the rim.

"Who else is here?" I asked as Lance and Gabriel took their seats and glanced at the menu.

"Oh, your other guests headed to the dance floor," Alissa explained.

I looked over at the raised area on the other side of the room where people were dancing to Billie Eilish's Bad Guy and my heart leapt as I spotted Roxy Vega dancing with her sister like she didn't have a care in the goddamn world.

She was wearing a red dress which hugged her perfect figure and showed off her long, bronze legs. Her dark hair was half pulled up in some kind of messy bun and trailed over one shoulder, looking like an artist's version of just fucked. My mouth dried out as I watched her, my heart beating faster just looking at her. I knew I shouldn't. I knew I should be angry she was here but a selfish, secret part of me wondered if she might just overlook our differences tonight. The few times I'd gotten close to her had been when she was relaxed like this.

"You invited the Vegas?" Lance asked suddenly as he spotted them too and I dropped into my seat, pointing at the first thing I saw on the menu so that Alissa would leave us alone.

Gabriel smiled widely. "Yeah, they know how to party."

"How the hell would you know that?" I asked. "You literally just met them."

"Maybe psychically," Gabriel replied dismissively like I was the one acting weird, but I didn't see how he could just claim vision friendships with people and act like he didn't have to put in any fucking groundwork to actually make that into reality.

"I don't think we should really be out drinking with students," Lance said warily, his gaze still on the Vegas who hadn't looked our way yet.

"Students like Darius?" Gabriel asked with a snort of laughter.

I almost said *I'm different,* but realised that would sound a bit odd.

"I guess…" Lance said and I was surprised when he didn't raise more objections. "I mean, we're all together, there's nothing inappropriate going on and no one can see us here. So I suppose it doesn't matter."

Alissa returned with our drinks, smiling widely as she laid them out between us.

As she stepped away from the table, the Vegas appeared.

They fell still as they spotted us, Roxy's gaze narrowing while Gwen's eyes widened in surprise.

"Fuck, Gabriel, when you said we were coming out with your friends, I assumed it would be people we didn't know. Not tweedleass and tweedledipshit," Roxy said, folding her arms and pushing her tits up in the process. Her eyes were lined in black and her lips painted a deep red to match her dress. I didn't think I'd ever seen a girl I desired as much as her and I couldn't stop myself from drinking in the sight of her even while she stood insulting me right to my face.

"Believe me, if we'd known this place had such low standards, we wouldn't have come here either," I deadpanned, unable to resist the urge to bite back at her.

Her gaze cut to mine and her eyes swept over me slowly, seemingly drinking in the sight of me just as I was her. That illusion was shattered though as she looked away again dismissively, not rising to the bait and ignoring me yet again. That shit was getting old fast and I gritted my teeth in irritation as she proceeded to act like I wasn't even fucking here.

"I didn't know it was your birthday," Gwen said, her eyes on Lance like she was surprised by the news.

He gave her a half smile, seeming a little embarrassed. "I don't usually like to celebrate but Gabriel and Darius decided to surprise me with a night out so…"

Gabriel and Darius? What the fuck? I organised this whole thing and that asshole just gate-crashed it!

"Well, happy birthday," Gwen said, dropping down into the seat beside him and pressing a kiss to his cheek. He turned towards her as she did and she almost caught his mouth. She blushed as she drew back, looking flustered and turned to give her sister a pointed look.

"Oh, yeah, happy birthday," Roxy said, placing her hands down on the table and leaning forward to kiss Lance too. The red lipstick print she left on his cheek was about as far from his mouth as possible and she drew back the moment she'd delivered it.

Gabriel jumped up and pulled the two of them into a hug over the table and Roxy laughed as she was crushed to his broad chest like they really were old friends. I didn't get it. They'd only met him a week ago and he was their damn teacher, why were they instantly acting like they were best friends, offering out hugs and laughs and somehow making me feel like I was the odd one out at a party *I'd* fucking organised?

He released them and waved at Alissa to bring us more drinks as he sat down again and the girls followed suit.

Roxy cast a look my way for a moment before reaching over and snagging the cocktail stick full of cherries from her sister's glass. Gwen made a half assed complaint as Roxy smirked at her.

I couldn't tear my gaze away from her mouth as she slowly drew a cherry off of the stick and pulled it between her lips. The girl was seductive without even fucking trying. I was getting hard just looking at her and she still wasn't looking at me, her eyes on Gabriel as he started going on about some game he wanted to play. I gave his words enough of my attention so that I'd know the rules while continuing to watch Roxy fucking Vega eating cherries.

"It's simple. We come up with dares and take it in turn to do them. Anyone who chickens out or can't complete it has to drink a shot of Sourache-"

"What's that?" Gwen asked.

"It's a shot that tastes like absolute shit and is imbued with magic that makes your entire body ache for a whole minute," Lance explained. That didn't really cover the fucking awful experience you got from drinking Sourache, but I decided not to expand on it. They'd find out for themselves soon enough if they lost the game.

"So, when you get a dare you can pick one other person to help you complete it if you want to. But if you fail with help, then you have to take two shots," Gabriel finished.

"Okay, but you might as well prepare yourselves to lose because me and Darcy are gonna whoop your asses," Roxy taunted.

"Well there's a first time for everything," I said mildly.

Roxy's eyes lit with the challenge as she glanced my way, but her attention quickly diverted back to Gabriel as she went back to ignoring me.

The Dragon stirred beneath my skin and I fought off the urge to growl. People didn't ignore me. It rubbed against every ingrained part of my nature to allow her to continue, but snapping at her wasn't going to work. So I'd make it my mission to get her attention tonight whatever way I could.

I smirked as I thought of that, getting to my feet and heading away from the table to track down our chaperone. Alissa spotted me before I made it more than a few steps and I ordered a tray of Sourache shots for the game before turning back to the table.

I dropped into the seat beside Roxy and she exhaled irritably as I threw my arm around the back of her chair.

"So who's picking the first dare?" Gwen asked, tucking a lock of her dark blue hair behind her ear.

"I dare Roxy to be nice to me tonight," I said and the others all looked between us.

150

She sighed impatiently. "Pass. Give me the sour shot thing," she said.

Gabriel laughed way too loudly in response to that and the others joined in too. I grinned at her, just glad to have forced her to actually respond to something I'd said and ready to keep pushing her for more. Because I couldn't fucking help it. If she was here and looking like that then every inch of my attention was going to be on her whether she wanted it or not.

Alissa delivered the tray of Sourache shots for our game and Roxy leaned forward to snare one. She eyed the violent green liquid with a raised eyebrow for a moment before tipping it into her mouth and swallowing it in one.

Her back straightened and her hand gripped the table as she fought against the urge to cry out from the effects of the shot and we all laughed. Gwen stared at her sister with her lips parting, reaching out to pat her back like she was wasn't sure how to help her.

The minute wore out and Roxy released a breath as her posture relaxed and she barked a laugh.

"That stuff is fucking awful," she said. "But it's still less painful than fulfilling that dare would have been."

I laughed before I could stop myself. That girl had bigger balls than half the guys I knew. Max practically started crying if we made him take a shot of Sourache and Seth howled the whole time its effects were in place. Roxy barely broke a sweat and came out swinging on the other end of it.

This night may not have been going the way I'd planned. But maybe it was still salvageable after all.

ORION

CHAPTER TWELVE

"**Y**our turn, birthday boy." Gabriel smirked, leaning in to sling his arm around my shoulders, but I was more focused on Darcy's bare leg pressed up against mine and her black dress which had a v-cut dropping all the way down between her cleavage. I wanted to run my hands all over it while I tasted the strawberry daiquiri on her lips.

The waitress had brought us even more drinks, but I was nursing my bourbon. If I got drunk, my willpower was going to take a battering and I'd start plotting ways to get Blue alone. Which was risky as shit in a bar full of people and my current company. Then again…Darius was my best friend and Gabriel was my Nebula Ally…would they really sell me out anyway?

Fuck you, bourbon. You do not get a say in this. It doesn't help that that lusty bitch Venus is back in my chart today either.

Then again, it is my birthday…

The less people who knew about us, the better though. It meant there was fewer chances for slip ups and less people to get in trouble if it ever came out. No, it wasn't worth the risk.

"Orio." Gabriel shook me. "I said it's your turn."

"Right, yeah. What's the dare, Noxy?" I asked.

Gabriel gazed over the balcony down at the sea of dancing bodies below. "That guy." He pointed to a man standing at the bar with a red neckerchief and a moustache he was fucking twirling.

"You mean the douchebag?" I clarified.

"Yeah," Gabriel laughed, turning back to me. "I dare you to get that neckerchief from him without him realising."

Darcy laughed and I shot a smile at her. Her hand landed on my thigh beneath the table and my dick jumped to attention.

"Are you gonna do it?" Her big green eyes sparkled and the way she bit into her lip with excitement had me tumbling into insanity. *Fuck it.*

I tossed back my bourbon, gazing around the faces at the table as I picked an accomplice. The only one of them who wasn't smiling at me was Tory. She'd managed to create two inches of solid space between her and Darius despite how close his seat was to hers and she looked ready to leave. Darcy glanced at her with a frown and my lips pursed.

The only way my girl was going to stay here for the night was if her sister stayed too. And more than that…she was important to Darcy. I supposed I could make an effort for her. No matter how fucking uncomfortable that might be.

I pointed at Tory and her eyebrows shot up. "Come on, thief, I seem to recall you're great at stealing things."

She passed Darius a grin at that and he glowered back.

"Yeah Roxy's *real* good at deceiving people," Darius growled.

"Not as good as you are. Honestly, I don't think half your friends have realised you have no personality yet," Tory said airily then firmly went back to ignoring him.

On reflection, maybe bringing up the time Tory had burned his room down and stolen his draining dagger hadn't been the best move. But it was too late now.

I stood up and Gabriel sidled out of the booth to let me go. Tory tossed back her drink before moving to my side, her expression closed off as she approached me.

"So what's the plan, *sir*?" she asked coldly.

"You don't have to call me sir tonight," I corrected. "Come on." I jabbed her in the back to make her move toward the staircase and we headed down into the thronging crowd.

I leaned close to talk over the loud music. "You flirt with him and I'll get the neckerchief from behind."

Tory cracked a laugh, shaking her head at me. "That guy is gayer than the day is long, dude. So *you* flirt with him and I'll get the neckerchief." She slipped away into the crowd before I could respond to that and I scraped a hand through my hair, remaining in place.

Shit.

A waitress sailed by with a tray of shots and I grabbed a bright pink one, knocking it back and wincing against the powerfully sweet taste. Heat burned in my chest and I headed through the crowd toward the bar, the melodic thump of the bass pounding in my ears. I pushed through a group of girls who giggled and tried to snare me for a dance, but I waved them off and made it to the bar where the guy was leaning against it, still twirling his damn moustache.

Tory was already behind him, trying to get the barman's attention. She glanced over her shoulder, catching my eye and fighting a grin. I cleared my throat, stepping up next to the guy and letting my gaze slide down his dark blazer before dragging it slowly back up again.

"Hey," I said with a nod and half a smile.

His eyes whipped up and down me too and apparently I made the cut as he stepped closer.

"Hey." He smiled back and I caught Tory rolling her eyes at me over his shoulder. She mouthed *try harder* and I let my inhibitions fly away as I stepped closer to him. I wasn't going to lose at this. I fucking invented this game.

"Do you want a drink?" I offered.

He twirled his moustache again and I inwardly cringed. He shifted closer, reaching out to splay his hand across my chest. "Yeah I want something tall, dark and handsome."

"Well…order's up." I nearly cracked up as Tory fell into silent hysterics behind him.

The guy grinned, his eyes flipping to the crown on top of my head. "Oh my stars, is it your birthday?"

"Yeah." I shrugged and Tory shifted closer behind him. She reached up, brushing her fingers over the back of his neckerchief and the guy went to glance behind him. On impulse, I caught his face between my hands, forcing him to look at me.

A solid lump rose in my throat as I gazed at that bristly moustache which I had absolute no desire to get closer to. "I have a present I need help... unwrapping."

Tory met my eyes over his shoulder, reaching for the neckerchief again while biting her lip to stop from laughing.

"I have very nimble fingers," the guy purred and I bit down on the inside of my cheek as I pretended to be into that.

"Good, 'cause I've got a ribbon that needs *pulling*."

I'm gonna lose it.

Tory had the neckerchief undone and I knew I needed to give her one more second so I dragged him against me, leaning toward his ear as the scent of his musky aftershave overwhelmed my senses. "I'll come for you later."

"Yeah you'll come real hard for me," he growled, his hand pushing between us and grazing across my shirt. He pinched my nipple before I could do a fucking thing to stop it. *Argh.*

I lurched away, heading into the crowd where Tory was waiting, swinging the neckerchief and dancing to the music.

She grabbed my arm, her eyes bright with amusement. "Did he notice?"

"No. He was too busy tweaking my fucking nipple," I told her, serving me a few alarmed stares from the Fae dancing nearby as I rubbed my chest.

Tory fell apart, laughing as we headed back across the room. "You're not as much of a bore as I thought." She shouted over the thumping tune.

"I'm still an asshole though," I said with a smirk and she grinned.

"Yep." She snorted as we reached the balcony and headed through the shimmering stars blocking the view of the booth. Everyone was laughing and Darcy glanced between us with the brightest smile as Tory bowed dramatically and tossed the neckerchief at the heart of the table.

Gabriel jumped up to let me back in my seat and I turned to Darcy with a dark smile. "Your turn, Blue."

"What's the dare?" she asked as my gaze slipped down to her lips and my insides knotted up. *What I'd give for the whole world to freeze right now so I could steal a kiss.*

156

I glanced around the table, my gaze catching on Darius's frown. I didn't want to think he was having a shitty time because of our current company. Some of the most important people in the world to me sat around this table. Him included. I wished he could get along with them.

"I dare you to make Darius laugh," I said, taking a sip of my drink.

She grinned, a mischievous look entering her gaze. "Okay…will you be my partner?"

I nodded and she reached into her purse, taking out a pen and writing something on her hand. She held it below the table for me to read and I frowned as I read the word *sucker* a second before she cast a shot of water at my face. My head and shoulders were drenched and everyone started laughing, even Darius.

Darcy beamed at me triumphantly as I raised a hand to dry the water dripping from my hair with magic.

"I'm going to get you back for that," I warned, but it only made her smile widen.

She turned to her sister to continue the game and Gabriel threw me a wink, pushing my bourbon closer to me.

"Drink up, Orio," he said and I clinked glasses with him before tipping the whole lot into my mouth.

I was drunk. So fucuuuking drunk. And horny.

Plan of dreams: Step one…get Blue naked. Oh shit wait, I need more steps.

Darcy was dancing with her sister on the edge of the balcony while Gabriel ordered more drinks and I watched them with Darius at my side. Just fucking watched, like it was okay to watch. Definitely wasn't. But I was four bourbons and two Souraches too late to give a shit.

"I love you," I told Darius, slinging my arm around him. "You're so lucky, man. You could just go and be with Tory Vega. Just go and *be* with her."

"You're speaking out of your ass," Darius said, leaning into me. "Why does that make me lucky anyway? You hot for Tory? Cause I'll beat your ass."

He clenched my shirt in his fist and I blew out a breath of laughter. He half looked like he was joking and half looked like he meant it.

"I'm not, but you are. By the stars, go and tell her."

"Yeah." Darius nodded, bolstering himself up. "Yeah I'm just gonna walk over there and – and- for the love of the moon this is soft." He raked his hand down my shirt. "What's it made of?"

"I dunno, man. Cotton?" I plucked at the shirt and Darius leaned into me, bringing the seductive scent of his blood with him. "You smell like freshly baked bed... I mean *bread*."

"Do you wanna bite me, Lance?" Darius laughed darkly, catching my face between his hands and squeezing until my lips pursed. Then he angled my head toward the Vegas. "Your Source is over there."

My eyes hooked on Darcy's tight waist and the way her body moved in time with the music. I started to get hard for her and shoved Darius back. *He does not need to feel my boner. Not again.*

I stood up abruptly, my eyes set on my girl as my fangs lengthened. Gabriel appeared with my crown on his head, his silver-ringed eyes hooded as he made his way toward us.

"I'm checking out." He took off the crown, throwing it at Darius like his head was a hoop toss and it hit him right in the eye.

"Motherfucker," Darius hissed.

Gabriel rested a hand on my shoulder. "I'm gonna stardust home and screw my wife," he said loudly just as the music stopped between songs.

The girls laughed and I smirked at Gabriel, pulling him into a hug as I stood up. "Say hi from me. You know, after the screwing. Or is after weirder? Maybe before. No after. Definitely after."

"Orio I'm gonna be way too fucking busy to say hello from you." Gabriel grinned then his eyes drifted to the Vega girls and he angled me toward them. *Why does everyone keep pointing me at Darcy tonight? It's killing me.*

"Look after her," he said before heading over to say goodbye to them then stardusting himself out of there. All the teachers at Zodiac were gifted a weekly ration of stardust and I knew exactly what I was going to use the rest of mine for tonight.

Wait, did he say look after her*? Why not* them*?*

"After party at King's Hollow?" Darius offered. "The guys are there, but they won't care if you come. I'll tell them I need some time with my Guardian or some shit."

He definitely hadn't thought that plan through, but it also sounded like way too much of a sausage fest for me.

"Nah, I'm gonna head back. I'll take the Vegas so you can go straight there?" I offered.

Darius stood up, pulling me into a tight embrace, his muscles locking around me. The bond between us grew sharper and I clutched onto him. "I'm gonna miss you," I said out loud even though I'd meant to say it in my head.

"As much as Gabriel?" Darius asked, his forehead knocking against mine.

"You guys need to get a room," Tory interrupted and we stepped away from each other.

Darius bumped into the table as he moved toward her. "After party at King's Hollow?" he asked her and I looked to Tory hopefully on his behalf.

She swept past him as if he didn't exist, picking up her cocktail and sipping it through a straw. Darius clenched his fists, glaring after her and looking like he was about to pop a vein in his temple.

Darcy was still dancing on the spot and I grinned stupidly at her as her eyes met mine.

"Let's go." I took the stardust out of my pocket and Darius took out his own pouch. "Night Darius."

Tory glanced his way, her eyes pinned on him as he tossed the glittering dust into the air and disappeared.

"Ready?" I asked the girls as they grabbed their purses from the booth.

They nodded and I planted a large tip on the table before throwing the stardust over us.

We were dragged through the network of stars and my feet hit the ground outside The Orb. Darcy stumbled into me with a giggle and I was reminded of the first time we'd travelled by stardust together on the night of her Awakening. I steadied her before remembering to move away and looked to Tory.

"I can walk you back to your Houses," I offered, but Tory waved a hand at me.

"Walk Darcy back, I'm good. Night." She hugged her sister.

"Are you sure? I can come back with you?" Darcy offered.

"I need to sprawl across the whole bed tonight," Tory said with a grin. "See you tomorrow." She waved over her head as she walked off down the path toward Fire Territory and I turned to Darcy, suddenly getting my wish sooner than I'd expected.

"Blue." I smiled dreamily, tucking a lock of hair behind her ear.

She is so...everything. Does she know how everything she is?

She moved up into my personal space, tip-toeing to whisper in my ear. "Where can we go that's private?"

I slid my hands around her waist, half tempted to shove her up against the wall of The Orb and devour her right here. Her blood called to me like a Siren's song and I ran the pad of my tongue up her throat, making her laugh.

"I know..." I muttered, scooping her up and using my Vampire speed to shoot toward Jupiter Hall. It was closed up at night, but my magic unlocked the door and I ran inside, carrying her to the Cardinal Magic classroom and unlocking that too before hurrying in.

I cast a silencing bubble a second before her lips found mine. She tasted like sin and strawberries, making me groan.

"Do you know how many times I've wanted you in this classroom?" I asked between kisses, running my mouth down to her throat. She tilted her head to one side, clawing her hands through my hair as her thighs latched tighter around me.

"How many?" she asked breathlessly.

"Four million, three hundred thousand, two hundred and ninety eight – no make that ninety *nine* times." I hardened between her thighs and pleasure bounced through my limbs as I raked my fangs down her neck. By the sun, this *girl*.

I was just about to sink my teeth into her soft flesh when she pushed me back and dropped to her feet. She slipped away from me, running to my desk and jumping straight into my seat.

"What are you doing?" I growled, stalking after her as she grabbed a pen and paper from my desk, shielding it with her arm as she started writing.

"Nothing," she sang. "Look away Mr Grumpcakes."

"That's Professor Grumpcakes to you," I teased and she snorted a laugh. Her breasts were brushing my desk and a cascade of blue hair washed over it as she leaned in close to the page.

I approached slowly, my breathing increasing as I tried to restrain myself from flipping her over my desk and fulfilling the fantasy I'd been having a lot lately.

Darcy finally looked up, grinning like the Cheshire Cat as she started ripping the page into six squares. Then she stood, gathering them all into a pile and holding them behind her back.

"I don't know what you're up to, but it's getting me so hot," I growled, stepping closer to her until she pressed a firm hand to my chest.

"Well as you didn't give me a heads up that it was your birthday today, I've had to improvise on a last minute gift."

"Let me have it," I insisted, grinning darkly as I held out my hand.

She planted the pile of paper in my palm with a sexy as fuck look on her face. I had to drag my eyes away from her to pay attention to the gift.

The words on the first one stared up at me, bringing a wicked smile to my lips.

I O U

One kiss anywhere you like.

My pulse elevated as I flicked to the next one.

I O U

One strip tease.

"Oh fuck yes," I breathed, thumbing through the rest.

"There's only one condition," she said cheekily. "You can only use one at a time. Don't be greedy."

"I'm nothing but greedy when it comes to you." I grabbed her waist and she slinked away, holding out her hand.

"Well you'll have to control that. So...would sir like to redeem one of his vouchers?" she put on an overly posh accent and I barked a laugh.

I placed the strip tease request in her hand and she eyed it with a flirtatious smile. I dropped down into my office chair, opening a button at my neck as I watched her with hungry eyes.

She placed her purse down on the desk, taking her Atlas out of it and tapping away on the screen. I took the opportunity to trace the curve of her ass with my eyes and picture her bent over my desk again. A low and impatient growl escaped me and she glanced up with a grin.

Raise Hell by Dorothy played and as the heavy pound of rock music filled the air, Darcy hurried across the room to kill the lights. I was plunged into darkness a second before she cast a fireball which hung above her, twisting and turning, lighting the room in a deep red and gold glow.

"Ten House points to Aer," I said with a smirk, sinking lower in my seat and spreading my legs to get comfortable.

Her laughter rang back to me then she did a dramatic hair flip which brought a chuckle to my lips. She ground against Tyler Corbin's desk, rolling her hips to the music. She was trying to be funny, but fuck did it look hot too. Her dress rode up almost all the way to her panties and I sucked on my lower lip as she hooked her thumb under the hem, riding it high enough to give me a glimpse of her ass as she leaned forward over his desk.

She spun around, stumbling sideways and hitting the desk beside it. I chuckled but my amusement died away again as she turned toward me, striding up to my desk and leaning on it, giving me a look down her cleavage.

"Come here," I groaned, aching to be inside her.

She ignored me, crawling up onto my desk and sending a stapler and a pen pot crashing to the floor as she pushed them aside. Her dress rode up even higher as she knelt up then dragged it over her head and spun it above her before tossing it away. *Fuuuck.*

A tight lump pushed at my throat as I discovered she didn't have a bra on and only a tiny lacy thong. I was gonna go mad if I didn't get my hands on her soon. It was taking every ounce of willpower I had to remain sitting there.

She pushed her hands into her hair and rolled her hips to the music while I appreciated her body and my fangs lengthened to sharp points.

I was rock hard and desperate, shifting forward to rise from my seat.

She dropped over the edge of the desk and straddled me in the chair, keeping me in place. My hand slammed down on her back as I tried to drag her in for a kiss.

She twisted her head to stop me, sliding her palm down my chest and undoing buttons as she went. When she reached my waistband, her fingers curled around my belt and into my pants, grazing the tip of my dick with her soft fingers.

I thrust my hips with a groan and she smiled wickedly at me, removing her hand and taking hold of my belt buckle.

A heady giggle escaped her and she leaned in to rest her forehead to my chest.

"What?" I grunted, grazing my hands over her ass as more blood pumped south, making my head spin and my need for her grow even keener.

"It's just…this is Orion's belt," she started laughing harder and I grinned. Her blue hair tickled my chest and I reached up to bunch my hand in it, tugging backwards to make her look at me.

"It is. And Orion wants you to take it off right fucking now," I commanded and her lips popped open, desire unfolding in her eyes. She started pulling at it without another ounce of laughter, but I'd had enough of waiting.

I clutched her ass, standing and throwing her down on my desk, her hair fanning across it and making my dick twitch with need. I shrugged out of my shirt then tugged myself free of my pants.

Without giving her any warning, I ripped her panties aside and slammed into her. She cried out, her back arching as I dug my fingers into her waist, pleasure bleeding through every vein in my body. She was burning hot and fucking perfect, her muscles tightening around me as I claimed her with another hard thrust.

I shifted one hand to circle my thumb against her clit and she moaned loudly, the sound making me even harder as I pounded into her. I took her with powerful thrusts of my hips and she rubbed against my desk, branding it for-fucking-ever. How I was ever gonna teach in this room again without getting hard was tomorrow's goddamn problem.

Pleasure and adrenaline rolled through my body in a divine cocktail and a bead of sweat ran down my spine. I leaned down to brush my tong͏ her nipple before sinking my fangs into the swell of her breast. She moaned, her fingers clawing at my back as I drank her blood, getting high off of every mouthful. Her power tasted like candy and air. She was sweet and sharp and fucking delicious.

I pulled my fangs free and a bead of blood raced across her flesh, turning me on even more. I hooked my hand under her right thigh, forcing her legs wider then drove into her again, savouring the feeling of her body wrapped around me.

Blue shut her eyes with a cry of delight and I clutched her jaw with a growl.

"Look at me," I demanded and her eyes flew open, her pupils dilating. She came for me, her whole body bucking and her muscles tightening. I held her hips at the perfect angle, her body driving me to ecstasy as I stilled deep inside her, pleasure rocketing through me and making me unable to draw breath as I rode out the high of my release.

"*Yes*," she gasped, her hand curling around the back of my neck as she drew me down for a kiss. I didn't bother to return her breath to her with air magic. It felt too good to feel how destroyed she was beneath me, her limbs holding no strength at all as she tried to clutch onto me. I barely had any left myself.

I trailed my mouth along her jaw and braced my hands on the desk to keep my weight off of her.

She traced her fingers down my backbone, her lips brushing mine and sending a shiver scattering through my body. It had been so long since I'd felt content. But with her, I was starting to see glimpses of my old self, the guy who'd loved life, who'd had a future. And I hadn't realised how much I'd missed him.

"Happy birthday, Lance," she whispered and for the first time in fucking years, it really was a happy one.

DARCY

CHAPTER THIRTEEN

I was lost to a daydream about last night as I changed into my bathing suit for Water Elemental class. I wandered after Tory into the lagoon where rippling blue light fell across us and danced on the high cliffs surrounding the pool.

I bit into my lip as I pictured the way Orion had pinned me down, the muscles on his body gleaming and his-

Washer's hand landed on my arm and he stepped in front of me in a pair of tight red speedos. "Ooh naughty naughty, what are you thinking about I wonder, hm?" His hand sailed up my bare shoulder and flames flickered at the edges of my visions as he tried to push his power into me. Relief filled me when it didn't work and I flinched away from him in disgust.

He frowned, glancing down at his hands as if he'd made some error. "Been practising your mental shields, have you?" he asked, obviously disappointed.

"Yeah," I said brightly, loving my newfound Phoenix powers. "Guess you can't affect my moods anymore, sir." I shrugged then hurried away to join Tory in the warm water while she shot Washer a glare.

Geraldine waded toward us in her tight-fitting suit, her muscles on show and her large breasts bobbing as she moved. She tossed a lock of light brown hair over her shoulder as she arrived, a grin pulling at her mouth. "Well call me a Pegasus in paisley pyjamas, Darcy, did you just fight off professor Washer's gifts?"

"Yup," I said brightly. "Guess all that practising finally paid off." I didn't like lying to her about our Orders, but we didn't have much choice.

"I can't wait to see Max's face when-" Tory started but she was cut off by the devil himself as he jumped into the pool beside us. Water sprayed over us and he smiled predatorily at Geraldine as he closed in.

"When you what, little Vega?" Max asked Tory, arching a brow.

"When you realise your swimming trunks are transparent," Tory changed lanes with a smirk and Max quickly dropped his gaze to them, causing the three of us to burst out laughing.

He scowled as he looked up, folding his arms across the taut muscles of his chest. "Hilarious. Even if they were see-through, do you really think I'd have anything to worry about? Tell 'em, Grus." He glanced at her knowingly and she planted her hand on her hip.

"I don't keep a fil-o-fax of floppy fiddlesticks I've cadoodled with." Geraldine rolled her eyes.

"It wasn't floppy," Max huffed.

Geraldine waved a hand like she couldn't care less and Tory and I fell into silent giggles. "Besides, Lady Petunia has danced with many courtiers this week. How on the moon would I even remember what your floppy spatula looked like?"

"It wasn't *floppy*!" Max snapped. "And hang on a second, are you saying you've fucked a bunch of dudes since me? It's only been a week!"

"I'm not going to stand here discussing how many breadsticks I've dipped in my honeypot since yours, Max Rigel. It's none of your business."

Geraldine turned to walk away and my lips parted as Max caught her arm to stop her. He moved into her personal space, lowering his tone as if he didn't want us to hear. "Come on, you have to admit how good it was. Come to mine tonight so I can remind you."

"I have a date with a fine gentlefae tonight. I expect he'll see to Lady Petunia's needs just fine."

"Which Fae?" Max demanded.

"And why would I tell you that?"

"Because I'm gonna break his legs," Max growled.

Darius started wading toward his friend and Max released Geraldine, running a hand down the back of his neck. He cleared his throat, nodding to the Fire Heir as he arrived.

Darius's eyes flipped to us, clinging to Tory for several long seconds. Did he realise how obviously he was checking her out? His eyes were practically stuck to her cleavage.

Tory whipped her middle finger up between her boobs and Darius glowered and walked away again without a word.

Washer split the students into different classes and Tory and I worked side by side as he taught us how to create a wave by pouring our magic into the pool. We soon started to get the hang of it, sending out small waves across the surface one at a time.

"Very good," Washer commented. "Now make a nice big wet one for me."

I tried to school my expression but it was impossible not to wrinkle my nose around Washer and his gross ways of talking.

We sent out a few bigger waves and Washer clapped his hands. "Good and when you're ready you can do a big squirt like this." He pressed his hands into the water and a wave crashed over Tory and I, making us both shriek.

My hair was plastered to my skin and water dripped from me in torrents.

"Yes…just like that," Washer purred, taking in our soaked bathing suits before adjusting his tiny speedo and walking away toward Darius. He was bending forward in the water as he cast some magic and I almost called out to warn him.

Get up, idiot!

The second Washer's hands landed on his hips he straightened so fast that the back of his head smashed into Washer's nose. The professor stumbled back into the water and a laugh tore from my throat as his legs went over his head. Tory grinned and for a moment she shared a smile with Darius before they quickly turned away from each other.

"You like him," I teased, poking her in the arm.

She tutted. "I *despise* him."

"You think he's hot though," I said airily.

"Well who doesn't?" she said then cursed herself for saying it.

"I wonder if we'll ever get taught how to transplant personalities, then you'd be all set," I said as I cast another wave across the pool.

"Yeah," she said half-heartedly like she didn't really want that and I frowned at her. My sister was too stubborn for her own good sometimes. She probably liked Darius just the way he was. Asshole personality and all. If he'd just apologise for all the shit he'd done to her and started trying to make up for it...maybe there was something salvageable between them. Or maybe I was just too optimistic for my own good sometimes.

"How are things going with Caleb?" I asked.

"You're very interested in my love life this morning," she said with a grin then knocked her shoulder against mine. "Anyway you never did tell me who the mystery guy was you were meeting on the Lunar Eclipse."

I laughed nervously, dipping my fingers into the water again. Dammit, I wanted to tell her so bad. It was stupid that I couldn't. Tory wouldn't breathe a word to anyone. And after last night, it seemed like she'd bonded with Orion. At least a little bit anyway. But enough for her to not freak out the second I told her the truth? Probably not. She thought Orion was nearly as bad as Darius. She'd think I'd lost my mind.

I was saved from answering as Max suddenly sailed above the water on a wave as if he was surfing without a board, guiding himself along with his magic. He sped past us then circled Geraldine several times, cutting her off from Angelica as he gazed down at her with a seductive grin.

"Oh do stop being a giant mountain crack, Rigel!" she shouted then threw up her hands and cast an enormous wave which sent him flying and he disappeared under the water with a huge splash. He resurfaced with a roar of anger and the class started laughing at him as he drudged back toward Geraldine.

"I'm coming for you, Grus." He pointed at her.

"Ooh I'm shaking right down to my leopard print pantyhose," she said with an eye roll.

"You will be." He stalked away and Geraldine waved goodbye to him just with her little finger. "Is that supposed to be a reference to my dick?" he snapped.

"I didn't make any kind of reference," she said innocently. "Though maybe *you* think it looks like your floppy frankfurter as you mentioned it?"

"It was not *floppy!*" Max shouted so the whole class could hear. Darius shot him a confused look and Washer drifted his way as if he could sense some emotions coming off of him that he liked.

Max headed away in embarrassment and I shared a look with Tory. It looked like Geraldine had him well and truly wrapped around the little finger she was still wiggling at him. And I really hoped he kept trying it on with her, because this was freaking hilarious.

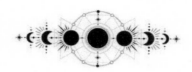

Dear Miss Vega,
Your presence is required in my office immediately.
Failure to attend will result in a severe docking of House Points.

Yours,
Principal Nova

I was frozen to the spot, reading and rereading that message as I sat in my room after dinner. It was nearly eight pm, so what the hell could she want to talk to me about?

My heart jack-hammered in my chest as I thought of the worst case scenario. But she couldn't have found out about Orion and I. We'd been careful.

Were we really that careful last night though?

What if someone had seen us sneaking into his classroom?

But then why would she wait until now to call me to her office?

I pushed my feet into my sneakers, tugging on a coat over my uniform before slipping out the door.

Please don't let it be about Orion. Please please please.

My hands grew clammy as I closed in on Pluto Offices where Nova's office was located. I hurried along even though I wanted to drag my feet or even turn around and run for the hills. But I had to face this.

It probably wasn't about Orion anyway. Maybe Tory had gotten the message too.

Why didn't I message her, dammit?

I cursed myself as I opened the door, heading into the atrium and following signs to Nova's office through a stairwell. I'd never been to it before, but I'd seen her heading in here multiple times. I jogged up the brightly lit stairs, running my fingers along the golden railing while trying to convince myself this wasn't about Orion.

I reached the top floor, rounding into the corridor and I stopped walking. Stopped breathing. Because Orion was standing there, anxiously scraping a hand through his hair. The second he spotted me, his face paled and he shook his head slightly in some signal. But god only knew what it was.

I moved toward him slowly, barely able to draw in breath as he rapped his knuckles against Nova's door.

Please god no.

He'll lose his job. Be power shamed. This will screw up his whole life.

I forced myself to walk through the door after him, stepping into the large room. It had dark red carpet, oak furnishings and a long window which overlooked Fire Territory in the distance. Nova glanced up from her desk, her fingers clasped together and a taut expression on her face. Every organ in my body felt like it was wrapped in barbed wire.

"Apologies to call you both here so late, but I'm afraid I have to follow protocol on a matter which has recently been brought to light." Nova gestured for us to sit in the two chairs side by side in front of her desk, her eyes flipping between us like she was hunting for something. I kept my features neutral, waiting for her to explain and trying not to panic. But holy hell was I panicking. Orion could probably hear my pulse as loudly as his own.

Nova stood, walking over to a printer across from her desk and fishing something from the tray. She returned to her seat and every hair on my body stood to attention as she placed a photograph in front of us.

It was from last night. Orion was leaning in close to speak to me and there was a stupidly bright smile on my face as I gazed up at him under my lashes. Worst of all, my hand was resting lightly on his arm and before us was a line of empty glasses.

No no no no no no no.

Orion cleared his throat, picking up the photograph then tossing it back down with a breath of laughter – *how is he freaking laughing right now?*

"Yes I know it's ridiculous," Nova said with a tired smile and I looked to her in confusion. "But I'm afraid I have to hear it from both of you."

"Hear what?" I blurted, breaking my silence and Nova glanced at me. "An explanation for this."

"It's obvious, isn't it?" Orion drawled. "I got ambushed on my birthday by the Vegas. This one in particular." He sighed like it wasn't the first time and I caught on fast, dipping my head in embarrassment to play along.

"Apparently the waitress was paid off to get a few incriminating photographs of Mr Acrux last night," Nova explained.

"Yes well, he was there. He was having a rough night and as you know about my situation with his father…" Orion trailed off and Nova nodded quickly.

"Of course, say no more," Nova said. "I'm afraid the photographs of Mr Acrux have been released to the press already. The one of you and Miss Vega has only made it onto FaeBook so far as I'm aware, but you should do all you can to have them taken down as soon as possible. You know how rumours can escalate."

"Of course," Orion agreed.

"So Miss Vega," Nova said sternly, shifting her gaze to me. "You followed your professor to a club? That's very inappropriate, you understand?"

"Yes," I said, keeping my head bowed low and feigning my shame.

"So why is a student taking such an interest in you, Professor?" Nova questioned him.

"Perhaps you should ask her that," Orion said lightly.

"Miss Vega?" Nova pressed. "Would you like to explain?"

I took in a breath, ready to act as best as I could as a blush burned into my cheeks, helping my case. "I have a crush on him." I cleared my throat, looking anywhere but at Orion.

Nova sighed, turning to him. "Well it wouldn't be the first time, would it? Whatever will we do about that face of yours." She tittered.

"I'll try growing a thicker beard," Orion taunted and I chewed the inside my cheek as I felt Nova's eyes scraping over me.

"Perhaps a wife would be a better option?" Nova teased. "I think Professor Prestos is still single, maybe you should ask her out? You'd make a lovely pair."

My insides squirmed and my hands tightened on the arms of my chair.

"I'm seeing Francesca Sky," Orion said lightly and my jaw clenched even though I knew it was a lie.

"Oh, I do love that girl. She was such a bright student," Nova said dreamily and I tried not to crack a tooth. Nova looked to me, leaning in closer. "I know it's normal to get urges at your age. And your hormones must be going haywire."

"I'm eighteen. I'm way past puberty," I said firmly, disliking her patronising tone.

"Of course, but your Order has recently emerged, that can be just as unsettling, my dear. Have you dated anyone since you arrived at the academy?"

Is she seriously asking me this right now?

"No. But I don't see how that-"

Nova cut over me. "Perhaps you should join one of the Order Mixers. If you find a regular mate, that can help to assuage some of these raging hormones."

"Sure... I'll think about it," I said, forcing a smile and she nodded, seeming satisfied.

"Do let me know if you're having any more issues. I can assign you a counsellor if you'd like?" Nova asked and I didn't like the way she said *issues*. Like she really did think there was something up with me. Maybe she believed the rumours the newspapers were circulating about me talking to invisible crows.

It struck me that if I was really honest with her, the newspapers would say a helluva lot worse about me. *Oh yes, Principal Nova, I should tell you that I am actually screwing the Professor currently sitting beside me, he's also been giving me secret lessons to harness the shadows which my sister and I were given in a crazy-ass ritual run by one of the High Councillors. Oh and*

I've been hiding my Order form which could be the most powerful to emerge in a thousand years. Nothing to lose sleep over though, right?

"That won't be necessary, thank you," I said.

"Okay, you're dismissed."

I stood and moved toward the door, wanting to get the hell out of there.

"Oh and Miss Vega?" Nova called and I glanced back over my shoulder with my fingers perching on the door handle. "If I get word of you hassling Professor Orion again, the consequences will be most severe."

"Yes, ma'am," I said, my throat tight as I slipped out of the door.

I was hot and cold, sweat beading on the back of my neck as I hurried down the stairwell, drawing in long breaths. I couldn't help but be rattled. How was I supposed to keep seeing Orion after this? If we got caught, it would be game over. K.O. Freaking Armageddon.

I spotted a sign for a bathroom and followed it, rushing into the women's and resting my hands on a sink as I tried to calm my nerves.

The idea of stopping things with Orion caused my heart to splinter and threaten to shatter into a thousand pieces. But what choice did we have? This was a warning. A *turn back now* sign with flashing lights ringing it and a blaring alarm which had been well and truly triggered.

I ran some cold water onto my hands, splashing it onto my too-hot cheeks. The door opened and a blur of motion made my heart jolt before Orion's arm curled around my waist and dragged me into one of the toilet stalls.

"What the hell are you doing?" I hissed as he cast a silencing bubble and gave me a heated look.

"I can hear anyone coming a mile off, trust me," he growled, his brows pinching together tightly.

I shook my head. "This is stupid, let me out."

"No," he snarled, gripping my shoulders to keep me in place. "You're thinking about calling time on this."

"What choice do we have?" I whispered despite the fact there was a bubble in place. But Nova was just upstairs – this was the definition of crazy!

"We'll be more careful. We shouldn't have gone out together last night."

"I know, but Gabriel invited us so-"

"He's reckless, but we can't be. He doesn't know what's between us, so he didn't think about the risk."

"*Lance*," I sighed, an ache building in my chest. "I can't bear what would happen to you if we got caught. It would kill me to be responsible for that."

"I'm responsible for my own actions," he said in a powerful tone that sent a rush of electricity down my spine.

"It's not worth it," I said as tears burned the backs of my eyes. Was I really calling things off between us? It didn't feel doable. Like the bond between us was made of solid iron.

"Yes it is," he said, dropping his head to try and steal a kiss, but I turned my head so he couldn't.

"This is crazy," I half laughed, half choked. But I looped my arms around his neck, the need to be closer to him driving me insane. "If we get caught-"

"We won't," he growled. "I can hear everything around us. We'll always be a step ahead."

"You don't know that. We weren't last night." I clawed a hand into my hair, anxiety tearing through my limbs.

Orion sighed, leaning in to speak into my ear. "I can't stop, Blue. I know it's fucking insane. But I've stopped caring about the consequences. This thing between us gets stronger every day and I can't fight it…can you?"

I inhaled at his words, the pounding of my pulse all I could hear in the pause that passed between us. The answer was obvious. It would be almost impossible to let go. It was as if the stars themselves were pressing me into his arms, holding me there and refusing to let go.

"I could try, for your sake," I said. It would hurt like hell, but if it saved him from the fate of being discovered I could do it.

"I don't want you to. In fact, I forbid it," he ordered and I rolled my eyes.

"Come on, Lance. Do you really think we can get away with this forever?" I breathed.

He locked his arms around me, crushing me to his chest. "You know… that's the first time you've admitted you want this to have a future."

I swallowed down the lump in my throat. Orion had made so many strong gestures toward me, but I'd been afraid of doing the same. Because deep down, I'd been terrified of facing the possibility of us ending. Every day was a gamble. And how long could we really carry on like this without being found out?

"I'm just so afraid that the second I tell you I'm all in on this, the sky will come crashing down around us," I said.

His fingers brushed the base of my jaw as a primal look entered his dark gaze. "Well say it and let's see," he said with a challenging smile playing around his lips.

I brushed my mouth over his in a feather light gesture as I gave in to my most desperate desire. Him. "I'm all in."

He winced, looking up at the ceiling as if expecting it to fall down. "Hm, nope the sky is still intact."

I slapped him on the chest and he released a low laugh before touching his lips to mine. It felt like a promise, one sealed by the stars themselves. It burned all the way through me and stole my breath away.

"We'll be more careful," he said as I stepped back, figuring we should probably leave this bathroom.

"No more public appearances," I agreed and he unlocked the stall to let me out, barring my way before he opened it.

"You go on ahead."

I nodded, stealing a final kiss before slipping out of the stall and heading into the corridor.

My heart was working overtime as I made it outside, taking in a lungful of fresh night air to calm my nerves.

I didn't know what the future held, but I hoped the heavens were on our side. I really didn't want to regret the decision I'd made, but it hadn't even really been an option to call things off. We were in too deep with each other and the universe seemed to be conspiring to keep us that way. I just hoped that meant the stars were on our side and would help keep this secret from ever coming out.

I soon reached The Wailing Wood and a shiver crept up my spine at the silence that greeted me. There were no students walking around. It was almost nine and curfew would kick in soon. My eyes played tricks on me as I caught shadows moving in my periphery. But every time I turned my head towards them, they were gone.

Just keep walking, there's nothing out here.

Except maybe a Nymph. Or a hungry Fae in their Order form. Or the Heirs.

Yeah, okay maybe I need to quicken my pace a bit…

I brought fire to my fingertips to illuminate the path and the tingle of my magic soon stole away my nerves. I was getting more and more confident with my powers every day. And even though I wasn't allowed to show my Order form, I sure as hell would be getting it out if a Nymph jumped me.

Crack.

I swivelled toward the breaking twig deep in the wood, upping my pace again and encouraging the fire to bloom in my hands.

A dark shadow stepped onto the track up ahead and I sucked in a breath, raising my hands to defend myself.

Seth's chiselled features came into view under the light of the flames in my hands and a smirk hooked up his lips. "Hey, babe."

He strode toward me and I kept my palms raised, glancing over my shoulder to check I wasn't being circled by more Heirs.

"You know it's not normal to lurk in a forest after dark, right?" I said and he released a low chuckle.

"It is for me."

"Some people would call that creepy," I pointed out, lowering my hands half an inch but not enough to let my guard down.

"Others would call it sexy," he mused and I couldn't fight the small laugh that escaped me.

"You're deluded." I recalled the last time I'd seen him in the dark at the Lunar Eclipse party. He'd seen Orion and me together, but he'd been so drunk I figured he'd forgotten most of that night anyway.

I went to move past him, but he caught my arm to halt me. His grip was gentle but it still sent my heart into a haywire beat.

"Let me go," I said firmly, staring up at him. He released me, giving me an innocent look.

"I just need your help with something," he said, releasing a dog-like whine. "Please?"

"What?" I narrowed my eyes.

He sighed, glancing away. "You clearly don't want to be a member of my pack. I guess a part of me hoped you'd come around to the idea, but..." He shrugged one shoulder and I drew back a step.

"So?"

"So, just challenge me and I'll kick you out of the pack. I'll get it done quick, you just have to cooperate." His brows raised hopefully and when I didn't answer, he caught my hand in his grip with a pleading whimper. "Come on, Darcy, my pack won't come back to me until I get rid of you. Please do this. I can't be alone anymore. You don't want to be with me, so let me be with them. I can't stand it anymore." He shifted from foot to foot, pushing a hand into his long hazel locks, a look of desperation flashing through his gaze.

My throat tightened at the sight of his pained expression and though I kinda liked the idea of torturing him a while longer after what he'd done to me, I also wasn't going to stoop to his level.

"Fine," I sighed. "I challenge you, Seth."

A baying howl rang out from the trees, then another and another, the voices filled with a keen excitement. I backed up in alarm, looking for that pitiful expression that had been there just seconds ago, but it was gone. Replaced by a cruel, demonic smile.

"Well thank fuck for that," he growled and my hackles rose.

I retreated another step and my back pressed to a warm body. I turned sharply, gasping as I found Seth's pack standing there in Fae form, shoulder to shoulder. They moved swiftly, circling around me and penning me and Seth between them.

"What are you doing?" I snapped, my pulse racing and my survival instincts kicking in hard.

"Turfing you out of my pack," Seth answered.

"We want our Alpha back!" Frank crowed from the front of the line, his muscular arms folded in front of his chest. "We'll have him as soon as you're gone."

"So just kick me out already," I demanded, fighting to keep my voice level. "I don't want to be his Omega anyway."

Seth pulled his shirt off and reached for his belt, tugging it free while his dark eyes remained pinned on me.

My mouth dried out and I glanced around at the wolves as they started to strip down too.

"You'll be out of the pack in a minute," Seth explained.

"What are you gonna do?" I hissed, trying to hold my nerve as the pack started shifting into their giant Wolf forms.

"I'm rising to your challenge... it's probably gonna hurt, babe." Seth kicked off his shoes and I stared at him with anxiety burning through me.

I moved to the edge of the circle, making my fire flare to scorching flames and trying to force my way through. I hit a magical barrier and stumbled back, fear dripping down my limbs as I turned to face Seth.

Seth sneered. "You can't leave until you've fought me. So fight me, Omega."

A chorus of howls rang out behind me and a shudder rolled down my spine.

I couldn't run. I couldn't hide. I *had* to fight.

I bit back the rising lump in my throat, digging for my courage as I planted my feet.

Seth dropped his pants then leapt forward, shifting in mid-air so his huge white Wolf form ripped free of his flesh and landed before me on four enormous paws. Panic slithered under my skin, but I held my ground, refusing to show how afraid I was.

I could shift. But then he'd see what I was up close. I'd risk Lionel finding out if Seth suspected anything.

Shit shit shit.

I raised my hands and the flames in my palms reflected in his huge brown eyes as he started circling me. The pack snapped their teeth, barking and howling intermittently, the noise setting my nerves on edge.

I'd fight him as Fae. If he was in his Order form, at least he couldn't use magic. But if he was going to kick me out, didn't I have to lose this fight anyway?

I didn't have time to figure that out as he lunged at me with a snarl

180

ripping from his throat.

I conjured a wall of earth to shield myself, jumping backwards, but he smashed through it like it was made of paper. His teeth were bared and ropes of drool clung to them as he raced toward me.

A scream escaped my throat as I darted sideways, shifting my magic to use air instead and pulling a tight shield in around me. Seth collided with it and the force sent me flying to the ground. I slammed into the mud, rolling onto my back as Seth placed his huge paws on the bubble of air which surrounded me.

The pressure of his weight made the air buckle and I threw up my hands with a yell of effort to keep it intact.

He tore at it with teeth and claws and I gasped as he broke through.

I winced, willing my magic to protect me. Instead of the slice of Seth's claws, I felt his weight crash into a soft tangle of vines encaging my body.

He started shredding them with his teeth and I sank my hands into the earth, willing more and more to grow while shuffling backwards along the ground. Moonlight spilled through the holes as Seth ripped it to shreds, hunting for me under the mass of greenery spewing from the mud.

I slipped out of the tunnel, leaping to my feet and the pack started barking. Seth was in a frenzy as he ripped and tore at the mass of vines caging the ground and I knew I only had seconds to act.

I ran forward with adrenaline chasing away my fear then dove onto his back, propelling myself with air magic. He reared backwards immediately and I conjured a vine into my hand, latching it around his throat and willing it to tighten.

He snarled furiously, whipping his head sideways and catching my leg between his powerful jaws.

I shrieked as he wrenched me from his back and I crashed into the earth again, pain ricocheting up and down my spine. My leg was bleeding and *fuck* did that hurt.

I groaned, pushing myself upright but Seth leapt onto me, pinning me down with his giant paws. The full weight of him pressed onto my chest and something cracked, drawing a pained groan from my lips. His teeth were bared as he leaned into my face, drool dripping onto my cheeks as I sank deeper into the mud beneath him.

"*No,*" I choked as another sharp crack sounded from my ribs.

I reached up to his face, clutching his furry cheeks between my hands and his snarling expression softened. His pupils dilated and a soft whine escaped him.

Fury bled under my skin as his claws ripped into my flesh and I poured fire into my hands, letting it tumble from my veins in an explosive wave.

Seth screeched with pain, rearing off of me and rolling in the mud to try and put out the flames which flared along his fur. Pain drilled into my body and I clutched my sides, trying to get up, but every movement caused a bolt of agony.

The fire fizzled out in my periphery and Seth padded toward me once more, rage pouring from his gaze. I conjured vines to slow him down but he broke through them like twigs, diving over me. Fear crashed over my heart as he locked his jaws around my throat.

Panic took hold of me and time seemed to slow. I drew in a breath of horror as he half lifted me off of the ground, his teeth nearly piercing flesh.

"Stop – it's over!" I shouted. "You win!"

He lowered me down to the ground in an instant and I winced as pain exploded through my ribs. In a heartbeat, Seth was at my side in his Fae form, kneeling in the mud, completely naked, his expression dark.

He leaned over me, sliding his hands under my top while I tried to push him back, but I was in so much pain it felt like I was about to pass out.

Warmth spread over my wounds and I took a long breath as the agony slowly subsided. Seth leaned closer, his hair falling around me in a curtain as the last of my injuries healed over.

"You just had to submit. It didn't need to be this way."

"You didn't tell me," I spat, venom building up in my gut.

"You had to figure it out for yourself," he sighed with a genuine look of remorse which confused the hell out of me, then he knocked his knuckles against my cheek before getting to his feet.

He shifted back into his Werewolf form and raised his head to the moon where it peeked through the canopy above. The sound of his howl was echoed over and over again as his pack surrounded him, nuzzling his sides as he took his position at the head of their line. Then he charged away into the trees and paws thundered across the ground as his Wolves followed him.

I pushed myself upright in the mud, shivering as the adrenaline drained from my body and the cold took its place instead.

I started walking back to Aer Tower, my uniform half shredded and totally caked in mud. For some strange reason I didn't feel that angry at Seth. Maybe it was the remorse in his eyes after it was over. Or maybe it was that I knew on some base level, that this was the way of Fae. And I was starting to realise there would always be fights like this, especially when it came to the needs of our Orders. It was our nature. But I just hoped the next time I was faced with an opponent, I'd come out on top.

CALEB

CHAPTER FOURTEEN

I pushed a hand through my blonde curls, restyling them after my run earlier as I strolled through the abandoned corridors of Jupiter Hall. I was late. But Orion was always late so I wasn't too bothered. I could have shot there with my gifted speed but I didn't. Orion never did.

My mind was on the hunt I'd won this morning. If I closed my eyes I could still taste Tory's blood on my lips, feel her hand as she'd pushed it into my pants and then- the fucking bell had rung. Honest to shit. And she'd left me in favour of fucking Tarot class. I'd hounded her all the way there and she'd laughed in my face when she really did head inside.

I groaned, wishing I'd saved the hunt for tonight when I could have monopolised more of her time. But like a fucking idiot, I'd used up my magic reserves last night while we were at King's Hollow so I'd needed the drink. At least that part had gone to plan.

I made it to the Cardinal Magic classroom and heard Orion's voice coming from inside already. *Fucking typical that he'd be here on time today.*

I eased the door open and slipped inside silently, shooting to my spot at the very back of the huge classroom between Darius and Seth.

I was leaning back in my chair, ankles crossed beneath the desk with my hands behind my head within less than two seconds, looking casual as fuck with a smug ass grin on my face.

"Ten points from Terra," Orion said, not bothering to raise his voice or even look my way.

"Asshole," I muttered, knowing he'd hear me and not giving a shit.

Orion's gaze flipped to me and he bared his teeth. I bared mine right back with a hiss. We both knew I was more powerful than him, we both knew I was stronger too. The only Vampires capable of challenging me were my mother and probably my younger siblings when they were Awakened. Though thanks to the advantages I'd been given as the oldest Heir with having my powers Awakened young and all the extra training I'd been given, my mother was the only real threat to me. And I wasn't planning on challenging her any time soon. So the only reason Orion got away with shit like that was because of his position as my teacher. It wasn't a good look for me to disrespect him, so he got some leeway with his shit.

We glared at each other for a long moment, the nature of our Orders pushing us into rivalry as the two strongest Vampires in the academy. Before either of us crossed the line into any kind of actual challenge, he turned away and continued with his lesson like nothing had happened.

Seth sniggered, offering a hand for me to high five between the desks and I did so with a smirk.

"Dickwad," Darius muttered but he was half grinning too.

"Why are you late?" Max asked from the other side of Seth.

"I was filling up my magic," I supplied.

"And getting a blowjob too, no doubt," Seth joked.

I snorted a laugh. "Unfortunately not."

Darius scratched at the stubble lining his jaw as he feigned interest in Orion's lecture. It was the only class where he bothered. Because of our early Awakening, we'd been taught most of the magical spells and lessons that the rest of our class was learning already. We tended to use the first parts of our classes to chat amongst ourselves while the others were given their work and then the teachers would come to us and get us to prove how well we could do the spell in question and set us something more advanced.

Orion was currently teaching the rest of the class about strengthening mental shields so that they could have a better chance at breaking off Siren lures or Cyclops invasion. I quickly tuned him out. My mother had made me work on mental shields every damn day for the last four years. She said it was important that Max and his family could never hold an advantage like that over us and she was right. I loved my friend and I trusted him, but I had to be able to know he couldn't overpower or manipulate me with his gifts if he ever tried or we wouldn't be evenly matched.

Seth stretched his arms high above his head, cracking his neck as he yawned widely.

"You guys can't even imagine how much fucking sex I had last night," he said.

"We know," Darius put in. "You've been going on about it all morning."

"And I can literally taste the lust on you," Max said with an exaggerated shudder.

I laughed. "I'm just pleased for you, man," I said. "You deserve to have your pack back again."

"They're so fucking apologetic," Seth said. "Honestly, I think Frank's still got lock jaw and Alice couldn't even walk straight when we got out of bed."

I glanced across the room at Frank, sniggering as he massaged his jaw. He could have healed that shit, but maybe he just liked remembering what had given him that injury too much to get rid of it.

"You wanna know the best bit?" Seth breathed.

"You've told us way too fucking much about all of it already," Max said.

"No, I held back on the *best* bit," Seth insisted.

"If you tried that weird nipple thing again I don't wanna know," Darius said.

"Fuck no," Seth said in disgust. "I told you that got weird fast. I'm never doing that again."

My laughter was a little too loud that time and Orion scowled at us. "Are you four looking for detention?" he snarled.

"No, sir," we all said like good little boys and he rolled his eyes as he gave his attention back to the class.

We stayed silent. He fucking meant it. *Asshole.*

I pulled my Atlas from my bag and looked over the notifications that had flashed up during the morning. There were the usual messages from the fan club despite the fact that I never replied, I'd been tagged in a bunch of FaeBook posts which weren't anything interesting. My gaze darkened as I saw one of them was yet another Pegasus porn group. I so wanted to be mad at Tory for that, but as soon as I thought of her I just remembered the way she looked pinned beneath me and I kinda forgot about it. It was fucking ridiculous. But she was fucking hot so I wasn't questioning it anymore.

Of course I didn't have any messages from her. She literally never messaged me unless I started it which was like...unheard of. I'd never had to chase a girl like this before.

I flicked my messages open and drummed my fingers on the desk as I decided what I wanted to say to her. Her temper burned so damn hot that I was forever treading a dangerous line. One wrong message could mean blue balls for a week. I couldn't risk it.

Caleb:

Hey, sweetheart. Do you wanna hang out tonight? X

I watched as the red ticks illuminated to let me know she'd read the message. She was probably trying to think up the perfect thing to say back to me. Agonising over it, debating it with her friends and trying to figure out how best to keep me-

Tory:

No.

For fuck's sake. Not even a fucking kiss.

Darius snorted a laugh beside me and I glanced at him as he didn't even bother to pretend that he wasn't reading my messages over my shoulder.

"She plays hard to get," I muttered then instantly wondered why I was making excuses to him.

He only smirked at me, shrugging his shoulders like he gave zero shits. We both knew he gave shits, but whatever.

Caleb:

You don't know what I'm offering yet...

Tory:

Is it a date or sex?

My heart leapt. Fuck yes. It was on. Date or sex? Date or sex? *Date or sex? Dammit I have no idea which answer she wants.* Most girls would want the date at least pre sex. But Tory wasn't most girls. I had to admit the idea of taking her out on a date was actually pretty appealing though. *Fuck it.*

Caleb:

A date. The best fucking date you've ever been on. ;)

Tory:

No.

I groaned as I leaned back in my chair and Darius laughed beside me. But I wasn't giving up that easily. I'd just change my answer then I'd have her.

Caleb:

That was a typo. It was meant to say sex. I can guarantee you the best night of your life...

I waited. Ticks came up. She'd read it. She wasn't typing. I tapped my foot impatiently. I could shoot over to her Tarot class in the space of about one minute and get the answer from her mouth myself. I'd probably earn myself that detention from Orion, but if it got her in my bed it would be worth it. Of course bursting in on her in her class might just put me back on her shit list. Then I'd have detention *and* blue balls. Fuck.

"Alright! I'll tell you!" Seth gushed like we'd all been desperately waiting for him to finish his story. "I made Maurice sit outside. In the fucking naughty corner! *All night!*"

We all started laughing just as a flash of movement caught the corner of my eye. A pineapple hit Seth square in the face and knocked him flying off of his seat with a curse.

Darius got up and offered him a hand as laughter rang out around the room.

"Detention, Capella!" Orion barked. "You were warned."

"What the thuck! You bwoke my nothe you thucking thycopaff!" Seth shouted as he got to his feet, blood running freely down his face.

He placed a hand over his nose and repaired the break with healing magic while scowling at our Cardinal Magic Professor who just glowered in response.

Max took pity on Seth as he slumped into his seat, drawing the blood off of his face and out of his shirt using water magic so that it hung in a red orb above him.

"Any Vamps wanna taste Capella blood?" Max called.

A girl in the front row leapt up as did a guy sitting off to the right of the room. I knew them vaguely but I'd never really wasted my time on learning the names of Fae who didn't matter.

The two of them glared at each other and Orion leaned back against his desk as the fight for dominance broke out.

They ran at each other and I watched with a bit more interest as the girl shot beneath the guy's attack and knocked him straight off of his feet. She leapt on him, punching him in the gut several times as he failed to fight her off before she threw vines from her palms and tied him down.

"Twenty points to Terra," Orion chuckled as she leapt up victoriously, opening her mouth for Max to deposit Seth's blood.

She moaned lustily as she drank it and I smirked at Seth. "You do taste pretty good," I said but he ignored me, his icy gaze locked on Orion.

Darius wrapped his arm around me, laughing as he sat back in his seat. "Roxy sent you a reply, Cal," he taunted.

I straightened my spine, leaning forward to snatch my Atlas from the desk to see what she'd said.

Tory:
No.

I groaned, leaning back in my chair as I dropped it to my desk again and Orion continued his lecture.

"Maybe she's not that into you," Darius teased and I flipped him off jokingly as he leaned back in his seat. I couldn't reply; Orion would put me in detention with Seth if I interrupted him again. It wasn't fair, but as Darius rolled his shirt sleeves up and I caught sight of the Libra sign branded onto his forearm I guessed he probably thought it was pretty unfair too. And I could suck up a little preferential treatment from time to time in light of that.

The class broke out into conversation as Orion set them to work and he shot up the aisle between the chairs towards us.

"So, as none of you need help with mental shields, I was thinking you could work on your illusions today," Orion suggested as he perched on Darius's desk and looked around at us like he hadn't just launched a pineapple into Seth's face. On that note, where *was* the pineapple?

Seth was glaring at the far wall, refusing to acknowledge him but Orion clearly gave zero shits about that.

I smiled at his suggestion. Illusions were brilliant magic. I'd managed to make Seth see a flea crawling over his arm a few days after his flea dip and practically given him a heart attack. I was more than happy to work on getting better at them.

"What kind of illusions?" Max asked.

"Voices. I want each of you to try and work on creating a full sentence in the voice of someone you know. It needs to be a convincing likeness or I'll mark you down. Cast a silencing bubble so you don't distract the others. Questions?"

We all shook our heads and he tussled Darius's hair before heading away, somehow locating the pineapple as he went and swinging it in his grip while it dripped blood to the floor.

I took the job of creating the silencing bubble for us and as soon as it was in place, Seth released a low growl.

"That motherfucker needs to remember who we are," he snarled, his eyes fixed on Orion's back.

"Leave it alone," Darius warned and Seth growled again.

"Maybe it's about time he was put in his place," he went on.

"I said forget about it," Darius commanded darkly.

"How about we start with the illusions?" Max suggested, a sense of calm seeping over us as he tried to diffuse the tension.

"Yeah okay," Seth said, his eyes flashing in that way they always did when he was about to go into full asshole mode. "Why don't you show us what Tory Vega sounds like in the sack, Cal?" he suggested.

I rolled my eyes, clearly not about to do that just as Tory's voice filled the space around us.

"Is it supposed to be that *small*, Caleb? I'm just not really sure how I could even make use of that."

I burst out laughing as I turned to look at Darius who was smirking triumphantly. "That's it, right?" he asked. "Or did I get the accent wrong?"

"I think you got a few of the words muddled," I replied, leaning back in my chair as I concentrated on creating my own illusion.

My version of Tory's voice held way too much enthusiasm but that kinda worked for what I was going for anyway.

"Holy shit, Caleb! I've never seen one that big! I'm just not sure I can handle you at all!"

The guys laughed and Darius rolled his eyes. "You wish," he said.

"Too right," I agreed.

"I've got a better one," Seth said as he created his own illusion.

"We're so sorry for all the bullshit resistance we've been putting up," Tory and Darcy's voices came in unison. "But we realise now that we can't fight the truth. The four of you are clearly superior. We will spend the rest of our lives bowing at your feet to show how much we believe that."

I snorted a disbelieving laugh while Max offered Seth a fist bump. Darius leaned back in his chair, folding his arms with a frown in place.

"That day will never come," I said with a shrug because it was true. The more time I spent in Tory's company, the more obvious it became to me. She wasn't the kind to bow, no matter the pressure put on her. And despite the differences between her and her sister, it was clear they were the same in that regard.

"If they won't drop to their knees willingly, then we'll just have to make them do it as planned," Max said.

"There's nothing holding me back now I've cut Darcy from the pack," Seth added in a low growl.

I pushed a hand into my hair, glancing at Darius. He was the harshest of us at times but he was also the most level headed. He wasn't afraid to change his mind if he had good reason to. And he wouldn't be swayed by the pressure of the group once his decision was made.

"You still want to go ahead?" Darius asked, his gaze trailing over the other two who were clearly eager, before landing on me.

I shrugged. "It's no secret that I like Tory," I said. "And if I'm honest I don't think any of this shit is going to work. Those girls weren't born to bow. Maybe we should be thinking about negotiation instead. They don't want the throne, maybe we just accept that?"

"That's not how Fae work," Max said. "If we want to claim our power, we have to be the most powerful. We have to prove it."

"But we aren't," I countered. "Not anymore. And if we keep pushing them into a corner then I think that one day they'll fight back hard enough to cause us real problems."

"You think they can beat us?" Seth scoffed. "We've got years of training and a lifetime of preparation on our sides. Brute strength can't top that."

"Those advantages won't last forever," I muttered. The girls were already learning to harness their powers. Give them five years, ten, twenty... with enough determination they'd match our skill and outmatch our power. Then they could come looking for payback whenever they wanted.

"Which is why we have to crush them *now*," Max growled. "We need to beat them so thoroughly that they don't ever dare to challenge us again."

I sighed, looking at Darius again. The others had made their position clear. It was on him now. If he sided with me, we'd have to hash it out. If he sided with them, I'd fall in with the group. It was how we'd always done it. We spoke our minds, gave our arguments then went with the majority. It meant I might not always like what we did, but we always presented a solid front. Unbreakable. The four of us united was a power that could never be challenged.

Darius turned his arm out and looked down at the skin there for a long moment. I followed his gaze to the cluster of zodiac symbols he had tattooed on his forearm. He'd surrounded the red Libra symbol with those of every other star sign not long after his father had linked him to Orion. I guessed it had been some kind of rebellion against that mark being placed on his flesh without his permission. He pressed his thumb to the Gemini symbol as he thought about what to do.

"Well?" Seth pushed, growing irritable.

"I'd have thought your orgy would have kept you in a better mood for longer," I joked, coaxing a grin from him.

"You can always come join us tonight if you're curious, Cal," he offered, kinda joking kinda not.

I smirked at him. "My interests are a little more singular at the moment, but thanks anyway. Maybe next time."

Seth smiled more genuinely at that.

"For fuck's sake, Darius, if you're this indecisive about what to do then take a few days to think it over," Max said, clearly getting a read on Darius's emotions. "I've got other things I want to achieve with this lesson anyway."

I followed his gaze across the room to where Geraldine Grus was practicing fighting off the lure of one of her Ass Club Sirens.

"Alright," Darius said. "We can meet at King's Hollow Saturday night and make a decision about the Vegas then."

The rest of us nodded our agreement and we let the subject go. Even Seth knew there was no point trying to push Darius into a decision when he wasn't ready to make one. He was stubborn as fuck and about the worst thing you could do if you wanted him to make a choice was back him into a corner over it. He'd just bite your head off, beat the shit out of you and still refuse to answer anyway.

"What's going on with you and the Ass Queen?" Darius asked as Max continued to stare at Grus.

"Nothing," Max ground out. "Yet."

"Seriously?" I asked. "You've got a thing for our biggest critic?"

"Says the guy screwing the girl who might steal our throne," he tossed back.

Darius growled at that comment but didn't say anything.

"You just like the idea of Grus," Seth chipped in. "Because she's an impossible challenge. You know she'd sooner cut her own tits off than let you in her panties."

The corner of Max's mouth hooked up a little, but he didn't say anything. Not that we needed any more than that to know exactly what it meant.

"No fucking way!" I said, looking over at Grus again. I strained my ears to pick up her conversation as she started flapping her arms about.

"-beaten off the lusty lurkings of the Siren king. So I'd like to think I've got this brain walling down to an art, little Andre! Don't doubt your own seductive skills because of my willpower wall!"

I drew my attention back to the guys as Darius spoke. "So why isn't she following you around like a lovesick puppy like they usually do?"

Max exhaled irritably. "She's fucking immune to my gifts. I'm pretty sure the only reason she hooked up with me in the first place was because the moon drove her into my arms and she's all into Celestial guidance. So unless Venus wants to do me a favour and send her my way again, I'm not sure she's going to give me another shot."

"So just choose another girl," Seth said with a shrug. "Take your fucking pick." He gestured to the room at large as if every single girl here would just drop their panties at the mere suggestion that one of us wanted them. I mean, it wasn't entirely inaccurate but there would certainly be a few who weren't interested. Probably.

"I don't want another girl," Max said simply, his gaze on Geraldine as Orion moved to talk to her.

"What the fuck is happening to us?" Seth groaned, swiping a hand over his face. "First you two are fighting over a Vega – a Vega who doesn't seem to want either of you half the time might I add. And now you're chasing the president of the fucking Ass Club, Max! I don't even recognise you guys right now."

"Weren't you all obsessed with Gwen the last time I checked?" Darius asked him.

"No. Well, not *obsessed*. It was a Wolf thing. She's not my Omega anymore so that's gone now..."

"Tory does want me," I protested irritably, my gaze falling on her goddamn refusal message again for a moment.

Darius scowled at me then picked up his own Atlas, clearly not intending to respond to that.

"And Grus wants *me,*" Max said adamantly, pushing to his feet. "She just doesn't want an Heir. I'll make her realise she's wrong about that. Then I'll get the girl *and* the Vegas will lose their fucking cheerleaders in one fell swoop. You assholes should be thanking me."

He strode away before we could respond to that and Seth rolled his eyes dramatically.

I watched as Max headed straight over to Geraldine's desk and focused my gifted hearing in on their conversation.

"Hey, Grus," Max said, perching his ass on the edge of her desk and looking down at her. "Do you wanna try out those shields on a real challenge?"

"I assume you intend to try and force lusty desires onto me, Maxy boy, but I'm really not interested in reacquainting myself with your wandering dongle so why don't you trot along?" she suggested and I snorted a laugh. That girl was weird and kinda annoying with all her royalist bullshit, but she was funny as fuck too. I just wasn't sure if it was intentional or not.

"What's wrong, baby? Are you afraid of what you might feel if you let yourself?" Max pushed, leaning closer to her.

She didn't back off, but it seemed more like a power play than in encouragement to his proximity.

"Fine. If you insist on philandering instead of educating yourself then I will make use of your bothersome presence. Feel free to exert your oh so impressive powers over me."

Max smiled widely and let his power go at full force. Pretty much everyone in the room stopped what they were doing and looked at him. Guys and girls alike moaned in a way that was way too sexual for the middle of a Cardinal Magic lesson and I spotted Damien Evergile rubbing his thighs excitedly.

Geraldine looked back at Max impassively, seeming close to bored and he growled as he upped the power again.

For a few seconds I was gripped with the urge to go to him, drop to my knees and offer him a blowjob, right before I slammed my mental walls into place more firmly and dismissed the idea.

"Fucking hell," Darius complained. "If she doesn't jump on him in the next five seconds I'm pretty sure the rest of the class will."

Geraldine slowly lifted her hand and I watched in amusement, expecting her to start caressing Max's thigh which was planted several inches in front of her on her desk. Instead, she curled her fingers, turning her hand back towards her as she inspected her nails, casual as fuck.

"I think I just fell in love with Geraldine Grus," I joked as Max's forehead furrowed with concentration.

Someone threw their panties at him and another girl started unbuttoning her shirt as she strode across the room with intention.

"That's enough, thank you very much, Mr Rigel!" Orion called. "I don't want to fill out the paperwork that would be required to explain why half of my class descended into a sex party."

Max growled with irritation as he withdrew the power of his gift and the room breathed a sigh of relief.

"Fifty points to House Terra for a truly impressive mental shield, Miss Grus," Orion added proudly and she beamed at him.

"Well hot cucumbers, I wasn't expecting that!" she cooed. "And perhaps the lump of perfectly toned sex pest might remove his fanny from my workspace now?"

"You heard the lady, Rigel," Orion said, pointing him back to his spot beside Seth with a smirk.

Max stood up but didn't leave, leaning close to speak with Geraldine. Obviously I could still hear him though. "Come on, Grus, I know you had a fantastic time the night of the Eclipse. I promise round two will be even better…"

"I'm afraid there won't be a round two," Geraldine replied dismissively, looking towards the front of the class like he wasn't breathing right in her ear. "Lady Petunia had her taste of forbidden fruit, but I'll be guiding her towards safer pastures in the future."

"Who the hell is Lady Petunia?" Max asked.

"*Now,* Rigel!" Orion snapped.

Max lingered another second, but Geraldine ignored him so he stomped back towards us.

A lot of the girls he passed reached out to him as he went, still feeling the effects of the lust he'd offered up and trying their luck, but he ignored them.

Marguerite jumped out of her seat and scurried across the room to retrieve her panties while glancing about like she was hoping no one had noticed.

"Is that the end of that nonsense then?" Seth asked as Max slumped down in his chair.

"No chance," he replied, his gaze still locked on Geraldine. "It's just the goddamn beginning."

Darius laughed and I exchanged a grin with him. I'd never known Max to set his sights on a girl and be disappointed, but I wasn't sure I liked his chance with Grus.

"A thousand auras says she ends up kicking his ass to make him leave her alone," I said.

"A thousand says she'll change her mind and be dropping her panties within the week," Seth said, shaking his head. "She won't resist him for long."

"Pfft," Darius shook his head. "A thousand says she'll break his heart without even trying."

"Harsh, man," I said, tossing him a cynical look as Max continued to watch Geraldine.

He shrugged his broad shoulders, tapping a pen against his desk. "Just calling it how I see it. Look at her ignoring him, that's just fucking cruel."

"Shut up, assholes," Max said. "You're all wrong anyway. Grus is feeling this too, I can tell. So it's just a matter of breaking down her walls. I'm gonna be so fucking irresistible that she won't be able to help falling for me."

"Sure," Darius said. "Let me know how that pans out for you though. Because thinking a girl feels something and knowing it are two different things. They're a fucking enigma wrapped up in a secret, cloaked in a goddamn layer of confusing as fuck. So if you figure out the key to them then feel free to share with the group."

"I think your problem with girls, or more specifically, *girl,*" Seth joked. "Isn't that she's an enigma or any such thing. It's got more to do with you being an asshole."

Darius growled but before he could reply, the bell rang to sound the end of class. He was up and out of his seat before any of us could say anything else and Max exhaled irritably.

"Nice job, Seth. Sometimes I think you've got the emotional compassion of a teaspoon," he said.

"I happen to like teaspoons," Seth replied with a shrug.

Darius strode out of the room with his Ignis circle closing in around him and I drummed my fingers against the desk.

"Is that all about Tory Vega?" I asked slowly, wondering how deep of a wedge she might be driving into our group. Our rivalry over her aside, me and Darius were getting on fine, but she was obviously causing a little tension.

"No," Max replied. "Something's been off with him since the Lunar Eclipse. I can't get a read on what exactly but he's been...darker. Like something's haunting him. I dunno. He's doing a good job at keeping me out of his head but I catch the odd taste of something strange on him."

"You think Lionel did something new to him?" Seth asked in a low voice. Most of the class were gone now but my silencing bubble was still keeping our conversation private.

"Has he been home?" I asked with a frown. I didn't think so, but he had plenty of stardust and it wasn't like I kept track of him at all times.

"I dunno," Seth replied. "But if something's getting him down then it's not hard to figure out who might be responsible."

"Maybe we should spend the night at the Hollow on Saturday," Max suggested. "Have some beers, get him to relax. He might tell us."

"Yeah and the sun might rise in the west," I muttered.

"We could ask Orion to come too," Max suggested. "For Darius."

"Fuck no," Seth growled as my lip curled back a little. "I thought you said we want to chill out. I'm not hanging out with that asshole any more than I have to."

"Fine," Max agreed with a shrug. "It was just a thought. You know how much Darius likes hanging out with him."

"He probably knows what's going on already," I added, looking at Orion as he took a seat behind his desk. "We could ask him."

"Yeah, I don't think he'd tell me jack shit," Seth said. "He just broke my nose with a pineapple."

"He's not going to break Darius's confidence," Max agreed. "We need to get it from the source."

"Fine," I said, finally standing and grabbing my bag. "We'll get it out of him Saturday night."

"Why are the three of you hanging around like a bad smell?" Orion called without bothering to look up at us.

I dispersed the silencing bubble and we headed for the door without another word. If something was wrong with Darius, we'd help him fix it. That was what we did. We looked out for each other. No matter what.

TORY

CHAPTER FIFTEEN

I raced through the corridors of Jupiter hall, my heart pounding as I sprinted at full pelt, knowing Caleb was closing in on me. The day was icily cold and the coat and hat had seemed like a great idea until I'd agreed to let a Vampire chase me. My hair was sticking to my scalp where I'd shoved it beneath the woolly hat and sweat coated my body beneath the jacket. I'd have thrown them off, but I'd caught sight of Caleb just before I'd darted into this building and I couldn't waste a second.

I turned a corner and half tripped over my own feet in my haste, cursing beneath my breath as I righted myself again.

A door flew open beside me and Orion was suddenly standing in my way. I stumbled to a halt and he silently pointed into his office.

My eyes widened in surprise and I took his offer of help without a word.

The scent of bourbon and the heavy bass of rock music greeted me as I moved inside and he pulled open a cupboard door for me.

I slipped into it wordlessly, throwing up a silencing bubble to hide my heartbeat and heavy breathing from my hunter. I eyed Orion between the slats as he took a seat behind his desk, lifting his drink to his lips and jotting something down like he didn't have a care in the world. Or a girl in his closet. I didn't know if this was a result of our bonding sessions over the shadows or just plain old weird ass behaviour, but I wasn't going to question it at that moment.

The door burst open and I held my breath as Caleb looked into the office, his curly hair was dishevelled and his eyes were wild with the thrill of the chase.

Orion looked up at him sharply. "What are you doing in my office, Altair?"

"Sorry, Professor," Caleb said, though he didn't sound sorry and his gaze was roaming the room expectantly. "I'm looking for Tory Vega, did she come this way?"

"Tory?" Orion asked in surprise, a faint frown pulling at his forehead before he smoothed it away just as quickly. "Are you tormenting your Source?" he demanded. "You know the Code."

Caleb snarled, baring his teeth. "No I'm not, *Professor*. If you have to know, we're playing a game. And as two consenting adults, that is completely up to us."

Orion fell unnaturally still as he glared back at Caleb. "You're hunting her?" he demanded.

"It was her idea," Caleb said, his voice taking on a defensive tone even though he maintained his aggressive stance. "And there are no rules against it."

"No. But there are very strong warnings against it, for very good reason-"

"Well maybe *you* wouldn't be able to handle it, but I'm perfectly in control. And if you don't mind, I've only got six minutes left to find her, so if she's not here, you're wasting my time." He didn't give Orion the chance to object as he turned and shot away with his Vampire speed. The door slammed shut behind him, rattling the picture frames which hung on the walls.

Damn cheater! He wasn't supposed to use his gifts.

Orion got to his feet with a growl, almost looking like he was going to give chase for a moment but his gaze slid to my hiding place and he leaned forward, pressing his hands flat to the desk instead. I made a move to come out but he shook his head sharply, halting me.

The look on his face made me think he was pissed as hell and I was beginning to wonder if I'd accidentally put myself at the mercy of a scarier

Vampire.

My heart rate was finally falling into a more even rhythm and I released a slow breath as Orion beckoned for me to leave the confines of the cupboard.

I lifted my chin as I stepped out, dispersing my silencing bubble and Orion's gaze scraped over me.

"Thanks," I said quickly. "But I should really get going before he-"

"Take a seat, Miss Vega," Orion commanded, his tone leaving no room for negotiation.

I hesitated, eyeing the door and wondering if I should just leave. This wasn't school hours and I'd only come into his office because he'd invited me. I hadn't broken any rules so he had no reason to keep me here.

"If you run, I will catch you. And perhaps you'd be better off not encouraging a second Vampire to hunt you today?"

I pursed my lips and dropped into the chair, slapping an insolent expression onto my face. I eyed the clock which hung behind him. If I stayed here for five more minutes, I'd win anyway so it was probably worth the lecture I could feel coming.

"What have I done wrong now?" I asked, the shadows stirring beneath my skin as if they sensed my discomfort.

Orion didn't sit and I didn't miss the fact that his position standing over me was designed to be intimidating. But in all honesty after everything the Heirs threw at me on a regular basis, a teacher with a grouch complex wasn't likely to frighten me any time soon.

"I'm guessing that Caleb hasn't made you familiar with The Vampire Code?" he asked, eyeing me like he was judge, jury and executioner all rolled into one.

"He came blathering about it to me a few weeks ago because he felt bad about watching the others half drown me," I said dismissively. "I told him I didn't give a shit about it."

"Well it might have been worth your while to listen. Or to at least look into it yourself before you started screwing him."

I raised an eyebrow at his judgemental tone and leaned back in my chair like it was a damn throne and I was the queen of the world. I'd been in enough interrogations in my time to know how to play this and I wasn't going to fall into the trap of losing my shit.

"I think that my sex life is my own business and it's pretty inappropriate of you to comment on it," I said slowly.

He let out a long breath. "I thought that maybe you and Darius might-"

My hand clenched into a tight fist and I practically snarled at him. "If I never set eyes on Darius Acrux again in my life it will be too fucking soon. I *hate* him for what he helped his father do to us. You should know that better than anyone as you were there too. Or am I supposed to pretend I don't remember that, *sir?*"

Orion actually had the good grace to look uncomfortable at that, dropping his gaze for a moment before he went on.

"You know full well that neither Darius or I had any knowledge of what his father was going to do to the two of you. Darius risked his own life in place of yours that night because of how he feels about you and-"

"Bullshit," I snapped, slamming my fist down on the arm of my chair and causing it to burst alight. *Okay, so maybe I'd lost my shit after all.* The flames tickled my flesh but at the look of rage on Orion's face, I managed to make myself smother them as quickly as they'd appeared. "The two of you have your own agenda against Lionel and when push came to shove, Darius let him toss my sister in that fucking pit. Me too. I'm not going to forget that any time soon."

"Won't you just talk to Darius? Perhaps then you-"

"I'd sooner gouge my own eyes out with a rusty spoon. Am I free to go or did you have another lecture you wanted to get back to about the Heir I actually give half a shit about?" I asked angrily.

Orion let out a long breath through his nose which implied I was testing his patience and I had half a mind to just get up and walk out and find out what he'd do about it. The shadows were growing restless, whispering to me, flickering over my vision for a moment before trailing away.

Orion narrowed his eyes at me, clearly deciding to return to his original topic. "There are rules in the Code which dictate the way a Vampire *must* behave but there are also recommendations which, while not being an outright law, we are highly encouraged to follow. One of those being that we do not indulge in the hunt."

"Why?" I asked, not really caring but wanting to distract myself from Darius fucking Acrux.

"Because what might seem like a game to you, is actually tapping into the most primal instincts of our kind. You are placing yourself in the position of prey. And the more Caleb lets his instincts guide him and his blood pump with the thrill of the chase, the closer he gets to losing control all together. You know how much stronger he is than you when he uses his gifts, what if he threw you against a wall so hard he cracked your skull? Or pounced on you from a great height and broke your neck?"

I shifted uncomfortably in my seat. "He's never done anything like that to me," I protested. Apart from that time he drove me up a mountain and I half thought he was going to kill me. But he didn't, so...

"Well let's assume that he's able to rein in the use of his gifts. What about the bloodlust? The chase builds the bloodlust from a desire to an aching *need*. Couple that with the fact that you're offering him your body too and you're basically making yourself into something irresistible to him in every way. When you enter into this game, the two most primal desires of his flesh are running away from him and he is pinning every ounce of his energy and attention into claiming both of them."

"Maybe I like having every ounce of his attention on me," I replied, though I couldn't deny the prickle of apprehension which ran through me at his words. I'd noticed the way Caleb got sometimes when the game didn't go his way or even when it did. He could be a bit rough with me, but never more than I'd been happy with. He'd never crossed the line.

Orion rolled his eyes. "He mentioned that he's on a time limit, care to elaborate?"

I considered telling him to fuck off, but I got the feeling he wasn't going to let me out of this office until we had this cosy little chat so I gave him his answer. "When one of us starts the game, he has fifteen minutes to catch me before it ends."

"And if he doesn't catch you?"

"Then he doesn't bite me. It was kinda the whole reason I suggested we start playing it. Contrary to what I'm sure you'd like to believe, being bitten isn't enjoyable and I'm not strong enough to fight him off yet so at least this way I have a chance." I shrugged.

Orion sighed heavily and dropped into his seat. "I understand why you might have come up with this idea but it isn't a good one. Even if Mr Altair manages to stop himself from biting you when he loses, it is likely to enrage him more than you can comprehend. And the chances are that that will result in him tracking you down again and biting you anyway."

"Maybe you're not giving him enough credit," I said slowly.

"And maybe you're giving him too much," he replied darkly. "My comments are not on *who* he is but *what* he is and I know full well what the call of blood as powerful as yours can do to a man."

I glanced up at the clock and a smile pulled at my lips. "Well perhaps we're going to find out how well Caleb takes losing," I said. "Because he just did."

Orion's lips twitched like that idea pleased him, but he stifled the look so quickly I couldn't be sure.

"Just be careful, Miss Vega. And don't expect any help from me again when you need somewhere to hide."

"So why did you help me this time?"

"I thought you were your sister-" he cut himself off like he shouldn't have said that and I raised an eyebrow at him.

"Playing favourites with your own Source?" I accused. "Good to know."

"Well if you would be kind enough not to cover your hair with a hat in future, we won't have this trouble."

"Thanks for the tip. I've just been dying for fashion advice from a teacher," I said, rolling my eyes as I stepped out into the corridor.

Before Orion could respond, a huge metallic crash sounded from outside and I hurried across the hallway to look out at the open courtyard which separated Jupiter Hall from The Orb.

Caleb threw a second giant fireball at the curving golden wall of the building and that metallic crash sounded again, echoing through the floor at my feet. He cursed loudly then shot away using his Vampire speed.

"Do you still think he can handle your game?" Orion asked knowingly beside me and I bit my lip on answering. Because as much as I didn't want to admit it, I wasn't so sure anymore. "You may think I'm just overstepping the line and trying to tell you what to do for no other reason than me being an overbearing Professor-"

"I'd have called you a grumpy old asshole," I put in, smirking at him.

He snorted a laugh and pushed his hands into his pants' pockets. "Less of the 'old' I'm only eight years older than you."

"Yeah so when you were my age, I was ten," I pointed out. "So you're like half my age again. Hence, *old.*"

Orion frowned like he didn't really like me pointing that out, but why would he give a shit?

"What? Were you hoping we might become besties and start braiding each other's hair?" I teased.

"I already have a bestie," he mocked back.

"Yeah. You have bad taste in friends."

He laughed again and for the weirdest moment it did kinda feel like we were friends. I mean, he was still my Professor, still an ass, still old…but we'd actually been through kind of a lot together too. He'd fought alongside Darcy against the Nymphs and he'd helped us with the shadows the moment he realised we'd been cursed with them. No questions. Even now when he was being a total downer on my games with Caleb, he was actually just trying to look out for me. And maybe I hadn't really given him any credit for all that. I'd just lumped him in with Darius and offered him up the same douchey behaviour the Dragon had earned from me. Besides, we'd actually had fun together on his birthday…

"I dunno if I've ever said thanks," I said slowly, giving him a sideways glance.

"For what, Miss Vega?"

"Can you maybe just drop that shit?" I asked. "At least when we're not in class. You know Vega wasn't even the name I grew up with, right? We just agreed to go along with it because our surname never really meant anything to us and people wouldn't stop with it. We have enough trouble trying to get people to accept our names are Tory and Darcy without us trying to fight the Vega thing too. But I'd really just prefer it if you'd call me Tory when we're doing our shadow shit or hanging out for your birthday or whatever. Okay?"

"Sure," he replied with a smirk that made him look smug as fuck. "So, will I be getting that bracelet soon or do you need time to figure out what colours might suit me best?"

I snorted a laugh. "You might wanna ask Darcy if you really want a friendship bracelet. She's good at shit like that. Me? I'll take you on a night out where I'll steal a motorbike from some entitled prick and take you on a joy ride then drink you under the table so we both wake up wishing we hadn't. That's the kind of friend I am."

"Sounds good. But I'm a borderline alcoholic so I seriously doubt you could drink me under the table," he joked.

"Well I've been drinking myself into a coma every night since Lionel forced the shadows on me just so that I can sleep without nightmares so…"

Orion's gaze narrowed on me and I realised I'd let my mouth run away with me there.

"Don't worry about it. I'll catch you later." I turned and walked away from him, but before I could get three paces, he shot around me and was in my face.

"The shadows shouldn't be that loud if you've been subduing them like we've practiced," he said, frowning at me. "*Are* you subduing them, Tory?"

The look he was giving me was concerned but it was calculating too. I might have been a bit harsh on him because of his connection to Darius, but I had good reason for that. He wouldn't want me toying with the shadows like I was. He wouldn't want me learning to control them as well as I was starting to. Because he wanted Darius to have the advantage.

"I'll try harder," I said sweetly. I'd been lying to teachers, foster parents, social workers and the cops my whole life. I was damn good at it and I slammed my defensive walls back up just as quickly as I'd let them slip.

Orion frowned like he wasn't sure he bought my act but I just raised my eyebrows at him, waiting for him to say it.

He sighed.

"Look, if you're struggling with them while you're in your House then you should go to Darius. I know that the two of you aren't seeing eye to eye right now but I promise you, on this he won't do anything other than help you."

I scoffed at that and stepped around him. "Thanks," I said dismissively.

The shadows could have me before I'd go begging for help at Darius's door. "But Mr Tequila is helping me just fine."

I walked away from him and this time he let me go. What else could he say anyway? This curse was mine to bear now and I'd deal with it whatever way I had to to survive it. Including embracing it.

It was dark as I made it outside and I released a breath that rose in a cloud of vapour as I started walking for Ignis House.

I checked my Atlas as I went, finding a few messages from Caleb asking for a rematch which I ignored. I half wondered if Orion might be right about him hunting me down again anyway but I wasn't going to sweat it. Caleb might be a douche who went along with his asshole friends whenever it suited him, but he'd also taken me up a mountain when he was pissed as all hell with me and hadn't hurt me. Well…not any more than I was comfortable with anyway. So I decided to trust him at least in that. I might make it a point to discuss the hunt with him in a little more detail the next time we were alone though, just to make sure we really were on the same page with it.

I started walking through Fire Territory and for a moment I thought I heard someone calling my name. I looked around, but couldn't see anyone on the path so I continued on again.

Gabriel dropped from the sky right in front of me, moving as fast as a Vampire and causing me to shriek in alarm.

"What the hell?" I demanded as he stood before me, tucking his giant black wings against his back.

"I did call out but no one ever looks up," he said with a shrug.

"Right." I frowned at him, wondering if there was a point to him dropping out of the sky and scaring the life out of me.

"I need you to do me a favour," he said.

"What's that?"

"I'm out of stardust for our Order lessons. So unless we can get any more, we won't be able to continue."

My gut dropped. Even though I'd only been flying for a really short time, the idea of not being able to do it felt like being caged. It was unthinkable.

"I don't understand how I'm supposed to-"

"I need you to ask Darius for some," he replied.

I balked at that idea. "No. Seriously dude, no. I've got money, I can pay for-"

"The Acruxes control all of the stardust. It's made by Dragons. Even if you bought it you'd still be getting it from them. Besides, I've *seen* what will happen if you ask him. He'll give it to you."

"Why?" I asked. "Why would he do that for me?"

"I don't know," Gabriel said in a way that sounded like he really did know. "I just know that he will. Beyond that there are two paths your conversation might take. Which way it goes will depend on the two of you."

"That's not helpful," I pointed out. "That's like saying 'here's a sandwich, this will go one of two ways, you'll eat it or you won't' and that's not a real prediction. Those were the only two options there ever were anyway."

"Not true. Maybe I'd smash it in your face and let mayonnaise run riot through your hair. I've been known to do that in the past."

I rolled my eyes, smiling despite myself.

"Maybe," I agreed. "So is there a time scale on me asking a favour of the asshole I've been ignoring for the past week and a half?"

"You just need to do it tonight," Gabriel assured me. "This side of midnight feels like it's guaranteed to get us the stardust so best make it before then."

"Fine," I groaned. "I'll do it."

"Good. Then we can all go flying tomorrow."

He didn't let me respond to that as he shot off into the sky and I tipped my head back to watch him go with a smile on my face. Okay, so at least knowing my reward for this painful interaction would be getting to soar through the sky. I could make myself do it for that.

I headed back to Ignis House with flying on my mind and hurried through the common room before going straight to my room. I was tired and sweaty and I needed a shower. Interactions with bad tempered Dragons could wait that long.

I glanced in the mirror beside my door as I flicked the lights on. I just so happened to like this hat. It had a little pink bobble and made me look cute. Which was ironic because I was anything but that. And I'd bought several other hats too, now that the weather was getting colder. So what if it covered up my hair? It wasn't my job to make it easy for grumpy Professors to tell me and

Darcy apart.

I tossed my coat and hat back in my closet and headed straight into the shower, telling myself that I wasn't stalling as I stepped beneath the flow of hot water.

I took my time washing my hair then faffed about blow drying it and moisturising my skin after I'd gotten out. When I couldn't even lie to myself about the effort I was going to to avoid heading upstairs, I sighed and yanked on a pair of baggy sweats and a crop top. I didn't put any makeup back on because I gave zero shits about how I looked. I wasn't going to make an effort for Darius Acrux.

With a huff of irritation directed at Gabriel, I stalked out of my room. It was half eleven so I really couldn't avoid it any longer and a part of me was wishing I'd just gotten on with it the moment I'd come back to the House instead of wasting time. But it was too late for that so I set my jaw and jogged up the stairs instead.

I stalked towards Darius's door, the old warning he'd given me ringing in my ears. I wasn't supposed to come here uninvited. But here I was.

I refused to flinch and raised my fist to knock on the door without hesitating.

"It's open," Darius called back because entitled douchebags didn't bother themselves with things like opening doors.

I took a long breath then opened the door.

Darius was sitting with his back to me on the three seater grey couch which sat to the right of his enormous room. The TV was on and he was watching Pitball match replays while drinking a beer from the bottle.

He didn't look around, his gaze staying fixed on the TV as a slow motion shot played through of a player having their head smashed into the dirt while their opponent stole the earth ball from him.

"Hi," I said loudly when he didn't seem inclined to turn my way.

His head snapped around instantly at the sound of my voice and he shoved himself to his feet.

"Hey," he said, hesitating on the other side of the couch. His gaze slid over me but I didn't know what he was looking for. He wore a white T-shirt and a pair of black sweatpants, his hair unstyled and still damp from a shower so I guessed we'd made a similar non amount of effort. Then again I'd known I was coming here and he hadn't so mine was more intentional.

"So, Gabriel said I had to come here," I said, not wanting him to think this was my choice. "He's run out of stardust for transporting us to our Order lessons…"

Darius raised an eyebrow at me and I ground my teeth as I realised he was going to make me actually ask the question.

I took a deep breath and forced myself to do it because I just wanted this interaction over.

"So, would you possibly be able to give us some?"

He still didn't respond and I bit my tongue on the next word.

"*Please.*" I smiled sweetly, offering him the same bullshit show I used to put on for my foster parents when they would question me on where I'd snuck off to all night.

Darius laughed at my display and moved around the couch, approaching me slowly. I fell still, holding my ground and not wanting to show an inch of weakness.

"Close the door," Darius directed.

I glanced over my shoulder at it. I didn't hate having that route to freedom available and I wasn't keen on giving it up.

"Why?"

"Because stardust is ridiculously valuable and there are thieves in this school. I'm not just going to give away my hiding place for it with the door wide open."

I pursed my lips and sent a gust of air into the door, knocking it shut while I tried to ignore the fact that I'd just locked myself in with a beast.

"You don't need to look at me like I'm a serial killer," he deadpanned, walking across the room to his bed.

He lifted the mattress and I snorted a laugh as he revealed the stash of silk bags hidden there.

"Something you want to say?" he asked as he took a bag from the stash.

"Well it's just you said you wanted to keep your stash hidden from thieves, but under the mattress is pretty much the first place anyone would look for something." I shrugged.

"I guess you'd know," he replied.

"I would," I agreed, holding his eye. I wasn't ashamed of the things I'd done to survive. "But I guess you *wouldn't* know what it was like to go two days without food, watch your sister shiver herself to sleep under a threadbare blanket and have to go out and get some money in any way you could just to make sure you didn't starve."

Darius frowned in response to that. "I didn't mean…sorry. You're right, I haven't got a clue what it's like to have to do something like that. Or to have to live like that. I shouldn't judge you for what you did to survive."

I raised an eyebrow at him. "I didn't realise that word was even in your vocabulary."

"Maybe you would have if you didn't ignore me all the time," he replied.

"Well maybe I wouldn't have to if you weren't such a consistently repetitive ass."

Darius opened his mouth to bite back at me but no words escaped him. His fist closed on the pouch of stardust and he forced himself to halt whatever words had been working their way up out of his throat.

"You know, I think that if you want to have this, you're going to need to do something to earn it," he said eventually.

"Like what?"

Darius cocked his head as he considered that. "Help me hide the rest of it somewhere a thief wouldn't check."

"You could just entrust it all into my keeping and I'd promise to keep it safe for you," I offered.

Darius smirked at me. "Unlikely. I might be able to understand what drove you to stealing from people. But once a thief always a thief, right?"

I shrugged because that was probably true. I didn't need to steal anything from anyone at the moment, but if the need arose I wouldn't exactly find it difficult to slip into old habits.

"Fine," I agreed because it was obvious he wasn't going to give it to me until he made me jump through this hoop.

I glanced around his fancy ass room, scoffing slightly at the solid gold headboard before walking straight past his bed and into his bathroom.

"Are you going to use my toothbrush again?" he asked as he followed me and I rolled my eyes, not bothering to respond. I guessed he was referring to the night I'd gotten way too drunk and ended up sleeping here, but I didn't remember brushing my teeth.

"You have a goddamn jacuzzi in your bathroom," I pointed out as I headed into the huge space. The walls were covered in grey and white tiles and the taps and toilet flush were solid gold. *Of course they are.*

"You were quite fond of that the last time you came here too," he said. "Do you wanna try it out?"

"Why, are you leaving?" I asked, looking back over my shoulder at him.

"Do you really want me to?" he asked in response.

I ignored the heat that ran down my spine at that suggestion and pointed at the base of the jacuzzi as I turned back to face him.

"Unscrew that panel and put your little stash in there. Most thieves won't dismantle something to check for hidden crap," I said. "Can I have the stardust now?"

Darius walked towards me, holding his fist out and opening it slowly in offering.

My heart thumped harder as he penned me into the corner of the room with his huge body but I refused to back away.

I reached out, my fingers gripping the bag half a second before he closed his hand around mine.

I flinched and tried to pull my hand back but he didn't release me.

"I think we need to talk," he said slowly.

"Let go of me," I said, my voice stronger than I felt inside.

"What is it you think I'm going to do to you?" he asked, hurt flickering in his eyes as he released my hand. "You're impervious to fire magic, I can't even use Dragon Fire against you. I'm hardly going to hit you or hurt you in some other way. I just want to talk to you before you run off and start ignoring me again."

"Oh, I don't know," I replied sarcastically. "We're in a bathroom after all, maybe you're going to try and drown me again? Or choke me? Or maybe you just want to try and draw me closer to you again just so that it will hurt even more the next time you push me in the mud or call me a whore."

216

Darius's lips parted but he didn't say anything else. He was frowning like he didn't want to own the fact that he'd done all of those things and more to me, but there was no denying it.

My heart was beating a frantic rhythm as I looked up at him while listing all the things he could so easily do to me and on instinct I reached for something to protect myself.

The shadows sprung to life within me without any need for further prompting. Darkness fell over my vision and I glared through it at Darius as his eyes widened with surprise. I inhaled deeply as the euphoric call of the shadows sang to my soul and drew on more of them to protect myself.

The whispering grew louder, promises of power, destruction and death breathed into my ears like the softest caress. Shadows spilled along my arms, cloaking my body and dancing between my fingers as I let them have their way.

It would be so easy to keep going. So easy to let them do whatever they wanted and feed my soul with the pleasure they promised me.

I took a step towards my tormentor, baring my teeth as I closed in on him and the shadows begged for his life. And after everything he'd done to me, why shouldn't I take it? I'd be protecting myself and my sister from the threat he clearly still posed us.

I reached out and caught his T-shirt in my grasp, fisting it in my hand while pressing my other palm flat to his chest right above his heart.

The shadows leapt forward, intent on their victim and lurching out to coil around his soul.

Power slid beneath my skin and Darius gasped in surprise as the shadows fed on his magic and gifted it to me. The heat of his fire burned beneath my skin and I moaned as it lit me up from the inside out.

It was like the purest taste of sin. I was consuming that which placed him above me, feeding on the very thing he wielded to hurt me.

"Roxy," Darius breathed, his hand cupping my cheek as he captured my gaze with his. "Fight it."

I blinked at him, wondering what he meant and why he wasn't trying to fight me off. Golden light danced on the edges of my vision as he let the barrier around his power fall away, leaving himself vulnerable to my shadows as they raced forward to devour everything that made him, him.

I felt like I was standing on a precipice, I could lean one way and let the shadows feast, take anything and everything from him. Or I could lean the other and fall back into his arms, let him pull me away from the dark.

The shadows deepened over my eyes and it felt like I was reliving every heinous thing he'd ever done to me, existing in the memory of each torturous moment I'd spent in his company. Just as I was about to let the shadows have him, another memory surfaced. I woke up in his arms, the heat of him surrounding me and the feeling of complete and utter safety enveloping me.

I gasped as I drew myself back from the shadows, throwing a cage up around the part of my heart where they resided and locking them away.

I stumbled forward and Darius's arms closed around me as he drew me against his chest.

The scent of him enveloped me, cedar and smoke mixing with something entirely him.

His fingers slid through my hair, his other hand stroking along my spine as I shuddered in his arms. My heart was thundering to a dangerous beat and I had to wonder if I'd really been in more danger of hurting myself than Darius by giving in to the shadows.

"It's alright," he breathed. "I won't ever let them have you."

"Why?" I forced out, reaching up to brush the tears from my cheeks. "You don't care about me. All you've ever done is hurt me, so why would you promise me something like that?"

I managed to push myself out of his arms and the places where his hands had been tingled with the memory of his touch like they missed it.

"I do care about you," he said, the frown on his face telling me he wasn't sure why and I sure as shit didn't know either. "And I'm...I mean, I shouldn't...I never should have..."

"What?" I breathed, looking into his dark eyes and hoping for...what? Something I didn't dare let myself hope for.

"You have to know I can't...I didn't...I never wanted to..."

"To what?" I demanded, needing him to say it. To just fucking *say it*.

He shook his head at me like the words burned too much to force past his lips. My temper rose again because even after everything, he wasn't going to own any of it. He wasn't going to apologise or say *anything* that might make even the littlest difference.

"Just say it," I begged.

He reached for me but I stepped back. I needed to hear it. No short cuts. Not after everything he'd done. If he wanted something from me then he had to fucking *say* it.

Darius frowned and I could see some kind of battle going on within his gaze, but I wasn't just going to stand here while he tried to figure it out. If it was this damn hard for him to say whatever the hell it was then he clearly didn't feel it strongly enough.

I plucked the bag of stardust from the floor where he'd dropped it and side stepped him, heading for the exit.

I made it all the way through the bathroom and to the door which led back to the hallway before he called out to stop me.

"Roxy, wait."

I paused, looking over my shoulder at him.

"What? I have somewhere else to be," I snapped even though I didn't.

"With Caleb?" he asked and I just frowned at him because that wasn't the case, but it wasn't like it was his business if it was. He seemed to take my silence as confirmation though and his gaze hardened.

"Do you have something to say to me or not?" I demanded.

"No," he growled. "Just skip off back to his bed like a good little blood donor."

"Nice." I wrenched the door open and stepped out into the corridor.

He called after me again but he could go fuck himself.

I started jogging and his footsteps followed me out into the corridor.

"I didn't mean that," he was saying but I didn't want to fucking hear it.

"You never mean any of the things you say or do to me, do you?" I shouted back. "But you still keep doing them."

I made it to my door and shoved my key into the lock, tearing it open just as he caught up to me.

I stepped inside and tried to throw the door closed in his face. His hand swung up to stop it at the last second.

"So that's it?" he demanded. "You're just going to run away from me?

Just going to go right back to ignoring me?"

"And you're going right back to tormenting me and making my life miserable, right?"

His eyes flashed with emotion but I was done, so fucking done.

With a wrench of energy, I forced the door shut between us and quickly turned the key in the lock.

"Roxy!" Darius shouted from the other side.

"That's not even my fucking name, asshole!" I screamed back.

He kept pounding on my door but I just backed away from it.

"You really want us to go right on back to hating each other?" he called through the wood. "Like nothing happened on the night of the Eclipse? Like nothing changed?"

"Nothing did change," I snarled. "I hated you then and I still hate you now!"

There was a long pause and in the silence that stretched I almost thought he'd gone until his voice came back to me again.

"Fine. If that's how you want it, then stay my enemy. But don't forget you asked for it."

He slammed his fist into my door and I leapt back as a crack split up the centre of the wood, but his retreating footsteps sounded a moment later, letting me know he was gone.

I sank down onto my bed, shaking all over though I refused to acknowledge it. Tears slid down my cheeks but I ignored them too. Because I didn't care about Darius Acrux. And he certainly didn't mean enough to me to make me cry.

DARCY

CHAPTER SIXTEEN

"Come to me..."

Shadows swirled around me, dark and alluring. They crept along my skin like warm hands and pulled, pulled, pulled me toward oblivion. I was safe, wrapped in a blanket of comfort as ecstasy trickled through my veins.

"Where are you?" I whispered into the void, my voice like satin as it slid from my tongue.

"Over here...closer...come to me..."

She sounded further away than before and my heart squeezed with the need to find her in the abyss.

"I can't see," I breathed, trying to swipe away the pressing black.

A hand caught mine and soft fingers latched onto me. My heart pulsed softly as I stepped forward, feeling her arms sliding around me even though I was still blind.

"Save me." Her breath dragged across my cheek, branding a cold kiss there that washed deep into my bones. For a moment I felt like I was standing with someone I knew, someone as familiar to me as my own flesh and blood. Then she was gone and the darkness swirled around me, its sweet pull drawing me after her.

I took a step, reaching for the whispers at the edge of my hearing, *desperate to find them.*

But then a memory found me of someone whose flesh matched my own, whose soul was built of the same essence as mine. Then another presence, a man with endless eyes who held me close and begged me not to go. And whoever they were drew me back a step, because there wasn't a realm in this universe I could go without them at my side.

I woke gasping, sweat plastering the covers to my skin. I threw them aside, stepping out of my bed and moving to the window. I pushed it wide and the icy morning air poured over me, rushing across my heated flesh.

The shadows receded into some ever-present space inside me. They'd always be there, waiting to tempt me into their arms.

I recalled the voice of the girl who'd tried to summon me to her. She'd asked for help. Was she some poor lost soul who'd stepped into the void and never come back?

I shuddered, pulling the window shut as the cold became too bitter. Frost clung to the window pane and the white sheen dusted the grass down below. It glittered like stardust as the rising sun spilled over it and I gazed at the peaceful scene until my heart returned to a normal beat.

My alarm went off on my Atlas and the sound of soft windchimes tinkled through the air. I dropped back onto my bed, tapping the screen to turn it off and opening up my horoscope.

Good morning Gemini.
The stars have spoken about your day!
Today will deliver many challenges on your doorstep, but take heart, the stars are glimmering in your favour. So long as you dig deep for the strength inside you and use the pull of Jupiter to prepare you for surprises, you could have a great day. Remember, the honey will be all the sweeter once you've faced the hive to take it.

It was cryptic as usual, but I was always on guard whenever it spoke about challenges and surprises. *Especially freaking surprises.*

I headed into the shower to wash away the clinging darkness of the dream and was soon walking down to The Orb in my uniform and coat. The wintery air brought my senses to life and by the time I reached The Orb, my face tingled with its icy caress. I needed to start wearing gloves and a hat soon, so an online shopping spree was in order.

Better not tell Tor, or she'll buy me the whole winter catalogue.

I smiled as I spotted her, already at our usual table surrounded by our friends. A suspiciously new looking cream scarf was wrapped around her neck and as I approached, I spotted the price tag still hanging from it.

I snapped it off, waving it under her nose. "One hundred auras for a scarf? You're gonna bankrupt us before we graduate," I teased.

She snatched the tag from my hand with a grin. "Have you seen our bank account? I couldn't bankrupt us if I tried."

"But you *are* trying, right?" I laughed.

Sofia giggled across the table, taking a bite out of her toast but she wasn't looking at us, she was staring at her Atlas.

"Is Tyler sending you dick pics?" Tory asked with a smirk.

Sofia glanced up, her cheeks colouring a second before Tyler appeared behind her, leaning down for a kiss. She quickly tucked her Atlas away and turned to press her lips to his and he fell into the seat next to hers.

"I don't send dick pics, Tory," Tyler said as he snatched an apple from the fruit bowl Geraldine had filled on the table. "The screen's not big enough to encompass *all* that."

"Ew," Tory laughed. I noticed dark circles ringing her eyes and frowned as I realised it was odd for her to beat me to breakfast. I guessed the shadows were keeping her up at night too.

"You okay?" I asked her under my breath and she shook her head.

"Didn't get much sleep." She glanced over at Darius. "And I had a bit of a run in with the Dragon asshole."

Before she could tell me more, Geraldine appeared with a large tray of bagels, nudging Tyler aside as she placed them down at the heart of the table and dropped into her seat opposite us. She looked a little frazzled and her usually perfect uniform seemed kinda ruffled. "Grape juice on a one-way flight to Alestria, I nearly lost an arm for these bagels this morning."

"What happened?" I asked in surprise.

"Max Rigel happened!" she huffed. "That bloated beluga whale needs to get the hint. He's swangling his way into my life at every turn these days. He laid siege to the entire bagel pile!"

"Please tell me you knocked him on his ass," Tory said hopefully.

Geraldine swiped a hand over her hair to flatten it. "Certainly. But not before he sent my skirt shooting up over my head with a jet of water. Gravy granules, does he have no shame at all? I had to teach him a lesson of course to try and drive the message home."

Tory elbowed me and as if on cue, Max Rigel stalked his way past us toward the exit of The Orb with jam dripping from his hair and what looked like a bunch of bananas sticking out the back of his pants. He snatched them out, tossing them to the floor and some sad sap of a girl hurried to pick them up, running to her friends' table where they preceded to start eating them. *Gross. Do they have no shame?*

I turned to grin at Geraldine and she lifted her chin, grabbing a wedge of butter and a knife for the bagels.

My gaze fell on Diego several feet beyond the table, holding a plate of eggs and toast, glancing our way with a look of uncertainty.

I nudged Tory and she glanced over at him, shrugging before returning to picking at her breakfast.

"He said he's sorry," I whispered. "I feel bad for him."

"Whatever, take in the stray if you must," Tory said. "But I don't recall getting an apology myself."

I chewed on my lower lip, standing and heading over to him as he drifted toward an empty table. Before I made it to him, Seth Capella stormed across the room, flipping Diego's plate up into his chest and ramming his shoulder against his before making a beeline to the buffet.

"Asshole!" I called after him but he ignored me.

I hurried to help Diego wash the eggy mess off of his shirt with the aid of my water magic, cursing Seth under my breath.

Diego's arms hung limply at his sides as if he'd given up on life. The guy seriously needed a pep talk. And it looked like I was the only one willing to give it.

"Just ignore him – and all the Heirs for that matter," I said.

"How has that worked out for you in the past?" he asked with a frown.

"Fair point." I broke a grin and his shoulders relaxed as he returned it. I nodded over at our table with a hopeful look. "There's room for one more."

"Your sister looks like she's trying to melt my head with her glare."

I glanced over at Tory, silently communicating that she back off. She rolled her eyes in response then slapped a too-cheery smile on her face instead.

"She's just having a rough morning," I said to Diego with a shrug. "Maybe if you apologised about before…"

He nodded, shifting from foot to foot then he leaned in closer and whispered to me, "I've been meaning to but…well she scares the cagada out of me, chica."

I snorted a laugh, taking his arm and guiding him over to the table. "Ignore that resting bitch face, it's totally an act." Okay not totally, but he didn't need to know that.

We arrived behind Tory and I tapped her on the shoulder when she didn't turn around. She sighed dramatically, her stare hardening as she swivelled to look at Diego.

I clutched his arm tighter, sensing he was about to bolt.

Diego cleared his throat several times, then finally choked out a garbled apology, intermittently falling into his native tongue.

"Okay okay," Tory waved a hand. "You're giving me a headache so I forgive you and all that jazz." She pointed at the empty seat on her other side and Diego smiled as he dropped into it.

Geraldine pushed the bagel tray toward him with a motherly look. "You're as skinny as a dieting toothpick, Diego. Tuck into my buttery bagels."

He grabbed one and we were all soon chatting like nothing had changed between us. Even him and Tyler seemed to get on just fine and for a second it felt like the shadows that lived in me had evaporated, leaving only the light of my friends shining through my skin like rays of the sun.

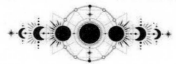

It was our first Numerology class and I was excited to learn about another magical faction as we headed into the classroom half way up Neptune Tower. The room was built of grey stone walls, the bricks exposed and the air cool. On each wall were seemingly random numbers including eleven, seven, three, thirty three and seven hundred and forty seven. They were etched deep into the stone as if they'd been carved by a giant blade and where the cuts had been made, glittering crystal was revealed within.

Tory, Diego, Sofia, Tyler and I all sat on one of the long desks at the back of the room, taking out our Atlases and textbooks.

Professor Faun was a stocky man with dark skin and short dreadlocks which hung over the shaven sides of his head. He had a handsome face and a crooked smile that made me warm to him quickly.

"Numbers. Are. *Everything*." He pressed a button on his Atlas and jazz music began to play throughout the room. He clicked his fingers to the beat, shutting his eyes as he lost himself to it, sucking on his lower lip. "Mmm yeah."

I glanced at Tory and we both stifled laughs as Professor Faun sauntered his way between the aisles, moving in a strange, seductive sort of rhythm.

"I heard he's a Satyr," Kylie whispered from the table in front of ours. "They're so...sensual." She sighed like she was lost to some dream and a flicker of fire in my periphery made me realise the professor was giving off some vibe my Phoenix powers were shutting out.

"Everyone relaaax." Professor Faun released the top button of his shirt. "Get comfortable, shake out your limbs and enjoy the positive vibes of this space. We're all just spirits dancing in an endless sea of stars."

"Is he high?" I whispered to Tory and she snorted into her hand as Faun danced past us, his moves surprisingly good.

"Numerology is the music of the heavens. Each number is a note and they all work together to create one magical tune." Professor Faun cast a vine in his hand, shooting it across the room to flick the light switch so we were plunged into darkness. A disco ball above us immediately started spinning and the silvery light it cast merged into infinite numbers, all spinning around us across the ceiling and walls.

"Your soul is written in numbers," Faun explained like that made total sense. He funky-danced his way back up to the electronic board at the head of the room, tapping it to bring up the first slide.

Determining your birth path number and using its groovalicious meaning to discover your path in life and place in the world.

"Your first task is to work out your birth path number. Follow the equation on the board then I'll go around the room discussing each number specific to you and what it means." He tapped the board again and the equation appeared. I frowned, expecting some god-awful math equation, but luckily it was pretty simple.

Add up all the numbers in the month, day and year you were born.
For example:
01/18/1990

$$0 + 1 + 1 + 8 + 1 + 9 + 9 + 0 = 29$$

Add the number once again to learn your Birth Path Number:
$$2 + 9 = 11$$
$$1 + 1 = 2$$

I wrote out my birth date on my Atlas as everyone in the class set to work. After a minute, I came up with a Birth Path Number of one and was intrigued to learn what that might mean. Tory got the same obviously while Sofia got a six and Diego got a seven.

Professor Faun made his way over to us, seeming interested as he took in the number one Tory and I had written down.

"One is the number of achievers...leaders." His eyes ran over us and curiosity burned in them. "Many of Solaria's rulers have possessed this Birth Path Number."

"Well we don't plan on ruling anything so..." Tory shrugged.

"*Plans*," Faun spat out a laugh. "Plan away, Miss Vega. You will soon realise that all plans are futile. The only ones that matter are written in the stars."

"So technically we could find out if we're destined to rule or not?" I asked curiously and Tory rolled her eyes in my periphery.

I ignored her, fixing Professor Faun in my gaze. My sister seriously needed to be less cynical. We were at Zodiac Academy for god's sake. I didn't like the idea of my life being fated either, but if it was, I'd rather know that… and what freedom we had in our choices.

"Yes and no," Faun mused, rubbing the stubble on his jaw. "Numerology will give an indicator of the life you'll lead and can help guide you along your path. All of your power numbers influence your decisions. They're as bound to you as your DNA. If you are born to lead, then lead you will. But that doesn't necessarily mean you will rule Solaria."

"Good, because the day I bow to the Vega Whores is the day I hang myself from a tree in The Wailing Wood," Kylie said loudly, her joke punctuated by a snort from Jillian.

Faun turned to dock House Points and I muttered to Tory under my breath, "I think I just got my first real incentive to claim the throne."

Tory released a laugh and Faun whipped around to look at us with a questioning frown. We gave him innocent looks and he moved away to define Sofia's number, naming her as a caregiver and nurturer, likely to lead a career in health services. Diego's number seven denoted him as a seeker who looked for meaning in life, questioned things and had a spiritual nature.

Yup, when your grandma's soul is knitted into your hat, I guess that makes you one seriously spiritual guy.

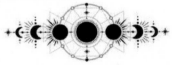

I headed to the Pitball Stadium after school hours with my heart thumping against my throat. Tory had gone back to her room for something, but the look in her eye had told me she had no intention of showing up for cheer practice. Did I blame her? Hell no. Being stuck on a squad with Marguerite and Kylie was almost as bad as being stuck on a team with the Heirs. Not that it was a competition or anything, but I had the awful feeling I'd just won.

At least there was a silver lining. One with muscles, incredible skill on the pitch and who actually liked me. And no, it wasn't Orion – a moody Vampire for a coach? No thank you. He wasn't going to go easy on me just because we were…whatever the hell we were. Nope, if ever there was a knight in shining armour awaiting me in the locker rooms, it was Geraldine Grus.

I reached the stadium, finding myself locked out and recalling Geraldine had a key the last time I'd entered this way – to rub Griffin shit all over Max's kit. A smile pulled at my lips at the memory and I wondered if we'd get a chance to mess with him again soon. The hashtag #poowhatyougottado was trending high this week and I often flicked through the FaeBook newsfeed to amuse myself with the mocked up images of Max. Someone had found a professional photo of him lying on a beach with his lips parted and had done a great job of adding a lot of poop to that pic.

I tugged at the door a few pointless times then blew out a huff and took my Atlas from my pocket. I was about to shoot Geraldine a message when an arm dropped around my shoulders. I jolted in surprise, finding Caleb there, steering me toward the door. "Stuck out here, sweetheart? I'll let you in."

"Oh…thanks," I said suspiciously. He might have been seeing my sister, but I was still wary as hell when it came to Caleb Altair.

He reached for the door then paused, turning to me with mischief sparkling in his eyes. "Of course…I'll want a favour in return."

I sighed, my eyes swinging to the sky. "Of course you do."

"It's just an itty bitty one," he said with a grin that could have melted most girls panties. Not mine because ew, my sister had been there. Which gave me blinkers just for him, along with any other guy my sister had laid a hand on. It was innate. He might as well have looked like a potato in a dress for how interested I was in him. Plus, you know, there was the completely mind-consuming hotness that was Lance Orion for me to focus on.

"What is it?" I glanced over my shoulder, hoping for any other team member to arrive who could let me in. Except maybe Seth…or Darius…or Max. *Yeah, anyone else would be great though.*

"I want the truth," he asked, his arm tightening around my shoulders. "Tell me what Tory's said about me."

I barked a laugh and his expression darkened.

"What?" he demanded.

"It's just…there's not much to report."

He scowled. "There must be *something*."

231

"I mean, she thinks you're hot." I shrugged and that seemed to lighten his mood a fraction.

"Tell me what she wants from a guy," he blurted, swinging me around to look at him. "What am I missing? I mean, look at me. What's not to like?" He pushed a hand into his hair and gave me an actual smoulder.

I pursed my lips. "How about not being a douche? Have you tried that?"

"I am trying," he said gently, his cocky shit suddenly falling away.

I frowned, suddenly finding the desperate look in his eyes kinda sad.

"Cal!" Seth jogged up to us and Caleb released me in an instant.

I glanced at the firmly closed door with frustration.

Just let me in, dammit!

Seth's eyes swung to me, his gaze dripping with disdain. "You're really trying out for the team?"

I clenched my jaw, a fire igniting in me at the disbelief in his tone. Sure, I hadn't exactly believed I was a great candidate either two minutes ago, but now he thought it, I was going to give my best shot at proving both of us wrong.

"Yeah, and? Can you just open the door?" I moved toward it and Seth stepped past me, unlocking it with his key.

He headed inside with Caleb in tow and I moved to follow just as he slammed the door in my face. An actual growl escaped me and I hammered my fist on the door.

"Open up!"

No response.

"Tory also said you've got the personality of a grape, Caleb!" I shouted after him, knowing he'd hear with his Vampire ears. It only made me feel one percent better.

My heart thumped in my ears as I reached into my pocket for my Atlas to message Geraldine. Except it wasn't freaking there.

My mouth parted as I hunted the area but nope, one of those assholes had freaking pick-pocketed me.

Deep breath, Darcy.

I gazed around for a solution to present itself but unsurprisingly none came to me.

Unless…

I stared up at the roof high above. It was currently open to the sky and though it was a seriously tall building, that didn't really matter to my air magic. It was just the fear of it failing on me that made me pause.

What am I gonna do? Fly up there like Wonder Woman and swoop down onto the pitch?

Holy shit I think I am.

Wait, does Wonder Woman even fly?

I pushed air from my hands before I could back out, propelling myself up the curving metal wall which arched toward the sky. A rush of adrenaline poured down my limbs as I hurtled up and over the open roof. The four quarters of the pitch gazed up at me from below. The team were assembling on it, jogging out of the tunnel which led to the locker rooms.

My stomach dropped the same second I did, the blast of air from my hands slowing so I started descending – fast.

Oh shit shit shit –

By sheer force of will, I held my scream in my chest, refusing to embarrass myself. Which lasted all of two more seconds as I crashed into the ground and slammed to my knees before everyone. It wasn't perfect, but it wasn't *totally* humiliating either – *win!*

Geraldine started applauding as everyone stared at me like a meteor had just crashed from the heavens. "Holy spaceballs!" she gasped. "What an entrance!"

Orion's brows were practically in his hairline, his arms folded and bulging against the fitted black T-shirt which labelled him as the Pitball Coach.

"Five points to Aer," he said with a smirk. "But it would have been ten if you made that landing, Miss Vega." Backhanded, but I'd take it. He glanced back up at the sky as if looking for another Fae falling from the heavens. "Where's your sister?"

"She's on her way." Total lie. I bet she was stretched out on her bed watching Faeflix right about now.

I spotted the cheer squad congregating at end of the pitch, stretching and flashing a lot of skin in our direction. Most of the guys were captivated by the show and Orion started directing them into sprints around the pitch to distract them. There were nearly fifty people present including almost thirty freshmen waiting to try-out.

"Your kit's waiting for you on the bench in the girl's locker room. Go get changed," Orion ordered. "And hurry or I'll remember how late you were to practise."

He was such a hypocrite, but damn it made me hot when he got all bossy like that. I didn't let him know it though, offering him an eye roll before heading down the tunnel into the locker room.

My kit was waiting for me and my Atlas had been left on top of it by whichever one of the Heirs had thieved it from me. I stripped down, shoving my stuff into a locker and was soon dressed in the navy and silver colours of the academy. I wore a pair of fitted shorts and as I wasn't an official member of the team, the academy letters were printed on the back of the shirt instead of my name. I pulled on the knee high socks and sneakers before jogging back out to the pitch where I was ready to freeze my ass off.

Orion immediately sent me off to do sprints with the rest of the team and I nodded, running to join the pack. After the comment Seth had made, I was determined to do my best today. I was gonna make myself a substitute. It was a reasonable goal. I'd played lacrosse in high school so I wasn't completely inept when it came to sport.

After four sprints, my legs ached, by eight my lungs burned, by fifteen my tongue was practically lolling. *Okay maybe I'm ten percent inept.*

Orion finally called time and though I'd not been the fastest, I hadn't been the slowest either. I could feel him assessing me and tried to stand straighter but holy hell I was dying.

Sweat clung to my skin and I drew in heavy lungfuls of air, wondering why I'd ever thought I'd get cold during this.

"Right team, line up in front of me," Orion commanded and the star players did as he said, the Heirs and Geraldine included. There were only eight of them, though I was sure a full team was made up of ten. I glanced around to see if anyone else would join them when Orion explained their absence.

"Our Airsentry, Ashanti Larue, lost her life in the battle that took place here. Subsequently, one of our Pit Keepers, Milly Badgerville, quit the team. So we're looking for official replacements. The Pit Keeper position is open to any Element, so stand to my left if you're trying out as an Airsentry and on my right to play Pit Keeper."

I hesitated as the subs and newbies split accordingly. Several people went for the Pit Keeper position and the rest lined up for the Airsentry, all of which were massive, broad chested girls and guys. I vaguely remembered it was a defensive position so hell if I was suited to that. Apart from being clumsy as shit, I couldn't tackle a Labrador, let alone someone the size of the Heirs in a match.

Pit Keeper it is.

Orion's eyes followed me as I moved into my chosen line and I swear he nodded his approval.

"Airsentries, you will each try to get a ball in the Pit while our new Keepers try to stop you. All of the main team will be playing defence to prevent you from scoring," Orion explained.

"Perhaps a demonstration from Solaria's finest Airsentry of his time," Geraldine suggested, eyeing Orion with a cocked brow.

"I don't think so, Grus," Orion said with an amused expression.

"Go on, sir," Justin Masters piped up. "Impress the newbies."

Max put his fingers in his mouth, whistling loudly in encouragement.

The rest of the team started chanting, "Go on sir, go on sir, go on sir!"

Orion's eyes flashed to me then he strode toward Darius, handing him his Atlas with an eye roll. "For fuck's sake, fine," he said, shaking his head but a smile was playing around his mouth.

"What ball do you want?" Darius asked as he eyed the screen, evidently able to control the Elemental Holes from it.

"Surprise me," Orion said, rolling out his shoulders. "Rigel, Grus, on the pitch."

Max and Geraldine jogged out either side of him and as Darius tapped the screen a fwooomph sounded an Airball shooting far up above us.

Orion ran for it, powering down the pitch and launching himself into the sky to catch it. He snatched the ball from the air and landed in a crouch. Max and Geraldine were already charging him down and he barrelled toward them, locking the ball tight under one arm and raising his other hand.

Geraldine cast a wall of earth, tearing it up from the ground, but Orion launched himself over it with a gust of air.

Max was waiting, casting ice under his feet. He leapt away from it, running on nothing but air as the two of them took chase.

Everyone started calling out in encouragement and I found myself doing the same as he sped toward the Pit. Max was hot on his heels and he leapt forward to take him down, but Orion swerved sideways at the last second.

Geraldine cast vines out to catch him and Orion leapt forwards, throwing the ball just as the vines caught him around the waist and he crashed into the ground. The ball fell into the Pit and I cheered in excitement as Geraldine released him and Orion sprang to his feet, muddy, bruised and looking hot as hell.

I wet my mouth as he jogged back to us with Geraldine and Max in tow.

"Right, enough time wasting," Orion said firmly, but a spark had entered his gaze. "Airsentry tryouts, head onto the pitch and try to get a ball in the Pit."

The Airsentries fanned out across the pitch and Orion took his Atlas back from Darius, tapping something on the screen.

"Two Keeper tryouts at a time. If you let a ball in, tag out. There'll be no rounds. Everyone on the main team is going to be playing defence so if you're tackled, get up and keep playing," Orion called and my heart beat quickened as I moved to stand beyond the Pit while two of the tryouts took up position in front of it.

"Good luck, little Vega!" Max called to me with nothing but poison in his eyes.

"Don't fall into the Pit again," Seth said with a smirk.

"You might not get out this time," Darius added before jogging after Caleb down the pitch.

Tension prickled along my skin as the team spread out. The Heirs were gazing at the Airsentry tryouts like easy prey and one guy actually looked ready to call it quits before the game had even started. I moved into the group of Keepers standing on the edge of the pitch and two of them jogged up to guard the Pit.

"Three, two, one!" Orion blew his whistle and the shrill sound combined with the thundering of feet across the ground. At a tap on his screen, balls shot out of the four Elemental holes in each corner of the pitch.

My pulse elevated as the main team raced to tackle the Airsentries and they ran to try and get a ball. I couldn't keep my eyes off of the Heirs as they took down player after player like it was as easy as breathing. Geraldine at least helped hers up while the Heirs leapt over their prey to make the next kill.

Darius was like a tank as he tackled players to the ground and some of them didn't move again once he'd got off of them. My jaw was dropping further and further as the Airsentries battled to reach the Pit and finally one girl broke through. Her bright blonde hair whipped out behind her as she ran, her arms smeared with mud and her eyes full of determination. The Heirs were busy taking other players down but Damien Evergile was hot on her heels, casting a pillar of fire after her.

She knocked the two Pit Keepers aside with a huge blast of water, directing it behind her as well to extinguish the flames at her back. With a shriek of excitement, she slammed the ball into the Pit and I released a whoop, the energy in the air electric.

The cheer squad had started up a routine, but I couldn't turn my attention from the apocalypse taking place on the pitch to watch.

"Tag out!" Orion barked at the two Pit Keepers before praising the blonde girl and sending her back to keep playing.

I glanced around, noticing a few of the Keepers had backed up and figured I might as well go for it. I headed to the front of the Pit with Elijah Indus, his jaw set in determination. He stood to the other side of the Pit and adrenaline tingled in my veins as Orion blew the whistle and more balls were launched onto the pitch.

I set my feet firmly on the ground, sensing the depths of the Pit behind me as I remembered the Heirs pushing me in there.

A dark haired boy broke free of the warring pitch, racing toward the Pit with a battle cry. I lifted my hands, focusing on the ground beneath his feet as I attempted to trip him up with earth magic. As he got within two yards, power exploded from my body and a huge tremor ripped through pitch. He yelled in surprise, crashing to the ground and the Earthball dropped from his arms with a dull thud.

A girl swooped down on it, picking it up and launching it toward the Pit. I threw up an air shield as Elijah tried to knock her over with a wall of ice. The ball bounced harmlessly off of my shield and a grin burrowed into my cheeks. *This is actually kinda fun.*

Seth charged someone down ten feet in front of me and my heart hammered as he scooped up their Airball and swung toward me with a vicious smirk. I gritted my jaw as he ran forward, fire burning in my veins as I faced him.

I half wondered if Orion would blow the whistle on him for taking a shot at the Pit, but he didn't. I couldn't even see him in all the madness and there was no way in hell I was taking my eyes off of the wolf closing in on me.

Seth threw out a hand and knocked Elijah flying. His power slammed into my shield a second later and I gasped, driving my heels into the ground and throwing every ounce of energy I had at it. I felt my shoes skidding in the mud as the pressure of his power forced me backwards. Everything he'd done to me manifested into my magic, pouring out of me in wave after wave. I wouldn't let him have this win. I refused to. Not after he'd defeated me in front of his whole pack, broken my ribs and nearly bitten my head off.

He'd spent a lot of his magic taking people down on the pitch, and through sheer force alone, I may have just had an advantage.

With a cry of exertion, I released everything I had into the shield and magic sparked around me, rising the hairs on my arms.

Seth launched the ball at me with another wave of magic propelling it. A boom sounded as it hit the shield and my magic fell a heartbeat later, but it had done its job. The ball bounced back and fell harmlessly into the mud with a wet slap.

It took me a moment to realise the pitch had quietened. The Heirs were watching me from where they stood. Darius had his foot resting on someone's back while Caleb was mid-way through choking another player out.

Orion's eyes finally found mine and he looked like he'd just been handed the holy grail.

"Tag out," he commanded and I nodded, moving around the pitch and finding the rest of the group looking like they'd already been told they hadn't made it onto the team. My breathing was wild and the excitement coursing through me was intoxicating.

Holy shit, I can't believe I pulled that off!

As the crazy game started up again, Orion shot to my side in a blur, steering me out of earshot of the waiting Keepers. "You'll have to work on your stamina," he said with a suggestive smirk. "Apart from that, it's clear you're made for this, Blue." He dipped his head to my ear for half a second. "Thought you might be." He stepped back and I stared at him with my heart pounding as I found a world full of faith gazing back at me. No one had ever looked at me like that. Like I was unstoppable.

"Keep going!" Orion called to the pitch. "I'll be back with a pissed off Vega Twin in thirty seconds." He disappeared with a flash of his Vampire speed and I bit down on my lip to hold back a laugh as he raced out of the stadium. Tory was not gonna appreciate that.

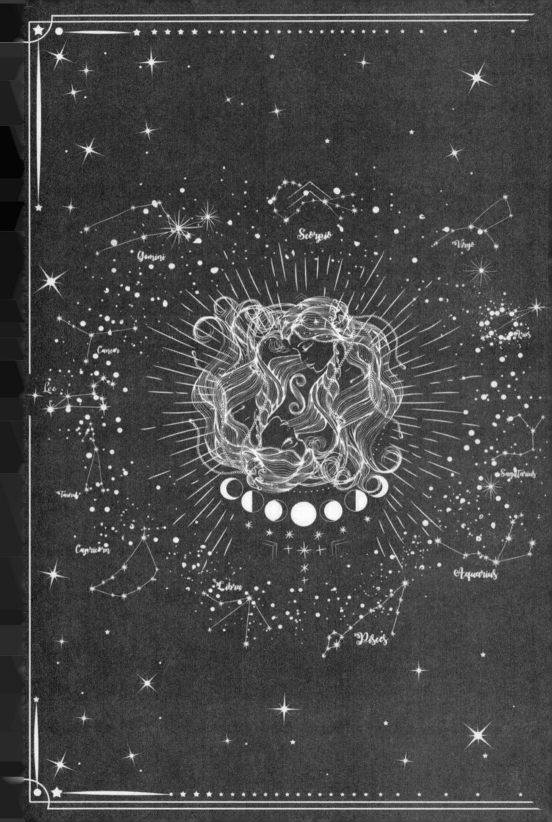

TORY

CHAPTER SEVENTEEN

I lay in my bed listening to Sweet Dreams by Beyoncé with my headphones on and my eyes closed as I finally found a little peace from the shadows.

I breathed out a sigh of relief as sleep called to me. I wasn't sure if it was because the sun hadn't quite set yet or just because I'd had a brilliant time flying with Gabriel and Darcy at lunch time which had blissed me out. But for whatever reason, I actually felt relaxed for the first time since the Eclipse. And I hadn't even been drinking. *Points to Tory.*

I hummed along to the song, my mind snagging on my own beautiful nightmare as I thought about Darius for a moment. I hadn't spoken to him since the slightly mortifying screaming through the door scenario and I didn't plan on it either. And yet for some reason, he still managed to work his way under my skin and into my daydreams.

I sighed as I tried to concentrate on falling asleep and forget about Dragons who were way too attractive for it to be fair. Not that I cared what he looked like…

A huge crash sounded, followed by the sound of splintering wood and I screamed as my eyes snapped open and my door was blasted right off of its hinges. I scrambled upright, throwing a shield of air up around me in a panic just as a blur shot into my room.

"You're late for cheer practice, Miss Vega!" Orion boomed, his eyes sparkling with excitement as he looked down at me.

"What the fuck?" I gasped as I scrambled upright and yanked my headphones off. "Are you insane?"

"It has been suggested before," he agreed with a dark laugh. "Now get your ass up and grab your shit. You've already lost fifty points for Ignis."

"Boohoo," I growled, strengthening my air shield so that he couldn't get to me. "I do hope my poor House Captain isn't too devastated. I can't imagine how he'll feel when I lose even more for not showing up at all."

"That won't result in further loss of points, Miss Vega, it will result in a trip to see Principal Nova to discuss your future at this school. You are required to take part in a club to keep your place here."

"Well then I'll tell her that I want to join the *Ass* Club and we won't have a problem anymore," I growled.

"No. *I'm* in charge of club allocation and she will stand by my decision. So either you get your pep in place or you get your ass out of this academy."

I glared at Orion as I tried to consider my options but he was clearly out of patience. A spurt of water shot from his palm and coated my air shield before solidifying into a ball of ice and locking me inside.

I gasped in panic as the cold of the ice reached me and a flare of fire burst from my skin to counter it.

The ice shattered and before I could make another move, strong arms wrapped around my waist and I was hoisted over Orion's shoulder.

I shrieked in panic as he shot straight towards my open window and leapt outside.

My scream carried across the whole of Fire Territory as we fell and Orion laughed as he used his air magic to slow our fall before we went splat.

The second his feet hit the ground, he shot away with his Vampire speed and I clamped my eyes shut to stop myself from puking at the combination of the insane motion and swinging upside down.

We came to a sudden halt and Orion dumped me on my ass on a wooden bench.

I blinked around at the girls locker rooms in confusion as he started backing up.

"Get changed and get out on the pitch in two minutes or its detention

242

with me every night next week," Orion commanded in place of a goodbye and he left in a blur of speed, a snort of laughter hanging in the air behind him.

"You're fucking insane!" I shouted after him as I shoved myself to my feet.

My chilled vibe was most definitely dead and worse than that, I now had to endure the torture that they called cheer practice.

Fuck a duck.

I ground my teeth as I stood staring at the black sports bag which hung from one of the hooks with *Tory Vega* sprawled across it in pink and silver sequins. *Sequins!*

I glanced at the door. *Surely detention would be preferable to this hell?*

"She won't make the cut anyway," Kylie Major's voice came from outside the locker rooms and I got the feeling she was calling out specifically to make sure I could hear her.

"I just don't understand why Professor Orion would do this to us," Marguerite lamented. "We're the school cheer squad. I've never even seen her crack a smile unless she's following up after some wiseass comment or just laughing at her own rudeness. She has no pep! *No pep at all!*"

I groaned because for once in my fucking life, I'd found something to agree with Marguerite Helebor over and it didn't make a single inch of difference.

Orion had abandoned his Pitball coaching to hoist me to this hell over his shoulder like a sack of fucking potatoes. This was serious. He meant it. I just didn't know why. Why curse me with this? Hadn't I admitted I thought he was marginally less of a douchebag the other day? Didn't that make us ever so slightly friendly? Was this one of those asshole boys club things that dudes did to each other for a laugh but girls did not find funny? Not one fucking bit...

I released a long breath and unzipped the bag.

If I'd thought the sequins were bad then I hadn't even begun to realise the level of hell I'd be participating in with the rest of it.

I slowly unpacked the contents of the bag.

One cheer outfit consisting of a navy and silver trimmed skirt which barely covered my ass and a matching crop top which showed off way more cleavage than made sense for a sport that involved jumping up and down so much. A pair of glimmering pom-poms which changed colour magically as I shook them unintentionally while tossing them down on the bench like they were contaminated. One pair of knee high navy socks with silver bows at the top of them. One can of *Ultraglitz* spray-on sparkle, whatever the fuck that was. One pallet of *Cheery Faevourites* face paint. A pack of sparkly pink hair ribbons. A tube of *Pegasus pink* lip gloss. And to top it off, a pair of glittering pink sneakers.

Fuck my life.

"Hurry up, Vega!" Orion yelled from somewhere outside and I growled to myself as I stripped out of my clothes and donned the cheer outfit. It felt the way I imagined peeling the skin from my flesh and wearing it inside out would feel. Not entirely pleasant.

Once I was in the ultra tight outfit, I moved to look at myself in the mirror by the sinks. It wasn't entirely horrendous. I mean, sure, my personality had been stamped out and any sense of individuality I may have wanted to cling to was being bleached away by the uniform singularity of being part of a team.

Tory was not a team player.

Fuck.

I eyed the hair ribbons for a long moment before taking one and tying it around my neck like a choker.

The pink lip gloss went in the trash and I topped up the blood red lipstick I'd chosen earlier after fishing it out of my jeans' pocket. It was the only damn thing I had on me aside from my key. Which I was guessing was useless now that I had no door.

I kicked the sneakers on reluctantly and fell still as I realised they were changing colour with every step I took. It was kinda cool…you know, for a ten year old.

I scooped up the fucking pom-poms with a growl and started heading for the door but before I could get there, an idea struck me. I paused, looking back at the sequinned bag as a smirk pulled up my lips and I hurried back to it.

My plan didn't take long, though it was a little awkward to complete with a mirror and no help but fuck it, it would make my point.

By the time I stalked back out onto the Pitball pitch I looked peppy as fuck – discounting the scowl I was sporting in protest of my abusive situation.

"Let's all have a round of applause for our latest cheerleader!" Orion called, drawing every fucking Fae in the stadium's attention to me.

Caleb stuck two fingers in his mouth and whistled at me. I responded with a single finger of my own before turning and stalking away from him and the other Pitball players to join the cheer squad. That's right, I had a fucking squad now. *Peachy*.

The mean girls lined up to stare at me, pouting their pink lip-glossed lips and folding their arms in a wall of plastic defiance as if they thought I wanted to be here or some shit.

"By all means, don't let me join up," I said as I arrived before them. "I give zero shits about this but Orion has forced me to attend. So if you want to kick me out then please do – I can still say I showed up."

"Oh no," Marguerite said coldly as she trailed her eyes over every inch of me, making it clear she found me lacking. "We won't be doing that. You came here to cheer. So let's see what you've got."

"I bet she can't even do a standing backflip," Kylie scoffed, covering her mouth as she spoke to Jillian beside her like it might stop her nasally voice from carrying.

I rolled my eyes at her before leaping straight into a backflip and landing it perfectly.

"At the last high school we attended in the mortal world they gave you a choice in what subjects to study and I chose the physical options over the academic ones," I said, yawning to let them know how bored I was. "Gymnastics was four times a week and we practiced inside so I didn't have to go out in the goddamn frost in the winter. It was a no brainer."

"No brainer's right," Marguerite scoffed.

I offered her a sweet as pie smile and she scowled at me.

"I don't like her," Kylie whisper shouted behind her hand to the other girls.

"Boo to the fucking hoo, I don't like you either. It's not really the point though, is it?"

Marguerite sighed dramatically, marking something down on her clipboard which might as well have been a self portrait for all the interest I had in it.

"Come on, girls. We have to persevere through the hard times. The stars have decided to challenge us with this…new recruit…and we will just have to get on with it. I know that the rest of you can shine brightly enough to dazzle the attention away from less desirable teammates."

I rolled my eyes and looked away from her to the far side of the Pitball pitch where Orion was making the team do sprints back and forth. Darcy looked about ready to bust a lung and I offered her a smirk as she started running my way.

She raised an eyebrow in response, glancing at the cheer squad as if to say *you've got it worse.* I cut my gaze to Darius as he raced away from me up the pitch like a stampeding rhino and shrugged to say *I'm not so sure about that.*

Darcy snorted a laugh and Orion spotted us.

"If you can exchange loaded looks with your sister then you can run faster, Vega!" he barked and Darcy groaned as she turned and started running for the far end of the pitch again.

My gaze slid to Orion as he took in my new, peppy as fuck appearance and he smirked at me like a goddamn psychopath.

"Very nice, Tory, I can see your inner pep shining through already," he called.

I scowled and flipped him off.

He barked a laugh. "Five points from Ignis. And you'd better start cheering if you don't want to lose more."

"You're a fucking sadist," I muttered as I turned my attention back to the cheer squad and his laughter followed me.

"We're going to have to think about the pyramid," Marguerite was saying. "It'll need a rearrangement now that we have an additional member." Her eyes fell on me as I stood at the edge of the group and folded my arms. "You should probably be on the bottom tier, Tory," she said sweetly. "So we can make use of your brawny arms."

She clapped her hands which apparently was some kind of signal because the other girls all ran and started building a pyramid. Seven of them kneeled in the sand at the edge of the pitch and Marguerite pointed to the end of the row, clearly expecting me to get down there beside them.

"No thanks, hun," I said sweetly. "There's only one thing I ever get on my knees for." I pushed my tongue into my cheek tauntingly and she practically spat a fireball at me.

"You don't get to choose what you do! You just follow orders!" she snapped.

"Says who?"

"I'm the captain, which means you *have* to!"

"Well, how about we just come to a little arrangement so far as my participation in this horror show goes? I'll pick and choose what I'm willing or not willing to do and you'll suck it up or I'll kick your ass again."

Marguerite glared at me, fire crackling between her fingers as she tried to figure out what to do with me.

"And I should probably remind you that fire doesn't hurt me," I said sweetly, glancing at the flames she was conjuring. "And as you're just a fire Elemental that basically makes you're powerless in a fight against me. Doesn't it?"

"If you don't fall into line, I'm going to talk to Professor Orion about getting you kicked off of the squad," she snapped angrily.

"Please do," I deadpanned.

Jillian released an unexpected laugh which she tried to cover up with a cough as Kylie glared at her.

With a growl of frustration, Marguerite turned and stormed away from the squad across the pitch towards Orion.

I smiled innocently at the rest of the squad and started playing with a handful of water which I conjured into existence, making it run between my fingers then hop from one hand to the other while ignoring the looks they were giving me.

"Do you think you could shoot yourself twenty feet up with your air magic?" a girl to the right of the group asked me curiously and I banished my water magic as I gave her my attention.

"Why?" I asked suspiciously.

"Well we've been trying to perfect a routine and we wanted a huge air leap in the middle of it. If we have a girl who can shoot herself that high and spin all the way down in a controlled descent then-"

"We don't need a Vega to take the central roll in our routine, *Bernice,"*

Kylie snapped. "I told you I've almost got it figured out."

"Let's see it then," I suggested, eyeing her as she tossed her platinum blonde curls.

"I said *almost,*" she snarled at me. "It's not quite ready yet."

"Oh, so you can't really do it then?" I teased.

Kylie's face turned a rather unattractive shade of beetroot as several members of the squad laughed at her expense.

"Fine. I'll show you, but don't go complaining that it's not perfect yet," she said, tossing her pom-poms to the floor.

Everyone stepped back to give her space but I held my ground, watching her impassively as she took a steadying breath and hopped up and down a few times.

She bent her knees and jumped up, directing her hands at the ground and shooting air magic from her palms to propel her up towards the sky.

She ascended about twelve foot off of the ground then turned one hand out so that she started spinning as she descended.

She put a little too much power into the air meant to turn her and it knocked her off balance, her descent looking more like a fall. The air magic she used to slow herself sent her tipping to the right and as she reached the ground, she fell straight back on her ass with a snarl of embarrassment.

"I *told* you it wasn't quite ready!" she said as Jillian clapped enthusiastically.

"And like *I* said," Bernice replied dismissively. "We don't have anyone capable of the move yet."

I smirked at Bernice as she eyed me up, twisting her dark braids around her finger.

"So are you gonna give it a try or are you too chicken shit?" she challenged.

I barked a laugh, smirking at Bernice as I stepped back, calling air magic into my palms. Perhaps this whole cheerleading thing wouldn't be entirely horrific with her on the squad.

"I'm not afraid," I said confidently. "I'm just not sure how to do it. I feel like imitating Kylie would be a mistake."

Bernice and some of the other girls laughed as Kylie glared at me.

"You just wanna propel yourself up in a straight line then come back down to land in exactly the same spot while spinning in place. Kinda like a pirouette on the spot as you fall," Bernice said. "So let's see what you've got, Vega."

I glanced up again, wondering if I was about to fall on my ass like Kylie had. But I'd been using my air magic like this a lot in our flying lessons and I was starting to get pretty good at knowing how much energy to exert to get the desired movement through the sky. I just had to hope it wouldn't be too different without wings.

"Okay then, but if I fall on my ass, I want you all to laugh louder than you did for Kylie," I joked.

Kylie folded her arms, smirking expectantly as she waited for me to make an ass of myself.

I rolled my shoulders back and called on my air magic, aiming my palms at the ground beneath my feet as I directed a blast of it to propel me skyward.

I shot into the air, way higher than I'd really meant to as I released too much power by accident. I must have been about forty foot in the air before the magic eased and I started falling again. I directed a small shot of air behind my back which got me spinning and the stadium blurred around me as I rotated again and again. The girls beneath me started cheering and a laugh spilled from my lips as I let sparks of fire magic fall from my fingertips as I spun. They whirled around me like I was a Tory shaped comet falling back to earth and I couldn't help but grin at the rush I got from using my magic for something so fun.

I hit the ground a little harder than I'd meant to, stumbling back several steps but managing to stay on my feet.

"Shit, Vega, you don't do things by halves do you?" Bernice cooed with a wide smile while Kylie glared at me like I'd just used her bleached blonde hair for toilet paper.

"Well she doesn't seem to be doing too badly to me," Orion's voice came from behind me and I turned to find him approaching with Marguerite at his side.

"Cheering isn't just about using flashy magic," Marguerite snapped.

"It's about school spirit, team work and being *cheerful*. She doesn't *fit*."

Orion folded his arms, looking like this debate interested him about as much as discussing a pimple on Marguerite's ass would.

"Well as you're *so* cheerful and friendly, I'm sure you will make it your mission to help Miss Vega fit in," he replied.

I glanced across the pitch to the Pitball team who were stretching their limbs out and I smirked as I realised that meant practice was over.

"Well, as fun as this has all been, it looks like it's time to go," I interrupted.

"She didn't even use any of her face paint to show her support for the team," Marguerite pushed. "She doesn't care about anything that we stand for!"

Orion looked to me like he was expecting me to deny that fact but I only shrugged. All the other cheerleaders had painted cute little slogans or names onto their arms and cheeks. Most of them had opted for the Heirs' surnames or initials but I was about as likely to start doing that as I was to change my name to Dorothy and fly on home to Kansas.

"That's not entirely true," I said with a smirk.

I turned my back on them and started walking away, flipping up the back of my skirt so that they could appreciate my use of the face paint I'd been gifted. Marguerite gasped in shock as Orion released a surprised laugh. I'd scrawled *bite me* across my ass cheeks where they hung out beneath the tiny pair of shorts which somehow counted as a uniform for this ridiculous sport.

"Don't be late for your next practice on Tuesday, Miss Vega!" Orion called after me.

I dropped my skirt and raised both middle fingers over my shoulders as I strolled away. I really wasn't cheerleading material. But if Orion was going to force me to attend then it looked like I was stuck participating. It didn't mean I was going to suddenly have a personality transplant though.

"Tory!" Caleb's voice made me pause just before I reached the locker room and I turned his way as he shot towards me.

"Hi," I laughed as he came to a halt, smirking at me with his hair falling into his eyes. Mud splattered up one side of his face and his Pitball kit was filthy and ripped along the hem.

"Hey," he replied with that smug as fuck grin that I kinda loved. Not that I'd ever tell him, but his overconfident bullshit was a pretty big turn on.

"Good training session?" I asked, reaching out to finger the hem of his ruined kit.

"Did you see the way I just tackled Max? He almost drowned in that puddle," he laughed, his eyes bright with excitement.

"Sorry, I was concentrating on my own rigorous training schedule and I must have missed it."

"I dunno if I've congratulated you on making the cheer team actually," Caleb said, his gaze drifting over my uniform slowly.

"I don't think congratulations are in order. More like commiserations," I sighed.

Darius, Seth and Max made a beeline for us as they walked off of the pitch too and I shifted back a step, meaning to leave. Caleb caught my wrist, halting my escape.

"Wait a sec," he said. "I wanted to ask if-"

"Looking good, little Vega," Max called as they drew in on us. "I hope you're practicing chants with my name in them."

"Oh yeah of course I have been," I replied brightly, shaking my pom-poms at him. "Max! Max! His hair's so shiny. It's just a shame his dick's so tiny!"

Caleb barked a laugh and Max rolled his eyes, cupping his junk. "I can easily prove that bullshit false."

"No need," I replied. "Geraldine told me all about it." I held my thumb and forefinger close together and offered him a smile.

Max narrowed his eyes on me then turned sharply. "Grus!" he yelled, drawing a look from Geraldine just as she bent over in a stretch. She eyed Max while folded in half, looking through her legs with her ass in the air.

"I'm currently engaged in a cool down routine and don't have time for chats with floppy flounders," she called back.

Max growled and headed over to her with determined strides while Seth and Darius continued to linger like bad smells.

I'd done a good job of keeping the hell away from Darius since screaming at him through my bedroom door but now his gaze was boring right into me from barely a meter away. I kept my eyes off of him though, acting like he wasn't there at all as I turned to Seth.

"Didn't I hear Orion saying you got the most scores in your practice match?" I asked him. "Does that make you the best on the team?"

Seth smirked, his chest puffing up as he re-tied his man bun. "Hell yeah I did," he replied. "And I'd agree that it probably does mean I'm the best."

Caleb scoffed, shifting his weight so he moved closer to me.

"Well that's hardly a measure of who's doing the best in a match," Darius pitched in. "Defensive players aren't trying to score Pits so you can't exactly judge the best player based on scores. Half the reason he scored so many was because I was on his team stopping the others from taking the ball."

I turned to Caleb like the fart hadn't spoken. "So, was there a point to you stopping me before I could go and change out of this hideous costume?" I asked him.

"Yeah. You're coming out with me tonight," he said boldly. Not asking. Telling.

I smirked at him while tossing up my responses. I wasn't sure if I should tell him to fuck off or just go with it. I didn't have any plans tonight and from the way Darcy's face was painted with exhaustion, I was ready to bet she'd be crashing the moment she got back to her House. She was still on the far side of the pitch, talking to Orion about something and half the reason I was even still stood here was because I was waiting for her.

"Am I?" I asked slowly. "And where are we going?"

"Don't you think you should be more careful around her until she's mastered her Order?" Darius asked.

"I think she's worth the risk," Caleb replied dismissively, his gaze not straying from me as he addressed me again. "So are you going to get ready or what?"

"Alright," I replied, smiling a little.

Caleb grinned and Darius growled loud enough to make me look at him for a moment despite my great intentions to ignore his existence. His eyes were dark and his posture tense, his arms folded over his broad chest. My heart jolted but I refused to balk as his gaze travelled over me, lighting fire beneath my skin everywhere his eyes landed.

The flames of my Order form flickered before my eyes and I blinked, turning my head away from him again as if I'd never looked at all.

"I'll meet you outside the stadium after I'm changed," I said to Caleb who grinned in response.

I turned away from him, joining Darcy as she trudged towards me, covered in mud and looking dog tired.

"Good try-out?" I teased as we headed into the girls' locker room.

"Surprisingly yeah. I made the team as a Pit Keeper!" Darcy announced, her eyes glowing with excitement.

"No way!" I gasped.

"Way. But I'm wondering how long that'll last because I'm aching in places I didn't know I had and I think my legs will fall off if I have to do those sprints every session," Darcy groaned before offering me a sidelong smile. "You look...peppy."

"Yeah," I agreed as I grabbed my bag and headed for a shower. "I owe Orion for this little slice of hell."

Darcy giggled as she moved into her own shower stall beside mine and our conversation was cut off by the sound of running water.

I soon emerged and dressed myself in the high waisted jeans and red crop top I'd been wearing when Orion came and snatched me from my room. I braided my hair over my shoulder and raided Darcy's bag for some makeup while she was getting herself dressed.

"Going somewhere?" she asked curiously as I moved to the mirror.

"Caleb's taking me out. Hopefully for food because I'm starved," I supplied.

"I thought you were just hooking up?" she asked. "Because this kinda seems like a date. Which after the carnival makes two..."

I rolled my eyes at her in the mirror as I applied my own red lipstick, the only damn thing I had on me. "Not a date. Just a...pre hook-up adventure."

"Riiight."

Darcy took her makeup back and tossed it in her bag, not bothering to put any on herself. "Well I've got a date with my pillow. Pitball is insane and I'm knackered."

I laughed and we headed out side by side. Darcy waved goodbye to me as we spotted Caleb leaning against the wall of the stadium, his leg kicked back against it as he perused his Atlas.

"Ready?" he asked brightly, standing up straight as he spotted me.

"Where are we going?" I asked as he threw his arm around my shoulders and we started walking. I didn't even have a coat so I called on my fire magic to stop me from shivering.

"It's a surprise," Caleb said, grinning like a Cheshire Cat.

"Is there going to be food at least?" I asked, my stomach growling.

"Yes," he agreed. "But I'm not telling you anything else so don't ask."

I sighed. I didn't like surprises. But I got the feeling he wanted me to keep prodding him about our destination while he had no intention of giving it away so I let it drop.

We followed the path through The Wailing Wood to the multi-storey car park where he kept his car and we took an elevator up to the Batmobile itself on the top floor.

"Don't you have a car that's less…" I waved at the ostentatious thing, not even sure what to call it. It was all black and so pretentious I didn't even have words for it.

"This is the only car I keep on campus," he replied with a frown, sounding a little offended. "Don't you like it?"

"It's fine," I replied. "Don't worry about it."

"So what would you rather we drive?" Caleb asked curiously as he unlocked the car.

"Well if we're taking our pick, I'd go with that," I said, pointing at a beautiful red super bike which was parked in a space opposite his car.

Caleb snorted a laugh. "Well I don't think Darius would agree to lend it to us somehow."

A prickle ran down my spine as I took a step closer to the bike. Of course it belonged to Darius, I didn't know why I hadn't realised that instantly. It was a limited edition, fucking perfect, nought to sixty in two point six seconds, absolutely lust inspiring beauty.

"Well, I could probably get her started within about ten minutes," I offered, my gaze running over the bike as my heart beat faster at the mere thought of riding it.

Caleb laughed like I was joking and dropped into his car beneath the door which swung up like a weird wing. And of course I was joking. Mostly. I wasn't going to steal Darius Acrux's bike. Probably. At least not while one of his besties was here.

I sighed and headed away from the bike to get into the car beside Caleb.

"Buckle up," he encouraged as the doors fell closed and he started the engine which purred like a hungry beast beneath us.

"No," I replied simply, ignoring the seatbelt as I made myself comfortable by sliding the window open.

Caleb eyed me curiously but didn't ask. And I was hardly going to offer up details of the night I almost drowned as a fun topic of conversation so we both just left it alone.

He flicked the radio on and a playlist started up, making me wince as the clash of an ultra loud beat pounded together with some weird techno vibe.

"You can pick something else if you don't like that," Caleb said, tossing me his Atlas so that I could choose a different playlist.

I scrolled through the options as he drove us out of the academy grounds and down the winding road towards Tucana. Everything in Caleb's playlists seemed to be one form of dance music or another. Apparently we were doomed to travel inside a mini rave despite my bleeding eardrums. I gave up on trying to find something good to listen to, realising our tastes in music were a bit too far from each other's for me to find a middle ground easily.

I settled for lowering the volume and trying to ignore the doof doof doof of repetitive drivel that Caleb was drumming his fingers along to on the steering wheel.

Before long, we were pulling up outside a huge bar with blacked out glass windows and a name which seemed to be written in symbols instead of letters and left me just as clueless to our location as I'd been before I arrived. Caleb shot around the car and opened my door for me, offering his hand like I was a proper lady and making me smirk as he hoisted me out of the car and into his arms.

"You can't park there!"

I looked around as the bouncer called out angrily but as Caleb turned to face him, the huge man dropped his gaze to the floor.

"Sorry, Mr Altair, I didn't realise it was you," he gushed, his bald head reddening.

"No problem," Caleb said with a shrug as he drew me past the long line of people waiting to get in and another bouncer instantly opened the door for us.

"I always wondered what it would be like to be one of those people who cut the queue like that," I said as we stepped into a posh atrium and a woman hurried forward to take Caleb's coat.

"And how did it live up to your daydreams?" Caleb teased.

"It made me feel like a total douchebag," I replied with a shrug and he laughed.

"Well get used to it. You're Roxanya goddamn Vega. You'll never queue for anything in your life, ever again." He took my hand and led me after the hostess as I frowned at his back. I wasn't entirely sure I liked the sound of that. So just because it turned out I'd had royal parents now I was going to get special treatment my whole life?

We stepped through a velvet curtain and the hostess led us to a VIP table behind a rope. *And so the doucheyness continues…*

I sat at a little round table and Caleb said something to the hostess, pressing a roll of aura notes into her hand before she walked away.

"So is this your favourite restaurant or something?" I asked, glancing about. My gaze fell on a stage at the far end of the room. We were raised above most of the other diners so I had a clear view of it. There was a lone microphone standing in the centre of it with a screen sat in front of it facing away from us.

"It's just a bit of a laugh," Caleb supplied.

A girl got up and walked onto the stage to a smattering of applause and a few hoots of encouragement from her friends. I shuddered a little as she headed straight for the mic and looked away from her again.

"So, I have a weird kinda hate thing that it might be worth telling you about if a band is about to start playing," I said, looking at Caleb.

"Oh?"

"Yeah. So, live music kinda weirds me out. I just find it so cringe when people sing at me and then there's the whole awkward social pressure to applaud and jump about in appreciation for how great they are. Even if you don't think they're great. It just makes me feel kinda…sick." I pulled a face as Caleb laughed.

"And how about when amateurs are the ones doing the singing?" he teased just as the girl struck up the first chord of We Are The Champions.

I fell still, my brain finally catching up to what this place was as I looked around at the stage and spotted the words to the song illuminated on the screen as the girl sung her heart out.

"Karaoke?" I asked in horror, looking at Caleb like I was begging him to make it not true.

He laughed and leaned forward. "You really hate it that much?" he asked.

"Fuck, Caleb, this is like…I don't even have words for it. It's like my worst nightmare come to life. Sorry to be a total fucking downer but can we just go somewhere else?"

"Seriously?" he asked with a frown, glancing down at the stage with a smile. "It's just a bit of fun, Tory."

I pulled a face. "Not my kind of fun."

"You just need to give it a chance. Once you've had a few drinks you'll be belting out Mariah Carey like no one's business."

I opened my mouth to protest but the hostess arrived at that moment with our drinks and food.

My stomach turned as she dropped a huge platter of slime in front of me, accompanied by a bright pink cocktail.

"What the hell is this?" I asked in disgust.

"Sushi," Caleb said with a frown. "I got you the chef's special. It's all freshly caught today and-"

"You know I don't eat animals, right?" I asked, picking up a chopstick and poking at something bright pink. It *wobbled*. I almost puked in my mouth.

"Not even fish?"

"No," I replied. "And especially not raw fucking fish." I shuddered again, dropping the chopstick in disgust.

Caleb laughed like this was all some big joke and not a total fucking disaster. I picked up my drink in desperation, ignoring the fact that there were goddamn flowers floating on the top of it and draining it in one. The achingly sweet taste of it sent my tastebuds haywire and I gagged a bit. Why the hell had he ordered for me instead of asking what I might actually *like?*

The next singer got up and started blasting out the Spice Girls. I was all for girl power but not when it was being butchered by a huge guy who looked like he was half transformed into a Werewolf and was wearing a sombrero.

I twisted my chair around the table so I didn't have to look at the stage but my skin was still itching with the desire to get out of here.

"I'll order you some vegetarian sushi," Caleb offered as he ate his own food with the chopsticks like a pro. I didn't even know how he was doing it but I was sure as shit that I wouldn't be able to.

"Will it be hot? And not slimy?" I asked, looking around at the other tables and losing hope as all I saw were tables and tables of slime balls.

"Well...maybe you'll like it if you give it a go?" he suggested.

I shrugged, knowing I wouldn't like it. I enjoyed food that was heavy on the carbs and fat and ideally piping hot. But I wasn't going to just write it off without even attempting to eat it, especially while he was giving me the puppy dog eyes.

The hostess hurried to replace my wet fish with wet vegetables and I tried not to sneer at the fresh meal. I gave the chopsticks three tries then just stabbed the closest weird, green *thing* onto one of them instead.

I forced it into my mouth and chewed slowly. Caleb watched with that smug look on his face like he thought I was about to start praising this cold, gross slime which I was fighting not to spit out. I eyed a napkin, wondering if I could do it before deciding even my sparse manners couldn't allow that and forcing myself to swallow. It was even worse on the way down.

I tossed the chopstick down and shook my head just as the possible Werewolf belted out the chorus in a key so wrong my ears wanted to bleed.

Hell. I was in hell.

"You don't like it?" Caleb asked in disappointment.

"Look, dude. You don't really know me and I don't really know you. I'm not into fancy, slimy food and listening to people sing live. I'm guessing you're not into a lot of the things I like. It doesn't really matter though, does it?" He was the one who'd told me he didn't want any kind of future with me anyway. I wasn't sure why he looked so disappointed.

"I guess not," he replied, twirling his chopsticks between his fingers. "Do you wanna ditch this place then?"

"Please," I replied with the first genuine smile I'd given him since we'd walked through the doors to this disaster zone.

Caleb grinned in return, tossing the chopsticks down and rising to his feet. I was up in an instant and the two of us headed straight for the door, much to the surprise of the hostess. Caleb cheered her up again with another wedge of auras and as soon as he'd collected his coat we were back outside and I was able to shake off the creepy feel of the place.

"What now then?" Caleb asked.

"Do you have any speedway tracks around here? Or motocross arenas?" I suggested.

Caleb arched an eyebrow at me and shrugged. "Maybe...I mean I could find out. Darius would probably know..."

"Maybe just scrap that idea," I interrupted. He was clearly about as into bikes as I was karaoke and the stars only knew where the hell we'd end up if he got advice from Darius about it.

"There's a stand-up club not too far away," Caleb suggested.

"That kinda causes me the same issues I get with live music," I replied. "Paintball?"

"At night? In these jeans?" His brow creased and I could tell he hated that idea.

"Never mind. Shall we just go drinking instead? And maybe I can find a burrito truck on the way?"

"You'll eat food prepared in a van but not delicacies made in a five star restaurant?" Caleb asked with a smirk.

"Well, we aren't all pretentious assholes," I teased. "And most of the best foods are prepared in vans."

"They're really not," he argued.

"Whatever. Let's just agree to disagree," I said with a shrug.

"About everything, apparently," he replied with a frown.

I smirked at him. "Why are you pouting, Caleb?"

"I'm not. I just wanted to have a fun evening with you and it's not really going to plan..."

"Well then why don't we just call time on this fiasco? You find me a burrito, I'll give you a blowjob and we're all good," I suggested.

"Seriously?" he asked, perking up at that.

"About the burrito? Hell yes. The blowjob? You just took me on what was arguably the worst date of my life. And I once went out with a guy who took me to a bridge over a ravine filled with junk so that we could 'look at the view' and he could do a drug deal. So I'm thinking no."

Caleb laughed and led the way to his car. "Maybe we can have a do over tomorrow? We could have breakfast together?"

"I'm not a morning person. Remember?"

"No."

"Like I said, you don't really know anything about me. Do you?"

"Apparently not."

We looked at each other awkwardly for a moment and I decided to break the tension. "But you *are* pretty good in the sack, so there is that."

"There is that," he agreed, smiling again as he pulled away from the kerb. "Maybe I can remind you just how good when we get back to the academy?"

I snorted a laugh without committing either way. "Maybe."

"I can work with that."

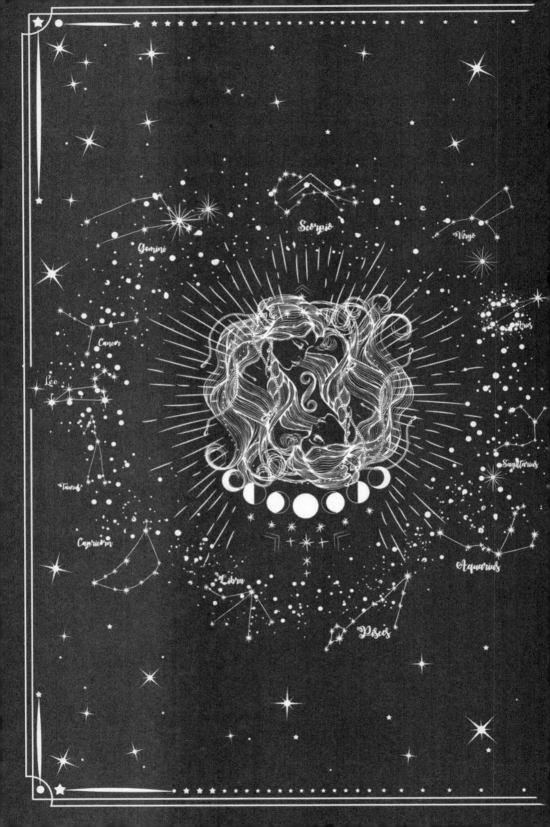

DARCY

CHAPTER EIGHTEEN

I tapped on Orion's bedroom window with adrenaline spiking through my body. I couldn't stop grinning when he pulled the curtain back then smothered my laugh as his eyes widened frantically. He pushed the window up, reaching out and snatching me inside with his Vampire speed. It was almost eleven at night but I'd checked to make sure no teachers were around before I'd snuck in. Besides, I was wearing a black sweater dress with equally black pantyhose and my hair was tucked into the hood of my dark coat. *Totally* invisible.

"You shouldn't have come here," he whispered anxiously, pushing the window shut and pulling the curtain so hard he almost ripped it down. I knew he was right. We'd only recently made a deal to be more careful, but we were so limited in when we could spend any time together that what choice did I have but to make reckless decisions? Meeting with him was *always* reckless.

I cast a silencing bubble as his arm tightened around my waist and he tugged me against his warm chest. I glanced up at him as my hand rested on his stomach, the heat of him wrapping around my icy skin. He still had his suit shirt on, the buttons loose where he'd removed his tie and giving me a glimpse at his muscular chest beneath.

"Am I in trouble?" I teased and he swung me around to dump me on the bed, leaning over me with a menacing smile. I shrugged out of my coat, reaching for him as my heart pounded with anticipation. I'd been going mad in my room thinking about him. Seeing him around school made my fingers itch for him, my soul burn for him. It was torture being so close but being unable to bridge the gap between us.

"You will be if you get us caught, Blue." He dropped his mouth to my ear, raking his fangs along my flesh and sending a hungry shiver through me. He growled like a beast and I arched into him, wrapping my hands around his shoulders and tugging at his shirt.

All of this pretending not to be together drove me insane. But I wondered if it was the thrill of this game we were playing that had me so hooked on him or if it was something more than that. All I knew for sure was when I was with him, it felt like the stars were singing our names.

"Yoohoo!" Washer's voice carried from somewhere and I leapt up so fast I nearly headbutted Orion in the face. He lurched backwards then hurried to the bedroom door, tugging it open a crack. "I can sense you in there, Lance. Mmm a lot of lustiness on the breeze. Have you got company?"

"He's talking through the fucking mail slot," Orion snapped and my heart beat unsteadily for a moment before I remembered we had a silencing bubble in place.

"My power reserves are low and I can always bring a sweetener. A bottle of your finest bourbon, hm Lancey? Let me in, don't be a prude."

I shuddered, pulling my knees to my chest as all the lust I'd felt a second ago totally and utterly died.

"Is little Franny with you?" Washer called hopefully and my neck prickled at that. It was pretty obvious Orion and Fran had slept together but the idea of them being in this actual bed suddenly made me stand up.

"Maybe you should tell him to go?" I suggested and Orion glanced at me with a frown.

"I'm not opening that door while you're here. He'll give up in a minute."

"There must be room for a little one," Washer implored. "Just a teeny weeny."

"Ew ew ew," I breathed and Orion threw me an apologetic look.

"Oh are you finished? I feel your lust fading – don't leave me out next time you naughty boy." Washer sighed heavily then Orion nodded to confirm he was gone a beat later, grimacing in disgust.

I felt like a layer of grime was sitting on my skin and I needed ten showers to get it off. He'd gotten one thing right. My lust was gone. Gone gone gone. And I couldn't see it coming back any time soon. From the look on Orion's face, he felt the exact same way.

"Drink?" he asked, skimming a hand over his beard as he surveyed me.

"Yeah, ten shots of tequila to burn that moment from my memory please," I said and he broke a grin.

"You got off lightly. One time, he stuck his teeny weeny through that mail slot."

"*No*," I gasped.

"Yeah, it only took a new door and ten counselling sessions to stop the nightmares though." Orion smirked and I broke a laugh as I followed him out into the lounge, unsure if that story was entirely a joke or not. *I definitely don't wanna know.*

I was pretty pissed at Washer for pouring a bucket of cold water on our moment alone, it wasn't like we got that many of them.

"Red wine okay?" Orion offered and I nodded as he disappeared into the kitchen across the open plan room.

I ran my fingers across the back of the couch, recalling the last time I'd come here. It seemed like a dream. It was one of the happiest moments in my life and I often used it to push away the shadows when I felt them drawing in.

As we definitely weren't going to jump on each other any time soon, I figured now was a good time to actually talk for once. I mean, we had so little time together that when we *were* alone my first instinct was to rip his clothes off. Sure, we talked afterwards but could we manage it now? Like a normal couple.

Yeah a Solarian Princess screwing her Vampire teacher who is firmly team Heirs is totally normal.

Orion returned to the room with a couple of glasses of wine, his intense gaze burning into me as I took one. I dropped onto the couch and kicked my shoes off, pulling my feet up underneath me. Orion sat beside me, though we still weren't touching thanks to Washer.

"Have you been practising holding back the shadows like I showed you?" Orion asked in full professor mode.

"Yeah, it's getting easier to hold them in…" I chewed on my lip.

"But?" he asked with concern.

I swirled the red wine in my glass, watching it spin around in a vortex of darkest crimson. "I keep hearing that voice. And when I'm dreaming it's like she's so close to me. I don't feel as in control. Sometimes…I want to go to her."

"You mustn't. Not ever." Orion's throat bobbed as I looked up at him and the fierce emotion in his eyes started a fire in my veins.

"I know. I'm trying, Lance," I said earnestly. "It's just when I'm asleep their power is all consuming. Have you been having any dreams?"

He shook his head in answer, a deep frown lining his forehead. He took a mouthful of his drink before placing it down on the coffee table with a look of contemplation. "What does the voice say?"

"She wants me to go to her." I shrugged. "I don't know why that voice in particular is so clear."

"No…me either. But I've been trying to find out. The problem is, texts on dark magic aren't easily available. Even the archives here at the academy don't keep books on it. It's a crime to have things like that in your possession and the ones I own don't have nearly enough information on the subject, but I think it must be because you and Tory formed a connection with her when you went into the shadows on the night of the Lunar Eclipse."

"How many laws do you break in a day?" I teased and he smirked, taking hold of my ankle and tugging so I laid my leg over his knees.

"Maybe I'm attracted to trouble." His fingers brushed against my calf and even the memory of Washer couldn't stop the electric energy that sparked along my skin in response.

I inhaled and he watched my lips before continuing to brush his fingers up and down my calf.

"Your sister isn't managing the shadows so well," Orion said, his eyes dark.

I nodded, my heart tugging at his words. "I know. I'm worried about her. Is there anything I can do?"

"Just make sure she's practising what we learn in our sessions."

"I do remind her, I just hope she listens." I sipped my wine as worry spun a web inside me. I didn't like the idea of her practising with the shadows on her own, but when Tory wanted to do something, it was pretty impossible to stop her.

"If she'll listen to anyone, it's you," Orion said and his words gave me hope. I just had to try harder to make sure she was getting control of them, but sometimes it felt like there was space growing between us recently. It was full of unspoken words and the weight of this secret I was keeping from her.

"How long have you been practising dark magic?" I asked, my voice hushed even though I knew no one could hear us.

"Since I was a boy – it's not the same as being Awakened. You don't need your Element to harness the darkness. My father taught me most of what I know. I never realised it was something other Fae didn't do until my parents made me make a magical vow with them to never tell anyone at the high school I attended. It only really hit home when my father died and we had to lie about how it had happened to the press."

"How did it happen?" I asked as sadness crept through my chest.

His brows pulled together and his gaze remained on the movement of his hand on my leg when he answered. "He liked to experiment with dark magic. He had a theory that magical Elements could be transferred from the dead permanently. He couldn't accept that they could only be borrowed temporarily. He was an air and water Elemental like me, but he dreamed of fire." He took a long breath, lost to some memory for a moment before continuing. "We used to collect bones together. He only ever wanted them from fire Elementals. And one day he decided to try and draw all of their magic into his body at once." He paused for a second. "I was there when it happened. The fire consumed him, devouring his body so fast I didn't even have a chance to say goodbye. All that remained of him was ash and bone."

"Lance," I breathed, my heart slicing to ribbons. "That's terrible."

"She'd never admit it, but it broke my mother. She tried to make me into him for a long time. But when I rebelled, she turned all that bitterness in her heart against me instead."

"You must miss your father," I said softly.

"Yeah, I know he wasn't a perfect man and…I mean this might sound fucked up, but some of the best times I ever spent with him was out digging up graves to steal powerful Fae bones." He glanced at me with a hollow smile and my heart beat harder at the idea.

"Holy shit," I breathed.

"Yeah," he said with half a laugh. "And that's not an easy feat, Blue. Graveyards in Solaria are highly guarded. Especially where powerful Fae have been laid to rest. And in an effort to be completely honest with you, Darius and I still use my father's old tactics to get our hands on bones for our practice sessions."

"But why?" I shook my head, my stomach knotting uncomfortably. "Is it all for power?"

"Yes and no," he said thoughtfully. "I made a pact with Darius a long time ago that I'd help place him on the throne and in the process, destroy his father."

My throat thickened as his fingers stopped moving on my leg. "But why dark magic?"

"Lionel is not only one of the most powerful Fae in Solaria, Blue, he's also cunning, methodical. He will have prepared for the possibility that his son might turn against him. It's how he is. So I gave Darius an edge against him in the form of dark magic. He's learning to harness the Elemental power of bones. Once he's mastered it, we have a plan in place for him to challenge Lionel for his position of power."

My heartbeat quickened with excitement and a little fear. "Do you really think he can take him on?"

"Yes. He will naturally become as powerful as him in time, but that isn't enough. He needs to destroy his father. He needs to wipe him from the world in a single fight. So when Darius is ready, I'll help him gain access to the bodies of the most powerful Fae Elementals in the history of the world. The problem is, the Celestial Councillors' family graveyards are the best guarded in Solaria."

"And do you really think Darius won't become like his father?" I asked, my voice quavering a bit as I recalled how he'd attacked my sister in the past.

Orion's jaw tightened and he leaned forward. "I know he has his flaws, but I swear he's not like Lionel. He regrets what he did to Tory even if he'll never admit it."

I knew Orion must really have seen some good in him. He wouldn't have placed the entire fate of Solaria on this plan if he didn't. But could I place the same faith in a guy who'd hurt Tory, who made it his personal mission to force us out of this academy?

I thought of him on the night of the Lunar Eclipse, how he'd tried to save us and something softened inside me ever so slightly. I didn't trust him, or even forgive him. But maybe there was hope for him yet.

I inhaled slowly. "Why are you telling me all of this? I mean…we don't exactly talk about it, Lance, but aren't I Darius's enemy? Doesn't that make me yours too?"

He reached out to take my hand. "I trust you instinctively, Blue. Since the first day we met, the stars have reeled you towards me and me towards you. Don't you feel it?"

I nodded, unable to drag my eyes from his as I was pulled into their glittering depths. "But why?"

His mouth twitched at the corner and he broke my gaze again. "There's only one reason that makes sense to me, but I could be wrong. Maybe I fear I'm wrong too."

"What?" I pressed.

Sure, I'd had thoughts about why this bond between us was so powerful, but I could explain it away through the intensity of a forbidden relationship. If I was being really honest with myself though, I knew it was more than that. I hadn't trusted anyone for years, why would my heart suddenly choose the most risky man possible for me to put my faith in? It didn't make any sense. Not unless there was more to it…

"I think….maybe…" Orion frowned then let the barriers around his magic down and I gasped as my power rushed to meet his. I moaned from the feel of it, his magic soaking into my blood and settling there like it was where it belonged. He felt like air and light and freedom.

"Lance," I said breathlessly as he caught my hand and more of his magic crashed into mine like two waves colliding in a stormy sea.

"I think the stars picked you for me, Blue. I think you're my Elysian Mate." His fingers intertwined with mine and I bathed in the caress of his magic, tipping my head back to rest against the couch as I absorbed his words.

Elysian Mates? Me and him? It made sense in its own way, but it scared me too. That fate was currently winding us together, making it impossible to pull away. And if it was true, it meant we'd already been tested and there were no doubt more tests to come.

"Are you sure?" I asked, my mind spiralling with the possibility.

"No." He shrugged one shoulder. "We'll find out sooner or later though, I guess."

I finally withdrew my power from his, my thoughts too hazy to focus on anything while we possessed each other like that. A low growl rumbled through Orion's chest and I smiled at him, tugging my leg back to fold beneath me once more.

"It goes against everything in my nature to be able to power share with you," Orion said with a smirk. "As a Vampire, I've always done things alone. It's not easy to let people in, especially not so deeply as to share magic with them. The only Fae I've ever managed it with are Darius, you and-" He halted mid-sentence, a flash of pain crossing his features and I sat up straighter.

"Who?" I whispered.

Orion shut his eyes as he seemed to wrangle some dark memory. It took me a moment to realise he was fighting the shadows and my breathing became more rapid as I shifted up beside him, laying my hand on his arm to try and coax him out of the darkness.

He released a breath, opening his eyes which were curtained by shadows. "Clara," he croaked. "My sister."

The grief in his expression tore me apart and I stayed close, waiting to see if he'd elaborate. The way he was being so honest made me think he'd tell me anything if I asked, but I didn't want to pull this from his lips. I wanted it to be his choice.

"Do you want to know what happened to her?" He reached out to tuck a lock of hair behind my ear, skating his fingers down to my jaw, his expression broken. I longed to fix the shattered part of him I could see gazing back at me but I had no idea how.

I nodded mutely, wondering if he could hear how fast my heart was beating.

"She was manipulated by my mother and Lionel," he said heavily. "After she graduated from Zodiac five years ago, Stella got her claws in her. She started working for the Acruxes like my family always did, but it wasn't like her. We'd spent years talking about the new lives we were going to build for ourselves. Neither of us ever planned to work for them."

"Why did she change her mind?" I questioned, picturing the girl I'd seen in the photograph at Lionel's house with her soft brown hair and freckly cheeks.

"Lionel...he...," Orion cleared his throat and I could see the rage swelling up in him toward the Dragon who ruled our lives. "He bonded with Clara, he made her his Guardian like I am to Darius. Then he let her drink exclusively from him as her Source."

My eyes widened in surprise. "She was a Vampire like you?"

He nodded.

"Why would Lionel ever let her do that?" From everything I'd learned about Fae, it seemed completely backwards for someone as powerful as Lionel to let any Vampire ever feed on him.

"Because he needed her to cooperate," Orion said, his voice empty. "He gave her the one thing Vampires can't resist above all else. The taste of pure power. It's a burden we have to bear, Blue. Vampires are a slave to it. It's a primal need. It's why we claim the most powerful blood Source we're able to. It's why your blood pushes me to the edge of insanity."

His eyes slid to my neck and I swallowed the growing lump in my throat as I tried to understand. It was sad to think that it had such a hold over an entire Order. Without blood, they were powerless. And in Solaria, being without power was worse than a death sentence. No wonder they hungered for it from the core of their being.

"So what did Lionel want her for?" I asked, part of me frightened of the answer.

"The same thing he wanted you and your sister for," he said in a snarl. "He took her to that very same place on the clifftop and called a meteor from the sky. She walked willingly into that pit for him while I was bound on my knees beside Darius. But when the shadows came for her, she didn't come back, the darkness killed her." He looked away and my heart splintered as I sensed the pain of that grief radiating from him.

I curled up beside him, resting my head on his shoulder and holding him, because there was nothing else I could offer. "I'm so sorry," I whispered, placing a kiss beside his ear.

His arm slid around my waist and he held me against him for what felt like an eternity. "Lionel forced the Guardian bond on me and Darius that night. He'll do anything to gain control over those around him. He figured I was the best man to look after his son and nothing was going to make him see otherwise. So he stole my life from me then stole my sister in the same breath. After that, he pulled some strings so I'd get a job here at Zodiac to watch over Darius and that's when we decided to fight back against him. It's been a long time coming, Blue. But I'll see Lionel Acrux dead if I have to tear all the stars from the heavens to do it."

A tear slid down my cheek and dropped smoothly onto his shirt. He turned to me abruptly, wiping his thumb across my cheek with a desperate frown. "Don't be sad."

"But it is sad." I wound my arms around his neck and he pulled me close, his steady breaths brushing against my ear.

"When Lionel brought you down into that pit, I relived my worst nightmare. I don't ever want to be in that position again. Powerless, unable to save you. But I realised you don't need me to rescue you, Blue. You and your sister came back from the dark without anyone's help. And Lionel should fear you both for that reason alone."

His fangs brushed against my neck and I could sense his hunger rising as he restrained himself.

I drew my hair away from one side of my throat, tilting my head to give him access to my blood. Orion groaned as he sank his fangs into my flesh and he held me tight to keep me in place. I sighed as the sharp pinch of his bite gave way to a dark pleasure only he could provide me.

"I want to help you stop him," I said with fervour. I'd stand against Lionel in any way I could. I'd feed Orion power to keep him strong and I'd even suck up my pride when it came to Darius Acrux if I had to. "We'll destroy Lionel for what he's done and make sure he never hurts anyone we love again."

TORY

CHAPTER NINETEEN

After another sleepless night haunted by the shadows, I managed to fall into a deep sleep right around dawn. By the time my alarm screamed enough to rouse me again and I crawled out of bed, I found a bunch of messages from Darcy and the others wondering why I'd missed breakfast. I groaned into my pillow, still feeling dog tired despite the sleep I'd managed to get. But I couldn't stay in bed any longer. At least I had a free period first thing today and I didn't have to worry about being late for class.

I shot a message to Darcy explaining myself, though it wasn't really that out of character. But she'd been a little overprotective ever since I'd admitted to dabbling with shadows and they'd started haunting me with more vigour. I didn't want her to worry, but it was nice having someone who did.

I got up and dressed quickly, pulling my headphones on as I started up a playlist and headed out of my room in search of food.

The sun was shining brightly again today, the sky blue above me as I walked, causing me to squint against the headache growing in my skull. I wasn't suited to missing this much sleep. Since I'd been given the shadows, I wasn't sure I'd gotten much more than three or four hours a night and with the alcohol I was consuming to try and drown the nightmares too, I was definitely suffering.

I pulled a pair of sunglasses from my satchel and put them on, withdrawing into my own personal cocoon where the sun couldn't assault me as the mellow soundtrack I'd selected helped me relax.

I'd missed breakfast, but the lunch options were already available in The Orb and I grabbed myself a sandwich and a coffee before taking a seat in an armchair beside a fireplace at the side of the room.

The warmth of the fire washed over me, tickling against my magic supplies and slowly topping them up. Now that I knew this was how I replenished my magic, it was kinda obvious. I felt a bit stupid for not realising it sooner, but then who didn't like sitting beside a warm fire when it was cold outside? I'd just thought the peace and tranquillity I'd felt around the flames was normal, not anything magical.

It was quiet inside The Orb, not many students bothering with this place in the odd hours between meals even if they did happen to have a free period too, but that suited me just fine.

Darcy sent me a message to say she was hanging out down by the lake with the Ass Club and I replied to say I'd join them after I'd eaten. I just needed to mop up a little of the tequila I'd consumed last night and I'd track them down. Maybe Geraldine would take pity on me and offer to heal away my self-inflicted suffering too.

I scrolled through FaeBook as I ate, laughing to myself as I spotted a Griffin support group with the subtitle how to say no to Fae with a dump fetish. The author hadn't quite had the balls to name Max Rigel but it was pretty obvious that the group stemmed from that rumour. The pranks we'd played on the Heirs just kept snowballing, delivering more and more rewards as time went on and I couldn't for a moment feel bad about it.

With that amusement tugging at my lips, I took a moment to send Caleb a suggestive photo of a Pegasus as it bent forward to graze.

Taunting him about it might have been dumb, but if he wanted to punish me for it I was pretty sure we could come up with an acceptable way for him to do it.

A prickle ran down my spine and I looked up as I felt eyes on me. My gaze fell straight on Darius Acrux as he strolled into the room and I immediately fell still as his focus zeroed in on me.

Darius stalked towards me and I fought the urge to straighten in my chair, acting like his presence was utterly irrelevant to me, despite the little flood of adrenaline which had just entered my veins.

He didn't bother with hellos and leaned forward to snatch my sunglasses from my face, tossing them down on the table in front of me.

My muscles tightened in response but I forced myself to remain still, pushing my tongue into my cheek as I gazed back at him impassively.

"It's too dark in here for sunglasses, Roxy. Are you hungover again?" he asked. "Maybe you need to work on your drinking problem."

I half considered biting back at him but I held my tongue instead, not wanting to give him the satisfaction of engaging in whatever strange game he was playing.

"Are you ignoring me?" he demanded, leaning forward to place his hands on the arms of my chair.

I was vaguely aware of students backing away from us, a ring forming as they watched to see how this would go down.

"What do you want me to say?" I asked, my voice bored as I pulled my headphones down to hang around my neck.

Darius growled at me. "I want you to bow your head when I walk into a room. I want you to learn your place and stick to it. If I say jump, I want you to say how high."

I leaned forward, invading his personal space just as he was invading mine, holding his eye. "I think," I breathed quietly, though I knew any Vampires in close proximity would hear us anyway. "That you made a mistake with me. You took me to your room when you saw me in pain. You looked after me when you should have left me to suffer. You brought me to your house to play on your bikes and let me find out your secrets. And then you realised that even showing me all of those parts of yourself weren't enough."

"Enough to what?" he snarled.

"Enough to change the way I see you. To make me hate you any less." He flinched minutely at my guess, just enough for me to think I was right about it. "But the bit I've been struggling to figure out, Darius, is why do you give a shit what I think about you? Shouldn't you want me to hate you like I do? Why are you so damn obsessed with me?"

"I'm not obsessed with you," he snapped. "I just want to get rid of you.

And I want to sit in this seat. So move."

I half considered fighting him over the chair but I wouldn't win and it was just a fucking chair. I pushed myself to my feet suddenly, forcing him to straighten and release his grip on the armrests as he scowled down at me.

I looked up at him impassively and I could see just how much that pissed him off. Barely an inch of space divided us and my heart was thundering a panicked tune but I refused to let him see me flinch.

I reached up, parting my hair and pulling half of it over my shoulder, twisting it in my grip as I looked at him. "Shall I start tying it in pigtails?" I asked innocently. "So that you can pull on them whenever you see me?"

"Be careful what you wish for, Roxy," Darius warned, reaching out to take my hair into his grasp. "If I pull on your hair, you'll be screaming my name in response." He tugged just a little and I snorted dismissively.

"Why don't you let that little fantasy keep you warm while you're sitting in my chair?" I asked, shifting aside and gesturing to the seat he wanted me to vacate so badly.

Darius narrowed his eyes at me as he dropped his hold on my hair and folded himself into my seat, leaning back and spreading his legs like his balls were so fucking big he couldn't possibly close them.

I pulled the edges of my skirt out to the sides and gave him a mocking curtsy. "Enjoy it, your highnass."

Before he could respond, I scooped my sunglasses off of the table where he'd tossed them, turned my back on him and shifted my gaze across the room to the red sofa where he always sat with the other Heirs. It was empty which was a damn shame because it looked really fucking comfy.

I smirked to myself as I strolled straight into the gathered crowd who parted for me like I was contagious and I cut a beeline for the red couch. My heart was pounding, my throat thick. I knew this wouldn't end well for me but I just couldn't bear to let him get away with his bullshit.

I put my sunglasses in my pocket and threw up a shield of air magic, strengthening it with everything I had in a tight ball around me as I closed in on the couch.

A defiant grin hooked up the corner of my mouth and I spun back to look right in Darius's eye as I dropped down into his usual spot at the end of the couch.

Everyone in The Orb fell deathly silent. Out of the corners of my eyes I could see them all backing up. My heart was racing and I held my breath, waiting to see exactly how far this asshole was willing to push me today.

One look in his eyes told me it was going to be really damn far.

Darius stood so suddenly that the armchair he'd taken from me fell to the ground with a clatter behind him. He stalked towards me, the crowd backing up so far that they were practically outside now, a ring of fearful eyes watching us from the edges of the room.

As Darius closed in on me, the shadows stirred beneath my skin, whispering promises of help and violence. But I didn't call on them, I focused on holding my air shield in place and waited for the attack we both knew was coming.

Darius snarled, his fingers flicking towards me so a gigantic fireball shot right at my face. It hit my shield and I gritted my teeth as it exploded up and over it, sending more magic to reinforce the spot that was coming under attack.

The moment my focus shifted to reinforcing that patch of the shield, another attack hit me from behind, more fire blooming as I sucked in a sharp breath and my shield crumpled.

I stumbled to my feet as his fire ripped through my defences but squared my shoulders, refusing to back down.

I didn't need to fear the flames but I doused them none the less, sucking the oxygen from the space surrounding me and holding my breath as the flames failed to get close enough to damage my clothes.

Darius smirked as he closed the distance between us, no longer held away by my shield.

I scowled at him as he drew closer. Why was he always hounding me? What made him think that he could just treat me like this whenever it suited him? Heat was building in my chest as my rage grew. I was so sick of his bullshit, so sick of being his victim.

The shadows stirred beneath my skin again and I was almost tempted to call on them. If the room hadn't been full of witnesses then I'd have done it. But as it was, I had to fight to hold them back as they licked between my fingers for half a heartbeat.

Darius hesitated for a moment, his gaze slipping to my hand. A wall of fire suddenly sprang up all around us, sealing us within a dome of his power and hiding us from the prying eyes of the students outside it.

He flicked his other hand and I felt a silencing bubble slide over my skin half a second before he started laying into me.

"Are you calling on the shadows again, Roxy?" he demanded. "Is that the real reason you were wearing those glasses?"

"No," I snapped. I hadn't lost so much control that I couldn't keep them hidden within my flesh.

"What is it, then?" he asked as if he had a right to ask me anything.

"Just fuck off, Darius," I snapped. "Aren't you supposed to be in the middle of pushing me about again? Isn't that how you get your kicks?"

"Yeah, it is," he agreed.

"Well come on then, big man, why don't you show me why I should be oh so terrified of you so that I can go back to my day, pretending that you don't exist."

Darius's jaw clenched. "Orion told me you've been drinking."

"So? That's my business, not yours. Why do you give a shit anyway?" I growled.

"Because the shadows are a problem for all of us. And if my father gets word of you wielding them then pissing *me* off will be the least of your worries. So if you're having trouble controlling them then we need to do something about it."

"Right. Because *he'll* actually kill me where you prefer to just make me so miserable I'm tempted to end my suffering for myself," I growled, ignoring his half assed suggestion of help. I wouldn't have to spend so much time trying to figure out how to strengthen my hold on the shadows if I didn't have to fear him and his family. It was his fault I felt the need to go to them so often, his fault they were gaining enough access into my psyche to be causing me problems.

"Fuck off, you're not suicidal," he replied dismissively. "Nobody burns as hot and cold as you do if they don't love life."

"You don't know anything about me," I snarled.

"Yeah I do. And that's what you can't stand," he replied darkly. "Because we're the same you and me. Both fucked up, broken pieces on a game board that's bigger than we can cope with. Both hoping to find some way of winning despite the odds being stacked against us all the damn time. Both addicted to things that push our boundaries and make us feel alive. Because at the end of the day, even feeling the worst of things is better than feeling nothing at all."

I glared at him, not wanting to admit for a moment the way his words resounded with something deep inside me. He was right though. I'd rather be sobbing with sorrow, screaming in fear, laughing until I was breathless or riding the very edge of a high than just keeping to the middle path. The thing I feared most in life was boredom. I didn't want to live an easy life, I wanted to blaze through an adventurous one and I'd choose to burn out entirely before I'd let myself whither in emptiness.

"So what?" I snapped.

"So I won't let you ignore me, Roxy," he snarled. "I'll have your attention even if I have to take it without your permission."

"Why?" I demanded. "Why not just go after someone else?"

"Because we don't get to choose our obsessions. And you're mine."

I stared at him in surprise, not knowing what the hell I was supposed to say to that while my heart pounded out of rhythm and my stomach did some kind of graceless somersault.

"What if I don't want to be?" I asked eventually.

"Then that's just tough." Darius flicked his fingers at me so suddenly that I didn't even have time to react before a blast of water hit me square in the chest.

The wall of flames fell away and I was propelled across the room, falling in a wet heap on the floor to a chorus of oooohs from the students who had stayed to watch our spat play out.

I shoved myself to my feet with a snarl of rage but Darius was already striding out of the room on the far side of The Orb, throwing a smug grin back at me just before he disappeared out of sight.

"Show's over, assholes!" I snapped at the crowd, raising my hand as I slowly drew the water out of my clothes and into a ball which hung before me.

A group of seniors were clearly filming my less than graceful recovery, so I tossed the water their way before turning and stalking outside too. Firmly heading in the opposite direction to Darius goddamn Acrux. Because fuck him and his goddamn asshole agenda against me. If he wanted my attention then I'd just work doubly hard at making sure he didn't get it. And more than that, I'd avoid him like the plague so he wouldn't have the opportunity to force his presence on me with another attack like that again.

As I headed outside, I checked my Atlas, groaning as I realised my free period was coming to an end and I had to go straight to class. I'd been hoping for a bit of time to chat to Darcy this morning about all things shadow, Dragon and Vampire related but it looked like it would have to wait.

Just before I could shove my Atlas away, I noticed a reply waiting for me from Caleb to my teasing about the Pegasass situation.

Caleb:
So the first time you choose to message me without me messaging you first, it's to send me that shit?

I frowned, wondering if he was right about that. Did I really never message him first? *Probably not.* I'd learned a long time ago not to give assholes too much attention anyway. Douchebags liked to think the world revolved around them and I'd have nothing better to do with my time than sending them countless messages. Which was not true.

Tory:
What's the matter, Caleb? Can't you take a joke? ;)

Caleb:
Maybe you just don't know how to be funny.

Tory:
Cry me a river…

Caleb:
Come to Terra House tonight.

Tory:

Why?

Caleb:

You know, this playing hard to get shit might get old eventually…

Tory:

That must be why you're about to call everything off then.

Caleb:

*Not likely. But I'm not going to keep asking nicely, maybe you'll respond better to commands - you **are** coming to stay in my bed tonight.*

Tory:

Wrong.

I smirked to myself and tossed my Atlas back in my satchel. No doubt I'd find a shit ton of messages from him later on or he'd just come to hunt me down in person. I honestly didn't know why he kept falling into the same trap but it was fucking hilarious so I kept on setting it up.

I didn't have any time left to meet up with Darcy and the others down by the lake so I headed straight for our lesson instead. We were about to have our very first Physical Enhancement class which I was actually pretty hyped about. I had my gym bag with my kit in it and Professor Prestos who taught the lessons was my Liaison so I already knew her semi-well despite the fact that most of our contact was carried out via email. She seemed cool though and I'd always done well in sports so I was hoping that this lesson would at least come pretty easy to me.

I headed through The Wailing Wood, taking the track which led north west towards the Pitball stadium where we'd been told to meet for this class. Apparently that wouldn't be the same every lesson though so I'd have to keep an eye on my schedule for changes in its location.

Darcy called out to me as the stadium came into sight and I fell into step with her, Sofia and Diego. I cast a wary glance at our woolly hatted 'friend', staying on the other side of the group to him. Darcy was more inclined to buy into his apologies than me. I personally found it hard to forget the casual way he referred to me as a whore or the general creepy ass fact that his hat had his grandma's soul knitted into it. I mean, what the actual fuck? You couldn't pay me to wear something like that. And I sure as shit didn't want it near me. What if she was in it, lingering amongst the head sweat, dandruff and loose hairs, whispering to him about the way my skirt was too short or my attitude too slutty for her liking? Not that I gave a shit what some dried up soul crust thought of me, but I still didn't want her near me. The idea of her grossed me out.

Professor Prestos was waiting outside the stadium in a tracksuit with a stopwatch hanging around her neck.

"Hurry up!" she called. "You've got four minutes to get changed and back out here. Every minute you're late will lose you a House Point!"

I flashed her a smile which she returned as I jogged past her into the Pitball locker rooms. We all focused on getting changed and I pulled on my own navy blue and silver trimmed tracksuit as quickly as I could. The sweatshirt had Vega emblazoned across the back of it and the sneakers that accompanied it had thick treads for off-road running.

We made it back outside just in time to avoid losing any points and waited for the stragglers. Prestos took the points she'd promised from them before calling out for all of us to follow her deeper into the woods.

"Today's lesson is an assessment," she called out. "There is a track through the trees, marked out by the bright pink arrows." She pointed at the first arrow and I craned my neck to see where it pointed, spotting a high wooden wall blocking the track ahead of us, ropes dangling down the length of it for people to use to clamber over the top. "This is a test of physical ability but I want to see proper use of magic too. The different obstacles can be overcome with one or two Elements or tackled physically. So each of you will have advantages at different stages of the course."

"But, Professor," Kylie called out, interrupting Prestos and earning herself a frown from our teacher. "The Vegas have *all four* elements, so they get an advantage at *every* obstacle. So shouldn't they have a handicap or something?"

Prestos laughed like Kylie had just told a hilarious joke. "Suck it up, Major. That's the world we live in. Those with the most power are always at an advantage in Solaria. It's up to those of you with less Elements and lower levels of power to find ways to utilise what you've got. Exploit friendships, Order gifts, anything you can to give yourself an edge. That's what it is to be Fae. And any pathetic whining about it being *unfair* will get you a meeting with Principal Nova about your place at Zodiac Academy. This is the best academy in Solaria. You guys are either here for a reason or you'll be gone before you know it. So Fae up and quit bitching or I'll see you in detention."

"Oh, I like her," Darcy whispered to me and I grinned.

Kylie folded her arms but raised her chin, clearly meaning to do as she'd been told.

"So for this challenge, I want you all to work *alone*. That means no waiting for each other, helping each other out or doing anything to hinder anyone else either. This is a straight race. You'll all start at once and I want you to run around the course as fast as you possibly can, using your magic to help you as and when you're able. I'll be ranking you on how quickly you can make it back to me. That will be your starting rank in this class and in each lesson following this, positions will change based on your performances. Top ranking students will earn privileges such as access to exclusive areas on campus. Low ranking students will earn themselves sessions in the gymnasium and after school classes to try and build you up. I wasn't joking about your places at the academy being at risk because of this class. At Zodiac Academy we are looking to educate the best of the best. If you consistently fail this or any other class, you can expect to lose your position here."

"I can't believe I could lose my place here because I'm not great at gym class," Diego groaned and I cast a glance his way.

"Well maybe now you'll be motivated to work out more," I replied.

"Hey, I'm not exactly tiny," he protested, folding his arms and clearly tensing his biceps.

"I didn't say you were. But in a school full of shifters with more muscles than is really fair, you're definitely a little light on the brawn." My gaze slid over a lot of the other guys in our class as I took in bulging biceps and broad shoulders everywhere I looked, it really wasn't a bad view.

Diego huffed and Darcy gave me a look that said I was treading the line of bitch. I replied with a look of *I know but I don't care* and she smirked at me.

"Okay, everyone! On my whistle…" Prestos gave a sharp blow on her whistle and we all sprang into action.

The moment we made it to the wooden wall, all of the air students including me and Darcy used our Elemental magic to propel us up and over it. Almost everyone else was forced to scramble for the ropes and climb it, though I did spot a couple of the more powerful water and earth elementals riding a column of water or earth up to the top too.

I landed in the thick mud on the far side of the wall and started running straight away. Darcy kept pace beside me and we raced towards the next obstacle. A wide river of mud fell away in front of us, ropes stretched out over it, tied between trees on both sides.

"Do we have to hang from them to cross?" Darcy asked, wrinkling her nose.

"Looks like it," I agreed. "We could try and use earth magic to make a solid path but I think the ropes will be faster here."

Darcy nodded at my assessment and I moved towards the closest rope, jumping to grab it then swinging my legs back and forth until I managed to hook an ankle over the top of it. I locked my ankles together as I dangled beneath the rope like a sloth on a branch and started hoisting myself along, crossing the mud with my hair swinging beneath me and my arms burning with the effort involved in dragging myself across.

I grunted as I dropped to the ground on the other side, looking around to see Darcy half way across behind me.

"Keep going, Tor!" she called. "Prestos said no waiting for each other!"

I hesitated for a moment before calling out in farewell and running on. Kylie and Jillian had made it over too and there was no way I was going to let them beat me.

I raced on around the track, fighting my way beneath nets which covered muddy ground, wading through freezing rivers, running through fires and many more challenges which seemed almost impossible. But with the use of my magic and hard persistence, I finally rounded the last bend and sprinted back to Professor Prestos who stood waiting with her stopwatch and clipboard ready, a smile playing around her lips.

"Good work, Vega," she said, jotting down my time. "You're first back."

I fell to the ground, panting to catch my breath with a big ass smile on my face. I was freezing cold, smothered in mud and about the happiest I'd been in a long time.

"I guess all that running finally paid off," I joked.

"Dedication in all things usually pays off at some point," Prestos agreed with a smirk.

We waited as I caught my breath and the sound of footsteps pounded towards us just as I got to my feet again.

Darcy sprinted around the corner, her cheeks flushed and blue hair flying around her face as she used her air magic to push her along even faster.

I started cheering her on, jumping up and down and clapping as she raced towards us and she laughed as she spilled over the finish line and collapsed to her knees in the mud, mumbling about dying from exhaustion.

"Good job, Vega," Prestos praised again, this time aiming her compliments at my sister.

Once Darcy caught her breath, we found a fallen log at the side of the track and took up our positions to watch the rest of our class make it back over the line. It took over half an hour for all of them to appear and Diego ran through among the last of the pack.

"Good first effort, class!" Prestos called out as we all gathered around. "You'll receive an email with your official ranking. It's no surprise that the Vegas made top spots as the most powerful students we've ever had attending the academy. But don't let that dissuade you. Plenty of the less powerful students have done well. Cygnus, you made fifty nine, despite the fact that you rank in the bottom quarter power-wise."

Sofia beamed at being called out and I slapped her a high five in celebration.

"Dedication, determination, delivery. Being Fae means fighting for your position. So just as those of you at the bottom of the rank need to step up and fight to claim a higher position, those of you at the top are going to need to work hard to defend yours. There's nothing easy about being powerful. It may seem that life at the top of the pyramid is all sunshine and roses to those of you at the bottom but remember: if you're the best there will *always* be someone who wants to challenge you for that place. You will have to fight to maintain your position every single day of your lives. Because you're Fae. That's what we do. And if you can't hack it, then I suggest you pack up and withdraw yourselves from the academy now. Because you've made it through The Reckoning which means the real work starts here."

Prestos looked around at the class like she was hunting for anyone who didn't make the cut and we all stood a little straighter, returning her gaze fiercely. When she was satisfied, she dismissed us so that we could all go and clean up before our next class.

"Wow, do you really think it's all going to get even tougher from here on out?" Sofia whispered as we made our way inside to the showers.

"I think I'm beginning to realise why the Heirs come at us so hard all the damn time," Darcy groaned, wiping a hand over her face which really just moved the mud around.

"Yeah, I get it," I replied. "And I think we've also come way past the point of no return with them. If we're destined to be locked in this power struggle with them for the rest of our lives then I say it's time we concentrated everything we've got on learning how to beat them."

"Hell yes," Darcy agreed. "One of these days, I'm going to be the one knocking them onto their asses in the mud."

I laughed, my power stirring beneath my skin as if it liked the sound of that. "I think it's time for us to accept who we are. We're the lost Vega Princesses, Heirs to our own throne and the most powerful assholes in the whole of Solaria. And I think it's time we stop letting other people tell us what that means and deciding it for ourselves."

MAX

CHAPTER TWENTY

"I hear you took Tory Vega out on a date, Cal," Seth said as he stood over Darius, spotting him on the bench press.

We were all working out in the gym that we'd set up in the lower level of King's Hollow so that we could have some privacy from the prying eyes of the other students. It was Saturday night and we were going to stay at the Hollow tonight, catch ourselves up on everything that had been going on in the last week with the Nymphs plus try and get to the bottom of what was eating Darius. Not that he was aware of that part of the plan which the rest of us had made. I shot Seth an irritable look as he brought up Tory Vega, who seemed like the worst subject choice if we were planning on getting Darius in a good enough mood to open up to us. Seth only shrugged, his nosiness knowing no bounds as always.

"Heard it from who?" Caleb asked, rising himself up into what must have been his hundredth pull up, using a bar grown from the roots of the tree we were standing within. This room was in the trunk of the huge tree which supported our hideout, hidden behind the staircase which gave entry to the main structure above. The wide space was lit with fires which burned brightly in sconces around the edge of the room.

"The Celestial Times," Seth replied with a shrug. "Though they didn't call it a date. They said you'd been seen charitably donating your time to showing Roxanya Vega around Tucana."

I snorted a laugh. That paper was so far up our parents' asses that they'd never dare release a story saying he'd been dating a Vega, even if they had a photograph of him screwing her.

"Oh, right," Caleb grunted.

"So…?" Seth pushed.

Darius gritted his teeth, his muscles bunching as he continued to lift the four hundred pound weight above his chest. I frowned at the weight, mentally psyching myself up to try and match it, though I knew I couldn't. Our Dragon brother was always going to be the biggest of us physically. Not that that stopped me from wanting to beat his ass one day.

A trickle of irritation was slipping from Darius at the change in conversation, his physical exertion making it harder for him to concentrate on keeping me out of his head.

"So?" Caleb asked, dropping to the ground and picking up a towel to wipe the sweat from his brow.

"*Was* it a date? Because I thought you were just screwing her," Seth pushed.

Caleb didn't hide the irritation from his features in response to that, but it was punctuated by the feeling of his annoyance washing over me. He hardly ever bothered to block me out. Unlike Darius, Caleb seemed happy enough for me to know how he was feeling most of the time.

"Well I decided to try out dating her," Caleb admitted. "But it was a fucking disaster so I'm not sure we'll do it again."

Darius let a little bit of amusement slip from him at that admission and I sighed as I picked up a kettlebell and started on some squats. That girl took up far too much of his attention. Caleb's too.

"I want the details," Seth said like an excitable fifteen year old girl who'd just been asked to prom. I snorted a laugh and he shot me a grin. "Where did you take her?"

"Fine," Caleb said, dropping down to sit on the end of the bench beside Darius's. "I took her to that sushi and karaoke place on the east side of town."

Darius barked a laugh as he placed his weight back on the rack and sat up. His muscles bulged from the workout, the Phoenix and Dragon tattoos which danced with each other on his back gleaming with sweat. "No wonder it went to shit then," he taunted.

Caleb narrowed his eyes on him in return. "Oh yeah? Why's that?"

"Well for one thing, Roxy doesn't eat fish, or meat, or anything pretentious that comes in tiny little squares. So I'm betting she thought sushi was fucking disgusting," Darius replied with a snort of amusement.

"Yeah she did," Caleb admitted irritably.

"And she doesn't really strike me as the type to enjoy applauding idiots for making fools of themselves. Or as the kind of girl who would like getting up on stage and enjoy being gawked at while she did her best rendition of some power ballad." Darius looked mildly disgusted by the fact that Caleb had even taken her there at all and I had to admit it didn't exactly seem like the best choice of venue.

"Well she likes having fun," Caleb replied defensively. "You know, pushing limits and stuff, so I thought I'd try pushing her out of her comfort zone."

"That's so far out of her comfort zone that I'd imagine she didn't even stay for an hour," Darius mocked.

Caleb pulled a face which was an admission in itself and I smirked at him.

"So you struck out then?" I asked, though I couldn't be too amused at his expense because Grus still wouldn't even consent to sitting with me at breakfast let alone going out on a date with me. In fact that whole situation was driving me crazy. I couldn't get the night I'd spent with her out of my head and she was acting like it didn't mean a goddamn thing to her. It was bullshit. Complete bullshit. But so far, there was nothing I could do to make her admit that.

Darius on the other hand had no issues with mocking him and barked a laugh, offering Caleb a shit-eating grin which was half asking for a smack.

"Well if you know her so fucking well then tell me where you'd have taken her, asshole," Caleb shot at him, rolling his eyes like he didn't think Darius would be able to do any better anyway.

Darius leaned forward, his elbows on his knees as he answered without even having to think about it.

"I'd take her over to Clearmont Park on the west side of town," he replied.

"You think she'd want to go for a walk in the park?" Caleb scoffed.

"No. I'd take her there because they've got the best burrito truck in town parked up by the main gates every Saturday night and she practically has an orgasm every time she eats Mexican food."

"Oh shit, that's right!" Seth piped up. "That girl totally makes sex noises when she eats!"

"She's louder than that in bed," Caleb replied, earning a scowl from Darius. "So is that the dream date you'd be offering her, then? Food from a questionable truck?"

Darius seemed in two minds over replying but eventually he did. "After we ate, I'd take her to the Everland Street parking lot just as it was getting dark."

"You think she'd want to hook up with you in a parking lot because you bought her a burrito from a restaurant on wheels?" Caleb scoffed

"No. Every Saturday there's a bike meet in that lot. And street races to win bikes. So I'd take her to that and after she'd beat every fucker there and won their bikes from them, I'd take her to Blue Lake," Darius added.

"Why? That bar isn't even on the west side," Caleb pointed out.

"I know. But they stock fifty different types of tequila and have over a hundred tequila cocktails on the menu. Plus they play good music and she loves dancing."

Caleb pursed his lips irritably.

"That does kinda sound like a perfect date for her," Seth said with a shrug. "Assuming she likes tequila."

"She does," Darius replied with enough confidence to say he was sure of that. Apparently he'd been paying rather a lot of attention to her because I had no fucking idea she could even ride a bike let alone the rest of it.

"Pity she hates you too much to ever agree for you to take her out then," Caleb shot at Darius who just shrugged in response.

"I never said I was going to ask her. But you asked me where I'd take her if I did," he replied.

"Well for someone who *isn't* going to ask a girl on a date, you seem to have thought pretty damn hard about what you'd do for one," Caleb accused.

"No I haven't. You asked and that's what I came up with." Darius replied and I only felt honesty coming from him, making me actually believe that. Which was worrying in its own way because that meant he'd been paying enough attention to Tory Vega to figure out all that stuff about her and know it so well he didn't even have to think about the answer before it sprang from his lips.

Caleb glanced at me for confirmation and I gave him a slight nod.

"Well why not?" Caleb asked with a huff of irritation. "She told me that the two of you almost hooked up on the Eclipse. And it seems pretty fucking obvious to me that you want her. So why haven't you tried to take her?"

I exchanged a look with Seth, wondering if this might descend into an argument. As far as I knew, the two of them hadn't actually discussed this so frankly before.

Darius stilled, his eyes dropping to his hands as he considered his answer. "I think she's hot but she annoys the fuck out of me too," he said dismissively but I didn't miss the tension in his posture. "Besides, even if she didn't and even if I hadn't done all of the shit I've done to her and she didn't hate me about as much as it was physically possible to hate a man, what can I offer her?"

"Don't tell me you've got an inferiority complex," I teased, aiming to keep the subject as light hearted as possible while exerting my gifts and spreading a sense of calm and friendship between us just in case. They would feel my influence touching them but I always took a lack of complaint as permission to use my gifts when it came to the other Heirs.

Darius smirked, giving Cal an exaggeratedly assessing look. "Well I can't really compete with that little boy lost thing he's got going on," he said. "And if she's all for blonde haired, blue eyed boys then there's not a lot I can do about it."

"Yeah, who the hell would want all of those muscles and the darkness and the tattoos..." Seth trailed off as he blatantly checked Darius out and we all laughed.

"I want the real answer," Caleb said before the subject got dropped. "What do you mean, 'what can you offer her?'"

Darius stood and started lowering the weights on the rack as Seth switched positions with him. "I just mean I can't exactly take her on a date like that, can I? Even if she *would* say yes, my father would lose his fucking mind if I was *seen showing her around Tucana,*" he said dismissively. But it was the kind of casual tone that sounded false.

Darius glanced my way, his mental shields reinforced again so it was damn hard for me to get a read on him. But as always when he spoke about his father, there was a darkness in his eyes.

"And she wouldn't say yes anyway so this is a pointless conversation. Like you said, she hates me." Darius's gaze darkened even further with that remark and for a moment I could have sworn I felt...pain. *Shit.*

Seth reached up to grip the bar but paused, looking up at Darius. "Lionel's never given a crap about who you were screwing before. So long as you're still engaged to Mildred, what difference would it make to him?"

"Don't be an idiot, Seth," I said, dropping the kettle bell and taking a seat beside Cal. Seth lifted the weight over his chest and started on his set. "The Vegas aren't just some girls. They could screw up everything. None of our parents would be pleased to think we were getting too close to either of them. Unless they were hoping we could exploit that relationship somehow." I cast a sidelong look at Cal who shrugged.

"Mom hasn't said anything that calculating," he replied. "But she hasn't discouraged me from spending time with Tory. She likes to hear how her magic is progressing and stuff, I think she believes keeping the Vegas sweet can't hurt in the long run. Just in case..."

"Just in case they rise up, claim their place and de-throne us?" Darius scoffed. "Don't worry, Father will kill them before that day ever comes. Why do you think I work so hard to keep them beneath us?"

I raised an eyebrow at that because it sounded suspiciously like Darius was trying to protect the Vegas by tormenting them instead of his motivations being about maintaining his own power. *Our* power. Protecting them from the wrath of his father seemed like a secondary priority to me. Everything I did to them was for the security of our throne. For us. For Solaria. The Vegas' protection hadn't ever really crossed my mind.

"Lionel wouldn't actually *kill* them though, would he?" I asked with half a laugh.

Darius pushed his tongue into his cheek, opened his mouth then closed it again. I caught a hint of frustration from him, but he didn't answer.

I exchanged a look with Caleb. There was something we'd been beginning to suspect about Lionel for a while, but none of us had had the balls to ask it outright. But I was sick of dancing around the subject.

"Is it that you don't *want* to tell us?" I asked slowly. "Or that you *can't?* "

"What do you mean, can't?" Darius asked, his eyes on the weight Seth was struggling with. Just as it looked like Seth might drop it, Darius reached out and helped him guide it to the rack instead.

"I *mean* does he Coerce you not to talk about certain things with us?" I pushed.

Darius looked up, catching my eyes as he opened his mouth. Silence hung for a long moment before he responded. "No one can use normal Coercion on me," he said eventually.

Caleb growled, reading between the lines just as I was. "And what about Dark Coercion?" he asked in a low voice. Dark Coercion was totally illegal, if we were right about Lionel using it then it meant he was deep into some really dodgy shit. There had always been rumours about the Acruxes using dark magic but it had never been confirmed. The Orions were tangled in it with them if you believed half the shit that was whispered about their families or printed in The Daily Solaria.

Darius didn't reply which was something of a response in itself. Of course, if he'd been Coerced not to tell us using dark magic then he wouldn't be able to anyway. His gaze gave away his frustration but as he looked my way, a glimmer of hope entered his eyes and he suddenly stopped blocking me out.

I inhaled sharply at the sudden assault of emotion pouring off of him, realising just how successfully he'd been blocking me out and for how long as I almost drowned in the feeling of it all crashing over me at once.

"There are some things I can't tell you, which is really fucking frustrating," Darius said, his voice rough. "But maybe you can guess what I'd like to say if you can feel it."

"So *is* he using Dark Coercion on you?" I almost whispered, my heart pounding at the implications which weighed heavily on the answer to that question.

"No," Darius replied. But it was a lie. I could feel the dishonesty, the frustration, his guilt compounding it as he was forced to lie to us.

"Holy shit," I breathed.

"Did he lie?" Seth asked, his gaze yo-yoing between me and Darius like he wasn't sure where to hunt for his answers.

"He did," I confirmed.

Darius's shoulders sagged and relief fell from him in a wave. I could only stare at him, my head spinning with all the implications posed by his answer. The next answer we needed to know was how long this had been going on for. And what he'd been forced to lie about. But it was going to be damn near impossible to figure that out if he couldn't tell us. We'd have to ask the exact right questions so that I could read the lies as they spilled from his lips.

"When did this start?" Caleb asked, his eyes wide with horror.

Darius frowned for a moment before seeming to realise he could answer that.

"Since I was Awakened. Since he started preparing me to take his place on the Council. Not that I believe he'll ever really let me take his place while he still lives," Darius ground out.

"So what does he stop you from telling us?" Seth asked, frowning as he seemed to realise that was a dumb question. "I mean, what kind of thing?"

Darius looked between all of us for a long moment then sighed. "The worst kinds of things," he said eventually, giving an answer that wasn't an answer at all. "Look, I know you guys want to help and I love you for that. But there *is* no helping me with my father. You can't stand against a Councillor, hell, you can't even expect your parents to. It would disrupt the balance of power, unsettle Solaria while the Nymphs are the strongest they've been in a long time. In the grand scheme of things, my misery isn't relevant."

Darius gave us a defeated shrug and turned, heading out of the room before we could say anything in response. His sneakers thumped up the stairs carved into the hollow trunk beyond the door and I looked between the others with a frown.

Seth whimpered and started pacing, his Wolf instincts making him restless.

"I don't like the way he just said 'my misery' like that's some kind of constant state he's in," he said. "I mean, it's not that bad is it? We haven't been so blind that we've just totally fucking missed the fact that Darius is actually that unhappy... Have we?"

I exchanged a loaded look with Caleb and pushed my hands through my mohawk as I expelled a breath.

"He's been blocking me out of his head for a hell of a long time," I said with a frown. "But he just let the walls down and...*fuck*, I think we really screwed up. He's not just miserable, he's a ball of anxious energy and darkness and pain. I don't even know how to marry that with the guy who makes me laugh every morning over breakfast and wrestles with me in Water Elemental. He's been hiding this shit for so long that I don't even think he knows how to drop the mask anymore."

"So what the hell are we gonna do about it?" Caleb demanded, getting to his feet like he was about to race after Darius that second.

"I..." I looked between the two of them and slowly shook my head. "I don't have a fucking clue. But whatever the hell it is, we'll do it. Give me a minute alone with him so I can see if he'll keep letting me get a read on his emotions. Maybe it'll be easier to figure out how to help him if I can get a clearer picture on the issue."

"Okay," Caleb agreed reluctantly and Seth whimpered again.

"One minute," Seth said. "Then we're coming up to deal with this. Together."

"Alright," I agreed.

They both nodded and I headed out of the room, following Darius upstairs.

He was sitting on the grey couch as I came up, still not shielding his emotions from me as he looked at something on his Atlas. Whatever it was was confusing him a hell of a lot. There was some lust, longing, anger, irritation and a hell of a lot of pain. I stepped closer and snatched his Atlas from his hand before he could stop me.

I flipped it around to look at it, expecting something from his father or maybe a newspaper article. I did not expect to see a photograph of Tory Vega in her underwear and a pair of filthy walking boots.

Darius snatched it back out of my hands with a possessive growl and quickly locked his screen.

"What the hell is that about?" I demanded.

"Nothing," he replied angrily.

I threw up a silencing bubble so that Caleb wouldn't hear my response. "Bullshit. I thought you said nothing was going on with you and Tory."

"It's not," he snapped. "She sent that to me the night of the Eclipse. I've got no fucking idea why and I can't ask her because all she's done since that night is ignore me unless I'm literally right in her face pissing her off so much that she has no choice but to give me her attention."

"Why are you so obsessed with her?" I demanded. "It couldn't come to anything serious even if she *was* interested. Not to mention all the fucking reasons why you shouldn't be getting close to a Vega in the first place. And Caleb-"

"I'm aware that he's seeing her," Darius growled, jealously and anger mixing with a tug of possession and hurt. "I don't need reminding."

"Yeah. Well I don't think he should be either. Those girls are nothing but trouble. For you, him, *us,* for the whole of Solaria! You shouldn't be agonising over her, you should be concentrating on getting rid of her."

Darius looked at me with a weird kind of desperation in his gaze. "I know," he growled. But with his emotions still wide open to me I could feel how much that thought tore at him. It actually hurt him to think about getting rid of her. "I don't know what's wrong with me, Max, I've never…I can't stop thinking about her and wanting her and hating her all at once."

I opened my mouth to respond but the sound of Seth and Caleb approaching up the stairs reached us. They couldn't hear our conversation from within the bubble but they'd want to know why we were keeping it private if I didn't drop it sharpish.

"You need to try," I said firmly. "Try and remember all the massive fucking world and future altering reasons we need the Vegas gone. Promise me you will."

"Fine," he ground out, sagging back into his chair.

My heart lurched as I felt a stab of hurt coming from him directed at me. He'd just tried to open up to me about his feelings for Tory and I'd shot him down. But what else could I say? Even the idea of him liking her was insane. It wasn't like he could ever have a future with her anyway and if he felt everything he was feeling about her now when they hadn't so much as kissed then what the fuck would he feel if he managed to start something with her only to have to end it when he married Mildred? I didn't want to hurt him, but he had to let go of whatever the fuck he was thinking or feeling about Tory Vega. And so did Caleb. I'd be telling him that too.

I dropped the silencing bubble as Seth and Cal walked in, casting curious looks our way.

"I thought you wanted to talk to me about my father?" Darius asked irritably, clearly ending the subject of Tory Vega. Which was probably for the best while Caleb was here anyway. This situation was so fucked.

"We want to talk to you about *everything* that's making you feel the way you are," I snapped back. "Because you've been hiding a whole chasm of fucking dark shit behind those mental walls of yours for way too long. We're your brothers. You can tell us anything! Don't you trust us?" I demanded, realising that I was feeling pain of my own too. How could he have been bottling this up for so long? I understood the Dark Coercion had tied his tongue on some things but to bury his misery the way he had was wrong on so many levels. We could have helped him with this a long time ago. He should have wanted us to. The other Heirs were my first port of call whenever I needed anything and I'd always thought that was the same for all of us. But this revelation made me reassess that. Did he really think he couldn't ask us for help when he so clearly needed us?

Darius held my eye for a long moment, his mental walls flickering in and out of place as he fought against the desire to block me out again.

He finally sighed, scrubbing a hand across his jaw as he left them down. "That's not it," he replied and the honesty in his words made me relax a little. "I just…didn't want to drag you guys into this. I can deal with it. Lance is helping me train and soon I'll be strong enough to challenge my father for his position on the Council. Once I can get rid of him, everything will be better. I'll be able to make my own choices, live my own life, help Xavier to… Everything will be better," he reaffirmed, clearly not planning on elaborating.

But I hadn't missed the fear that had come with the mention of Xavier's name.

I dropped into the armchair next to his position on the couch and Caleb moved around to sit beside Darius, exchanging a confused look with me.

Seth headed to the kitchen, grabbing four bottles of beer and handing them out before perching on the arm of the couch beside Darius. He reached out to pet Darius's hair and for once he didn't try to bat him off. I even felt a tendril of comfort coming from him in response to Seth's actions.

"Why are you so worried about Xavier?" I asked gently, begging him to answer and at least let us help with that much.

Darius opened his mouth to respond, but the fear he was feeling sharpened and he shook his head instead.

"Is that something you've been Coerced not to say?" Caleb asked.

"No…it's just, if I tell you, you'll be duty bound to tell your parents. I don't want to put any of you in that position."

Seth whimpered, looking to me like I might have some magic solution to that problem.

I chewed on my bottom lip, wondering what the hell it could be if he thought he couldn't share it with us for that reason. It made me think of my own secret. The one I'd kept from all of them. The one Tory Vega was holding for me.

My pulse hammered as I considered telling them about my lineage. Would they care? Would they support a claim pressed by my younger sister when she came of age just because she was legitimate and I wasn't? I didn't think so. And maybe I had held onto this lie for too long. Maybe it was time we all exercised a higher level of trust.

"What if we exchange a secrecy oath?" I suggested. "And I'll tell you all my secret too?"

Darius frowned, leaning forward in his chair as he looked at me. "What secret?" he asked.

I only smiled, offering him my hand as I summoned the magic I'd need to perform this spell. Once it was in place, we could tell each other the lies we'd been holding back but we'd be bound by the magic so that we wouldn't be able to speak of them again outside of this place.

"I'll tell you a secret as well," Caleb agreed, shifting closer, his leg

302

pressed against Darius's. The four of us were huddled so close together that it should have been uncomfortable but somehow it wasn't. This was the bond of our brotherhood. Darius needed us and we were going to show him that we'd be here no matter what.

"Me too," Seth agreed quickly.

Darius only hesitated a moment longer before nodding, clapping his hand into mine. We both dropped the barriers on our magic and I inhaled at the assault of his power as it wound its way beneath my flesh, forming a tide with my own magic so that the two washed back and forth between us. We were evenly matched but the heat of his fire magic flared beneath my flesh as my air power swept beneath his. Our water magic met and swelled, the power of it blooming as it joined for a little while.

Caleb reached out and clasped his hand over ours from the left while Seth gripped us from the right. As they dropped the barriers around their own magic, earth power rumbled through the bond too. I didn't think we'd ever all power shared together like this before. The four deep wells of our magic swelling and combining into something truly terrifying. We were a force of nature individually, together our power was cataclysmic.

"Shit," Seth groaned heavily.

Caleb chuckled and I grinned too. It was more than a little overwhelming, but it felt really fucking good. Even Darius smiled as the waves of energy slid between us and we were each caught up on a tide of power so raw it was intoxicating.

I worked on placing the secrecy oath over our power and could feel Darius, Seth and Caleb strengthening the spell as they cast their own magic into it too.

I wasn't sure if Darius would speak right away so I decided to open up first to show him how much I trusted him. "My mother isn't my mother," I said, my voice trembling as I spoke those words aloud for the first time in my life.

"What?" Darius asked, clearly surprised that my secret had been so heavy. Seth and Caleb both stared at me like they couldn't quite believe what I'd said and I barrelled on, wanting to spit it out before I lost my nerve.

"My father had to marry the woman you think of as my mother because of an arrangement for power. But he loved my real mother before that was decided. He kept her close and got her pregnant before his wife. They covered it up, pretended I was legitimate to hide the scandal. And I'm pretty sure my step mother poisoned my real mother to get rid of her after she'd had her legitimate children."

"But…" Darius frowned, trailing off as he thought over what I'd said. "Does she want you gone too? Do you think Ellis will challenge you for your place in time?"

"I'm not sure what my sister will do," I admitted. "I don't think she knows…but my stepmother has always forced competitiveness between us. There's no love lost between me and her and I expect that if my stepmother can't kill me off, she will want Ellis to challenge me eventually. I'm pretty sure the only reason I still draw breath is because Dad placed protections on me. He's made it clear that he wants me to sit in his place. He doesn't care about my legitimacy but the scandal it could cause…"

"I know," Darius growled. "But we would stand by you even if the whole world found out you were the son of a mortal, let alone being a bastard. What difference does it make anyway? Your power comes from your father. So fuck anyone who would give a shit about your blood not being pure enough. There's no better man or woman to sit in your father's place after you and if your stepmother thinks she can replace you with Ellis, she's fucking deluded."

"Too fucking right," Caleb agreed, looking straight into my eyes.

"I always thought your mom was an asshole," Seth added thoughtfully.

A warm smile spilled across my face and my grip on Darius's hand tightened. Why had I always been so afraid of the others finding out about this? I shouldn't have doubted them. I shouldn't have doubted *him*. But the Acruxes were well known for their pure blood beliefs. Darius was already engaged to his second cousin just to make sure they kept their line pure. Powerful. Dragons. I'd thought that might mean he held prejudiced beliefs too, but maybe it really meant he could understand my position better than anyone.

"Thank you," I said, looking around at my brothers, my heart swelling with emotion at the unfaltering loyalty and love in their eyes.

I looked between them, wondering which of them was going to reveal their secret next as the flood of our magic continued to sweep between us.

Darius seemed to want to speak, but he hesitated and Caleb stepped in to stop him from having to voice whatever was haunting him before he was ready.

"I almost killed a girl a few months after I was Awakened," he said, chewing on his bottom lip. "I let myself get too low on magic and we were drinking…she was all over me, begging me to bite her and I did. But I guess I was too drunk because I tore her skin too much and she just started bleeding everywhere. I didn't know how to heal someone magically then so I had to run for my Mom…" He cleared his throat before going on. "She got there just in time. Saved the girl and then paid off her family. She gave them this massive estate on the other side of the country and covered the whole thing up so it wouldn't cause a scandal. That's why she made me go home on the Eclipse, just in case… But I wouldn't do that again," he added defensively. "I'm careful now. I know it wouldn't ever happen again, but sometimes I still dream about her lying there, bleeding and bleeding…"

Seth whimpered sympathetically and Darius reached out with his free hand to clap him on the shoulder.

"We know you wouldn't hurt anyone like that on purpose," he said firmly.

"I've never been worried about you hurting me when you bite me," Seth added, grinning wolfishly and breaking the tension as Caleb smiled back.

"Good."

"Xavier emerged as a Pegasus," Darius breathed before Seth got the chance to offer up his secret.

We all stared at him for a long moment, shock rendering us speechless.

"Fuuuuck," Caleb said.

"I'll second that," I agreed.

Seth actually fucking howled and Darius dropped his head back with a groan.

"I don't know what to do. Father has him locked up in his room like a fucking prisoner. He won't let him out, won't let him join a herd or even transform at all. And every time he loses control of his Order form and turns into a goddamn lilac Pegasus he's…punished."

The last word seemed to stick in his throat and I got the feeling that was one of the things he wasn't allowed to say.

305

"You mean Lionel beats him?" I growled because I was so fucking sick of us having to pretend we didn't know about that shit.

Darius locked his jaw but the emotion I caught from him confirmed it.

"He never used to pay Xavier much attention but ever since he Emerged…"

"Fuck," Caleb said, even though it wasn't really necessary.

"We'll figure it out," Seth swore. "Somehow."

"He'd rather kill him than have the world find out what he is," Darius said and the hopelessness pouring from him broke something in me.

"That's not going to happen," I snarled. "I swear it."

"Me too," Caleb promised.

"The four of us can do anything if we set our minds to it," Seth said confidently. "We're the strongest pack Solaria has ever seen. The most powerful alphas of our generation all bound together through love and brotherhood."

The weight on Darius's shoulders seemed to ease a little in response to that and he sighed. "Okay. We'll figure it out together."

"Come on then, Seth," Caleb urged. "What's your secret?"

"Oh…well I always tell you guys the big stuff so mine's not really important…"

"Spit it out," I demanded, sensing his embarrassment as a smile tugged at the corner of my mouth.

"*Fine.*" Seth looked between the three of us and blew out a breath. "So I…*might* have tried that nipple thing again after all-"

"I don't wanna hear it!" Darius barked a laugh and reared back in disgust.

"I'm stuck between morbid fascination and total repulsion," Caleb admitted.

"No. Fuck no, I don't need to hear anything else about you and that weird suckling thing. This secret session is officially over," I said.

Seth grinned and we all drew back, releasing our grip on each other and drawing our own magic back under our flesh.

My skin felt raw as I settled back into my own body, the power within me familiar and deep but no longer all consuming.

I looked between my brothers as a moment of silence passed between us following our revelations, feeling closer to them in that moment than I ever thought I had before.

"We need to focus on building our strength," I said slowly, turning over the various issues we were contending with. "Lionel is by far the biggest problem we've got."

"I don't think he'd do anything against the other Councillors," Darius said with a shake of his head. "Or you guys either. At least not unless he was utterly sure he could challenge them and win. So unless something changes…" He trailed off like that could actually happen and I frowned.

"He's our problem either way," I said firmly.

"Your issues are our issues," Caleb agreed, gripping Darius's shoulder.

"We stand together in this like we do in everything else," Seth said, nodding firmly.

"So what are we going to do?" Darius asked, a faint glimmer of hope shining in his eyes.

"*First*," I said. "We need the Vegas out of the way. They're distracting us from bigger issues. I say we go ahead with our plans to destroy them once and for all at Halloween. Once their reputations are destroyed and their confidence is battered, we won't have to worry about them anymore. They'll know their place and stick to it rather than cross us again."

"I agree," Seth said firmly.

Caleb frowned but didn't voice his protests on Tory's behalf again. All eyes fell on Darius.

"Fine," he said eventually, though I didn't miss the flicker of heartache the word cost him. "Let's just get it over with. The Vegas have had enough chances to bow willingly."

We turned to Caleb. He was outvoted; this was the part where he would fall in line.

Caleb's lips parted and he pushed himself to his feet. I could feel the arguments he wanted to make brewing beneath his skin but he held them back until he choked on them, stalking away from us to get another beer from the ice chiller.

He took the top from the bottle and drained the beer in one long drink, tossing the empty bottle in the trash.

"Fine," he said darkly. "But this had better be the end of it. If it doesn't work, then we need to think about other options."

"It'll work. There's no way they'll be able to bounce back from this like they have everything else. No one will ever forget it," Seth said excitedly.

I was grinning too and I got up to claim a second beer for myself. "Let's get drunk," I suggested. "We need a night off."

"Fuck yes," Darius agreed, catching another beer as I tossed it to him. "Let's drink until we forget who we are."

I snorted a laugh, wondering if he really was aiming for that. It would be pretty damn hard to achieve, but I guessed sometimes it was nice not to have to think about the pressure on us. Or the responsibilities put on us that went hand in hand with our claim. Being an Heir wasn't even something we had a say in. We *were* the most powerful Fae of our generation. It was on us to prove that point, but it would never stop being true.

We were born to rule.

I just hoped that when we sat on the Celestial Council, we'd still be able to do this. That we'd still be as close as we were now, still love each other as brothers. Because there was nothing more important to me than the three men in this room. And one day, we were going to rule the world together.

TORY

CHAPTER TWENTY ONE

Attention Students!
Tonight is the official celebration of Halloween.
The sun is currently travelling the path of the Via Combusta – The Burning
Way – between the fifteenth degree of Libra and the fifteenth degree of
Scorpio. On Halloween night, the malefic stars will be triggered by the peak
of the sun's path, bringing on chaos and bad luck. It will also corrupt those
on the verge of darkness.

Here are some pointers to get you through the event…

1. The faculty and I strongly encourage you to resolve any feuds you are
currently in the middle of and make amends with your enemies. We don't
want any more bloodshed on our hands than is absolutely necessary. Please
remember that if you're bleeding on school grounds it may be better to
take an external route to get help rather than passing through buildings to
minimise the clean up required afterwards.
2. Those of Orders with predatory inclinations such as Werewolves,
Dragons, Nemean Lions and Manticores are advised to refrain from shifting
during these hours as those urges will be keener. Eating a fellow student
will earn you a sentence in Darkmore Penitentiary and the FIB won't take

Halloween as an excuse.

3. Vampires are encouraged to feed and fill their reserves before the moon rises and the malefic stars come in to play. The Uranus Infirmary will not be stocking any extra supplies of blood for infusions.

4. Stay indoors and away from those who have caused you strife in the past to avoid any resurgence of emotions which may result in an altercation.

5. If students are truly fearful of their dark nature overriding their actions during this time, please speak to Professor Orion who can provide magic-restricting chains to tether yourself in your room until the night is over.

We must all be Fae enough to face this annual astrological event. If not, perhaps you should consider whether your place at Zodiac Academy is deserved.

Yours,
Principal Nova.

I re-read the announcement Principal Nova had sent around the school for the third time and snorted a laugh as I tossed my Atlas back down on my bed. This school was insane. It clearly stated in that message that Halloween was going to make the students violent and dangerous and yet there was no mention of us avoiding the party or of extra staff on call to look after us. Nope. It was down to us to own our inner monsters and keep them on a tight leash or face the consequences. And after the insanity that had come to pass under the influence of the moon during the Lunar Eclipse, I wouldn't be taking one of these warnings lightly again.

It would probably be safest for us to just stay in tonight, avoid people who had caused us strife in the past…like all the Heirs and all their followers for example. But screw that. Because tonight's party sounded epic on a whole other scale. And my costume was a stroke of pure, unadulterated genius. I just hoped Caleb could take a joke because if he couldn't then I wasn't going to be getting lucky tonight. But that was a risk I was willing to take. Because Sofia was even going to provide the glitter for me. And I couldn't wait for her to arrive.

I picked up my Atlas again, about to message her to see where she was just as another message flashed up on it. My heart did that annoying half back flip, half wither and die thing it liked to do whenever I saw Darius just as his name flashed on the screen.

Darius:

All Ignis House students are reminded that tonight is the Halloween party in the Earth Caverns. You know the rules by now for an event like this – show up or ship out!
Our whole House will be in attendance and you WILL be in costume.
Any fucker letting the House down will answer to me.
See you on the dance floor!

I bit my lip, remembering the way I'd responded to his last House message and wondering what the hell I'd been thinking to send him that goddamn photo. At least the crazy moon wasn't at work tonight. My actions would be entirely my own. Although if I was drinking then I had to admit that that probably wasn't much of an improvement. Drunk Tory did make a lot of very questionable choices. But she also tended to have a fucking awesome time so I wasn't going to be too hard on her. Shame could wait for tomorrow. Tonight I'd be having the time of my life.

My Atlas pinged again and I looked at the message in surprise.

Darius:

Don't I get a reply this time?

I frowned, wondering why the hell he might think I'd message him back. I had literally told him to his face on multiple occasions that I hated him, so what the hell was he even thinking?

Darius:

I can see you've read that...

Darius:

And that…

Tory:

Stop hassling me, stalker.

Darius:

What, no photos in your underwear tonight?

Tory:

I'm pretty sure it's your turn to send me something.
Also, fuck off.

I locked my Atlas and tossed it back onto my bed just as a knock sounded at the door.

Darcy threw it open without waiting for me to answer it and I grinned as Sofia and Geraldine followed her in. It was a bit of a squish, but we were determined to all get ready together before heading to the party.

"Holy huckleberry, I'm as excited as a banana with its peel off!" Geraldine gushed as she started heaping pots of face paint and makeup onto my desk while Darcy moved to hang their costumes from the edge of the doorframe which led into my en-suite.

Geraldine had dyed her hair turquoise to match her outfit and it actually looked damn good on her.

"I've started a trend with my weird hair colours," Darcy joked, eyeing my rainbow streaked locks with a grin.

"I don't think I can pull this off long term," I replied, running my fingers through my hair and watching as pastel pink, purple, yellow, green and blue layers passed before my eyes. "This will wash out with the counter-dye, but I am pretty pleased with how it turned out."

"You look utterly spiffing!" Geraldine complimented with a wide smile.

Sofia had dyed her hair a yellowy orange colour for her Nemean Lion outfit and had already back brushed it and filled it with hair spray so that it stood around her head in a mane.

"We're all going to look amazing," Darcy said enthusiastically and I nodded my agreement.

My eyes widened as Sofia lifted a huge pot of honest to god Pegasus glitter out of her bag with a grin and I clapped my hands excitedly.

"Are you sure you wanna do full body?" Sofia asked sceptically. "You'll be washing glitter out of your ass crack for a month."

"Worth it," I announced, tugging my clothes off as I prepared to be painted. "I might end up naked with someone tonight and I don't wanna have weird blobs of un-glittery skin!"

Darcy snorted a laugh and Geraldine's eyes widened before she turned away to start applying her own makeup.

"Okay. Well I've been practicing the spell to make it stick to your flesh. If I do it right, it'll just feel like an extra layer of your own skin until you use the counter spell to remove it. It won't smudge, sweat, peel or rub off before then," Sofia announced proudly.

"Okay," I grinned excitedly as she moved forward and began painting the thick layer of pink, silver and purple glitter onto every inch of my skin.

"Galloping galoozas, I still can't believe you're going to party like a Pegasus right in Caleb's face," Geraldine gushed. "You are too daring for your own good my lady!"

"I don't know what you mean," I replied innocently, batting my eyelashes which flashed as glitter caught in the light at the movement.

"You are sure he isn't going to flip out on you over this aren't you?" Darcy asked, looking at me with concern.

"Ermmm…" I looked in the mirror as Sofia's glitter application skills concealed my torso beneath a layer of sparkles and I shrugged. "I mean, what can he really say? I chose to go as a Pegasus. No one says he has to hook up with me while I'm looking like this. And if he *did* want to and that *did* kinda prove that he maybe has a bit of a Pegasus fetish after all, is that really my problem?"

The other girls laughed and I waited patiently as Sofia covered my back, the paintbrush cold along my spine.

My Atlas pinged on the bed and Darcy gasped a moment later.

"What?" I asked.

"I'm getting serious déjà vu," she groaned. "Because it seriously looks like you're sexting Darius Acrux *again*."

"Pfft," I replied. "Unless one of you has snapped a pic of me having my ass painted and sent it to him, I don't think so."

"This time it's one of him, not you."

I looked over my shoulder and glanced at my Atlas in her hand then looked away again just as quickly.

"Oh god, please tell me we're not about to see a dick pic," Sofia groaned.

"Of course not," I replied, looking at Darcy again. "Is it?"

"Oh give me a gander!" Geraldine exclaimed. "I do like an eyeful of man meat from time to time."

"Fuck, Geraldine," I gasped. "Man meat?! Seriously, you can't call a guy's junk man meat. Or banana drama for that matter."

"Well what shall I call it then? His long Sherman?"

"No!" I gasped. "Someone help me out here!"

Sofia was pissing herself with laughter and Darcy looked like she was almost crying.

"Dingle dongle?" Geraldine suggested and I cracked up.

When I could form words again, I took my Atlas from Darcy's hand and glanced at the screen.

Darius:

One new photo.

"It's not going to be a dick pic," I said, my finger hovering over the message.

"It is," Geraldine countered. "I can feel it in my waters."

"It's *not,*" I insisted. "It's just a…well I don't know what exactly, but not a dick pic. Probably. Maybe. Like, sixty three percent."

He wouldn't send me a dick pic.

Would he?

I tapped on the message and it opened to a picture of Darius with his shirt off, stacked muscles drawing my focus and making me bite my lip as I tried not to look too much. He was wearing some kind of insane costume which consisted of a cape which seemed to be on fire and had flames painted onto his skin around his tattoos and up the sides of his face. He was such an asshole but he really was pretty. Damn.

"Well I'd lick his lollypoppet," Geraldine cooed and we all started laughing again.

I locked the screen once more and tossed it down on the bed. He wasn't getting a reply because I wasn't messaging him in the first place. And I was going to delete that photo...later.

"You should," I agreed. "Because I don't want his lollypoppet or his pocket Rodger or his umgo bongo anywhere near me."

"Perhaps I should. I could start work on collecting the full set of Heirs as notches on my bedpost," Geraldine joked.

For half a second I almost snapped at her. Like some small, insane, teeny tiny psycho deep down inside of me wanted to tell her to back the fuck off of Darius even though I knew she was only joking. But in that half a second I thought of him as mine and I didn't want her or anyone else near him. Which must have meant I really was crazy.

I cleared my throat, dismissing that insanity as I looked back at the mirror to appreciate my ever more sparkling skin.

Sofia finished painting and placed a hand on my stomach, the tingle of magic dancing along my skin at the contact as she cast the spell to stop the glitter from shifting.

"Done!" Sofia announced proudly and I grinned as I moved to look at my sparkle-tastic body in the mirror by my door.

I didn't even have nipples anymore. I was just one big, glittery explosion of colour. I brushed my hands over my skin and none of the makeup moved one bit. It didn't even feel sticky, more like wearing a face pack over every inch of my body.

"Maybe I should just go naked," I joked. "You can't see anything anyway."

"Yes!" Geraldine gushed as the others said. "No!"

I laughed, moving across the room to collect my silver underwear and I pulled it on followed by the white dress. It was strappy and short, leaving as much of my glittery skin on show as possible while still covering up the parts that counted.

Darcy had already gotten changed into the little black dress she was wearing as part of her costume and she tied a floor length red cape around her shoulders next so that she looked like a Vampire from the mortal stories.

Geraldine had pulled on an emerald green mermaid tail skirt complete with sparkly scales and she matched it with a seashell bra which somehow made her boobs look even bigger than usual. Darcy moved to tie Geraldine's long, turquoise hair in a fishtail braid over her shoulder, clipping little seashells into it as she went.

I grabbed the curling iron and set to work styling my rainbow hair as Sofia changed into the skin tight Lion jump suit she was going to wear to complete her outfit. She only did the zip up half way, leaving her cleavage on show.

Once I'd finished my hair, I placed the golden Pegasus horn hairband on my head and stepped into my stilettos.

Sofia painted whiskers onto her cheeks and Darcy added a drip of fake blood to the corner of her blood red lips to complete her outfit.

"Well bite my begonia and call me a sea urchin, don't we all look spiffing?" Geraldine exclaimed, clapping her hands excitedly.

"Can you take a photo of me in my costume so I can send it to my friend?" Sofia asked, handing me her Atlas.

"What friend?" Darcy asked as I took the photo and handed her Atlas back.

"His name's Phillip, apparently," Sofia replied as she typed out a message and sent it off.

"What do you mean *apparently?*" I asked with a frown.

"Oh. Well he's recently Emerged as a Pegasus but he comes from a pure blood family of Dragons so he's kinda stuck in isolation, hiding who he is. He's pretty lonely...I'm just trying to help him as much as I can but really, he needs to get away from his family and join a herd..." She pouted her lips and shrugged. "There's not much I can do about it while he refuses to do that, but I can be a friend."

"That's...really shit," I said, my brow pinching as I thought of Xavier Acrux. Was there a chance that there was someone else in the same position as him or could she be talking to *him*?

"Yeah," Sofia agreed with a sigh.

"Have you seen a photo of him?" I asked.

"Err, well no. Because he's hiding who he is, so…"

"That sounds dodgy to me," Darcy said. "What if he's really some gross old dude, or-"

"He's not," Sofia interrupted. "I got his number from a member of his family who wanted to help him. I know he's hiding who he really is, but I trust everything else about him. He's just lonely."

I nodded in acceptance and decided not to voice my suspicions about Xavier. If it *was* him and he had chosen to hide his identity from her then I couldn't blame him. He was terrified of his father. So was I for that matter.

"Shall we move our scabooses?" Geraldine suggested excitedly, shimmying her chest so that her seashells clattered together.

"Hell yes." I grinned as we turned and headed out of the room.

I left all of my shit where it was, not wanting to carry a bag and Sofia took my door key for me as I locked up, placing it in a pocket of her jumpsuit.

We made our way across the school grounds, more students flooding around us dressed in weird and wild outfits as we all headed for the Earth Caverns where the party was being held.

It was cold out but I used my fire magic to keep myself warm as we walked.

Geraldine called out to any *Ass* Club member she spotted along the way so that by the time we arrived at the party, we were surrounded by a huge group who all greeted us enthusiastically and tried to get as close to me and Darcy as possible.

We headed down into the underground tunnel which led to the main cavern, the sound of a thumping bass drawing us on and a million twinkling lights lining the cave roof, making the whole place look magical.

Geraldine and Sofia headed off to get some drinks as we arrived, but I cut a line straight to the dance floor with Darcy. We started dancing right away, finding a spot between the writhing bodies of the other students and grinning as we fell straight into the rhythm of the music.

Just as the second song started up, a strong arm hooked around my waist and I squealed in surprise as I was hoisted straight off of my feet and carried across the room at high speed.

Caleb dropped me a little way down one of the side passages and shoved me back against the cave wall, sending a spike of pain down my spine as he snarled at me. He was wearing an outfit that left his chest bare and his hair looked like golden leaves beneath the crown on top of his head.

"What the fuck are you dressed as?" he growled, placing both palms to the wall either side of my head so that I couldn't escape.

"*Ow,*" I snapped, raising my chin to look him square in the eyes. "What the hell, asshole?"

"I asked you a question, Tory," Caleb growled.

"A fucking hippo," I replied. "Can't you tell?"

"No. Because it looks to me like you're some kind of weird fetish version of a Pegasus."

"Well you'd know," I mocked and he bared his teeth.

"This shit isn't funny. That's my reputation you're fucking about with."

"Oh lighten up," I said, rolling my eyes. "Who gives a shit if you want to screw a Pegasus? It's just a joke, Caleb. I thought you were supposed to be the funny one?"

"Well maybe this isn't something I want to laugh about," he growled.

"Why?" I pushed. "Don't you like it? I've covered every inch of my skin in it…"

Caleb's gaze dropped down over my outfit and he swallowed thickly.

I could see his resolve weakening and I edged closer to him. "How did that rhyme go again? Are you horny for the horn?"

"No," Caleb snapped, shoving away from me and backing up to put some distance between us. "Just go back to the party, Tory. I can't be around you tonight anyway."

"Why?"

Caleb's lips parted like he had something to say to me, but eventually he just shook his head and shot away again, leaving me alone in the dark.

I scowled after him and headed back towards the lights of the party. A little piece of me was disappointed that he couldn't take the joke. But a bigger piece of me didn't give a shit. If he wanted to go and pout in a corner about his precious reputation then that was on him. I had every intention of having a fantastic night dancing with my friends and I didn't need any men for that.

DARCY

CHAPTER TWENTY TWO

The music thumped in my ears and set off a wild excitement in my body as I took in the incredible magic in the cavern. The stalactites far above glittered and flashed, the crystals and minerals brought to life by a pulsing light which seemed to emit from within the rock itself. At the far end of the cave, a stage was built from a pillar of earth where a DJ with devil horns and a red mask was lost to the trance of his own set.

The ground had been wielded to build stone chairs and tables around the edges of the space and the floor was lined with a springy moss. The walls were covered with vines that moved like snakes in every direction, all of them coated in neon flowers which released puffs of glitter every few seconds. It was beautiful, captivating and made me want to learn how to wield all of that insanely cool magic.

Tory led us off the dance floor and over to a huge drinks table where a bright green punch was flowing through a fountain of ice. I grabbed a glass which was also made from ice and delicately held in a nest of vines, filling it from one of the streams that trickled over the lowest tier. I took a sip and my tastebuds crackled and popped as the sour drink swept over my tongue. A zing of adrenaline ran through my veins in response and I eagerly took another mouthful as the magic in it continued to spark throughout my body.

"Well flick my nipples, that tastes wonder-tastic!" Geraldine exclaimed, refilling her cup the moment she finished it.

"What's that about your nipples, Grus?" Max's voice made me turn and my heart stuttered as I spotted the other three Heirs standing beyond him in a tight circle. I couldn't help but admire their incredible costumes. Each of them had come as the Element of their House, looking like an artist had used their bodies as a canvas.

Max's scales were in place below his waist, but his chest was bare and someone had painted silver and blue swirls all across his skin which glittered like moonlight. His broad shoulders were covered with seashells and in his hand was a huge golden trident that looked sharp enough to skewer someone. His mohawk was dyed a deep navy colour and a crown of glittering blue gemstones perched on his head.

Seth was dressed as air. His long hair was dyed icily white and fluttered in a breeze I couldn't feel; the crown atop his head was a silver ring of spikes that glinted sharply. His shoulders were covered with feathers which hung over his muscular chest and his trousers were made of some tailored white material, buckled with a large silver belt inlaid with clear crystals.

Caleb wore the colours of earth. His blonde locks had been transformed to look like golden leaves, swept back beneath a crown of bronze. He wore a dark cape woven from moss and ivy which hung from his shoulders by a bronze plate.

Darius looked forbidding in his fire costume. His shoulders were covered in armour which appeared to be made of coal and a flickering blue fire rippled along it. His hair was swept back beneath a crown of gold and red flames seemed to flicker within the metal itself. The tattoos on his chest intermittently lit up, flaring like a flash fire before returning to deepest black.

"You don't do things by halves, do you?" I said to Max and he shrugged.

"We had a photo shoot for the press, little Vega. They wouldn't let us do anything less than perfect."

"You've really got to work hard at keeping up that douchebag reputation," Tory commented with a smirk, but Max shrugged it off, looking to Geraldine. His eyes raked down her mermaid costume, settling on her breasts for a long moment before he glanced up with a grin.

"We match," he pointed out and I eyed Geraldine, wondering how she was going to react to his attention.

"Princess Mer-Geraldine would never be seen dead with some common hagfish," Geraldine said dismissively and a snort escaped me.

Max's jaw clenched. "I'm not a hagfish, I'm Poseidon, king of the sea."

"Oh, well why would the mighty King Poseidon wear a hagfish costume?" Geraldine asked with a frown and Max's eyes flared with rage.

"He's not - I mean, I'm not. *It's not a hagfish costume!*"

A few girls giggled as they walked past him and his cheeks coloured. He glanced over at the other Heirs, looking like he was about to walk away but for some reason he didn't.

He cleared his throat. "How about a dance?" he offered her before shooting a glare at me, Tory and Sofia. "Or a chat alone?"

I could see the Heirs growing impatient as they looked over at us and I caught Seth's gaze unintentionally. He smirked, his eyes trailing over my costume with a dark intrigue. Darius was staring at Tory while Caleb was talking to a blushing girl with a drink in his hand and boredom in his eyes.

"No thank you, sea urchin," Geraldine said lightly, wafting Max away like he was a servant in her own royal court.

When Max didn't move, staring at her in complete disbelief, Geraldine sauntered away from him and we promptly followed, laughter escaping us as we put some distance between us and the Heirs.

We moved onto the dance floor and grouped together as we started swaying to the pounding beat. I took another swig of my drink and let its magic take over, raising my hands in the air and staring up at the colourful ceiling above.

I was aware of the crowd closing in around us and more than one guy tried to break our group apart and pull us away to dance. Geraldine was soon in the arms of a guy dressed like a Minotaur with massive horns protruding from his head and a fur cape hanging from his shoulders. Sofia danced with Tyler who was shirtless with brown wings strapped onto his back and a bird mask over his face. I guessed he was a Caucasian Eagle. It seemed like most guys at the party had opted for the half naked look to show off all their muscles. I wasn't exactly complaining, but there was only one half naked set of muscles I really wanted to be looking at.

Tory and I were left together, dancing to the endless beat, each of us taking it in turns to fetch drinks from the fountain. My mind was a haze of happiness and I wasn't even bothered when the Heirs seemed to ring around us, each of them sporting a pretty girl grinding all over them. Caleb slipped away from the girl he was with, drained the beer in his hand then made a beeline for Tory.

"Dance with me," he basically commanded her and she rolled her eyes.

"I'm busy dancing with my sister," she called over the loud music.

I wafted her away. "It's fine, Tor, I'm gonna go look for some water anyway."

"Are you sure?" she asked as Caleb wound an arm around her possessively.

"Yeah, I'll be back in a bit." I headed away and she moved into his arms with a look that said she was gonna give him hell for his bossy tone.

The throng of bodies was kind of suffocating and my mouth was parched by the time I reached the drinks table. I hunted for some water, finding an elaborate ice bucket at the end full of bottles. I swiped one out, drinking the whole lot in one go. I sighed my relief as I tossed it into the trash and my eyes fell on Seth as he exited the crowd, my skin prickling as he swept past me to grab some punch.

I strode away from him, heading back into the crowd but immediately felt a hand latch around my wrist. I growled, turning sharply, expecting to find Seth there but instead I found a tall man with a thick black cloak and a psycho killer mask over his face.

"Having fun?" he asked and my heart fluttered at the sound of Orion's voice and the scent of cinnamon sailing over me.

His chest was bare beneath the cape and I didn't know what the hell he'd come as, but it was freaking hot.

"You're not allowed to be here," I tip-toed up to speak in his ear.

He turned me around, pulling me back against his chest to dance and I melted into the arc of his body. "I wanted to see your costume," he purred and I grinned, grinding back against him as his hand slid around to my stomach, drawing me tighter to him.

"And what do you think?" I asked airily.

"I'm guessing you're a Vampire, but I don't see what the cape has to do with it."

"I'm Count Dracula," I said like it was obvious.

"Who?"

"The most famous Vampire ever," I said.

"Makinos the Devious?" he asked in confusion.

"What?" I laughed and his grip on me firmed.

My heart stuttered as I gazed at the sea of students around us, knowing this was reckless but I was lost to the feeling of him so close to me.

I turned around to face him, linking my hands behind his neck as the press of bodies pushed us closer and closer together. I could feel him watching me beneath the mask, sending a delicious kind of heat deep into my belly. As our bodies moulded, I felt the hard length of him digging into my hip and a grin pulled at my mouth.

Need grew in me as I danced against him, my breathing becoming rapid as he rested his hands on my hips and guided my movements. His fingers were digging in harder and harder and I was starting to lose my mind with how much I wanted to kiss him.

I glanced up at him under my lashes and in an instant, he snatched my hand and dragged me off of the dance floor. I nearly tripped over someone's long scaly tail as I hurried after him, but his grip was so firm that it kept me upright.

We emerged from the crowd on the other side of the cavern and my heart thundered an excited tune as Orion led me briskly into one of the passages which split off from the main cave.

The music fell to a distant drone as we hurried along into the pressing darkness. My breaths came in rapid pants as Orion's fingers locked between mine. I was blind in the tunnel but with his Vampire sight, I guessed he could see just fine.

He halted me suddenly, throwing me back against the cave wall, the sound of his mask hitting the ground coming a moment later.

He pinned my arms against the cold stone and I moaned even before he kissed me, his mouth bruising as his tongue pushed between my lips. He crushed me to the rock with the hard plain of his chest, grinding against me so I could feel how much he wanted me.

His fangs suddenly sliced into my lip and I gasped as my blood spilled into his mouth and a heady groan escaped him.

"This is risky," I said between kisses as he reached down to push his hand beneath the hem of my dress. "You're always telling me to be careful, you're such a hypocrite."

"I know," he growled as his fingers found my panty line and my thighs parted for him. "But I can't help myself. I have a craving for you I can't sate, but I sure as hell want to try."

His hand dipped beneath my panties and I rolled my head against the wall as his fingers found me hot and ready for him. He pushed two inside me with a low growl and my cry of pleasure rang around the cave roof.

"Fuck, silencing bubble," I gasped, choking away my moans.

He lifted his free hand, casting it in an instant along with an amber light orb above us so I was rewarded with the sight of his blazing eyes. He flicked his thumb over the sensitive flesh at the apex of my thighs and pleasure skittered through me once more. I clung to his shoulders, falling apart in his arms as he continued to torment me, but I needed more than this. I had to have all of him.

I reached for his waistband, stroking him through the material of his pants and he swore between his teeth. I unzipped his fly and freed him, curling my fingers around his smooth length and drawing a deep growl of desire from his lips.

He pulled his hand free from my panties, tugging them down and I immediately stepped out of them. He hooked one of my legs over his hip and my stomach clenched in anticipation a second before he drove himself into me. Another cry escaped me as pleasure punctured every nerve ending in my body.

I held on to the back of his neck as he laid siege to my body, my ass pressed firmly to the wall as he held me in place and pounded into me again and again.

I could hardly catch my breath as the friction between us grew hot enough to start a fire. I wrapped my other leg around him, my hips rocking in time with his as I met him thrust for thrust.

His hand slid to my throat as he angled my chin up to steal a kiss. His fangs sliced into my lower lip and I tasted blood as it soaked between our tongues, his hips moving faster as he drank from me, consuming me in every way possible. He groaned in ecstasy and the sound sent me haywire.

I fisted my hand in his hair, on the edge of nirvana as he wrung pleasure from every inch of me. It was only a second more before I came apart, pleasure washing through me like falling dominoes, setting off a chain reaction of pure bliss in every part of my being.

Orion followed me with a powerful thrust, filling me entirely as his fingers bit into my hips.

His mouth found mine and laughter rolled between us as I held onto him for support. My legs were shaking and I was pretty sure I'd fall right on my ass if he let me go.

He finally stepped back and I sagged against the wall, pushing my dress down as he zipped up his pants and gave me an infectious smile I simply had to return.

I moved to pick up my panties from the ground when the sound of someone clapping made my heart freeze and my lungs hollow out.

I twisted around as pure horror raced through every inch of me.

Seth walked up the tunnel toward us, looking like an angel in his feathery outfit, but a demon stared out of his eyes.

I stilled beside Orion, my mind going a hundred miles a minute as I tried to think of some explanation for this.

How much did he see??

Orion waved his hand to disband the silencing bubble around us, his rigid posture and bared fangs making my pulse quicken.

Holy shit what do we do?!

"I thought I was going crazy," Seth mused, pausing a few feet away as his eyes swung between us then fell to my panties on the ground. "But I should always trust my instincts."

"Seth it's not what you-"

"Don't lie to my face," Seth cut over me in a vicious snarl.

"Don't do anything stupid, Capella," Orion warned in a deadly calm tone. His muscles flexed and Seth's did in turn.

Reality hit me with a brutal punch to the gut.

He's going to tell. He's going to destroy Orion's life and all because of me. How could we have been so stupid?

Seth broke a laugh that was anything but friendly. "Like what? Tell

Principal Nova?"

Ice seemed to bind itself to my limbs as I stared at him, pulling me into a panicky state. "Please, Seth. Don't tell anyone."

Orion reached for my hand, his fingers wrapping around mine in a show of solidarity. I couldn't bear to look at him because I could feel him accepting this fate. But I refused it. I would *not* say goodbye to him because of Seth fucking Capella.

"Why would I tell anyone?" Seth asked innocently and for a second I was sure I'd misheard him.

He stepped closer with a cruel smile, moving up into Orion's personal space, a wolfish growl resounding in his chest.

An animalistic tension passed between them and I sensed it was taking everything Orion had not to strike at him.

"I own you now, *sir*. And I own your little bit on the side too." Seth looked to me and my throat thickened. Venom slid under my skin and my Order form rose like a fiery beast within me.

Flames licked along my arms and lit up the chamber in blood red tones.

Seth eyed me impassively but when I stepped forward, he squared his shoulders to face me.

Orion tugged me back a step and Seth smiled in satisfaction as the flames extinguished along my skin. I couldn't fight him, neither of us could. Because he was right, he did own us with this secret. We were bound to him by it unless we let the truth come out, but I couldn't bear for that to happen.

"Maybe I'll tell Nova myself and save you the bother," Orion said coldly.

"*Lance*," I hissed frantically. "You can't. I won't let you."

Seth watched our interaction with interest before looking to Orion. "You're bluffing. Because we both know there's more at risk than just your job or even your reputation. Which is why I'm kinda surprised you'd fuck a student, *Lance*. Was a bit of Vega pussy really worth it?"

Orion swung at him in a blur of motion, pinning Seth to the wall by the throat. "Don't you talk about her like that you piece of shit!"

Seth blasted him off of him with a powerful shot of air and Orion stumbled back with a snarl.

Seth flattened the ruffled feathers around his throat with a scowl. "Touch me again and I *will* fucking tell. It's not sinking in, is it? You'll both do what I say, *whenever* I say. Otherwise you can face the music, Professor."

I glanced at Orion with fear in my heart. "What else is at risk?"

Orion frowned deeply, not answering me and I hated that my answer came from Seth.

"Don't you get it, babe? You're a Solarian Princess, a fucking Vega Heir." He started laughing and it was a horribly callous sound that echoed off the walls. "Orion could go to prison for manipulating you."

"But he didn't," I gasped, shaking my head in denial.

The way Orion was avoiding my gaze made me terrified and when he spoke, his voice was hollow. "It depends what the papers say and what the Solarian Court believes. Even memories can be manipulated with magic, a Cyclops couldn't prove it for sure. So if there's enough doubt..." He shook his head, not finishing that sentence and pressure closed in on me from all sides.

I couldn't breathe. I couldn't face that happening. Not ever. I'd convince everyone in court that he didn't manipulate me. I'd make sure of it.

But even then...he'd still be power shamed and from the little I knew about that, it was one of the worst fates in Solaria. A Fae stripped of rank, forced to the bottom of the food chain. In a world where everything was about power, how could Orion ever bear it?

I turned to Seth who was giving us the only other option; do as he bid and our secret would stay between us.

"What do you want from us?" I demanded and Seth smirked.

"The short answer? Anything I fucking fancy."

A storm was rising around Orion but I placed a hand on his arm, begging him with my eyes. "We have to."

"*Blue*," he breathed, his gaze cracking with desperation.

"Please," I begged, knowing he'd face the court instead, but this had to be better than that. Even if the idea of doing as Seth told us repulsed me, I'd rather that than let Orion take the fall for our relationship. "If he tells Nova, we'll be ripped apart."

Orion's throat bobbed and sheer panic swept across his expression at my words. He squeezed my fingers in agreement and the tension ran out of my shoulders. "If he asks anything sexual of you, you will not fucking agree to it."

My mouth parted in horror at the idea that Seth would even think of doing something like that and I turned to him in alarm.

"I'm not a monster," Seth said with a taut frown. "Now fuck off back to Asteroid Place, Professor. Darcy's coming with me."

Orion didn't move, our hands still locked together.

"Did I not rub the lamp right?" Seth mocked. "I wish for you to fuck off." He snapped his fingers impatiently and Orion growled dangerously, bringing my hand to his mouth and laying a kiss on the back of it.

"You have to go," I said softly, seeing the conflict in his gaze.

I pulled my hand from his and his jaw ticked as he remained standing there a few seconds longer. He strode up to Seth with his fangs bared. "If you hurt her, I'll kill you. I don't care if you're an Heir or if I end up in Darkmore Penitentiary for the rest of my fucking life. I'll take any fate for her, so just remember that when you're playing your little game, Capella." He rammed his shoulder against Seth's then shot away with his Vampire speed in a blur.

My heart stuttered as I was left alone with my mortal enemy. His gaze dripped down to where my underwear still lay on the ground and my insides ripped to shreds.

"Put your panties on, babe. I can't wait to hear you tell everyone how good it felt to fuck an Heir."

SETH

CHAPTER TWENTY THREE

Darcy glared at me with a poisonous hatred in her eyes and I stared coolly back at her.

This is what you get for refusing to bow to me and for fucking a teacher like no rules apply to you in this world.

I moved towards her, taking in the smeared fake blood around her mouth, her ruffled hair and the bite mark on her lip that Orion hadn't had time to heal. I reached out to it and she flinched back.

"I'm healing it," I stated and she gritted her teeth, letting me press my thumb to her lip. I sent a flare of healing magic into her skin then dragged my thumb across her mouth to coat it in fake blood and lipstick, pulling my hand back and smearing it over my lips.

"What are you doing?" she hissed, looking disgusted and to be fair, it was pretty gross, but totally necessary.

"No one's going to think you screwed me if there isn't a little evidence."

"Why do you even want people to think that?" she snapped. "It's screwed up."

"Because it's fun, babe. And also because of the way it makes you feel. Like shit." *Which is how I've felt around you for a long fucking time. I'm owed some payback.*

And maybe, just fucking maybe, I was a teensy bit hurt I'd known she was screwing someone else, but I'd doubted what I'd seen the night of the Lunar Eclipse. It just kept circling back to me though. I'd tried waiting outside her Liaison sessions a couple of times, but Orion kept that room firmly silenced.

Still, a nagging thought inside me had willed me to keep looking. And then what do ya know? I'd seen her wrapped in his arms on the dance floor. Not that I'd been sure with his disguise in place, but I had a gut feeling. And I was determined to see the truth at last. So I'd given them long enough to compromise themselves then followed them down here. And that was the best decision I'd made in a long ass time.

Admittedly, I was still kinda surprised. Because Darcy always seemed like such a good little girl. And yet deep down, she was bad and twisted. But if she craved excitement like that, she didn't have to go and break Solarian law to get her kicks. *I mean seriously, a fucking teacher, Darcy??*

I pushed a hand into my hair, messing it up enough to be believable while Darcy surveyed me with a dark scowl. I was glad she felt something for me. Something that burned her up on the inside and couldn't be ignored. She deserved this. Because this was what she did to me in reverse.

"So who else knows about your secret? Tory?" I guessed and her face paled.

"No," she said quietly. "I didn't want to risk bringing her into this."

I released a low whistle. "Lying to your sister, that's low."

"Screw you," she snapped.

I was genuinely surprised. I imagined she would have mentioned that little piece of info to Tory, but apparently not. So one of the infamous twins was keeping secrets from the other. Maybe their united front was breakable after all.

"Here." I held out my hand for her to take and she reluctantly complied.

I yanked her toward me and she braced herself against my chest, pushing away from me. "Now's the part where you can let out a bit of that rage on me, Darcy. No need to hold back, if we actually fucked it would be rough as hell." I offered her my cheek and her brows arched.

"You want me to hit you?" she asked with way too much hope.

"Hit, scratch, bite, go nuts. But don't blame me if it turns me on."

Her palm smashed across my face and holy fuck she actually had a decent arm on her. I blew out a breath of laughter and she hit me across the head then clawed her nails down my arms with a furious snarl.

I backed up, smirking as she came for me like a hungry wolf, slamming her small fists into my chest. I caught her wrists when I'd had enough, grinning as her eyes spat venom at me.

"Come on then, babe." I slid my fingers between hers and tugged her along. "Let's go have some real fun."

She remained quiet as we walked and I stole a glance at her as tears glittered in her eyes. The way the two of them had reacted had been a bit surprising. Orion giving me a death threat over her made me think he had at least some kind of feelings for her, but Darcy? She couldn't like him like that. He was just some asshole teacher with failed dreams. I mean sure, he was ripped as fuck, magically powerful and I'd had plenty of my own wet dreams about him, but whatever.

"Smile babe," I instructed. "If your friends don't believe you – and that includes your mouthy sister –my tongue might start to loosen…"

She blinked up at me, setting her jaw. "I'm not going to pretend I like you as a person. Tory would never believe that anyway."

"Agreed. You're drunk and you hate-fucked me, cool?"

"Fine," she huffed. "But how long is this game going to last, Seth?"

"As long as I say it does." I shrugged and she blew out a breath of frustration.

We arrived back in the main cavern and I kept her hand firmly in my grip as people looked our way. Their eyes slid over our appearance and whispers were exchanged. I felt Darcy bristling beside me then she quickly hid it under a mask of indifference. I released her hand, pressing my palm to the small of her back instead and guiding her toward her friends across the room.

My heart sank when I realised I couldn't tell the other Heirs the whole story about this. I had to keep their affair a secret until I'd had my fun or Darius would tell me to stop for the sake of his pal Orion. But shit, I wasn't going to keep it completely to myself. I just wouldn't tell them what I had on her.

The fun had barely even begun tonight. By the end of the evening, Darcy and Tory Vega would be ruined. What we had planned was going to pull the rug out from under their feet. And now that I had control over one of them, things would be even easier. The night couldn't have gone more my way. And although Halloween was one of the most chaotic days of the year, I currently had Jupiter in my chart and that was the luckiest planet of them all.

Caleb spotted us first, his arms around Tory as they danced together. Even though he'd been pissed as all hell when he'd first seen her costume and had sworn to stay away from her all night. *Good job there, Cal.*

Darcy put on a casual expression and I was surprised at her acting skills. But then again, she had been fucking a teacher for who knew how long and no one else knew about it.

"Hey man," Caleb called, his eyes running over me and Darcy as the cogs worked behind his eyes.

Tory turned and I felt Darcy tense ever so slightly beside me.

Tory glanced between us like she couldn't work out what she was seeing. "Are you okay?" she blurted and Darcy glanced at me, her jaw tight.

"I'm fine, can we talk though?" she asked her sister, but I caught her arm before she could even think about leaving me out of this show.

Tory eyed my hand on Darcy's arm like she was about to rip it off.

I hooked my hand around Darcy's waist as she hesitated, pressing my mouth to her ear. "Don't leave them in suspense, babe."

She pushed away from me, shooting me a glare before moving to stand with Tory. "I did something stupid." She looked to me with pursed lips. "Him."

Tory's mouth fell open. "What? No you didn't," she refused.

"I did," Darcy sighed. "I need a drink." She tried to walk away but Tory caught her arm, shaking her head in disbelief.

Caleb's eyebrows shot to his hairline and he looked to me, silently communicating his question of *did you actually screw Darcy Vega?*

I shrugged innocently, but when I got a moment I was going to share this with him and he was gonna laugh his ass off.

Geraldine Grus appeared out of the crowd with an armful of punch and Darcy grabbed one of the cups, tossing it back and wiping the remaining fake blood from her mouth.

"Fried cannelloni, you could cut the tension here with a cake knife. What in the rave cave is going on?" Geraldine asked.

"Darcy says she screwed Seth," Tory said in disbelief and Darcy looked like she wanted to crawl into a hole in the ground and die. I smirked, absorbing her reaction and drinking in her discomfort.

Hurt for me, babe.

Geraldine's mouth fell slack and she passed another drink to Darcy who chugged the whole thing again.

"Did you choose to?" Tory demanded like she couldn't believe anyone would fuck me willingly.

I growled in anger at the accusation. *Fucking Vega.*

"Yeah," Darcy said, eyeing more of Geraldine's drinks hopefully. "It's not like I like him. It's just sex."

Tory frowned as if she didn't recognise her sister and that was probably the harshest blow I could have dealt Darcy. I almost felt bad about it. Not quite though.

Max and Darius arrived, obviously sensing drama and I nodded to them in greeting.

"Well spread me on a slice of honey wheat bread," Geraldine breathed, handing another drink to Darcy, but she didn't touch this one. "We've all gone down under to play on an Heir's dickeridoo. But you can put the instrument down, Darcy. I for one would never play it again in my life."

"Did I just get rejected again?" Max grumbled.

"I need some air." Darcy pushed her way through the crowd and Tory stormed after her.

Something bitter settled in my gut but I ignored it, clenching my jaw and turning to the Heirs. I'd won. This was a good thing. And I wasn't going to let anything ruin the sweetness of my victory.

Geraldine realised she was left alone with the four of us and promptly turned away with her head held high.

"Dude, did you really screw Darcy Vega?" Caleb asked in complete disbelief.

I cast a silencing bubble around us, a smile pulling at my mouth. "No," I revealed and they all gave me their undivided attention. "I've got something on her. Now she has to do what I say."

"What did you get?" Darius demanded.

I mimed zipping my lips. "Can't tell you that just yet, brother. But I will. All in good time."

Caleb rolled his eyes. "Just tell us, man."

"Be patient," I said simply. "And enjoy the show."

Max clapped me on the back with a look of excitement. "Right, well I'll get it out of you later, but right now we need to get on with the plan."

"Agreed," Darius growled, his eyes dark. "Come on." He moved forward and the crowd parted for us without any encouragement. Our silencing bubble moved with us as we went, keeping any nosey assholes from listening in.

"I don't know about this, guys," Caleb said and Darius growled deep in his throat. The tension between them made me uncomfortable. I hated having rifts in our pack.

I nuzzled against Caleb and he glanced at me with a frown as I tried to make him relax.

"We won't let it go *that* far," I encouraged.

"Pfft." Max turned to us with a scowl. "We'll let it go as far as it needs to." He glanced away again and I shared a look with Caleb that said I had his back. I knew the boundaries we had to walk within here.

Darius led us into a passage leading off from the main cavern and as soon as we were in the dark, he ran his hand across the wall, searching for the concealment spell we'd put there. A soft glow emitted from his palm then the crevice in the wall appeared, revealing where we'd stashed the potions in preparation.

Darius held onto the four vials, his gaze flipping between them. There was a deep red one, a dark purple one and two clear concoctions which were the antidotes to the coloured potions.

I swiped the purple one from his hand with an antidote and pocketed them. "I can deal with that easy enough."

"Caleb, you do it." Darius held out the other potion to him, but Caleb shrank from it.

"No way, bro. I'm not getting involved."

"Your ass must be getting pretty chafed up on that fence you're sitting on," Max growled. "You can't have it both ways. You're with us or you're with them."

"I'm not *with* them," Caleb said coolly. "But I'm not fucking with Tory."

"By the stars," I sighed, a low whine leaving my throat. I hated all this tension. Why were things so difficult these days? "Once the Vegas are out of the running for the throne, you can still mess around with Tory. It won't matter," I implored. "But we'll only get their submission if the whole world loses faith in them."

This was what we'd decided. So long as the Vegas had support, from their friends, from each other, from Solaria, they could dream all they liked about sitting on our throne. So we needed to take the air from under their wings.

Caleb nodded firmly. He wouldn't stop us, but he wouldn't help us either. "I'm not sticking around for it though," he added and he shot away from us before we could protest. So much for standing together.

"Fine, I'll fucking do it." Max snatched the potion from Darius's hand. I noted that Darius hadn't offered to do it either, but in fairness he probably wouldn't get near Tory without her ripping his head off. He kept the other antidote when Max didn't take it, pushing it into his pocket with a frown.

Max jerked his head at me and I walked away with him, glancing back at Darius as he scowled in the direction Caleb had taken. My heart hurt to know things were tense between them. I wanted to fix it, but I knew Caleb had no intention of cutting Tory out of his life altogether. We were all starting to accept that the Vegas were a pretty permanent fixture in our lives for the foreseeable future. But that was why it was so important to get them to submit. We needed to deal with this now before they got any stronger, any better trained.

"You're hurting," Max commented.

My skin prickled at his words. I never shielded my emotions from him, but at that moment I suddenly got defensive. "It's just Caleb and Darius, I hate that they keep fighting."

"No…it's not that," Max said in a low tone. "I felt it back on the dance floor. Is this about Darcy Vega?"

Her name sent ice trickling down my spine and I clenched my jaw, refusing to answer.

"If you're pining for her-"

"I'm not," I snarled more aggressively than I'd intended.

Max threw me a look, his eyes softening. "I get it, man," he said in an almost whisper. "I mean, I'm not exactly keeping my own shit together right now."

"Because of Grus?" I guessed.

I saw the way he looked at her, the way he kept talking to her, spending time in her general area. I'd never seen Max try so hard with anyone and none of us had called him out on it because we were pretty much all dealing with the same longing for forbidden fruit.

"Yeah," he grunted. "I feel like a fucking hypocrite. But Grus isn't a Vega..."

"Well I've got my Vega locked down," I said firmly.

"Right. *Your* Vega. Do you hear yourself? For the love of the moon, we need to all keep our heads."

"I know. I'm totally fine," I said firmly.

"Don't lie to my face," he said sadly and my stomach knotted. "I can feel it. And I'm not judging you, but whatever it is that happened between you and Darcy tonight is clearly bothering you. So find a way to deal with it."

"I am." And that was the truth. I had the perfect way to deal with it. I'd torture both her and her pet teacher until they were in fucking agony. That *was* dealing with it.

A growl rumbled through my chest and Max brushed his hand over my arm, drawing some of my anxiety into himself. I sighed as he pulled it away, loosening the thorns wrapped around my heart so I could breathe easier.

"Thanks," I murmured as we headed through the crowd.

I spotted Tory by the drinks table with a group of her friends and nudged Max in her direction. Darcy was nowhere in sight and I frowned as we arrived before the rest of them.

"Stay the fuck away from my sister!" Tory called, pointing at me in a way that was definitely a death threat.

I rolled my eyes. "Chill out, babe. You think you're the only one who can fuck around with an Heir and that's okay?"

"Caleb isn't like the rest of you," she hissed and Grus nodded her agreement beside her.

"Whatever. You don't know him," Max growled defensively. "We've been friends our entire lives. He will *always* pick us in the end."

Tory placed her drink down on the table, marching toward me with furious strides. She pulled up short in front of me and I folded my arms, gazing down at her and waiting for her anger to pour out.

"You're just a sad little mistake she won't even remember," she said venomously and Max slipped away beyond her.

For some reason, her words actually stung. It wasn't like I'd even screwed her sister, but I suddenly saw how much this girl detested me shining out of her eyes. On some level, I'd always thought of our back and forth as a game. This was just how Fae had to behave. I didn't hate the Vegas on any real level. It was just politics. But both of them despised me to my core. And something about that didn't sit right with me.

Max suddenly reappeared, clapping a hand to my shoulder. "Come on, let's go." His intense look said he'd successfully put the potion in Tory's drink and I strolled away with him as she returned to her friends. She swiped her drink from the side and took a sip and I pulled Max to a halt. "Watch her. If it goes too far, give her the antidote."

"Darius has it."

"Well go get it from him," I insisted, my heart pounding overly hard. *Are we going too far with this shit?*

I shook off the feeling, nodding in goodbye to Max and hunting for Darcy. I spotted her at a table with a bottle of water, sitting opposite her weak ass friend who always wore a hat. Couldn't recall his name. The guy's costume consisted of a couple of weird horns protruding from that awful fucking beanie and a brown T-shirt. *The fuck is he supposed to be? A horned turd?*

"Fuck off," I told him as I arrived and the guy had the gall to glare at me and not move.

"Go away Seth," Darcy demanded, her hand tightening around the water bottle in her grip.

"I need a word," I said firmly, a note of threat to my tone.

"I don't want to talk," she hissed and there was that look of hatred again.

"Well I do." I grabbed a chair. "Let's all have a nice little chat about our night then. I saw something interesting in one of the caves earlier…"

Darcy shot me daggers then turned to her friend. "Can you give us a minute? I'll come find you."

He frowned, looking uneasy but complying as he dropped out of his chair. "I'll be right over there," he said like that would be of any help to anyone.

I cast a silencing bubble around us and Darcy took another swig of her water. "What do you want?" she asked icily.

"I want you to drink this." I placed the little vial down in front of her, casting an illusory spell over it so the rest of the room would see nothing but another bottle of water.

"What – *no*," she gasped, pushing it back toward me, her eyes wide with fright.

She went to stand up but I caught her wrist. "It's not a request, babe. You know the deal, do as I say or Orion will pay the price."

"How can you be so awful?" she breathed like she really wanted to know the answer to that. The truth came to my lips, though she'd never get it.

I was raised to be ruthless, to step on heads and force other Fae down beneath me. It was the way of the Wolf and the way of Fae. With those needs combined, I was the fiercest Alpha in the entire world. One chink in my armour could mean me falling from grace. And without my throne, what did I have?

"Just drink it," I said in a flat tone, swallowing any and all emotion I had toward doing this. I could go to a dark place in my mind when I had to. Switch off. Check out. And that was where I needed to go now.

She shook her head. "What is it?" she asked like she actually thought I might poison her.

"Do you really think I'd kill a Vega Princess? I'm not a fucking idiot."

"Then what is it?" she snarled.

I sighed, uncorking the vial and dabbing a bit on my finger before licking it off. "See, not poison. Now drink." The potion tingled along my tongue and I swear the feathers around my neck shifted. *Fuck, this shit is strong.*

Darcy lifted the vial to her lips and I wondered whether she was really so self-sacrificing for another Fae. Did she actually care about the dude that much? I mean shit, the only people I'd drink some random potion for were the other Heirs or my mother.

Darcy shut her eyes like this decision physically hurt her then took a sip, then another. I shifted in my seat then snatched it away on instinct.

"That's enough," I muttered, stoppering the vial and stuffing it in my pocket. She was supposed to drink it all, but whatever. That shit was strong. It would be enough.

"Watch out for those ravens," I said, planting the thought in her head.

I slid out of my seat, giving her a lingering look as she stared after me in fear.

I ran a hand through my hair as anxiety rose its head in my chest. With a slow inhale, I forced it deep down into that locked box inside me where all my other uncomfortable emotions lived.

I moved back into the shadows at the edge of the cave, taking out my Atlas and spotting the other Heirs doing the same in preparation.

Tory was back on the dance floor, swaying to the beat, her hands in the air. My gaze flipped to Darcy and she flinched suddenly as if something had appeared in front of her. "What? No, I can't talk to you...you're not real." She scrunched up her eyes and shook her head. "No go away, go away."

A few people close by started watching her and I smirked.

"Shoo, birdy." Darcy wafted thin air with her hands, knocking her water bottle over. "All these birds just need to go somewhere they can fly free, its not safe in a place like this." She shook her head again, lost to the potion.

A second later, she screamed in alarm, jumping out of her seat. She held her hands above her head, ducking down and casting flames in her palms.

I started recording as she stumbled back into a group of people and pointed above her. "The ravens! They're everywhere! What can I do?" she cried in alarm. The potion would give her hallucinations for at least half an hour and we'd have plenty of footage by then.

She clamped her hands to her ears, garbling about the birds and people started laughing, taking out their own Atlases to record her. For some reason, I didn't laugh along. In fact, I didn't feel much at all.

I glanced over at Tory, finding her grinding against Milton Hubert before reaching for his friend too and guiding his hands around her with a moan. The two guys moved closer to her in excitement as she rubbed herself against them. The potion would make skin to skin contact feel fucking orgasmic and she was probably too drunk already to question it. My throat thickened. She was meant to act like a slut, not actually fuck anyone. If things went too far, someone was gonna have to swoop in with the antidote.

She placed their hands on her own shoulders and threw her head back as she delighted in the touch of the men around here. When Geraldine got close, she grabbed her hands too, whipping her dress off to give her access to more skin. *Oh fuck no.*

"Your highness!" Geraldine gasped and Max intervened, practically steamrolling her away before she could assist Tory. My heart pounded harder as I felt this getting out of control. The hat guy Darcy had been sitting with went over to help, but Tory just wrapped her arms around him too. He looked kind of terrified, but she wouldn't let him go.

Darcy fell to the ground in my periphery, air magic swooping out around her and knocking people off their feet. "What do I do about the birds?! Help me!" she begged.

People screamed as they ran away from the magic pouring from her and I hurried toward her, scooping her from the ground, feeling eyes on us as I clutched her to my chest. A bunch of students were recording us from every angle as Darcy looked up at me, her eyes wild and her pupils dilated. "The ravens. Do you see them? They're right behind you." She was breathing wildly and I held her tighter with one arm.

The crowd started applauding me for helping her as I pushed through them, glancing over my shoulder and searching for my friends. Darius was closing in on Tory so I knew he'd deal with her.

I carried Darcy out of the main cavern then started jogging along toward the exit. She continued to garble about ravens all the way back to Aer Tower.

I soon brought her to her room, fumbling her keys out of her purse and nudging the door open when I had it unlocked.

I laid her down on her bed, taking out the antidote and holding it to her lips. "Drink."

"They're still here," she muttered through the haze of her mind. "The shadows are all around me." She blinked and for a moment I swore darkness swirled in her gaze. This potion was some crazy shit.

I tipped the vial into her mouth and she spluttered but managed to swallow it down. She clung to my hand, flinching every time a vision flared up. "They're going to hurt me," she gasped.

"They're not. It's not real," I said firmly as her fingernails bit into my skin.

"Make them stop," she begged, rearing up and resting her head against my chest. I stiffened before slowly closing my arms around her. She wouldn't remember this anyway. Between the potion and the alcohol she'd consumed tonight, I might as well have been a ghost sitting here with her.

"Please," she whispered, her hands curling around me. "Make the Heirs stop."

My heart jolted as I held her, her words washing over me and making me feel like the biggest asshole in the history of the world. I tried to force that feeling down too, but it wouldn't go anywhere.

"They will," I said gently. "Just bow, Darcy."

"I can't…bow," she said, the call of sleep making her voice soft. I laid her down on the pillow and a couple more words slipped from her lips. "*I won't.*"

Her eyes fluttered closed and I realised I was still holding her hand.

I stared at her for far too long. The Vegas, to the very core of their beings, had iron wills. It was why we were trying this different tactic. But the frightening thing was, I saw my own will mirrored in hers at that moment. Even on the verge of oblivion, she fought. She refused to give in. That wasn't going to change. Just like the other Heirs and I were never going to give in.

I pulled my hand from hers and drew a blanket over her before slipping out of the door and shutting it firmly. I lingered there for ten whole seconds, at war with my emotions. I finally managed to bury them deep in the pit of my soul and walked away, plastering a smile on my face as I headed back to the party.

I'm Seth Capella. I'm not weak. I don't break for anyone. And I certainly won't break for a Vega.

DARIUS
CHAPTER TWENTY FOUR

A growl spilled from my lips as I stalked through the crowd of writhing bodies with my gaze firmly set on Roxy Vega. Heat coiled from my skin, hot enough to make everyone flinch away from me as my fire magic begged me to release some of this anger from my flesh. But I didn't have anywhere to aim it. Because the reason for my rage sat firmly on my shoulders. I'd chosen to go along with this. I'd made yet another strike against her, even though I was beginning to feel like these attacks wounded me more than her. She'd barely spared me a glance all night. I didn't even know what I wanted from her anymore, but the way she kept ignoring me was driving me insane.

I cut a beeline for her, her glittering skin making it easy to keep my eyes on her between the throng of bodies.

She was dancing with her eyes closed, her head tipped to the cave roof and her body simultaneously grinding against Milton fucking Hubert and that douchebag friend of hers in his fucking beanie hat. If I didn't cut this shit short fast, that fucking potion might have her doing more than just dancing suggestively.

"Roxy," I called, loud enough for the assholes surrounding her to hear me and back the hell away.

Roxy's eyes fluttered open as her dance partners abandoned her with fearful looks my way and she pouted like I'd just stolen her favourite teddy bear.

"What's up Dari-ass?" she asked, laughing at her own joke as she continued to dance on her own.

My gaze raked over her hungrily. She was almost unrecognisable with her skin covered in silver Pegasus glitter and her hair dyed to look like a rainbow, but she looked good enough to eat.

I couldn't help but admire her balls, turning up here, wearing that even though she knew it would rile Caleb up. And despite his feelings on the subject, I couldn't help but think of it as pretty damn funny. It made her look like some kind of ethereal creature, mysterious in her beauty.

She didn't dance alone for long, her gaze fixing on me as she moved straight towards me.

My lips parted in surprise as she coiled her arms around my neck, pulling her near naked body flush against my bare chest.

A moan of ecstasy escaped her and my heart leapt as I caught hold of her and tried to peel her back off of me. As much as I'd fantasised about holding her like this, I didn't even take any pleasure in the moment. She wasn't herself, that damn potion was making her act this way and I needed to get rid of the effects of it fast.

"I got you a drink," I said, holding out the tequila shot which held the antidote to the potion we'd slipped her.

She eyed it for a moment before taking it from my hand and knocking it back.

As the potion took effect, she slowly stopped dancing, stepping away from me and frowning around herself like she wasn't quite sure what was going on. It should really just feel like sobering up a bit and I was hoping that was what she'd put it down to.

I bent down and retrieved her dress from the floor, holding it out for her as my gut writhed uncomfortably. We'd wanted to make sure we got good footage of her dancing with plenty of guys, but if I'd thought for a second the potion would make her act like *that* I never would have let her drink a drop of it.

Roxy took her dress from me and pulled it on with a slight frown like she couldn't work out how she'd ended up out of it in the first place.

Part of me wanted to turn away and leave her here rather than face the shame of what we'd almost just let happen to her. But I couldn't just abandon her here while she was looking so confused. I needed to make sure she got back to her bed. If I just knew she was safe tonight then I could put this whole mess down to a terrible fucking idea and forget about it. I'd stopped her before anything too bad had happened anyway. So I would just have to convince myself there was no harm done. Even if I did feel like a sack of shit right about now.

"This party's getting old. You wanna head back to your dorm? I can walk you," I offered, wondering if she was about to tell me to fuck off. Or if I'd have to toss her over my shoulder and drag her back there against her will. Either way, I was more than done with letting the assholes at this party gawp at her and I needed to be sure she was safe.

I held out my hand and she raised an eyebrow as she looked at it.

"Truce?" I offered. "From now until tomorrow we can just pretend to like each other. Or at least not hate each other."

The moment stretched and I grew a little self-conscious as my hand hung in the space between us.

"Maybe I'm always pretending to hate you," she said eventually and I stilled as she reached out and took my hand. She looked up at me from beneath lashes which sparkled with the colours of the rainbow and my heart pounded at the impossibility of that suggestion. Because whether I wanted to admit it or not, the idea that she might not hate me appealed to me in a desperate kind of way. "Or maybe I'm not," she added, snuffing out that little ray of hope just as quickly as she'd offered it.

I didn't know why the hell that made me smile, but it did.

I curled my fingers around her small hand and drew her through the crowd towards the exit. She was still half dancing as we went, laughter spilling from her lips as she caught sight of a few members of the Ass Society who'd chosen to dress as Sirens with a dump fetish. They'd painted scales on their bodies and then smeared big clods of brown mud over themselves to finish the look. I was guessing Max hadn't spotted them or I imagined they'd be dangling from the roof by their ankles by now.

I half wondered if I should confront them over it just as Roxy gripped my arm and pointed in the opposite direction, laughing again.

I followed the line of her arm to see two girls who had dressed themselves up as the Vegas. They were both wearing dresses that looked like they would have been at home in The Savage King's court and had towering crowns on their heads. They'd added sashes to their costumes with the names Gwendalina and Roxanya scrawled over them and were putting on a good show of drawing attention to themselves.

"Doesn't that piss you off?" I asked Roxy in surprise, turning to look down at her.

"Oh lighten up, Darius. If you can't laugh at yourself from time to time then you're going to end up spending a lot of your life taking offence over things that really don't matter." Roxy rolled her eyes at me like I was ridiculous and I frowned as I tried to accept the fact that she genuinely didn't care.

Before I came up with a response, she tugged her hand from my grip and slipped away from me between the crowd.

I cursed under my breath and darted after her. By the time I caught her, she was half way up the long tunnel which led back out of the cavern.

"I'm covered in glitter," she pointed out like I might not be able to see the fact that her whole body was covered in the shimmering silver substance.

"I noticed," I replied.

"Well I'm gonna go wash it off," she announced.

"Sure. We'll be back at the dorms soon and then you can have a shower."

Roxy sighed like that answer disappointed her, but she didn't elaborate. We made it out of the cavern and she looked up at the sky for a moment, pursing her lips as she thought about something. My heart pounded wildly as she looked my way and a smile captured her lips. Roxy didn't smile at me. Certainly not since the Eclipse. And I couldn't really blame her for that. But until that moment I didn't think I'd let myself appreciate how much it would mean to me if she did.

In the next heartbeat I realised why she was though as her wings burst from her back, punching holes into her dress as red and blue flames licked along the feathers and she flexed them to their full width. She stopped the transformation into her Order form there and I couldn't help but be mildly impressed that she'd managed to learn that much control in the short time since she'd Emerged.

"Catch you later, dude," she said, laughing as she leapt into the sky and started flying for the moon.

Shit.

"Where are you going?" I called after her as she beat her wings and climbed towards the heavens above us.

"Swimming!" she shouted back before flying away with a laugh like escaping from me was just so damn hilarious.

Fuck.

I unbuckled my pants and kicked my shoes off before rolling my clothes into a ball so that I'd be able to carry them.

A ripple of energy coursed along my spine as I called on my Dragon and a moment later, my claws slammed into the dirt as my Order form ripped free of my flesh.

I grabbed the bundle of clothes in my mouth before springing up into the air to chase after Roxy Vega.

Branches battered at my wings, catching on my scales as I fought my way out of the canopy and eventually I burst into the sky with a growl burning along my throat.

I beat my wings as I flew higher, turning my head until I spotted the fire of Roxy's wings in the distance.

With a powerful flap of my wings, I took off after her, chasing her through the sky as she headed towards The Orb and the other buildings at the centre of campus.

I started gaining on her but before I got close enough to catch her, she dropped out of the sky and disappeared from sight.

Cursing internally, I raced after her, diving for the ground as I reached the spot where I'd last seen her flaming wings.

I headed straight for the curved roof of The Orb and the metallic structure echoed hollowly as the considerable weight of my Dragon form came to rest on top of it.

I twisted my head left and right as I tried to spot her but she was nowhere to be seen.

Cursing to myself, I leapt down to the ground, transforming back into my Fae form just before I landed between The Orb and the crescent shaped building that housed Lunar Leisure and the pool. I glanced that way, spotting the door ajar and frowning as I wondered if she'd really meant it when she'd said she was going swimming.

I grabbed my clothes from the floor, dragging my pants back on quickly before kicking my feet back into my shoes. I jogged over to the open door, pausing to look at it as I spotted two little wooden picks abandoned in the keyhole.

"Roxy?" I called, stepping into the dark building and out of the cold night air.

There was no response but I carried on, stepping into the huge gym and passing the various pieces of weight and cardio equipment before heading on towards the pool.

As far as I knew, Roxy hadn't come here since the night Max and I had trapped her beneath the water and my gut twisted uncomfortably as the scent of chlorine awoke memories of that night in me.

I stepped out onto the dark tiles which lined the pool and stilled as I spotted Roxy floating in the centre of the water with her eyes closed. Her dress was abandoned alongside her shoes at the edge of the pool but she'd kept her silver underwear on for her swim.

A huge cloud of glitter was spreading away from her body as she lazily swept her arms back and forth and I guessed she'd used magic to undo whatever had been holding the glitter in place on her skin.

"Are you just going to stand there staring or are you coming in?" Roxy asked without opening her eyes.

I cleared my throat, moving closer to the edge and trying not to think about what I'd done to her the last time we were here.

"Or maybe you've come to finish what you started last time?" Roxy asked, her mind clearly following the same trail as mine.

"If you're worried about that then why did you come here?" I asked.

She sighed before dropping beneath the water and swimming towards me.

I watched her as a long trail of glitter was left in her wake and she slowly surfaced right in front of me, placing her arms on the edge of the pool as she looked up at me with her big, green eyes. There was something about the way that she looked at me sometimes that made me feel like she could see through every wall I put up, spot every lie and piece of armour I wore and look straight upon the creature which hid in the depths of my soul.

"I came because all I want is to be free. And fear shackles you just as easily as chains if you let it. So do your worst…or don't. I can't control what you choose to do, but I *can* choose what *I* do."

Before I could reply, she climbed out of the pool, letting the water run down her body and take the glitter with it.

I couldn't help but stare at her as she stood in her underwear, her eyes dancing with the fire of her Phoenix as she looked up at me like she was waiting for something. But I seriously had no idea what that might be.

A part of me wanted to reach for her and my gaze drifted to her mouth as my imagination got carried away for a moment, but I managed to take a step back instead.

Roxy looked up at me, pushing her hands through her wet hair which was still coloured like a rainbow and drawing the water out of it with her magic. She siphoned every drop from her body and underwear before heading past me to grab her dress and push her feet back into her stilettos.

"When was the last time you ever did something just for the hell of it?" she asked me teasingly as she started walking backwards, drawing me after her as she headed towards the diving boards.

"What do you mean?" I asked.

"Like, when did you last do something pointless, with no ulterior motives?"

"I'm hanging out with you now," I pointed out.

She scoffed lightly. "Oh so you've got zero agenda with me, have you? That'd be a first."

I held my tongue because she was right. I did always have an agenda when it came to her, though sometimes, like right now, it seemed like I wasn't even sure what that was. I was supposed to be getting rid of her, but the idea of that tore me in two at the same time as me knowing it was necessary.

"Come on." She grabbed the ladder for the high board and started climbing with a hint of laughter in her voice.

I frowned as I watched her go, wondering what the hell she was even doing while knowing whatever it was, I wanted to be doing it with her.

I followed her all the way up to the top where she stepped out onto the diving board above the water.

She walked forward carefully then dropped down to sit on the very end of the board, her legs swinging beneath her over the water.

I moved to sit beside her, leaving an inch of space between us despite the fact that I wanted to pull her close. I sighed, running a hand over my face. This whole thing was so fucked. I'd set her up tonight, gone out of my way to hurt her yet again but here I was, sitting in the dark with her, aching to touch her, stealing glances at her like some kid with a crush. Why was everything so difficult with her? It should have been simple, no matter what she looked like or how hot I thought she was, I shouldn't have been agonising over the idea of getting rid of her.

Maybe once it was done, I'd be able to move on from this, forget about her. But as she leaned back to lay on the diving board and the white dress she was wearing rode up, revealing the bronze skin of her thighs and another glimpse of her underwear, I knew that was an empty hope.

I'd never hungered for someone like I did for her.

And it wasn't just the way she looked, every time she bit at me or fought back against me, the beast inside me raised its head. She was more than just some girl who posed us a threat. She was a real challenge, unafraid of me no matter what I threw at her and capable of matching or even besting me in every way. I'd never met a girl like her before. She was my equal. She had no interest in my power or my name so every piece of attention she threw my way was earned by *me*. She actually cared about who I was over *what* I was. And even though she hated what she found most of the time, she still saw me. And the idea of that was as exhilarating as it was terrifying.

"Is Xavier texting Sofia?" she asked all of a sudden and my lips parted at that strange question.

"Yes," I said eventually because it seemed pointless to lie to her about it. "He can't tell her who he really is, obviously. But I wanted him to have someone of his kind to talk to, some contact with a herd…" I trailed off because giving him the phone number of one girl to message seemed like a pretty pathetic way to help him, but I didn't know what else to do.

"I take it Lionel still won't let him reveal his Order to anyone?" she asked.

I laughed but it was a hollow, empty thing. "Never."

Roxy pursed her lips like that pissed her off but she didn't add anything else.

"And how's your lovely fiancé?" she asked, a smirk playing around her mouth as she changed the subject.

"Fuck knows," I replied on a growl. "Father keeps mentioning getting her to transfer here from her academy so that we can get to know each other better. I heard him saying he expects us to get married the year after I graduate..."

The horror of that idea haunted me most nights before I slept. The worst thing of it all being that I knew I'd end up going through with it if I couldn't challenge him by then. He'd just use his Dark Coercion to force me if I tried to refuse anyway.

"Why don't you just run away?" she teased. "Is your precious throne so important to you that you'd trade your happiness for it?"

I smirked at her as I lay down too, turning my head to look at her in the dim light. She swung her legs back and forth and the board bounced beneath us.

"Where should I go?" I asked. "The Azerian Desert? Or the Polar Capital? Maybe I should just go to the mortal realm and set myself up there?"

Roxy shrugged like those ideas weren't entirely insane. "Better that than a life in chains," she said simply.

I parted my lips to respond but what could I say? It was anything *but* simple. I'd been born to rule, everything I was, everything I'd endured to get to this point was all in the aid of that. I could never be satisfied with a simple life, hiding in the shadows. Besides, I had responsibilities here. To my brother, the Heirs, Solaria as a whole. I wouldn't just turn my back on them.

Roxy yawned widely and I was reminded of what Lance had told me about her struggling to sleep since the shadows had been forced on her. I hadn't struggled too much with them yet, but then I had years of practice with dark magic and learning to keep the shadows at bay.

"Shall we go back to our dorms?" I asked, forcing myself to look away from her to the pool which was now filled with so much glitter that I wasn't even sure how the hell anyone would clean it out. I imagined there would be a very angry janitor in here tomorrow.

Roxy shrugged but got to her feet, the diving board flexing beneath us as I stood too.

I took her hand and she looked at me in surprise as I tugged her towards the edge. She only hesitated for a moment before letting me guide her closer to the drop and I smiled as I caught her around her waist, hoisting her into my arms.

She shrieked but it wasn't in fear, her voice lined with laughter as I held her close and leapt off of the diving board.

Roxy cried out, her arms winding around my neck as we fell, but before we could hit the water, I flexed my fingers, forcing it to fall under my command. A column of water flicked up like a whip, winding around us and shifting us over the pool before depositing us on the edge of it.

Roxy's eyes widened at my use of magic and I smirked at her as I started walking towards the exit.

"You're so fucking smug," she mocked but her tone was teasing.

"I can't help it if you're impressed by me," I replied and she rolled her eyes.

"I'm not impressed by that. If you want to impress me, you'll have to do something better than that."

"Like what?"

She shrugged, her arm shifting around my neck and the touch of her fingertips against my skin sending energy darting down my spine. "I'm not the one who has trouble breaking the rules," she teased, pushing out of my arms so that she could walk beside me.

I instantly missed the warmth of her body against mine but if she felt the same, she didn't let it show.

We walked back out of Lunar Leisure in silence and I watched her from the corner of my eyes.

"I don't have my dorm key," she announced as we made it back out into the cold air outside. "Sofia has it..."

"So come and stay with me," I replied instantly, wanting her close despite all the reasons that I shouldn't.

Roxy turned to look at me and the heat in her gaze made my heart pound and my resolve weaken. I couldn't help but wonder just how drunk she must be to be spending time with me like this. And if I was being totally honest, I was pretty sure she must have been close to wasted. Because Roxy Vega wouldn't give me the time of day if she was sober and right now she was looking at me like I was the only person in the world.

"I dunno," she said slowly. "There's a *lot* of stairs to climb to get all the way up to your fancy ass room. Maybe I'll just curl up on the floor outside mine and wait for Sofia to show up."

I barked a laugh and an idea occurred to me. An utterly ridiculous, absolutely irrational idea. But the mere thought of it made my heart pound faster and I couldn't help but be tempted by the possibility of proving to her that I didn't just blindly follow the rules all the time.

"I left my window open," I said slowly. "I can give you a ride up there."

Her eyes widened as she realised what I was offering. And sure, she could just use her own wings to fly up there but riding on a Dragon was practically against the law. Especially if you asked my father. He could banish me from the Dragon's guild if he found out. I could hear him now, *Dragons are not pack horses*. But I didn't give a shit. I'd break that rule for her. Hell, I was beginning to wonder if I wouldn't break a few more for her too.

A slow smile crept across Roxy's face and she moved nearer to me. "What are you waiting for then, Dragon boy?" she teased. "You'd better take your pants off."

I barked a laugh and stepped closer to her as I unbuckled my belt. I couldn't quite figure out if I was drunk or going insane but I had to admit I liked it.

Roxy's gaze fell to my movements and I paused as I unzipped my fly.

"Are you literally gonna stand there and stare at me while I get naked?" I asked.

"Like you did when you burned all my clothes off of me on my first day?" she countered, arching a brow at me.

I pushed my tongue into my cheek and dropped my pants, but her gaze stayed fixed on my eyes.

"If you could bring my clothes I'd appreciate it," I said slowly and she nodded seriously like I'd just tasked her with something really important.

"Could you get in trouble for doing this?" she breathed.

"Why do you sound concerned about that?" I teased. "I'm pretty sure trouble's what turns you on."

Roxy laughed and my heart leapt at the sound of me making her happy.

I turned away from her, taking a few steps to make sure I had enough room before drawing the Dragon free of my flesh.

My skin tore apart and the huge beast which lay within me sprang free, my claws gouging lines in the path as I shifted into my Order form.

Roxy gasped in surprise but she didn't back away. I turned my head to look at her and she stooped to grab my abandoned clothes before slowly approaching. She looked so small and delicate standing beneath me as I towered over her as the king of beasts, but there wasn't any fear in her gaze as she moved closer. Only excitement.

I dropped into a crouch and lowered one of my huge, golden wings so that she could climb up onto my back.

My skin tingled as she clambered on, a trickle of adrenaline entering my limbs at the knowledge of defying my father like this and with a Vega of all people. He'd probably be having a mini heart attack right about now if he sensed it.

Roxy made it onto my back, her thighs tightening around me and her hands gripping one of the huge spines which protruded between my shoulder blades.

Hold on tight, Roxy.

With a powerful leap, I spread my wings and took off into the night. Roxy whooped excitedly, her grip on me firming as I flew higher and higher, the academy shrinking away to nothing but pinpricks of light beneath us as I beat a path straight to the stars.

Once I was high enough, I tucked my wings close to my body and free fell straight towards the ground again.

Roxy screamed as we plummeted and I released a plume of Dragon fire as my own excitement grew with hers, the flames whipping around us and away into the night.

I snapped my wings out before we could hit the ground and shot skyward again, spinning in circles and bathing in the laughter that spilled from her lips as she clung on for dear life.

I finally headed back towards Ignis House, carving a path through the sky to my bedroom at the highest point of the glass structure.

I landed carefully, gripping onto the building with my talons and creating a bridge with my wing for her to use to get in through the window.

Roxy jumped inside and I pushed off of the building, turning in a wide circle as I headed back towards the window once more.

I flew straight at the opening, shifting back into my Fae form just as I reached it and jogging several steps as I landed inside.

Roxy had moved across my room and taken a seat at my desk, kicking her feet up onto it and giving me a look at her long legs as she hooked a letter off of the pile to the left of the wooden desktop.

I moved to my closet, pulling on a pair of boxers and sweatpants as she tugged the letter from the envelope with a dramatic flourish. I didn't move to stop her, that pile was full of fan mail which I basically just let sit there endlessly without bothering to read it. There were a few too many weirdos in Solaria who liked to write to me and I was generally of the opinion that I was better off not reading the things they sent me most of the time.

"*Dear Darius,*" Roxy purred, dropping her voice seductively. "*I recently read the article published about you in Fae Weekly, and I have to say, I did not realise you were so fond of baking* – is that true?" Roxy asked, looking up from the letter with an eyebrow raised at me.

I rolled my eyes. "They asked me what new hobbies I'd taken up recently and I said that as a joke," I supplied, dropping down onto my bed so that I could watch her as she continued to read.

"Yeah, of course. I doubt you can do anything for yourself like that," she mocked and there wasn't really much I could say in protest because it was true. I'd grown up in a house that had more servants than family members residing in it. The idea of me baking was pretty ridiculous. She lifted the letter again as she kept reading. "*I will admit, I did enjoy perusing the photographs included with that piece too. Particularly the one of you running on the beach with the other Heirs* – oh she has a point there, I saw that and you did look hot," Roxy commented, making my heart lurch in a strange way. But she continued as if there was nothing at all odd about her admitting she found me attractive. "*I've included a gift with this letter in the hopes that when you catch the scent of me from it, you may seek me out and hunger for me just as I hunger for you.* What does she mean a gift?" Roxy asked, hooking the envelope back off of the desk and drawing another piece of paper out of it.

"Ohmagawd!" Roxy shrieked, dropping the letter and leaping to her feet in disgust. "There's hair taped to that and it did *not* look like head hair!"

She backed away from the letter so quickly that she lost her balance in her stilettos and I reached out to catch her as she fell back towards me.

Her weight collided with me and I laughed as I tipped backwards onto the bed, pulling her with me.

I rolled her over, pressing her back so that she was pinned beneath me and she looked up at me, laughter tumbling from her lips. I fell still. My heart was pounding and my gaze slid from her eyes to her mouth.

"I must be fucking insane to be alone with you like this," she breathed. "You'll probably just go right back to making my life hell tomorrow."

I frowned at that comment even though it almost seemed like she was joking. "And you'll go right back to hating me," I replied.

"I haven't stopped."

Silence fell between us and I shifted back an inch. "There's probably good reason for that."

Her brow furrowed but I didn't elaborate. She'd realise what we'd done when the story broke tomorrow. And as much as I was aching to close the distance between us, I couldn't do it. Not when I knew she'd regret it as soon as she found out about what me and the other Heirs had done...

I shifted back suddenly, getting to my feet and grabbing my Atlas from the pants she'd dropped beside my bed.

"I'm just going to have a shower," I said, backing away from her. "You can watch TV or whatever you like."

"Okay…" she replied, not bothering to hide her confusion as I walked into the bathroom. But it didn't matter if she thought I was behaving strangely. I just needed to get hold of Seth before he sent those videos to the paper.

I closed the door and locked it before pulling up the messages on my Atlas.

Darius:

I don't think this is the right way to deal with things after all. Don't send those videos.

Seth:

Right. Just the small issue of the fact that I already did it about an hour ago. And they just sent me the link to the story on their website...

Fuck!

I snarled, tossing my useless Atlas away from me like it was personally responsible for that story making it out to the press already. Like I hadn't just fucked everything up again. Like I always fucking did.

I headed into the shower, setting it hot and letting it scald my skin as my anger at myself reared up inside me and a deep growl left my throat.

By the time I'd calmed down enough to return to my room, I found Roxy fast asleep in my bed.

I approached her slowly, dropping down to sit on the edge of the mattress with my thoughts warring amongst themselves.

She reached out sleepily, taking my hand in hers and pulling me down to join her. And I let her. Because I was weak and selfish. And because I knew this had been my last chance to prove to her that I could be more than just the asshole who made her miserable and I'd fucked it up. It felt like this had been a test and I'd failed before I'd even begun.

I lay down and she curled against me, laying her head on my chest and fitting so perfectly into the curve of my body that it was like she'd been made to fit there.

The ache in my chest lessened as I held her close, my fingers toying with the rainbow coloured strands of her hair as her heavy breathing fluttered against my skin.

I wasn't even sure if I'd be able to sleep. Because I knew that in the morning this peace would be shattered. And once again, I only had myself to blame.

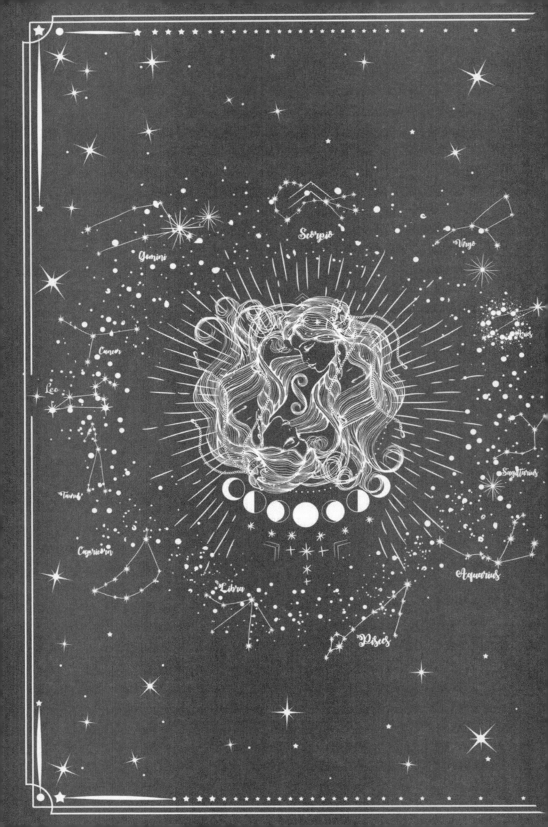

TORY

CHAPTER TWENTY FIVE

For the second time in my life, I woke feeling warm, safe and content in someone's arms. Though unlike the last time, I remembered enough of last night to know precisely whose bed I'd just woken up in.

Darius's arm held me close but his grip was loose, his breathing steady as he slept.

I opened my eyes slowly, looking at my hand where it lay on his chest. The edges of his tattoos called to me and my fingers twitched with the desire to trace the lines of them across his skin

Instead of acting like some kind of lovestruck lunatic, I pushed myself upright and ran a hand through my hair as I looked down at him.

He looked so peaceful in sleep, all of the hard lines of his usual scowls and glares replaced with a softness that was hard to marry with the man I knew him to be.

I scooted away from him, my head throbbing from the alcohol I'd consumed last night as I looked around for some way to tell the time.

I spotted his Atlas laying on his nightstand and touched the screen to illuminate it. My lips parted in shock as I saw it was almost eleven am. I hadn't woken in a cold sweat, I hadn't started screaming so loud the guy in the next room had to come pounding on my door to shut me up. Hell, I couldn't actually remember hearing the call of the shadows at all during the night. And

I'd slept for at least ten hours. I hadn't managed more than four in a row since the night of the Eclipse.

For a moment, I wondered if it was the drinks I'd had but in all honesty, I'd been putting away that much alcohol most nights in an attempt to banish the shadows when I slept.

No. That wasn't what had kept them away from me. And I was willing to bet the comfy ass mattress wasn't the culprit either.

My gaze slid over Darius again and I chewed on my lip as I considered that. The duvet was pooled in his lap and his bare chest revealed the myriad of tattoos which covered his skin. There were dark flames dancing up the left side of his chest and figures rose from them in a way that was either filled with hope or pain depending on the way I looked at them.

I shifted away again, pulling my eyes from the art on his skin and feeling like a bit of a stalker for staring so much.

My head spun dizzily again and I reached out for the top drawer of his nightstand, hoping to find some painkillers lurking there to save me from my hangover.

Instead of painkillers, the drawer held a sheaf of paperwork but before I could close it again, my gaze snagged on the title. It was a copy of a letter from his financial adviser and the top page detailed a summary of the last year's charitable contributions he'd made.

I read the names of the charities he'd given money to with interest.

True You Centre for Fae with Order Disassociation
One Stop Women's and Children's Shelter
The Pegasus Herd Relocation Association
Re-life Fund for New Identities for Fae Escaping Power Abusive Homes

He'd donated tens of thousands of auras to each of the charities and done it all under a false name so none of the credit came back to him. I re-read the names again, noticing the fact that two of them were to do with Xavier and wondering if the two women's shelters were relevant to him too.

"What the fuck are you doing?" Darius's hand locked around my wrist so tightly that it hurt and I gasped, dropping the page I'd been reading as well as the ones beneath it as I tried to tug my arm out of his grip.

"Ow," I protested, twisting around to face him and finding his eyes full of rage. "Let go, you're hurting me."

"Is this why you stayed here last night?" he accused. "So that you could snoop through my things while I was sleeping?"

"What? No! I was looking for painkillers for my hangover and-"

"What the fuck is a painkiller?" he demanded and for a moment I could only blink at him stupidly before realising that of course they didn't have drugs like that in Solaria. Everyone here used magic to heal things like headaches but in my hungover state I'd just fallen back on default methods, not to mention the fact that I was yet to learn how to use healing magic anyway.

"It's a mortal thing," I muttered, yanking on my arm again.

"Bullshit," he snarled, his gaze falling on the papers which were now scattered all over his carpet. "I should have known you wouldn't have been spending time with me without a motive."

"I didn't have a motive," I snapped. "You're the one who asked me to come back here. I didn't want to look at any of your fucking stuff. I just-"

"You probably should have put out if you wanted to wear me out enough to get away with this shit," he said coldly, his grip on my arm tightening painfully as that statement sent a dagger of ice into my chest.

For a moment I could only stare at him, wondering how fucked up his life must be if he seriously thought the only reason someone might have wanted to spend time with him would be to get something out of it.

His gaze was dark and full of anger and I could see he'd convinced himself of this bullshit story no matter what I said. And why should I even have been justifying myself to him anyway? I'd told him the truth of it and if he didn't want to hear it then that wasn't my problem.

"You're hurting me," I repeated when he still didn't let me go.

He released me suddenly, shoving my arm away from him so that I almost fell off of the bed. I stumbled to keep my balance and backed away from him as the shadows rose beneath my skin hungrily.

His accusing gaze followed me as I made it to the door and I gripped the handle behind my back.

"Don't come looking for me the next time you get too drunk to take care of yourself," he said coldly and the knife he'd driven into my gut twisted sharply.

I hadn't come looking for him and he knew it. He'd sought me out like he always did and like a fucking idiot I'd fallen for his charm. But this was going to be the last time.

"Fuck you," I hissed, pulling the door open and stepping back into the corridor. I swung the door shut between us and jogged away from his room as fast as I could without full on running.

I hurried down the stairs and headed straight for Sofia's room where I started hammering on the door as soon as I arrived.

"We're busy!" Tyler's voice came from beyond the door and I growled in frustration.

"I need my door key so press pause on the banging for thirty seconds please!"

Sofia's laughter came in response to that and a moment later the door opened a crack. I caught a glimpse of Tyler's bare chest and a cushion pressed over his junk as he shoved the key into my hand.

"I'll meet you in The Orb in half an hour!" Sofia's voice came from the depths of the room as Tyler pushed the door closed again.

"More like an hour," he replied cockily.

"Pfft, you wish," Sofia laughed and I smirked to myself as I headed away to my own room.

As soon as I got inside, I headed for a shower. The rainbow hair dye I'd used for my Pegasus costume had come with an anti-dye potion and I was ready to return to my brunette glory. Besides, rainbow hair was a little too cheery for my personality, especially as I'd woken up on the wrong side of the wrong goddamn bed today.

My Atlas pinged as I made it to the bathroom door and I paused, glancing at it to discover a bunch of messages from Darcy.

I frowned as I clicked on them, finding demands for my whereabouts and a plea for me to meet her in The Orb as soon as I could. I sent her back a quick message to say I was having a shower and she replied to say she'd have lunch waiting for me.

We were seriously in need of some twin on twin time anyway. I still couldn't believe she'd pulled a Tory and hooked up with that asshat Seth and I needed to make sure she was okay with what had happened now that it was the cold light of day.

I wasn't entirely sure if something more was up with her or not so I made my shower as quick as possible and dressed in a black sweater and red skirt before slipping my Atlas into my pocket and jogging down to The Orb.

I arrived at the same moment as Max showed up and he gave me a wide smile, standing back to let me walk through the door ahead of him.

"Have you woken up with a personality transplant today?" I joked as I stepped in ahead of him.

"No, little Vega. It's just a beautiful day. Have you by any chance read The Celestial Times today?" he asked innocently, though the twinkle in his eyes made me think that question was anything but innocent.

"Erm, no," I replied. "I don't really read it all that often. It's full of fluff pieces about you and your buddies or bullshit about me and my sister more often than not, so I don't bother."

"Well, I suggest you make an exception. Just for today." He grinned widely and strolled away from me before I could reply, making a beeline for the Heirs' red couch where Seth and Caleb already sat.

My gaze snagged on Caleb for a moment, but he just frowned as he spotted me before looking away again. Last night he'd alternated between avoiding me and dancing with me before he bailed on the party altogether. I got that he hadn't found the whole Pegasus thing funny, but the issue I had with that was that he was wrong. That shit *was* funny. Stupid funny. And he needed to stop pouting like a little bitch about it and learn to laugh at himself from time to time.

I turned away from the Heirs, hunting down Darcy and the *Ass* Club and finding them sitting together on the far side of the room.

Before I could get close to them, Caleb shot through the room and snatched me off of my feet and carried me straight back out of the room.

"What the hell?" I demanded as he set me back on my feet at the back of The Orb, caging me in against the wall with his arms, his hands pressed flat to the curving structure either side of my head.

"I've had my family's PR guy on the phone to me this morning," he said in place of a greeting.

"So?" I demanded.

"*So,* he had to intercept a photograph of you and me dancing together last night while you were wearing that fucking Pegasus costume before it got to the press."

"Well I didn't send it," I replied, rolling my eyes. "And who gives a shit anyway?"

"After those fucking rumours you started, quite a lot of people give a shit. I can't have those kinds of whispers going around about me."

"Whatever, dude. That shit was funny. Still is. It's not my problem if you can't take a joke. Besides, you were the one who came and danced with me after saying you couldn't hang out with me all night. So take it up with yourself." I shrugged and tried to step away from him but he growled, not letting me go.

"You might not get it yet, but for people like us reputation is *everything,"* he said darkly. "Although I think you're about to realise that too."

"Are you threatening me?" I asked, narrowing my eyes.

"It's too late for that," he replied dismissively. "But I mean what I'm saying Tory. You need to cut that shit with my reputation. I don't think you're getting the message-"

"It's coming through pretty clear," I countered, narrowing my eyes. "You already told me once before that I wasn't good enough for you. And now you're calling me an embarrassment too."

Caleb's gaze darkened but he didn't deny what I'd said. "I just don't think you get me at all sometimes," he growled.

"Oh I get you. Your reputation means more to you than having a laugh or happiness or basically anything fun. And if I'm damaging your public persona so hard then why don't you just stay away from me?"

"Maybe I will," he bit back.

"Maybe you should," I agreed.

We glared at each other for a long moment and he swiped a hand over his face as he backed away from me.

"Look. Tory…this whole thing we've had going…I just don't see how we can keep it up. I don't think we should keep hooking up like we were."

I rolled my eyes at him. "Good. Because I don't need this kind of drama from some guy who isn't even my boyfriend."

"So we're breaking up?" he confirmed, his brow furrowing like that didn't appeal to him but he seriously needed to check his facts because we'd never even been together.

"Shit dude, you can't break up with someone who was never yours in the first place," I said, shaking my head as I walked away from him.

He didn't follow me and I kept going until I was back inside where I headed straight for Darcy and the others for a second time.

I could tell something was wrong even before I'd made it to the table and Darcy looked up at me with tears brimming in her eyes.

"What's happened?" I asked, hurrying forward and sitting down beside her.

"They've...Tor, the fucking Heirs set us up last night," she breathed. "And they sent videos and photos to that goddamn rag, The Celestial Times. Here, look."

She passed me her Atlas and my brows raised as I spotted two photos side by side, one of me in my underwear sandwiched between Milton Hubert and Diego in a dance that looked about thirty seconds from becoming a threeway. And the second was of Darcy looking like a crazy person as she tugged on her hair and seemed to be screaming something at a rock.

My lips parted as I read the headline.

Rumours of the Vega Twins' Instability and Sex Addiction Confirmed.
By Gus Vulpecular

Reports have been confirmed tonight that the return of Gwendalina (Darcy) and Roxanya (Tory) Vega has been blighted by the truth of their mental deficiencies.

Though the Fae of Solaria rejoiced at the return of the lost Royals earlier this year, it turns out that their arrival may be nothing more than the appearance of two damaged and unstable girls.

371

In the attached images and footage, you will see that Gwendalina is indeed convinced that she can converse with inanimate objects. Eyewitnesses said, she was heard offering a non-existent raven a piggyback and at another moment, she tried to buy an invisible crow a bow tie. By the end of the night, she had entered into a full blown argument with a rock who she claimed stole her sombrero and tried to set the imaginary creature alight.

Meanwhile, in more footage from the same party, Roxanya (Tory) Vega can be seen gyrating against two of the six men she took back to her room that night. While polyamory is widely accepted amongst Werewolves and other pack Orders in our society, this constant change of sexual partners and reports of her demanding wildly outrageous acts from the men she seduces under threat of her using her royal name to slander them if they don't participate, is more than a little abnormal.

The article went on but I gritted my teeth, slamming the Atlas down on the table with a snarl of rage.

"How did they do this?" I asked angrily. I could remember most of last night, but the images included of me in that article went beyond Drunk Tory promiscuity and I sure as shit couldn't remember doing any of that. In more than one of those photos I was all over Diego. *Diego!*

Hell no. Even drunk Tory wouldn't hook up with him. Especially after the things he'd said to me and my sister. *Especially*, especially while he was wearing that fucking soul hat. There wasn't enough tequila in the world to make me forget his grandma was up in there whispering fuck knew what to him at any given moment.

"Alas, I believe they slipped you a-something," Geraldine said, looking moments from tears. "And Seth made Darcy drink a potion which gave her hallucinations, allowing them to obtain the footage they required of her too."

"I'll fucking kill them!" I yelled, jumping to my feet, my rage white hot and blinding. "C'mon Darcy let's show them exactly how much power the Vega twins have got."

I looked around, expecting to find Darcy beside me but she was still in her seat, her eyes wide as she shook her head. She caught my wrist and tried to tug me back down into my chair.

"There's no point, Tor," she said and my mouth fell open in surprise. Darcy may not have been as hot headed as me but she never backed down from anything. And she sure as shit wouldn't just bow her head and take this lying down.

"What?" I asked, because in all honesty I couldn't process the fact that she was still in her seat.

"I just…" Darcy trailed off, looking over towards the Heirs' couch where Seth and Max sat looking so fucking smug that I wanted to scream. Caleb had joined them again too but he was scowling off into the distance, not looking our way like he had zero interest in their latest game.

"C'mon," I demanded. "Let's go kick the shit out of them!"

"I don't see what starting a fight will achieve," Darcy said vaguely, her gaze darting to the Heirs and back. "The story is already out so…"

"So what? They made you look like you were three peanuts short of a bag, Darcy! I'm not going to just sit back and let them spread rumours like that about you!"

"I know," she said. "But it doesn't really matter, does it? I mean, how many people even read that paper?"

"What paper?" Tyler asked as he and Sofia appeared hand in hand, looking at me as I stayed on my feet, ready to bust a blood vessel at any moment.

"The Celestial Times has printed some utterly bamboozling lies about our great and noble ladies," Geraldine said, her own anger making her voice quiver. "I'm just about ready to slap a slippery salmon myself!"

Tyler and Sofia frowned in confusion and Angelica passed over the Atlas which still had the article open on it.

I was practically grinding my teeth to dust in my mouth as I tried to think up some way to get back at that pack of smug assholes. It wasn't going to be rumours and pranks this time. I'd be going for the damn jugular.

"My mom can spin this," Tyler said quickly. "Print a story that paints this in a better light. I'm telling you, she does this kind of thing all the time. Within a week everyone will be wishing they could talk to rocks and begging to have a sex addiction like the Vegas. Do you want me to ask her to set up interviews for you? Maybe photo shoots too?"

"*Yes*," Darcy said, sounding relieved. "See, Tor? We can fix this without having to go against the Heirs."

"It's not enough," I growled. "I'll do whatever interview your mom wants Tyler, but it's *not* enough! I want them bleeding at my fucking feet!"

Darcy looked like there were a thousand things she wanted to say to me, but she glanced around at everyone else, her gaze falling on the Heirs before she finally shook her head.

"No," she said in a voice so soft it shouldn't have made much of an impact, but it felt like a blade that she'd just plunged into my back.

My lips parted and pain splintered through me as I failed to understand what the hell was going on with her.

I looked away from Darcy, unable to look at her while I was feeling like this.

My gaze fell on the Heirs' couch again just as Darius walked over to join the others. Max leaned over to say something to him and Seth pointed our way. Darius's gaze found me and a dark smile pulled at his lips.

He thought he'd won. They thought they'd beaten us. But there was no way in hell I was leaving it at this.

"Fine," I snapped, tearing my gaze away from the Heirs so that I could look at my twin again. I couldn't remember any time in our lives when we hadn't stood together, when she'd let me down like this. "I thought it was you and me against the world, Darcy," I breathed, tears stinging the backs of my eyes.

"It is," she said helplessly, but if that was the case then why wasn't she standing with me now?

Darius's booming laugh carried to me across the room and something broke apart inside me.

"Well if you don't want to fight back against them for this then that's up to you," I snarled as I took a step away from the table. "But I for one am going to tear those assholes apart. And I plan on starting with that motherfucking Dragon."

I turned and stormed from the room before she could respond, my heart breaking into a thousand pieces. And not because of the lies the Heirs had told about us. But because for the first time in my life, I truly felt alone.

DARCY

CHAPTER TWENTY SIX

I rushed out of The Orb, needing space and air and fucking *anything* to make this pain inside me go away. I walked blindly, tears fogging my vision and making me want to scream. More than that, I wanted to rip the Heirs apart with my bare hands. But I couldn't. Not with Seth hanging a sword over Orion's head. He'd destroy him. But Tory…I'd just let her down so badly. I'd hurt my own flesh and blood. I'd abandoned her when she needed me, with the aim of protecting someone else. But the consequences for Orion were too steep, I couldn't attack Seth and let him ruin his entire life.

"Hey Vega Whore!" a girl shouted and I recognised Marguerite's voice with a pang of dread.

My heart hammered as I spotted her with Kylie and a group of their friends walking toward me down the path. Kylie's eyes were puffy and red and pure hatred seeped from her expression as she glared at me.

I clenched my jaw as they came to a halt before me and ice froze the inside of my palms as I prepared to defend myself.

"Do you think you're special because Seth Capella dicked you?" Marguerite said with a cold laugh and Jillian and the others sniggered. "He probably thought pity fucking you would make you stop following him around."

"Shut up," I snarled, anger rising in me like a wild beast.

"What are you gonna do to make me?" she hissed, raising her hands so flames coiled in them.

"Sethy wouldn't touch you unless he was blind drunk!" Kylie suddenly piped up, her lower lip quivering.

I wished I could deny that I ever screwed him, but they would all just question him about it. He'd know I told the truth and then what would he do? Seth was volatile, unpredictable and vicious. There was no doubt he'd tell Nova about me and Orion if I admitted to his lie. But that didn't mean I had to be kind about him.

"Maybe you should stop caring about a waste of space asshole like Seth," I shot at Kylie. "He chewed you up and spat you out, and frankly he couldn't get a girl off if he had a map and a vibrator so I really don't see what the fuss is about." If my reputation was going down the drain, then so was his.

I marched forward as Kylie's hair exploded into a sea of snakes, all hissing at me venomously. "Slut!"

I'd had enough of this. I blasted a path through the centre of their group with a gust of air and darted into it, but before I got through, someone made the ground lurch at my feet.

I crashed to my knees and my spine tingled with the urge to shift as anger spilled into every corner of my body. I swung around and found Kylie standing above me. I raised my hands to fight off the attack I expected, but she did something much worse than blast me with magic. She spat in my face and I jerked backwards in shock.

Her group of friends roared with laughter and all of them hurried off down the path toward The Orb. I trembled from head to toe, rising to my feet and pulling my sleeve over my hand as I rubbed the spit from my cheeks. My chest felt like it was cracking, breaking open and ready to unleash a torrent of pain into the sky.

I started running and made it to The Wailing Wood before I came apart, slipping between the trees and choking down a lungful of air as I pressed my back to a huge oak and slid to the ground. I cast a silencing bubble around myself and screamed until my lungs were raw.

My Atlas was pinging and pinging and a part of me wanted to smash the damn thing. But eventually, when my heart stopped hurting enough for me to breathe, I took it out and stared numbly at the screen. Orion had messaged me a hundred times since last night and though I'd answered to tell him I was okay, that was all I could really say. And that was a lie anyway. How was any of this okay?

It looked like he'd seen the article and I tapped on his latest message with an ache in my chest.

Lance:

I shouldn't have left last night. This never would have happened.
Where are you? I need to see you.

I answered by sending him my location on a map and shut my eyes, resting my head back against the tree. Maybe he'd have an answer to this because I sure as hell couldn't come up with one. All I knew was that letting my sister down like this wasn't an option. So I'd tell her the truth, come clean about it all. She deserved that. And at least then she'd know why I couldn't strike back at the Heirs, not until I could sort out this mess with Seth.

Orion appeared in a blur and I disbanded my silencing bubble as my heart thumped with the relief of him being here. He was dressed in sweatpants and a T-shirt, his hair dishevelled and his eyes red from lack of sleep. He dragged me to my feet in an instant and wrapped me in his arms. We were hidden here behind the huge tree trunk so I didn't have to fear being seen.

I came apart, tears escaping me as I clung onto him, wondering how a single day could have caused so much destruction. If I'd heeded that warning Nova had sent out about Halloween, maybe we wouldn't be in this mess. The stars had been volatile and we'd both ignored them in favour of some time in each other's company. *Stupid. Idiotic. Moronic.* There wasn't a word strong enough for it. We'd been reckless time and again and our luck had finally run out.

He held me until the tears dried up, kissing my hair and murmuring soothing words.

"I have to tell Tory," I said, stepping back and wiping the tears from my cheeks as I clung on to the resilience in me. "It's the only way to fix things between us. She'll understand and then we can work out what to do together."

Orion swallowed thickly then slowly nodded. "You're right...I'll tell Darius too. He'll talk to Seth and make him back off and keep him from telling anyone. I won't let him hurt you."

Hope glimmered in my heart as I nodded and he moved closer, his expression broken and full of regret. "I'm so sorry for coming to that fucking party."

I shut my eyes, shaking my head. "We've both done stupid things to be together. We could have been caught a hundred times."

"But of all the Fae in Solaria," Orion growled, clawing a hand into his hair. "Why did it have to be Seth fucking Capella?"

"I know," I sighed heavily. "Is there any way to undo this?" I didn't really expect an answer, because I knew there wasn't one, but darkness swirled in Orion's gaze and anxiety prickled my spine at his next words.

"There's one thing I could try but..." He shook his head.

"What?" I begged.

"Dark Coercion," he said thickly. "But the consequences of casting it on an Heir to the Solarian throne are unthinkable."

"Then don't," I said immediately, clutching his hand. "You can't risk breaking the law again, Lance. It's not worth it."

"For you, anything's worth it," he said and my heart broke because I knew he meant it and it was almost too much to bear. "Do you wish you'd never come to me, Blue?" he asked and I knew what he was referring to. The night I'd broken into Asteroid Place and banged on his door with blue hair and high hopes, telling him I wanted him.

"Don't say that," I said in horror. The shadows pressed closer in my mind and I felt them spread between us for a moment like they were feeding on the dark emotions we were feeling. I pushed them back, focusing on the man in front of me who owned my heart and who I knew would do anything in the world to protect me. "I can't regret it. But if you get arrested because of me, I'll never forgive myself."

"You must," he growled like it was a decided fate.

"Don't you dare give up," I demanded, fire burning hot in my veins and chasing away the cold.

"I'm not, but Blue...if this all falls apart, you have to do as I ask. You have to let me take the fall alone."

"*No*," I snarled, rage crashing through my chest like thunder. "I'm just as responsible as you are."

He lifted a hand, running his thumb along the line of my cheekbone, not saying another word. I could feel this argument wasn't settled, but I didn't want to fight right now. I had to try and fix this shitstorm which had hit my life in the past twenty four hours.

"If I was a stronger man, I'd tell you to stay away from me. I'd break this off and let the dust settle until Capella had nothing to hold against us. There's no video, no evidence, and his memory will fade in a year or so. It wouldn't stand up in court even if they used a Cyclops. There's a point where memories become inadmissible in court."

"I don't want to stay away," I whispered, because I knew it was impossible for me to. I felt bound to him like the stars had wrapped golden thread around us and refused to let us go. In the very root of my bones, I knew we belonged together.

"Good. Because I'm not a better man," he said in a low growl, his eyes full of shadows. "I'm the devil and I want you. I want you like I've never wanted anything or anyone. And I will fight to make you mine, no matter what it takes. No force in Solaria will rip us apart."

I stared at him in awe of his words, lost to the power of them. I clutched his hand and nodded firmly. "I'll fight for you too, Lance Orion. Whatever it takes."

"Whatever it takes," he echoed and a clap of power sparked between our hands. I sucked in a breath of surprise and a sad sort of smile pulled at his mouth.

"Looks like you just struck a deal with me, Blue. No backing out now, not unless we want the stars to turn against us too."

"Hell, I don't need any more enemies. Especially not amongst the stars." An empty laugh escaped me.

"Agreed," he said grimly.

"I'm going to go find Tory," I told him, not wanting to wait a second longer and he nodded, squeezing my fingers.

"Do you want me to come with you?"

"No," I breathed and fog rose before me in the air. "I need to do this alone. She's my sister and I've hurt her. I have to make things right between us."

"Okay." He leaned in, pressing his ice cold lips to my burning hot ones and I melted for half a second, stealing the brief second of peace he offered me. "Go," he urged, then he was gone in a blur of movement and I stepped out from behind the tree with hope in my heart.

I hurried along the frosty ground, stuffing my hands into my coat pockets and urging more of my fire magic into my veins. I headed for Ignis House, hoping Tory had gone there but I'd search the entire campus until I found her anyway.

Before I reached the end of the trail leading toward Fire Territory, a shadow stepped onto the path, haloed by the hazy morning sun. Rage swam in my blood as I came face to face with Seth Capella once more.

"Thought you might have headed this way," he mused, walking toward me. "Looking for your sister, right?"

"What do you want?" I snarled, refusing to answer his question. I took my hands from my pockets and brought fire to my fingertips in preparation of an attack.

"Well a thank you would be nice. I did tuck you into bed last night after all, babe." He smirked and poison trickled down my spine. I'd never hated a person as much as I hated him. None of the Heirs compared. He was my personal enemy. My fucking nemesis and some deep, innate part of me wanted to destroy him Fae on Fae.

"How kind of you after you spent the hours before that destroying my damn life."

"Yeah about that...I'm here to make things even less enjoyable for you."

Panic swirled in my gut, but I fought not to let it show on my face. My tongue felt too heavy as he stepped forward and I immediately took a fighting stance as he slinked toward me like a predator.

"See...the thing is, I can't have you running off to Tory and ruining all of my fun, babe." He pushed a hand into his dark hair, the white washed out of it from last night. His cocky smirk grew and a bloodthirsty creature awoke in me. "Caleb was listening in when she asked you to come at us earlier and I know you said no because of what I'd do if you did. And that's the way things are going to stay."

He drew closer, his shadow falling over me and it felt like he'd just blotted out all the light in the world.

"Don't do this," I hissed. "I have a right to tell her."

"You *did*." He shrugged casually. "But I just took that right away from you."

I lunged forward on instinct, a growl tearing from my throat as I brought up a fistful of flames. My knuckles crunched as they slammed against a solid air shield I couldn't see and a cry of pain escaped me.

"Fuck you!" I roared at him and my shout was echoed back to me from far away. I squared up to him as he continued to smile, my Order form rising, begging to be unleashed on him. "One day I'm going to crush you under my heel," I promised. "I'm going to deliver every ounce of pain on you that you've delivered on me and everyone I love."

"Love?" he toyed with that word, his tongue wrapping around it like it was as sweet as candy. "I assume you mean your sister and not your plaything professor?"

I tsked, refusing to answer that. It was none of his business what I felt for anyone.

I glanced over his shoulder, still determined to head to Ignis House to see Tory and make this right. But I could see Seth wasn't going to allow it.

"I wonder what they'll say about Orion in the papers. Do you think they'll call him a pervert or a monster? Both maybe?"

"Stop it," I spat. "He's none of those things."

"You never know what papers will print about people," he said, hinting at today's news article.

"Do you think I care what people say about me? What *you* say about me?" I moved up as close as I could get with his air shield barring my way to him. "You're nothing, Seth Capella. You're just a boy kicking his toys out of the pram because I bother you. I get under your skin and you can't handle that like a man. This isn't facing me like Fae, it's pathetic. And if you think you've won, you are so wrong. The stars are on my side because they see you for the worthless creature that you are. And they'll pay you back through me."

The smile had fallen from his face to be replaced by a dark scowl, one filled with pain and bitterness and something darker than even the shadows lurking under my skin.

I turned to walk away and he caught my wrist in a vice-like hold. I shook him off, letting fire flash up my skin to burn him away and he flinched back with a wolfish snarl.

"Don't walk away from me!" he roared but I didn't look back. I moved faster and faster, taking out my Atlas and calling Orion, clinging onto my final ray of hope.

We can still fix this.

There's still a chance.

He answered on the first ring. "Did you find her?"

I cast a silencing bubble around myself to keep our conversation private.

"No," my voice cracked. "Seth found me first." I relayed what had happened and could practically feel Orion's fury pouring down the line and into me.

"I'll talk to Darius."

"Do it soon," I pleaded. "We have to stop Seth."

"We will, Blue, I promise. I'm looking for him now."

I sighed, some of the heaviness leaving my lungs but not nearly enough. The shadows were creeping into my bones and it was getting harder to fight them off.

"Are you alright?" he asked when I said nothing.

"It's the shadows," I said honestly.

"Try to breathe, relax. They're feeding on these emotions. Don't fall into their trap."

"I'm trying." I shut my eyes as I walked, their sweet caress tangling around me.

"Come to me…I'm here, just a little further."

Orion was talking but I was falling deeper and I couldn't get out. My eyes wouldn't open and a sticky weight descended on my bones.

"So close, reach for me. We can help each other."

A tranquil calm fell over me and I relished its embrace as it stole away the fear in my heart and the desperation I'd felt just moments ago. The darkness sang to me like a lullaby and I wanted to climb into its hold and never come back.

"Darcy!" Someone was shouting but I couldn't think who, the darkness was getting thicker and I was moving further and further away from the world, drifting through a sea of black.

"Wake up, Miss Vega!" Someone shook me and I jerked out of the dark, finding Orion's inky eyes boring into mine.

I was on the ground, gazing up at the canopy fanning out above him. The sound of girls giggling caught my ear as a group of students headed by.

"You're all in detention!" Orion barked at them and their laughter stopped dead. His frantic gaze fell back to me and I blinked hard, pushing him back in fear of anyone else suspecting something between us except a normal student/teacher relationship.

"Shit," I hissed, rubbing my head where I must have hit it on the ground.

Orion quickly healed it then helped me to my feet. I stepped away even though there was no one else on the path now, but it wasn't worth the risk.

"Thank you," I sighed then realised my silencing bubble was still in place and quickly disbanded it. "Now go find Darius," I demanded and he frowned.

"I've been looking everywhere and he's not answering his fucking Atlas." He glanced over my shoulder. "I'll find him. We'll talk later," he murmured and I nodded before he shot away again.

I looked behind me, spotting more students moving down the path, the easy smiles on their faces tying a knot of jealousy in my gut. What would it be like to attend this academy with no shitty Heirs ruining your life at every turn?

I shook off the pointless feeling and hurried along with the intention of looking for Darius too. I didn't know how he'd react to this news, but I trusted Orion. And if he thought Darius could sort this mess out for us, then I believed him. But seeking him out for help when I couldn't ask my sister for it was a bitter pill to swallow.

If I'd just gone with my gut and told her initially, none of this would be happening. I hadn't wanted to drag her into my mess, but she was my twin. She'd stand by me through everything even if she didn't approve, even if she thought the idea of me and Orion was insane.

I'll let you know everything soon, Tor, and then I'll never lie to you again a day in my entire life.

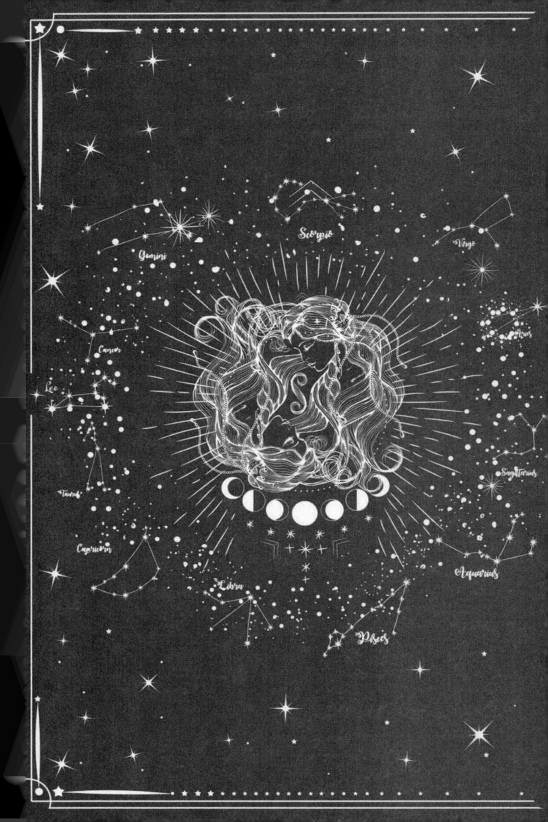

TORY

CHAPTER TWENTY SEVEN

The wind howled around me as I strode around the lake, dark thoughts twisting through my mind and calling on the shadows as I tried to figure out how best to strike back at the Heirs.

Especially Darius.

Stupid fucking Darius with his stupid fucking face and his lying mouth and his massive fucking bed and his goddamn jacuzzi and every beautiful, perfectly crafted motorbike the world had ever seen with none of the appreciation for how they ran. He didn't deserve to have so much. I wished I could take it all away from him. Every single thing.

I stopped still as a thought occurred to me.

There is one thing I can take from him pretty easily though…

I quit my aimless pacing and turned north, cutting a path through The Wailing Wood and heading straight for the parking lot which stood by the main gates. I may not have been able to take the Heirs on in a straight fight yet, but I could sure as shit hit them where it hurt.

My hair billowed out behind me as the storm picked up intensity, my red skirt whipping around my thighs and a chill prickling against my skin. But this was no natural gale, the wind was dancing to the tune of my power, rising up into a whirlwind around me as I channelled my rage into my air magic, needing an outlet for some of this fury.

My heart was beating to a frantic rhythm and my jaw was set in a hard line.

Darcy may have been willing to let the Heirs get away with this shit, but I wasn't. Not anymore. Not when they painted such pretty lies and worked so damn hard to destroy us.

The parking lot appeared ahead of me and I pulled my black sweater off, tying it around my waist so that I could unleash my wings.

Gabriel had focused our Order lessons on us learning to only half transform so that we could keep our Phoenix nature hidden and now calling on my wings alone was almost easy.

They burst from my back with a surge of magic and the pure heat of them washed over me as they caught alight. For a moment, I bathed in the warmth of the fire as it stoked my magical reserves before banishing the flames so that my golden feathers caught the sunlight without them. This way if anyone spotted me, I was less likely to be recognised. The Heirs had minions everywhere and I didn't want them to know what I was doing until it was too damn late for them to stop me.

With a hard beat of my wings, I took off. The raging winds I'd called to life swept beneath me at my call, pushing against my feathers and lifting me ever higher.

I flew straight towards the parking lot, tucking my wings tight as I made it to the top floor where the Heirs kept their cars and landing inside.

My boots pounded across the concrete as I headed straight down the line of priceless vehicles and I set my gaze on the gleaming red super bike at the end of the lot.

I approached it quickly, banishing my wings again so that I could move more easily into the small space beside it where I dropped to my knees.

I pulled a hairpin from my hair and a savage smile tugged at my lips as I quickly started tugging at the wires for the ignition so that I could hotwire this beauty.

It took a bit of time for me to work around the immobiliser and for a terrifying moment I almost set off the alarm, but I was finally rewarded for my efforts as the electrics suddenly came to life and I jumped up to start the engine.

As my thumb pressed down on the ignition, a tingle of magic swept across my skin and the hairs rose along the back of my neck. I stilled, frowning as I tried to figure out what the hell that had been. There was something about the power of it that had seemed familiar and yet I knew it wasn't mine. It must have been something placed on the bike, but what?

A distant roar sounded and I snapped around, looking out of the parking lot and over The Wailing Wood just in time to see a huge, golden Dragon send a plume of fire into the sky in the distance.

Oh shit, that was a magical alarm hardwired to an asshole.

I glanced at the bike, half considered bailing on my plan, then kicked my leg over the saddle instead.

The deep purr of the engine rumbled between my thighs and with a twist of my wrist, I was speeding down the exit ramp with the wind tugging through my hair.

I circled down the ramp at high speed, the lot turning into a blur around me as I focused all of my attention on getting the hell out of here.

The bike rode like a dream, even better than I'd imagined. It took the ramp like I was on a speedway and before I knew it, I was heading straight towards the exit.

A barrier stood in my way and my heart lurched as I lifted a hand for a moment, casting a fireball at it as I maintained my speed.

A huge crash sounded as the barrier was destroyed and I sped straight through the dying embers of the fireball as I shot out onto the road which led off campus. But instead of turning for the gate and freedom, I swung the bike right, aiming straight back for the heart of the academy grounds.

My pulse was banging to the beat of a war drum in my chest and Darius roared again from the sky ahead of me as he drew closer.

I looked up, my hair whipping back over my shoulders from the speed of the bike as I inched it faster and faster and I spotted him flying straight towards me above The Wailing Wood.

Darius's beady Dragon eyes were locked on me and his rage could be felt building in the air all around me as I shot straight towards him.

I gritted my teeth, refusing to show even an inch of fear while real terror rose within me at the same time. But I wouldn't back down. Not this time.

He'd pushed me too fucking far. What was with all of the bullshit last night where he pretended to give a damn about me and took me back to his room? He'd already set me up by then. He'd known what he'd done to me and Darcy and yet for a moment he'd made me think…

I gritted my teeth, a snarl of pure rage escaping me as I refused to follow that train of thought any further.

I sped down the path towards the edge of the trees. All I had to do was get beneath them before he could make it to me.

Darius roared again as we closed in on each other, each of his razor sharp teeth on show for a moment that seemed to stretch out forever as I sped straight towards him.

I shot beneath the cover of the trees just before he could reach me and the roar he released in response set the ground trembling beneath my wheels.

A smile bit into my cheeks and I laughed like a mad woman as I tugged the throttle back, shooting along the path which led into the depths of The Wailing Wood as I caught glimpses of Dragon fire and golden wings beyond the canopy above me.

I threw a silencing bubble up around me to hide the sound of the bike just as I took a sharp left, veering towards Air Territory.

I wasn't sure I'd ever ridden so fast in all my life. It was exhilarating, terrifying, liberating and utterly freeing. I was unstoppable. Like a force of nature that even a Dragon couldn't capture.

My momentary cockiness was burst like a bubble as the sound of a wolf howling filled the trees around me.

"She's heading for Aer Tower!" Max's voice called out between the trees and I twisted my head, spotting him riding on Seth's back in his huge white Werewolf form as they chased me too.

I threw a hard shield of air magic up alongside the silencing bubble before he could cast any magic at me and dragged the throttle back even further.

Seth might be as fast as a hell dog in his Order form but he was no match for the beast beneath me and I was soon pulling away from them as I sped on down the path.

But I wasn't in the clear, there was one Heir who could match my speed and I hadn't caught sight of him yet.

I shot out of the trees and took a hairpin turn towards Aer Tower. I dropped the silencing bubble as I spotted students on the path ahead of me, needing them to hear me coming so that they would get out of my goddamn way.

Screams filled the air as I rode fast between the bodies, weaving back and forth at high speed to avoid them and riding right past Aer Tower.

A roar filled the heavens behind me and heat brushed against my skin as a huge ball of Dragon Fire shot overhead.

I twisted in my seat to look over my shoulder, spotting the enormous golden Dragon closing in on me. Seth and Max were racing along the path behind me too and the adrenaline in my veins burned with white hot energy as I quickly looked back at the path ahead of me to take the next turn.

I shot around the corner, opening up the throttle as the crowd of students disappeared and I took the path which led straight to the cliffs above Air Cove.

Darius bellowed his rage at the sky again and I felt the lick of his flames curling over my air shield.

Fire can't hurt me, asshole.

Suddenly the cliff appeared ahead of me, the blue sky opening up above it and calling me on.

Almost there!

Caleb appeared in a flash of movement, blocking the path ahead and gritting his teeth as he wielded the earth to do his bidding.

The ground quaked and trembled beneath me, the bike bucking on the uneven terrain as an earthquake shuddered through the ground.

I almost fell off but I managed to cast air at the last moment, righting the bike as my heart leapt in panic.

Darius roared again right behind me, so close that I could practically feel Dragon breath on the back of my neck.

I turned the bike sharply, aiming it at the horizon and throwing my hand out to force the earth to create a smooth path ahead of me.

I loosed the throttle, drawing it back as far as it would go and the engine bellowed beneath me as I shot straight towards the edge of the cliff.

Caleb fought to regain control of the earth and Seth howled his fury behind me as Max threw his air magic at my shield, trying to break it open. But it didn't matter. They couldn't stop me.

The ground bucked beneath me just as I hit the edge of the cliff and the bike took off.

A whoop of excitement and fear tore from my lips as I soared out over nothing and the huge drop beneath me sent my gut spiralling with vertigo.

I stayed in the saddle until the bike began to fall then leapt out of it, my wings bursting from my back with Phoenix fire burning blue and red along the length of them.

I beat my wings and watched as the bike fell and fell and – CRASH! It slammed into the rocks which protruded from the sea with an almighty bang, the beautiful bodywork destroyed in one fell swoop. It didn't explode like in the movies though and that was disappointing. With a flick of my fingers, I sent a fireball chasing after it and a huge explosion tore from the machine as the flames found the gas tank.

For a moment I felt a pang of guilt for the beautiful piece of machinery as it died but the roar of absolute fury that tore from Darius's throat a moment later made it worth it.

A wave of Dragon fire washed from his mouth, punching through my shield and coming straight for me. I yelled out in surprise, throwing my arms up and casting a wall of red and blue Phoenix flames between us just before his fire could touch me.

The Dragon and Phoenix fire burned gold as it merged but the power of my flames consumed his with a flare of white hot energy.

Before he could come at me again, I turned and shot away from him, flying fast and hard with the aid of my air magic to speed me on.

Caleb and Max were shouting back and forth and the four of them raced after me as I powered away towards Fire Territory with my heart in my throat and victory burning a path down my limbs.

They were mad as all hell, but I was as fast as lightning with the wind I was casting behind me and if they wanted to punish me for what I'd just done, they were going to have to catch me.

The barren landscape of Fire Territory didn't offer up many potential hiding places but as I swept over it, I spotted a cloud of steam hanging thickly in the distance. Where Water and Fire Territory merged, the Shimmering Springs sprawled out in pools of hot water which created a maze of paths and caverns far too narrow for a Dragon to navigate.

I sped towards them, tucking my wings and extinguishing the flames which lined them as I dove into the cloud of steam.

Darius roared somewhere behind me but he wasn't close.

I dropped to the ground and started running down the little alleyways between the pools, the thick steam making it hard for me to see as I ran on. I banished my wings so the weight of them wouldn't hold me up and my shoulder blades tingled as my Order form withdrew beneath my flesh again.

I cast a silencing bubble around me to hide myself further and spotted a narrow cave cut into the side of the rocks.

I darted into it and dragged my black sweater back on to hide myself better as I leaned back within the shadows.

For several long moments the only thing I could hear was the frantic pounding of my heart but then Seth's voice came on the wind.

"She probably ran straight out into Water Territory!" he called just as he stepped onto a path in the distance. The other Heirs moved close to him and I noticed that he and Darius had put their clothes back on. I guessed either Max or Caleb had carried them for them while they hunted me which was a shame because this would have been even funnier if the two of them had been running all around campus with their dicks flapping about as they tried to find me.

"She's probably run back to the Ass Society at The Orb," Max put in.

"I'll head there and check," Caleb said, shooting away before the others even replied.

"When I find her, I'm gonna fucking destroy her," Darius snarled, his eyes flashing with rage.

"What do you want us to do?" Seth asked him, seeming unsure of how to best go about tracking me down.

"Go and hunt in Water Territory and check back at her room in Ignis house if you don't find her there," Darius growled. "And if you *do* find her, hold her until I get there. This is personal."

"Oh this is gonna be good," Seth said excitedly before turning and running away with Max right beside him.

Silence stretched as Darius stayed where he was, turning slowly as he looked all around at the maze of paths which led between the hundreds of little pools and waterfalls which made up the hot springs.

"Roxy!" Darius bellowed suddenly. "I know you're still here somewhere. Come out and face me like Fae!"

My spine straightened and I gritted my teeth at that challenge and I only hesitated for a moment before stepping out of the shadows. Because what the hell else was I going to do anyway? It wasn't like he'd forget about this and hiding any longer would only be delaying the inevitable. This fight was coming whether I liked it or not.

Though in that moment, the fire in my veins said that maybe I *did* like it. I was sick of him pushing me around and treating me like shit. It was time for me to stand and face him like Fae. And if he knocked me on my ass then that was fine. Because I'd just get right back up and come at him again. And again. Until he was the one staring up at *me* from the dirt.

I waved a hand to dispel my silencing bubble and strolled straight towards him. "Are you looking for me?" I asked innocently as he whirled around to face me.

The rage in his eyes burned right into my soul and for a moment my bravado faltered. But only for a moment. I might have been terrified of Darius Acrux, but I wasn't going to let him know it.

"You must have a death wish, Roxy," he growled, striding forward and closing the distance between us until there was nothing more than an inch of space dividing our bodies.

"I've just got a no more assholes wish," I countered. "And I'm not going to put up with your bullshit anymore."

"Well wishes like that don't come true in Solaria, Princess. And if you're going to stand up and fight me then you'll be the one paying the consequences."

"I think you're the one who'll end up paying, oh mighty Fire Heir, because your flames can't hurt me and your power can't match me. So why don't you just give up now before I end up dragging you through the dirt in front of the entire Kingdom?"

Darius snarled right in my face, leaning close threateningly and I slammed my palms into his chest, knocking him back a step with the force of my hatred.

His eyes flared and he shoved me right back. My back collided with the rock wall behind me, a faint hiss of pain shooting along my spine, as he came straight for me.

I glared at him, raising my chin defiantly, daring him to do his worst as he reached out and snatched a handful of my hair into his grasp, tugging on it hard enough to tilt my head back. A gasp of pain parted my lips and his mouth collided with mine a moment later as my heart leapt at the unexpected turn of this argument.

For several long seconds I was thrown, tossed into the flames as my lips parted for his without question and his tongue invaded my mouth. He kissed me hungrily. Possessively. Claiming every piece of me for his own and a moan was dragged from me as my knees buckled and I was filled with the overwhelming urge to give in to exactly what he wanted from me. Let him take me, use me, own me, have every piece and break them all apart just because he could.

I was submerged in the cage of his arms and the temptation of his flesh. But he hadn't managed to drown me before and I didn't plan on allowing it now.

With a wrench of determination, I jerked backwards, parting our lips through pure force of will.

The second I was free of him, I swung my right hand at him, slapping him square across his jaw as rage ate me alive.

Darius stared down at me in surprise for a long moment and pure, unbridled hatred lit the air between us. We glared at each other, each waiting for the other to make the next move.

Steam from the hot pools swept between us, shrouding my view of him and making my heart pound with panic as I wondered what I'd find in his gaze once it cleared.

The mist blew away again and the tingling of my lips drew my gaze to his mouth.

We stayed utterly still, my chest was heaving with deep breaths and about a thousand insults sat waiting on the tip of my tongue. But I held them there, reaching into the space between us instead and fisting my hand in the material of his black T-shirt as I yanked him towards me again.

His kiss almost burned me as the heat of this moment brought our magic to the surface of our skin and energy raced through every small point of contact between us.

His body pressed to mine, driving me back against the wall as I gasped into his mouth and his tongue took me captive.

His hand came to my jaw as he pinned me in place, his hips grinding against mine so that I could feel how hard he was already through the layers of material that separated us. It sent a wave of delicious temptation through me as I was forced to clench my thighs together and fight the urges raised in my flesh by his touch.

I dragged the material I was still fisting lower, yanking on it so hard that I heard it rip. Darius growled against my lips and I moaned hungrily as he kissed me harder and my hands made it to the tear in his T-shirt before pushing inside. My heart pounded as I swept my palms across the firm muscles of his chest, my fingertips pressing down firmly as I explored every curve and ridge.

His hold on my face tightened as I touched him and his hand slipped to encase my neck.

I inhaled sharply, breaking our kiss for a moment as he tightened his grip. He pinned me in place with his hand around my throat, taking the chance to shift his attention from my bruised lips to run a trail of kisses down my neck which were punctuated by drags of his teeth across my flesh. I leaned back a little, half meaning to shift his grip from my throat and half wanting to give him more access to it. He refused to release me as he bit down right below where his thumb held me, just hard enough to hurt but not quite enough to break the skin.

I moaned in protest, jerking my head back as I pushed my hands further beneath his ruined T-shirt.

Darius yanked on my hair again to hold me still and sucked on my neck hard enough to leave a mark.

I groaned in frustration as he continued to use his position to leave marks on my neck without kissing my lips again.

I stopped the exploration I was making of his body and raked my fingernails down his perfect chest, feeling his skin break beneath the pressure I exerted.

Darius growled at me and the sound of it sent a wave of fear and anticipation racing down my spine and heat flooding between my thighs. I arched into him, my breasts pressing against his chest and he gave in to me, returning his attention to my mouth again.

I moaned as he kissed me, releasing his grip on my neck so that he could find my breast, his hand grasping through the thin material of my sweater as my nipple hardened in response to his touch.

The grip he still held in my hair tightened to the point of pain which felt so fucking good I cried out. I pushed at his ruined T-shirt, shoving the material up until he was forced to break away from me to rip it over his head.

He released my hair but the moment his shirt hit the ground, he stepped forward again and pushed my skirt up, catching the backs of my thighs and hoisting me up into his arms. I parted my legs so that he could step between them and he drove me back against the rock wall again, hitting it hard enough to knock a cascade of gravel tumbling down on us.

His fingers dug into my ass as he held me against him and I locked my ankles behind his back, squeezing my legs together so that he was pressed against me as firmly as possible. I could feel how hard he was as he ground up against me through his jeans, the rough material grazing my inner thighs in a way that set my blood pumping.

His kisses were setting me alight, my whole body bowing to the carnal desire I'd felt for him since the very first time I'd seen him.

He was still all the things I hated about him but he was also my own personal brand of hell. And I'd been sinning for a long time, waiting for him to punish me.

Darius pinned me against the wall with his body and shifted his hand beneath my skirt until he reached the lacy material of my black panties.

His fingers twisted around the side of them, tightening into a fist as he gave them a sharp yank.

I gasped as he ripped them off of me, the material cutting into my thigh before it broke.

His hand moved between us and I gasped he pushed a finger straight inside me.

He groaned hungrily as he felt just how much I wanted him, pushing a second finger into me and drawing them in and out at a perfect pace which had me panting in his arms.

I raked my hands through his black hair as I kissed him again, dragging him against me like I wanted to devour him whole.

I could feel him smiling in anticipation against my mouth as he kissed me again and I drew his bottom lip into my mouth before biting down hard enough to draw blood.

Darius yanked his head back, pushing his tongue against the bite on his lip as his eyes swum with dark promises which coiled their way through me.

He drew his fingers back out of me and I groaned in disappointment as he watched me with a gaze so heated it set every inch of my flesh on fire.

My grip landed on his biceps and my gaze dipped down to take in the sculpted perfection of his chest and arms and the swirling ink which covered them.

A twist of black flames ran over his shoulder and I moved my hand, scoring the line of the tattoo with my thumbnail as he watched. His powerful shoulders tensed and he dropped me to my feet suddenly, stepping back so that the heat of his body was lost to me.

He hooked his thumb into his belt as he began to pull it loose and I stepped forward, knocking his hands aside as I took it from him instead.

I yanked on the belt, slipping it free of its buckle and dragging it out of its loops.

Darius's hands found my waist and he pushed them beneath the base of my sweater, his fingers sweeping across my skin beneath the material. He snatched the hem into his grip with an impatient growl before yanking it over my head.

He groaned at the sight of my lace bra which matched the panties he'd already destroyed and revealed my hardened nipples pressing through it.

I dropped his belt with my sweater and undid the button on his fly, kissing him again as I made him walk back several steps and I pushed my hand inside his jeans.

Darius growled as I took the full, hard length of him in my hand, my pulse hitching with anticipation as I felt the size of him. I began to move my hand up and down as his kisses moved along my neck again, trailing fire across my flesh.

He caught my wrist suddenly, pulling my hand out of his jeans and spinning me around so that my back was pressed to his stomach. He pinned my arm across my body and I pushed my ass back against him at the sound of his pants hitting the ground behind me.

His dick pressed into my ass and I ground back against it, groaning at how hard he was and knowing my body was reacting just as keenly to his.

I tugged an arm free of his hold and reached back over my shoulder, gripping his neck and turning my head so that I could kiss him again as he roughly pushed at my skirt. It fell down my thighs and I stepped out of it, kicking my boots off in the same movement.

Darius gripped my hip and pushed me forward like he was planning on bending me over the rocky ledge of the pool beside us but that wasn't going to work for me. I wouldn't be turning my damn back on him.

I twisted in his arms, smacking his hand off of me as he tried to fight against what I wanted. He snatched my wrist into his grasp to stop me from smacking him again and a growl escaped him which had my heart thundering to a heady beat.

"No," I snapped.

"You want me to stop?" Darius asked, his voice rough with desire.

My gaze travelled over his naked body and I bit my lip hungrily as I took in every mouthwatering inch of him.

"Don't stop," I replied but I still wasn't going to let him bend me over that rock.

He assessed my body with just as much need in his gaze and kissed me hard as he drove me back towards the pool.

This time I let him move me as I shook his hand off of my wrist and clasped the back of his neck with my hands, gripping so hard that I knew I was marking him with my nails.

The pain only seemed to drive him on as his rough stubble bit at the soft skin of my face.

He caught my waist, his fingers bruising as he lifted me over the rocky wall and carried me into the hot pool.

My feet hit the bottom as the blue water lapped around my waist, gravel brushing across my toes as I backed up with Darius hounding after me, his kisses growing more urgent, his hands grasping at my breasts beneath my bra as I ran my hands all over him.

He hooked an arm around my back, pulling me flush against his body while still urging me backwards.

The hot water washed around our waists and he kept walking as he kissed, sucked and bit my neck and I clung to his shoulders, tipping my head back to give him more access.

At the back of the pool a small waterfall tumbled down a glistening rock face and he shoved me back against it, gripping the backs of my thighs so tightly that it hurt as he hoisted me back into his arms and I hooked my legs around his waist.

He broke away from kissing me and looked straight into my eyes half a second before claiming my body with one powerful thrust of his hips.

I cried out as the full, hard length of him drove inside me, filling me completely and sending my thoughts scattering.

He didn't give me a moment to adjust before pulling back and slamming into me again.

The constant trickle of the waterfall tumbled over us, slipping between our bodies so that our skin slid against each other. I moaned in need, my body demanding more as he shifted his mouth over my collar bone towards my breasts which were straining against the thin fabric of my bra, the only barrier left between us.

His mouth landed on my nipple over the lace, his teeth raking at the material as he growled in frustration. I gasped as he slammed into me again, yanking the strap of my bra down to give him the access he wanted.

The next thrust of his hips was met with his mouth claiming my nipple. He bit down and I hissed in pain and pleasure, dragging my nails across his shoulders in response, demanding more of it.

Darius growled again and I could feel the vibrations of it deep inside my body as he thrusted into me again and again.

I cried out, my muscles tightening around him as he kept up the relentless pace. My head was spinning and curses spilled from my lips as I matched the movements of his body to mine.

My nails gouged lines across his back, his neck, his shoulders. His mouth was everywhere, kisses that made my toes curl followed by bites which made me cry out. I was as savage as he was, tearing into his flesh while claiming all the pleasure I wanted from it.

My whole body was alight with his touch and even as I felt him driving me towards the edge, I knew it wouldn't be enough. I wasn't sure I'd ever get enough of the feeling of his body against mine.

He released my breast and shifted up to claim my lips again, pushing his tongue into my mouth and devouring the cries which were spilling from my lips as he kept up his relentless pace.

It was like he needed more of me despite the fact that he was taking it all already and I was giving it willingly.

I gripped his shoulders as his fingers dug into my thighs and I had to break our kiss to take a breath as my heart slammed against my ribs, fighting to keep up with his demands on my flesh which were making my entire body tremble with want and need.

The whole world narrowed to the feeling of him inside me as I tightened around him again and a cry fell from my lips as pleasure unlike anything I'd ever known crashed through my body.

Darius followed me over the edge, groaning into my neck as he found his release too.

Our chests were pressed against each other's, our heavy breathing the only sound to pass between us as he leaned his forehead to the rock wall beside me, his rough cheek scraping against mine. He still held my legs up, our bodies still connected as I fought to catch my breath and water continued to tumble over us.

I slid my hands from his shoulders, running them down slowly until my palms rested against his chest.

He turned his head and I moved to meet his kiss even though I'd already taken what I'd wanted from him.

This kiss was slower, deeper, his lips skating across mine in a gentle caress which was a million miles from the punishing passion which we'd both just succumbed to. I arched my back against him, reaching up to stroke my fingers along his jaw as we lingered a little longer in the moment.

When he finally pulled back, he caught my eye and something in his gaze seemed to call to me. Like he needed me to see him. The real him. Just for that second. I wondered if I was giving him a true glimpse of me in response as I brushed my thumb along his jaw and he tilted into my touch like he ached for it. Enough to let me know he craved the feeling of my touch on his skin.

My thumb made it to his chin and I withdrew my hand, frowning slightly at myself for touching him that way.

Our breathing evened out and Darius lowered my legs back down to the bottom of the pool as he stepped back, breaking the contact between us.

He looked down at me, his dark eyes full of questions and a glimmer of something I didn't want to address.

I bit my lip, wondering briefly why I'd just given into temptation with him before pushing that thought aside. I could beat myself up over it later, right now I needed to deal with the Dragon in front of me.

His gaze hardened as he looked at me, the anger which couldn't be sated by what we'd just done returning to hang between us.

I scowled at him in response, pulling my bra strap back over my shoulder as I fought to wrangle my thoughts away from the wanton desires of my flesh.

Darius took another step back, the pool lapping around his waist as I stayed where I was with the waterfall cascading over my shoulders.

He opened his mouth to say something but I got there first, striding towards him through the water.

"This doesn't change anything," I said aggressively, knocking my shoulder against his arm as I passed him.

"Thank fuck for that," he replied darkly.

I ignored him, heading for the edge of the pool and my clothes so that I could get the hell away from him.

As I gripped the edge and started to pull myself up, a gust of wind drove down on me and I flinched instinctively, looking up as water fell over me like raindrops, spilling from Darius's Dragon body as he soared away.

I watched as he banked hard and twisted out of sight into the clouds, brushing my thumb across my swollen lips.

My body was still tingling with the memory of his and I frowned as I headed over to reclaim my clothes.

Darius Acrux was probably the most pig headed, arrogant, infuriating man I'd ever met. But he was fucking mind blowing in the sack.

ORION

CHAPTER TWENTY EIGHT

I was perched on the top of Mercury Chambers which gave me a view towards Fire Territory. Anxiety was winding around my insides like barbed wire as I searched the skies for any sign of Darius returning after he'd flown across campus, looking like he was in the middle of a hunt.

A roar tugged a breath of relief from my lips and I caught sight of him flying back toward Ignis House, his golden wings shimmering under the winter sun. I swung my legs over the edge of the building, sliding down a drain pipe at high speed before shooting off across campus.

I pulled up short outside Ignis House, gazing up at the sky as I beat him back here. Darius soared above me, shifting just before he reached his window to land inside.

I shot around the side of the building as the sound of students chatting headed this way. Darius's room was at the top of the structure and it probably wasn't a great look for me to go strolling through the common room and into his bedroom. I took a deep breath and leapt up, gripping one of the thin crevices in the glass panes that made up the immense building and pulled myself higher using my Order strength to scale the wall. I soon made it to his window, jumping smoothly inside and hearing the shower running from the bathroom. I pulled the window shut and moved closer to the raging fire which was burning in the hearth, casting a silencing bubble around his dorm.

I tugged my Atlas from my pocket, finding a message there which must have come through just moments ago.

Darius:

I want to see you too, where are you?

"Right here," I called to him and the shower shut off. A second later he appeared in sweatpants, his hair wet and his eyes flaring with some dark emotion. He had scratches and bite marks lining his skin and my brows pinched in surprise.

"What happened?"

He grunted, then lifted a hand to heal them without a word.

"Where have you been?" I asked, my throat tight, not voicing what I really meant. *I needed you.*

Darius was as stiff as a brick wall and as he dipped his head, I realised something was wrong. Really fucking wrong.

"What is it?" I dashed forward in a blur, resting my hand on his arm. My skin had prickled and hurt a while ago, though not seriously enough for me to be concerned, but now the Leo tattoo on my inner arm was pulsing uncomfortably.

He locked me in an embrace and my heart pounded harder as I clutched him against me, the bond between us drawing us together and making me ache.

"Roxy," Darius growled in the deadliest of tones.

I slowly released him, stepping back. "I should have guessed." He shook his head marginally, the tension in his body making me worry. "What happened? Did you hurt her?" I asked carefully, wondering if I needed to go and find her.

"No. I mean yes... but not like that."

"Like what then?" I pushed.

"We fucked," he spat like he was saying he'd killed her.

"By the stars, Darius." The stress rolled out my body in a flood. "Well that's great, now you can drop all of this pretence."

"Pretence? What fucking pretence, Lance?" He shoved his way past me, throwing himself down on the bed and tucking a hand beneath his head as he blew out a long breath.

"I mean, you and her, this whole ridiculous feud you've been so focused on. Now that you've both finally given in to what you really want, maybe-"

"Maybe nothing. When we were together I felt so connected to her, like our souls were trying to tear their way free of our flesh to press against each other. It wasn't just good, it was completely overwhelming, I swear I can still feel the imprint of her skin against mine and taste her kisses on my lips…" He trailed off like he didn't even have words for it and I began to wonder if he might really be able to understand about me and Darcy. Because he practically could have been describing the connection I felt with her and I was beginning to hope that he wouldn't be angry with me after all, that he might even be able to see where I was coming from. "Then after we'd been together, she kissed me like… I dunno, like she meant it. Like it wasn't just sex and she felt the same way that I did and I thought that things had changed between us…for all of about ten seconds anyway," he added hopelessly.

"But they hadn't?" I asked with a frown.

"Not for her apparently."

"How can you be sure of that? Did you even talk to her, or-"

"She looked me dead in the eye and said it," he growled, anger rising in him so fast that I wasn't sure what to say. "I hate her more now than I did before I screwed her."

"What?" I asked in confusion, moving towards him and dropping onto the end of the bed.

"She tears me apart normally, but now I've let her in, I've gone and given her more pieces of me to chop up."

"Come on, it can't be that bad."

He looked up at me with a scowl like I didn't know anything. Like I was so fucking clueless.

"Do you have any idea how much I want her? How much it feels like I *need* her sometimes? It's like she's burrowed her way beneath my flesh and taken root in the depths of my soul. I hunger for her and ache for her and for the briefest moment, it felt like maybe she felt the same. Like all the anger and hatred between us had just been covering up everything else we desired.

Like just maybe I could have something good like that, something pure and honest and just...*mine.*" He released a breath like the weight of the whole world was on his shoulders and for a moment I couldn't find the right words to offer him. Because I did know how that felt. When I was with Blue, it seemed like nothing else even mattered. And when she looked at me like I was the only man in the world for her, it made me feel complete and happy in a way I couldn't put into words. I couldn't imagine how I would feel if she rejected me, if she pushed me away despite the passion that blazed between us.

"Are you sure she meant what she said? I've watched the way she is with you, I've seen the feelings she tries to hide-"

"Don't," he breathed. "Please don't try and give me hope when I know there is none. I've never met anyone like her. She doesn't care about who I am or how much power I hold, she's not interested in my money or my family or anything like that. I was an idiot to think that she might have seen something else in me though. There is nothing else."

"That's not true," I growled. "She's a fool if she can't see everything else you have to offer."

"I might crave her, Lance, but I despise her because of it. It's like she holds my heart in her fist and squeezes it just for fun. I wish the Vegas had never come back here. I wish they were still lost in the mortal realm and we could all be saved from the fucking hell of their company."

A snarl rolled from my throat on instinct. "Take that back."

Darius sat up with his own growl in response and his hand clutched firmly around my arm. "Why? What difference does it make to you? The only thing you'd lose out on if they weren't here is a regular blood Source."

"Shut the fuck up," I snapped, rising from the bed and beginning to pace. Darkness curtained my vision and a void opened inside me. "You know, if you pulled your head out of your own ass for once, maybe you'd realise that the best thing in the world just happened to you."

"You can't be serious?" he scoffed, standing up as fire flashed in his eyes.

"Wake up, Darius!" I barked. "If you get over this bullshit hatred you think you feel for her, you'll realise she's not only perfect for you, but her and her sister are the best fucking solution to your father we've ever had."

He gaped at me, silence stretching through the air and ringing in my ears.

"You can't be suggesting…" he trailed off, shaking his head like he refused to believe my mind would even go there.

"Share the throne," I demanded, my voice filling every space in the room. "Share it and all your problems go away."

"*No*," he gasped, looking at me like I'd betrayed him. But I hadn't. He just couldn't see what was staring him right in the face. "Who the fuck do you think you are suggesting that after everything we agreed before you went to get them from the mortal realm?"

"I know what we said back then. That we agreed the best thing to do was to make sure they could never rise to power. But that was before we knew them. Before I realised that they might be just what Solaria needs," I insisted.

"When I told you what me and the other Heirs had agreed to do to them, you swore you would stand by me. *No matter what.* We agreed that I had to do *anything* it took to make sure they didn't threaten my position. To make sure that they didn't interfere with our plans to eliminate my father," Darius snarled and shadows swirled in his gaze.

"Things change, Darius," I growled. "We never could have guessed that they'd hold the power they do, the strength of character, they're Phoenixes for the stars' sake! They *will* rise to power whether you agree to it or not! I'm only suggesting that you consider allowing it to happen united rather than waiting to find out which of you will end up crushing the others!"

Darius stared at me like he didn't even know who he was looking at and I bristled in anger as he refused to even try to understand what I was saying.

"Do you have any idea how much fucked up shit I've done to them to make sure they never rise to claim the throne?" he demanded. "I've played my part in this, I've struck at them again and again, even when it tore me apart to do it, even when it's made her hate me like she does! There's no way she would ever forgive me for what I've done and it's all because of what we *all* agreed and now you're just backing out on it and leaving all of the blame on my shoulders because you hid behind your little teacher badge and didn't do any of it! But you're just as bad as me and you know it, the difference is, you can get away with all of it because none of the suffering caused to them was by your hand. You left all the dirty work to me!"

"Are you fucking serious?" I yelled back. "In what world did you get the impression that I was alright with Seth cutting off Darcy's hair? Or you and Max almost killing Tory in that pool? When we talked about making sure they didn't rise up, I never knew it would equal that kind of savagery!"

Silence rang out between us and we stared at each other like we were standing on opposite sides of some great divide. I'd never argued with him like this. Never disagreed so wholeheartedly. And I could feel the pain of this feud ringing right down to my bones through the bond we shared. It pulled at my core, unravelling me like a ball of twine and darkness fed on every part of me that came undone.

"Wow. I've always known that I couldn't trust many people in this world, but I always thought you had my back, Lance. But maybe the only reason you're here is that mark on your arm," Darius spat bitterly.

"I'm your friend," I snarled, my fangs growing as I pointed a finger at him. "Don't throw that shit at me."

Something snapped in his eyes and I knew he'd lost the plot. "You're not, you're just some asshole my father bound me to. You wouldn't be here if he hadn't, you'd be on the other side of Solaria living out some prissy Pitball dream."

His words punctured something deep inside me and I tried not to be hurt by them, but it was no good. They sliced and teared at that piece of me I'd held onto since the day Lionel had bound me to him. The piece that still wanted that free life. I'd never once blamed Darius for that and we'd been friends long before I'd been forced to watch over him. And if it had never happened, I'd still have been there for him, I still would have given him this advice. Still would have helped him defeat his father, because I loved him like a brother.

"You're deluded if you think that," I said coldly, darkness sweeping through me as the shadows fed on the rage in me, multiplying it, making my insides burn.

"Well I must be deluded about a lot of things. Because apparently I thought you'd stand by me through anything. I thought you'd do anything to get me on the throne."

"I'm not asking you to give it up!" I roared, my hands starting to shake with rage. "I'm saying you're being too damn stubborn to see other options. The Vegas are more powerful than you. And I would take an educated guess that at least one of them cares about you. Don't you see, Darius, *this* is the perfect time to make an alliance."

Darius strode forward with the menacing gleam of his father in his eyes. "I wouldn't align myself with them if every star in the heavens begged me to. I'd rather die than share a throne with the daughters of The Savage King. Or have you forgotten what he was responsible for?"

"They're not like him and you know it," I growled. "Are you like *your* father, Darius? Do you judge yourself by the standards *he* set?"

He didn't answer, turning away from me and walking to the fire. Smoke was curling around his body and the temperature in the room was growing unbearable.

"What did you want to talk to me about anyway? I left my Atlas here so I didn't get your messages."

My mind turned to Darcy and my heart hurt thinking of everything she'd been through since Seth had discovered us. I needed to protect her. I had to pick up all the shattered pieces he had left in his wake. I couldn't put into words the anger I held for that asshole. I'd tear his throat out and drink every drop if I could.

I sighed, a heavy weight pressing down on me. I observed my friend with a tug in my gut because for the first time since I'd known him, I wasn't sure I could rely on him. Not for this. Not after he clearly hadn't changed his mind about the Vegas at all. In fact, it sounded like he hated them even more than he had yesterday. It had gotten personal with Tory and now he couldn't handle it. And if he thought I was betraying him by suggesting he share the throne with them, he'd think of me as even more of a traitor if I told him I adored one of them.

I remained silent for a long moment, warring with myself over what to do. If I told him and he flipped on me, he could make this worse. He could let Seth torture Darcy. And something told me that right then, he just might.

"Nothing," I muttered, moving to the window.

Darius glanced around with a taut frown. "You sent fifty messages, it clearly isn't nothing."

"Well I'm just a traitor now aren't I, Darius, so why would you care what I have to say?" I shot out of the window before he could reply, acid sliding through my veins and greasing my lungs.

I didn't stop running until I got back to Asteroid Place, slowing to a halt outside my chalet.

"Pizza?" Gabriel's voice startled me and I glanced up to find him sitting on the roof of my house with his wings spread and a pizza box in his hand. No one but a Harpy could sneak up on a Vampire. "I thought we could watch the game together."

"Game?" I muttered in confusion.

He jumped off the roof, landing gracefully beside me with a frown. "Orio, are you ill? Starfire are playing the Red Suns in the league!"

Shit. Pitball. And not just any Pitball. It was my favourite team playing their rivals. I'd forgotten all about it. It was the first time in years I'd almost missed a game.

Gabriel cocked his head. "Are you alright?"

"Yeah." I cleared my throat, putting on an expression that didn't say the world was ending. There was nothing else I could do now anyway. I needed a new plan to fix this mess, but a Saturday afternoon with my Nebula Ally watching Starfire destroy the Red Suns sounded like an escape I sorely needed. Especially with the shadows lurking so close. If I didn't distract myself from them soon, it was going to be nearly impossible not to give in to their call.

I led Gabriel around the side of the chalet and unlocked the door before pressing my hand to the door to disable the magical locks too. I heard Washer singing just beyond the door of his own house behind me and quickened my movements.

"Come on, come on," Gabriel murmured.

I swung the door open and had one foot inside when Washer called out to us. I groaned internally, turning back to face him and finding his leathery orange body staring back at me. The yellow speedo he was wearing left nothing to the imagination. And as hard as I tried to avoid looking at it, I swear it was trying to catch my eye.

I didn't have much time for anyone in this school, but I had to make small talk with the faculty if I didn't want Nova pulling me up on being a miserable asshole who 'brought the mood of the academy down a notch'.

"Oh hello boys," Washer said brightly. We might have been a hell of a lot younger than him, but boys we were not.

"Brian," I said politely, tipping my head to him as I let Gabriel inside to put some distance between him.

"I was just popping to the pool for a dip."

"I can see that," I said dryly.

"Won't you join me? Gabe is already half naked I see," Washer said keenly, eyeing Gabriel's heavily tattooed chest.

Gabriel spread his wings defensively. "Not for swimming."

"Can't I convince you?" Washer swung his hips and I didn't know what the hell he was trying to achieve. If it was to make my balls jump up inside me then he could have a gold fucking star.

"We're gonna watch the Pitball game," I said.

"Oh…well I'll just dunk my dipper then come join you."

"Er-" He strolled off before I could finish that thought and I growled under my breath, figuring this day couldn't get any worse.

I shut the door more sharply than intended and a crack splintered up the middle of it.

"What's up, man?" Gabriel frowned.

"Just girl stuff," I sighed, knowing I had to give him something. He wouldn't let it drop otherwise.

"Francesca?" he asked, though something in his tone made me think he didn't suspect her.

"Yeah," I lied because who else could I fucking say? Linda from accounts?

"Do you wanna talk about it?" he asked.

"No," I said, moving to the kitchen and taking out a bottle of bourbon and two glasses. I headed to the couch where Gabriel had banished his wings and pulled on the shirt which had been tucked into his jeans.

He flipped open the pizza box on his lap and held it out to me. My stomach felt like a lead ball so I waved him off, pouring a double – alright a triple – shot of bourbon and taking a large swig. I'd laid off of the day drinking a lot recently and I knew exactly who that had to do with. I'd even laid off of the night drinking for the most part. But now the world felt like it was about to fall out from under my feet and I couldn't go to the one person I wanted to in the whole world and drown myself in her sweet company.

So I turned to my old friend Mr Bourbon. He'd been there for me through Clara's death and all the bullshit years after. He took away the terrors that clawed into my dreams at night. He listened to me ramble about the past and didn't talk back. Didn't even comment, just rolled down my throat and placed me in a semi-coma.

Gabriel hadn't been around much since he wasn't from around here. Plus he had his hands full back home. He had his own shit to worry about and I didn't wanna put this on him. I *couldn't* put it on him anyway. *Oh by the way, Noxy, I'm screwing a student and now one of the Celestial Heirs has found out and is blackmailing us over it. Also, I have the Fifth Element and I practise dark magic on a regular occasion. I've been teaching the Heir of the scariest motherfucking Dragon on the whole planet how to wield it too. Nothing to worry about though, right?*

Sometimes, I thought prison was probably a star-chosen fate for me.

I switched the TV on and turned it up as it showed a pre-game interview with Ryan Luxian. He was an Airsentry and a fucking legend. I'd looked up to him through all my years at Zodiac Academy. I could remember the days I'd wanted to be like him, but I couldn't remember how that felt anymore. Where those dreams had lived was now just a hollow space that bled from time to time.

Gabriel slung an arm over the back of the couch as he devoured his second slice of pizza and turned to me. "So are you going to talk about it or will I have to make you?" He cocked a brow and I rolled my eyes.

"I don't want to bore you with my personal life."

"That's what Nebula Allies are for. Besides, if anyone has had girl drama, it's me."

"Too right," I couldn't help but agree. "But this is different. It's not like what happened between you and Elise."

"Okay then, answer me one question and I'll let it drop."

"Fine," I said, sipping my bourbon again.

"Is it on the same level of fucked up as what I went through?"

A ball rose in my throat. Gabriel had been through some serious shit.

My situation was bad, maybe even just as bad, but I simply couldn't go into it. "No, Noxy. It's not. I'll figure it out."

"I'm here for you, whatever it is." The intensity of his gaze made me shift in my seat. Sometimes it felt like he could see right into my soul. I almost considered opening up to him, but he'd be in serious trouble if it all went to shit for me. The FIB would question my closest friends, bring them in for Cyclops interrogation. I couldn't implicate him in it. I wouldn't even have considered letting Darius in on it for the same reason, but now that Seth knew...

Fucking Capella.

The game kicked off and I was glad of the distraction as we fell into watching it. I'd finished two glasses of bourbon by half time and was already filling my third. Everything felt a whole lot better behind a veil of alcohol.

"Yes – go on Nakimos! Run him down!" Gabriel shouted and I tried to muster the energy to join in. It was a close match and a really great game, but my mind just kept slipping back onto Blue. I realised I hadn't told her about Darius's answer yet and maybe that was because I didn't want to disappoint her. I slipped my Atlas out of my pocket, finding a few anxious messages from her and guilt pricked my gut.

Lance:
Sorry, Blue. Darius can't help us.

Darcy:
What happened??

Lance:
I'll explain when I see you next.
I'm sorry...I'll find an answer I promise.

Darcy:
We'll find one together.

Lance:
I'll come stay with you tonight.

I pictured her wrapped in my arms, her body moulded to mine while I tried to get enough of how good it felt to be that close to her. The thought brightened my mood a little, but her answer sent my happiness skittering away again.

Darcy:

It's too risky to come here. Seth could come looking to get some evidence.
I'll see you soon xx

I groaned but it was lost to the noise of Gabriel shouting a line of curses at the TV.

Soon? How soon?

My heart sank as I realised it wasn't going to be easy to spend a full night with her again. I tried to drown away the misery of that thought with another mouthful of bourbon, but doubted it would work that quickly.

Gabriel turned to me, looking baffled. "Did you not see that?"

"Huh?" I murmured, my eyes still on my Atlas.

"The Red Suns scored two Pits in a row. Holy shit, Orio, you must be in love with this girl because I've never seen you ignore a Starfire game."

Love?

I had a physical reaction to that word which felt somewhere between an aneurism and an elbow in the gut. I'd never been in love. And I'd only cared for so many people in my life. I could count them all on one hand. And if I was being entirely honest, I only really needed three fingers.

I spluttered something incoherent and that was just great because Gabriel looked like he'd hit the nail on the head.

"I remember when I first realised I-"

"Don't," I cut him off. "Stop right fucking there Noxy. I'm not in love. I'm just…in trouble."

"Same thing," he pointed out and I smirked.

The worst thing about denying it was that it felt like a lie. Which wouldn't have been the most terrible thing in the world if we hadn't been in this current shitstorm of a situation. Loving her felt like a promise of a future. And I couldn't give her that promise.

Gabriel thumped his knuckles against my shoulder with a dark look but before he could say anything, a knock came at the door.

"Coooey!" Washer called and my insides coiled into a tight knot. "I've brought nibbles! I made some of my famous chocolate covered balls this morning. They melt in the mouth like an orgasm."

"For the love of all the stars," I growled.

"We should ignore him," Gabriel said and I nodded.

"I can see you in there."

I jolted as I spotted him at the kitchen window, cursing myself for leaving the blind open. His naked chest was pressed to the glass and as he stepped back, he left two nipple marks on it.

"Argh, how am I supposed to clean that shit?" I grumbled.

"Water magic and a rag on a long stick?" Gabriel suggested and I snorted a laugh.

I got up with a sigh, pulling the door open and Washer walked into my house in nothing but his speedos. He must have dried himself off with his water magic but that didn't explain why he was going around like that in the middle of winter. He had a bowl of the aforementioned chocolate balls that I wouldn't be touching with any part of my body, least of all my mouth. He placed them on the table, bending right over in Gabriel's face and making him shrink back into his seat at the sight of his tanned ass.

I dropped back onto the couch, expecting Washer to take the armchair but no. Of course he didn't.

Washer wiggled his way between us then flung his arms over the back of the couch and spreading out so his armpit hair was almost touching my shirt.

Yep. Fuck no. I'm out.

I stood up, heading to the kitchen to get a glass of water. I was kind of regretting the bourbon. I didn't want to drink while Blue needed me. The least I could be for her right now was sober.

I spotted Washer's hand reaching up to touch Gabriel's hair and shot a tiny, controlled gust of air magic at it so his finger strained as he tried to close the distance. "I bet your wife has licked every one of those tattoos, hm?" Washer asked.

"You talk about my wife like that, you lose teeth. Any more questions?" Gabriel asked sharply.

"Just one…" Washer purred. "Are the rumours true about you…do you really share that svelte body with other-"

Gabriel ripped Washer out of his seat, slamming him down on the coffee table with a snarl. "What did I just say?" He held a fist to Brian's jaw and I folded my arms to watch the show.

"A-apologies," Washer stuttered and Gabriel slowly dropped his hand.

"Get out," he commanded and I flicked my finger to wrench the front door open for Washer to leave.

Gabriel released him, dropping back on the couch as Washer scrambled to his feet.

"It was just a question." He pouted innocently.

"Goodbye Brian," I said flatly and he rolled his eyes.

"You're such a spoil sport, Lancey. We could have so much fun together. All three of us could. Our new boy has obviously experimented, haven't you Gabe?"

"OUT!" we barked at the same time and Washer scurried out the door. I tried my best to ignore the way his speedos had slid firmly up his ass crack, but the stars were not on my side today. *Maybe put that in my horoscope next time, yeah? A little bit of a heads up would save me weeks of nightmares.*

I headed directly to the bowl of chocolate balls Washer had brought, carrying them to the trash and dumping them straight into it.

"Is he always like that?" Gabriel asked, wrinkling his nose.

"Sometimes he's worse."

"Noted."

I eyed my couch, making the mental decision to buy a new one.

"Want to help me burn a couch?" I asked and Gabriel grinned at the idea, a spark of mischief entering his gaze.

"We need a fire Elemental, why don't you ask Darius?"

"No," I grunted, my heart twisting. "I've got a fire crystal." I headed to the kitchen drawer to fish one out and Gabriel gave me that look again which said he could see right through me.

"Don't ask," I begged of him.

"I won't," he said sadly. "But when you're ready to start talking, Orio. I'll be waiting."

DARCY

CHAPTER TWENTY NINE

Another night of the shadows calling to me left a heavy feeling in my gut. I'd been awake since dawn and spent a few hours sketching, though every time I tried to draw something carefree I found myself twisting the image into something darker. The tangled roots of a tree became a writhing mass of snakes, the shimmering sunlight on the roof of The Orb became dark, jagged cracks I shaded in thick black tones. It didn't give me much relief and I soon tucked the images into my drawer with a sigh.

What I really wanted to do was talk to Tory. I'd written out a hundred messages to her last night before deleting them all. I'd fretted long into the night, wondering if there was a way to tell her about Seth without him finding out. But then I thought of the consequences of him discovering that I'd gone against him and I started fretting again. But the longer I hesitated to talk to her, the longer I went without my twin. And it was almost unbearable.

I practised controlling my Phoenix fire for a while, letting the blue and red flames gather in my palms, feeling the call of their immense power as it writhed under my skin. It whispered promises of revenge and the hotter it grew, the more that urge swelled in me. I let the flames circle up my arms, playing with it like a living thing as it wound around me, kissing my flesh with pockets of heat.

My Atlas pinged and I swiped it up, finding a message from Tyler.

Tyler:

My mom's sending a crew to do your interview this evening. Tory smashed it at hers last night! A car will be waiting to pick you up at the campus gates at 6pm.

My heart sank. Tory hadn't told me she'd gone to do the interview already. I wished I could have been there.

I shot a reply to Tyler, confirming the meeting placing and taking comfort in the fact that I'd be doing something proactive against the Heirs. Something they couldn't bite back at me for. I was a Vega twin and I was perfectly entitled to give interviews to the press when invited.

My Atlas pinged again and my gut dropped as I spotted Seth's name on the screen.

Seth:

Come up to the common room.

Two little ticks told him I'd read it so I couldn't pretend I hadn't seen it.

Seth:

Two minutes and counting.

Fury blazed through me as I stood up, claws scraping at my insides over being summoned by an Heir. It was worse than him beating me down, worse even than him cutting my hair off. He'd stolen my will from me. My ability to fight back. He was dangling my darkest secret over my head. It felt like being collared and leashed and no part of me could accept that.

But Seth was an idiot. Because this couldn't go on forever. One way or another, we'd escape his hold on us and I vowed to be ready for when that day came. My Phoenix fire flashed hotter along my arms and I pulled it back into me, soothing it and begging it to be patient.

I'll release you on him one day and he'll regret ever making me his target.

I tucked my Atlas into my jeans' pocket and headed out the door. Chatter sounded up in the common room as I climbed the stairs and my jaw clenched as I entered. Seth was lounging in his favourite grey chair by the fire across the room, his pack surrounding him. Some of them were spread across the couch opposite while others perched on the arms of Seth's chair and rubbed at his shoulders or ran their fingers through his hair.

I tutted under my breath, moving through the room. Seth's gaze fell on me and a dark smile pulled at his mouth as I slowed to a halt in front of him.

"You called me, your dogness?" I said, plastering on a polite smile and the Wolf pack started growling at me.

"Yeah, we were all about to play dress up. Thought you might wanna join in," Seth said smoothly as the beautiful Alice stroked his chest and grinned.

"Dress up?" I questioned. *Please don't get me involved in some weird-ass pack thing I don't understand.*

"How are we going to get a Vega to do it?" Frank asked in confusion, looking to Seth from beneath a sleeping girl on the couch.

Another tall guy with caramel skin and a thin moustache nodded his agreement. "Yeah, let's just pick some random freshmen. Where's that hat guy?"

"No Maurice. This particular Vega will do whatever I tell her to," Seth said with a triumphant smirk and his pack gasped, howling and barking excitedly. My gut sank as I looked between them all, trying to figure out what I was in for.

"Why?" Alice asked her Alpha, leaning in close to his ear.

My chest tightened as I stared directly at him, silently begging him not to tell.

"It's a secret," Seth said then mimed zipping his lips.

"I can get it out of you," Alice said, placing a kiss by his mouth and sliding her hand lower down his chest.

He nudged her away and rose from his seat, the members of his pack all stilling as they looked to him in anticipation.

"Turn around," Seth commanded me, but my feet wouldn't move. I didn't want to turn my back on this animal.

He twirled his finger in the air, giving me a pointed look and I forced myself to turn, releasing a slow breath to try and calm my pounding heart.

He moved close behind me and my skin prickled as his body heat washed over my back. "Wolves are hunters by nature, babe. We like to chase little furry creatures and eat them for lunch."

"Well it looks like I don't fit the bill," I said thickly, stepping forward but he caught the back of my jeans and tugged me back.

"Not yet." I could hear the smirk in his voice and my heart pounded unevenly. He yanked my top up a few inches and I stiffened, jerking forward again. He hooked me back with a low growl that resonated deep in my bones.

"Hold your shirt up to here," he instructed.

I reluctantly did as he said and he pressed a finger to my lower back, making a shudder roll through me. He started painting an image there, though I had no idea what it was as a tingle of magic swept over my skin.

"Maurice, show me the constellation again," he demanded and movement in my periphery said Maurice was moving closer.

Seth continued to paint what I guessed was the constellation on my back and a cold feeling ran beneath where his finger touched.

"Transformation crystal," Seth ordered and a second later something freezing cold pressed to my spine.

I cursed, lurching forward and spinning to face him. My Order form sprang up from the depths of my body and sparks showered from my hands, spraying over Seth as I lost control of it. He yelped as the embers burned holes in his fancy blue shirt and his eyes turned to two pits of fury. I couldn't concentrate on him a second longer as a wave of ice rolled across my lower back. Another freezing blast shot up my spine and flickered over my scalp.

"What have you done to me?" I gasped, placing a hand on a chair to steady myself as the strange feeling engulfed my body.

The Werewolves all jumped up, looking excited as they watched me, rubbing shoulders and nuzzling each other.

Something endlessly soft pushed down the back of my jeans and I reached around with shaking hands to feel what it was. I inhaled sharply as I tugged it free, craning my neck around to try and see it. I gasped as I spotted the pom-pom sized white rabbit tail poking out the top of my pants. I pulled at it in alarm and yelped as it yanked on my tail bone.

"Ah!" I swung around and the tail followed me as I released it. Seth's wolf pack fell apart with laughter and the darkness in his eyes lifted as a genuine smile graced his lips. He hurried forward, his smile still growing as he pushed his fingers into my hair. I caught his wrists on a knee-jerk reaction, my palms flickering with flames.

"Get off," I snapped.

He hissed between his teeth. "Back off the fire," he demanded and I pulled it down into my core with everything I had. "There," he said, taking my hand and guiding it up to touch something on my head. Two soft ears flopped over my hair and panic ran through me.

"Get rid of them!"

"But you look so edible, babe," he said like he was really enjoying this. He caught my hand and pulled me across the room toward a large mirror on the wall. As soon as the other students caught sight of my tail and ears, they roared with laughter, snatching out their Atlases to record me.

My cheeks flushed hot as Seth planted me beside him, slinging his arm around my shoulders as we stood in front of the mirror. I rushed forward to inspect what he'd done, from the grey ears dangling from the top of my head to the fluffy white rabbit tail which had appeared above my ass. That wasn't even the worst of it. Whiskers were sprouting from my cheeks and my eyes were changing too, my pupils overly large so I looked like some sort of cartoon anime character.

"Seth!" I barked, rounding on him. "You'd better get rid of this."

"Sure sure…later. Now give me your Atlas." He held out his hand. "Can't have you looking up any counter-spells."

"I won't," I insisted. I did *not* want to be parted with my Atlas even if I did have to go around like this. And I especially didn't want it in the hands of this asshole.

Seth held out his hand with a lazy expression and I noticed eyes on us from around the entire common room. A growl rumbled in my throat and heat spread over my shoulder blades as my Order begged to be set free.

"One day I'll burn you alive," I whispered, moving closer.

"But until that unlikely day, you have to obey me." He flipped his hand demandingly and I huffed furiously, snatching my Atlas out of my pocket and slamming it into his palm. "Off you go, little rabbit. I can't promise my pack won't chase you while you're looking so delicious." He winked, walking away to re-join his wolves and his pack fell on him, nuzzling him as they all had one big laugh orgy, hugging and kissing and giggling. It was ridiculous.

I was relieved when they all flopped back down into their seats, clearly having no intention of chasing me right then.

I glared at them for a second longer before turning and storming from the room.

I jogged down the stairs, taking them two at a time as tingles ran along my entire body. *How far is this transformation going to go?!*

I missed a step as I sped toward my corridor and gasped as I nearly crashed to my knees, catching myself on the bannister at the last second. I righted myself and hurried to my room, quickly opening the door and slipping inside.

Part of me wanted to just stay there and hide, but another part wanted to fix this. Undo what Seth had done and take the smallest of wins for myself. Who knew how long this was going to last anyway? If I didn't stop it, I could be sitting in Cardinal Magic on Monday morning as a Fae sized bunny covered in grey fur with big Thumper feet.

I grabbed my winter coat, pulling it on and stuffing the tail up the back of it out of sight with a groan of shame. Then I pulled the hood up and tucked my ears right back so there wasn't the slightest chance of them poking out.

I checked my reflection in the mirror, horrified as my whiskers brushed the edges of the hood. I clutched it tighter around my face and hurried out of the door. Without my Atlas I'd have to go to the library to do some research, but it was a Sunday, there'd probably be a ton of Fae there studying. I'd have to try and hide this from them even though I knew pictures of me were going to be plastered all over FaeBook soon enough anyway.

I somehow made it out of Aer Tower without anyone else seeing me. Rain swirled in the air around me as I bowed my head and ran all the way to Venus Library and spilled through the door.

Students looked up and the librarian gave me a sharp glare as I clutched the hood close around my face to hide my whiskers.

She frowned as I hurried past her and slipped into the first aisle, hunting through the books.

What am I even looking for – a de-bunny crystal??

I found a few books on transformation and carried them to a dark corner at the far end of the aisle then pushed through a door into a reading room. I sighed a breath of relief as I found the space empty.

I switched on the golden lamp on one of the tables and took a seat, dumping the books down in front of me. I started scanning through the contents pages, hunting for what I needed, though I wasn't sure quite what that was.

Someone opened the door and I bowed my head, cursing my luck as I tried to keep my face hidden. I stole a glance at them and spotted Diego as he carried a huge tome in his arms. He moved along to the next table, facing away from me as he dropped into a chair.

"Hey," I hissed, but he didn't respond. "*Diego.*"

Nothing.

I sighed, getting to my feet and hurrying over to him, realising he had headphones on under his hat as he bobbed his head to some tune.

I tapped him on the shoulder and he looked up. "Ah!" he fell backwards off his chair, lifting his hand defensively. Air magic swirled around me and threw my hood back in the gust. "Devil rabbit!" he screamed as my big floppy ears swung around my face.

"Diego it's *me*," I said in frustration, pointing at my blue hair.

"Darcy?" he gasped, his eyes trailing over my features as he relaxed.

I held out a hand for him but as Diego reached for it, I squeaked in horror as I realised it had turned into a furry grey paw. *Ohmagod no.*

Diego scrambled upright, tugging his chair with him and gazing over me. "What happened to you?"

"*Seth,*" I spat his name. "Can you help me find an antidote?" I asked desperately, glancing down at my other hand which I discovered was also a grey paw. I groaned, dropping my head back.

"Of course, chica. Or should I call you coneja?" he chuckled and I didn't have to ask to know what that meant.

"Come on, before I start sprouting fur all over the place." I hurried back to my table and Diego followed, dropping down opposite me. He picked up one of the books I'd gathered, glancing at me with a snort of amusement.

A smile tugged at my mouth and I cracked a small laugh, shaking my head at the craziness of this situation. I tried to turn the page in the book I'd been reading, but my bunny paw wasn't made for it.

I had to let Diego do most of the reading as I struggled to turn pages and I grew anxious as we failed to find an answer to my problem.

I chewed on my lip as I thought of the obvious solution.

"Can I borrow your Atlas?" I asked Diego. "I think we need the help of someone who knows how to fix this before I start craving carrots." *Actually a carrot does sound pretty good right about now - oh shit.*

"Who?" Diego frowned as he passed me his Atlas.

I sighed, realising my lack of thumbs meant I couldn't use it. "You'll have to do it. Message Professor Orion."

"What? No way am I calling that sanguijuela," he cursed.

"Diego please," I insisted. "He'll know what to do."

"So will a bunch of other Professors," he grumbled, tugging at his hat in irritation.

"Just do it," I pressed and he muttered under his breath in Spanish as he tapped out an email to him.

"He probably won't show up anyway. That guy is a son of a-"

"Bitch?" Orion appeared in a blur of motion, folding his arms and glaring down his nose at Diego as the door swung slowly closed behind him. He looked tired, his hair unkempt and his eyes dark. "Well I can't argue with that."

Diego lifted a brow, clearly surprised by not having his head bitten off for the comment.

Orion glanced over at me and my heart freaking stalled as his gaze slid down to the bunny ears, whiskers and paws I was sporting. His mouth twitched at the corner and he lifted a hand, scrubbing his knuckles over his mouth as he continued to stare like he was trying not to laugh.

"Enough staring, can you help me, sir?"

"Someone used a transformation crystal on you?" he guessed and I nodded.

"Yeah, Seth Capella."

His eyes turned to pitch at that. He rounded on Diego, plucking him from his chair by the collar of his shirt and pushing him toward the door. "Go to Mars Laboratories and ask Professor Shellick for a Malachite crystal and some Nightsugar powder."

"Why can't you go?" Diego blurted.

"Are you talking back to me?" Orion snapped.

Diego shook his head, backing up at Orion's fierce expression.

"Tell him I sent you."

Diego nodded and hurried away and I was left with Orion looking at me like I was a tasty snack.

"Don't laugh," I begged.

"I'm not going to." He lifted a hand and I felt the pressure of a silencing bubble slip out around us. "Do you have a cotton tail?" he asked, seeming hopeful.

"What does it matter?" I asked.

He grinned, prowling forward. "Maybe I want to see it."

I pressed my back to the bookcase behind me, shaking my head. "No way."

"Take your coat off," he urged.

"No," half a laugh escaped me. "I don't want you to see."

"Tough." He lunged forward, ripping my coat off and flipping me around. My eyes whipped to the door, but I guessed he'd hear someone approaching anyway.

A low chuckle escaped him as he tweaked my tail.

"You're such an asshole," I laughed. I tried to turn around but he held me in place, gently tugging up the back of my shirt. His fingers brushed over whatever Seth had painted there and a low growl escaped him.

"What is it?" I asked, my nose twitching. *Oh hell, I'm gonna have a button nose in a minute.*

He dropped my shirt and I turned around, leaning back against the shelves to hide my tail again.

"He's marked the Lepus constellation on you. Do you know what that is, Miss Vega?"

"I didn't realise I was in a class, *sir*."

He grinned darkly. "You should know your constellations by now."

"I'm gonna take a wild guess and say it's a rabbit?"

"Correct. A moon rabbit to be precise. And do you know what other constellation chases it in the sky?"

Why was I getting a pop quiz right now?

I chewed my lip, trying to picture my star charts. I'd memorised the places of all the star sign constellations but Lepus was obscure. "Umm..."

"The hunter," he answered for me, stepping closer, his fangs lengthening as he smiled. "Orion."

"Oh." I gave him a flirtatious look. "Well I don't fancy his chances against this rabbit."

"No?"

"Rabbits can be vicious." I bared my teeth and a hungry looked entered his gaze.

"I like them bitey." He moved forward, leaning in close and making my breathing stall. "Shall I lock the door so we can live out this little fantasy?"

"*Your* fantasy. And no, you've got issues." I smirked, slipping away from him. "Besides, you won't find it such a turn on when I morph completely into a pet rabbit."

"By the stars, maybe not. But if you *were* a little bunny I could keep you in my pocket and carry you everywhere. That doesn't sound so bad."

I folded my arms, giving him a stern look.

"Well I'd never have to worry about you getting into trouble again, would I?" He smiled darkly.

I raised my brows at that. "But you *are* the trouble."

His mouth pulled down at the corner, clearly not taking that joke well. He stiffened suddenly, then waved a hand to disband the silencing bubble and a few seconds later, Diego stepped back into the room.

He held out a shiny green crystal and a little pouch of what I guessed was the Nightsugar powder – whatever the crap that was.

"He docked ten house points from me for disturbing him." Diego frowned.

"How unfortunate," Orion commented dryly, taking the items from him and spinning a finger to instruct me to turn around again.

"You could give them back," Diego muttered.

"I could, yes," Orion agreed.

"So will you?" Diego asked hopefully.

"No."

I shot a glare at Orion over my shoulder, giving him a pointed look as Diego dropped down into a seat with a huff. He eyed my whiskers with a grin then rolled his eyes.

"Fine, five points to Aer," Orion tossed at Diego.

"He took ten."

"I know." Orion lifted my top and my skin tingled as he pressed his fingers to the base of my spine. He rubbed something gritty onto my skin which I guessed was that sugar stuff, massaging it over the area where Seth had painted the constellation. When he was done, he pressed the crystal to my spine and my back arched as a shot of heat splashed over my skin.

"There," he announced, dropping my top and I turned, reaching up to my ears and smiling as they started to retreat.

"Oh thank god," I breathed.

"I'm not a god, but I can see why you'd make the mistake, Miss Vega." Orion winked and I snorted a laugh, serving me a glare from Diego. Guess he wasn't over his hate for Orion.

Diego tapped his pen on the table, giving Orion the stink eye as he waited for him to leave. He started doing it so vigorously that the pen launched from his fingers and shot toward me, bouncing off my chest and dropping to the floor. I picked it up and held it out to him. His fingers closed around it, brushing mine and I gasped as blackness crashed over me, stealing away everything around me.

I could still feel Diego's hand and latched onto it in alarm as I spun through a vortex of darkness.

"What's happening?!" I yelled but no sound came out. I felt like I was moving at a thousand miles an hour through an eternity of nothingness.

I slowed suddenly and the shadows swirled, brushing along my skin and twisting around me in an embrace. Diego's grip tightened and his voice drifted to me as if from far away. "I'm here, chica. Don't let go."

"What's going on?" I gasped.

"The shadows took hold of us when our hands met. Both our powers have combined, can't you hear it?"

"Hear what?"

"Silence," he said and I realised he was right, the whispers were gone. "I've never been this deep, the power you possess must be immense."

"How do we get out?" I asked, trying not to panic, but this didn't feel like the usual pull of the shadows. It felt like diving into a pool of ink and closing the lid behind me. There was no lulling tug, drawing me into the deep. There was just perfect stillness and an endless void.

"I'm anchoring you," he said, but I didn't know what that meant. "Someone wants us here. Someone from the Shadow Realm. You'll be able to hear them while I block out the other voices." His voice quavered and my heart stuttered in response.

I knew who it was. Who it had to be. The same girl who'd called to me so many times. I felt her presence draw near then a soft breath fluttered against my cheek.

"Finally," she whispered. "It's been so hard to reach you." I felt fingers against my arm, but they were almost ethereal, passing through me like the hand of a ghost.

"Who are you?" I asked nervously.

She laughed softly and the musical sound echoed all around us. "I am nothing and everything."

"That's not an answer," I pressed.

"A name is just a name. Here, they call me the Shadow Princess."

"Who's they?" I asked, wishing the blinding darkness would lift so I could see her.

"The people of the dark," she whispered, a note of fear in her voice.

Something yanked at me deep in my gut and I almost lost my grip on Diego's hand.

"There's not much time," the girl whispered frantically.

That same tug of magic ripped through me and I clung to Diego's hand as hard as I could, sure I'd be drawn away if I let go.

"Tell me what you want," I begged.

"Help," she said, her voice breaking. "I need help."

"How can I help you?" I asked, though I wasn't sure I wanted to. She was just a strange voice in the dark, I wasn't going to trust her.

"You must build a bridge from here to the Fae realm so I can escape. But there's only one time of year it can be done. It's drawing close, I can feel it."

"El puente de las estrellas," Diego breathed in awe.

"Yes, the bridge of stars," the girl translated, a note of desperation to her tone. "At midnight on the last night of the year, the veil between worlds will be at its thinnest. That's when the bridge can be built. Please, you must find a way to do it."

Before I could answer, another powerful wave of magic tried to pull me from the depths of the dark. I gasped, gripping onto Diego's hand as I tried to stay.

The shadows swirled and light shone in my periphery. I turned to find Orion blazing through the ether, a light burning in his palm as he reached for me. His gaze shifted from me to the girl standing before us and I saw her in the glow, her freckly cheeks and youthful features seeming almost translucent.

Her form receded into the dark as tendrils of shadow coiled around her, chaining her and drawing her back.

"Lance!" she called, her eyes widening.

He caught my hand, lunging for her in the same movement, but the shadows prevailed, stealing her away.

She knew him. But how?

Orion clutched me to his chest, snatching hold of Diego and a vile, twisting, wrenching feeling made my head spin.

I blinked awake, finding myself on the floor of the reading room, my hand still wrapped around Diego's who was lying beside me. He groaned and I sat up, almost head butting Orion who was holding my other hand. His face was pale, his features pinched.

"Lance?" I whispered anxiously, biting my tongue as Diego sat up beside us. "Sir?" I corrected and his eyes focused on me. "Are you okay?"

He nodded once, rising to his feet and pulling me after him, his face deathly pale.

Diego stood, rubbing the back of his head with a frown. "Who was she?

She knew you," he said to Orion.

"I don't know," Orion said, but I sensed he was lying. He looked haunted, terrified. "This stays between us, you understand?" he growled at Diego who pursed his lips before nodding. Orion strode to the door, wrenching it open and shooting away without a word.

Anxiety rippled through me. "I'm going to go lie down for a while," I said to Diego. "The shadows drain me."

"Are you alright?" Diego asked frantically. "What just happened, I mean, that was crazy chica."

"I know." I rested a hand on his arm, unsure what else I could say.

"I can walk you back to Aer Tower if you like and we can talk about what happened?" he asked hopefully.

"I think I just need to rest, but we'll talk later." I headed out of the door with zero intention of returning to my room. I was going to hunt down Orion and get answers. The only problem with that plan was that I didn't have my Atlas and I couldn't go strolling into Asteroid Place in broad daylight.

As I walked out of the library into the freezing air, I was grabbed by strong hands. My stomach lurched as Orion shot across campus in a blur of movement and I winced against the powerful wind dragging over me.

When he stopped, my head was spinning and it took me a second to realise I was in his office in Jupiter Hall. He locked the door and cast a silencing bubble before turning to me with an intense expression.

"You *know* who she was," I stated.

He nodded, visibly swallowing. "Yes," he said on a breath of disbelief and a note of hope. "It was Clara…my sister."

My lips parted and my heart pounded out of rhythm. "Are you sure?"

"Yes – *fuck* – yes, I'm sure." He started pacing, scraping a hand through his hair.

"Is she alive?" I breathed, unable to tell. She'd seemed so intangible, like she wasn't quite there.

"I don't know. I think so. She wasn't just some soul…"

"She asked for my help," I said, watching him pace. "She said something about building a bridge of stars on the last night of the year." I shook my head, the words sounding crazy coming from me.

He halted, looking to me with a furrowed brow. "She thinks she can come back?" He rubbed a hand over his face then started laughing, his expression transforming into something hopeful and desperate. "That means she's alive. She's fucking alive!"

He ran at me, lifting me into his arms and kissing me hard. His laughter was infectious as he spun me around and I clung to his shoulders, sure I'd never seen him so happy.

"It's really her?" I asked, my heart lifting.

He skimmed his thumb across my cheek as he nodded. "Yes, it's her. I'd know her anywhere."

He placed me down and I rested my hand on his chest, his heart drumming excitedly beneath my palm. His smile lit a fire in my chest which blazed with heat. After everything we'd been through, it felt incredible to find out some good news. That his sister was alive, trapped in the shadows, but able to return.

"I'll help you bring her back. Whatever it takes, Lance," I promised, never wanting him to lose the light that was currently glowing in his gaze.

His eyes swum with emotion and he clutched me to him, the tension running out of his posture. "I don't know how this is possible. I haven't done anything to earn the grace of the stars."

I looked up at him, his words cutting into me "How can you think that? Lionel stole your sister from you, he bound you to a life you didn't choose. The stars owe you everything."

Orion's eyes glimmered with that thought. "Well whether the stars want me to have her or not, Blue, I will bend them to my will and build a bridge out of them to bring her back. On New Year's Eve, Clara *will* come home."

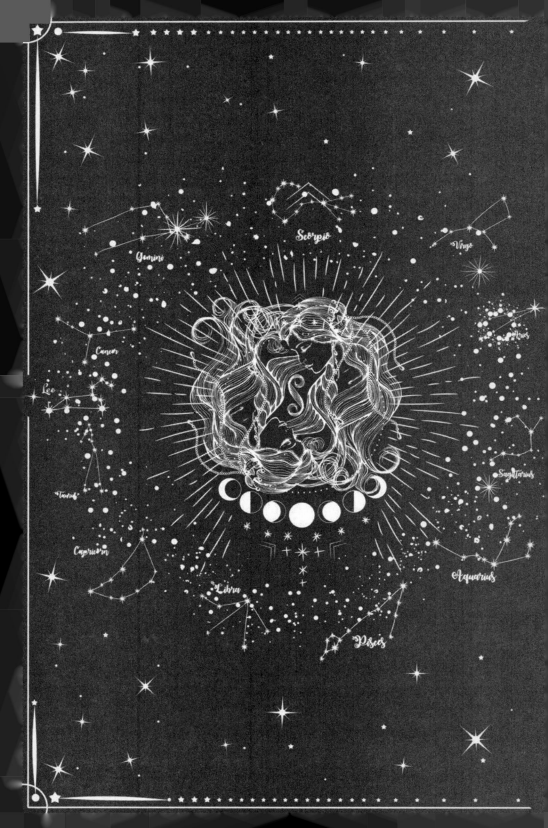

TORY

CHAPTER THIRTY

There was something wrong with me. Like deep seeded, right down in the marrow of my bones, *wrong*. I'd always known it. Given two options, I always made the choice that would hurt me, always picked the thing that was bad for me. I tried to justify it by claiming I just hated to be bored. That I'd rather have something hurt or terrify me than feel nothing at all. But maybe, when you looked really closely at all of the choices I made, it turned out that there was a simpler explanation than that. I just didn't know how to be happy. And perhaps sometimes I believed I didn't deserve to be either.

"Come to me..."

I tipped my head back, looking up at the ceiling in my bedroom as the shadows coiled around me. They slid beneath my skin like the taste of purest ecstasy and I moaned as I called them closer, bathing in their dark power.

Darkness twisted between my fingers and rose up around me. I could feel it thickening with each inhale, taste its black power on the air surrounding me. And it was hungry.

I flexed my fingers and the shadows rolled from me, slipping across my bed and dropping over the edge to pool on the floor beside me. The floor was so thick with them that all I could see down there was a chasm of deepest night.

I turned towards them slowly, pushing my bare feet out in front of me until they were hanging over the edge.

My heart pounded solidly in my chest, my ears rang with a distant warning, telling me not to slip so far into them. But in that moment, I wanted to feel the embrace of the darkness more than I feared its hold on me.

"Join me..."

I pushed my feet over the edge of the bed and dipped them into the shadows. Their touch was cold and slick, like submerging my toes in a spill of oil.

Everywhere they caressed came alive with pleasure so intense it blinded me. I moaned loudly, the pure, electric energy of the dark power calling to me on a base level. It saw all the harsh and hateful parts of me and praised them, found every dark and malevolent thought and stoked a fire beneath it. The shadows didn't wish for me to be a better version of myself. They called for me to do my worst and applauded when I did.

I slid from the bed, slowly submerging myself in the shadows as they whispered my name and kissed my flesh.

I lay flat on the floor, inhaling deeply as the darkness flooded my skin and moaning my pleasure as I accepted it. It snaked around my legs and tied itself around my arms and as darkness curtained my vision, I found myself standing on a precipice.

A girl stood before me wearing a dress made entirely of twisting darkness. A crown of thorns and shadows sat upon her head, cutting into her flesh so that blood shone wetly on it in the purple light of the sky above us. Her hair was a soft hazel and her eyes wide with understanding as she smiled knowingly at me, extending a hand to me in offering.

She took a step back so that she hung suspended in the air above the great drop with a wind I couldn't feel sending the shadows which coated her flesh swirling all around her.

"Come to me, Tory...soak yourself in the power of the shadows."

Her voice echoed through the air around us, rich with promises and expectation though her lips didn't move. But I knew it was her I could hear, like her mind was communicating directly with mine. She could give me all the power I might ever desire and free me from the shackles of my Fae life.

"You're all alone now. But the shadows are always with you, they won't hurt you if you give your heart to them…"

My lips parted, my soul aching to say yes.

I took a step forward, my toes curling over the edge of the cliff. The drop beneath me was impossible to judge, the void filled with shadows, darkness and a raw power which seemed to beat with a pulse of its own.

My own shadows rose like a coming tide within me and my back arched as pleasure crashed through me intensely.

I reached out, my gaze finding hers as I looked at this princess of the shadows who was offering me the world.

My fingertips brushed hers and I was on the verge of jumping just as flames rose beneath my skin.

The shadows inside me recoiled as my Phoenix blossomed and every inch of my flesh burned with it. But it didn't hurt, it woke me up and through the flames dancing before my eyes, the girl's face shifted, peeling back to reveal razor sharp teeth and eyes as black as pitch.

I gasped in fright and tried to snatch my hand back away from her.

"Save me!" she demanded forcefully.

I shook my head in fierce denial, gasping as my flames roared with life beneath my flesh.

Her grip tightened, her fingernails lengthening and cutting into my wrist as she tried to pull me over the edge.

A growl tore from my throat as I dug my heels in and I shook my head fiercely.

"No!" I snarled.

Phoenix fire flared bright and strong as I willed it to come to my aid and the shadow princess screamed as it burned her where she still gripped my wrist.

She tore her hand away and pain flared as her fingernails raked down my wrist and my blood spilled along my skin.

I stumbled back, falling as I lurched away from that precipice but instead of feeling the hard bite of stone against my spine, carpet greeted me instead.

I gasped as my eyes snapped open, my heart thundering a panicked tune as I stared around at my room at the academy. The shadows had disappeared and I lay panting as I tried to make sense of what the hell had just happened.

"I'm so lonely…"

I shook my head to clear it of the girl's voice. I couldn't help her. I didn't know how. And I certainly wasn't going to join her in the shadows to save her from being alone.

My skin was slick with sweat, my hair sticking to me as I got to my feet. I felt shaky, drained and for a moment I had trouble locating my magic within me.

When I finally latched onto the flare of power which sat deep within my chest, I let out a sigh of relief.

The pale light of dawn spilled in through my window and I stood looking at the rising sun for a long moment before an ache on my wrist made me look down.

My left wrist was torn open in gouges that had undeniably been made by fingernails and blood slid from the wounds in a steady stream which painted red lines over my hand and fingers before dripping to the pale carpet beneath me.

I cursed, lifting my arm as I headed into the bathroom where I quickly set the shower running.

I stripped out of my pyjamas and headed straight inside, washing my wrist as I tried to figure out how the hell a shadow manifestation had managed to give me a real wound. I had thought the Shadow Realm had just been in my head, that I could see it but not really touch. But it looked like I was wrong about that.

When I finally shut the shower off, my wrist was still bleeding. I frowned at the stinging wounds. They weren't deep but for some reason they wouldn't heal over enough to stop the blood from oozing out of them.

I cursed my stupidity for falling for the lure of the shadows and quickly bound my wrist with a washcloth to try and stem the flow.

I dressed in my uniform and gathered my school books together before snatching up my headphones and setting a playlist running at random.

I headed down to the common room and grabbed a cup of coffee before taking a chair beside the raging fire to the side of the room so that I could refill my magic supplies before class.

The heat of the flames washed over me as I sat there, letting my gaze fall out of focus as I considered messaging Darcy.

I hadn't heard from her at all last night and this tension between us was like a physical wound. I didn't understand what was going on with her and I couldn't work out why the hell she wouldn't tell me.

I hadn't even told her about hooking up with Darius and the very real possibility that I must have lost my goddamn mind. It didn't seem possible to me that we were in this position and yet here I sat, alone, not understanding why she was behaving the way she was or why she hadn't even replied to the messages I'd sent her last night.

I bit my lip and pulled my Atlas from my pocket, setting down the cup of coffee that had gone cold in my hands.

I pulled up my messages to her and sighed.

Tory:
I hate this. Can we please just talk it out?

My wrist tingled painfully as I twisted it to use my Atlas and I frowned as I peeled back my make-do bandage to find blood soaking through it.

The common room had slowly been filling as I sat there and I looked up as I felt someone watching me.

I stilled as I found Darius's gaze fixed firmly on me, his brow furrowing as he took in the blood soaking through the washcloth bandage I'd made.

For a moment I held his eye, my flesh tingling at the memory of the way he'd made me feel when I'd finally given in to the heat between us. I'd seen him a few times since but he hadn't spoken to me or even acknowledged me at all. In fact I had gotten the distinct impression he'd lost interest in me now that he'd gotten what he wanted, and that was fine. Just so long as that extended to him tormenting me too, although I somehow doubted that. Either way I'd gotten the message loud and clear. I'd just forget our one off moment of madness had ever happened and hope that he did too.

Darius took a step towards me with a look in his eye that I couldn't quite work out but if it was anything like usual, I could only imagine he planned on hassling me. I got to my feet, grabbing my bag and striding straight out of the room.

I couldn't deal with him today. Not with my heart aching over Darcy and my skin tender from the touch of the shadows. I didn't need him taking pot shots at whatever the hell else I had left.

I headed into the cold air outside Ignis House and started walking up the path to The Orb. I wondered if Geraldine might be there yet. If she was, I could ask her to heal my arm, but as the cold trickle of blood dripped between my fingers I wondered if that was the best idea. How was I going to explain that to her? I didn't want to lie to her any more than I had to about the shadows and it didn't seem very likely that I'd somehow done this to myself.

I paused in the middle of the path and sighed as I pulled my Atlas from my pocket. Orion had given me his personal number in case I ever needed help with the shadows and though I'd never used it before, I was fairly sure this counted as needing his help.

Tory:

I've got a bit of an issue I need to see you about.

Lance:

Has something happened? What have you heard?

I frowned at that weird response. What would I have heard?

Tory:

I just need help with something.

My message was ridiculously vague but I guessed sending details about the shadows back and forth wasn't the best idea.

Lance:

Okay. I'll meet you at my office in five minutes.

I tugged my blazer down over my wrist to hide the blood as much as possible then carried on up the path. I soon reached The Orb and the rest of the buildings at the heart of campus and headed straight into Jupiter Hall before climbing the stairs and walking to Orion's office.

The door was open as I arrived and I stepped inside with a prickle of discomfort running along my spine.

Orion was sat behind his desk, his shirt only half buttoned and his normally perfectly styled hair a mess. He got to his feet as I stepped inside and threw a handful of air magic at the door to knock it closed behind me. A silencing bubble fell around us a moment later and I arched an eyebrow at him as he looked at me with concern.

"Shit, dude, you could have gotten dressed properly before meeting me," I joked but he didn't even seem to hear me.

"What's happened?" he demanded. "Did Seth do something, or-"

"Seth? What's that asshole got to do with anything?" I asked in confusion.

Orion eyed me for a long moment, a little tension leaving his posture before his eyes fell on my wrist.

"What's that?" he asked with a frown.

"The reason I'm here," I said, pushing my sleeve back and pulling the bloodstained washcloth off of my wrist. "I was hoping you could heal it for me?"

"You messaged me at the crack of dawn to come and help you with a *scratch?*" he asked in disbelief.

"It's like eight, dude," I pointed out. "We have Cardinal Magic in half an hour so I assumed you'd be awake. Besides, I wasn't sure if I should ask anyone else to help me with this."

"Why not?"

I pursed my lips, preparing for the tirade I was pretty sure I was about to receive from him.

"Well, last night I must have, kinda...*accidentally*...given in to the shadows. A bit."

"You what?" Orion asked, his gaze lighting with concern instead of the anger I'd expected.

"Yeah. Well, I kinda sank into them and then it was like I was in this whole shadowy realm and that girl was there – the one who keeps calling us. She tried to make me stay." I held my wrist up as evidence and his scowl deepened.

"You fell so far that she was able to do this to you?" he asked in horror.

I cleared my throat. "Well. I made it back didn't I? So, no harm done and all that. Maybe you could just heal this and we can go on like nothing happened."

"Do you know how serious this is, Tory?" he asked me, stepping forward with an intense look. "If you were that deep in, it's a wonder the shadows didn't consume you. Especially once you started bleeding. It's a miracle you made it out without help."

"My Phoenix kinda burned me free," I said quietly, feeling like a little girl who'd been caught out doing something wrong.

"Well thank fuck for that," he growled. "What the hell had you feeling so hopeless that they managed to call you to them while you slept?"

I stilled beneath his penetrating gaze, my jaw locking tight.

"Can you heal me or not?" I asked, ignoring his question.

Orion reached out and took my wrist in his grasp but his gaze stayed trained on mine. I kept my chin up and my mouth closed.

Green healing magic encased my arm and I waited as it got to work at trying to fix the damage to my arm.

Orion grunted in discomfort as his gaze fell from mine to his work on my arm.

"*Fuck.* Whatever caused this injury held the power of darkness deeply within it," he gritted out.

"What does that mean?" I asked as his grip on me tightened and my blood oozed between his fingers.

"That it's going to be a bitch to heal. And it'll take a hell of a lot of magic to do it too."

I chewed on my bottom lip as he worked, sweat lining his brow as he pushed more and more magic beneath my skin.

After several long minutes, he drew his hand back and I sighed with relief as I found the wounds healed over. Orion used his water magic to clean the blood off of me and I was surprised to find the scratches had left pink lines on my skin. I'd never seen healing magic fail to remove all evidence of an injury before.

"That's all I can manage for now," Orion said, dropping back to perch on the edge of his desk. "I'm practically tapped out."

"It was that hard to heal?" I asked in surprise, Orion was pretty damn powerful so for it to have taken that much from him was surprising.

"The shadows aren't a joke, Tory," he growled and my spine straightened as the anger I'd been waiting for surfaced.

"Yep. I got that," I said, stepping back towards the door.

"I'm not sure you do. Darcy told me you've been practicing with them alone, even though you've been warned about the dangers of them."

My lips parted as a little tendril of betrayal found me at that admission. So she wouldn't talk to me about whatever the hell was going on with her but she'd spill my secrets to Orion?

"Well, I get the impression I'll need them if I ever want to stop your asshole bestie from making my life hell," I replied icily.

"You intend to use them against Darius?" he asked in surprise, a flare of protectiveness coming from him as if I'd just threatened to kill his Dragon buddy.

"Only when I have to," I replied.

"You know how dangerous the shadows are. You shouldn't be playing around with them like some stupid little girl!"

Anger licked along my limbs and I scowled at him as I made it back to the door.

"Well it's not like I asked for them, is it?" I snapped. "But if they're what I need to defend myself from that prick then I'll be using them."

Orion's jaw ticked. "Darius told me about what happened between the two of you yesterday," he said.

Heat spread across my cheeks at that admission and I clenched my fists angrily. "Nice. So he's gossiping about me with his little friends, is he? I'm sure he's really damn pleased with himself for getting what he wanted from me."

"That's not true," Orion said hastily. "He's not talking about you with anyone like that. He only told me that the two of you were together. He needed to talk to someone about-"

"Save it," I snapped. "I don't wanna hear about how I was stupid enough to let myself become the latest notch on his bedpost."

"Is that really all you think you are to him?" Orion asked sadly and I bristled at the implication that I was somehow missing something here.

"At what point would I have gotten any other impression? When he shifted and flew away from me as fast as physically possible? Or when I saw him at dinner and in the common room last night and he didn't speak a word to me, let alone look at me? Why would I give a shit anyway? I got what I wanted from him too so now we can just forget all about it."

"Tory-" Orion began just as the bell rang to announce the start of class.

"I'm going to be late," I said, catching the door handle and tugging the door wide.

"Your first lesson is with me, you're hardly going to be in trouble for being late," Orion snapped, knocking the door shut again with a gust of his magic.

I folded my arms, narrowing my eyes on him as I waited to find out what the hell he wanted from me.

"Darius isn't a perfect man but he is a *good* man. At the heart of him, everything he does is in aid of what he believes to be right. And he might be pig headed and arrogant and his own worst enemy half the time but his actions are rarely selfish. You can't begin to imagine the sacrifices he's made to his own happiness in pursuit of stopping his father and protecting Solaria from the Nymphs."

"Is there a point to this manifesto because I'm pretty sure we don't get to vote for our great and powerful Councillors so I don't see why you give a shit about my opinion of him."

"You're both as stubborn as each other," Orion muttered, swiping a hand over his face. There were bags beneath his eyes and as I looked at him a little more closely, I realised he was wearing the same shirt he'd been in for class yesterday. I'd thought he looked a mess because he'd hurried here while getting ready, but on closer inspection it seemed more like he hadn't slept at all.

"Are you alright?" I asked slowly, taking a step back towards him.

Orion looked up at me in surprise then glanced down at his wrinkled shirt. "Not entirely," he admitted, giving me an assessing look before going on. "Yesterday, your sister got into a little trouble with the shadows herself. She accidentally touched Polaris's hand and his connection to the shadows threw her in the deep end too."

"What?" I gasped, moving closer to him with a prickle of concern moving beneath my skin.

"She's alright. She didn't go as deep as you did by the sounds of things. But she saw the Shadow Princess too and…well, when I followed to pull Darcy free of the darkness…"

"What?" I demanded, the glimmer of fear and excitement in his gaze making me desperate for his answer.

"The Shadow Princess is my sister, Clara," he breathed, his gaze filling with hope. "And she needs our help to return to the Fae Realm. She's been in the Shadow Realm all these years so for her to hurt you…she must be deeply corrupted by them. But she can come back from that once she's free of them. It will take time, but I can help her."

My lips parted on a protest, my memory of her fingernails biting into my skin rising fast. She'd tried to pull me into the dark with her. She'd wanted me to drown in the shadows and the thought of setting her free had the hairs raising along the back of my neck. But what was I supposed to say? If it was my sister stuck in the Shadow Realm, I'd sell my own soul to free her. And perhaps my own fear had coloured the way I'd viewed what had happened to me. She said she was lonely. Maybe she wasn't trying to drown me, she just couldn't bear to be alone any longer.

"Shit," I breathed because I couldn't even begin to think of what else to say.

Orion's gaze was lit with a fierce determination and how could I blame him?

"We'll help her then," I said firmly, banishing my own doubts. Because I couldn't even imagine the pain of losing a sibling and if there was even the slightest chance that I could help him get her back then I'd do it. No matter what.

Orion grabbed me so quickly that a gasp of surprise escaped my lips just as I was locked in the iron embrace of his arms. It took my brain half a second to realise he was hugging me. He was relieved. He clearly hadn't been sure if I'd agree to helping him on this, but it really didn't seem like much of a choice to me.

I half laughed as I hugged him back, patting his shoulder awkwardly when he didn't let go right away.

"This is kinda inappropriate, dude," I joked and he barked a laugh as he released me.

"Sorry," he said sardonically. "We wouldn't want that now, would we? Although I think the FIB might have a few other things they'd like to investigate me for before hugging a student made it to the top of the list."

"We're really late for your class now, you know?" I said, glancing at the clock behind him.

"Right. You head on down there and I'll catch up when I'm not in yesterday's clothes," he agreed.

I laughed at him and headed out of the room, tugging my sleeve down to conceal the pink scars on my wrist as I headed to Cardinal Magic.

The rest of the class were all inside, waiting at their desks as I arrived and they looked my way as I entered, checking I wasn't Orion before turning their attention back to chatting amongst themselves.

Darcy straightened in her chair as she spotted me, her eyes widening and half a smile pulling at the corner of her mouth. I returned it a little hesitantly and dropped into my chair beside her.

"Hey," I said awkwardly. I never had an awkward moment with her in my life.

"Hey," she replied in a small voice.

Silence stretched between us and I frowned before throwing a tight silencing bubble up around the two of us, not giving a shit if it was rude to cut Diego and Sofia out of our conversation. We needed to talk. Right now.

"So were you just ignoring my messages on purpose then?" I asked, trying to keep the bite out of my tone but she winced like I'd shouted.

"Sorry. I...Seth took my Atlas," Darcy said, not offering any further explanation than that.

"Was this when you were hooking up with him again or just while you were hanging out like besties?" I asked irritably.

Darcy chewed on her lip but only offered me a shrug.

I let the silence spread, waiting to hear what she was going to offer me by way of an explanation but she just started fiddling with her pen like it was the most interesting thing in the world.

"So are you going to tell me what the hell is going on with you?" I asked when I couldn't take it any more.

Darcy looked at me, tears brimming in her eyes like something was horribly wrong. I reached out and took her hand.

"You can tell me *anything*, Darcy," I promised her. "I'd stand by you if you told me you'd been on a killing spree and had developed a taste for human hearts. So just tell me."

Her lips parted, she took a deep breath, her gaze held mine and she slowly started shaking her head.

"I'm so sorry, Tory," she breathed. "But I can't tell you. I just...*can't.*"

Pain splintered through me as her grip tightened on my fingers like she knew I was about to walk away from her, but what the hell did she expect me to do? Just sit here and accept the fact that the only person I'd ever had stand by me through everything in my life just didn't trust me enough to tell me when something was going on with her?

"I've never in my life kept secrets from you," I breathed, hurt lacing my words as tears stung the backs of my eyes. "You know every dark and ugly thing there is to know about me and I've never hidden an inch of it from you. But if you really don't feel like you can trust me then fine. Be that way."

Darcy's lips parted with horror and some of her tears spilled over her cheeks but she still didn't say a word.

I got to my feet so suddenly that my chair fell back, hitting the floor with a loud clatter that drew looks from all around the room. I burst the silencing bubble I'd put up around us, ignoring the stares I was getting from everyone as I headed through the huge room with determined strides, coming to a halt in front of Tyler Corbin's desk in the front row.

"Swap seats with me," I demanded and something about my tone or the look in my eyes made him agree without even cracking a joke.

He gathered his stuff and headed to the middle of the room and I dropped into his chair with heat prickling along my spine and pain tearing my heart to shreds.

Orion finally appeared in his fresh clothes, his brow dipping as he noticed the new seating arrangement. But I ignored his probing stare, dropping my eyes to my Atlas even though the screen was blank.

After a brief pause, he started the lesson but I couldn't hear him beyond the ringing in my ears.

The shadows shifted beneath my skin, hungry for the agony I was feeling and I let myself sink into their embrace just enough to numb the pain.

The darkness called to me with the promise of oblivion and for the first time, I found myself truly tempted to give in to its call.

CALEB

CHAPTER THIRTY ONE

I leaned back in my chair on the couch in King's Hollow, flicking through the FaeBook feed on my Atlas. A post caught my eye and I got sucked into it.

Tyler Corbin:

Arghhhhhh! Don't wanna share this but FML I need to.

So I head to Lunar Leisure thinking I'll spend a little time in the steam room – my ass was killing me since I pulled a glute in Physical Enhancement and I didn't want some random Fae's hand on my butt cheek to heal it (#theresonlyonefaeforme). SO, I head to the steam room and no one's about so what's a guy to do? Go in naked of course.

I strip down, hanging low (#hunglikeahorse), and head inside getting all steamy and shit - and it is steamy as fuck in there. Like, I couldn't even see my hand in front of my face steamy. I walk over to the benches, blind as a Halayan bat, then turn and sit down...on a steamy, warm fucking LAP! So I jump up like there's a fire under my ass (#therewasactuallyadick) but my glute gives out and I slap right down into it again.

That's when I feel it (#nothisdick but also #notnothisdick) his SIREN LURE. This guy is some Siren asshole trying to feed on me!

So I thrash like a beached dolphin and garble off something about my pulled glute in explanation for the double dip. He helps me up – thank the stars – and then his hand (#hisfuckinghand) slams onto my ass and he heals away my muscle ache.

I turn. The mist swirls. I see him, he sees me. #wesonaked

And then I die. I mean, actually die. Because it's a teacher – a fucking teacher! #GUESSWHO!?!?!?

Comments:
Marsha Walker:
Oh my stars, Tyler!!! Was it Washer??????????? Did he slip it in??
Tyler Corbin:
For the love of the moon! Of course he fucking didn't!!
Ashlee Olson:
Noooooooooooooooooooooooooooooo! #washoffwasher
Chelsea de Araujo:
Literally just threw up everywhere. #RIPcherrymuffin
Sofia Cygnus:
Baby no!
Brian Washer:
Now now, Corbin, I don't see what all the fuss is about. We're just two adults who had a little mishap. Nothing to be embarrassed about. How's that glute of yours feeling now? Nice and supple?
Lucie Baudry:
Are you sure it wasn't Caleb getting horny for the horn??
Amy Sawyer:
#couldhavebeenworse #steamyweany #wetwillies #brainwasher

What the fuck?? I was half amused, half traumatised on Corbin's behalf and half pissed off about that horny for the horn comment.

I glanced over at Seth who was lounging beside me watching some documentary on wild elk and half salivating as the herd bolted at the sight of a wolf. I tried to show him the post but he seemed to be in some kind of trance.

Darius sat in the armchair to my right, his jaw tight and his gaze fixed on nothing as he sipped at his fifth – no, *sixth* beer and thought about whatever was eating him.

He'd been damn pissy since Tory had trashed his motorbike and though he'd told us he'd found her and dealt with it, he hadn't exactly explained how. And it seemed like whatever had taken place between them had just made him feel worse about the whole thing. I'd already asked him if he was okay four times since we'd gotten here and I was willing to bet he'd punch me if I asked again, so I'd dropped it. Seth had too, aside from the occasional whimper he tossed Darius's way. There was no point in us pushing at him when he was like this though. And he'd locked Max right back out of his head ever since that day as well so he couldn't even get a read on what was going on.

Although Max wasn't here right now anyway. He was off chasing Geraldine Grus. Not that he'd admit it. But he'd taken up a lot of new routines recently which all put him in her general vicinity as often as possible.

I looked over the stories which were trending with just enough interest to confirm that the rumours the Vegas had started had well and truly died. No more mention of Pegasus fetishes or Griffin dump baths or flea ridden Alphas.

The only stories appearing were of Darcy Vega talking to ravens no one could see and of Tory Vega screwing every other person in the academy.

We'd won.

And that should have felt fucking brilliant.

But whenever I saw Tory sitting on her own in The Orb at meal times and Darcy looking half a second away from tears, I didn't feel particularly victorious...I just felt like a shitty person.

I sighed, raising my hand to turn my Atlas off just as a news notification flashed up.

Trending now: The Vega Twins give their first official interviews...

My eyebrows raised in surprise; the twins hadn't shown the faintest bit of interest in talking to the press before now. Why would they have suddenly decided to talk out while the press was full of hateful stories about them? A prickle of unease ran along my skin. If they'd chosen to do some retaliation piece insulting us and protesting their innocence, they were about to find out just how well that kind of thing would be taken. Denial stories never went well, even worse if you were stupid enough to try and blame someone else for your problems. But they had no press experience, no PR people to help them with this kind of thing, so I wouldn't have been surprised if they'd done it.

I'd meant it when I'd told Tory how important reputation was. And even though I'd known that our plan would finally push them out of our way for good, I still felt a little shitty about it. Those labels would be attached to them forever now. Even more so if they'd been foolish enough to lash out in response.

I steeled myself for what I was about to find as I clicked on the link and my mouth fell open in shock as I found it.

The truth about us – an interview with our lost Princesses...

The title was punctuated by two images which had clearly been taken on professional shoots. Darcy was standing in a woodland clearing under the moon, dressed like some kind of ethereal goddess as she reached an arm out to stroke the feathery head of a raven sat in the branches above her. Another of the huge black birds sat on her shoulder and the trees behind her were filled with them. She didn't look insane, she looked beautiful and kind, a knowing smile tugging at the corner of her lips and a glimmer of honesty in her eyes.

The second image was of Tory sitting on the edge of a huge bed with a group of eight ripped guys all laying behind her in their underwear. She wore a silk silver dressing gown which fell open a little to reveal the edge of her black bra. Her bronze legs were crossed but positioned in such a way as to show off every perfect inch of them. Her perfectly made up features looked almost doll like as she turned wide, green eyes on the camera, her red lips parted in a way that spoke of sex. The stylists had curled her brunette hair and it spilled around her shoulders and screamed just fucked and brought to memory the way her skin had felt pressed against mine.

I groaned as I realised what this was. They hadn't been stupid enough to bite back at these rumours, they'd found someone to spin them for them.

After a brief introduction, the piece started on Darcy, more photos of her in the woods surrounded by ravens and looking exquisite sat alongside a story about her work in animal shelters and her particular fondness for helping to rehabilitate injured birds. There were jokes about the way she sometimes spoke to them in her dreams or even when she was drunk because she was always trying to think up ways to help them.

It sounded totally fucking plausible and also made her look like a damn saint.

My jaw tightened as I scrolled on to the second half of the piece. If I'd thought Tory looked hot in the first photo, I hadn't been at all prepared for the orgy that would be taking place in the rest of them.

Image after image filled the screen of her in her underwear, pillow fighting with the male models on the huge bed and laying in the midst of all of them as they trailed their fingers over her perfect skin.

It didn't look sordid or depraved, it looked hot as all hell and I found myself wishing I was one of the guys in that bed. One of the images was of her alone with a seriously attractive model as he pinned her back against a wall, her dressing gown slipping off of her shoulder, her eyes screaming *kiss me* as he trailed a hand along her jaw.

It made my gut clench uncomfortably, jealousy writhing beneath my skin as I thought for the thousandth time about calling her or messaging her and trying to figure out how I'd fucked everything up between us so spectacularly.

Her part of the story was all about living with a sex addiction. They'd even spun it into a sob story about her upbringing in the mortal world where she'd always craved love and protection, saying she was really hunting for her true mate, just hoping to fall in love. She'd donated money to various mental health and addiction charities and truly hoped no one judged her too harshly. The article finished on a quote from her. *"I just want to be loved."*

I bit my lip as I clicked on the comments, knowing exactly what I'd find before I did but needing to confirm it.

Laura Frost:
I love the Vegas twins!!!
Vikki Wilson:
I wish I had a raven for a best friend!
Gemma Vincent:
One look at Tory Vega and I'm pretty sure I'm a sex addict too…
Cassie Farrow:

I can't wait for you two to take back the throne! You're so real and
relatable!!

Stephanie Gomez:
I'm going to dye my hair blue just like Darcy!!

I groaned, knocking my head back against the couch as I let my Atlas fall limp in my hands.

"What's up?" Seth asked, dragging his gaze away from the TV to look at me.

I bit my tongue, glancing between him and Darius who was looking my way too.

"The Vegas…" I said slowly, knowing this was going to kick off the shit storm yet again.

"What about them?" Darius growled.

"Well…they've kinda spun the stories we put out about them. And I'm pretty sure their reputations are stronger than ever…"

"What?" Seth demanded, finally wrenching his entire attention off the TV as he snatched my Atlas from me and scanned the article. "*No,*" he gasped, looking like someone just took a shit in his Faezerati. "Who the fuck have they got on their PR team?"

"What is it?" Darius asked, reaching for my Atlas, but Seth didn't give it up.

Darius growled irritably and got to his feet, stalking around the back of the couch to look over Seth's shoulder.

"What the fuck is she wearing!" he yelled, snatching the Atlas out of Seth's grip and swiping through the pictures with such force he was in danger of breaking the damn thing. "Every Fae in Solaria will see this! Each one of them will have photos of her in her fucking underwear if they want them!"

"Well the photos we leaked were of her in her underwear," I said with a vague shrug, the fact that Tory had exposed her body for the public to see didn't seem like the most pressing issue to me.

"They weren't the same," Darius growled. "They were grainy and dark, taken from a distance. And I tried to stop Seth from sending those to the press too."

"Did you?" I asked in surprise. He'd seemed all for the plan when I'd tried to protest against it. The idea that he'd tried to back out at the last minute kinda pissed me off. The whole thing I'd had going on with Tory had fallen apart after that night. If he'd opened his mouth sooner then it might not have happened.

"And who the fuck is that?" Darius snarled, ignoring me as he pointed at the model Tory looked about thirty seconds away from kissing...or screwing...and if I was supposed to believe the shit in that article then maybe that was exactly what she'd done.

"Who the fuck cares!?" Seth yelled. "He's just some low magic asshole who can only make money out of being hot. It's the least issue we have with this! Can't you see what they've done? They've spun the story, no one's gonna care about that shit we spread about them now. Instead of ruining their reputations, it's made Darcy look like a fucking animal saving saint and Tory-"

"I'm calling my lawyers and getting them to take every fucking photo of her dressed like that off of the internet," Darius growled.

"She clearly took part in that shoot and must have signed off on the use of those photos," I replied with a frown. "There's no way they're taking them down unless she retracts her permission."

"Well then I'm going to find her and make her fucking retract it," Darius growled, ripping his shirt off and stalking towards the window.

"Wait!" Seth called after him, getting up too. "We should all go. I wanna find out who the hell is helping them with this. These stories should have ruined them permanently, but they've somehow managed to twist them about to look like they were no big deal with one fucking interview."

"Fine," Darius growled. "She was in the Ignis common room earlier, she's probably still there." He tossed his pants off and jumped up out of the window without saying anything else.

"C'mon," I said to Seth, heading for the exit.

We jogged down the stairs and made it outside just as Darius took off in his Dragon form overhead. We watched him fly away above the tree canopy and Seth growled. "I should have thought to ban Darcy from doing this shit," he said bitterly.

"Are you gonna tell us what you have on her?" I asked for the hundredth time but his only reply was a smug grin.

"In time. But I'm having too much fun holding her secret over her to let it out yet."

I rolled my eyes at him before grabbing his arm and hoisting him over my shoulder. I shot through the woods and all the way through Fire Territory, arriving outside Ignis House before Darius and spotting him flying towards his room. I dropped Seth back to his feet and he grinned at me, pushing a hand through his long hair to tame it after our run.

I shot a ball of fire at the entrance to the House and we headed inside, jogging up the central stairs to the common room.

Tory was sitting on her own by a fireplace in the corner and we stalked towards her instantly.

We came to a halt standing over her but she didn't even look up at us, leisurely turning a page in the heavy book which sat perched in her lap.

"Why are you all alone, Tory?" Seth mocked. "Are you and Darcy still not talking?"

She still didn't look up but raised a finger at us to make us wait for her attention.

Seth growled and the corner of my mouth twitched with amusement. I didn't know how she managed to make giving no shits look so damn good but she seemed to do it effortlessly.

"We want a word with you, sweetheart," I said, reaching out to pull the book from her lap.

She sighed irritably, snapping the book shut on my fingers and making me snatch my hand back.

"I'm busy," she said, raising her eyes to look at me so fucking slowly that I got the impression she could hardly be bothered to acknowledge us at all.

"We wanna talk to you about the interview you and your sister did for The Daily Solaria," Seth said.

"Are you looking for an autograph then?" she asked casually.

"We want to know who you've got doing PR for you," Seth snapped.

Tory yawned widely, stretching her arms out and not replying.

Before either of us could add anything, Darius stalked into the room wearing a pair of sweatpants and moved to join us.

"Oh look, it's raining assholes," Tory said in a bored voice.

"We get it, you spun the story," Darius said, his voice harsh. "Now call The Daily Solaria and get them to take down the photos."

"Why?" Tory asked, her gaze locking on him coldly.

Darius ground his jaw and folded his arms. "You don't need to have half naked photographs of you everywhere to make the story work."

"From the man who published a picture of me in my underwear without asking me?"

"If you wanna blame someone for that then you can blame me," Seth offered, giving her a wolfish grin.

"Whatever." She shrugged dismissively. "It's my body, I'll do what I like with it. What possible reason have you got to come here and ask me not to?"

I glanced at Darius because I was kinda wondering the same thing. He was acting like some kind of overprotective boyfriend and I got that Dragons were all possessive and shit, but there was no solar system in which he could claim possession of Tory Vega.

"Tell us who you hired," Seth demanded again, saving Darius from giving an answer he clearly didn't have.

"No one," she replied, rolling her eyes. "We just gave an interview on the truth about those rumours. So unless the three of you are here to offer me a four-way to help out with my sex addiction then maybe you could all just fuck off?"

"You don't have a fucking sex addiction," Darius snarled.

"Don't I?" she asked innocently. "What other possible reason would I have for screwing so many waste of space assholes?" Her gaze flicked from him to me for a moment and I straightened my spine. I hadn't really spoken to her since we'd called time on the whole thing we'd had going on but I'd daydreamed up various ways to try and get her to change her mind about it. The look in her eyes right now made it pretty fucking clear how far I'd get with that if I made any attempt to talk to her any time soon though.

To my surprise, Darius didn't have an answer for her either and he just growled at her again.

"You think you're so fucking smart don't you?" Seth said, taking a step towards her and she got to her feet, glaring at the three of us like she didn't give one shit that we were all standing before her like this.

"Yeah, I do," she replied.

"Well now everyone knows for sure that you're a whore and the only friends your sister can make are ones that can't talk back."

Tory's gaze darkened so quickly that for a moment it almost seemed like an actual shadow curtained her vision.

"Fuck you," she snarled, pointing right into Seth's face before aiming her finger at me. "And fuck you." She turned to point at Darius last. "And fuck *you* up the ass with a rusty spoon."

She slammed her shoulders into me and Darius, forcing a path between us before striding away towards her dorm.

I frowned after her as she went and the second she was out of sight, Darius strode away too.

"I'm going flying," he called back to us without bothering to say goodbye.

I sighed, wishing we'd never gone through with that stupid goddamn plan. It hadn't even worked now so what was the point? All of this hatred between us and the Vegas was making my head spin.

"For fuck's sake," I muttered, dropping into the chair Tory had just vacated.

"What's up?" Seth asked, sitting opposite me.

"It's just all for nothing now, isn't it? And I've fucked up my whole deal with Tory for no good reason."

"Is she really that good in the sack?" Seth teased. I smirked at him knowingly and he leaned forward, casting a silencing bubble around us. "Wanna tell me about it?"

I groaned, leaning back in my chair and pushing my hands through my hair. "I don't even know if I have words for it," I said. "But it was like the whole combination of the hunt and her blood and her body…"

"Well I can give you a hunt if that's what you're craving," Seth offered.

I looked up at him in surprise. "You wanna let me hunt you?"

"Fair warning, though, if you want to bite me at the end of it, you'll have to overpower me," he said.

"You're serious?"

"Why not? Am I gonna be getting laid when you catch me like Tory did too?" Seth's smile widened and I wasn't entirely sure if that was a joke or not but I laughed anyway.

"I dunno, man. Her blood is unlike anything I've ever tasted and the way I feel when I hunt her down…I'm not sure if it would really be the same with someone else…"

Seth rolled his eyes at me. "Fuck that. You get off on the hunt as much as the girl. Besides, you don't have to be careful with me, I like it rough."

My smile grew despite myself and my fangs started tingling in anticipation. I leaned towards him, my gaze skimming over his neck and taking in the way his pulse hammered against his skin. I was actually pretty tapped out power wise, but I hadn't gone after Tory for a drink despite her still being my Source. I didn't want to rescind that claim on her, but I knew that if I asked her for a hunt now the answer would be no and just grabbing her in the middle of The Orb and taking her blood by force didn't appeal to me somehow. I swallowed thickly as I thought about taking part in a hunt with a prey who could really run from me and found myself nodding.

"Okay then," I agreed. "If you're sure?"

"I haven't got anything else to do tonight," Seth replied with a shrug like asking your friend to hunt you down and bite you was no big deal. "So you wanna tell me your little rules?"

"I usually give her fifteen minutes to run and I can't use my speed to catch her," I replied. "If I can't find her before the time runs out, I can't bite her."

"Pfft. New rules. You give me two minutes head start and use your gifts as much as you like. When you catch me, you're gonna have to overpower me to bite me." He got to his feet and pulled his shirt off. "Any objections?"

"No," I said, shaking my head as I watched him unbuckle his belt.

Seth grinned as he kicked his shoes off and my blood heated with the promise of the hunt as I sat watching him remove his clothes.

"You sure you don't want this to end in sex?" Seth teased as I continued to watch him.

For a moment I was reminded of the time he'd kissed me in the Shimmering Springs last year. We'd both been drunk as fuck and had been starting up on a three way with a girl from his pack, but for some reason she'd left and the next thing I knew, his mouth was on mine and I was pulling him closer and... I cleared my throat as I banished that memory and drew my eyes past his muscular chest and up to meet his gaze as I laughed.

"Well I do have a thing for brunettes," I joked.

Seth smiled widely as he dropped his pants. "Catch me if you can." He shifted suddenly, his Fae form giving way to his huge white Wolf and causing several of the other people in the common room to shriek in surprise.

He turned and ran out of the room and I got to my feet, crossing to the window and watching as he appeared outside.

He raced away across Fire Territory, running north east towards the grassy plains of Air Territory and I smirked as I watched him bounding away at full speed.

The two minutes seemed to drag on endlessly and my body filled with expectant energy as I waited to give chase. My fangs were tingling and the blood lust rose in a way that ached to be sated.

I watched the seconds tick down on a clock across the room and the moment his two minutes were up, I shot from the room at full speed.

I raced through the barren landscape of Fire Territory and up the hill towards the huge grassy plains that made up the landscape of Air.

My pulse pounded in my ears and my fangs snapped out, aching for blood as I looked all around for my prey.

Once I'd gotten as far as I could imagine him making it, I paused in the middle of the plain, looking around at the long swathes of brown grass which brushed my waist as it swayed in the wind.

I narrowed my eyes, turning slowly as I tried to spot him hiding within it.

A spurt of movement came from the corner of my eye and I turned just in time to see Seth pouncing out of the grass.

Two huge, white paws collided with my chest and I fell back to the ground with an oomph as he knocked the air from my lungs.

He snarled in my face and I released a bark of laughter as I formed a lasso from the long grass, winding it around his neck and yanking him off of me.

Seth yelped, severing the rope with a snap of his powerful jaws and lunging at me again.

I made the earth tremble beneath his feet and shot around behind him, leaping up and landing on his back.

Seth growled, spinning in a circle and twisting as he tried to get his teeth into me to yank me off of him.

I leaned away from his jaws, summoning vines to tie his mouth shut in a thick muzzle.

A deep growl left his throat and my heart pounded with the pure unbridled joy of the hunt.

I lunged forward, aiming to sink my teeth into his shoulder and force him back into his Fae form.

Before I could find my way through his thick, white fur, he dropped to the ground and rolled, crushing me beneath him. He shifted back to his Fae form before I could recover, pinning me down with his hips and throwing a punch straight into my jaw.

Pain flared through my mouth and I tasted blood as his knuckle split on my fangs.

I groaned as the earthy, rich taste of his blood washed over my tongue and threw a punch back at him, catching him in the side and knocking him off balance as he aimed for my face again.

Seth snarled at me, his Wolf nature showing through as he hit me again, the pain of the blow only urging me on.

With a surge of my Vampire strength, I reared up, wrapping my arms around his waist and flipping him beneath me instead.

Seth hit me again and I was pretty sure he cracked a rib as a spike of agony raced through my body, but I didn't slow in my attack.

I grabbed a fistful of his long hair, yanked his head aside and drove my fangs straight into his neck before he could stop me.

Pure fucking ecstasy rolled through my body and I groaned as I drank deeply from the vein in his neck.

Seth laughed as the strength fled from his limbs under the influence of my venom and his fingers twisted into my blonde curls as he pulled me closer.

My power reserves filled with the heady taste of his magic and I finally withdrew my fangs, my grip on him loosening as I drew back an inch.

"Fuck, Cal, I can see why you get off on that," Seth breathed, his bare chest rising and falling beneath me as I stayed on top of him for a long moment.

"You have no idea," I replied with a smirk.

Seth's hand landed on my waist and he slid it up beneath my shirt, his fingers hot against my skin.

I frowned at him a second before healing magic spilled through me and the pain in my ribs was washed away.

The corner of his mouth twitched and I slid my hand out of his hair to heal the bite on his neck in return.

"Come on then, put me out of my misery. Was I as good as Tory Vega?" Seth's gaze slid from my eyes to my mouth and a tingle ran along my skin as I considered his question.

My mind ran over the hunts I'd taken part in with Tory. They'd been hot as all hell, but the fight at the end of this one had made the beast inside me sing with pleasure. I'd always had to be careful to hold myself back with her in case I hurt her but with Seth, the rougher I was, the harder he fought back. I'd just released the full extent of the power of my Order for the first time in my life and it felt fucking incredible.

"Better," I replied. "Maybe I should hunt you more often."

"I won't let you win next time," Seth replied, pulling his hand back out from beneath my shirt.

"You didn't let me win anything," I growled.

Seth's only response was a smirk and I got to my feet, offering him a hand up as my gaze slid down his muscular body which was shining with sweat from our fight.

"You wanna go get drunk at the hollow?" he asked, pushing his hair back out of his face as the wind blew around us. He didn't wait for my response before shifting back into a Wolf and racing away towards the trees.

I stood for a moment as the force of his magic tingled beneath my skin and my flesh prickled with the fading spell of the hunt.

Breaking things off with Tory Vega might have been a terrible fucking call, but if I could keep on hunting Seth like that then maybe it wouldn't be so bad.

DARCY

CHAPTER THIRTY TWO

As December crept around, the academy transformed before my eyes. Half a foot of snow coated the ground and the entire campus had been decorated for Christmas. It wasn't just festive, it was like a winter wonderland on speed.

The water Elementals had cast beautiful ice sculptures outside all of the buildings and gleaming icicles hung from every roof and window ledge. The Pegasus herds had worked with them, adding glitter to the beautiful creations, including an archway in front of The Orb which was as clear as glass and featured each of the Elemental symbols.

The fire Elementals had set ever-lasting fires burning all along the pathways which hovered above the snow and were charmed not to melt it. They'd even set up a huge tepee in Fire Territory where students could get mulled wine and cider in the evenings and sit by a roaring fire pit inside.

Usually, I loved Christmas, it was my favourite time of year, but I didn't feel like I could enjoy any of it without Tory.

The weeks had slipped past with us barely talking and I was worried how we were ever going to fix things between us. Seth tormented me as often as he could and gave me daily reminders that he would only keep my secret if I played along. It was driving me to insanity. And Orion was on the verge of snapping too. He still wasn't speaking with Darius and I knew it was putting a serious strain on him. The bond between them was causing him physical pain, but he was too stubborn to go and talk to his friend.

I sat in The Orb in the early hours of the morning, drinking a hot chocolate and nibbling on a cinnamon bun as I thought over what to do. It was the same every day. I'd wake up early, anxious about all of my problems and not knowing how to handle any of them. The one good thing I had to hold onto was the information Orion and I were gathering about building a bridge for Clara. She still called to me in my dreams most nights, begging me to save her.

After what Orion had told me about the wound she'd given Tory, I was anxious about bringing her back. But he felt sure he could draw the darkness out of her once she returned to the Fae realm. The shadows had consumed her, but I'd watched her eyes light up when she'd seen her brother. It had brought her a pure moment of hope. Like she was just a lost girl, desperate to come home. If it had been Tory trapped in the darkness, I knew I'd do anything to pull her out of it. And if Orion said he could help her when she was free, then I believed him.

I had to hope Tory was coping with the shadows. She wouldn't talk to me about them at all now and sometimes I caught sight of them coiling in her eyes. But while we were arguing like this, I simply couldn't get through to her.

I checked my horoscope as it arrived, wondering if it held any clue of how to solve the problems hanging over me.

Good morning Gemini.
The stars have spoken about your day!
With Neptune in your chart, you must ride the turbulent waves it sends your way. Although it may seem as though the planets are working against you at times, there may be a glimmer of hope yet if you pay attention to the changing tide.
Your soul feels divided and you may be tempted to fix the unhealed wounds which ail you today. Without the sun, the moon cannot shine, but be warned, timing is everything and if you get it wrong, your day could take a turn for the worse.

I poured over the words, hunting for clues hidden between the lines.

The A.S.S soon arrived and I gave up and moved to join them.

When the bell finally rang, I headed to Practical Astrology which was held in the classrooms at the bottom of Earth Observatory. Though I loved learning about the ways of the stars, I was always uncomfortable around Professor Zenith who taught the Astrology classes. She wasn't just an advocate for the Vegas, she had to shout about us in front of everyone plus give us preferential treatment. It was the last thing I wanted.

I arrived at the base of the immense building of shining black stone, the dome of the observatory at the top of the tall tower casting a shadow over the ground.

As I filed inside with the other students, I spotted Zenith standing before the elevators, her jet black hair cascading over her shoulders and her pointed features angled right at us. "We'll be having today's lesson on the fourth floor. I'd like you to do some observations of Zodiac Academy's Horometer. Follow me." She turned and we all moved after her into the large elevator, shuffling close together.

I spotted Tory through the crowd and my heart twisted in the way it always did when I saw her. We hadn't ever fallen out like this before. Sure, we'd had the odd disagreement over the years and we'd fought sometimes as kids, but this felt different. Like a solid wall had been built between us and I didn't know how to get past it.

Sofia stood with her and threw a look over her shoulder, her eyes meeting mine and a frown pulling at her brow. I offered her a small smile and she returned it before turning to say something to Tory.

The doors reopened and I followed the rest of the class as Zenith led us down the curving corridor. The whole building was shaped like an upright tube so there weren't any corners. To my left was a row of full length windows that looked back down over campus. A group of juniors from my House were having a snowball fight, propelling the compacted balls at each other with shots of air. The attacks were vicious, especially as none of them seemed to be shielding themselves.

"Hey chica," Diego said, moving to my side.

"Hey," I breathed as Zenith led us up to two huge metal doors then turned back to face us.

"The Horometer is kept at the centre of this building and the walls which surround it all have a thick layer of iron built into them. This blocks any Celestial signals that could impede the readings of the machine. Every horoscope you receive on your Atlases each morning is divined by this incredible instrument." She placed her hand against a scanner on the wall and magic flared beneath her palm. The doors hissed then slid apart and intrigue filled me as I headed after the rest of my classmates into the room.

As I slipped through the door, an icy chill swept over my skin. A mist hung in the air, veiling my view and I shivered, letting my fire magic sweep through my veins and chase away the cold.

The doors slid shut behind us and we moved around a metal platform which ringed the edge of the room. A railing stood in front of us and as I moved to the edge of it, the mist started to disperse. From within the depths of it an enormous golden model of the planets appeared, each slowly moving around the gleaming golden sun at the heart of it. Above and below, the domed ceiling and floor glistened with a million stars. The constellations glimmered brighter than the rest, each marked out with lines of silver.

I clutched the icy railing as I stared down at the beautiful machine, watching as the planets slowly moved around, hovering on nothing but air.

Zenith came to a halt on the other side of the room and called out to everyone. "When new students arrive at the school, their name and birthday are entered into the Horometer, then each day after that it will chart the stars for you and give you the most accurate horoscope in Solaria. This device was made for the academy by one of the most gifted horologists in history. Lillian Foresight was a notable Fae of her time and even worked here at the academy for a few years before being granted a position at the Court of Solaria to offer predictions to the nobles."

"Oh this one's no good for you then, Darcy," Kylie's hushed voice reached me and I glanced over my shoulder as the back of my neck prickled. She stood nearby with Jillian and a few more of her vile friends. "You need a *Whore*ometer to give you a *Whore*oscope. I don't think they keep one on campus." Her friends fell into silent fits of giggles but Kylie fixed me with a dark glare without even breaking a smile. Hatred seeped through her gaze and I knew she was still furious about me sleeping with Seth. I would have been more than happy to tell her I hadn't, but she'd probably go running to him to rat me out.

I rolled my eyes at her instead and trained my attention back on what Zenith was saying.

"-and a Horometer can even be used to discover some types of Star Bond."

My ears pricked up at that and she suddenly had my undivided attention.

"This control panel is designed to read the energy of souls and is fairly effective in deciphering whether two Fae share a divine bond. Of course, in the case of Astral Adversaries, it would be quite the challenge to have them stand side by side in a room together to test them. And Elysian Mates can never be predicted. But a Nebula Ally is easier to detect. So let's have a demonstration. Where are my two wonderful Vega girls?"

My heart pinched as her eyes fell on me then she beckoned Tory from further down the walkway. I sighed, moving away from Diego as I walked around the platform to where Zenith was standing before a large screen on a podium.

Tory stood on her other side, looking disinterested and refusing to meet my eye. For a second, shadows swirled in her gaze and my throat constricted as it remained there. Luckily the room was dark, but if anyone looked too closely at her, she'd give away the darkness sleeping beneath her flesh. Or perhaps it wasn't asleep at all...

The shadows finally receded and the tension ran out of my shoulders.

"Now," Zenith said brightly, directing us forward. "Please place one hand onto the screen side by side. You'll feel a little zing then the Horometer will begin its assessment. Do not take your hand off the screen or the results will be void."

I nodded, placing my hand down and Tory sighed before doing the same. We were shoulder to shoulder and yet I'd never felt more distance between us. It hurt like hell. She wasn't just my sister, she was my other half. And without her, an entire piece of me was absent, leaving a bloody wound behind.

My thoughts were cast aside as the Horometer hummed loudly down below and the constellations on the ceiling and floor began flashing and sparking.

A shot of energy rushed up my arm and I gasped as a floating feeling seeped over me, making the hairs on my arms rise to attention. The feeling intensified and suddenly all I could see were the stars above and below, some of the constellations fading while others became brighter and brighter. Gemini was burning as white hot as the sun and I could barely look at it as a sharp ringing sounded in my ears.

All at once, the lights began to fade and the screen turned green beneath our palms.

"That's it girls, step back," Zenith instructed excitedly and we did, moving either side of her once more as she bent forward to look at the screen. A symbol appeared in silver and blue, like two interlinked moons.

"You're Nebula Allies," she gushed and a smattering of applause sounded around the room. "But of course you are, I could have predicted it myself."

I looked to Tory and she met my eye for half a second, then her lips pursed and she turned away, walking off into the crowd.

"Who else would like a go?" Zenith asked, patting me on the back, not seeming to notice the tension between Tory and I.

I moved away, my chest aching as I was parted from her once more. It didn't even surprise me that we were Nebula Allies. How could we not be? No matter how different we were, our souls were the same. But right now, we were anything other than aligned.

Pairs of friends and random classmates took it in turns for the Horometer to assess them, but there was only one other pair of Nebula Allies in the room. A guy and a girl who'd been dating for a few weeks.

I moved to join Diego again as another couple stepped up to the panel and a strange look of concern entered his eyes. "Chica, your sister is in trouble."

"What?" I breathed, quickly casting a silencing bubble around us.

"It's the shadows," he murmured even though he didn't have to be quiet. "I can see them. They surround her. With you, they simmer, with her they blaze. She is embracing them, not fighting them."

Horror filled me and I looked over to Tory, almost able to sense the cloud of darkness hanging around her.

"What can I do?" I asked Diego.

476

His brows pulled together. "She has to fight them herself. You need to encourage her to push them away. If she falls into them, she'll never come back."

"She won't listen to me," I said anxiously. Our dark magic classes had been tense. Between her hating Darius and her not talking to me, every time we went to that cave, I could almost feel the shadows trying to feed on those dark emotions. Sometimes I found it harder to push them away there than anywhere else. And if Tory wasn't fighting them at all…

"She's your sister," Diego said softly. "She will listen to you."

"I'll try again," I swore, because I wouldn't just leave her to battle this alone, even if she didn't want to talk to me.

We were soon heading back out of the room and I lingered by the door, waiting for Tory to appear, determined to speak to her now rather than later.

I caught her arm as she tried to slip out the exit and she turned to me with a frown.

"Are you okay?" I asked and she glanced at the students filing past us.

"I'm fine." She moved into the hall and I followed her, casting a silencing bubble around us. "Diego saw the shadows around you. He said it looks like you're embracing them, Tor, is that true?"

Tory shot Diego a glare as he headed down the corridor with Sofia and Tyler. She glanced back at me as pain flashed in her gaze. "It's none of your business what I'm doing."

Her words stung, but I persevered, knowing how thick she wore her armour when she was hurting. "I just want to help. If you're falling into them, you have to tell me. You have to try harder to shut them out."

"So you want me to tell you all of my shit, but you won't tell me yours?" she asked sharply.

I dipped my head, trying to find the words to answer her. "I would if I could," I breathed and she halted as the last of the students slipped into the elevator. Zenith didn't even reprimand us, just left us to our conversation as she took the elevator downstairs with the class.

"What's going on with you, Darcy?" Tory asked like she really needed to know and I wanted to tell her so badly it hurt.

I chewed on my lip, my secrets hovering on the tip of my tongue, but I was trapped. I was so scared of everyone finding out about Orion, of him losing his job, ruining his life. Besides everything with Seth, if I was questioned about it, they'd surely question my twin too. They'd assume she knew. A Cyclops would pull the truth out of her head and then what? Would she get in trouble too? I could already see the newspaper articles about me splashed everywhere. I could face that if it came to it, but I was terrified of dragging her down with me.

"I…" I trailed off and Tory rolled her eyes.

"Forget it," she tutted before walking off down the corridor and shoving the door to the stairwell open with a blast of air.

My throat was overly tight and I pressed back against the wall as I tried to catch my breath.

Please give me a solution, stars. I need help.

They didn't reply. Which wasn't surprising but worth a shot. My horoscopes were getting less helpful by the day, like my fate was balancing on a knife's edge. But it was starting to seem like the choice had already been made. Like the fall was inevitable. I just hoped I was wrong.

I headed outside where more snow had begun to tumble from the sky. Tory was long gone and Diego and Sofia walked a few steps ahead of me as we wound along the path.

A herd of Pegasus swept overhead and sprinkled glitter across the white carpet beneath them, neighing happily as they soared up into the snow clouds.

I drew an air shield around me and warmed it with my fire magic, soaking in the heat.

I had a free period and figured I'd devote it to the library. I'd been spending a lot of time there recently and knew I was using books and overworking as a way to escape from the stress of life right now. But while the answers to my problems were evading me, I was going to feed my brain as much about magic and astrology as I possibly could. It made me feel less powerless and every new spell I learned, meant I was one step closer to being a match for the Heirs one day.

I waved goodbye to Sofia and Diego as they headed to The Orb and took my Atlas from my bag. Seth had given it back eventually but only after he'd turned my hair pink and made me shout *Seth Capella has a huge dick* at the top of my lungs in the Aer House common room. Two bottles of Fae hair dye and a mega size bar of chocolate later had made me feel one percent better about that. But it wasn't nearly enough. Every time I was close to him, my Order form rose on instinct and sometimes I could almost feel myself losing control of it. It wasn't in me not to fight back, but I had to swallow down that need like some nasty medicine. Only it didn't make me better, it made me more ill.

I'd noticed he was being clever about the pranks he pulled on me. Half of them never made it to FaeBook and he rarely did anything while I was at The Orb or anywhere within earshot of my sister. He knew that if he had me do anything over the top in front of her, she'd realise I was under his control. So far, his plan was working in his favour perfectly. Not only did he have me under lock and key, he'd driven an even bigger wedge between me and Tory.

I had a message from Orion waiting on my Atlas and heat spread through me as I tapped on it. Through all of this, at least I had him. Someone who knew all of my secrets but was bound by them too. Together, we'd figure this out and we'd cut Seth Capella down when we did. Most weeks, we only spent our Liaisons together alone in fear of Seth finding us elsewhere, but it was getting more and more difficult to spend so much time apart.

Lance:
Guess what I'm eating...

Attached was a photo of a peach and a smile pulled at my mouth. Before I could reply, he sent another message.

Lance:
Wish it was yours ;)

I started typing out a reply but my foot caught on something and I gasped, crashing to my knees and only just stopping my Atlas from smashing on the ground.

I scrambled upright, glancing over my shoulder and finding a long vine stretched across the pavement. I rubbed my grazed palm with a curse, stuffing my Atlas into my pocket as I searched for the culprit. Seth dropped from a tree beside the path, a shower of snow cascading from the branches as he landed before me.

"Oh it's you, I thought it might be Washer as you were lurking in a tree like a pervert," I said coldly, turning my back on him and striding away.

He growled as he jogged to my side, linking his arm through mine and brushing his chin against my head. I jerked away but his muscles tightened so I couldn't escape. I hated to think I was getting used to this, but Seth was becoming a daily irritation.

"I don't need to lurk in trees to perve on people," Seth said.

"You just do it out in the open then?" I guessed airily.

"That's not what I meant," he said in annoyance.

"Sounded pretty clear to me." I shrugged and he glanced at me from the corner of his eyes, mirth glittering in his gaze.

He lifted a hand, casting a silencing bubble around us and I sighed.

"What do you want now? Isn't this game getting old yet?" I demanded.

"If it gets old, you and your professor better be worried," he said casually.

I yanked my arm free of his hold, turning to stop him with a scowl. "So it's inevitable then, is it? You're just going to mess with us until you're bored then throw Orion to the wolves?" This was what I'd been afraid of, that I was just buying time with all this bullshit.

"Interesting choice of words," he said with a smirk. "And no, it's not inevitable."

Despite not trusting a thing that came out of this mouth, I couldn't help but hope. "Then what's going to happen when you're done screwing with us?"

"I haven't decided yet. Maybe I'll let you live happily ever after." His face was unreadable, but I was sure he had no intention of doing that. It was just a way to keep me playing along. But if this really was just leading to it all coming out then why shouldn't I fight back?

With the way he was looking at me, I could tell he sensed what I was thinking.

"I mean it," he said. "There's a chance I'll take this secret to the grave. It depends how nice you are to me." He started walking again, catching my arm to pull me along once more.

"Be *nice* to you?" I said incredulously like he was asking me to lasso the sun from the sky.

"That's my next request, yeah," he said simply, shooting me a taunting grin.

I shook my head, looking away and tugging at my arm again. The only thing that had kept me sane while he tormented me was that he didn't seem to mind if I shot curses at him the whole time. Being rude to him was the last slice of free will I had left.

"What's the point? It won't be real," I said. "Do you really enjoy torturing me that much?" I didn't look at him as he answered. I couldn't. I felt sick to my stomach with how much I hated him.

"Yes," he said.

I shook my head, baffled by him. "Why?"

It wasn't just a question about this. It was a why for everything he'd done to me. Every cruel dig and hurt. I understood establishing dominance as Fae, but this didn't feel like that anymore. It felt personal. Like he hated me just for being me. And as much as I didn't like Seth or want anything to do with him, knowing that fact still needled its way under my skin. Like the stars were screaming how wrong it was that he treated me like this and wouldn't let me forget it.

He opened his mouth but I could already sense the lie he was about to tell.

"The truth," I growled.

His jaw tightened and he glanced away. A long pause passed between us and I eyed the library up ahead, wondering if I could just cut free of him and spend my free period how I wanted.

His eyes darkened and his beautiful features twisted; he looked like an angry God with a wrath to unleash and it made my heart judder with fear.

"I hurt you, Darcy Vega, because you hurt me every day just by existing." He threw out a hand and a powerful gust threw me back against the nearest tree, knocking the air from my lungs. Thick vines wrapped around me, binding me there so tight I could barely move a muscle.

481

I yelled curses at him as he marched away down the path, his shoulders rigid and destruction seeming to pour from the depths of his being. He wanted me to be nice? I'd rather gouge my eyes out with the sharp end of a stick.

I wriggled hard, trying to get a hand free to cast magic and several groups of students decided then was a great time to walk by. Laughter rang through the air as I fought to get a hand free, fury sizzling through my blood.

I finally loosened my hand and released a flash of fire to break through the binds. Then I shoved the remains of them off of me and strode back to the path.

Ice-cold water crashed over me and I gasped in horror as Max appeared amongst a group of girls. "Woops, my bad. I thought you were on fire, little Vega."

I saw red.

Rage coiled up inside me and sprang free.

I couldn't hurt Seth but I *could* throw my fury at one of his asshole friends. Fire burst from my hands and Max threw out a hand to shield himself. I fuelled it with a flare of Phoenix power and it flashed hot in his face before he got it under control with his Element.

The girls around him swore at me and Max scowled as he appeared behind a cloud of smoke. A snort escaped me as I realised I'd burned his eyebrows clean off and several of the girls started pointing and frantically jumping up and down.

"What?" he gasped as I started laughing.

One of the girls produced a pocket mirror and I backed up, desperate to see his reaction but knowing I was five seconds from a counter attack. And he'd probably take more than my eyebrows in retaliation.

"Are you surprised? I can't tell..." I called.

He made a noise like a strangled frog as he took in his singed forehead then two chasms of rage opened up in his eyes. "VEGA!"

I fled, shielding myself with air as water cascaded over me and Max released a battle cry behind me. I cast earth magic as I ran, creating a tangle of thorny bushes to try and slow him down.

My heart thumped wildly but the exhilaration felt amazing after weeks of being trodden on by Seth. I laughed louder so he could hear me and his shout of fury came in response.

I made it to the library, wrenching the door open and flying inside, receiving a sharp look from the librarian at my soaking wet clothes. I spotted Geraldine and a whole gang of the A.S.S sat around a circular table and she waved me over.

"Wet wilberwillies, what happened?"

"Max Rigel," I panted, glancing over my shoulder. "I need to hide."

"Quick, under here." She pointed beneath the table and I grinned in thanks as I dropped to my knees, crawling under quickly.

The library door banged and Max's legs appeared marching toward us.

"Which way did she go, Grus?" Max demanded.

"I don't know who you mean, you blown up seashell fart," she said lightly to a round of sniggers from the table. "And where in the name of Frangelica the fifth are your eyebrows? Did they sprout legs and run away from the frightful fish boy who grew them? I mean, I could hardly blame them."

I swallowed the laugh trying to rip from my throat.

A weight slammed down above me and I guessed it was Max's palms against the wood. "Come on, Geraldine, give her up and I'll make it worth your while."

"Well unless pointing out the direction the true queen took on her divine mission to evade your fish breath means you would turn into a pile of barnacles, I can't imagine there's anything in the expanding universe you could offer me to give her up."

Max growled furiously then stepped away from the table. "I don't have fucking fish breath," he muttered as he stalked away with a snarl and the laugh I'd been holding in my lungs finally tumbled from my chest.

If there was one way to make my day go from shit to walking on a goddamn rainbow, it was burning off an Heir's eyebrows and living to tell the tale.

TORY

CHAPTER THIRTY THREE

I walked along the path to the Pitball Arena in my ridiculous cheer uniform with frost crunching beneath my sparkly sneakers and my mind half invested in the shadows. Darkness slid beneath my skin, the touch of it welcome and terrifying at once. But I was like an addict; every time I pulled myself away from them, my reality closed in too sharply around me and I was drawn back to the strange comfort they offered me.

I'd never been particularly good at making friends. We'd moved from school to school so much as kids that I guessed I'd just gotten jaded about the whole social aspect of it. There were only so many times you could listen to people swearing they'd write and call you only to never hear from them again before you began to get cynical about the reality of those friendships. And now that the one person I'd had for my whole life was actively lying to my face and avoiding me the whole time, I couldn't help but pull away from the friends we'd made here too. I wasn't an idiot anyway; it wasn't like people liked me on my own merit.

Darcy was the one who formed those kinds of bonds easily and I was just the snarky, regularly rude addition to our duo. So when I saw the Ass Club and our other friends sitting together with Darcy, I just left them to it. It wasn't like she wanted me to. She'd even asked me to come back and sit with them on several occasions. But I couldn't bear to be in her company while these lies sat between us. And apparently she preferred our separation to sharing the truth with me. So I was alone. And the shadows fed on loneliness.

The only person I spent regular time with these days was Gabriel. We were going flying after practice tonight again and it was the only thing that was going to get me through the hell of yet another hour in Marguerite and Kylie's company.

"Come to me…"

I made it to the doors to the stadium and paused, leaning against the wall beside them and closing my eyes as I dipped into the shadows again, hearing Clara's voice more clearly as I gave in to the dark.

"Help me, Tory. I'm so alone…"

I knew that feeling, but I didn't want to dwell in the shadows with her just for company's sake.

"Roxy?" A hand landed on my shoulder and the heat of Darius's magic pushed against the barriers of mine.

I spun around, knocking his hand from my skin and meeting his eye as the shadows slowly retreated.

"What the hell are you doing?" he hissed, grabbing my waist to tug me away from the doors around the side of the building.

He was wearing his Pitball kit, the navy blue and silver bringing out the warmth of his skin tone and the dark of his eyes and for a moment I just stared at him.

"What do you want?" I asked, my voice hollow as the shadows kept me numb. "Haven't you taken enough from me already?"

His brow furrowed at that and he tugged on my waist again, shifting me along even as I dug my heels in. His skin was warm against my stomach where he touched me and I realised I'd forgotten to use my fire magic to keep me warm as I walked over here. I was only wearing my cheer outfit and it was goddamn freezing out.

"You were chasing shadows again, weren't you?" he hissed.

"How can I chase them when they live in me?"

"Roxy, if you keep doing this, you're going to kill yourself," he growled. "Is that what you want?"

"Well it's what *you* want, isn't it? So why are you complaining?"

"You still think I want you dead?" he asked incredulously like he couldn't understand me at all.

"How am I supposed to know what you think? You only speak to me to torture me."

"That's not true," he ground out.

"Isn't it?" I tried to call for the shadows so that I didn't have to face the emotions that were flaring at the feeling of him so close to me, but they seemed out of reach somehow as he held me tightly.

"I'm not the one who said they didn't think anything had changed between us after-"

"Darius?" Max's voice cut him off and he turned to look over his shoulder at his friend.

"I'll be there in a minute," Darius said, turning from Max dismissively and pinning me in his gaze again.

"Orion will have our balls on a platter if we're late," Max insisted and Darius growled.

"Just go," I said, rolling my eyes. "Being alone is kinda my thing now anyway."

I tried to slip past him but he caught my hand, halting my progress. "Wait for me after practice," he said in a low voice.

I looked at him for a long moment, the shadows slipping further away as he gripped my fingers tightly between his. His dark eyes shone with what I could have sworn was concern and I was more than a little tempted to take a step closer to him despite all the reasons I had not to.

"Fine," I agreed eventually. It didn't seem like he was going to let me go until I did anyway.

Darius almost smiled at me in response, slowly releasing his grip on my fingers and heading away to join Max.

I trailed behind them, pushing my fire magic into my skin and calling on my Phoenix to help banish the cold from my limbs.

"Hey."

I turned at the sound of Darcy's voice and found her walking up behind me in her Pitball kit. Her blue hair was tied back and her shoulders were squared like she was heading into battle. Which I guessed was sort of true when you thought about the brutality of the game.

"Hey," I replied.

Awkward silence reigned where she chose not to confide in me yet again and I didn't even know what to say to the girl I could hardly recognise anymore.

"Were you just talking to Darius?" she asked.

"He wants to see me after practice," I said with a shrug.

"Why?"

"He didn't really say." Information shared. From my side anyway.

"Oh."

"Yeah."

We headed into the locker rooms and I hung my sparkly Tory Vega bag from a hook as Darcy deposited hers.

"Have a good practice," she said as I headed for the door.

"Unlikely," I replied dryly before walking out to join the cheer squad.

Six weeks of being part of the team had done nothing for my enthusiasm for the sport, though I had to admit that I did enjoy the performance and learning the routines. It was the company I took exception to. Every session meant enduring insults and name calling. Not to mention the fact that they constantly tried to sabotage me and cut me from the better roles in the routines. It meant that any chance I may have had to actually enjoy the challenge presented by the sport was well and truly stamped out.

I walked over to join the squad and Marguerite turned my way as I approached, her gaze instantly falling to my stomach where I'd scrawled my slogan for the day using the face paint I was required to use for each session. Lucky for me, Orion didn't seem to have an issue with the things I chose to write on my body despite the fact that Marguerite complained about it to him every single session.

"Professor!" she called on cue, folding her arms and pouting angrily. "This is getting beyond a joke!"

Orion shot towards us from the far side of the stadium, clearly hearing her with his bat ears and tilting his head as he inspected the slogan I'd chosen for today.

Suck my dick and bite my balls!

Orion snorted a laugh and I smirked at Marguerite tauntingly.

"She doesn't even have a dick!" Marguerite moaned.

"Wanna check?" I asked, cupping my imaginary balls.

"*Sir!*" she gasped as if Orion might jump in to save her from the hell of my company if she only asked often enough.

"Five points from Ignis for the bitching," Orion said, pointing a finger at her like she was the most irritating person he'd ever met. "And ten points to Ignis for creativity," he added, smirking at me.

My lips twitched with amusement.

"Sir, as Cheer Captain I have to insist that certain standards be upheld. Is this the kind of shameless behaviour we want the other academies to think we encourage when they play against us?" Marguerite demanded indignantly.

"You're right," Orion replied thoughtfully. "You and Tory clearly have very different visions for the team."

"So different!" Kylie piped up.

"So I think I've got an idea to solve it," he said.

"You're kicking me off of the team?" I asked hopefully as Marguerite and her followers all brightened at that idea too.

"Oh no. I've thought of something better than that. I suggest that we have two cheer squads. One led by Marguerite and the other by Tory. You both work on routines and practice separately, then before the next match, you show the team what you've got and they vote for which one of you gets to support us in the match."

"Fuck that," I muttered.

"You can't expect half the girls to be lumbered with *her*!" Marguerite said in outrage.

"I won't make any of you do anything you don't want to. You can all choose which team to be on. Vega or Helebor." Orion looked around at the other girls and chattering broke out between them as they considered their options.

"No offence dude, but none of them are gonna want to be on my team," I said. "And I'm not exactly filled with team spirit so I'm not sure I'm really the best fit for-"

"I dare you," Orion said, shifting closer to me conspiratorially.

I pursed my lips, the corner of my mouth twitching with amusement as he used that damn game against me.

"Fine. Practicing on my own will suit me just fine anyway," I agreed with a shrug.

"Okay then." Orion moved to stand between me and Marguerite. "Line up behind your chosen captain and let the work begin."

Kylie and Jillian instantly stepped forward to join Marguerite followed by several of the other hangers on but the rest of the squad hesitated.

"Do you promise to make our routines killer?" Bernice asked me, arching a brow in assessment.

I shrugged a shoulder. "The more difficult the better," I agreed. "If I'm going to participate in this… *sport* then I'll be playing to win." Besides, there was a definite lure to the idea of knocking Marguerite off of her high horse.

Bernice grinned like that was exactly the answer she'd wanted and headed forward to join me. That seemed to open the flood gates and several more girls headed my way too. The rest of the team quickly chose a side and I was surprised to find it a pretty even split. About twenty girls on each team.

"You'll need team names," Orion said.

"Easy. We're Team Twinkle," Marguerite said with a cocky grin.

"Team Winkle?" I asked. "Why would you wanna name yourselves after a tiny dick?"

"*Twinkle!* With a T!" Marguerite snapped.

"Why are you shouting winkle at me?" I asked.

"By the stars, I hate you," Marguerite snarled and I snorted a laugh.

"We're the Vixens," Bernice put in which was probably a good shout because my thoughts were along the lines of 'Heir Hating Bitches' but maybe that wasn't as catchy.

"Done," Orion said, smirking at me like he just couldn't get enough of the ridiculousness of having me play this part. "I look forward to seeing your routines when they're perfected."

He shot away from us again and Marguerite scowled at my new squad. "You'll all be sorry you backed a Vega when you have to sit in the stands and watch us perform at the match," she hissed before turning and stalking away with the rest of her squad in tow.

I watched them go impassively before turning back to the girls who surrounded me and finding them all staring at me expectantly.

"What?" I asked, raising an eyebrow at them.

"This is the part where you tell us what to do," Bernice said.

"Oh. Erm… well how about we spend some time figuring out what moves we all want to include in the routines, make sure everyone can showcase their best stuff and think about what combos we might be able to pull off? Then I guess we'll need to figure out some music-"

"And the cheers!" a girl at the back piped up.

"Right. Maybe we can focus on more team based encouragement instead of Heir ass licking?" I suggested because there was no way in hell I was going to be jumping up and down and praising Seth Capella's luscious hair or Max Rigel's thick thighs. I'd been refusing to participate in those cheers since I'd been forced onto the team in the first place and I had no intention of jumping on the ass licking train now.

The other girls all agreed enthusiastically and I grinned as we began to practice.

By the time Orion blew the whistle to call time on our session, I was actually enjoying myself.

I headed for the locker rooms but before I could get there, Caleb shot into my path.

"Hey, sweetheart," he said, pushing a hand through his mud splattered curls and looking like a male model squeezed into a sports kit.

"Hey yourself," I replied with a smile.

"So, I've been thinking," he said slowly.

"Don't go doing yourself an injury," I deadpanned and he smirked.

"About something in particular."

"And what's that?"

"It's been weeks since I've bitten my Source…" His gaze slid from my eyes to my neck and I raised an eyebrow at him.

"And why's that?" I asked. It wasn't like I'd missed the fact that there had been decidedly less teeth in my throat recently, but I hadn't thought of it as something I wanted to draw attention to. Besides, I'd hardly spoken to Caleb at all since we called time on us hooking up.

"Well… I thought that you'd probably say no to me hunting you seeing as we decided to put a stop to the other perks of that game. And I've developed a bit of a thing for the hunt," he admitted, taking a purposeful step towards me.

"So who are you hunting these days?" I asked curiously. I hadn't particularly noticed him with another girl regularly, but I couldn't say I'd been paying much attention. And I didn't spend that much time in The Orb at the moment either.

"I've developed a taste for Wolf," he said, moving closer again. "But I will admit that I still crave the taste of you from time to time."

"Is that so?" I bit my lip as I took a step back and he hounded after me, moving into my personal space.

"Yeah. So I thought, it couldn't hurt to ask…"

"Ask what?" I backed up again and the corner of his mouth twitched into a smile as he followed.

"If I can hunt you again?" He turned the big eyes on me and I tilted my head as I considered it.

I really hadn't been having very many meaningful interactions with anyone lately and I had to admit that the thrill of the hunt got my heart pumping. I'd even developed a bit of a taste for the pain. There was something really exciting about it. But it also turned me on and I wasn't sure I wanted to fall back into Caleb's bed.

"I dunno if that's a good idea…" I said slowly.

"Because you think you won't be able to resist me if I hunt you?" he teased and I rolled my eyes. But in all honesty, there might have been some merit to that. I needed a distraction from the shitty state of my life and the call of the shadows and hooking up with him could be just that. But that didn't make it a good idea.

"Maybe," I agreed with a shrug of my shoulder.

Caleb smiled so fucking widely at that that I was half tempted to punch him just to wipe the smug look off his face.

"Don't get too up yourself over it," I said. "It's just because I'm a sex addict, remember?"

Caleb's brows pulled together at that, but he seemed to decide against commenting on it.

"Okay, well how about a test? You run from me and I'll bite you when I catch you. If it doesn't work for you, I'll promise not to do it again. And as a sweetener, I swear I'm not going to try to get in your panties either. This time."

"Well that does improve your offer considerably," I teased.

"Go on then, sweetheart. *Run.*" His fangs snapped out and I gasped in surprise as I turned and ran from him.

I sprinted across the Pitball pitch and headed for the locker rooms, running straight through them and outside.

Caleb caught me the second I passed through the doors, whirling me around and shoving me back against the cold wall of the stadium.

"You changed the rules," I breathed.

"Yeah." Caleb's hands were cool against my waist as he pressed me back and I tipped my head to give him access to my throat without even trying to fight him off.

I inhaled sharply at the slice of pain as his teeth cut into my skin, arching my back as I savoured the pain, feeling every piece of it and letting it rule me. I felt like I'd been stuck in a rut recently, doomed to repeat the same old shit day in, day out. His bite was like waking up. And as pathetic as it was to admit to myself, it felt pretty damn good to have someone's undivided attention on me for once. I'd felt so lonely recently that even a few minutes of feeling like the most important person in someone's world meant a stupid amount to me.

Caleb released me, stepping back as he wiped a drop of my blood from the corner of his mouth.

"Do you wanna stop being my Source?" he asked, releasing his hold on me.

My lips parted. I should have been saying yes. Hadn't I hated him biting me with all the fury of hell when he'd first started doing it? But then, had I ever really hated the way it felt? Or was it more the indignity of having no say in it? Because I could easily admit I had a bit of a taste for pain, especially when it was mixed with pleasure.

"No," I said finally and Caleb gave me the biggest, shit eating grin I'd ever seen. "But it's gonna be on my terms, Vampire boy," I added before his head got so big it exploded.

"How do you figure that out?" he asked.

493

"Because I'm pretty sure I can fight you off now."

"I'd like to see you try," he teased.

My lips twitched into a smile and I called on my Phoenix flames, commanding them to line my body in an impenetrable coat of fire. I even had enough control over them to save my clothes from them now too.

"You think you could bite me now?" I taunted.

Caleb's smile slipped and a sigh escaped him. "I doubt it. But I can always creep up on you. Catch you later, Tory."

He shot away from me before I could respond and I rolled my eyes as I headed back inside to grab my kit bag.

Darcy was just about to leave as I entered the room and she hesitated as I passed her by.

"I'll see you later, Tor," she said in a small voice.

"Yep," I agreed without looking at her because it hurt too much to watch her walking away from me all the damn time when all she had to do to end this feud between us was open up to me. And that wasn't something I'd ever had trouble doing with her. So I guessed she just didn't really care about me enough or trust me in the same way. Which just felt fantastic.

Her footsteps trailed away and I hooked my bag over my shoulder before heading back outside.

Darius was leaning against the wall beside the door to the guys' lockers as I emerged and he straightened as he spotted me.

"You actually waited." I pointed out stupidly. But I honestly never knew what to expect from him at the best of times so this was its own brand of confusing.

"I said I would."

"You did," I agreed.

Darius moved closer to me, his gaze skimming over me and landing on my neck.

"You're bleeding," he said, reaching out to heal me but he paused before he touched me. "Is that a bite?"

"Oh, right…yeah, Caleb-"

"So you and him are a thing again now?" he asked and I couldn't for the life of me figure out what he thought about that.

"No."

His gaze trailed over my face like he was searching for a lie and I shrugged.

"Why would you care if we were anyway?" I asked.

I swear he actually bit his tongue to stop himself from answering me.

He stepped forward slowly and pressed his fingers to the bite on my neck. The sting of the wound flared through me and I stilled, expecting him to heal it but he just stood there for a long moment instead.

"Do you really get off on my pain so much that you can't help but cause me more every chance you get?" I asked.

"Yeah," he replied. "Maybe I do."

"That's fucked up," I muttered.

"Well I've never claimed to be anything else. Are you going to talk to me about the shadows?"

"What do you want to know?" I asked.

"Are you drawn to them because of me?" he asked.

"Just because you're obsessed with me, it doesn't mean the feeling is mutual," I replied dismissively.

Darius snorted a laugh. "Heaven forbid," he agreed. "But I meant because you want to use them against me."

"Maybe I just like the way they feel," I said, not answering his question, partly because I wasn't sure I had an answer.

"Well, can you do me a favour?" he asked just as he pressed healing magic beneath my skin to remove the bite Caleb had given me.

"What?" I asked cautiously.

"The next time you want to drown in them, tell me about it."

"Why?"

"Because if you're going to drown then I'm going to drown with you." He released me and walked from me before I gave him an answer and I frowned at his back as he strode away.

I didn't know what the hell I was supposed to make of that declaration. Did he crave the kiss of the shadows too? Or was he really just offering to hold my hand if I fell?

DARIUS

CHAPTER THIRTY FOUR

Walking away from Roxy Vega felt something akin to being kicked in the balls. It was an all consuming kind of pain which wouldn't let my attention waver from it. I'd wanted to spend longer with her, but I honestly wasn't sure if my company would help or just make everything worse.

We didn't really talk to each other anymore or bite at each other or fight with each other. Hell, we didn't even look at each other anymore. Or more accurately, *she* didn't look at *me*. Because I sure as hell looked at her enough.

I woke early in the mornings and waited for her to appear in the common room just so that I could be sure the shadows hadn't consumed her in the night. I noted the bags under her eyes and the way she always sought out Milton Hubert right after she grabbed a coffee with three sugars. At first I'd thought there was something going on with them, but when I'd confronted him about it, he'd finally admitted that she asked him to heal her hangovers.

Which somehow was even worse than having to watch her with another guy. Because it was just another sign of how much she was struggling. I'd tried to talk to her about it a few times but up until today, any time I'd attempted to approach her, she'd just run from me. And not in fear, not in any way that I could perceive as a sign that she'd finally decided to bow to me. But in a way that said my company was the last thing she desired. And I couldn't really blame her for that. But it made trying to help her practically impossible.

I'd asked the students who were housed in the rooms closest to her dorm to keep an eye on her and report anything strange back to me. A few of them had told me she woke up in the night screaming pretty regularly. But when I'd tried to ask her about that, she'd taken it as some kind of attack and had just started placing a silencing bubble around her room every night so that no one would be able to hear her scream anymore. I knew because I often walked to her door in the middle of the night and pressed my hand to it, reaching out with my own magic until it brushed against hers and reassured me that she was okay. Or if not okay, then at least alive.

I glanced down at my fingers and found them stained with her blood from where I'd healed her. I only wished I could fix the wounds inside her as easily as those marking her flesh.

She'd said that there wasn't anything going on between her and Caleb now and that had filled me with a heady sense of relief which I had no real right to feel. Because as much as a fucked up little part of me liked to pretend I had some hold over her, I knew it wasn't really true. This crush or obsession or infatuation I felt for her didn't give me any rights to her. I hadn't earned any kind of say in her life. Not that that meant I craved it any less. But I had to remind myself of that fact. Because if Cal was biting her again, I was more than willing to bet he'd be looking for more than that from her. And I really didn't have any valid reason to object to that. What could I say to her about it anyway? *Don't be with him because we were together once. For one, too brief, earth shattering moment, you were mine. And I never should have let you go.*

That would probably go down about as well as it did when I tried to convince my Father not to beat me. She'd clearly chosen to forget all about us being together. And the pain of her rejecting me out loud, of having to hear her spell it out would just break the pathetic little part of me which still liked to cling to the idea that it had actually meant something to her. Because it had meant more to me than I could easily put into words. And despite the agony that it caused me to look back on that moment and realise it was well and truly gone, I wouldn't trade the memory of it for all the auras in the world.

I blew out an irritable breath as I strolled through The Wailing Wood. I didn't know what the fuck was going on with me. I didn't pine after girls. I'd never once in my life felt like this about one. But I couldn't help it. The only thing I could do was lock it up tight and refuse to let it show.

My Atlas started ringing and I pulled it out of my pocket, tossing up a silencing bubble out of habit before I answered it.

My heart lifted as I spotted my brother's name on the caller ID and I smiled as I said hello.

"Have you made any progress on busting me out of here yet?" he asked jokingly like he did every time we spoke.

"Working on it," I promised, which wasn't a lie. It also wasn't something I'd made any progress with.

"How's Mother and Father?" I asked, not because I really gave a shit but because I was really asking if the asshole head of our household had been turning his rage against my little brother again recently or not.

"Fine," he replied and I released a slow breath because that meant he hadn't had to endure too much in the last few days. "Although Mother did do something strange the other night."

"Oh?" I asked curiously. Mother didn't do strange. In fact, she didn't do a lot of anything. She just kind of floated around the house in a push-up bra and designer dress and looked pretty whenever Father decided to trot her out in public. Sometimes I wondered if she'd always been like that or if it was a role she'd fallen into since becoming a Councillor's wife. I knew she was magically powerful in her own right, but she never used her magic for anything beyond making herself look pretty or healing our wounds if we'd gone a round against Father.

"Yeah. She kinda, came into my room at like three in the morning and I just pretended to be asleep, in case…" He didn't need to finish that sentence because I remembered what it felt like to be woken in the middle of the night by Father when he came home drunk and mean and pissed off.

"What did she want?" I asked.

"She came and sat on my bed and she just…cried. She stroked my hair and sung me that lullaby she always used to sing when we were kids. You know the one about the man in the glass house who couldn't get out?" Xavier said.

I frowned as I came to a halt and I moved off of the path, leaning against a huge oak as I gave all of my attention to the conversation.

"Do you think she was just feeling nostalgic?" I asked.

"No. Well…maybe. But before she left, she said something. More like whispered it actually, so I'm not totally sure I heard it right…"

"What did she say?" I asked curiously. And the fact that I was curious about something Mother had done was more than a little strange to me.

"I *think* she said. 'I wish I could tell you.'"

Silence fell between us and I frowned down at my Pitball boots as I tried to figure out what that could mean.

If I knew her better then maybe I'd have had a chance at figuring her out, but in all honesty she'd always just been this kind of background adornment to our home. I was only ever glad of her company when she healed the injuries Father gave me. But now that I could do that myself, I didn't even need her for that anymore.

"Do you remember when we were kids and she used to chase us all over the house?" Xavier asked slowly. "Remember we'd play hide and seek and we always hid in the pantry and every time she found us she'd gasp in surprise and go on about how clever we were for hiding so well?"

I frowned as that story stirred some memories in me. "Kinda," I admitted. But it had been so long since she'd done anything like that with us that it was hard to say if it had even been her at all. "Maybe that was just one of the nannys though."

"C'mon, Darius, you remember," Xavier urged. "I'm younger than you and if I can remember it then you definitely can."

I grunted in agreement. "She used to use her earth magic to grow those glowing flowers in our bedrooms so that we wouldn't have to stay alone in the dark all night."

"Yeah!" Xavier said enthusiastically as I reminded him of that. "And she was the one who first showed us how to use a tray to slide down the stairs!"

I snorted a laugh as I remembered that too. We'd done it on the main stairs in the central atrium. She'd spilled off of the tray at the foot of the staircase, her long brunette hair tumbling around her as she laughed her head off and we giggled in appreciation. Her dress had gotten all tangled around her legs and we'd both jumped on her, tickling her with cries of joy. I must have been about six and Xavier four. We'd been happy. At least in that moment. And maybe more besides.

"But then Father came home with Tiberius Rigel for dinner and they saw her laying on the floor like that…" Xavier added.

I frowned as I remembered that part too. We'd all fallen silent, the fun torn from the house the moment our father had set foot in it. He hadn't actually done anything about it though. Only smiled as if he were in on the fun too. But his eyes had been hard and cold in that way I'd known to fear even then. Mother had apologised as she'd scrambled to her feet and we'd all hurried away from him, leaving him to talk business with Max's dad.

"She never played with us like that again," I muttered.

I could vaguely recall begging her to join in our games for a while afterward but the more times she politely refused, the less often we'd asked until I'd just sort of forgotten that she'd ever been a part of our fun in the first place. She'd slowly withdrawn from us more and more over the years following that and had eventually become the vapid creature we now knew.

"Did you ask Tory Vega out yet?" Xavier asked, changing the subject abruptly to hassle me about that.

"I never should have told you I hooked up with her," I muttered irritably. Though in all honesty I'd needed someone to talk to about her because I was burning up with all the things she made me feel and while this argument still sat in place between me and Lance, I didn't really have anyone else.

The other Heirs wouldn't be happy if I told them. Cal would be jealous, maybe even hurt, despite the fact that he'd told me to go after her if I wanted to on multiple occasions. Max clearly thought the lot of us should avoid the Vegas at all costs and Seth still took great pleasure in tormenting them whenever he could, so they clearly wouldn't be the most helpful or sympathetic of people to talk to.

"C'mon, man," Xavier groaned. "I'm literally cooped up in a tower here like a sparkly Rapunzel. The closest I come to having my own life is by hearing about yours."

I sighed, unable to refuse him when he played that card, but before I could answer, my Father's voice sounded in the background.

"Who are you talking to?" he demanded.

"It's just Darius," Xavier replied defensively and I ground my teeth at the note of fear in his voice.

"Your brother has more important things to do with his time than waste it conversing with you. Hand it over," he ordered. A moment later, his voice came more clearly as he spoke into the phone. "Have you mastered semi-permanent illusion placement yet?" he asked, naming the latest piece of magic I'd been working on in Cardinal Magic. No matter how busy he was, he always kept up to date with the class reports my Professors sent him daily. He couldn't have me falling behind in anything and embarrassing him.

"I've just finished Pitball practice," I replied. "I'm heading back to my House to get on with my assignments now."

"Then you don't need this kind of distraction, do you?"

The line went dead before I could respond and I tried not to let myself get caught up in concern for what he might be doing with Xavier now. He didn't sound the kind of angry that ended up in bruised flesh and broken bones, just the usual level of pissed off he exhibited around my brother these days.

I pushed my Atlas back into my pocket and sighed.

The Libra brand on my arm was itching and burning, driving me to go and seek out my Guardian. It had been too long since I'd spent any quality time with Orion and maintaining this argument with him was only hurting us both. My own stubbornness was the main culprit in keeping us apart. He'd clearly decided that I'd acted unfairly which was about as bad as shitting on his doorstep when it came to a Libra. And I actually agreed with him. I'd been a total fucking dickwad and only my own stubbornness was keeping us apart.

It was time I sucked it up and stopped this nonsense. It was affecting our training, our preparations to help Clara cross back over, even our sleep now as the bond between us constantly woke me with the urge to go to him. Enough was enough. I may have found it hard to admit when I was wrong, but I cared about Lance enough to suck up my pride. It was past time I owned my shit and apologised.

I turned back the way I'd come and headed through the trees in the direction of Asteroid Place. My heart felt lighter even just knowing my destination and the brand on my arm tingled in anticipation.

I approached the gated community and stuck to the shadows, using the dark to hide me as I circled around to the back of it.

I walked up to the iron gates and cast a column of water into existence beneath my feet so that it lifted me up and over them.

I landed on the other side and jogged toward his house. My skin was buzzing at the knowledge of finally fixing things between us and I couldn't help but grin as I upped my pace even more.

I was flat out running by the time I spotted his house and I sprinted up the alley which divided his from Washer's.

The door flew open just before I reached it and Lance's eyes were wide with excitement as he held his arms wide. I crashed into him and we wrapped our arms around each other and damn near fell over with the force of our collision.

"I'm sorry," I growled as I locked him in my arms and a part of me wished I'd never have to let go.

"I'm sorry too," he agreed, his beard scratching my cheek in the best way.

We stumbled into his house without releasing each other and I kicked the door shut behind us. Fuck knew what anyone would think if they saw us like this.

"*Fuck*, you smell so good," I groaned as the scent of cinnamon enveloped me.

"I'm really having to fight against the urge to kiss you right now," he joked, though as he said it, I was half tempted to turn my mouth towards his.

This fucking Guardian bond!

"I think if we just give each other blowjobs we'll be all good," I laughed and he nuzzled into me.

"By the stars, that doesn't even sound like the worst idea," he groaned and I laughed harder.

"I don't think you're just some asshole my father bound me to," I growled because those words had haunted me ever since I'd let the poison of them spill from my lips. "I was angry, but I never should have said that. You have to know that's not what I think of you."

"I know," Lance replied roughly. "And I'm sorry I tried to force the idea of sharing the throne with the Vegas on you like that. It wasn't my intention to yell at you about it or try and force a choice on you. I just think that-"

"I can't...please can we not discuss the Vegas tonight?" I begged. "They haunt me too often as it is."

Lance drew back just enough to eye me with a slight frown. I knew we needed to have this conversation at some point, but I wasn't going to change my mind about sharing my throne with the Savage King's daughters. Lance sighed as he seemed to realise that going into our issues now wouldn't solve anything and he gave me a small nod. It was almost Christmas and I just needed for the two of us to be okay. We could hash out this shit another time. Besides, I understood he just wanted to help me by presenting every possible solution to my problems with the twins, but I was sure he'd never really believed we'd share the throne.

"Of course," Lance agreed with a tight smile as he let the subject slip off the table for now. "I'm just so glad to have you back."

"It's been fucking killing me. I don't know why I didn't just suck it up sooner," I said in a low voice as I forced myself to release him and we moved further into the house. "I've just been so angry at myself for so many things recently and I...I guess I just didn't want to take ownership of any of it."

"Your father raised you to be ruthless and take no prisoners. He taught you never to bow or back down or apologise for your actions. I should have come to you," Lance said, gripping my face between his hands so that I couldn't look away from him. "I just didn't want you to think the only reason I came was this damn mark on my arm."

I shook my head and he dropped his hold on me. "I know our bond is more than what was forced on us," I said honestly. "I love you like a brother. You mean more to me than most real members of my family."

"Well let's just be glad we aren't related," he teased. "Because if we both had the temper of a Dragon then we'd probably have a lot more of these arguments to contend with – and the blowjobs would be extra wrong."

I snorted a laugh, scraping a hand through my hair as I let out a breath of relief. For the first time in weeks, my heart felt light and some of the tension in me eased. "You were right when you said I'm my own worst enemy," I muttered. "It seems like the only choices I've made recently have been for the worse."

"Well, I've been doing a damn good job of making bad decisions myself recently too, so I can't exactly stand in judgement over you." Lance led the way to the couch and dropped down onto it, topping up the glass of bourbon that sat on the coffee table and offering it to me before drinking from the bottle himself.

"You wanna explain that?" I asked, shifting closer to him so that our legs were pressed to each other's. After weeks of avoiding each other aside from classes, Pitball practice and our work with the shadows, the bond craved this connection between us and I knew from experience it was easier to give in to it than to try and fight it.

Lance looked at me for a long moment then sighed. "I do. But not now. Now I just wanna enjoy some time in your company and quite probably spend the night spooning you in the totally platonic, utterly fucking ridiculous way that this bond needs."

"*Fuck*, that sounds so good," I groaned, knocking my head back on the couch with a breath of laughter.

"Shall we watch a movie?" Lance asked, switching on Faeflix and hunting one down.

"That sounds like its own kind of heaven," I admitted because I really needed to spend some time just doing nothing and forgetting about all the shit in our lives. Tonight there would be no Nymphs or Councillors or politics or Vegas. Just two fully grown men watching action flicks and quite likely holding hands throughout. Which was pretty much the best kind of night I could imagine having right now. And as Orion reached out and took my hand, I felt myself grinning like a kid at Christmas and all of my problems seemed a little more bearable.

DARCY

CHAPTER THIRTY FIVE

I lay on my bed, frowning at a Numerology equation while my stomach grumbled for lunch. It was a Saturday and the chatter on campus gravitated around everyone's Christmas plans.

I didn't want to think about Christmas approaching when Tory and I were still arguing. She was the only constant I'd had for every Christmas since I could remember. It didn't matter what house we were in, which foster parents did or didn't celebrate with us. It mattered that every Christmas morning, we'd wake up and share it together. Me at the crack of dawn and Tory an hour later once I'd finally dragged her out of bed.

When it snowed, we built snowmen, had snowball fights and made a sled out of a metal tray. We'd stay outside until our fingers and toes were frozen and our noses bright red. It was our way. And I didn't care how old we were, I still wanted to wake up on Christmas morning and do all of those things with my only flesh and blood in the world.

I sent Tory a message, my heart thumping as I tried to decide what to say.

Darcy:

If I could tell you what's going on, I would. Please don't shut me out Tory. It's Christmas soon. We're going to be here alone at the academy, but that won't matter at all so long as I have you.

I could see she was typing a reply, the dots appearing then disappearing as she rewrote her answer several times.

Tory:

I don't understand why you can't trust me with this.

Darcy:

It's not about trust.

Tory:

Clearly.

I sighed, trying to figure out how to fix this. If I said too much about why I couldn't tell her, she'd figure out I was being threatened. As painful as it was, the best way to protect her was to pretend I really didn't want to share this secret with her. But that felt as good as hammering a nail into my heart.

Something glittered in my periphery and I swung around, inhaling sharply as Orion appeared amongst a cloud of stardust which quickly vanished into the ether.

"Holy shit," I breathed as I took in his appearance. He wore smart trousers and a crisp white shirt, his hair styled and a dark blue flower in his hand which was the same colour as my hair. It looked like a lily, the petals large and the dusty white pollen shimmering.

"Are you surprised?" he asked and I sprang off the bed, wrapping my arms around him and stealing the kiss I'd dreamed of for days. His mouth was warm and inviting and his grip on me tightened, my toes almost leaving the ground.

"I'm definitely surprised," I said with a grin as I drew away.

He held up the flower, twirling it between his fingers with a smirk and handed it over.

I took it, heat invading my cheeks. "It's beautiful."

"It's average. You on the other hand…" He pulled me in again, plucking the flower from my grip and tossing it down on my desk. "Look absolutely kidnappable."

"Wha-" Before I could finish that word, Orion tossed a handful of stardust over us and I was sucked into a galaxy of stars.

I tumbled through the fabric between worlds and nearly crashed into Orion as my feet hit solid ground. I was definitely getting better at landing though.

I looked around and forgot to breathe as I took in the space around me. We were beneath a huge weeping willow, the thick fronds hanging around the edges of the wide clearing underneath it. Frost coated the branches in sparkling blue and a chandelier of pure ice hung down above us with orbs of golden light glimmering within it. Beneath it was a table and two chairs carved from ice and covered with thick fur blankets. Food filled every corner of it and a bottle of wine stood at the heart of it. The ground was covered with a fluffy white layer of snow and a frozen stream ran through the heart of it like a sheen of glass.

"It's too much, isn't it?" Orion broke the silence. "I knew it was too much but I just kept adding icicles..."

"Lance it's incredible," I turned to him, in awe of what he'd done. He took my hand and a hundred words came to my lips, but none of them made it out. Not a single one of them was good enough to express how much this meant to me.

He created little worlds that belonged just to us. Beneath a swimming pool, between the sheets, under a willow tree. He could make anywhere ours and shut out every other living thing.

His throat bobbed and a vulnerable kind of smile pulled at the corner of his mouth. "I've not really dated a girl before. Not like this. Not the proper way. But with you, making you smile like that...it's everything. A few months ago, I would have looked at myself now and thought I was losing my fucking mind. You make me wanna dress up trees, Blue. I'm one hundred percent a lunatic for you. And I don't give a damn."

I smiled giddily, committing every part of this place, this moment, his crazy-ass speech to memory. It was our kind of perfect.

"Way to make a girl speechless." I bit my lip and he grinned wickedly.

He unfurled his fingers, planting a piece of paper in my hand and I looked down at one of the IOUs I'd given him for his birthday.

IOU

One day date.

"I was supposed to organise the date for *you*," I said, glancing up at him.

"Well I don't play by your rules, Blue." His lips hooked up at the corner and heat splashed through my chest. I didn't tend to play by his either so I couldn't argue with that.

I tip-toed up and brushed my mouth over his in the lightest, sweetest of kisses as his fingers slid between mine. He guided me to one of the seats and I dropped into it, eyeing him with a playful smile as he moved to the other chair.

He felt so far away and a blush was clawing its way into my cheeks. I wasn't really a formal dinners kind of girl and he didn't strike me as that kind of guy either.

He surveyed me for a second with a frown. "This isn't really *us*, is it?"

"No, but I know how we can fix it." I jumped up, grabbed the blanket off of my seat and laid it across the ground.

He grinned, standing and we gathered the food onto the blanket to make a picnic of it. He uncorked the wine with his teeth and I relaxed, dropping down beside him on the ground. *Much better.*

I opened my palm, encouraging a fire into it then placing it gently over the snow beyond the blanket. The snow started to melt and Orion took my hand, shifting up beside me. "If you don't want the snow to melt, you can protect it like this…" His magic butted up against my skin and I let my barriers down so his power washed through me.

I felt him guiding magic to my fingertips and the rush that swept through me was intoxicating. He showed me how to protect the snow from the heat and I soon felt the two Elements of fire and water working in harmony together.

Orion pulled his magic away again and I sighed as the raw energy of him left me.

"So I have some news," he said as he held out a bowl of stuffed olives to me.

I took one, crunching down on it and enjoying the bitter taste. "Oh yeah?"

"Darius and I made up," he said.

"That's great," I gasped. "So you can tell him about us and-"

Orion shook his head, lines forming on his brow as the words died in my throat. He sighed, dropping his gaze to the ground. "He apologised for being an asshole, but he didn't bring up anything else I'd said when we argued. If I tell him about us, I think it will just shatter his confidence in me entirely..."

I took his hand, my heart clenching into a tight ball. "I don't want to drive a wedge between you and your friend."

"It's not your fault," he growled, looking me in the eye. "He needs to learn the error of his ways. He has to come to terms with his feelings about your sister. Now they've slept together he might eventually-"

"Wait – *what*?" I gasped, my mouth dropping right open.

Holy crap, she screwed Darius??

Orion's brows arched. "I assumed you knew."

"Tory won't talk to me, how could I know?"

"It was a while ago." He scrubbed at his beard with an apologetic look.

"Yeah, well it seems like forever since Tory and I have been on good terms." I frowned, my soul aching for the company of my twin. "I guess I get it. Why would she share this with me when I'm keeping so much from her?"

Orion took my hand, squeezing gently. "I've been reading the cards, there's hope yet, Blue. Don't stop trying with her."

I smiled hopefully, wanting to believe that so much. "Of course I won't. It's so stupid anyway, if I'd just told her about us from the start, I could have saved all of this from happening. She slept with Darius for god's sake, why would she care about me being with you? And even if she did, she still wouldn't cut me off over it."

"It was for more reasons than that, you were trying to protect her from getting wrapped up in this."

I sighed, hanging my head. "I know and now I've screwed everything up instead."

Orion tugged me close, taking hold of my chin to make me look up at him. "We didn't know things would get this far. And besides, I was the one who warned you against telling her."

"Well I usually don't let you boss me around, so now we know why that's a bad idea," I teased, pushing his arm playfully.

He grinned wolfishly and pulled me closer. "Maybe I like it when you rebel anyway, it gives me reasons to punish you." He nuzzled into my neck and his fangs against my skin made my thoughts hazy. "Do you remember when you threw me off Aer Tower and I caught you in the stairwell?"

I nodded, biting my lip at the memory. "That was kinda hot in hindsight."

"Fuck hindsight. Do you know how many cold showers I've had to have because of you?"

A laugh fell from my lungs and I leaned into his arms, stealing a kiss and letting my worries tumble away. The magic of this place was captivating and I wanted to enjoy this stolen moment of pure peace, even if I knew it wouldn't last forever.

We made our way through the food and I was soon full, laying back on the blanket with my hand resting on my stomach. Orion used his air magic to lazily send the plates and leftovers back to the table then fell down beside me, cupping his head with his hand.

I gazed up at the glittering canopy above and happiness washed over me.

"Where are we?" I asked, wondering for the first time.

"This is on the edge of the Airvale Estate. My family home. My sister and I used to play here as kids."

"This is where you grew up?" I asked, suddenly itching to head out from under the willow tree and see it for myself.

"Yeah. Stella's away in the city so the house is empty - just like her heart."

I laughed and he leaned forward to brush a lock of hair behind my ear.

"So I guess you won't be having a cosy Christmas at home with your mother?" I asked.

"I'd rather eat iron nails and wash them down with a pint of acid."

I frowned. "So what will you do?"

"Probably stay at the academy. Unless Lionel ropes me into some festive fun at the Acruxes'."

"Maybe we'll see each other then if you stay at Zodiac," I said, but my heart was too heavy at the thought of not spending it with Tory to enjoy that idea. We *had* to make up before then. I couldn't bear to spend it without her.

Orion eyed me in confusion. "Hasn't anyone told you?"

"Told me what?"

"You and your sister will be expected to spend it at the palace. It's been prepared for your arrival."

"Are you serious?" I breathed, my heart pattering wildly. I'd wanted to go and visit the palace the second I'd heard about it, but I'd never have expected to actually stay there – even if we did technically own it now. And over Christmas no less.

"Yeah. I would have said sooner, but I figured Grus would have mentioned it. Her family have been involved in the preparations."

"Knowing her, she probably wanted it to be a surprise on Christmas Eve," I laughed, but my smile died as I considered what it would be like to step into my birth parents' home. The place I must have been once as a baby. It was completely surreal.

"Do you not want to go?" Orion asked, surveying my expression.

"I just…don't know what to expect I guess."

"Think Acrux manor times a thousand."

"Oh my god," I breathed. "Have you been there?"

"Once. I went with Darius for a tour while a photographer took pictures of him." He leaned in and pressed his lips to mine, making me forget my worries in a flash. "You'll like it, Blue. It's fit for a queen."

I raised a brow. "But not a queen you'd kneel for," I said airily. "You'd only get on your knees for a king or four."

"In my defence, I only gave Darius a blowjob one time while I was drunk so it really doesn't count," he joked.

I fell apart and he grinned, running his mouth down to my throat. His fangs skimmed my pulse and a hungry growl escaped him. I clutched his shoulders, titling my head to the side in offering and he dug his teeth into my skin without a moment's hesitation. I arched into him as he drank, my eyes fluttering closed as his hand found my wrists and pressed them into the blanket. He knew he didn't need to hold me down, but I was pretty sure he got off on it.

When he tugged his fangs free, his pupils were dilated and he was breathing heavily as he gazed down at me.

"What do I taste like?" I mused, quirking up a brow.

"Like power and fire and melted sugar."

"That's very specific." I grinned.

"I've spent a lot of time thinking about it." He bared his fangs as he smiled and my heart dissolved like a tablet fizzing in water.

"Can I see your house?" I asked, glancing hopefully at the branches surrounding us.

"Do you want to?" he asked, rolling onto his back with a frown. "It's just a house."

"No…it's a piece of you." I reached over to trail my fingers across his jaw. "I'm collecting the set."

He smirked at that, taking my hand and shooting to his feet, pulling me up with his Vampire speed. "You convinced me."

"It didn't take much," I taunted.

"You make it difficult to say no to, Blue."

He took the lead, guiding me to the edge of the tree and pushing the fronds aside with a sound like clinking glasses. I slipped through the gap and gazed across a plain of snow to where a beautiful house was nestled between two hills. All was still, even the air barely blew against my cheeks as I stepped onto the powdery snow beyond the willow.

The frozen stream wound up to the house and passed beneath an old waterwheel on the side of it. It was picturesque, like a modernised farmhouse with iron brick walls and painted red window frames.

Orion cast a wind behind us as we walked, veiling our footprints in a dusting of snow. I threw him a questioning look.

"Just in case," he explained.

"What would your mother do if she found me here with you?" I asked, unsure if I should be more worried about that possibility.

"Disown me. Oh wait, she already did that." He chuckled, but a growl left my throat on instinct.

"She's an idiot."

He squeezed my hand, but said nothing in response.

We approached the house and Orion moved to the front door, pressing his palm to it and shutting his eyes as he concentrated. A glimmer of light flickered across the door, then it opened with a click. "She hasn't stopped me from gaining access so I guess she still trusts me in some way."

He pushed it wide and gestured for me to go in ahead of him. I moved into the hallway which was large and cold with dark floorboards and paintings of electric storms in frames on the walls. An iron stairway curved up at the centre of the space and the exposed brick archways gave glimpses into other rooms around us.

Orion took a moment to remove the snow from our shoes with his water magic and deposited it outside. Then he pushed the door closed and gestured for me to explore.

I smiled, slipping away into the huge kitchen where a large red Aga stood heating the space. I ran my fingers across a wood-topped kitchen island and glanced up at Orion mischievously.

"Which one was your seat?"

He pointed to the one at the end and I brushed my fingers over that too. He moved forward, a frown pulling at his brow as he touched a chair at the opposite end. "This was my dad's." He stepped forward, skimming his fingers over the next one. "And Clara's." His hand remained on that one and his jaw ticked as he stared at the empty seat.

"We'll get her back," I promised and his gaze lifted to meet mine.

He nodded once then turned and strode from the kitchen. "Come on, there's one place I'd like you to see."

I hurried after him across the large hallway and up to a wooden panel in the wall. He pressed his hand to it and a flare of magic sprawled across the wood as he pushed the secret door open. A staircase was revealed running down beneath the house and a cold wind blew up around me, sending a chill through to my core.

"Where does it go?" I asked excitedly.

"It's where Dad used to experiment with dark magic." His eyes rippled with shadows and a shiver ran across my skin as I followed him into the narrow space, heading down beneath the house.

He cast a light orb ahead of us and my lips parted as we arrived at the bottom of the stairs. A large stone chamber spread out before us. One side held an old desk and the other was full of chests and shelves.

Darkness washed over me in a torrent and I gasped as a powerful sense dragged through the depths of my body.

"Close…so close," Clara's voice filled my mind and Orion turned to me in alarm as I lurched past him. *"You'll need it to set me free."*

The shadows were wild, wrapping around me, trying to pull me along.

"Blue?" Orion braced me, but I pushed away from him, a river of darkness guiding my footsteps as I moved toward one of the old wooden chests across the room. I dropped to my knees and pulled it open, rifling through the contents. Orion's voice sounded faraway like it was behind a barrier and I couldn't make out the words.

My hand snagged on a box and I pulled it out, setting it down on the ground. The shadows flittered away as if on a breeze and everything came sharply back into focus. Orion was kneeling beside me, his hand resting on the carved wooden box I'd taken from the chest.

"What's going on?" he asked anxiously.

"Clara said we need this to bring her back."

Orion's eyes searched mine, frantic with hope. He flipped open the box and stardust stared up at me, twinkling faintly, the strength of its immense power writhing through the air. It was no normal stardust, I could tell simply from the aura it gave off. This was the stardust that could allow a Fae to travel to the Shadow Realm. The kind Lionel had created the night of the Lunar Eclipse. The memory of that night seemed to cling to this dark material before me. I knew it like it was bound to my soul. And maybe in some way, it was.

"This is…genius," Orion breathed. "I'd thought perhaps that normal stardust would be enough, but this will open the path completely."

He hurried around to the chest, taking out a jar and scooping a measure of the dark stardust into it.

A door sounded upstairs and we both froze. Like literally, turned to goddamn ice sculptures because holy *shit*.

"Did you shut the hidden door?" I breathed, fearing his mother would see it open upstairs.

Orion nodded.

"Let's just stardust out of here then," I whispered hurriedly.

"We can't," he growled. "The house has a ward around it to stop anyone from stardusting directly into it or out of it. It's a security measure."

"Shit," I hissed, getting to my feet and Orion did the same.

"I can distract Stella while you sneak out the front door," he said, looking like the last thing in the world he wanted to do was talk to his mother.

I caught his hand, a wild energy building in my veins. "Screw that, let's run for it together."

His eyes glittered at that idea and he moved across the room into the stairwell in silent agreement. I hurried after him and felt the pressure of a silencing bubble slipping over me.

"Stay close," he murmured.

We reached the top of the stairs and I squeezed up next to Orion's broad frame as we peered out of the slim cracks around the door which gave a view into the hallway.

Stella came into sight in a tight red dress and killer heels. "You can hang your coat and gloves over there," she spoke to someone I couldn't see.

My heart thumped wildly as another woman stepped into view. Something was oddly familiar about her, though I was sure I'd never seen her before. Her dark hair was short and tightly curling, her face gaunt, but her small stature didn't take away from the flicker of power which seemed to emanate from her. She wore a thick black coat and a pair of ugly knitted gloves, leaving them on despite Stella's direction.

"I won't be staying long," the woman said in a throaty tone. "I'm just here for my portion of the dark stardust."

I glanced at Orion, sharing a concerned look. If they came down here, we were in serious trouble. Orion might have been able to explain away why he was in his family home, but how was he supposed to explain why a Vega Twin was accompanying him?

"Coffee first, Drusilla," Stella said. It was an order and though Drusilla looked reluctant to comply, she followed Stella into the kitchen all the same.

A ragged breath escaped me and Orion pulled me closer. "Time to go."

I nodded, steeling myself as he pushed the door open. We waited for a tense second before stepping out into the hall.

"-and how is your son getting along at the academy?" Stella's voice carried to us.

"Diego's worthless, he won't do anything I say," Drusilla said coldly and my mind reeled. "I wish I'd had a daughter. Much more compliant."

My mouth fell open. That was Diego's *mother*?

"Well I wholly agree with you there. Since I lost my baby girl, my son has been nothing but a thorn in my side. I swear he tries to upset me on purpose."

I crept along at Orion's side and he slipped the front door open, pushing me out before following.

"Let's run," he announced and he snatched my hand as we fled into the snow, whipping me off of my feet into his arms. I covered our tracks with a gust of air while he took the stardust from his pocket. "That tree is the boundary." He pointed up ahead and he shot toward it at high speed.

Adrenaline sailed through my veins as we came closer and closer to making our escape.

The second we passed the tree, Orion threw a handful of stardust into the air. I was wrenched into the abyss, spinning through a sea of stars before landing back at the academy in an instant. We were in his office and I laughed as I realised we'd gotten away unnoticed.

"What about the food under the willow tree?" I asked. I didn't imagine Stella would be taking a stroll that way any time soon, but it was possible.

"I'll go back for it later," Orion said then cupped my cheek and pulled me closer. I could feel his heart pounding as I rested a hand to his chest and I gave him a sideways smile.

"Looks like Diego's family is as messed up as mine," he sighed. "I suppose I could go *slightly* easier on him…"

"He has a good heart," I said softly.

He nodded, his lips tight like this was still difficult for him to accept. "Sorry today was a disaster."

"It wasn't," I said honestly, drawing him closer by tugging on his shirt. "I loved it."

"I love *you*," he countered and the world paused as the weight of his words slowed time itself.

"Lance," I inhaled, a feeling of raw happiness threading itself into my heart.

"This isn't the way I was going to say it and I'm still not sure that I should have…" His brows pulled together. "I don't know how long we have, Blue, but my heart will be yours whether we're together or not."

Tears pricked my eyes because the idea of us being torn apart was just too unbearable to face right then. I leaned up and pressed my lips to his, drowning in the way he made me feel. Because of course I loved him too. How could I not have realised it until now?

A knock came at the door and Orion pulled away as our moment was stolen from us. I hadn't even gotten to say it back to him.

Orion frowned, moving to the door and I dropped into the seat at his desk, rearranging my features to boredom.

He opened the door and Professor Perseus poked his head in the door. "Ah, Lance, I wondered if I could pick your brain about a few air spells I've been thinking of adding to the syllabus?"

"Of course. Miss Vega was just leaving."

I stood and headed to the door and Perseus gave me a friendly smile. I glanced back over my shoulder, my gaze meeting Orion's in a silent goodbye before I slipped away.

"Remember to practise those star charts!" he called after me in a stern voice.

A grin pulled at my mouth as I headed back to Aer Tower, unable to wipe it from my face for the entire walk. By the time I reached my room, I felt totally high.

He loved me. Lance Orion *loved* me. And I loved him back with every corner of my heart and all the spaces in between.

I opened the door and my happy moment came crashing down around me as I found Seth sitting in my desk chair, blue petals scattered over his knees and across the floor.

I immediately put up a tight air shield, my teeth clenching as I stepped into the room. "What are you doing here?" I demanded.

"Shut the door," he said casually, ignoring my question.

I resisted until he gave me a warning stare and I nudged it closed as my heart thrashed wildly in my chest. I stared at the destroyed flower with rage simmering beneath my flesh. He had no *right* to touch it.

"You should really get a magical lock on your door, babe. Someone unfriendly could get in…"

I scowled, folding my arms and disguising my discomfort at him being here with fury. "What do you want?"

He took something from his pocket and placed it down on the desk. My tongue thickened at the sight of the Aquarius Moonstone I'd used to infest him with fleas.

"I thought it was time to let you know that me and the other Heirs figured out what you and your sister did. *All* of what you did. The Pegasus rumours about Cal, the Griffin shit in Max's Pitball kit, the fleas you used to alienate me from my pack…"

I swallowed the rising lump in my throat, staring at him unblinkingly. "So this is payback for that?" I guessed, wondering if I finally had the reason for why he was tormenting me.

"Not really," he said casually, swinging himself from side to side in my chair.

My heart hardened into a cold ball as he stood up, gazing down his nose at me. I kept my chin high, staring right back at him. I might have been smaller, but I knew my own strength now. He couldn't intimidate me with height alone.

"The news article was payback," he explained. "But you just couldn't let it lie, could you?" A growl escaped him and fire magic tingled along the inside of my palms. "You had to go and twist that story and fuck with us once again."

The article had blown up since it had been printed and we were even starting to receive fan mail because of it. Barely a day went by on FaeBook where someone didn't mention how compassionate I was or how strong Tory was for facing her addiction. It had had more of an impact than we ever could have predicted.

"The thing is, Seth, you keep expecting us to just roll over like trained dogs. When are you going to realise we're never going to break?" I hissed the last word, the tension between us crackling through the air.

"I own you, Vega. And yet you *still* can't seem to behave." He strode toward me, tilting his head down as his gaze trickled over me. His hand shot out and fire flashed from my palms in warning. His hand closed on the door handle beside me and a grim smile pulled at the corner of his mouth. "And now the world has acknowledged your power, I guess you really are a worthy opponent." He opened the door and I stepped aside, frowning at the back of his head as he disappeared down the corridor.

I shut the door and locked it, trying to understand what way that guy's head worked. Was he praising me or threatening me?

My eyes fell on the petals on the floor and the answer was clear. He wanted my life to fall apart just like that flower had. And he wanted to be the one who did it. A pretty thing crushed in his fist. But I wasn't fragile, I was a weapon forged in fire. And it looked like he'd realised that at long last.

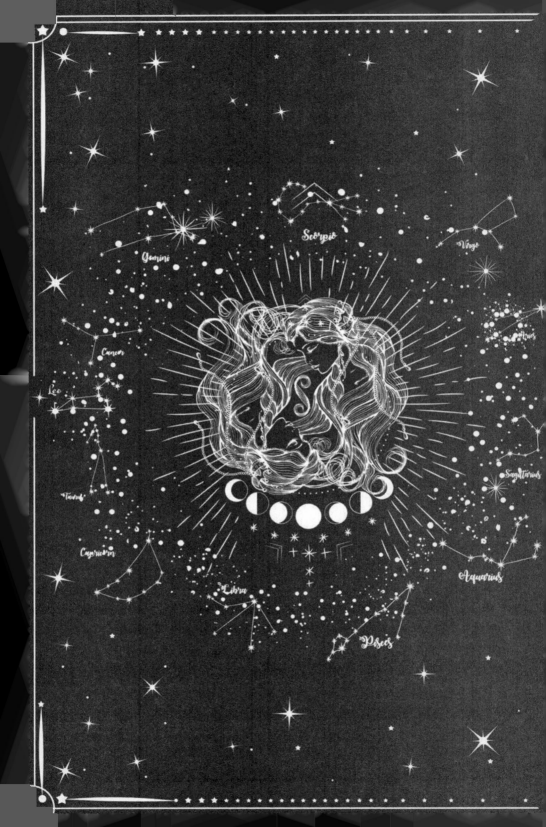

TORY

CHAPTER THIRTY SIX

Good morning Gemini.
The stars have spoken about your day!
Today may bring an unexpected surprise your way and the following
upheaval could lead to a dramatic change in your circumstances. Try to have
an open heart and give way to forgiveness when anger rears its head and
you will find yourself waking up to a brighter sun tomorrow.

I chewed over that little nugget of non information and tried to figure out what it meant. The shadows still clung to me after yet another night of listening to Clara's whispers. Sometimes I felt the lost girl was the only person I'd ever met who truly understood me.

I frowned as that idea started to take root. It wasn't true. Darcy knew me better than anyone and the suggestion that some Shadow Princess could even begin to compare was utter nonsense. It wasn't my thought at all. It was a shadow trying to take root in me. Trying to spread its poison beneath my skin and draw me away from my reality so that I would embrace the call of its master. I wondered if that was what had happened to Clara.

My Phoenix shifted beneath my skin and the kiss of its flames chased the shadows away again.

I finished buttoning my shirt and moved to look out the window.

The snow really was beautiful; the glistening white landscape spread out as far as I could see, looking even more magical than usual beneath its touch.

I yawned as I turned away from the window and moved to grab a coat and hat from my cupboard. I didn't strictly need to dress for the weather with my fire magic, but I felt like embracing the season today. I wanted to feel the bite of frost on my cheeks and see my breath rise into a cloud of vapour before me.

I pulled my thick, navy coat on and pulled my hat down over my ears before swinging my satchel over my shoulder and heading out.

Milton Hubert was heading out of the common room at the same time as me and he smiled as he moved to walk by my side.

"I've been thinking," he said, casting a sidelong look at me.

"Oh yeah?" I asked.

"Well, I can't help but notice that for someone who claims to be a sex addict, you don't actually seem to be getting laid very often."

"That's a super odd thing to have noticed about me," I pointed out.

He snorted a laugh. "I don't think you understand quite how many guys I have asking me about how to get on your radar. They know we're friends and seem to think that means I'm also your pimp, or maybe they want me to be their pimp for you... Either way, it drew my attention to the fact that there doesn't ever seem to be anyone coming or going from your room and you don't stay away from the House overnight anymore either..."

"Maybe you shouldn't believe everything you read in the papers," I teased.

"Like articles given by you, about you?" He smirked at me and I shrugged.

"Those are the most misleading of all. Why don't you tell your little buddies that I'm in recovery? I'm fifty days celibate today actually and about to receive my coin at my sex addicts anonymous meeting."

"Is that so?" he laughed.

"Depressingly...yeah I think it actually might be." I pursed my lips as I considered that. I hadn't been with anybody since that mental break I'd had at the Shimmering Springs with Darius. That absolutely unforgettable, I-might-just-dream-about-it-every-night-for-the-rest-of-my-life slip in sanity that I liked to pretend hadn't happened. Even thinking about it now had me biting my lip and I wasn't really sure what to do with the surge of heat tingling along my spine. Because Darius Acrux was absolutely not a mistake I was going to make twice. Certainly not while I was sober. I definitely wasn't going back there…like fifty four percent. *Dammit.*

"Well if you want any help with that, I've got a list of options for you," Milton joked.

"Gee thanks, I'll keep that in mind."

We approached The Orb and my Atlas pinged in my pocket.

Caleb:

Five minutes, sweetheart. You might wanna run ;)

My heart leapt as I read the message over for a second time. That wasn't the rules we used to play by. And he didn't seem to be giving me a choice in whether or not I wanted to play either. Which should have totally pissed me off. But I had actually been missing the games we used to play. I was getting tired with my routine of boredom and solitude and if a hot Vampire wanted to chase me about and drink my blood then who was I to say no?

"I've gotta go," I said to Milton as I glanced around, looking for any signs of Caleb. "I'll catch you later."

"Okay…" he replied, but I didn't have time for explanations and I turned away from him, jogging straight towards the closest building which happened to be Jupiter Hall.

I pulled my hood up and tucked my hair beneath my hat as I started running in the hopes that it might mean less people recognised me. Caleb's fan club would be more than willing to sell me out to him for the chance that a moment of his pleasure might be aimed at them.

The lower level of Jupiter Hall seemed busier than usual for this time of day, so I turned away from it and hurried up the huge stone staircase to the next floor instead.

I headed down the wide corridor and glanced over my shoulder, checking for any sign that I was being followed and smirking to myself as I failed to spot anyone.

I kept my pace quick but didn't run as I carried on down the long corridor, releasing a breath of laughter.

I took another step just as a door flew open beside me and a blur of motion announced the arrival of a Vampire.

I shrieked in surprise as strong arms wrapped around my waist and I was hoisted off of my feet.

We shot back inside the room and the sound of a door slamming came from behind me as the world spun and the scent of cinnamon assaulted me.

My ass hit a desk and I blinked in surprise as Orion shoved me backwards, pushing my thighs apart and moving between my legs as he pressed me back on to the desk.

"*Fuck.* I've been waiting to do this for so long," he gasped as his mouth moved to my neck and his fangs brushed against my skin. I recoiled in shock, my heart hammering with fear as confusion almost drowned me. What did he mean he'd been waiting to bite me? Had I just stumbled into some weird Vampire blood claiming war that he was waging with Caleb?

Orion's grip on me tightened as his fangs brushed my neck again, but instead of biting me, he kissed me, his mouth moving on my skin as his weight pressed me down.

What the fuck is happening right now??

I squirmed beneath him, trying to shove him back as my brain scrambled to figure out what the fuck was going on.

"Professor!" I snapped, shoving him again as he pushed his hands inside my coat and started tugging at my shirt buttons. My skin crawled as he pawed at me and I wriggled more, trying to push him off but he groaned like he thought I was pawing him back.

"You wanna play that game? Have you been a bad girl then?" Orion laughed darkly and my heart thundered in a panicked beat, but my brain was quickly catching up to the insanity taking place here and there was no way in hell my body was going to be taking part.

I opened my mouth to tell him to get the fuck off of me just as he wrenched me into his arms again and lifted me back off of his desk.

The world blurred again and the next thing I knew, he'd thrown me back against the book shelf to the side of the room. My eyes widened in horror as he crushed me with his body and I stared at him in what was quickly becoming full blown rage.

"What the fu-"

His mouth hit mine and I slammed my lips shut, grinding my jaw as I squirmed back against the bookshelf, my hands finding his chest as I tried to shove him back. But he was like a wall of pure fucking muscle.

Orion pushed my coat roughly and my hood fell off, taking my hat with it so that my brunette hair tumbled around my face. He jerked backwards, his eyes widening with surprise and what looked like pure horror.

"Oh shit," he breathed just as I kneed him in the balls as hard as I fucking could.

"*Fuck!*" Orion wheezed as he staggered back and I swung at him, punching him straight in the jaw.

"What the actual fuck?" I yelled at him as he backed up, holding a hand out to ward me off as he cupped his battered junk with the other hand.

"Wait," he gasped just as the door flew open behind him.

Darcy stood there, her lips parting with shock as she stared between me and Orion like she couldn't quite figure out what she was seeing.

I ripped a book off of the shelf behind me and threw it at Orion's head. "Run, Darcy!" I gasped, throwing another book at him. "He's lost his fucking mind!"

"What?" she breathed, taking a step closer in spite of my instructions.

"He's had a brain transplant with Washer, but decided to go full on gropey in his creepy ass Professor Pervert role!"

"Oh shit," Darcy breathed, stepping into the room, throwing the door closed behind her and tossing a silencing bubble around us. Her face paled and pure alarm washed over her features. "It's not what you think, Tor."

"So he didn't just snatch me out of the corridor, try to yank my clothes off and put his fucking mouth on me?" I demanded, throwing another book which hit Orion in the head.

"Ow! Stop throwing my fucking books!" he hissed, still nursing his manhood.

Darcy's eyes widened in panic as she looked to Orion. "No, Tor, you don't understand. He wasn't attacking you! He must have thought…"

"She had a goddamn hat on," Orion gritted out before turning a glare my way. "I told you about wearing fucking hats before!"

"What? Have you got a hat fetish or something? Because maybe you should be molesting Diego in that case instead of me!" I hefted another book into my grasp but Darcy put herself between us.

"No! I thought you were your sister," Orion growled, glaring at me like this was somehow *my* fault.

"And how is you dry humping my sister any better than…" I cut my tirade short, my gaze sliding from him to Darcy as her bottom lip started trembling.

"This is what I couldn't tell you," she breathed. "Me and Lance-"

"*Lance?*" I repeated, looking at Orion again like he'd just grown a second head.

"Don't look at me like I'm some old pervert," he snapped.

"You are," I replied instantly.

"He's only eight years older than me, Tor, you've had boyfriends older than him before," Darcy said, rolling her goddamn eyes at me like *I* was the one who was acting like a crazy person here.

"Well they turned out to be shady assholes too," I bit back.

"That's not because they were older than you, it's because you have terrible taste in men," she growled and my eyes widened as I realised she cared about this enough to actually go to bat for him over it.

I stared at her for a long moment then flicked my gaze back to him. Orion looked like he didn't know whether to be angry, relieved or afraid and he stepped closer to my sister, taking her hand in his as if to say he'd stand by her no matter how this played out.

"I don't…I mean, how did you…*when* did you…?" I waved my hand between the two of them as my nose scrunched up in horror, all kinds of old school porno scenarios running through my head. Like him keeping her back after class for being a naughty girl, or her bringing him a shiny red apple and offering to do *anything* to get a better grade in his class.

"We…" Darcy looked at Orion like she wasn't even sure if she should tell me and he let out a low breath as he finally stopped cupping his junk like it might fall off. He gave her a slight nod and tension seemed to drain from her shoulders as she went on. "We've always had a connection-"

"Yeah I know you thought he was hot by the way you drooled in his classes. I want to know at which point he decided to start molesting you?" I demanded.

"I'm not some fucking predator," Orion growled.

"Says the Vampire," I bit back.

"It's more than just some physical connection," Darcy said quickly, shifting so that she was slightly between me and Professor Humpsalot like she thought I might lunge at him at any given moment. And that didn't actually sound like the worst fucking idea in the world. He'd clearly been forcing her to lie to me about this. *He* was the reason I'd been alone for so long. And to think I'd actually begun to think of him as something less than an asshole.

My lip pulled back and Phoenix fire sprang to life in my hands, scorching his precious book and making his face twist with anger.

"I'm going to fucking kill you," I swore, taking a step forward.

"No, Tory!" Darcy moved between us and her own fire flickered along her arms as she faced me down. "Just *listen* would you? Instead of making assumptions! If you could ever just control your temper you wouldn't have half the problems you do!"

I stared at her in shock, the flames in my palms flickering uncertainly. I didn't think she'd ever shouted at me like that in our entire lives. The fact that she clearly felt so strongly about this was enough to make me pause and with a grunt of effort, I banished my flames. The book in my hand smoked slightly and Orion blanched like it physically hurt him to look at it. I had no idea why. It was titled Advanced Numerology, so I was really doing him a favour.

"Well start talking because if you can't convince me that he's not some kind of sex pestering, brain washing, secret keeping, dirty old pervert then I'm gonna fucking burn his balls off right here and now."

"What the fuck?" Orion snarled but Darcy ignored him.

"Okay, okay, just *listen*. I think it all started the moment we met really. We have a connection, Tor. He gets me in ways that no one else ever has. And I trust him so implicitly that it's like my soul knows I should. And we tried to fight what was happening between us because we know it's not allowed. But then, that night when we all went to the party at the Acrux Manor, we just...gave in." She shrugged helplessly. "And I know it's crazy and insane and against the rules and that both of us could get into so much trouble because of it but...I can't just turn off the way I feel about him. I can't deny what my heart wants and what I *need."*

Tears glimmered in her eyes as she pleaded with me to understand and I could see the depth of her feelings shining in her gaze. But that didn't mean he felt the same. Didn't mean he hadn't manipulated her or brain washed her or used his position as her Liaison to abuse her trust.

"Now *you*," I snapped, glaring at him. "Tell me what you want from my sister and don't you dare fucking lie about it."

Orion looked at me for a long moment before his gaze slid to her.

"Darcy is *everything* to me," he breathed. "She's all I think about and all I want. I see so much good in her and she somehow brings out the best in me. And if you feel that you can't keep this secret for us or like you have to tell the authorities about what's going on between us, then I understand. Because you want to protect her as fiercely as I do. But even if we're torn apart, even if I went to Darkmore Penitentiary and had to live out the rest of my days behind bars, I'd never regret a moment of it. Because my life was empty before I loved her. And parting us won't change the way I feel for her."

My lips parted, my heart beating to a heady rhythm as the honesty in his voice called to me. There was no way he could fake that look in his eyes. No way he could lie that convincingly. He loved her. And as I looked at her and took on the wild panic in her gaze, the desperate need for me to understand, I realised that she loved him too. This wasn't some sordid affair. It was real.

"Why did you lie to me about this?" I asked in confusion. Did she really think I would have blabbed if she'd just confided in me?

Darcy's eyes glimmered with tears. "At first I didn't want you to be implicated if it came out. But then Seth found out at Halloween and I decided to tell you anyway...but he blackmailed me not to. He's been holding this secret over us, making us do all kinds of things with the threat of telling everyone. Lance would be power shamed for loving me, Tor. And worse..."

"Love," I breathed simply. Because what else even really mattered in this world? I stood looking between the two of them again as I tried to figure out what else to say and suddenly wondering how I hadn't seen it before. "Okay... But what the hell are you going to do now?"

They exchanged a look and Darcy shrugged. "We just have to keep it secret. Then hopefully, once I graduate and a bit of time has passed..." Her cheeks coloured with embarrassment and I got the feeling she hadn't voiced that plan before, but Orion looked like he was trying hard not to grin at her words so I was guessing he liked the sound of it.

I lowered the book in my hand and dropped it to the floor.

"Can you stop damaging priceless books please?" Orion muttered and I couldn't help but laugh.

"You assault me, blame me for wearing a hat then tell me you're in love with my sister and the most pressing issue you have is my treatment of some old books?" I snorted a laugh.

"*You* assaulted *me,*" he protested.

"What did she do?" Darcy asked in confusion.

"He was trying to shove his tongue down my throat so I kicked him in the balls," I said with a smirk.

"You didn't just kick me in the balls, I think you fucking broke them," Orion snarled and Darcy laughed. "It's not funny."

"It is pretty funny," I contradicted.

Darcy laughed harder and suddenly she threw herself at me.

"Can you forgive me, Tor? I was just so afraid of what Seth would do. He can't figure out that you know about us – he's been using this to drive us further and further from each other. I didn't know what to do, but it cut me apart being away from you. I'm so, so, sorry." She squeezed me so tight that I could hardly breathe and I crushed her back with just as much force.

"I'm sorry for not trusting that you had a good reason to lie to me," I whispered back. "And I swear on everything I am that we'll find a way to make Seth Capella pay for this." My gaze slid beyond her as we pulled apart and Orion shifted uncomfortably as I looked at him.

"You get one shot to do right by her," I warned, pointing at him. "And if you fuck it up, if you hurt her or break her heart, then I won't just kick you in the balls. I'll *castrate* you."

Orion shifted his hands before his junk protectively, clearing his throat as he glanced at Darcy. "Fucking hell, I think she actually would," he muttered, like I was insane.

Darcy offered me the brightest smile in the world as she answered him. "Yeah, she totally would."

DARCY

CHAPTER THIRTY SEVEN

It was the last day of term and life was good again. Well, as good as it could be with Seth Capella hanging an axe over my head at every turn. But now Tory knew the truth, it was completely liberating. It wasn't planned and I was still worried about her being dragged down with me if it all went to hell, but maybe the stars had made the decision for us. And that *had* to be a good omen.

I spent a decent portion of my morning floating around my room on a gust of air, singing Power by Little Mix while mentally putting my middle finger up at Seth. Tory had begrudgingly agreed to pretend she didn't know about me and Orion even though she wanted to cut Seth's balls off for it. But those balls had *my* name on them.

I also had another reason to be happy. Because if the palace belonged to me and Tory for the Christmas holidays, then I had no reason not to invite Orion to stay with us. It had actually been Tory's idea which was totally insane. I couldn't get over how onboard she was with this, but since she'd told me the details about hooking up with Darius I guessed she couldn't really judge. And though I knew she was beating herself up over what she'd done, a part of me knew that she felt something for Darius she couldn't explain. And whatever it was, she had to work through it herself.

We'd have to wait and see how empty the palace really was, but it sounded like there would be whole wings of it going unused, so hiding Orion would be no problem even if there were staff hanging about the place. I hadn't told him just yet, I wanted to surprise him with it this morning. And I had the perfect surprise in mind.

I made my way down for the farewell breakfast before everyone headed home for the holidays, leaving my bag packed and waiting in my room. We'd received an official letter from the Gruses saying how excited they were to receive us at the palace. I had the feeling we were in for something extravagant, but Geraldine wouldn't breathe a word of what we should expect.

I soon arrived in The Orb and my brows jumped up at the sight of the incredible Christmas themed display surrounding our usual table. Geraldine and the rest of the A.S.S sat around it all wearing huge silver hats shaped like stars with *Merry ChristmASS!* printed across them. The table was covered in a layer of snow and plates of pastries, bagels, cooked eggs, toast, cereal and pitchers of juice and coffee filled the space. Snowflakes fell continually over it, melting before they reached the surface and I marvelled at the water magic.

"Merry Christm*ass* Queen Darcy!" Geraldine said as she spotted me then she looked over my shoulder. "And happy holid*ass* Queen Tory!" She snorted, falling apart with laughter. "Do you see what I did? Instead of saying A.S.S I made it into the word *ass*!"

"Oh I never noticed it spells that before," Tory said with a smirk.

I glanced over my shoulder at my sister and couldn't help but pull her into a hug the second she got close. She laughed, beaming at me as she stepped away and we were immediately accosted by two Ass members who placed plastic golden crowns on our heads. The words ASS Queens were etched into the front of them and I caught Tory's hand before she could take it off, snorting a laugh. She rolled her eyes but left it in place, dropping down into a seat at the table.

I sat beside her and I revelled in the Christmas spirit around us, but the thing I was most happy about was having my sister back at my side.

Diego had a sour expression on his face, picking at a piece of tinsel hanging from his Ass hat, looking about as merry as a Christmas elf who'd just gotten the sack.

"What's up?" I asked him, swiping up a sugary almond croissant and taking a bite out of it.

Sofia glanced over at him, but was quickly distracted by Tyler who was trying to explain a card game to her.

"Nothing," Diego mumbled.

"Must be something," I pressed. I hadn't told him about seeing his mother at Orion's family home. Orion still didn't trust him enough to discuss things like that and I felt more cautious around him these days too.

"I don't want to go home," Diego said sullenly, swirling his spoon around a bowl of cereal which had turned to mush. "We don't even celebrate Christmas and Mamá will just spend the whole time reminding me why I'm such a disappointment to the family."

I frowned, looking to Tory. "Maybe you could come to the palace with us?"

Tory gave me a sideways glance that said *oh please god no* and I gave her one back that said *but his mother's a total bitch, Tor.*

She rolled her eyes in agreement, taking a large bite out of a bagel.

"Do you really think I could?" Diego asked hopefully.

"Gambling grapes down to their last dime," Geraldine gasped as she listened in on our conversation. "It's the Vega Princesses' grand return to The Palace of Souls which has been empty for eighteen years, Diego Polaris! It wouldn't be suitable for you to join them on this landmark occasion."

"I doubt Mamá would have let me anyway," Diego said with a sigh.

I frowned then looked to Geraldine with concern. "Is it really going to be that big of a deal?"

"Yeah because I really just wanna go chill out in a big house with a sauna and swimming pool for days, so..." Tory shrugged.

Geraldine stood up then jumped onto her seat. "It won't just be a big deal. It will be the creamiest spongiest cake, filled with Faeberry jam and sugar dimples; the icing will be made of honey nectar from the largest queen bee to ever spread her wings in Solaria! The cherry on top will be the juiciest, most succulent fruit to ever touch your lips!" She stepped right onto the table, uprooting a bowl of hash browns. "It will be a devilish divinity of dapperness! The bells of Nunong will ring into eternity to crystallise the moment for generations to come! The nuns of Galhoun will cry the Vega name into the

535

everlasting night! The Councillors will have the wobbliest, weakest of knees as they try their hardest not to succumb to their most desperate urge to kneel at your feet and pledge the throne to the true royal asses they belong to! For a single momentous moment, no one in Solaria will remember the names Acrux, Rigel, Altair or Capella, for the Vegas will have returned!"

"The Vegas have returned!" The A.S.S roared, throwing their fists into the air.

I was speechless as I stared up at her, her hand planted on her heart, her other hand held aloft with flowers blooming from her fingertips.

"So no biggie then?" I said and Tory snorted, her shoulder knocking against mine as the A.S.S fell into hysterics.

I hurried to Orion's office with a late assignment in my hand as a total excuse in case I bumped into any teachers along the way.

I'd messaged him telling him to meet me here after getting changed in my room. He was gonna freak when he saw what I had under my coat. Because the answer was a big fat nothing. Apart from my knee high socks and snow boots, I was going full commando.

I arrived outside his office, knocking on the door excitedly.

"Come in," Orion said formally and I smirked, taking hold of my zipper and pulling it half way down as I stepped into the room.

Principal Nova was sitting in the chair opposite him, her back to me and I pulled the zipper up so fast I got my hair stuck in it. *Ahhh!*

Orion gaped at me just as Nova swung around in her chair, raising a single dark eyebrow. She frowned as I struggled to release my hair while trying not to reveal the fact that I was butt naked beneath this freaking coat. *Why stars, why??*

Orion's lips were so tightly pressed together I wasn't sure if he was fighting a laugh or if he was about to lose his shit.

"Why are you standing there like a lemon, girl?" Nova questioned as I got my hair free and cleared my throat. "What do you want?"

"I er, just had this Cardinal Magic assignment to hand in." I waved it as proof, moving forward to pass it over to Orion. His eyes narrowed as he took it and he leaned back in his seat.

"Which is late, so ten points from Aer," he said coolly.

Asshat.

I pursed my lips and nodded, moving back toward the door.

"Merry Christmas, Principal," I added before I exited.

"And you, Tory," she called and I sighed as I moved into the corridor, shutting the door behind me.

Well at least that wasn't horribly embarrassing. Oh no wait…it was.

I headed along the corridor and stepped outside where snow was beating down in fluffy white tufts. I stuffed my hands into my pockets, the cold rippling up under my coat and sliding over my naked skin. I urged fire magic into my veins and relaxed as it took away the chill.

A growl sounded somewhere close by and I gazed out into the thick mist formed by the snow as it beat down on the ground in front of me.

Two Wolf's eyes appeared amongst it and Seth leapt out of a drift in his huge white Order form. He knocked me back against the doors of Jupiter Hall and licked me right up the centre of my face. He ran off with a howl that sounded a helluva lot like a laugh and a blur of wolves dove out of the snow, racing after him across campus.

"Merry Christmas to you too, asshole," I muttered, pulling my sleeve down to wipe the drool off of my face.

I started wandering back to Aer Tower, the world quiet as the snow muffled everything around me. Tory and I were being picked up by Geraldine's father in an hour, but I'd wanted to spend that time with Orion. If Nova didn't budge her ass out of his office soon, I wasn't even going to see him before we left.

I loitered all the way back to the tower, checking my Atlas for any messages to say the coast was clear. But apparently it wasn't.

I trailed back up to my room with a pout, pushing through the door and kicking it closed.

Orion stepped out of my bathroom and I squealed in excitement, running forward to kiss him. He held me close, running a hand through my hair as snowflakes melted into it and he released a warm gust of air to dry it out. "I feel like Peter Pan. Always sneaking in your window."

"I leave it open just for you." I grinned.

"Well Wendy…want to come to Neverland? The lost boys miss you." He pulled me against his hard-on and I laughed darkly.

"They don't seem that lost," I teased.

"You'd better check just in case," he murmured and I tip-toed up, kissing him gently while running my hand over the serious bulge in his pants. He groaned against my mouth and I stepped back, unzipping my coat and letting it fall to the floor at my feet.

"*Fuck*, Blue," he gasped as he took in my body before stalking forward and pushing me down onto the bed.

I lost myself in his passion for as long as we had, but when my phone started pinging and I was on my third orgasm I knew it was probably time to call it quits. Orion lay beneath me looking ready to fall asleep as I jumped out of bed and ran around pulling on clothes and brushing my hair. He soon perked up, watching me with a delicious smirk that kept tempting me back to him.

When I was dressed in dark blue jeans and a cheesy Christmas sweater that said *Jingle All The Fae* across a Pegasus in a sparkly hat, I jumped on top of him and planted a wet kiss on his lips.

"I have an invite for you," I said as his hands rested on my hips.

"Does it involve me defiling this ridiculously adorable sweater?" he asked, tilting his head to one side with a hopeful look.

I smacked him on the chest with a laugh. "No. It involves you stardusting to the palace grounds and me sneaking you inside under a rug or something."

His smile fell away, replaced with a wide-eyed look. "The palace? I can't, Blue."

"No one would see you. I'm sure there's plenty of places to hide."

His gaze flickered with temptation and I leaned down, brushing my mouth along his jaw. "And we'd have lots of old, dusty rooms where you could defile this sweater."

He released a low laugh, clutching me tighter. "Well how can I say no to that?"

"You'll really come?"

"Yeah I'll come," he said with a filthy expression that gave it a double meaning.

"You're a bad influence," I teased.

"Says the girl who shows up at my office wearing nothing under her coat." He raised an eyebrow, giving me the stern teacher look and I gave him the innocent student one in return.

I sat up and he swore as I crushed his dick, scooping me off of him so he could get up. "By the stars, between you and your sister, I'll have no manhood left intact."

I giggled as he tugged on his boxers and I got to enjoy the show as he pulled on the rest of his clothes. A knock came at the door before he had his shirt done up.

"Just a sec!" I called, wafting Orion toward the window.

"Let me in – Geraldine's done something terrible!" Tory begged and Orion shrugged at me, stepping into the bathroom just in case.

It was the strangest thing being able to be open about this with somebody – besides a vindictive Werewolf asshole.

I let her into the room and closed the door before Orion reappeared from the bathroom, still buttoning his shirt.

Tory stared at him then looked to me, then the bed. "Ew, dude!"

Orion just smirked and she stared mock-angrily back at him.

"Sorry," I said guilty, glancing down at the bundle of glittering pink and purple material in her arms. "What's that?"

"It's hell stitched into a goddamn dress is what it is. *Two* dresses to be exact. Geraldine wants us to wear these to the 'grand returning' or whatever she keeps calling it. But *look* at them." She wafted them so the skirts unfolded, holding up the two gowns which were hideous beyond words.

Huge frilly bows and miles of netting clustered together on each puffy disaster.

"I'm not wearing it," Tory announced. "I'm going to burn them, Darcy." A wild light lit her eyes and sparks crackled along her skin. "Burn them with me, we'll say it was an accident."

Orion moved forward, plucking the dresses from her hands. "Let's not get hasty, little arsonist. Remember what happened the last time you lit something on fire?"

I thought of Darius's room and Tory sucked on her lower lip innocently while I started laughing.

"Just wear something else," Orion continued. "Problem solved."

"Then we'll insult her. She said she made these herself," Tory sighed dramatically.

"Oh god, we're going to be in the news wearing them, aren't we?" I said, staring at the monstrosities.

"I'll die first," Tory said passionately.

"Just wear what you like and put an illusion over them only Geraldine can see." Orion shrugged like that was so simple and I gave him my biggest eyes.

"You mean you'll do it for us?" I asked sweetly.

His eyes slid over me. "Yeah, of course Blue."

Tory's brows lifted as she gazed at him. "The weirdest thing about all of this is you being nice, you know that right?"

Orion's gaze darkened as a wicked look fell over his features. "It's not a permanent fixture."

"We'll see." Tory hurried to her suitcase, zipping it open. "I bought a bunch of stunning dresses for our palace stay, Darcy."

"Of course you did," I laughed as she produced two beautiful gowns from the depths of her luggage; one a rich navy and the other a deep plum. She passed me the navy one and I hurried to my closet to pick out some underwear and shoes.

"I'll leave you to it," Orion said, backing up to the window. "I'll head to the gate to cast the illusion on Grus." He shot out of the window in a blur of Vampire speed and I hurried forward to close it behind him.

We were soon dressed and heading down to the edge of campus where students were filing out of the large gate or jumping into cars as their parents arrived to pick them up. A few Professors milled around and I spotted Orion amongst them chatting with Gabriel.

Sofia and Diego hurried over to say goodbye and a pang of sadness hit me.

"Have a great Christmas," Sofia said, adjusting the powder pink earmuffs on her head. "I'll miss you."

"You too." I squeezed her then she moved to embrace Tory.

Diego had a small bag in his hand and a frown pinching his features.

"We'll be back before you know it," I said gently and he nodded, pulling me into a hug.

"Stay safe, chicas," he said, looking between us before heading away toward a black Faeyota. The driver's window rolled down and my heart ticked faster as I caught sight of his mother, her expression pinched as she took in her son. She said something to him between tight lips and he hurried around to put his bag in the trunk before climbing into the back seat. The car did a U-turn, driving past us slowly and I got the feeling we were being watched from within the blacked-out windows.

"Well ride my pelican and call it Fanny Sue," Geraldine gasped and I turned, spotting her approaching with the entirety of the A.S.S at her back. She wore a violet gown which was nowhere near as hideous as the ones she'd made for us and a shiny A.S.S badge was pinned over her large bosom. "Don't they just look like the shiniest crayons in the pack!?" she called to the club and they started clapping. "The dresses are just ravishing on you both if I do say so myself."

I glanced over at Orion who shot me a wink before turning back to Gabriel. *Bat ears.*

"Thank you, they're beautiful," I said, hugging her and only feeling one percent shitty about not wearing the ones she'd made. But I did not wanna arrive at the palace looking like a ball of cotton candy.

"Are you ready to dilly dazzle your way into the palace?" Geraldine asked excitedly, glancing over her shoulder at someone.

I spotted her father, Hamish, moving out of the thronging crowd, smiling kindly at us. He wore a tan suit paired with a bright tie that matched Geraldine's dress.

"Bless my sally sack – oh pardon my language." He bowed low. "It's just so wonderific to see you both again. Are you ready to go?"

"Yep," Tory and I said in unison and my smile widened.

Hamish took a pouch of stardust from his pocket and I glanced over at Orion to catch his eye again, giving him a small smile in goodbye.

A rumbling engine caught my ear and Hamish paused what he was doing, looking over at the road as three cars headed down it led by a pale grey motorbike.

"Dammit, he replaced it already," Tory muttered as Darius pulled the throttle and raced out of the gate to a round of applause.

I rolled my eyes as Caleb's black douche-mobile rolled up next and he lowered the window, pointing at Tory. "Merry Christmas, sweetheart." He raced away before she could reply, but she smiled after him, shaking her head.

Max pulled up next in a dark blue Aston Minotin, gazing out at Geraldine. "Have a good one, Grus. Looking hot as fuck by the way." He winked and Hamish straightened his spine, waving his fist after him.

"That slippery sea trout," he said indignantly.

"Don't worry daddypops, he just wants a twirl with a true gentlelady."

"That he does my bubbakanoosh," Hamish said, nodding firmly. "You remember what your Momma always said to do with men like that though, don't you?"

"Cut off their fingers then their dingers," they said in unison and I snorted a laugh, sharing a look with Tory.

Seth drove up in a gleaming white Faezerati and I folded my arms as he predictably coasted to a halt too. Was this the line for the asshole parade or something?

He was wearing a pair of sunglasses like a complete dick and pointed his fingers at us like a gun, pretending to shoot. "See you soon, Vegas." He drove off with a roar of his engine.

"Right. Let's get this chimp on the chipper, shall we?" Hamish tossed the stardust into the air and I was yanked away from the academy in a swirl of stars, my stomach spinning from the journey and from what awaited us at the end of it too.

My heels hit the ground and Tory caught my arm before I fell over in them. I threw her a grateful look, but was immediately blinded by the flash of cameras. A roar of questions filled my ears and I realised we were on a red carpet leading up to an immense golden gate at the top of a set of steps.

Either side of us, reporters were held back by barriers as they clamoured to get our attention. A man in a suit bowed low and took our bags from us then shot away in a blur of Vampire speed.

I couldn't take my gaze off of what lay beyond the gate. The palace climbed toward the sky, its sheer walls reaching up to create a huge gothic tower at the heart of it, its roof narrowing to a point which looked sharp enough to pierce the sky. The walls were pale grey and more towers reached up symmetrically on both sides of the imposing building. None of the roofs were coated in snow as if someone had taken the time to melt it all away. The windows glinted in the sunlight and excitement rolled through me as something about this place called to me like a distant memory.

"The Vegas will be taking no questions," Hamish said firmly and I noticed he was speaking directly to Gus Vulpecula with his dark red hair and foxy features. He was looking at us like a meal he wanted to spend time chewing over and I scowled at him in kind.

"Will you be partaking in the age-old royal traditions?" called a woman with a flowing mane of golden hair.

"Will you be doing a speech on Christmas morning?" another woman shouted.

"Are the press going to be allowed inside the palace?" a small man begged.

"How are you planning on spending your time here?" I spotted Tyler's mother who'd done our article for The Daily Solaria with her dark blonde hair and kindly features. Tory and I moved over to her despite Hamish's muttered complaints.

"We want to learn more about our relatives while we're here," I said into her microphone.

"And we want to relax," Tory added. "We've been working our asses off at Zodiac."

Laughter sounded from a few members of the crowd and Hamish ushered us toward the gates where two guards in black uniforms stood on either side of it. A silver fire symbol stood out on one of their breast pockets and the other guard had earth. I raised my brows as they bowed low and opened the gates to a cheer from the crowd. I glanced back from where we stood up on the steps and realised a sea of civilians were gathered beyond the reporters, trying to get a look at us.

They waved excitedly, jumping up and down and I lifted my hand, a surprised laugh escaping me. Tory raised her hand to wave too and the sound of roaring applause filled the air.

"The true queens have returned!" someone yelled, then the chant was taken up by the rest of the crowd.

A blush spilled into my cheeks as Hamish guided us through the gates and I took in the long path ahead which divided an immaculate garden on either side of us. Snow lay on the ground, but the path had been cleared so the edges of it were perfectly defined.

In front of us was a domed fountain with two huge stone wings spreading out from it like an angel was knelt beneath the water. I was rendered speechless as we headed past it and climbed up an immense set of steps toward wooden doors which were taller than The Orb.

They opened as we approached and Geraldine squealed her excitement behind me. We stepped into an entrance hall with a vaulted ceiling and an incredible stairway of dark wood. The banisters were intricately engraved with the different Orders and at the top of the first level was a beautiful wooden carving of a Harpy woman. Her hair flowed down her back as she looked up at something high above her, her eyes seeming to brim with love.

I turned my gaze to follow hers and found the entire ceiling painted with an enormous Hydra. The black beast took up the whole of the ceiling, its multiple serpentine heads gazing down at the woman below. A tingle of discomfort ran along my spine as I realised this was my first glimpse of The Savage King and his wife. Our true parents.

"I'm sure you'll want to explore every nook and cranny," Hamish said excitedly. "You're welcome to stay in any room you like, but the porter will have brought your things to your mother's rooms. Just follow the wings, they'll take you there." He pointed to the back wall where a little set of silver wings were delicately painted. I spotted another set further up the stairs to the left and my heart pitter pattered.

"I'll come find you for dinner later," Geraldine said. "Have a sniff and snaff and see what's what." She beamed, heading through a door to one side of the immense stairway and disappearing through it.

"This place is…" I started.

"Insane," Tory finished.

We walked up the stairs slowly and I reached for her hand, suddenly needing the closeness of my twin at such a huge moment in our lives. She took it without complaint and I squeezed her fingers as we approached the ornate carving of our mother.

"She looks like us," I breathed.

Tory shrugged. "Maybe a bit."

I glanced at her with a frown. "You don't like it here."

"It's not that," she murmured, dropping her eyes from the statue. "I just don't need to know about a mother and father who dumped us in a whole other world. They screwed up our lives before we'd even started them."

"I know," I sighed. "But I still can't shake the need to learn about them." I turned my eyes to the forbidding painting far above us. "I can't imagine having a father who was as cruel as they say he was. I'm scared to know what he did, but I think I need to know too."

"I get it." She smiled encouragingly. "So while you're learning all about how much of a dick Daddio was, I'll be hunting down the swimming pool and catching up on some sleep."

I laughed and we moved up the stairs, following the silver wings through incredible hallways and past murals of the palace which featured the different seasons. There was an energy in this place that seemed to hum within my veins. It was like the stars had waited a long time for us to return here and now they were waiting for something unbelievable to happen.

We made our way through old gothic spaces and finally found our mother's rooms. I pushed through a silver door where two wings split at the middle and my heart stuttered at the sight beyond.

We were on a balcony that looked down on a huge swimming pool below. It was carved from rock, a waterfall flowing from a hill which must have been made by earth magic. Steam coiled up towards a glass ceiling far above and the soft thrumming of harp music caressed my ears. Living trees clung to the edges of the pool and grass and flowers grew up the side of the hill.

"I think you found that swimming pool, Tor."

She grinned widely and we headed down the sloping stairs which curved around to the floor below. Doors led off of the walls in a hundred directions and I itched to look in every one of them.

I spotted our bags sitting outside two doors on opposite sides of the pool and hurried forward, entering my room. Anticipation filled me as I stepped into the space; the walls were made of dark glass with water swirling through them and a glimpse of a balcony called to me beyond a huge bed.

Tory suddenly caught my hand, wheeling me around with a grin. "This is all ours!" she yelled in joy.

I whooped with her and she tugged me along to the pool, kicking her heels off as she went. I kicked mine off too and our laughter rang off of the glass ceiling far above as we leapt in fully dressed.

The hot water wrapped around me and I breached the surface with a grin, still clutching onto Tory's hand. A strange thrumming resounded through the water and I gasped as I recognised what it was. I glanced at Tory who had the exact same expression on her face.

"Over there." I pointed to the waterfall and we swam across to where the water frothed and bubbled beneath the torrent. We raised our free hands, our magic flowing between us as we parted the falls and a hidden cave was revealed beyond it.

We let go of each other, climbing up inside and the curtain of water fell down behind us. The rock itself gave off a deep blue glow and everything in that small space screamed with magic.

"Here," Tory said excitedly, moving to the wall at the back and placing her hand on it. I moved there too, resting my hand down beside hers on instinct. A hole appeared in the rock, the concealment spell seeming to unlock at our combined touch.

Inside were two ornate silver rings, one with a G engraved on it and the other with an R. Behind them, standing against the wall was a Tarot card.

My heart beat harder as I leaned in and took the card while Tory scooped up the two rings.

"I think they're for us," she breathed. "Roxanya and Gwendalina…"

I eyed the card from Astrum which was of The Sun, its meaning now memorised from my Tarot Classes: Goodness, truth and beauty.

I turned it over, Tory moving close beside me as adrenaline rushed into my blood.

Welcome home dear Princesses.
Seek well, search deep.
This house hides a secret within its walls.
Where wings meet justice, your blood was saved.

"What does it mean?" I breathed and Tory shook her head.

"Cryptic as always. I guess we'll have to hunt the walls for secrets," she said dryly. "Or sit by the pool and wait for the secrets to unveil themselves to us. I'm easy." She turned and dove back into the water, leaving the two silver rings and the card with me.

I clutched them all close to my chest, my adrenaline spiking as the mysteries lurking in this place seemed to surround me. Well I for one, was going to keep an eye out for those secrets.

TORY

CHAPTER THIRTY EIGHT

I woke up on Christmas Eve in a bed that I could truly call my own for the first time in my life. Or at least for the first time that I could remember. We'd never had a real home. Never spent more than two Christmases in the same place. We'd only ever been additional extras to traditions that didn't belong to us.

I wondered what it might have been like to have had Christmas here with our parents. Would they have been like the other Councillors, more concerned with us showing strength and power than love and compassion even at the time of year meant for it?

I blew out a breath and pushed those thoughts away. They were pointless anyway. What did it matter if our mom would have always woken us up on Christmas morning with a kiss or if our father would have refereed our snowball fights?

They didn't get to do any of the things they might have planned to do with us. Good or bad. So what was the point in imagining up scenarios that probably bore no resemblance to the reality that had been stolen from us anyway?

I yawned as I stretched my arms out wide and swept them across the enormous mattress I'd slept on. It was practically big enough for five people. I didn't know whether to think my parents had just had way too much money or if they'd been partial to an orgy or two.

The bed frame itself seemed to have been made out of solid silver and the room it sat in was the most lavish place I'd ever seen. Stone vines grew up and over every surface, flowers in full bloom all over them and looking so realistic that I could only assume someone with the power of earth magic had grown them then turned them to stone.

A huge window sat at the far end of the room spanning the entire wall and holding two glass doors in its centre which led out onto a wide balcony that overlooked the gardens.

I yawned again as I sat up amongst the nest of blankets I'd slept in. They were so silky soft that it had felt like sleeping on a pile of feathers and one glance at the silver clock hanging on the wall told me that I'd fallen back into old habits in my comfortable surroundings.

It was half ten which meant I'd most likely missed that breakfast Geraldine had been going on about last night. I felt like three percent guilty about that but in all honesty, the fact that I'd managed a lie in despite the shadows lurking was nothing short of a miracle.

I crossed the room to the walk-in closet where I'd tossed my suitcase last night and pulled the door wide.

Lights flicked on automatically inside and I glanced at the huge space filled with rails and rails of clothes. I guessed no one had thought to remove our parents' things after they'd died, but the end result was this slightly creepy feeling that they were still here.

I stepped over my suitcase as curiosity nagged at me and I moved between the racks of elegant ball gowns and designer shoes.

I trailed my fingers along some of the dresses and the faintest smell of rosewater stirred the air. I paused, my eyes falling shut as the strangest sense of warmth and safety slipped over me. Like I was being held tight in someone's arms and nothing in the world could touch me.

My eyes fell open again and the almost-memory faded, though I was left with a sense of déjà vu as I stepped further into the space.

Maybe the ghosts who linger here remember me...

At the far end of the closet, a huge mirror stood taking up the whole wall. It had a frame of intricately carved wood which held images of a Hydra and Harpy dancing around each other. In some, the Harpy embraced the Hydra and in others they just seemed to be having fun.

I followed the pattern of the images up along the frame and paused as I spotted two new creatures dancing with them. The Phoenixes soared above them as the Hydra tilted all of his heads back to watch and the Harpy's eyes glimmered with tears of pride.

"That's impossible," I whispered, my breath fogging the glass of the mirror before me. *How could someone have known what we'd be?*

A strange pulse seemed to hum through the air around me and I bit down on my bottom lip as my gaze slid from the carvings to the glass of the mirror itself. It seemed perfectly ordinary, my reflection staring back at me with wary eyes. But something deep in my gut told me it was anything but that.

"Tory?" Darcy's voice snapped me out of the momentary daze I'd fallen into and I turned to look back towards the bedroom.

"In here," I called in response, my breath fogging the glass again. Which was strange because it wasn't cold in here.

"Sorry, but I had to come. Geraldine's losing her marbles down there and they seem to have some kind of weird ritual way of eating Christmas dinner that they need to teach us about before tomorrow. Though why on Earth it matters what order we eat our food in is beyond me." Darcy poked her head into the closet and I looked at her in the reflection. "What are you doing in here?" she questioned with a frown.

"I think I've found something," I said slowly. "Look, here. There's carvings of our mother and father and then…Phoenixes…"

"What?" Darcy stepped over my suitcase and headed towards me at a quick pace. She was dressed in a dark blue gown which exactly matched the shade of her hair.

"Look." I pointed up at the Phoenix carvings and Darcy leaned around me to inspect them.

That strange pulse in the air seemed sharper now that she was here too and my gaze fell back on the glass.

"How can that have been there?" Darcy asked. "It doesn't make sense. No one knew what we'd be before-"

I reached out and placed my palm flat on the glass and a thump of energy slammed through my chest, echoing off of the walls of my power and drawing on the energy which lay dormant inside me.

"Touch the glass, Darcy," I breathed, not knowing why but feeling sure that this needed her magic too. Just like beneath the waterfall.

Darcy frowned at me then slowly raised her hand and placed it alongside mine.

I inhaled sharply as some deep power coiled its way around my magic and tugged on it hard enough to create a bridge. As soon as I released my hold on my power, it started flowing straight out of my hand and into the glass, merging with Darcy's as the image of the two of us standing in the closet faded away to nothing. It was replaced by an image of a beautiful woman walking through a busy marketplace as she gathered exotic fruits into a large basket. The sky was brightest blue above her and the air was thick with heat. Yellow sand marked the cobbled street she walked along and the sense of the exotic place filled me with a strange kind of longing.

"Is that our mother?" Darcy breathed beside me. And as the woman in the image turned her face to look up at the sky, I realised she was right.

There were some resemblances to us in her features. Her dark eyes were framed by thick lashes, almost like a mirror image of ours and something about the set of her full lips seemed familiar too.

"Yeah," I agreed. "But what is this?"

Darcy shrugged as the image shimmered and changed. Our mother was walking along grand halls, carrying the fruits she'd bought in the market laid out on a wide platter. She approached a set of double doors and paused outside as she heard voices.

"Are you sure about this, my liege? It could cause a mighty batch of pickle sauce if the stars aren't in agreement."

I frowned as I recognised that voice. I could have sworn it was Hamish Grus.

"Question me again and I'll have your head along with the Emperor's," a dark voice growled in response.

Our mother's lips parted in shock and she took a step back but the door was flung open before she could escape.

The man who towered over her was powerfully built and darkly attractive. His strong jaw was lined with stubble and his brown eyes fell into a scowl as he spotted her standing before him.

"Do you know what we do with spies in Solaria?" our father growled, magic crackling between his fingers as he took a step towards her like he intended to flay the skin from her bones.

"It's you," she breathed in response, not seeming the slightest bit afraid as she stepped closer to him.

She kept walking, closing the distance between them until she was only inches from him.

"Lady, step away from his majesty!" Hamish barked and I spared him a glance. He was at least thirty years younger than the man we now knew, his moustache darker and frame a little slimmer.

Our mother didn't look at him, but pressed the plate of fruit into his arms as if he wasn't standing there threatening her.

"On the darkest day and longest night, I'll guide you home with love so bright," our mother whispered, her gaze locked on our father's. She reached out a hand and pressed it to The Savage King's chest. He stilled, the magic in his hands blazing, but he made no move to force her away. She slid her hand up over the fine silk shirt he wore, trailed her fingers over his neck and paused as she held his jaw in her hand. "I've *seen* the life we're destined to share. Would you like to see it too?"

Our father's gaze darkened and he parted his lips, seeming to be about to refuse her.

A knowing smile lit our mother's face.

"The truth will change the world," she insisted.

Before the King could reply, magic flared beneath her fingertips and his lips fell slack as she showed him visions of the future she'd seen for the two of them.

We were gifted the sight of them too and my heart beat faster as we caught glimpses them sneaking around a palace with white walls to meet each other in secret, stealing kisses beneath the stars, tangled in the sheets and flying through the clouds in their Order forms.

Our father was a cold man but when he was alone with her, he smiled, laughed, loved. We saw glimpses of a lifetime of happiness between them. Of her calming his foul moods and tempering his rage time and again.

I could feel our mother's emotions as they were attached to the visions. Their love would save her homeland from the wrath of The Savage King. Instead of conquering this beautiful land of sunshine and sand, he would marry its Princess and bring her home to rule at his side. Their love would save countless lives, not only here but in Solaria too. She'd seen it all. Like their destiny was unavoidable and the power of it greater than all the magic in the world.

It didn't matter that he was a madman who had ordered more blood and death than any King or Queen in the history of this world, she would love all of the parts of him that no one else ever saw. She would find the good amongst the hate and bring him closer to the light.

We saw the two of them being summoned beneath the stars and answering the call of destiny as they chose to be Elysian Mates, their souls bound together in love for all of time as their eyes were ringed with silver.

And though she chose him for her own heart's sake, she also chose him for the sake of everyone who fell under his power. Because with her at his side, the future was brighter, paths clearer and more inclined towards peace and prosperity.

There was so much love and passion in the future she showed him that it set an ache burning in my chest. We even saw her with a huge belly as he planted kisses against her skin and spoke to the babies growing inside her. Then we were shown the two of them cradling tiny twins close like their whole world began and ended with the little lives they'd created together.

The visions faded and I almost withdrew my hand, but the mirror shuddered against my palm and the scene shifted to show me something else.

Our mother woke in a cold sweat, dread pouring from her in waves as she hurried to the huge cot where two sleeping babies were snuggled close together.

A tear tracked down her cheek as she looked at us, panic blinding her as the vision she'd seen filled her with fear.

"What is it, love?" our father asked from the bed, pushing himself up onto his elbows.

"Blood," she breathed. "And fire and death. I still can't *see* any way around it."

"I told you, I'll never let that come to pass," he growled, pushing out of bed and striding towards her so that he could pull her into his arms. "I'm the most powerful Fae in all the world. No one can get to us. No one can hurt our children."

Our mother clung to him desperately, shaking her head like she just couldn't believe him and we were gifted another glimpse of her visions.

There was a shadow hanging over our family and no matter what she or our father did, death was coming for them. Every time she tried to change it, the shadow only moved closer. She saw a row of five graves, tiny coffins, fire, fear and screaming. But she couldn't see the threat itself. It was cloaked in darkness, fear embodied and no matter what choice she made, it still came true.

Every choice but one...as she fought to wrangle her visions, she came up with a single option which didn't end in the total annihilation of our family.

One night, while our father slept, she took a pouch of stardust and travelled to the mortal realm with me and Darcy hidden beneath her cloak.

Tears poured along her cheeks as she appeared in the house of a mortal family who had twins the same age as us.

She woke the people who she had selected to raise us and fear prickled along my spine as she Coerced them not to notice any difference in their babies. She told them to love and protect us and raise us to be strong in spirit and mind.

She sobbed as she left us there, taking their children in our place as she returned to the Palace of Souls.

I almost snatched my hand away from the glass. I couldn't understand how she could be so callous as to trade our lives for those of two innocent mortal girls. But before I could draw back, a final vision came to us.

It was me and Darcy sitting on the throne. Peace ruled in Solaria, the people were happy and the balance of power was restored. A dark shadow stood against us in the distance, but together, we just might have a chance of beating it and saving the people of Solaria. But without us, all hope was lost.

The vision faded and I staggered back as my heart pounded.

"Were they…did she store her visions in there for us somehow?" Darcy asked, chewing on her lip as she tried to process everything we'd just seen.

"She thought that we were Solaria's only chance of standing against the shadows," I replied in a hollow voice. "That's why she made us Changelings…"

I didn't know what to make of everything we'd just seen but a small, pathetic, aching part of me which I never liked to admit existed was tearing open. Our parents had loved us. Wanted us. They'd died wishing for a life with us. And that knowledge meant more to me than I'd ever imagined it could.

"She loved us, Darcy," I murmured. "Our father did too…no matter what else he was or what he did. Our parents wanted us."

Darcy burst into tears as she threw her arms around me and I felt myself trembling in her arms.

I hadn't wanted to find out more about the people who had brought us into this world when we'd come here. But now that I had, I realised how much I'd needed to know.

There were so many stories and rumours about them, so much hatred for the things our father had done and the monster everyone claimed he was, that I hadn't even imagined the idea that he might have loved his family. Or that the woman he'd married had been making him into a better man, saving the world from the worst of his nature.

"By the light of Uranus, Tory Vega, if you miss the luncheon I shall be most disappointed!" Geraldine called from somewhere back out in the bedroom.

I released Darcy and swiped the tears from my cheeks as I tried to compose myself again.

"What's all this hullabaloo?" Geraldine gasped as she appeared in the doorway and I half laughed as she caught me out.

"It's just a lot being here, I guess. We're feeling a bit overwhelmed," I said.

"Yeah," Darcy agreed. "It's…a lot."

"Of course it is!" Geraldine gasped. "And here I am like a badgering Brenda trying to make you slot into the roles of perfect Princesses when I should have realised you needed time to adjust to being back home!"

"Home?" I questioned in a small voice. How could I look at this place as my home? The palace was bigger than a small town. And yet…there was something weirdly comforting about being here.

"We've never really had a home before," Darcy said, sharing a look with me that said she wasn't so sure about this either.

"Well you do now," Geraldine said firmly. "Our Princesses were lost for far too long. But now you're home and the Kingdom of Solaria is rejoicing as our most powerful line is restored. The Fae world is built on a foundation of strength and power. And now we have our most powerful family back. There may be those who wish to keep you down or see you fall, but the true Queens are rising. The line of Vega is intact once more. And when you seize full control of your destiny, even the stars won't be prepared for the might you possess."

My lips parted on what should have been a protest but instead, I could only look at my sister as the strength of Geraldine's words washed over me.

We'd never asked for this destiny, never wanted this power or a throne or to be pitted against the Heirs. But it was ours all the same.

We'd been born to rule over this kingdom and the strength of our father and love of our mother ran through our veins.

We were the most powerful Order of Fae that had been seen in a thousand years. We were the first Fae to possess all four Elements in living memory.

So maybe it was time we stopped denying our birth right. Because the Vegas had been born to rule. And I was sick of being forced to bow.

DARCY

CHAPTER THIRTY NINE

I was curled up next to Tory in her bed as midnight came and went. Christmas Day was coming and I was so glad to be spending it in our usual way, sleeping in one room, ready to wake at dawn together – or at least, I'd be waking at dawn and prodding Tory up too.

Tory was breathing softly, but sleep wouldn't come so easily for me. My mind was spinning with thoughts and questions about our mother and father. I needed more answers and the walls themselves seemed to hold them, whispering in hushed voices I couldn't quite hear.

I let my eyes fall closed, thinking of my mother, recalling her face from the mirror vision she'd gifted us. She'd known we'd walk in this palace again one day and unravel the secrets she'd left for us. And I knew there was more to find.

Pale light filtered through my lids and I cracked an eye, finding the moon had broken through the snow clouds beyond the glass doors which led onto the balcony. We'd left the curtains open to watch the snow pile up on the stone rail.

The whispers grew louder and I had the strongest sense that I wasn't imagining them at all. The walls really were speaking, or maybe it was the stars. Either way, something was calling to me, pulling me from the warmth beneath the covers like a Siren's song.

I dipped my feet into a fluffy pair of slippers and willed heat into my veins to banish the chill beyond our bed. I moved to the window, the moon looking brighter than I'd ever seen it, nestled amongst a blanket of stars which shone like diamonds.

"What is it?" I whispered like a crazy person, but I'd experienced too many strange things since my arrival at Zodiac not to believe in this. "What do you want to show us?"

Something caught my eye in my periphery and I turned to find Astrum's card laying on the foot of our bed, the picture of The Sun glowing like a fire burned within it.

I moved towards it tentatively, my heart hammering as I picked it up and warmth crackled through my fingers. I turned it over to reread the message and heard the last line in my head, spoken in my mother's voice. *"Where wings meet justice, your blood was saved."*

My throat thickened as a small set of painted wings on the wall lit up under the moon's rays, guiding me toward it.

"Tory," I hissed, hurrying to wake her.

"I don't wanna wear the Ass hat," she murmured and I shook her arm.

"Get up," I urged and her eyes squinted open.

"Darcy? What's going on?"

"I think our mother wants to show us something," I breathed.

She woke up fully, slipping out of bed and I pointed to the shining set of wings on the wall as she gave me an *are you insane?* expression.

"Look," I urged.

"Shit," she exhaled.

We moved toward it and I reached out, brushing my fingers across the embossed silver paint. The glow instantly died and another set of wings lit up beside the door. I inhaled deeply, turning to Tory who gave me a nod, sliding her hand into mine.

"Let's go," she said firmly.

We stepped out of the room and the crash of the waterfall surrounded us, along with the stifling heat of the pool. Another set of wings lit up on the other side of it and we hurried across the space toward it. As Tory pressed her fingers to it, another one glowed above a door to our right.

We jogged towards it and I pushed it open, revealing a dark corridor beyond. Tory cast a flame in her palm and I did the same as we stepped into the pressing black. The walls were illuminated as we walked, showing large paintings in gilded frames. Our mother and father featured in many of them, but there were other relatives too, all staring out at us.

At the far end of the corridor, a huge picture encompassed the entire wall. Our parents stood side by side, each of them holding a baby in their arms. My mouth parted at the way they looked at us, love pouring from their expressions.

"Seek well, search deep." Mother's voice filled the air and I stilled.

Tory looked to me, her wide eyes telling me she'd heard it too.

Another set of wings glowed to our left as we turned into a large ballroom. The ceilings were made of glass and one of the walls was too, looking out onto a patio under a huge sloped roof. The floor was so polished I could see our reflection in it as we walked, heading to the silvery wings in the far corner of the room. Beside it was a painted set of golden scales which ignited with the same power.

"Where wings meet justice, your blood was saved."

I pressed my hand to it and frowned when it continued to shine. Tory moved forward, touching her fingers to it as well and a ripple of energy flowed along my arm.

A click sounded and a secret door swung open in the wall, revealing a dark passage with icy walls.

"Oh my god." I leaned forward to look inside but the second I did, a wave of heat enveloped me. I was dragged into a vision of blood and death and fire.

Servants were strewn on the floor while four guards tried to hold a door closed at the end of the room. Smoke plumed beneath them and the scent of burning filled my nose.

One of the guards cast thick vines to hold the door in place while the others readied magic in their palms to fight whatever was trying to break through it. The walls shuddered as an immense weight fell against it and fear crashed through my heart as I stared unblinkingly at the scene.

Somewhere, a baby was crying and a woman was screaming, the

horrible sounds tangling in my skull.

Another door flew open to my left and my heart halted at the sight of Professor Astrum. He was much younger, but his hair was already grey and falling around his shoulders. His hand was locked around a child's who ran a step behind him.

"This way, don't panic dear boy," Astrum soothed him.

The door broke open and the guards were thrown aside by a huge tree-like arm as three Nymphs spilled into the room. Terror clutched my heart as the guards battled to destroy them but that awful sucking, rasping filled the air as the monsters took hold of their magic. Fire flared behind the beasts, climbing the walls and devouring everything in its path.

Astrum darted toward the secret door in the wall, guiding the boy's hand forward to press against it. I looked down at the child with his raven hair and familiar eyes. I wasn't sure if I really knew him or if the memory was tugging at emotions inside me, making me feel what Astrum had felt that day.

"This will lead us out of the palace," Astrum promised. "Don't look back!"

The two of them disappeared into the tunnel and the second the door closed behind them, the vision evaporated.

I gasped, leaning against Tory as the strength of the memory took a chunk of my power with it.

"Who was that?" Tory breathed and I shook my head, having no answer.

The door swung shut and the magic around it faded as it locked once more.

We tried pressing our hands to it to pull more memories from its depths, but the silver wings were quiet, the secret passed on.

I woke early on Christmas morning with a smile pulling at my lips, drinking in the beautiful room around me and the amber sunlight pouring across the bed. After last night, I was filled with hope. I didn't have all the answers, but every minute spent here seemed to reveal something more to us and I was sure the palace had more to unveil.

Whoever the boy was that we'd seen in the vision, he had to be important somehow. I just couldn't connect the dots though. It was as if my mother and Astrum had conspired to bring us this information, storing their memories in walls and Tarot cards and waiting for us to find them. But what did it all mean? We were surely still missing pieces of the puzzle.

I hurried out of bed and grinned as an idea came to me. I slipped onto the balcony, pushing fire magic into my blood to banish the cold as I stared across the incredible view. A high wall ringed the palace grounds and I could just glimpse a city beyond it with gleaming sky scrapers. I made a mental note to ask Geraldine where exactly we were in Solaria. We could have been a thousand miles from the academy or two and I decided to get a map of the world as soon as I could. I'd been so locked inside the academy bubble, that I hadn't spent nearly enough time thinking about what lay beyond its walls.

I scooped up a snowball from the edge of the balcony and moved back inside, knowing this could potentially start world war three, but what the hell? I took aim at Tory, launching it at her and it exploded over her face.

She shrieked, leaping to her feet and her eyes narrowed on me. "Oh you're so dead!"

She sprang off of the bed and I darted outside with a whoop of excitement, scooping up more snow and using my air magic to propel it at her. She laughed, raising her hand and casting a flash fire which melted it mid-air before picking up a handful of snow and launching it at me. It smashed against my chest and our laughter carried into the sky as we continued the fight until we were soaking wet and smiling our heads off as we headed back inside.

I soon went back to my room to get ready for the day, admiring the beautiful glass walls where water washed through them in a slow and never-ending circle.

I showered in the ridiculously lavish en-suite and dressed in a sparkly white sweater dress with a snowman on it – because hey, it was Christmas. I paired it with some knee high socks and pinned one side of my hair back with a silver clip.

My Atlas pinged in my bag and I took it out, biting into my lip as I found a message from Orion.

Lance:

Merry Christmas, Blue. Looks like I'll be spending it with you anyway. I guess you've heard the news?

I frowned, tapping out a reply as I headed out of the room to find Tory.

Darcy:
What news?

Lance:
You'll see…

Cryptic bastard.

I found Tory out in the hall wearing black jeans and a tank top.

I snorted a laugh. "Is that your idea of being Christmassy?" I teased.

"No…" She lifted something in her hand, waving a shiny star clip at me and pushed it into her hair. "Ta dar."

"Jingle balls no!" Geraldine called from the top of the stairs. I looked up, finding her in an incredible midnight blue ballgown complete with Cinderella gloves and her hair twirled up into an intricate bun. "You must wear dresses fit for royalty!"

She started running flat out down the stairs which was pretty impressive in those heels and she came to a halt in front of us, shaking her head. She looked radiant, her skin seeming to shimmer under the lights and her earthy eyes were glittering.

"What does it matter?" Tory asked with a shrug. "It's just us."

"Gobble my nobble," she breathed, tugging anxiously at her dress. "I didn't want to say anything too soon in case I brought Daniel Downer to the party."

"What are you talking about?" I pressed, a knot forming in my chest at her expression.

"It is a royal tradition for the Vegas to dine with the High Councillors and their families, and it has been decided that that tradition will be upheld in honour of your first Christmas back at the palace," Geraldine said then held her breath, gazing anxiously between us.

"You mean Lionel Acrux will be here?" Tory balked, looking horrified.

"And the Heirs?" I gasped.

"Yes." Geraldine bowed her head in shame. "I wished only for you to enjoy the time given to you before their arrival. But now I see what a salty flapjack I've been."

I sighed, resting a hand on her arm. "It's fine. And you're right, it would have spoiled the days we've spent here knowing they were coming."

"God, how long are they gonna be here for?" Tory asked, her brows pinched.

"For the afternoon and...the evening and then...the night also." Geraldine cleared her throat. "They leave tomorrow at dusk."

"Well we'd better get ready I guess." I looked to Tory, realising what Orion had meant. He must have been accompanying Darius and his family here. And that fact descended on me like a lead weight as I realised we might not get any time alone together after all.

Trust them to spring it on him out of the blue as if he had no life of his own. I guessed that was what Lionel wanted though; everyone around him on a tight leash.

My gut clenched at the idea of seeing that puffed up Dragon bastard again after what he'd done to us. We'd have to pretend we didn't remember what had happened on the Lunar Eclipse, act completely normal. Well, as normal as we could manage in the company of a man who would see us dead in a heartbeat. Especially if he knew we possessed the Fifth Element just like him. And that we were really Phoenixes instead of Fire Harpies. We were the biggest threat his family had ever known and he could never find that out. Not until we were trained well enough to protect ourselves.

Geraldine stayed with us as we headed into Tory's room to get changed.

Tory glanced at me with a thought dancing in her eyes. "That closet has a bunch of royal gowns in it." She pointed to the one where we'd seen the vision in the mirror.

My lips parted. "You mean our mother's gowns?"

Tory shrugged one shoulder, some part of her unable to say that word even now. "They're just going to waste."

"This moment is made up of all my dreams," Geraldine gushed and I turned to see tears swimming in her eyes. "The Princesses wearing their mother's dresses – it's getting me all wet-eyed and wobbling." She wafted her hands under her eyes and I frowned, nudging her softly to draw a smile from her. "Go!" she begged. "The anticipation is eating my innards."

I laughed as I followed Tory into the closet, taking in the beautiful array of dresses around me.

I thumbed through the rail to my right while Tory looked at the one opposite.

"Do you think they'll fit?" I wondered aloud, plucking an incredible rose gold dress off of the rack and holding it against me.

"Looks like it will," Tory said, picking out a heart-stopping ocean green dress.

I tugged my sweater dress off and pulled on my mother's one, getting lost in miles of netting as the huge skirt fell around my ankles. Tory moved forward to lace up the back, the bodice strapless with a corset style that cinched in my waist.

I helped Tory into the green one, the lacy straps sitting delicately over her shoulders. The skirt swept out behind her as she twirled and the colour made her dark green eyes glitter.

We headed back into the bedroom and Geraldine burst into tears.

"Oh don't, you'll ruin your make up," I hushed her, hurrying forward. She used her water magic to guide her tears straight out of her eyes so they didn't make her mascara run, swirling around us in the air as we tried to soothe her. It was completely weird and totally cool.

"You just look so magnanimous," she said, holding a hand to each of our cheeks. "I'm the luckiest lady in the whole of Solaria. I feel like I'm floating upside down on a cloud covered in Faeflies."

"We wouldn't get anywhere without you, Geraldine," I said seriously and we all clutched each other in a tight embrace.

Geraldine led us out of our mother's rooms and into another huge wing of the palace. We passed through immense dark halls which had a forbidding air to them and screamed of our father. I could feel his presence in this part of the palace like he was still pacing the corridors in a foul mood. I longed to know why he had such a cold heart. What had happened to him to make him so cruel?

It seemed so brave of my mother to accept him as hers despite everything she must have known about him. I hoped she'd been happy, but from the looks of the memories we'd seen, it seemed she was. Maybe it was impossible for Elysian Mates to be anything but happy with each other. And that made my mind catch on Orion and wonder if we really could be destined for one another like my parents had been.

We arrived outside a set of wooden doors, the iron handles shaped as two snake-like heads of a Hydra.

A couple of guards moved forward to open the doors and I straightened my skirt, suddenly feeling like we were about to be scrutinised from head to toe.

The doors pulled open and I forgot to breathe. We were at the top of a beautiful staircase which sloped down into a vast throne room. The ceilings looked half a mile high and blue stained glass windows let in a cold kind of light.

Purple fires roared in several fire places and I had the creeping feeling of standing in some dark lord's lair. And I supposed I was. It was imposing, intimidating. And I imagined that was exactly how The Savage King had wanted his guests to feel. Even the fact that we entered up high like this atop a staircase meant we had to look down on anyone gathered below.

My gaze fell on the enormous throne sitting in the shimmering blue light which filtered down from the windows in straight shafts. It was made of dark stone, the wide seat rising at the back and splitting into fifty Hydra heads, their long necks winding together and reaching toward the ceiling. Two of them curved around to create the arms, their two-pronged tongues protruding and their sharpened fangs on show. All of their eyes were inlaid with sapphires which glinted under the light falling on them. It spoke of the power of the man who'd sat on it. It was a threat to anyone who challenged him and a statement about the magic which must have lived in him. It was also a sharp reminder of the way of Fae. The strongest ruled the land. And that would one day be us.

The doors opened at the far end of the throne room and a line of guards marched ahead of a group of people. The Councillors were dressed in fine clothes, the four of them walking in a line side by side. Behind them were the Heirs, each of them in smart black suits and bow ties. Orion was beyond them in the same attire, making my heart tumble as I took in his fine clothes and swept back hair. His arm was linked through Catalina Acrux's who wore the most low cut dress ever, the swathes of white silk looking almost like a wedding dress. Behind them was Xavier with a large group of what I guessed were the other Heirs' siblings and the Councillors' partners.

They all stopped at the base of the stairs and Hamish appeared beside them, ushering us down.

I glanced at Tory and we locked hands as if on instinct, walking down the steps side by side while every eye in the room scoured us. I lifted my chin as Lionel stared at us coolly, his jaw ticking as we approached. There was an awkward pause where it seemed appropriate for either party to bow, but neither of us did. I could feel it set the tone as the Councillors exchanged looks. We hadn't said a word about it and yet both Tory and I had clearly decided this intuitively. We were owning our power, our names. Besides, this was *our* home, which made them *our* guests.

Hamish cleared his throat, hurrying forward and I glanced over my shoulder, realising Geraldine had remained at the top of the stairs.

"You look wonderful," Seth's mom, Antonia, broke the silence first, seeming like she was itching to reach out and touch us. Her gown was pale blue with intricate little white flowers all over it, the colour enhancing her soft features.

"Beautiful," Caleb's mother, Melinda, agreed. "For a moment I thought I was seeing your mother twice." She smiled kindly and the knot in my chest eased a fraction. Her rose red dress hung off her shoulders and hugged her figure perfectly.

Max's father, Tiberius, stepped forward, holding out his hand to us. "It's a pleasure to see you both again." He looked regal in a dark blue suit and a white cravat.

We took his hand in turn, exchanging pleasantries before the air was cut with the sharpness of Lionel's voice.

"Well I'm famished," he said coldly, looking to Hamish. "Will we be made to stand here all day?"

"No, High Lord. We can move this pumping party bus straight into the dining room, hm?" he offered, looking nervous as he dabbed at his brow.

Lionel nodded curtly, barely sparing us a glance as he headed after Hamish, taking the lead despite the fact that I was sure we should have.

The Heirs slowed before us next and I couldn't help but notice how handsome they all looked. For once, they resembled the princes they were, but the hardness in their eyes made me uncomfortable.

"You look amazing, Tory," Caleb said, moving forward to place a kiss on the back of her hand. "Will you walk with me?"

He offered her his arm and she threw a glance over at Darius before nodding quickly and walking ahead with him. Darius immediately stalked after them with a scowl and my gaze flitted over to Orion beyond Max and Seth. His eyes burned a hole right into me and warmth spread down into the depths of my bones. I longed to force my way past the Heirs, shove Catalina and her fake boobs onto her ass and take her place beside him.

Probably not the best idea.

I forced my gaze away from him and back to the Heirs just as Geraldine appeared at my side.

Max's throat bobbed as he stared at her. "Looking good, Grus," he said and Seth rolled his eyes. "Will you walk with me?" He offered his arm and Geraldine surveyed him closely.

"I suppose I do need a dapper chap on my arm today," she said airily, moving forward to link her arm through his and Max looked like he'd won the lottery as they headed away.

Seth held out his arm for me and I pursed my lips. "I'm good." I stepped past him but he caught hold of me.

"Come on, babe. It's Christmas. Truce for today, yeah?"

I frowned at him, but let him take my arm, knowing he still had the power to pull the trigger on me and Orion any time he liked. And wouldn't that just make this day go from wonderful to fan-freaking-tastic?

"You look stunning by the way," Seth said and my frown deepened in suspicion. "What?" he questioned my expression as we headed through a doorway and along a wide corridor.

"When you say something nice, it usually means you're planning to do something horrible."

Seth knocked his shoulder into mine, his fingers brushing against my skin in his wolfish way. I twisted my hand away to stop him and a low whine escaped him.

"It's just a compliment today," he swore. "I love Christmas, I'm not going to ruin it by being a dick. Besides, this is your home. I know how big of a deal this stuff must be to you."

I gaped at him, wondering if an alien had abducted the real Seth Capella and replaced him with a fake. "Alright who are you and where's the Wolf asshole gone?" I raised a brow and he snorted a laugh. He looked boyish and young in that moment, his hand sweeping back to fix a loose lock of hair into his bun.

"He's still here, babe. Just sleeping."

I lowered my voice as I answered. "Okay."

"Why are you whispering?" he frowned.

"I don't want to wake him up."

"That's it, that's it, remember the old Vega ways!" Hamish called from up ahead. "Spiffing, oh quite magical."

I tried to peer around the corner ahead, wondering what was going on. We turned and found a beautiful stone arch parting us from a brightly lit dining hall. The archway was built of two interlacing wings and was inlaid with glittering clear jewels which pulsed with light every time a couple stepped under it.

Lionel moved beneath it with Melinda and leaned forward to place a kiss on her cheek. My brows pulled together as they walked on and Tory and Caleb stepped in after them. Tory tried to keep going, but Hamish caught her arm and pushed her back.

"Gravelly gingersnaps!" Hamish gasped. "My lady, you cannot step through the archway without sharing a kiss with your companion. The stars will curse you with bad luck for the remainder of the day if you don't, but gift you with good luck if you do. Your mother's arch awakens every Christmas for just this thing."

My heart twisted at that fact, the sweetness in my mother's arch sullied by my own companion.

Tory huffed then Caleb dipped in, caught her waist and pressed a kiss to her lips. Darius stood behind them with his hands in his pockets, looking like he was about to go full Dragon on them. I couldn't help a smirk as Tory danced away and Caleb hounded after her like a love-sick puppy.

Hamish caught Darius's arm. "You won't mind walking a fellow through, will you?"

Darius scowled, but guided Hamish rather forcefully under the arch, waiting while Hamish leaned in and kissed him on the cheek. Darius moved on but Hamish waited on the other side to direct people through.

Max and Geraldine were next and she flipped her hair like she didn't give a damn as they moved under the arch. She immediately planted her lips on his while he was still rolling his shoulders and puffing out his chest in preparation. Then she was gone just like that and he stood staring after her like a fish out of water.

"Off you trot, Mr Rigel." Hamish swept him away.

He waved me and Seth forward and my stomach dipped as I realised he was going to put his mouth on me. Because there was more chance of me turning into a snowflake and floating away on the breeze than me putting my lips on *him*.

"Swap with me." Seth turned around sharply. "You'll go through with me, won't you Aunt Catalina?" he asked sweetly.

Her face turned sour as she dug her nails into Orion's suit sleeve possessively. My brows jumped up in surprise as Seth caught her arm and towed her toward the arch, giving her no choice despite her tight-lipped protests. I stood in front of Orion with a burning need to get closer to him, glancing over my shoulder as Seth kissed Catalina on the cheek then threw me a not-so-subtle wink.

What. The. Actual. Crap?

Orion's eyes glowed keenly as he took my arm and guided me toward the arch.

"Hello Professor," I said politely, my heart quivering like a leaf in my chest. I didn't know why I was such a hot mess, I'd only seen him a few days ago, but some deep part of me needed his company like my lungs needed air.

"Miss Vega," he said curtly.

Had Seth seriously just gifted this moment to us, or did he really not want to kiss me that badly?

We stepped under the arch and I looked up at Orion with my heart in my throat and my pulse absolutely everywhere. He leaned down, pressing his lips to my cheek close to my ear.

"You look indescribable," he murmured so quietly I barely caught it.

His lips left a scorching mark behind and I didn't know how such a simple touch could leave me so weak, but I felt it tearing at the edges of my soul.

He linked his arm with mine and we walked into the spectacular dining hall where a huge table awaited us.

"This isn't how I planned to spend Christmas," I whispered.

"Me neither," he murmured, throwing a glance at the Vampires in the room to check they weren't listening. "It's gonna be really awkward when the mailman shows up with my extra large sex toy delivery."

I laughed loudly in surprise and several of the Councillors looked our way.

"Is it an extra large delivery or an extra large sex toy?" I asked between tight lips as they returned to their conversations.

"You might find out later if the stars are kind to us." He grinned widely then Catalina appeared, pulling him from my arms and my heart sank into the pit of my stomach.

I walked up to the end of the table where Tory sat between Darius and Caleb, both of their arms pressing against hers though they had plenty of room. She pouted, driving her elbows into them to make them back off and I threw her a sympathetic smile. That shit was hashtag awkward.

I dropped down between Seth and Max opposite her as the Councillors filled the middle of the table and Orion and the rest of the family members filed the other end. I could tell whose Seth's siblings were because they were all over each other, barking with laughter and nuzzling against one another. He had six of them in total, four girls and two guys. Xavier was crowded in between two of the girls, looking a bit out of his depth as they leaned over him and played with his hair. The rest of the Heirs' siblings were all talking easily like they were old friends.

Max turned to me with a lazy smile. "How are you enjoying your palace, little Vega? Are you having wet dreams about all the power that lived here once?"

"I don't get wet dreams about power, is that something you struggle with?" I asked sweetly.

Max chuckled, nodding his head. "Can't say it hasn't happened."

What's happened to the jerky mcjerk crew today? They're being nice. And it's creeping me out.

"Dinner is served!" Hamish called and I looked up, finding a host of waiters spilling into the room holding silver platters filled with a feast for kings – and queens.

I was still kind of shell-shocked about the turn this day had taken. This had definitely not been how I'd planned on spending Christmas. Though I couldn't help but admit, I was kinda curious as to how this was going to play out.

TORY

CHAPTER FORTY

"It's so nice to reclaim the old palace traditions," Melinda Altair's voice reached me and I glanced down the table to the Councillors. It hadn't escaped my attention that no one had taken a seat at the head of the table and I got the feeling that that was the place reserved for the King. Or maybe the Queens. Either way, no seat had been placed there and no one was mentioning it.

"Yes. It's a nice gesture to welcome the lost Princesses back and let them be a part of things," Lionel replied, lifting a fork full of some fancy food to his mouth.

"*Let* us?" I asked with a laugh, raising my voice to make sure there was no chance of them missing my words. "Just whose palace are you in again?"

Lionel paused with his fork half way to his lips, his gaze boring in to me as I casually sipped on my champagne.

Darius cleared his throat in warning beside me, but I ignored him. I wasn't going to let these assholes steamroll my Christmas and then make out like they were doing me some kind of favour by being here. If anything, they should appreciate the fact that we hadn't kicked them out.

Lionel smiled but it didn't touch his eyes. "Well that's an interesting question," he replied. "Because there are some who say that the Palace of Souls should belong to the most powerful Fae in the Kingdom, not just be blindly handed down within a bloodline."

I nodded like he'd made a fair point and he pushed his appetiser into his mouth.

"Of course, we *are* the most powerful Fae in the Kingdom," I mused. "So I guess it would be ours whichever way you looked at it."

Darcy caught my eye across the table and she seemed to be stuck between laughter and horror at me baiting our enemy like that. I shrugged one shoulder minutely and took another long sip of my drink.

"So if you weren't sitting here having dinner with all of us, what exactly would you be doing with your day, sweetheart?" Caleb asked me, drawing my attention away from the Councillors.

Everyone seemed happy enough to let the subject drop there before it could fall into any kind of disagreement and I turned away from Lionel's acidic gaze.

I shifted my eyes to Caleb and speared some food onto my fork. The wrong fork. Because I didn't give two shits about the ridiculous royal eating traditions and if the uninvited guests at this table thought I was a savage for using the wrong cutlery I couldn't care less. "I dunno. We've already had our snowball fight and that's pretty much our only tradition. So maybe just watching TV or looking around the palace."

"What kind of tradition is a snowball fight?" Darius asked on my right, drawing my attention around to him.

"The only kind you can have when you've got no money and never spend a Christmas in the same place twice," I replied in a sweet as pie voice while scowling at him.

He nodded his head but he was frowning at the same time. "So you never had more than one Christmas in the same place?"

"We had two with the Felbrooks," Darcy put in from across the table.

"Yeah," I agreed. "But they made us eat in the kitchen while they had their family over in the dining room, so…"

"You were sent away from them?" Darius asked in a low growl.

"Actually, you could call *that* our Christmas tradition," I said lightly. "It's tradition for us to feel unwanted on Christmas Day. And thanks to you guys, we get to feel like that this year too. Even though it's the first time we've actually got our own house to celebrate in, you all still made the effort to make sure we didn't miss out on the feeling of being an unwelcome addition to the festivities. So thanks for that."

"Tor…" Darcy said in a low voice and I glanced at her for a moment, offering her an apologetic smile before dropping my gaze to my food.

For some unknown reason, tears were burning the backs of my eyes and I wasn't going to let these assholes see that so I just concentrated on my meal as an awkward silence descended on our part of the table.

Seth cleared his throat uncomfortably and waved over a waiter with more champagne as a soft whimper left his throat.

Great, now I'm the one ruining Christmas.

"You're not unwelcome," Darius murmured so low that I wasn't sure anyone else could hear him. "And I'm sorry we're ruining your day."

I looked at him in surprise, my lips parting as I tried to figure out what I was supposed to say to that. I hadn't even known that word was in his vocabulary, let alone that he was capable of aiming it at me.

"You're not ruining it," I replied slowly, trying to shrug off the feeling that something had been stolen from us by this ambush of a meal. "It's not like we had some other amazing plans…"

He caught my eye and for a moment I felt like he really understood something about me. His gaze trailed to his father then back to me before he spoke again.

"It's funny, you spent every Christmas wishing you could spend it with a family who wanted you there and I spent every Christmas looking forward to these formal meals so that I didn't have to spend too much of it in the company of mine."

His hand shifted on the table and his little finger grazed mine. My stomach fluttered at the unexpected contact and I bit my lip as I found myself hooked in his gaze with his dark eyes boring into my soul as if he could really see me.

"Well maybe Christmas just sucks whatever way you do it," I whispered conspiratorially. "And it's only ever perfect in the movies."

"This year isn't shaping up too badly so far," he countered, his gaze sliding over my face and pausing on my lips which I sharply remembered pressing to his flesh not so long ago.

My skin prickled and I looked around as I felt the touch of Siren magic brushing against my skin. The heat faded from my veins and I found Max watching the two of us with a slight frown. My Phoenix Fire quickly burned through his magic and I rolled my eyes at him for trying to steal my lust as I returned my attention to my food.

"Why don't you girls pick something for us to do later if you want to make a new tradition?" Max suggested casually. "You could bring Grus too…" I followed his gaze down the table to where Geraldine was talking excitedly with some of Seth's sisters. I caught the words *getting down with the candy cane of shame* and snorted a laugh to myself.

"I can ask her," I said slowly. "But I'm pretty sure she's hooking up with someone later…"

"Who?" Max demanded and Darcy caught my eye in confusion. I twitched my lips in amusement and she caught on, quickly adding to my lie with one of her own.

"Oh yeah, she's been seeing one of the servants," Darcy said enthusiastically. "She said she's never had someone rock her coconuts like he can…"

Max's mouth fell open as he stared around at the wait staff who were coming and going in outrage. "Bullshit," he snarled. "Some fucking waiter is not better in the sack than *me.*"

I snorted a laugh and Darcy smirked into her carrots.

"Is it that guy over there?" Max demanded and I followed his arm to a huge waiter who was carrying four trays at once and making it look easy.

"No, but he's hot," I agreed, checking him out. "Maybe I should ask him to come and fluff my pillows later…"

"I can do that for you if you need help with it," Caleb piped up and Darius set his glass down hard enough to rattle the cutlery.

I glanced at him in surprise but he wasn't looking at me, he was scowling at the hot waiter who seemed to notice and promptly left the room.

"Is it that guy?" Max demanded, pointing out another stacked waiter.

Is that some kind of requirement for working here or something? 'Wait staff needed, previous experience preferred, thick thighs appreciated and stacked abs a plus…'

"No. It's him," Darcy said and I smirked as she pointed out one of the smallest guys in the room who just so happened to be about twenty years older than us too.

"Fuck off," Max said in denial. "There's no way she'd trade me in for him!"

"She said he's got hidden talents," I added with a wink.

"Yeah," Darcy agreed. "And a huge-"

Max pushed himself to his feet with his gaze locked on the poor waiter and me and Darcy both burst into laughter.

"You're joking?" Seth asked in amusement as Max lowered himself back into his chair with a frown and Caleb barked a laugh.

"That wasn't funny," he groaned.

"Yeah it was," Caleb disagreed.

"Cut him a break," Darius said, leaning back in his chair as his eyes glimmered with mirth. "It's hard when the girl you like won't give you the time of day. One minute he thought they were all on then the next she's back to ignoring him and hating him and…" He trailed off as we all looked at him and his gaze slid over me. "And he doesn't need us laughing at him too," he finished slowly.

"Thanks, brother," Max grumbled as he set to work attacking his potatoes.

"Why don't you just try being honest with Geraldine if you like her?" I suggested. "Just tell her what it is you like about her and maybe she'd be more open to-"

"I'm not making a fool of myself for anyone," he muttered in response and I dropped it.

"So what have you two been doing here for the last few days?" Caleb asked us, changing the subject.

"Mostly just exploring our palace a bit," Darcy said and I quirked a smile at her.

"Yeah, sorry dude, but I'm decidedly less impressed by your fancy house than I used to be," I said with a smirk at Darius and he actually grinned.

"Right. Now you've got a palace so you think you're so much better than us mere Heirs," he joked.

"Well…we *are* Princesses so…"

Darius laughed and for a moment I just stared at him with my lips parted. Where were the douchebags who tormented us all around campus? Was this some kind of Christmas miracle or something? Had a little elf come and crawled up all of their asses to fill them with Christmas spirit this morning? Whatever the reason, I wasn't going to question it.

"Of course, if you officially abdicate the throne, you won't be able to toss the term Princess about quite so casually," Lionel said loudly, drawing my attention back to him further down the table.

"If we do what?" Darcy asked with a frown.

"We don't need to discuss this at Christmas," Antonia put in as she drained her wine. A waiter instantly refilled it and the rosy tint to her cheeks made me wonder how many she'd put away already.

"Well it's not like we have much chance to speak with the girls while they're obtaining their education," Lionel contradicted. "So it seems like as good a time as any to float the idea."

"The idea of us renouncing our claim on the throne?" I clarified, my spine straightening at the suggestion of us turning our backs on our birth right. I'd never said I wanted to rule over Solaria. But this place, the things we'd already discovered just from being here for a few days, it was in our blood. I didn't want to turn my back on the first link I'd ever really had to our parents without even having the chance to explore it fully.

"Well, you have made it clear on several occasions that you have no desire to rule. If you renounced your claim publicly, gave up your holding on the Palace of Souls and the throne, then-"

"No," I said simply.

Darcy shot me a concerned look across the table for biting at him but fuck it. That asshole was already out for our blood and I wasn't going to pander to the idea of him taking our palace from us too.

"Come now," Lionel said on a laugh that seemed like he'd had to force it into existence from the pit of his ass and was anything but friendly. "I know it must be nice to indulge in the fantasy of this place, but we aren't talking about taking your inheritance from you. The gold in your parents' accounts and the other properties they owned would still pass to you once you graduate. And didn't you say before, that you held no desire to claim the throne?"

I pursed my lips, my gaze falling on Darcy because we *had* said that on multiple occasions. But that was before. Before the Heirs had tortured and tormented us for months. Before we'd really understood what it was to be Fae. Before Lionel Acrux had stolen us away from the Academy and risked our lives to take possession of the shadows. And after suffering through all of that and coming out fighting on the other side, I was a lot less inclined to release our claim on the throne our parents had left for us. Especially to someone like him.

"Let the pudding party commence!" Hamish Grus called loudly and I was saved from answering by a tide of waiters who descended on the tables and started clearing our plates to make room for dessert.

I leaned back in my chair as the serving staff worked to gather everything from dinner and a warm hand landed on my thigh beneath the table.

Darius's grip tightened as he leaned close to speak to me and I felt a silencing bubble slide over the two of us.

"I thought you knew better than to bait my father," he growled in my ear, his stubble grazing my jaw as he leaned in close enough to make a prickle of heat run down my spine. "Do you have a death wish or something, Roxy?"

"Why?" I breathed, turning just enough to catch his gaze in mine. The space between our mouths barely existed at all as I kept my eyes locked on his. "Are you going to punish me for being bad?"

Darius's pupils dilated at that suggestion and I turned away from him dismissively as he dropped the silencing bubble before anyone could notice it. He didn't take his hand off of my leg though.

My gaze trailed over the amazing desserts that were being loaded onto the table. There were mounds of profiteroles, cheesecakes which glittered with magic, every kind of pie and tart and cake imaginable plus ice cream, sorbets and syrups in every flavour. My mouth watered at the mere sight of them and I wasn't entirely sure where to begin.

Darius still hadn't withdrawn his hand from my thigh and I looked at him from beneath my lashes, wondering what he was thinking.

He didn't return my gaze, but his hand shifted on my leg as he found the slit in my dress and pushed his fingers beneath the material.

My breath caught in the back of my throat at the feeling of his warm skin against mine, a thousand sin filled memories of the two of us in the Shimmering Springs crashing over me and rendering me speechless.

"So what traditions do *you* usually follow when you're not coming to the palace for Christmas?" Darcy asked the Heirs as she started loading a selection of desserts onto her plate.

"Well we always have it together," Seth replied. "We usually rotate whose house we go to and this year it would have been at mine."

"But that was before we found our lost little Vegas," Max added, his voice coloured with amusement.

"We usually eat together with everyone like this and then after the press photographs-"

"That what?" I asked in disgust. Were we going to be expected to give up part of our day to the press??

Darius laughed darkly, leaning forward to pile dessert onto his plate with his right hand while shifting his left further beneath my skirt.

My heart leapt as I tried to remember what I'd been saying and Darius shifted his fingertips across my inner thigh.

"Yeah, sorry sweetheart but that's part and parcel of being one of us. Photo ops are kinda mandatory at all times," Caleb laughed before taking a mouthful of his chocolate cake and placing his hand on my left knee.

I froze. My plate was still empty and the guys either side of me were both touching me in a way I absolutely shouldn't have been allowing. Yet here I was, still sitting there, not pushing them off of me.

I bit my lip and reached forward to pile some profiteroles onto my plate and speared one on my fork as I tried to figure out what I was supposed to do. The obvious solution was to push them off of me. But as Darius shifted his hand a little higher, I found myself tipping my leg towards him, inviting him closer instead.

Caleb caught my eye and smirked at me as he slid his hand up my leg too.

For some reason, until that moment I hadn't really considered the fact that I'd been playing with fire by hooking up with two of the Heirs. I'd never really considered Darius to be an option because of the hatred that flared between us until we'd let that spill over into lust. And with Caleb it had always been clear there was no future in it, so I hadn't really seen the harm in what had happened between me and either of them. But as Caleb shifted his hand an inch higher again, I got the feeling I was about to find out what it was like to be slap bang in the middle of a love triangle. Minus the love part. I guessed that would be a lust triangle then. Which actually didn't sound all bad aside from the fact that two sides of the triangle were unaware of each other's participation in this particular interaction.

Although that was clearly going to change in about thirty seconds because Darius's hand had just paused in its ascent beneath my skirt as his fingers brushed against the line of my panties.

My breath caught as my heart beat harder and my core filled with a molten heat which definitely wasn't going to be sated by his hand just laying on my flesh.

My eyes slid to meet Darius's and there was a question in his gaze which had a blush rising to my cheeks. My gaze fell on his mouth and I couldn't help but think about the passion of his kisses on my lips.

Caleb shifted his hand higher and my heart leapt as his knuckles knocked against Darius's.

I dropped my fork with a clatter and practically leapt out of my seat as a low, possessive growl left the back of Darius's throat. Caleb's lips fell open in surprise like he didn't know what the hell to think and I absolutely wasn't going to have that conversation.

"Bathroom break," I announced loudly as people all along the table turned to look at me in surprise. I spun around and swept away as fast as I could without actually running.

I glanced back at the table and found Caleb and Darius scowling at each other like they both couldn't make sense of what had just happened and I wholeheartedly agreed with them. Because when I'd woken up this morning, I'd had zero Heirs on my radar and now two of them seemed inclined to seek out my attention again.

My heels clicked loudly as I strode straight down a long corridor outside the dining hall, vaguely hunting for a restroom but mostly just trying to get the hell away from that awkward as fuck interaction. And hot. It had been awkward and hot. I could admit that to myself as my pulse continued to pound and heat danced along my spine.

I opened a door at random but instead of finding a restroom, I found myself in a huge chamber with portraits lining the walls and a large stone chair at the centre of it. This chair wasn't like the throne in the throne room. It was made of glass and covered in glimmering silver gemstones which mapped out the constellations.

I walked towards it slowly, my curiosity piqued as I looked around at the portraits which hung from the walls. They depicted men and women of various ages, some with crowns on their heads though plenty without. As I drew closer to the chair, I spotted a portrait of our mother amongst them. She was looking up at a midnight sky, her gaze serene and a silver tiara perched in her hair.

"Do you have the gift of The Sight?" a dark voice sounded behind me and I spun around to stare at Lionel Acrux as he drew closer to me.

"Not really," I hedged, my heart leaping as I realised I was alone with him.

Shadows stirred beneath my skin but I forced them back, willing them away so that he wouldn't notice. I called on my Phoenix instead, relaxing a little as the warmth of my Order licked against my skin from the inside out.

"Pity. This is the Royal Seer's Chamber, though none currently hold that position. Your mother was the last great Seer of our generation. There are plenty of others with the gift of sight of course, but none who could See so clearly as her... however, even that wasn't enough to save her in the end." Lionel drew even closer to me and I stilled, refusing to show him my fear as he came to a halt at my side, looking up at the portrait and seeming lost in memory for a moment. "She was a truly beautiful woman," he said slowly, his gaze sliding from the picture to me. "That's one thing you and your sister *have* inherited."

He reached towards me and tucked a lock of my dark hair behind my ear, his cold fingers sliding along my jaw and down my throat.

I narrowed my gaze on him as he withdrew his hand and a shudder ran down my spine.

"Were you looking for something?" I asked coldly. I wasn't going to pretend to feel anything towards this man aside from contempt.

"I just wondered how you were settling into the palace?" Lionel asked casually.

"It feels like home," I said, surprising myself with the ring of truth those words held.

"Well don't go getting too comfortable."

"Same to you," I replied darkly while a small voice in the back of my head screamed at me to shut the hell up.

Lionel lunged at me so quickly that I couldn't even try and fight him off before his hand locked around my throat.

"Don't test me, *girl,* " he hissed as he drove me back until my ass hit the glass chair in the centre of the room and he was leaning over me.

I gasped, my fingers curling around his as I tried to dislodge his grip on me.

"If for one moment it seems to you as though I'm not in full control of your destiny, then check again. You and your sister only draw breath because I desire it to be so. You only study at your academy and screw your way through half the men you meet because *I* allow it. You only sit there and challenge me and speak out the way you do because I have chosen for it to be the case. And if at any moment you push me too far, then it would be oh so simple for another *tragedy* to occur in the Vega household." Lionel's grip on me tightened bruisingly and Phoenix fire flared hot beneath my skin, only staying contained in my flesh through pure force of will.

"What the hell is that supposed to mean?" I hissed through the tightness in my throat as he continued to squeeze.

"Your mother was the greatest Seer in generations," Lionel breathed. "And yet she couldn't escape her own death. Seers can't see Nymphs because they hide in the shadows. But then whoever could have predicted that they'd get into the palace?"

I stared at him as I tried to figure out if that was supposed to be some kind of threat.

"I tried to save them, you know. Your father was my friend…"

"I didn't know The Savage King had friends," I said, curious despite myself. If he'd been there the night my parents were killed, then maybe he would know who that boy was that Astrum had saved.

"Perhaps he didn't by the end."

I stared at Lionel, willing him to share more of what he knew with me, but it seemed he was done with this conversation. He shoved me away from him so that my back collided with the glass chair behind me and the air was driven from my lungs.

"*Forget this conversation,*" Lionel growled, his voice thick with Dark Coercion as shadows danced before his eyes and spilled between his fingers. "*And start showing me a bit more respect among company.*"

Phoenix fire ran hot beneath my skin as it burned through the pull of his commands and I scowled at him as he walked away from me with a swagger to his step like he thought he was the king of the fucking world.

Just as Lionel reached the door, he turned back to look at me with a cruel smile twisting his handsome face.

"*Oh, and feel free to break my son's heart the next time he comes looking to crawl between your thighs,*" he added, shadows coating his words again as he tried to compel me to fall to his will. "I was going to command him to stop chasing you, but I think this might just be better. When you cut him open and make his wretched heart bleed for you, his hatred will only grow stronger. And when it comes time for us to destroy you and your sister once and for all, he'll be only too willing to play his part."

The door clicked shut behind him and I remained in place with my heart hammering and my mind whirling. He hadn't been careful in choosing his words because he'd thought he could make me forget them, but I still wasn't sure if he'd actually told me anything or not.

Whatever way, it had only solidified one thing in my mind: Lionel Acrux was our enemy and he was working against us just as surely as we needed to work against him.

The afternoon had been filled with a photo shoot which dragged on for a few hours as photographers took shot after shot of us with and without the Heirs and Councillors. We sat around a fake dinner table and exchanged fake gifts. My cheeks hurt from fake smiling and I was just about done with this whole

Christmas sham by the end of it.

All I'd wanted was a day with my sister, not this freak show of falsehood. But apparently we didn't get a say in these things. At least not while the Councillors were able to press their decisions on us.

By the time the evening rolled around and we'd changed into new gowns for the Christmas ball, I was just about ready to quit and head for bed.

"It's Christmas, Tor, no need to look so sad," Darcy teased and I turned to smirk at her. Her new dress was silver and shone like starlight as she moved.

I'd opted for a black halter dress which fell to my feet and was tied down my back in an intricate series of laces. My blood red stilettos showed beneath it as I walked and raised me up a good few inches so the Heirs couldn't tower over me so much.

The music drew us closer to the ballroom and I forced a little smile onto my lips as we walked.

"I'm not sad," I said. "I'd just been looking forward to a few Heir free days and now we've been lumbered with the Councillors too. And I get the feeling that this is going to be our lives now. Always having to do things we don't want to. We've got responsibilities when all I want is freedom."

Darcy laughed like I was joking and maybe I was in part. We definitely had a lot more here than we used to have in the mortal realm and I wasn't ungrateful for that. It just seemed like a lot of what we had now came with strings attached.

We descended the grand staircase and entered the ballroom to a round of applause.

I rolled my eyes at the ridiculousness of it and cut through the dancing bodies in search of the bar.

Before I could make it, strong arms caught me and I was whirled in a tight circle as the room spun and I suddenly found myself in the middle of the dance floor in Caleb's arms.

"Happy Christmas, sweetheart," he said, dragging my body flush with his as we started dancing.

"Merry Christmas, asshole," I joked, letting him keep me as we moved in a slow circle to Have Yourself A Merry Little Christmas by Bing Crosby.

"So do you wanna explain what happened at dinner earlier?" he asked me. "Because Darius doesn't have much to say on the subject."

"What can I say?" I shrugged. "I'm a sex addict."

Caleb snorted a laugh. "I haven't seen much evidence of that myself, recently."

"Never say never," I teased. "But I don't belong to you Caleb so if I choose to get my kicks elsewhere then that's up to me."

"Mmmm."

That wasn't much of an answer, but he didn't seem pissed at least.

"Just how many guys am I currently competing with?" he asked casually.

"You tell me, Caleb. You're the one who set me up to look like I'm screwing every guy I meet. So maybe now I am."

"I don't believe you," he said, turning me in a circle beneath his arm.

I snorted a laugh and I made it back into his grip as he pulled me close again. "Good. But honestly, would it make any difference if I was?"

He hesitated for a moment then shook his head with a chuckle. "No. I think I'd want you even if I was one of ten."

I rolled my eyes at him and stepped back as the song ended. "Just not long term. Right?"

His jaw ticked. "No. Not long term," he admitted.

Just what every girl wants to hear on Christmas. You'll do for now, sweetheart, you're just not the girl I want to end up with. Be still my beating heart.

"You know what, Caleb, I'm kinda beat. I think I'm just gonna go to bed," I said, stepping back as another song started up.

"Do you mean alone?" he asked.

"For tonight, yeah."

"And what about tomorrow night?" he asked with a smirk.

"Why don't you text me in the New Year and I'll think about it," I teased.

"You can count on it," he assured me and I shook my head as I walked away from him.

I spotted Darcy dancing with Orion and gave her a quick wave to let her know I was leaving. Geraldine was dancing with Max and I decided to leave her to her own Heir drama as I turned and slipped out of a side door in hopes that no one would see me escape.

I started humming The Pogues Fairytale of New York beneath my breath as I tried to figure out my way back to the entrance hall using the unfamiliar corridors.

It was quiet beyond the ballroom and cool too, the hairs rising along my bare arms as I walked.

I frowned in confusion as I came to a heavy wooden door with a crown etched into the wood at the end of the corridor, wondering if I'd taken a wrong turn somewhere.

Curiosity won through and I stepped forward and opened the door.

My eyebrows rose as I realised I'd made my way into the huge throne room somehow. I found myself looking at the back of the enormous chair carved with fifty Hydra heads where it sat on a raised platform so that the King could be above the people at all times.

The room was dark but a single, pale blue light spilled down on the throne.

I almost turned back but curiosity tugged at me. I wondered what it would be like to sit upon the throne that the Heirs were so desperate to claim as their own. What was so important that they kept treating us the way they did just to keep it for themselves?

I took slow steps towards the throne, my heart beating faster as I approached it and adrenaline tingled through my limbs. This felt naughty, forbidden, like I was doing something that might get me into trouble and yet... I lived for this feeling. For the freedom of choosing to do things I shouldn't. Making bad choices and owning them. And I just couldn't resist the temptation the throne presented me with.

I rounded the huge chair and my breath caught in my throat at the sight of the man I found sitting there.

Darius leaned back in the throne, his legs wide and one arm slung carelessly over the armrest as the other cupped the back of his head. He'd run his fingers through his hair, breaking it free of the product he'd used to style it so that dark strands fell loose over his forehead. His suit jacket was abandoned on the floor before the throne and he'd untied his bow tie, leaving it hanging loose around his neck with several buttons of his white shirt open.

My lips parted as his gaze fell on me and for a moment I was lost for words. This was the man who'd tortured and tormented me, made my misery his goal and watched me fall into the shadows at his father's orders. I hated him. I wanted to hate him so badly it hurt. But in moments like this I felt like I was just lying to myself.

"What are you doing here?" I breathed, my quiet voice echoing in the stone room.

"I couldn't watch you dancing with Caleb," he said, holding my eye and just owning how he felt for once.

"Why?" I asked, still not moving despite the fact that a smarter girl would have run by now.

He shifted in his position on the throne and I looked up at him as he moved to lean his elbows on his knees as he gazed down at me.

"Because you're in my head all the time. You pulse through my blood with each beat of my heart. I live for every scrap of attention you offer me and suffer through every moment you spend ignoring me," he said darkly, holding my eye the entire time.

"I thought you hated me?" I asked.

"I do," he agreed. "Because you represent everything I want and everything I can't have."

"You want me?" I asked slowly, taking a step towards him despite the dark energy which coiled around him.

"You know I do," he replied simply as if anything about us was simple.

"No I don't. I know you like to hurt me and tear me down," I said. "I know you want to control me and take from me and make me bow at your feet."

"I do," he agreed, not even trying to deny any of it. "And I think a fucked up part of you likes it when I do those things."

"Fuck you," I hissed, but I still hadn't left.

"I think you like it when I hurt you because on some level you believe you deserve it."

"Why would I feel something that fucked up?" I snarled.

"Because we're the same. Every time my father hits me or hurts me or chains me, a little piece of me relishes the pain. Because I know I deserve it. For not getting Xavier away from him. For not stopping him from claiming the shadows. For letting him hurt you and your sister." Darius frowned like he didn't like thinking those things about himself, but I could feel the honesty in his words too. And for some strange reason, I did understand what he meant.

"I was the reason no one ever kept us," I said in a low voice, like admitting this out loud might make it even more true. "I was the loud one. The rude one. The one that no one liked, let alone loved. I actually overheard one of our foster carers asking social services to find me a new placement while they offered to adopt Darcy alone. I could have told our social worker that I'd agree to that. I could have let her be happy instead of dragging her down with me. But that's what I do. I'm the one who stopped her from having Christmas traditions or friends who lasted more than a semester. I'm the one no one has ever wanted long term..."

Darius was looking at me in a way that made my heart beat faster and I wasn't really sure what to make of it. I didn't know why I'd just told him that. I'd never even shared those feelings with Darcy much. She always just disagreed if I tried to point it out and I loved that she cared about me enough to ignore my flaws. But it didn't make it any less true.

"That's why you push me even when you don't have to," he said. "You want me to punish you and you want to hurt me in return," he pressed, not caring that my scowl was deepening and my hands were curling into fists at my sides. "And I think you get off on seeing me in pain."

"How have I ever hurt you?" I snapped.

"You hurt me every time you ignore me. You hurt me every time you spend time with Milton or that douchebag with the hat or Cal or any other fucker who catches your eye."

I pursed my lips at him. "Maybe you've been believing your own bullshit. I'm not the one who told the world I was a sex addict."

"You did actually," he pointed out, clearly meaning that interview I'd done for The Daily Solaria.

"Only because you gave me no choice."

He stared at me for a long moment. "I had that model fired."

"What?" I asked with a frown.

"The one in that photo shoot with you. The one it looked like you really did screw."

"Wow. You're insane," I said harshly. "That poor guy probably really needed that job."

"He didn't need to take his work so fucking seriously," Darius growled.

"What the hell is this, Darius?" I asked him angrily. "What is it you want from me? Because you're acting a hell of a lot like some scorned lover, but we never even made it off the starting line so I don't understand why-"

"Neither do I," he growled. "But when I see you, all I want is to lay claim to you. I want you to be mine and I know you never will be and it's making me even more fucked up than I was to begin with. That's why I hate you. Not because I'm supposed to or because my father wants me to, but because you represent every freedom I've never been given. It's like you were designed entirely to taunt me and toy with me and crack me open and I won't let it stand."

"So what do you want from me?" I demanded. "Do you want to sit up on that throne with me on my knees before you. Would that end this feud between us?"

"I don't know."

I stared at him for a long moment with heat building in my skin and an ache of longing warring through my body. I might still hate him, but I wanted him too. When my nights weren't possessed by the shadows they were haunted by dreams of him. Of the taste of his lips and the touch of his flesh. He watched me like he didn't know what to expect from me and I placed my foot on the first step of the raised platform which held the throne. There were three in all. To make sure that whoever sat up there would look down on anyone who stood before them. And if that was what he needed from me so badly then he could have it.

I would never bow to him, but he could have me on my knees.

As I made it to the second step, Darius sat up, looking at me like he was hoping I had some answer for him when in reality I was more fucked up then he even knew.

I could see that ache in him, that need, that hunger which drove him to do all the things he did to me. And I wanted to claim it and cover it up with something else. I'd take his pain and burn it down with lust and maybe both of us would feel better. Just for a little while.

I held Darius's gaze as I slowly lowered myself to my knees in front of him.

"I'll never bow to you," I breathed as the cold stone at the foot of the throne bit into my skin. "But if you like me on my knees then there are better things that I can do down here than kiss your feet."

Darius sat up straighter as I placed my hands on his knees and slowly pushed them up the insides of his thighs.

His gaze was fixed on my movements and my heart started pounding as I watched the reaction I was causing in his flesh.

This man who sat before me on a throne with a will of iron and the temper of his Dragon was fast falling prey to my movements. I may have been the one on my knees, but he was the one who was submitting. I was in control of this, of him, of the lust in his gaze and the need in his flesh. I could offer up pleasure or pain to him or a mixture of both in whatever quantities I desired. And knowing I had him at my mercy set every inch of my flesh alive with a need of its own.

I slid my hand up over his crotch, smiling darkly as I felt the rock hard ridge of his arousal waiting for me.

"Is this what you want from me?" I taunted him as I slid his fly down and pushed my fingers into his boxers.

"I want everything from you," he replied fiercely and in that moment I was willing to let him have it.

I released him from the confines of his pants and a breathy moan escaped me as I took in the full, hard length of him. I'd hardly even touched him yet and the desire in his gaze was enough to set my whole body alight.

I pushed up further onto my knees and slowly took the length of him into my mouth.

Darius groaned as I drove my lips down his shaft, my tongue circling as I slowly withdrew again.

"*Fuck*, Roxy," he hissed through his teeth as I took him in again, my own body humming with need as I felt him growing even harder, swelling with desire as I took control of him.

His hand fisted in my hair and I moaned as he pulled me down harder, driving himself into me possessively as I moaned in excitement at the knowledge of how much he was enjoying this.

I took him in and out of my mouth again and again, savouring the taste of his desire and the way his body was falling prey to mine. Every time a moan of excitement left me, his grip on me tightened like he wanted to own me with this action, but I was the one who was owning him. My fingers bit into his thighs as I upped my pace, working him towards a climax that I could feel building in the tightness of him in my mouth.

"Stand up," Darius commanded suddenly, pulling me back off of him by my hair and tipping my chin back so he could look at me.

He reached for me, catching my arm with his free hand and dragging me up into his lap so that I was straddling him with my dress hitched up over my thighs. His mouth found mine and he kissed me so hard I forgot whose air I was breathing, his tongue pushing into my mouth and his lips bruising as I wound my arms around his neck. I rocked my hips over him so that I could feel every hard inch of him straining between my thighs and pulled him closer like I was trying to devour him.

Darius yanked me back by my hair so that he could look me in the eye and he swiped a thumb across my mouth where my red lipstick had been smudged.

"I don't want you on your knees. I want you fighting me and hating me and fucking me like you mean it. You're Roxanya Vega and you weren't built to bow to anyone," he growled passionately.

"You want me to hate you?" I asked in surprise.

"I want you to feel for me. And I'll take hate if that's all you're offering."

He kissed me again and this time I didn't hesitate as I kissed him back, my hands finding his shirt buttons as I began to yank them open.

Darius caught the hem of my dress and started tugging it up. The back of it was laced with six different ties and it had taken Darcy about ten minutes get me into it. It snagged on my waist, cinching tight and wouldn't go any higher.

He grunted as he yanked harder and I broke our kiss with a curse as the material cut into me.

"Ow," I snapped.

"Why are you wearing something that's so hard to take off?" he demanded.

"Because I don't actually plan on hooking up with assholes all the time, it's just something that keeps happening to me," I growled.

Darius looked at me for a long moment and the corner of his mouth hooked up just as I felt the heat of his magic building in his skin.

"Wait," I warned. "This dress belonged to-"

Fire magic flared in his palms and I yelped as his flames burst to life across my back and he tore what was left of the dress off of me. Fire might not have been able to hurt me, but it did a number on my poor dress.

"What the fuck?" I snapped as he looked over my blood red underwear with a heated gaze.

"Did that piss you off?" he asked.

"Yes," I snarled.

"Then show me how much," Darius dared.

I shoved him back against the throne so that his shoulders hit the back of it and a dull thud echoed around the stone room. I'd already unbuttoned half of his shirt, but I wrapped the material in my fists and ripped the rest off of him with a snarl of anger that sent buttons flying.

Darius laughed and I bit his lip hard enough to draw blood.

I pushed his torn shirt off of him and broke our kiss to press my mouth to those tattoos that I'd dreamed about way too many times.

Darius moved his hand between us, pushing his fingers down into my panties and groaning as he found me just as ready for him as he clearly was for me.

I was already panting with need as he circled his fingers around my opening, teasing me, taunting me and refusing to give me what I wanted.

I gripped my legs around him more tightly, the heels of my stilettos digging into his thighs and drawing a grunt of pain from him.

His fingers circled within my panties again and I was pretty sure he wanted me to beg, but that wasn't going to happen.

I pushed away from him, leaning back as my hands moved behind my back and I unclasped my bra, drawing it off of me. Darius groaned as he pulled his hand back out of my panties and pushed me back so that he could gain access to my breasts.

He sucked at my nipple, dragging it between his teeth in a way that hurt so good I cried out. My voice echoed off of the stone walls of the throne room and I wondered what would happen if anyone found us here like this. A Vega and an Heir screwing on the throne we fought over so desperately.

I gripped his hair in my fist and kissed him again as he shoved his pants down, revealing every inch of his body beneath me.

He was like something drawn straight in the image of a god, every curve of his body drew me in, from the broad slope of his shoulders to the perfect cut of his abs and the flawless lines of his face. I was drunk on the sight of him and the feeling of his body against mine.

He was like a drug and I felt like an addict going back for another hit. I knew that he was poison, but I just couldn't stop myself from taking a bite.

Darius lifted me up and my nails bit into his biceps hard enough to draw blood as I held myself off of him and he dragged my panties down.

He kissed me again, his stubble raking across my jaw in the most delicious way.

I drew back, my gaze locking with his dark eyes as I lowered myself down onto him.

My breath caught in my chest as every inch of him slid inside me, filling me up in the most perfect way.

He watched me as I took him in, his eyes burning with a fierce hunger as his hands gripped my ass and he pressed me down so hard that I moaned in pleasure.

"You're so fucking beautiful, Roxy," he breathed and the sound of that name on his lips sent a flicker of anger through me.

That's not my fucking name.

I rocked my hips, riding him hard as my knees bit into the cold stone of the throne we sat on and my stilettos bit into his legs. He could have ripped the shoes off of me, but I got the feeling he was savouring the pain just as much as the pleasure. His hands were everywhere as he met each of my thrusts with a sharp jolt of his own hips, drawing cries from my lips which echoed so loudly I was surprised everyone in the palace hadn't heard us.

My hands fisted in his hair, my nails cutting his skin as I punished him and punished myself and tried to take out every inch of frustration in my flesh on this beast beneath me.

His kisses were bruising, his grip unwavering. He pulled my hair and bit my breasts and for each slice of pain he dealt me, I was rewarded with a jolt of pleasure.

Darius drew water magic into his hands, coating his fingertips in ice as he ran his hand down my stomach.

I gasped as the bite of the cold sizzled against my skin which was burning with the power of my Phoenix.

Goosebumps rose everywhere he touched me and I groaned as he moved his fingers straight down onto the perfect spot at the apex of my thighs.

I swore at the slice of cold against that sensitive area and Darius devoured my curses as he kissed me again.

His frozen fingers started moving at a heady rhythm in time with each powerful thrust inside me and every muscle in my body tightened with expectant energy.

The mixture of the cold of his fingers and the heat of him inside me was making my head spin and I ached for him to release me from the torment of my flesh. We were both panting with need and exertion and as he growled with desire, I felt the sound of it vibrating through every inch of my flesh.

With one final, punishing thrust of his hips and stroke of his thumb, he sent me toppling over the edge and I clung to him as his name fell from my lips and my whole body writhed with the most intense pleasure I'd ever felt.

He followed me into oblivion, his grip in my hair tightening to the point of ripping some out as he held me against him and spilled himself inside me with a growl of pleasure.

I sagged against him, our heavy breathing filling the space as I pressed my forehead to his and tried to recover from the earthquake that had just taken place in my body.

Just as I was starting to catch my breath, Darius dropped the shields on his magic and I automatically lowered mine in response.

The sensation of his power flooding through my flesh sent every sensitive nerve ending buzzing with pleasure again and I cursed as my body fell prey to his once more.

His arms wrapped around me and he drew me into a kiss unlike the others we'd shared. His tongue pushed into my mouth almost slowly and his hands slid up my spine as I gave in and it didn't just feel like lust anymore. It felt like the sky was falling in and the earth was splitting apart and the only two things left in the world were the two of us.

My fingers trailed up his chest until I was cupping his jaw between my hands and I felt like this kiss might just consume me entirely.

We finally broke apart, pulling our magic back into ourselves as we tried to catch our breath.

"You're going to be the ruin of me," Darius growled in my ear and I pushed myself back just enough to look down at him.

"Not if you destroy me first," I breathed in response as I painted the lines of his jaw with my fingertips.

He pushed my hair away from my face and inched me back so that he could look deep into my eyes. "Is that what you think I'm trying to do?"

I gazed back at him for a long moment, half wanting to hurt him, half wanting to kiss him again. There was still so much fucked up shit laying dormant between us. So many things we'd said and done that I found it hard to see him as anything, but a predator even now.

"I don't know,"I replied honestly.

"Maybe that's a good thing," he muttered.

He leaned forward like he might kiss me again but I drew back, gripping one of the Hydra heads as I climbed off of his lap and moved to retrieve my clothes.

I pulled my underwear back on then took his shirt from the floor and put it on over the top of it as he'd destroyed my dress.

He pulled his pants back on and I watched as he refastened his fly.

We looked at each other for a moment like there might be something else we should say, but what was there really?

We hated each other and that frustration had overflowed into sex. Again.

No big deal. And I planned on reminding my thundering heart of that as many times as it took until it returned to a normal pace.

I blew out a breath as his gaze hooked on my exposed thighs and I snatched my ruined dress from the floor.

There really wasn't anything else for us to say so I just turned and walked out of the room, heading up the staircase before hurrying back through the empty corridors of the palace towards the Queen's wing.

I was going to have to admit my latest indiscretion to Darcy as soon as I saw her and she was going to have a fucking field day over it.

DARCY

CHAPTER FORTY ONE

A knock came at my door and I woke with a groan, shifting under the weight of a heavy arm. I drew in a breath, realising Orion had stayed the night when we'd definitely planned for him to leave before dawn.

"Darcy!" Tory called through the door. "Open up."

I released a breath of relief, slipping out of bed while Orion sank deeper under the covers. I put on his shirt, hurrying to the door and dispersing the silencing bubble we'd cast last night. "Are you alone?"

"Yeah," she replied and I let her in, shutting the door quickly behind her.

She was dressed in a white winter coat with a faux fur hood, a sparkle in her gaze.

"What's going on?" I asked.

"The Heirs have challenged us to a snowball fight, *that's* what's going on," she said with a manic grin. "It's our game, Darcy. We'll smash them!"

I laughed excitedly. "Oh I'm in."

Orion shot to our side in a blur, his boxers in place. "I need to see this."

"Just one thing…" Tory bit down on her lip, glancing at Orion like she wanted him to go away. She raised a hand, casting a tight silencing bubble around me and herself.

"What's up?" I frowned as Orion folded his arms with a look of irritation.

"So I maybe, kinda hooked up with Darius again last night."

Do not judge my sister. Do not, do not, do not.

"Are you sure you know what you're doing?" I asked in concern. "He hurt you, Tor…" *Like drowned you in a swimming pool!*

"I'm totally in control of it. Cross my heart."

I nodded, relaxing a little. She could handle it.

Tory dropped the silencing bubble and glanced at Orion.

"Yeah, so I lip read that whole thing," he stated. "I'm glad you're making him happy." He smirked.

"Dude!" Tory balked. "Not cool."

"You just made it so easy when your tongue lolled out as you said *Dariuuus*," Orion taunted and she shoved him in the arm.

I snorted a laugh, unable to help myself and Tory's gaze whipped onto me accusingly.

"You should have seen Blue's face when I told her you hooked up with him the first time." Orion barked a laugh and Tory's eyes widened.

"What so you and Darius just gossiped about me like a pair of girls? Then you told my sister before I had a chance to?"

"*Technically* you could have told me but we were ya know…not talking." I shrugged innocently.

"That's true. And anyway, Tory, it wasn't like Darius told me about the size of your dick or anything," Orion mocked and her eyes flared with a challenge.

"You're right, that's just what me and Darcy do with the guys we screw. I know alllllll about you and your sordid little ways, sir."

"With your sister," he deadpanned and Tory's nose wrinkled.

"Ew, can we stop this conversation like right now?" I insisted, but they ignored me.

"Not the point," she hissed. "And you can tell Darius if he describes a single freckle on my body, I'll cut his balls off."

"What is it with you and cutting people's balls off?" Orion's brows pulled together. "Just go for the jugular, you savage."

Tory cracked a smile and the two of them beamed at each other like good friends. It felt freaking amazing to see them looking at each other like that.

"Right, get dressed – they're waiting for us," Tory said excitedly.

"Sure, right after I do a few of those sordid things to your sister," Orion called and she clamped her hands over her ears as she ran out the door, her laughter calling back to us. I wasn't sure I'd seen her this happy in a long time. But give my sister an opportunity to thrash the Heirs with snow and that equalled one smiley Tory. Or maybe it just had to do with the triple D she'd gotten last night (Darius's Dragon Dick).

"How sordid?" I turned to Orion with a playful smile.

"So fucking sordid." He hounded forward and I squealed as I ran for the en-suite, racing into the shower as he shot after me.

We were extra late to meet the Heirs by the time we got ready to leave, but I was hella satisfied.

I wore a khaki green jacket and warm gloves and Orion shot back to his room to fetch new clothes.

When I exited my room, he was waiting on the stairs dressed in a leather jacket, jeans and boots, looking divine and like he'd been standing there waiting for me for ages. *Damn Vampire.*

"Tory's gone ahead," he explained.

We headed through the palace and out of the main entranceway, finding Tory chatting to Xavier beside the Heirs, all of whom were standing around on the stone steps which led down from the palace.

"Where the hell have you guys been?" Darius balked.

Oh shit.

"Er-" I started and Seth raised his brows, enjoying the show as I fumbled for an excuse.

"Well I bumped into Darcy and she insisted she knew the way out, but ten wrong turns later and here we are," Orion said smoothly and I pursed my lips.

"Yeah plus we passed this bookshelf and Orion saw some Numerology book on it and basically had to stop and have an orgasm over it," I said with a shrug.

"Ha, that's so you," Darius laughed. "Bet it was a *real* smooth hardback."

"Yeah, and the spine was so curvy," Orion played along and I bit my lip on a grin. "I could have fingered those pages all day."

"Alright enough with whatever the fuck is happening right now, let's head to the woods." Max pointed toward the western corner of the grounds, taking off to lead the way.

The walk was almost a mile there and I started to wonder if this was just going to be another Heir prank to add to my collection. But I was pleasantly surprised when we arrived in a wide clearing at the heart of the pine wood and no one sprang an attack.

"Right, it's on. I'm not walking a step further," Tory said, moving to my side.

"Hang on, you two can't team up," Max said, folding his arms.

Tory placed her hands on her hips and I raised my brows. "Why not?" we said at the same time.

"Because you do that mind communication thing that gives you an edge," Max said firmly. "You can be the team captains."

"Well..." I hesitated and Tory pouted.

"Done. That's the deal or no game," Seth said, waving us apart.

"Fine," Tory gave in and I shrugged.

The other Heirs exchanged looks, but didn't argue, lining up with Orion and Xavier for us to choose from.

"Youngest picks first," Orion called and I smirked.

"Alright, I pick you Professor," I said, looking to Tory with a challenging grin and she shot me one right back. Orion flashed to my side with a burst of Vampire speed, scooping up a snowball and freezing it in his palm to a solid lump of ice.

"Woah, psycho pants. Are we aiming to kill?" I asked and he smiled lazily, the hardened ball rising above his palm on a perfect tornado of air.

"Everyone here can shield." He shrugged.

"Err, I'm not Awakened, I don't have my magic yet," Xavier called.

Orion barked a laugh. "Fair point." He let the ice return to snow. "You sure you still wanna play?"

"Oh I'm not just gonna play. I'm gonna destroy," Xavier said with a fire in his eyes.

"Come on, pick someone Tory," Max encouraged, bouncing on his heels excitedly.

"Caleb," she said lightly and Darius's usually carefree expression evaporated. His eyes narrowed on Caleb as he joined Tory's side and flung an arm over her shoulders. She promptly shrugged it off, but that did nothing to soothe the rage in Darius's eyes.

"Darius," I picked and Tory shot me a *oh you're gonna play dirty are you?* expression and I flung one back that said *I'm taking no prisoners, Tor.*

Like hell was I gonna turn down having a Dragon on my team. Even if he was a douchebag ninety nine point nine percent of the time.

"Didn't realise you were so competitive, Blue," Orion murmured as an icy wind gusted around us, his tone telling me exactly how much he liked finding that out about me.

I glanced at him with a smirk. "When it comes to snowball fights, I'm merciless."

"Can you bring that team spirit to the next Pitball session?" he taunted.

"If you help me win, I'll bring it to *every* Pitball session." I held out my hand and he took it, his lips hooking up as a clap of magic rang between us.

Darius had Caleb locked in his sights already and I smothered a laugh, looking to Tory to see who she was gonna pick next.

"Max," she said. "Let's see what the Water Heir can do with all this snow."

"Shit," Lance muttered. "Xavier's a liability, but fuck Seth right up the ass."

"I heard that," Seth said with a scowl.

"Dude," Darius shot at Orion with a look of confusion, but he avoided his eye.

I frowned, looking at my final options. I didn't really know Xavier, but the fact that he had no magic wasn't exactly a good sign. But did I want Seth Capella on my team? Hell no. And did I want the excuse to kick his ass in a snowball fight? Hell yes.

"Xavier," I blurted.

Seth pouted and headed over to Tory who immediately cast a silencing bubble around her team.

I did the same, turning to discuss tactics.

"We should all pick one target," Orion said and I held up a hand to stop him right there.

"*I'm* the Captain," I said, smiling sweetly. "And Xavier hasn't got magic so he can't take on someone on his own."

"If one of you shields me, I've got a solid aim." Xavier wiggled his eyebrows hopefully.

"I love you, bro, but I'm not gonna hold your hand through this, I'll be too busy pummelling Caleb's face with snow," Darius said with a dark grin.

"He's a Vampire, you won't land a shot on him," Orion said. "I'll take Caleb."

"Fine, Roxy's mine," Darius said with a smirk, seeming to warm to that idea suspiciously quickly. I pursed my lips, knowing exactly what he and my sister had gotten up to yesterday and hoping he wasn't going to hurt her. Because it was obvious she felt something for him even if she'd never admit it to herself.

"That leaves Max and Seth," I said thoughtfully.

"Max will ride Seth," Darius said. "I bet my claim on it."

Orion nodded firmly, getting that Captain look in his eyes again which said he wanted a win. "We can take them."

I glanced over my shoulder to see Seth was already stripping down and I turned to Xavier with an idea. "How about you change into your Order form and I...ride you? If you're okay with that?"

Xavier turned as pale as a sheet and I immediately knew I'd said the wrong thing.

"Oh I-I can't," he stammered, shaking his head and glancing over his shoulder like someone might appear right behind him.

"We're almost a mile from the palace," Orion said with a shrug. "No one would see. Just don't fly."

Darius scrubbed his knuckles against his jaw, his brows tightly knitted. "I mean, it would be good for you, Xavier. You must be desperate to shift."

Xavier chewed on his lip and it hurt me to see how uncomfortable he was at the idea of something so natural. His father had so much to answer for and it made me furious on his behalf.

"You don't have to if you don't want to, but this is *my* home, Xavier. And if you want to shift, then you shift."

Xavier looked to his brother with so much hope in his eyes it kind of broke my heart. Darius laid a hand on his shoulder, a smile pulling at his mouth as he nodded.

"Father's not going to leave the palace, he's too busy snooping around, trying to dig up dirt on the Vegas."

"He's what?" I breathed, but Darius waved me off with a laugh.

"What's he gonna find? That you're expanding your bird sanctuary to take in misguided toads?" Darius grinned at me in a way that was totally without bullshit. He was sharing an in joke with me. A freaking *in* joke.

I snorted a laugh then shrugged. "Alright, are you doing this Xavier?"

"I'm doing it," he said like he still wasn't sure, but he reached for his shirt.

"Wait, not yet," Orion said seriously. "We should run into the trees, split up and circle back on them. Keep Xavier for the element of surprise." He bobbed on his heels and before I could tell him off for stealing my captain hat again, my stomach screwed up into a ball at him looking so damn cute. Besides, it was an awesome idea.

I pulled my eyes away from him, adrenaline pumping through my veins. "Okay, Lance buy us time to get away with your water magic then run like there's a fire up your ass – which there probably will be," I said, realising I'd used his first name but it didn't look like the other two had noticed.

"As you wish, Captain." He pushed a hand into his hair as his eyes dragged over me.

He was definitely getting off on this.

"Ready?" Tory called and I turned to her, nodding as I dropped the silencing bubble.

Seth was in his huge white Wolf form and Max was climbing up onto his back. Caleb had his sights set on Darius, but he didn't have the Element of water. Which made Max and Tory the strongest on their team. Of course, I didn't see how we'd land a hit on anyone who possessed fire. And come to think of it, she did have three Heirs on her team and I only had one. But a powerful and trained teacher had to count for at least one Heir - maybe not the Pegasus who was afraid to shift though. *Better an underdog on the team than an assdog though.*

607

"GO!" Max roared and Seth charged forward.

I turned fast and fled for the trees at Xavier's side. The earth trembled violently and I glanced over my shoulder as Orion cast a huge wall of snow at the other team and Seth and Max collided with it. Orion shot off into the trees and I ran faster, thankful at last for the bi-weekly Pitball sessions and Physical Enhancement lessons which had kicked my butt into shape.

Darius darted off between two thick boughs and I spotted him climbing up one of them with impossible ease. *Monkey Dragon!*

I kept at Xavier's side while he tore clothes off and bundled them in his arms.

A baying howl cried out behind us and I increased our pace before dragging Xavier behind a huge pine.

"Are you ready?" I whispered hopefully.

He nodded, placing his clothes at the base of the tree and turning his back on me, revealing his bare ass. I glanced over my shoulder, casting a tight air shield around us as I listened for approaching footsteps.

"You okay?" I asked, my heart pounding as Xavier hesitated a little longer.

"Yeah, I just – I don't get to do this much so er – here goes." He leapt forward and a glittering lilac Pegasus burst free of his body.

I stared at his beauty in awe and he snorted happily, trotting toward me and rubbing his nose against my shoulder. Another howl sounded behind us and I moved to Xavier's side. He lowered a wing to let me climb up and joy filled me as I settled myself on his back.

"Let's win this thing," I said determinedly and Xavier neighed in excitement, rearing up and making me cling on for dear life before he shot forward into the trees.

He was crazy fast, the world a blur as he tore along the snowy ground, kicking up white dust behind us. I realised he was circling back the way we'd come and I gathered a storm of air around us, preparing to whip up the snow and hurl it at the first opponent we saw.

Laughter escaped me as Xavier weaved through the trees so smoothly it was like we were flying, his hooves barely touching the ground. A yelp somewhere to my left made me whip around and I spotted Darius on top of Tory, having jumped from his tree perch. My laughter rang higher as they wrestled on the ground, rubbing snow into each other's hair and laughing like they didn't hate each other's guts.

A blur of white shot in front of us and I screamed as Max raised his hands atop Seth and a tidal wave of snow rose behind him. I released the storm around me, throwing sheets of snow at him in an attempt to uproot him from Seth's back. Max took a full body hit but kept his balance, clearly not shielding as he used his magic to lift the huge line of snow behind him even higher.

His eyes locked on Xavier and he grinned widely. "Look at you, little dude! Fucking ace. Now let's see how fast you can run!"

I squealed in excitement and alarm as Xavier spun away from them and I heard the whole hillside of snow racing after us.

Seth barrelled ahead of the wave as Max raised both arms, gathering up every bit of snow he could to add to his wall.

Two blurs sped by and I guessed Orion and Caleb were having their own high-speed version of the game as snow sprayed out from them.

"Go!" I begged of Xavier and he didn't need encouraging twice, tearing through the woods like a hurricane.

I whooped to the sky as we outpaced Seth, but the rumbling of all that snow behind us didn't ease. I glanced back, finding Seth and Max had peeled off, getting out of the way of the snow as it crashed through the trees and came after us at double speed.

"Shit!" I yelled, glancing over my shoulder and raising a hand. Fire bloomed in my palm and I threw huge balls of it at the wave, not holding back as I melted away as much of it as I could. It was terrifying and exhilarating but it wasn't enough to save us.

"Hold steady," I begged of Xavier, letting go of his mane and carefully turning around to face the other way. *Shit shit shit, this is stupid and reckless and so much fun!*

I raised my hands higher, calling on the deeper power within me, my Phoenix flames curling around my hands. I let them fly and two burning channels of red and blue fire tore into the snow, melting huge holes right through it.

The wall suddenly collapsed and I cheered in triumph, turning myself around and patting Xavier on the shoulder. He whinnied happily, slowing to a trot as we circled back towards the clearing where we'd started the game.

Tory came tearing out of the trees as we arrived, pummelling snowballs at us with air magic and Xavier lifted a wing to block them. I laughed, jumping down and scooping up snow, leaving my shield down as I propelled them back at her. Xavier trot-danced around us then turned his ass towards Tory and started kicking up snow with his back hooves.

"Xavier!" she cried through her laughter, throwing out a wall of fire magic to melt the snow he was tossing at her.

An arm locked around my waist and I screamed as a Vampire ran with me across the clearing. I realised it was Caleb as he slammed us into a tree then shook it hard to dislodge all the snow from the branches. He was gone in a flash and I was too late to stop it as it crashed over me, leaving me in a freezing pile up to my waist.

His laughter rang around the woods as he zipped about the place then an *ah!* sounded a second before him and Orion appeared at the centre of the clearing. Orion had frozen him up to his neck in solid ice and amusement ripped through me as I waded out of the snow to join the others.

Caleb clenched his jaw as he released his fire magic and the ice began to steam. But it was clearly strong enough to keep him in check for a bit longer.

"Get him!" Tory cried despite the fact that he was on her team.

Me and Orion joined in as we started pummelling his head with snowballs.

Xavier neighed his amusement, shaking his mane so glitter fell around him on the ground.

Darius appeared behind Tory with a huge snow ball held above her head, but as he saw what my sister was doing, he lowered it and looked at Caleb frozen at the centre of the space.

"A snowman," he said brightly, walking forward, lifting his huge snowball up again.

"Darius," Caleb warned. "Don't you d-"

Darius planted the huge ball of snow over his head and I fell apart with laughter, dropping down to the ground as I clutched my side. Seth and Max arrived but neither of them continued the game, falling apart with the rest of us while Caleb thawed his way out. Fire flared at last and the snow and ice dissolved around him, leaving him soaked and scowling. It didn't last long as he split a grin then jumped on Darius, tussling his hair and the two of them fell into a playful wrestle in the snow.

Orion dropped down beside me and I fought the urge to rest my head against his shoulder, sharing a smile with him instead.

Xavier trotted off into the woods and I guessed he was going to get his clothes as the game came to an end.

"We win," I sang.

"Err no, this is just half time," Max said, dropping down to sit beside Seth as he pulled on his clothes. He reached over, drawing the water out of them without a word and Seth nuzzled him in thanks. Everyone set about drying each other and I smiled as the peace of the moment washed over me. *I wish it could always be like this.*

The Heirs' Atlases pinged all at once, but none of them took them out.

"Oh is it time for you all to take your crazy pills?" Tory taunted and Darius hid a smirk with his thumb.

"No, sweetheart." Caleb stood up, stretching his arms above his head. "That means the press are here."

Their Atlases pinged again and Seth got to his feet with a frown. "And *that* means my PA is doing her nut because I'm not standing right next to her ready to take interviews. Fucking Sharon."

Their Atlases continued to blow up with messages and I took mine out, finding several texts from Geraldine. I'd left it on silent mode and hadn't even thought to check it.

Geraldine:
Cradle-snatchers in the night! The press will be here in thirty minutes - have you returned from your morning dalliance?

Geraldine:
Bugger my backpack! Where are you and your sister? Fifteen minutes!!

Geraldine:
I've laid out dresses in your rooms but flip my bits you're cutting it close, your majesties!!

Geraldine:

That vagabond of a Vulpecula is here!! Come show him what real royalty look like and ram your prowess down his raisin hole!

Geraldine:

The throne room awaits you! Its empty womb is now fertile and ready for its new queens – come hither and implant it with your greatness!

"Implant it with your greatness?" Orion murmured as he leaned over my shoulder.

I snorted a laugh, knocking him away. "Excuse me snoopy snooperson, I have a throne room to impregnate." I stood up and everyone frowned at what I'd said. "Geraldine," I added in explanation. "Come on, Tor. We have to go."

Tory pursed her lips as she stood up. "Do we really have to entertain some boring reporters all day?"

"You do if you want the public backing you, little Vega," Max said, getting to his feet too. "So maybe you should stay here." He winked, starting to walk across the clearing and the rest of us followed.

We soon arrived back at the palace, slipping in through a servants' entrance in the west wing so no one would spot us. The halls were quiet as we headed along, none of us quite sure where to go as we roamed the winding corridors.

Everyone's Atlases started pinging again, but no one took them out. I didn't even check mine because I knew we were late as hell anyway.

"Stop," Caleb and Orion said at the same time.

"What? Why?" I asked, but the other Heirs fell eerily still, looking to Caleb as he listened to something.

I moved closer to Tory, sharing an anxious look with her as the air around us became laced with tension.

"Fuck," Orion breathed, his eyes whipping to me, filled with a swirling terror.

"What is it?" Tory demanded.

A blood-curdling scream sounded from far away, chilling me right through to my core.

"What's happening, what can you hear?" Max pressed a hand to Caleb's shoulder, his face twisting as he drank in his emotions.

Caleb and Orion shared a look and my heart slammed into top gear. Before either of them answered, they sped past us in a blur, throwing themselves against the door at the end of the hall. Vines burst free from Caleb's hands, spreading out across the wood while Orion froze the lock and the edges of the doorframe.

I raised my hands on instinct, panic crashing through me in waves. "What's happening?"

A huge weight slammed against the door they were holding shut and my shoulder bumped Tory's as we pressed against one another in alarm.

Darius, Seth and Max moved to stand on either side of us with their hands held high and Xavier stood a step behind.

"Get in your Order forms!" Orion shouted as another shuddering slam sounded against the door.

A rasping, sucking noise filled the air and fear dug into my heart with icy talons.

"*Nymphs*," Xavier gasped behind us.

I shed my coat and Tory did the same. I had a halter neck sports bra beneath my clothes out of habit these days and as I pulled my top off, my wings burst free of my back the same moment Tory's did. The Heirs moved forward as our fiery wings spread out behind us, heat sizzling through the air.

I locked hands with Tory, memories of the last battle we'd fought coursing through my mind. I was afraid, but I wasn't going to run. Our power could kill them. We were a weapon that needed to be used. But how had they gotten into the palace? And how many of them were here?

Seth leapt forward, shifting into his Wolf form and scales crawled across Max's skin, peeking out beneath his clothes. Darius stood firm, fire blazing in his hands.

"Xavier, shift!" Tory urged.

He hesitated a second longer before bursting into his Pegasus form and bowing his head, lining his horn up with the door as he nudged his way between Tory and Darius.

"Move back!" Caleb caught Orion's arm, dragging him away from the door, the two of them stumbling as the Nymph's powers started to take hold of their magic.

I glanced around for another door, but this was the only way forward. Geraldine stood somewhere beyond this corridor, plus the servants, the press. We couldn't just run, we had to fight, we had to *help*.

"We can take a couple of Nymphs," Darius snarled as Orion joined him with a firm nod.

Seth growled in agreement, bending down ready to pounce as the doors trembled with another heavy crash.

"You'd take them better in your Dragon form and it's safer anyway," Orion muttered.

"I'll shift when there's room to fly," Darius replied, his jaw set.

A huge crack splintered up the centre of the door and Tory's magic flowed into my veins while mine flowed back into hers.

Our Phoenixes were wide awake and ready to burn the world down.

"Get ready!" Orion barked and I raised my free hand higher as red and blue flames chased each other in my palm.

The doors split open and a beast straight from the Shadow Realm stepped through, its towering height throwing a sheet of darkness over us. Its body was gnarled like bark and its red eyes glowed with bloodlust as it reached out its probed fingers and tried to suck the magic right out of us.

The full force of its power slammed into me and I felt it locking down my magic. But it couldn't touch my Order powers. And I knew the strength of our fire could destroy it.

Tory squeezed my hand and we released our power at the same time, the chaotic whirl of flames spearing towards our enemy. The energy we created between us merged into an ice blue jet which ripped straight into the Nymph's body. It exploded into a shower of ash and I gasped at the devastation we'd caused united.

Seth charged forward as another Nymph stepped into the shattered doorway, launching himself into the air and tearing out the creature's throat. Tory and I ran forward, unleashing a monstrous whip of fire which severed the Nymph's head from its shoulders before it burst into a shower of soot.

A horrible screeching noise sounded somewhere up ahead and I winced against it as another voice joined it, then another and another. The Palace was infested. Our home was under attack.

"We have to destroy them," Tory growled powerfully and I nodded in agreement.

"Let's go," I breathed.

We ran forward and the rest of our group followed as we rounded into a long chamber.

"I know where this leads, come on!" Darius called, charging ahead of us.

Orion hurried to my side and the gentle brush of his shoulder was enough to calm my racing heart a fraction. Xavier cantered on behind his brother and Max took a seat on Seth's back once more.

When Darius opened the huge door at the end of the chamber, Caleb shot to his side, the two of them moving through it together. The clash of a battle sounded beyond the door, the shriek of Nymphs and the wail of Fae ringing in my ears.

We sped after them and my heart hammered as we spilled into the enormous throne room.

The Councillors were locked in battle with fifteen Nymphs, their rasping, sucking power raking against my ears. Antonia had shifted into her chestnut Werewolf form and Max's father, Tiberius, had his shining jade scales on show. I couldn't spot Lionel or Melinda in the fray. Bodies were strewn across the flagstones in piles of ash, but I couldn't tell who they were.

My heart jack-hammered as the Heirs split away from us, racing fearlessly into battle.

Xavier charged straight at a Nymph, skewering it on his horn before Antonia ripped its throat out and it scattered into ash.

"Darius!" Orion called and they shared a nod as Darius tore through his clothes, exploding into his incredible golden Dragon form. Four scaly feet slammed to the ground but not for long as he stretched his wings and took off into the air, circling around to the vaulted ceiling and releasing a ferocious blast of Dragon Fire down on the head of a Nymph.

"Fly," Orion ordered us. "Go." He squeezed my arm then took off in a flash before I could stop him. He brought a Nymph to its knees with his

Vampire strength and Darius circled over to finish it, their moves so smooth it looked like they'd done it a thousand times.

"Come on." Tory released my hand and I flexed my wings, taking off and flying up above the surging battle below.

I spotted a group of Fae by the back wall as two Nymphs closed in on them, stealing their magic and dragging it into themselves.

I pointed them out to Tory and we swooped down on them, our hands brushing. As our power collided, we released it down on the Nymphs, turning them to dust before they could take another step toward their prey.

Relief filled me as we circled above and the group stared up at us, pointing and gasping as they recognised us.

A horrible scream ripped through the air and panic seized my heart as I recognised Geraldine's voice. I turned, hunting for her in desperation and spotting her on her back beneath a Nymph. Her father lay beside her unmoving and pure terror filled me as Tory and I raced to help.

A battle cry filled my ears and Max dove on the Nymph's back, locking an arm around its throat and yanking backwards with all his might.

Geraldine scrambled away, tugging her father's arm and my heart lifted as he stirred, crawling after her.

A bellowing roar of pain echoed around the room and Tory glanced over her shoulder in a panic.

"Go help Darius," I urged and she nodded, darting off in the direction the roar had come from.

I swooped down on the Nymph Max was holding, my jaw clenched with rage. This beast had tried to hurt my friend.

"Max let go!" I demanded and he dropped from the Nymph's back, slamming to the ground the second I let my powers fly. Two twisting ribbons of hellfire tore the beast apart and I came to land, holding out a hand to Max and helping him up. He caught my eye and a strange sense of camaraderie passed between us for an endless moment.

A groan of pain sounded and I turned to find Geraldine clutching a bloody wound on her arm. Max ran to heal her and relief skittered through me. I gazed around the devastation and I could see the strength in everyone as we fought united. Together, we were unstoppable. Together, we could win.

A Nymph's arm rammed into my ribs and I was thrown across the room, gasping for air as stars burst in front of my eyes. I hit the ground in a corner of the room and pain spiked through my spine as I tried to move, but couldn't. My ears buzzed and my vision blurred as I battled to regain my senses.

The Nymph who'd attacked me moved closer, its head cocked and a vile clicking noise sounding from its tongue. My heart trembled as its shadow fell over me.

My arms wouldn't move, my fingers twitching but something was horribly wrong. Fire curled around my hands, but I couldn't direct it as the Nymph leered over me, a hungry look in its gaze like I was a feast to be devoured.

A lump pushed at the base of my throat as fire crawled out from my skin, desperate to reach the monster before me, but I couldn't wrangle it to my will. I couldn't move, my body wasn't responding. Terror reached into my core and took me hostage.

I couldn't fight. I couldn't even scream.

A shadow appeared in my periphery, colliding with the Nymph as it reached out its probed hand. Orion punched a hole through its chest, and the beast screeched so loud, the windows shuddered.

He brought it to its knees by brute force, taking hold of its head and tearing with all of his might. A crunch sounded and the Nymph exploded into embers, dancing around Orion in the air as he turned to me with a desperate fear in his eyes.

He dropped to his knees, pushing his hand beneath me and I gasped as pain splintered through me once more.

"It's okay, I've got you," Orion said gently and I nodded, trusting him to fix this.

I shuddered as warmth spread out beneath his palm on my back and sighed as the pain ebbed away, my spine healing under the intensity of his power. He sagged forward as exhaustion took him and I reared up, clutching him to me.

A protective growl escaped me as I encouraged Orion to his feet and pushed my hair from my neck. "Drink," I demanded, yanking him against me. He dug his fangs into my throat and started swallowing my blood as fast as he could.

I stared around at the devastation over his shoulder and fear took root in me as I realised we no longer had the upper hand.

Antonia was pinned down by the foot of a Nymph while Tiberius desperately tried to get her free. Geraldine fought fearlessly between her father and Max, but they were being forced into a corner and I could see their strength waning by the second.

The death rattle of the Nymphs echoed through the air and pounded through my skull. Someone in their Nemean Lion form had been impaled on the end of a Nymph's probes and blood was pouring across the floor like a river. The more I looked, the more death I could see, the more lifeless bodies and hopeless faces.

"Blue," Orion whispered with a note of fear as two Nymphs turned our way.

I gritted my jaw, seeking out my sister across the room. Her eyes locked with mine in understanding and at the exact same moment, our Phoenix forms burst fully from our flesh. Fire scored away my clothes, wrapping around me like satin, draping over my limbs and caressing my body.

I stepped in front of Orion and stretched my wings out to shield him from the two Nymphs who wanted us, the flare of my fire reflecting in their lifeless eyes.

With a yell of rage, I raised my hands, scoring the air apart as my Phoenix fire blazed, forming wings of its own and destroying two Nymphs without so much as a thought. The fierceness of my power was overwhelming as it cut through the hearts of monsters, speeding through the room and taking out the creature who had Antonia in its clutches.

Tory destroyed two of the Nymphs advancing on Geraldine and Max and Darius swooped down after her, lifting another clean from the ground and tossing it through a huge stained glass window. The crash rang in my ears. Then the tinkling sound of a thousand shards filled the room as they cascaded over a Nymph and sent it straight into oblivion.

My eyes were drawn to the staircase as Lionel Acrux, Catalina and Melinda Altair came spilling out of the door. The three of them were covered in ash, their fine clothes ruined and their eyes wheeling between me and my sister.

Another Nymph fell prey to my fire and a feeling of invincibility coursed through my blood and made me heady. I wasn't just powerful, I was power embodied. My Order form was a dominant being that was matched only by the indestructible force which was my sister.

A ragged breath left me as Tory finished the final creature across the room, her hands still glittering with sparks as she hovered above the throne.

Darius came to land with a thud, shifting back into his Fae form.

Silence reigned for a long moment then a cheer went up from someone which was quickly joined by others. Members of the press flooded out from their hiding places and servants huddled in corners hurried to join them, clapping and praising us. It took me a minute to realise some of them were chanting "Vega Queens, Vega Queens, Vega Queens!"

Geraldine took up the chant with her father, pushing Max aside as he tried to check her for injuries.

I spotted Gus Vulpecula creeping out from beyond the staircase, a sheepish look on his face. His rust-red hair was dishevelled and coated in dust, his wide eyes taking in the ash of the fallen Nymphs in shock.

Xavier hurried to Darius's side, whinnying frantically. Lionel's gaze fell on him as he descended the stairs, abject rage written into his features.

"Xavier is hiding," Darius said loudly before Lionel could say anything, pretending the Pegasus beside him wasn't his brother. "He's safe, Father."

Lionel inclined his head ever-so-slightly, but the look he gave Darius said he was still in trouble.

Tory moved to land beside me and I pulled her into my arms, so glad we'd made it through this unscathed. Our fire still wrapped around our bodies, saving our modesty and as we hugged, it flared brighter.

"How did they get in?" Hamish asked, wrapping an arm around Geraldine's shoulders.

"The wards have fallen around the palace. They must have wielded some truly powerful magic to manage it," Lionel answered, taking control of the room as all eyes fell on him. "But as we know, they have managed it before…"

"Are there any more of those frightly freaks in the wings?" Hamish asked.

"They're all dead," Lionel confirmed.

"Thanks to the Vegas," a servant girl said, wiping tears from under her eyes. "We can't thank you enough."

Lionel's face turned to stone. His eyes scraped over us and my heart pounded out of tune. "Phoenixes," he snarled, the word slicing the air to ribbons. "You aren't Fire Harpies at all."

The Heirs looked between us in a mixture of horror and surprise.

Oh shit.

Orion caught my hand, lunging for Tory's in the same instant. He hissed as our fire burned him and I immediately took control of it so he wouldn't be hurt by it. He still held on tight to Tory and I could see her wrangling her own flames around him so they caressed him instead.

"What are you doing?" I hissed.

"I'm taking the Vegas somewhere safe," Orion announced, his voice filling the room.

"You are duty bound to my son," Lionel said in a deadly voice.

Darius folded his arms, giving Orion a small nod. In an instant, stardust fell over us and we were yanked away on a whirlwind of lights. I gasped, hating to leave when so many lay dead on the ground. So many lives lost, Fae who'd served our family, who wanted me and my sister to sit on the throne.

My heart ached as we landed in Orion's office back at the academy, my mind spinning as I tried to process what had just happened.

"I had to take you, the palace has been compromised," Orion said in a dark tone. "The only place in the world you're safe now is within these walls. And not just because of the Nymphs. Lionel knows what you are. It's only a matter of time before he tries to kill you."

"Shit," Tory breathed.

"We need to fight back," I gasped.

"Not yet," Orion said in warning. "You're not anywhere near ready."

"We just turned those Nymphs to ash, maybe we are ready," I argued, fire still blazing around me and coursing through my veins. I didn't know if it was the adrenaline from the fight, but I felt ready to take on the world right then.

"Yes! Let's cook us a Dragon," Tory said determinedly.

"You don't know what he's capable of when he releases his full power," Orion growled. "I've seen it. Your fire might turn Nymphs to dust, but Lionel is a fully trained Fae. And not just any Fae. He's one of the most powerful Fae in the world."

My blood chilled and I realised he was right. We might have had this powerful fire, but what about our magic? We couldn't even do any kind of advanced spells yet. Lionel could probably kill us in a thousand ways we didn't even know existed yet.

"You're just stopping us so Darius can have the chance to take him on," Tory accused. "You know if we make a stand, we'll win."

"Don't presume to know the way I think," Orion growled forcefully and Tory frowned but nodded in acceptance.

I took her hand, drawing her closer with a sigh. "We have to be sensible or we'll end up dead."

"But you will face him with me?" she asked hopefully.

"Of *course*. When we're trained. When we're ready."

"It's time you started thinking about allies," Orion said in a low tone. "You need to build relationships that will help you politically."

"You mean the Heirs," Tory said scathingly.

"Do you?" I pressed and Orion nodded.

"Whose side are you on?" Tory narrowed her eyes.

"I'm on the side that stands against Lionel Acrux," he said, his jaw tightening and my heart thumped unevenly at the strength in his gaze. "It's the only side that matters."

TORY

CHAPTER FORTY TWO

My room at the academy seemed to echo with an empty kind of hollowness as I lay in my bed. The whole place was deserted as almost everyone spent the holidays back at home and the quiet here was more than strange.

I didn't mind the solitude though after the horror of the Nymph battle. And at least here the reporters couldn't hound us. I'd already had to ask for a new Atlas ID because mine had been leaked and I'd been inundated with emails, calls and texts from every fucker and their old aunt Deirdre wanting to know more about our roles in the fight. We'd agreed to do another interview with Tyler's mom in the new year just to give them something, but other than that we'd decided not to comment. The whole of Solaria seemed to be praising us as heroes and hailing the return of us as their Queens and it wasn't like we could just offhandedly deny that we were back to claim our throne.

On the other hand, we could hardly stake a claim either. Lionel had been trying to get in touch too and Orion said that the only reason he hadn't already shown up here to demand answers from us was because he was needed to head up the war effort with other Councillors. It hadn't even been twenty four hours since the fight at the palace, but there had already been six more reported battles against our enemies across Solaria since then.

A part of me was just glad that we didn't have to take part in those fights, but another part ached to get out there and help. We had power which was so potent against the Nymphs and it felt wrong for us to be hiding away while others risked their lives trying to fight them without our fire.

But Orion was right. We weren't trained. We hadn't even begun Elemental Combat lessons yet. And Lionel just might be out for our blood. So it was best we stayed here.

I shifted uncomfortably as I tried to find my way to sleep, but it was proving impossible. My mind was just too full of everything from the battle to all the things we'd discovered in the palace about our parents and our heritage.

For a little while I'd begun to let myself think of the palace as my home, but I was beginning to wonder if I'd been deluded to feel such a connection to a building. I didn't know why I'd felt such a bond to it, but it had almost seemed like the walls themselves had hummed with a familiar kind of energy.

I pulled my Atlas from my nightstand and sat up as I searched the internet for my answer. It didn't take long for me to find a few articles on the way the Palace of Souls had been built. Each generation of Vegas had added to the construction with their own magic, imbuing the place with the very essence of their power as well as adding to the structure itself. So I guessed I had my answer. The magic of my ancestors ran through that building just as their blood pumped through my veins.

"Come to me..."

I dropped my Atlas into my lap and looked up as if I might see the owner of that voice looking back at me. I hadn't heard her calling to me at all while I'd been in the palace and I wasn't sure if that had to do with the place or the fact that I'd been too happy there to even think about the shadows. There had been plenty of drama thanks to the Heirs and Councillors showing up, but I'd still been enjoying myself even then.

At least I had been until the attack.

"The hour is drawing closer. Build the bridge..."

The Shadows shifted beneath my skin and I closed my eyes as a little wave of pleasure trailed after them. I might not have been tempted by the shadows while we were in the palace, but here they seemed to call to me all the damn time.

My eyes fluttered shut and for a moment I saw her. The girl who called to me and begged me to save her from the dark. Orion's sister didn't look much like him apart from her eyes which burned with the same intensity as his.

"The time draws close," she hissed, reaching for me.

My limbs grew cold and the shadows wrapped themselves around me more tightly.

Pain cut across my forearm and I gasped as the shadows rushed tighter and ecstasy spilled along my flesh.

I was vaguely aware of the fact that I was bleeding, that I'd cut my arm open with a shard of ice to let the darkness in, but I couldn't draw my attention away from the pleasure long enough to care.

Pain carved into my arm again and I moaned as more pleasure raced after it. It almost seemed like the shadows had taken hold of my body and were guiding my actions to draw me closer to them. But it felt so good that all I wanted was more of it. More and more until it swallowed me up and I was consumed by it.

"Roxy!"

Fire blazed around me and suddenly I wasn't alone in the dark anymore. A man stood with me, shrouded in flames with giant golden wings sprouting from his back.

His hand took mine and I was dragged from the shadows so fast that my head spun.

I drew in a shuddering breath as I found myself lying in my bed with Darius straddling me, his grip tight around my wrists and his flesh hot with the power of his fire Element. Healing energy danced along my arm, closing my wounds.

"Are you back?" he asked desperately, his gaze locking with mine as his eyes burned with a wild kind of panic.

I drew in a deep breath, panting as I tried to get my bearings again. "What happened?" I asked, frowning as I tried to figure out how I'd gone from sitting in my bed to almost drowning in the dark in the space of a few minutes. Or had it been hours? I felt so lost, like I wasn't sure what way was up or what my own name was. There was just one, solid thing tethering me to this place and he was staring at me like he didn't know whether to kill me or kiss me.

I made the decision for him as I reared up and pressed my mouth to his, groaning with need as he met my kiss with a passion so dark I felt like I was drowning all over again.

Darius's grip on my wrists tightened painfully as he pinned me down, driving me into the bed and kissing me so hard it seemed like he was trying to steal something from me with the brutality of it.

He drew back suddenly with a growl of anger, locking me beneath him with both his grip and the fire in his eyes.

"I just dragged you back from the clutches of the shadows," he snarled. "Why the hell were you feeding them your blood?"

I frowned at him as I tried to figure out what had happened. "I don't know," I breathed eventually. "I don't remember..."

"Well try harder." The fire in his gaze was catching and I could feel my own temper rising up to meet his.

"I told you, one minute I was just sitting in my bed and the next I could hear Clara calling to me. I don't remember much after that except waking up with an asshole on top of me."

"From what I gather that last part is pretty much standard for you," he snapped.

"Fuck you."

"Again?" he taunted and my Phoenix bristled with anger as I squirmed beneath him, trying to free myself from his iron hold.

"Not likely," I snapped. "I'd sooner burn all the skin from my body than let you touch it again."

"That would be why you just kissed me like that then," he said with a smirk which said he thought he owned me.

"Get the fuck off of me," I demanded, yanking on my wrists as I tried to buck him off. He had about thirty seconds before I was gonna call on my Phoenix to light a fire right beneath his balls.

Darius laughed without any humour and shoved himself upright before stepping back to lean against my desk. "Get up and get dressed. You're coming to King's Hollow to explain to the other Heirs exactly why you hid your true Order form from them. I suggest you play the dumb little mortal card and claim you didn't know. Because if you can't convince them, you'll be answering to the Councillors."

"Maybe I don't plan on answering to anyone," I replied, pushing myself up so that I could stand and face him. He was still so much taller than me that I had to tilt my head back to meet his eye but I didn't care. I wasn't going to let him stand over me like my superior.

"Well your plans don't mean shit to the Celestial Council. And they don't mean much to me either. I'll drag you there if that's what it takes. So are you gonna get dressed or are you wearing that?" Darius's gaze slid over my baggy sweats and crop top like they genuinely offended him and I was more than tempted to keep them on just for that reason.

I sighed loudly to let him know he was the most irritating person I'd ever met. "Fine. Are you gonna just stand there and watch me get changed?"

Darius hesitated like he might really have been thinking he'd do that then rolled his eyes as he headed for the door. He paused before leaving me to it and looked back with a frown.

"If you've lost control over the shadows then we need to do something about it. Do you swear you didn't intend to cut yourself?" he asked, the asshole portion of him hidden again for a moment.

I pursed my lips, half tempted to lie to him but the truth was more terrifying than the idea of trusting him with this small sliver or honesty.

"I didn't," I replied. "I really don't know what happened…"

Darius frowned. "I'll talk to Lance and we'll figure out what to do."

The door closed between us with a snap before I could reply and I decided to ignore the little part of me which was wondering why he even cared.

I shot a message to Darcy, warning her that the Heirs wanted to see us incase Seth was headed her way too. I was guessing Orion had stayed with her last night and I doubted she wanted the Wolf asshole catching them in the act again.

Sadly, I was too late to save her from that fate and her reply told me that she was already walking to the Hollow with Seth now.

I tossed my clothes off and snatched a bikini top from my drawer before pulling on a pair of high waisted leggings too. I grabbed a sweater from the cupboard and moved to my window with a smirk.

If the Dragon asshole required my presence at the Hollow that was fine. But I didn't have to endure the walk down there at his side.

I climbed up onto the window ledge and threw the window wide with a laugh.

My back tingled as I called on my wings and I leapt off of the ledge with a whoop of excitement half a second before they burst from my flesh.

The golden feathers blazed with fire which warmed my skin and drove out the final dregs of the shadows as I flew hard and fast straight towards the heart of The Wailing Wood.

I laughed aloud as the wind clawed through my hair and pushed at the feathers of my wings.

All my life I'd ached for a pure kind of freedom and I found it in its simplest form when flying through the clouds. My skin buzzed with the joy of the flight and I could feel each and every burden I carried just slipping away from me as I spun and soared through the sky.

A huge roar sounded behind me and I turned with a laugh as I spotted Darius taking chase in his stunning golden Dragon form.

I dove from the clouds and shot straight towards the centre of the forest.

The air stirred behind me as he drew closer and his powerful wings sent my hair swirling with each beat.

Darius turned sharply, diving into the trees as he spotted King's Hollow before I could and I gave chase. He landed on the roof of the enormous tree house with a thump and I dropped down before him with a smirk.

He looked at me for a long moment, his bright, golden eyes watching me through the reptilian slits of his pupils. His nose bumped my chest and I reached out on instinct, running my fingers over the glimmering scales between his eyes.

"I like you so much better when you can't talk," I mused.

He snorted derisively and I was shrouded in smoke for a moment. By the time it cleared, Darius stood before me in his Fae form. "But then you wouldn't be able to bite back at me with such force, Roxy. And as much as you might claim to hate that, I think we both know it gets you going. You might hate me. But you like hating me way too much to want it to just stop."

He didn't wait for me to reply before lifting a hatch in the roof and dropping inside.

"Dipshit," I muttered.

I withdrew my wings and a shiver ran down my spine as they disappeared again and I pulled my sweater over my head.

I dropped down into the treehouse, following Darius and finding the space inside empty aside from him. He'd pulled on a pair of black sweatpants, leaving his chest bare as he headed into the kitchenette and started up the coffee machine.

His back was to me and I frowned as my gaze lingered on the two biggest tattoos which ran over his broad shoulder blades. I'd never really looked at them closely before but as I did, my lips parted.

"You have a Dragon and a Phoenix fighting on your skin," I pointed out like he might not already know. Fire danced across the space between the two beasts, licking against each other in a raging inferno.

"Well don't go thinking I got a tattoo for you, Princess," he taunted. "You might be a fucking tom cat in the sack, but I had that tattoo long before I ever set eyes on your pretty face or got my hands on your body."

"I didn't think you'd gotten a tattoo for me," I snapped, moving closer to him as he turned to face me. "I just think it's a weird coincidence."

"You never struck me as the kind of girl to turn all stalker on me just because we've hooked up a few times," he said, watching me over the rim of his coffee cup as he took a long sip.

"Oh please, I'd sooner stalk a fart on the wind than start mooning over you," I replied, rolling my eyes. "You should get over yourself, Darius."

"Maybe *you* should get over me," he countered. "Because you're the one who had their tongue half way down my throat ten minutes ago."

"Well don't worry about it because it won't be happening ever again," I promised.

Darius set his coffee cup down and moved towards me suddenly, walking so close that I was forced to back up against the wall to try and escape him.

He rested his hand on the wall beside my head and leaned down close so that his mouth was mere inches from mine. My heart pounded out of rhythm from his proximity but I kept my expression set to unimpressed as I held his eye.

"You can deny it as much as you like, Roxy, but you and me are going to happen over and over," he promised, the scent of him wrapping around me and the heat of his flesh blazing so fiercely I could feel it despite the inch of space dividing us. "So no matter how much you hate me or despise me or wish you didn't want me in any way at all, there's no stopping it. You don't feel fire like that and just let it burn out."

The sound of a door opening came from downstairs and Darius shoved away from me like he hadn't said a word.

I glared at the Phoenix on his back as he walked away from me, collecting his coffee and taking a seat by the fireplace. He flicked his fingers towards it and a fire burst to life just as the others all appeared.

Darcy looked less than impressed as she walked into the room with Seth's arm wrapped around her shoulders and Max on her other side.

Caleb's jaw was set in a tight line and he frowned at me as he came in last.

"Good, we're all here," Max said darkly as he looked between everyone and took a place standing before the fire.

Darcy shrugged out of Seth's grip and moved to sit on the couch while I stayed on my feet with my arms folded.

"Sorry we're a bit late, Darcy begged to give me a blowjob on the way here and it seemed rude to refuse," Seth said casually, dropping down beside my sister as if he didn't notice the shudder of disgust that ran through her at his words.

I rolled my eyes at him, biting my tongue on flat out calling him out on his bullshit. "Well no doubt it took her a while to find your tiny dick in amongst that big old Werewolf bush she told me you've got going on down there," I replied mockingly. I might not have been able to call him out on his lies while I was supposed to still be in the dark about the truth between Darcy and Orion, but I'd soon figured out the best way to disarm him. I just made out that Darcy had shared all kinds of unflattering details about him with me and he couldn't really argue against them unless he wanted to admit to his lies.

Seth growled but didn't rise to bite back at me and Darcy smirked at me gratefully.

"Why were you lying about the truth of your Order forms?" Caleb demanded, ignoring our back and forth as he cut to the reason we were here.

"We weren't," Darcy replied innocently, giving them the story Orion had suggested we stick to after we'd returned to the academy last night.

"All we knew was that we had wings and some kind of crazy fire magic," I added with a shrug.

"We weren't the ones who said we were Fire Harpies," Darcy said with a nod. "And it's not like we know anything about Orders, let alone extinct ones."

"I don't really see what the big deal is," I finished.

The Heirs exchanged loaded looks and Darius just watched the fire.

"You don't see what the big deal is?" Max asked incredulously and I could feel his Siren gifts trying to find a way past my Phoenix fire, but it danced beneath my skin and kept him out as easily as breathing.

"Orion said something about it being why we're impervious to fire and about it guarding us against mental magics like Siren spells," Darcy said thoughtfully. "Which is handy, I guess."

I almost laughed out loud and had to raise a hand to cover my mouth and fake a cough. Caleb narrowed his eyes on me like he didn't buy it, but what could he really do?

"So you just expect us to believe you had no idea?" Caleb scoffed.

"In the same way that we had no idea that we were Fae or that magic even existed or that we were Princesses? Yeah I expect you to believe we were once again left in the dark about our true natures. Sorry if you think we were secretly planning a Phoenix bonding session without you or whatever, but I don't really see what you think we would have been trying to achieve by lying about what we were." I arched an eyebrow at him and folded my arms like I was pissed about being here and had zero idea what he meant.

Darcy nodded firmly in agreement and I almost smirked at the sense of déjà vu that gave me. I couldn't even begin to count the amount of times I'd lied like this to foster parents, teachers, social workers or even cops while Darcy bit her tongue and agreed with a firm nod, knowing she was too much of an open book to front out a bare faced lie if she spoke too much.

"Fine," Darius said, piping up at last. "It doesn't matter anyway. So what if they're Phoenixes? Their magic still can't rival ours, but they're handy in a Nymph situation. I don't think they need to have a discussion with our parents about it if that's all they know. Do you?" He looked between the other Heirs and they seemed to agree with him, albeit a little reluctantly.

"I thought you'd be the most pissed about this," Max said, frowning at Darius. "They're impervious to fire. Even Dragon Fire. Doesn't that mean-"

"It doesn't mean anything," Darius said with a shrug, lying so damn well that I had to believe he'd been at it as long as me. And when I considered the monster who'd raised him, I guessed I could imagine why he'd be good at that. "They might not burn, but they can still drown." Water slid between his fingers in a clear threat and I bristled internally as he casually suggested that of all things. He might have been trying to cover for us to some degree, but it was only because that served him and his vendetta against his father. He didn't give a shit about us. He clearly held no remorse for any of the things we'd suffered at his hands. He'd almost drowned me once and he would clearly do it again if he felt he was justified in doing so.

"Can we go, then?" Darcy asked, pushing to her feet.

The Heirs looked like they might protest, but I didn't see how they could.

"So long, asshats. We'll leave you to your dastardly plans," I said casually as the two of us strode for the door and none of them made a move to stop us.

Darcy and I stayed silent as we made our way out of King's Hollow and she tossed a silencing bubble up around us as we headed away from them at a fast pace.

"Do you think we did enough to keep the Councillors away from us?" she asked, worrying at her bottom lip.

"Hopefully," I agreed. "But if we have to face their questions too, we're ready. Even Lionel's Dark Coercion can't breach our mental walls so we can do it if we have to."

Darcy's Atlas pinged and she drew it from her pocket, her expression softening as she saw who it was from and I rolled my eyes at her. This thing with Orion was making her all gooey. It was adorable in a slightly terrifying way. Because as much as I loved to see her happy like that, I just couldn't see how they were going to make this last long term. At what point would it be acceptable for them to be open about their relationship? We had to survive four years at the academy with him as her teacher and even if they weren't caught, then how could they suddenly say they'd decided to get together after the fact?

"He's asking where we are," Darcy said as she typed out a reply. "Apparently Gabriel's seen something about New Year's Eve and-"

A blur of motion shot towards us and I flinched as Orion came to a halt before us, his eyes bright and hair disheveled. He wore a Solarian Pitball League shirt and sweatpants and looked younger than usual. When he took his teacher's hat off completely like this, I could see the two of them working as a couple so much more easily. I just had to forget the whole teacher thing and it was as clear as day.

"Gabriel had a vision about me for New Year's Eve," Orion said excitedly, taking Darcy's hand as he looked between the two of us with hope shining in his eyes.

"And?" Darcy asked. "Has he seen us getting Clara back?"

"He can't see the shadows, they don't show up in visions," Orion said with a frown. "But he saw me heading down to the cave and he said he got a sense that something huge was coming right before my future was lost to the darkness!"

"That doesn't sound like a good thing, dude," I said, raising an eyebrow.

"Of course it is," he replied, shooting a frown at me. "It means we were there using the dark magic to create the bridge. He's seen us doing it. It must be the right time."

"But he couldn't see whether or not it worked?" I asked dubiously.

Darcy shot me a warning look as Orion frowned at me.

"Of course it's going to work," he growled. "Haven't you noticed how strong the call of the shadows have been since we came back to the academy? Something big is coming, this has got to be it. We're going to save my sister!"

I bit my lip and looked to Darcy for the answer because I was coming up short. Yeah, I'd noticed the call of the shadows was stronger than it had been, but it was hard to say what that meant. Was it because we were drawing close to something huge like pulling Clara back into the real world? How the hell was I supposed to know that?

"Are we ready to build the bridge?" Darcy asked, squeezing Orion's fingers encouragingly.

"Yeah, but we'll need to wield the shadows together. I've been studying a lot of ancient texts on it, I'm confident that I can do the right spells. But it'll be easier with more power. So the four of us will have to work together on it. I'll tell Darius too. It'll be like power sharing for the three of you, you'll all just channel the shadows through me and with our combined strength, we'll be able to build a bridge strong enough for her to cross back."

He looked so damn sure and so damn hopeful that I felt myself nodding in agreement without needing to consider it further. If this was what it took to get his sister back, then I was all in. I just hoped he was right about the meaning of Gabriel's vision because if I found out that my future was lost in darkness, I sure as shit wouldn't be looking so damn cheery about it. But he clearly knew more about dark magic than me and if this vision had convinced him, then it convinced me too. We were going to get his sister back and with a bit of luck, the shadows might not draw me so much once she wasn't stuck there to call on me.

"Okay. So what do you need us to do?" I asked.

"I'll make all the preparations," Orion said, his attention sliding to whatever that meant. "You just need to show up at the cave before midnight on New Year's Eve. Make sure your magic is fully replenished and wear something warm. Gabriel said there's a blizzard coming."

"Okay," Darcy and I agreed at the same time.

Orion gave us both the biggest fucking grin and I almost laughed. I didn't think I'd ever seen him smile like that before. He pressed a kiss to Darcy's lips briefly then shot away from us, sending a flurry of snow up around us as he went.

"I guess we won't be partying the new year in then," I said with a smirk.

"Nope. It looks like we'll be spending it in a dark cave, making Orion's dreams come true," she agreed with a wide smile.

"Well, when you put it that way, I can't think of anything I'd rather do," I laughed.

DARCY

CHAPTER FORTY THREE

The campus was alive with music, laughter and parties. I could hear it all from my room way up in Aer Tower. I'd decided not to join in with the fun tonight. New Year's Eve had an entirely different agenda for me and I wasn't going to let Orion down when he needed me most.

I'd stupidly told Geraldine I was sick and she'd offered to bring me all kinds of potions and remedies to heal me. I'd had to admit I wasn't feeling up for partying tonight instead and made a mental note that being sick didn't qualify as an excuse amongst Fae. Not when they could heal ninety percent of illnesses.

At nine o'clock I was going stir crazy and by ten, I was losing my mind. I paced my room, started some cheesy romance series on Faeflix then returned to pacing again.

Darkness kept creeping into my mind and dragging at my thoughts. I had to fight it back, breathing deeply and focusing on the anchor of love that kept me from falling into its clutches. My sister, Orion. Between them, I was unbreakable. The shadows couldn't have me. And they couldn't have Orion's sister much longer either.

"Come to me..." Clara's voice sounded and I swallowed thickly.

"We're coming," I promised. "We're going to save you."

Anxiety swirled in my gut as I checked my messages. Tory was in her room too, waiting for me to give her the green light. From the sounds of it, she was as anxious as me.

I checked FaeBook just for something to do, dropping down onto my bed and drawing my knees to my chest. There were pictures of the Heirs spread all over the newsfeed. There was one of Max being held upside down in The Orb, his face entirely covered with a bubble of water while he drank from a keg through a long straw.

There was another of Caleb shirtless with a girl taking a shot out of his belly button and another of Seth standing on a table, lifting a naked girl above his head with nothing but air magic. It looked like things were getting seriously wild tonight, especially when I spotted a photo of the faculty looking like they were in the middle of a game of strip poker. Washer was fully nude, his back to the camera (thank you stars) but Principal Nova sat in front of him, her eyes wide and trained on his junk. *Gross.*

I decided to head down to the beach a bit earlier than we'd planned to meet, getting too nervous to wait any longer. I was already dressed to go in jeans and a tank top, so I pulled on my coat and pushed my feet into my snow boots.

My pulse spiked as I mentally prepared myself for what I had to do tonight. I didn't know what to expect except that we had to go into the shadows again. I had to hope the training we'd had with Orion would be enough to keep us all safe, because the pull of the shadows was stronger than I'd ever experienced them before. Their allure was stronger, winding through my limbs and caressing my veins. I could almost hear the whispers calling to me, urging me into their endless depths.

I headed out of my room, the sound of a heavy bass pounding up in the common room as I hurried to the staircase.

"Hat boy, hat boy, hat boy!" a group of people were chanting and I relaxed when Diego's laughter followed. Whatever was happening up there, it sounded like he was onboard with it.

"Save me…" Clara's voice brushed against my ears.

I shivered as I headed downstairs, pulling up the hood of my coat to try and remain as invisible as possible.

I slipped outside past a group of giggling girls wearing fake wolf ears and made my way along the path in the direction of Air Cove. Snow was falling thickly before me, but the paths were lit by fires which blazed all across campus to help people find their way.

I kept the cold at bay by flooding heat into my veins, but I couldn't do much about my racing heart.

What if this doesn't work? Or what if it does but Clara's been lost to the shadows too long to make the journey back?

My spine tingled with worries as I rushed along, but as I closed in on the cliff, those thoughts were replaced by hope. Orion had been broken by the loss of his sister; if there was anything I could do to place her back at his side, I'd do it. Maybe the shadows were a gift in this sense. And maybe the stars were shining kindly on us for once. I just had to focus on my training and give him all the power I could to make this happen.

But what then? Could Clara really return to normal life amongst the Fae? Wasn't the press going to go mad when they found out she'd seemingly come back from nowhere?

Orion and I hadn't spoken about anything beyond bringing her safely back to the Fae realm. But if we were questioned, we couldn't admit to using the shadows. And what would Lionel do when he discovered the truth?

My mouth grew dry and I realised the only way we could get away with this was by keeping her a secret. She'd have to stay hidden from the world so no one ever looked into her return. Because if the FIB started looking into it, I imagined Orion would be the first to go under investigation. I didn't know what the punishment was for using dark magic, but I didn't imagine it was a light slap on the wrists.

I reached the top of the narrow path which cut down the side of the cliff to the beach. The world was loud out here, the roar of the waves and howl of the wind making my pulse elevate as snow tumbled down around me. I could almost feel the change in the atmosphere as midnight drew nearer, the magic in the air making the veils between worlds thinner. And it was time to use it to our advantage.

"Can't we just talk about it, Sethy?" Kylie's voice reached me out in the mist and I darted down onto the path, dropping into a crouch in the darkness.

"There's nothing to talk about," Seth replied, their footsteps drawing closer.

"You have to pick a mate one day, why not me? We have a connection," Kylie said, her tone giving away that she was bordering on drunk.

"I can't just pick a mate, that's not how it works for Werewolves. I'm sorry it's not you, babe, but you've gotta get over it."

Their shadows fell over the path as they walked by in the direction of The Wailing Wood and my heart ticked faster as I caught sight of the back of Seth's head. He was guiding the snow away from them with air magic so it bent around them in a dome.

They moved away and I released a slow breath, heading down the path and picking up my pace again. I stepped onto the beach and started walking to the cave, casting an air shield to keep the heavy snowfall at bay.

A figure stepped out from behind a boulder and Orion smiled hopefully as he spotted me. I increased my pace, jogging to his side and clutching his hand. "Are you ready?"

He pulled me toward the hidden cave. "I have everything we need, but I'm not sure I'll ever be ready for this really."

I squeezed his fingers then released him as he took a shining draining dagger from his pocket and traced it over the cliff wall in ritualised movements. The illusion fell away and my heart thrashed against my ribs as I followed him into the dark cave.

I lit a fire in my palm, letting it grow and grow and releasing it to burn at the heart of the cave floor. Orion cast an air shield around the edges of the space, keeping the wind and snow out so the place had a chance to warm up in the heat of my fire.

He dropped a pack from his shoulders, moving to kneel on the ground and I lowered down in front of him. He laid out the jar of dark stardust we'd stolen from his mother along with his draining dagger, a cloth filled with dry herbs and a silver leaf which looked as delicate as glass.

A thrumming energy in the air made me shiver and I found my eyes slipping closed as the shadows called to me again. Orion rested a hand on my knee and I blinked them away, taking a slow breath as I looked at him.

"They're close tonight," I breathed and he nodded, a serious expression pulling at his features.

"Are you sure you want to do this, Blue?"

"Yes, I want to help," I said firmly. "But Lance, what are you going to do once she's here? The world can't know she's back, people will ask too many questions. The FIB could find out what we did. Or what if Lionel comes for her?"

His brow creased and a look of distress entered his eyes. "I know," he sighed. "I'll hide her. I own a place on the outskirts of Tucana where she can stay."

"But what if someone sees her?" I breathed. "She can't stay there forever, she'll need a new identity, a new life."

"Once her magic is restored, she'll be able to change her appearance with an illusion."

"She's going to need you," I said gently. "Who knows what effect this has had on her..."

"I'll look after her," he swore, his jaw ticking. "I'll do whatever it takes to protect her. I owe her that and so much more."

"You did everything you could to save her," I said softly as my heart tugged apart for him.

His eyes dropped to the ground and darkness consumed his features. "Not enough."

I could almost see the shadows twisting around him and shifted closer with concern. "Let's get her back."

His eyes brightened and he glanced up at me with a desperate hope shining from them. It hurt me to think of him being torn away from his sister. If I'd lost Tory like that, I'd be doing everything I could to bring her back too.

"If the shadows become too much, I want you to pull yourself out of them," Orion said in a low tone. "Leave me if you have to and get out of here."

"No," I growled. "I'm not going anywhere, I can handle it."

"I know you can." He brushed his knuckles over my cheek. "But I won't risk you for anything."

"If it gets dangerous, we can stop," I said. "But I'm not leaving you."

He frowned, but gave in with a small nod, seeing that I wasn't going to back down. He took out his Atlas and his forehead furrowed. "Darius hasn't replied."

"Neither has Tory," I sighed as my brows pulled together, taking out my own Atlas. I pressed call on her name and lifted the device to my ear as I waited for her to answer. It rang on and on, but she didn't pick up and my stomach knotted with concern. Orion tried to call Darius but received the same response.

He checked the time, cursing under his breath. "There's only a small window of opportunity for this," he said furiously. "We have to start soon."

"They'll come," I promised, knowing Tory wouldn't let him down.

"They'd better," Orion growled.

The fire flickered before me and darkness seemed to seep into its depths, turning it to a dusky purple colour. I inhaled slowly, the power of the shadows closing in on me once more. They were here, winding through our bodies and pulling at our souls. I could feel them trying to guide me away again on dark wings, but I clenched my hands into fists until my nails nearly broke the skin, forcing myself out of their clutches.

Orion released a low groan as they affected him too and I shifted closer to him so we could fight them united, gripping his hand tightly. I felt them withdraw as I let the barriers of my magic down and our power washed together like a singular, powerful entity.

I checked the time once more and my worry started to escalate.

"Where the fuck are they?" Orion snarled, fury bleeding from his expression.

"They'll be here," I encouraged, looking to the cave entrance, expecting to see them at any moment.

Come on Tory, where the hell are you?

"We have to start soon, there's no other chance for this," Orion snapped.

"Get everything ready," I said, trying not to let the anxiety into my voice, but I wasn't sure I managed it.

Orion frowned darkly as he spread out the materials before him. "I don't understand why Darius would let me down like this tonight of all fucking nights."

I glanced toward the cave entrance again, my pulse thundering in my ears. We didn't have long left and I had no idea if the two of us would be strong enough to do this alone.

Please hurry, Tory.

DARIUS

CHAPTER FORTY FOUR

I sat in King's Hollow alone as I waited for the message to meet Orion and the Vegas so that we could free his sister from the Shadow Realm. My knee bounced with unspent energy and I half wondered whether I should take a flight in my Dragon form to expel some of it.

The New Year's Eve party down at The Orb was well underway and I probably should have just gone down to it with the other Heirs rather than wait here alone, but I just hadn't felt like partying tonight.

My mind was full of all the things we'd been practicing to bring Clara back from the shadows and I couldn't afford to let myself get distracted. Lance was relying on me. The loss of his sister had devastated him and the hope which I'd found living in his eyes since discovering she might not truly be gone was something I couldn't ignore. He needed me tonight like I didn't think he ever had before and I was going to be there for him no matter what.

I glanced at the clock for the thousandth time and pushed myself to my feet with a jolt of shock as I realised it was almost midnight. I'd been sat here all night waiting to meet him and yet somehow I'd just lost a huge chunk of time. My heart pounded unevenly as I struggled to understand how I'd gone from waiting around to late in the blink of an eye.

I frowned at the clock, double checking the time on my watch as I tried to figure out what the hell had happened. I'd just lost over half an hour of time and I couldn't account for it at all.

"*Shit.*" I pulled my Atlas from my pocket as I strode towards the door and my frown deepened as I spotted six missed calls from Lance. "What the…"

My head snapped up as the strangest thump of drums seemed to call to me through the window and my gaze fell on the raging snow storm outside.

I dropped my Atlas and it clattered as it fell to the floor. It started ringing again behind me but I'd already made it to the window.

I frowned at the snow as it swirled in a mini vortex beyond the glass, twisting in a flurry which looked more than unnatural as it seemed to part to create a path for me which headed away south through the trees.

I grabbed the window and pushed it open, climbing out through it and standing in the deep snow which had gathered on the wooden walkway outside.

I was high up in the trees, looking down over the forest as the strange tunnel through the falling snow stretched out ahead of me.

The thumping beat of some huge drum seemed to rattle the very foundations of the earth and pulse right through my body so that my heartbeat leapt in time with it.

The cold air brushed at my exposed skin as I stood there in my jeans and black T-shirt, but the idea of turning back to claim my coat felt impossible.

There was no going back. Only forward. This path had been made for me to follow and the strange magic calling to me wouldn't release me until I did its bidding.

I blew out a long breath, a cloud of vapour rising in front of me as the heat of my fire Element blazed beneath my skin and warmed me from the inside out.

With a surge of determination or quite possibly madness, I gripped the wooden railing before me and leapt over it.

I fell down the two floor drop at a fast pace and landed in the snow at the foot of King's Hollow with a solid thump. It should have hurt like hell, but somehow it didn't and I pushed myself up from my crouch as the strange magic surged around me again.

The blizzard grew fiercer beyond the pathway, fat snowflakes swirling through the trees so thickly that I couldn't see any distance into them at all.

The only way which was clear was the path ahead of me and the pounding of drums grew louder as I took my first step that way.

A frown tugged at my brow as I tried to remember what I'd been doing tonight. There was somewhere I was meant to be, something I was supposed to be doing...

The thought came and went with the breeze as I strode on through the trees towards my destination.

A memory tickled at the edges of my mind of me being called from my bed by Max's Siren Song when I was sixteen. I'd followed the lure of his call out into the dark then too, but something about the heavy beat of this music and the strength of the magic compelling me told me this was no Siren Song.

With every step I took, my heart beat a little harder, my steps grew more urgent, nerves stirred in my gut. It was like I knew in my veins that there was somewhere important I was meant to be and excitement was rising in me the closer I got to my destination.

I finally made it out of The Wailing Wood and followed the path painted by the magic further south.

On and on I walked, my footsteps never deviating from the trail, my heart pounding with anticipation as I drew closer to the end of this path.

There was something achingly important about this moment. Something which held my fate in its hands and locked it up tight. I knew it in my gut. This magic was no trick or ruse to lure me somewhere. It was pure. The magic of the stars in their simplest form.

Destiny.

I headed into Fire Territory, taking an unfamiliar route into the craggy rock formations until I found myself descending into a wide ravine.

The snow had formed banks against the rock faces either side of me but in the centre of the long space, a wide circle of red stone was clear and waiting.

My gaze tilted to the sky as the heavy snow clouds parted impossibly right above that spot.

My lips fell open as I drew closer, my gaze locked on the circle of black, star-filled sky as it appeared miraculously right above that clear spot of ground.

My boots hit stone as I stepped into the circle and my heart pounded to a reckless rhythm. Because I suddenly knew exactly what this was. I was here to face the most important question of my life and my heart was jackhammering in my chest as I watched the sky in fascination.

Two constellations weren't sitting where they were supposed to be. It was as if the heavens had rearranged themselves for this one moment and the stars which made them up glowed even brighter than usual as they came together, so close they were almost touching. Leo and Gemini. I'd recognise those constellations anywhere. And if the sky was rearranging itself to bring them together, then it could only mean one thing.

This was a Divine Moment. The stars had guided me here and they'd be bringing someone else to join me. Someone who was perfect for me in every way. Who pushed me and challenged me. Who made my heart beat harder and my flesh prickle with desire unlike anyone I'd ever known.

She was my mate.

The one the stars had selected for me. My one true love. And after tonight there wouldn't be a force in the universe that could ever tear us apart again.

The soft sound of footfalls approaching through the snow pulled my attention down from the stars as I looked towards the far side of the ravine.

The blizzard had closed in again and I couldn't see any more than a shadow moving amongst the snow as she drew closer to me. But I didn't need to see her. I'd known who was coming from the moment I'd looked up at the stars.

Hell, if I was being honest with myself, a part of me had known this was coming from the very first moment I'd laid my eyes on her.

Roxanya Vega was the daughter of The Savage King. The girl I should have hated without even having to try. She was a thorn in my side and a challenge to everything that had ever mattered to me. She made me angry like no one I'd ever met before, made me hate her with a passion which was unequalled by anything I'd ever felt. But despite everything that had passed between us, I'd never once been able to deny how much I wanted her.

The few times she'd let her guard down around me and let me in, I'd felt like the whole world had stopped spinning just for us. I'd held her when she was in pain, tasted raw lust on her lips, watched her rise from the shadows and rescued her from the dark. And she'd rescued me too. Before she'd come into my life I'd been stagnating, hardening and growing into a man I'd sworn I never wanted to become. But she was like a breath of fresh air. When she looked at me, it was like she really saw *me*.

Despite my privileged upbringing, I'd had very few chances to make any real decisions for myself. My father governed everything I did like a puppet master pulling my strings. He'd planned out a life for me which I was destined to lead no matter my own wants or desires.

But he couldn't control this. He couldn't twist this fate. The moment we both accepted this bond between us, our destinies would be sealed and we'd be bound together forever.

Elysian mates. Unbreakable. True love.

I'd never taken anything for myself like this before. Never had something purely because it was the deepest desire of my heart. But that was what she was.

Roxy Vega was the piece of me that was missing. She was everything I should have realised I needed sooner. If we hadn't gotten so caught up in hating each other, we could have already had something to build the foundation of this on. But none of that mattered. Because from this day on, I'd be hers and she'd be mine. And I'd do everything and anything it took to prove to her that I could be worthy of her love.

The snow whipped around the clearing and my heart thundered a desperate tune as her footsteps drew closer.

My breath caught as she stepped out of the blizzard and her gaze fell on me.

Her full lips parted, snow clung to her long hair as it fell around her shoulders and the brightness in her eyes made me want to stride straight up to her and pull her into my arms. But the fear in her gaze held me still. She didn't know what was happening. She didn't understand the importance of this moment. But I did. I knew. And as I looked at her, I couldn't help but feel the most overwhelming sense of happiness. Because I'd never had anything like this. Something pure and untouched by my father or the Council or the Heirs or my responsibilities… something that was just *mine*.

The blizzard raged around us and we stood in the centre of the storm as this immortal moment held us both hostage.

It was time for us to choose our fate.

And I didn't think I'd ever had such an easy decision to make in my entire life.

I'd wanted her to be mine for so long that I couldn't remember a time when the idea of it hadn't consumed me. And it had been for this. All of it. Everything we'd faced together, every fight and disagreement, every single moment leading us here. We'd faced more tests and challenges than I could count to get us here, but we'd made it.

Now all we had to do was grab this moment with both hands and claim it for our own.

It wasn't a decision, it was fate. And for the first time in my life, it felt like destiny was on my side.

ORION

CHAPTER FORTY FIVE

"They're not coming," I spat and something broke in Darcy's gaze as she realised I was right. Even if they were on their way, they weren't going to make it in time.

Fuck Darius for doing this to me. I'd given everything of myself to him. My whole life was bound to his, but the one time I needed *him*, he couldn't show up.

"We can do it alone," Darcy's voice called me out of the dark place I was descending into.

I looked to her, finding a fire in her eyes so fierce, I knew she was right. She was all I needed, but placing the weight of this task solely on me and her made my chest tight.

"Do it Lance," she demanded. "Our magic is enough. We've fought battles together, we can take on the shadows too."

I squeezed my eyes shut for a second, fearing how much pressure this would put on her body and soul.

"We can't wait any longer," she demanded. "Do it *now*."

I finally gave in, praying she was right and grunted in agreement. My anger at Darius snaked through me, devouring everything in its path, but I forced it back to focus on what had to be done.

I snared her in my gaze, preparing to give her an order that I would force her to obey. "When we go into the dark, follow me, Blue. And don't ever let go of my hand."

"I will," she breathed, firelight flickering over her face.

"Swear it," I growled.

"I swear."

I crushed the silver leaf with the dried Withermore seedlings, the sun-baked Nightshade and the charred Starweed, scattering them on the cave floor before me and Blue. My heart thundered in my ears as I picked up the draining dagger and turned to the girl I loved.

"I don't want to hurt you," I said gently. I hated practising blood magic with her. Every training session had been torture, but she had to do it. It was the most powerful way to learn to retreat from the shadows when they coaxed her into their arms.

I locked my fingers around her tighter as she plucked the knife from my hand and cut a line up the centre of her palm without a moment's hesitation. She shuddered, passing it back as blood dripped from her skin and made my spine prickle at the sight.

Once we went into the shadows, I wasn't going to let go of her. And I knew in the depths of my soul that I'd keep her safe before anything else. I would have done this alone if I could have, but I needed her magic combined with my own to be capable of this. And even then, I couldn't be entirely sure it would be enough. I couldn't believe Darius had let me down like this and I would have expected more from Tory. My heart started knotting up again and a furious snarl fell from my lips.

I snatched the dagger from Blue, cutting my own palm and holding my hand out over the herbs, squeezing to let the blood flow. Darcy lifted her fist beside mine and blood seeped between her fingers, dripping down onto the dry mixture. Ecstasy rolled along my limbs and Blue sighed as the same pleasure invaded her veins.

I took a pinch of the dark stardust from the jar and tossed it on top of the herbs, battling to keep my thoughts straight as darkness trickled into my mind. The pieces of the silver leaf caught light, a blackish fire crackling across the ground and devouring every piece of the seedlings, the Nightshade and the Starweed with it. All that remained was our blood, and my heart thumped solidly in my chest as the fire caught on that too, growing brighter and brighter until I winced against the light of it.

I snatched hold of Blue's hand as the shadows washed over us, crashing into my veins more fiercely than they ever had before. I kept her near, her presence grounding me and keeping my mind sharp amongst the shadows. Her magic tumbled through my veins like a force of nature and kept the shadows from climbing too deep inside me. I pressed my own strength into her body, willing the darkness away from her with everything I had.

I was falling, whirling through an abyss so vast I could feel it weighing on my very soul.

After an endless moment, my feet collided with hard ground and I dragged in a breath of air that felt too thick, too heavy, too stale.

Darcy materialised beside me and I took in the desolate world around us. My lungs laboured in this place and with a feeling of horror, I realised we weren't in the dark between worlds anymore. We were standing in the Shadow Realm.

I stepped forward, searching the deserted horizon. This world was bleak and barren, the sky an empty grey thing with nothing but a pale light glowing beyond a smog of clouds. No wind stirred my hair or brushed my skin. I wondered if we were entirely here at all. The only thing that felt real was Blue's hand clutched in my own and I had the feeling it was more important than ever not to let go.

Whispers rushed into my ears and sang lullabies to me, drawing me into their arms. I turned to look at Darcy and struggled to push the shadows out as they clawed into my veins and filled my chest with an agonising pleasure.

My gaze snared on someone beyond her and my lungs weighed down like lead as I looked upon the face of my sister.

She looked different than the last day I'd seen her in the Fae world, her body slim and clad in a dark cloak made of shadow. Her skin was pale and she'd lost weight but it was her. Really her.

"Lance?" she breathed, the word close and far away at once. She reached out to me and I ran toward her, tugging Blue after me in my desperation to close the gap between us.

My heart hollowed out as Clara reached up to caress my face, the warmth of her skin opening up a wound inside me that had never truly healed.

"Is it really you?" Tears slid down her cheeks and I dragged her against my chest, still holding onto Darcy in an iron grip.

Clara's arms wrapped around me as she fell against me, her tears sliding onto my neck. She was so painfully real it hurt. She'd been here during all the years I'd mourned her. But how?

"How are you alive?" I begged as she pulled me closer in desperation. How alone she must have been here. She must have craved the touch of another Fae, wasting away in the shadows. It was enough to break me apart.

Darcy kept hold of my hand but gave us as much room as she could, gazing around the desolate land with wide eyes.

"I don't know," Clara breathed. "I don't know how real I am, Lance. I don't know if I'll survive coming back to Solaria. But I'd rather die trying than stay here another second."

I gripped her tighter, terror coating my insides as I considered the possibility that I'd gotten my sister back only to lose her all over again.

"The spell will work," I growled, pouring my heart into the words. Because it *had* to work.

"If it doesn't..." Clara looked up at me and I rubbed away her tears with my thumb, my body hurting at finding her here like this. So small, so lost. She had always been so strong, now she looked weak, broken.

"It will," I said through my teeth. "I'll make sure of it."

"Just in case," she whispered, tip-toeing up to press her lips to my cheek. "I love you with all my heart, dear brother. I've thought about you all these years. I've missed you. But sometimes darkness has to have its way and its owned me for such a long time..."

"Lance," Darcy said cautiously. "We should go." She gave me an anxious look, then turned to Clara hesitantly. "I'll help you get back."

"It's going to take a lot of magic," I said as the whispers called to me again.

The three of us released soft sighs as the shadows wrapped around us and sang our names. I took Clara's hand, holding the two of them close and vowing not to let go until we were standing in the cave at Zodiac Academy.

"Now, Blue," I encouraged and she let her eyes fall closed. Her magic washed into mine alongside the power of the shadows that lived in her and she let it all run formlessly into my veins to lend me strength.

I started to pull us through the dark, forming a bridge with my mind and visualising it as clearly as I could, wielding the shadows around us.

Starlight danced beneath my eyelids and feathers seemed to brush over my skin as I called on the power of the heavens to help us.

I spoke the words I'd memorised from the old texts I'd studied, guiding all of mine and Blue's power into my voice. "Nocturnae sidera nobis dirige nos. Quid opus aedificare. Ut quod oportet."

The power of the spell drained our magic fast, eating it up and spitting it out in the form of a white hot light around us. The shadows drank it away as quickly as it came and I knew it needed more fuel.

I tugged on Clara's magic but only a hollowness answered. She hadn't fed in all these years, she had nothing to offer, her power long since diminished. Darcy's magic flooded into me with more force and I gasped, realising she'd been holding back. Her strength was intoxicating, rolling through my veins and gifting me everything I needed to continue the spell.

"Stellae de zodiaci, accipere virtutem meam: da mihi virtutem quoque partum a ponte inter mundos!" I called to the sky, the stars blinding me as they twisted to my will, bowing under the immense power pouring from Darcy into me.

A weightless sensation spilled through me and the shadows curled around my hands, trying to break my grip on my sister and Blue. I roared in effort, practically crushing their fingers in my grip as I refused to let go. The darkness couldn't steal them from me, I'd die before I released them into its clutches. They were two of the most precious Fae to me in the entire world and I'd give anything to bring them home.

Their nails dug into my skin as they held onto me and my vision swum with a mixture of dark and light as we careered into the void between worlds.

I never stopped speaking with the stars, fearing they'd turn away for one moment and leave us here, casting us into an eternal chasm of black.

"Post velamentum autem amo ducere. Tolle eas Solaria, tolle eas in domum suam. Detrahet me in eos!" My voice echoed back to me over and over and light flared beneath my feet.

A million stars seemed to bind together and I walked over the galaxy as it guided me forward, the immense power of the bridge humming in the air around me. I couldn't see Darcy or Clara beside me, but I felt them there as I clung onto them, moving along the bridge built for us by the stars.

My feet hit solid ground and I was blinded as the light fell away, branding a mark onto my retinas. I still had two hands in my grip and relief hit me so hard, I couldn't breathe. I blinked away the ghosts floating before my eyes, looking from Darcy to Clara to make sure they were okay.

My sister's lips formed a perfect O as she took in the cave she stood in. The cloak of shadows was still wrapped around her and I guessed she'd learned to wield them during all the years she'd spent alone in the Shadow Realm.

She dropped to her knees suddenly and I released Blue, falling down beside her as terror crashed through my chest.

"Are you alright?" I pulled her into my arms and she tilted her head back, her face ashen, but her eyes alight with joy.

"I'm free," she gasped, her chest rising and falling as she drew deep breaths into her lungs. "I forgot how good the air tastes here." Tears washed over her skin and I clutched her against me.

Darcy stumbled down beside us and I looked to her in alarm. "Are you okay?"

"I'm fine," she said unsteadily. "My magic is gone...I can't even reach my Phoenix. It's like it's sleeping."

"It'll come back, you need to rest. I'll start a fire to replenish you," I added, looking to where her last one had gone out, leaving a blackened mark beneath it. "Thank you," I said earnestly and Darcy nodded, blinking back her own tears as she looked to Clara where she was cradled against my chest.

So long as her heart continued to beat, I knew my sister would be okay. And as I listened to the familiar thrum of it in my ears, nearly five years of grief lifted from my shoulders, bringing a part of me back to life which had long since been lost.

TORY

CHAPTER FORTY SIX

Snow swirled all around me and I looked about in confusion as I tried to figure out what was happening. I felt like I was trapped in a bubble in the centre of the storm. The blizzard raged outside of this little globe of peace but inside it, barely a snowflake stirred.

"Roxy?" Darius breathed and I looked up at him, wondering if he'd done this to me.

"Why am I here?" I asked, tipping my head back so that I could look at the stars which shone in the odd circle of space above me.

It didn't make sense. My brain couldn't process it. All I knew was that some deep magic had taken me hostage and led me here. To stand before the man I hated so desperately it hurt.

My gaze fell back to Darius like I just couldn't bear to look away from him for long. He was wearing jeans and a black T-shirt, clearly no better dressed for the blizzard than I was in my blue leggings and crop top. But the magic that had called me from my room hadn't given me a chance to even consider grabbing a coat. I wasn't even wearing shoes. My fire magic flared beneath my skin, warming me against the elements and I guessed his was doing the same for him.

"We…this…" Darius looked up at the stars again for a moment like they might be able to help him with the answer to my question. "I think that this is our… Divine Moment," he said slowly like voicing his opinion on this madness actually frightened him.

I scoffed lightly, my gaze raking over him like I was hunting for the punchline. But he didn't laugh. He didn't even smile, he just took a slow step closer to me.

"You mean you actually think the two of us could be Elysian Mates?" I asked incredulously. Because how could he believe that? How could he really think that two people destined to love each other with the fierceness of the sun could hate each other with the strength that we did? "We're more likely to be Astral Adversaries."

Darius frowned at my words like they'd cut him open.

"This isn't a joke, Roxy," he breathed, inching closer to me. "It's not something either of us can choose. The stars picked us for each other. They've been challenging us and driving us together at the same time. That's why we keep colliding the way we do, why you're all I think about… Don't you think about me too?"

"You mean when I fantasise about ways to hurt you for all the things you've done to me?" I asked darkly even though it was a lie. Because I may have thought about him like that more than once, but I'd also dreamed about him night after night. I'd fantasised over him and daydreamed about him and I'd beaten myself up over it a thousand times. Because he wasn't some prize to win, he was my own personal hell. He'd made sure of that at every opportunity.

"I mean, like the way I lie awake at night, remembering what it felt like to hold you in my arms. How still the world felt, how pure that moment was between us. How I imagine I can still smell your perfume as my eyes fall closed and how I reach across my bed in the night wishing you were really there. Or like the way my heart beats harder when you walk into a room and my throat thickens when I try to think of the right things to say to you. How I fight to get your attention in any way I can because I can't bear it when you ignore me."

My lips parted and I didn't know what to say. Because he was making the way he treated me sound so different to the way it felt when he did it.

"You've hurt me more than anyone I've ever known," I breathed.

Darius swallowed hard, taking a step closer as his gaze took me hostage.

He was so strong and so solid, like this unstoppable force of nature which had decided to come crashing into my life and had tried to tear me apart so many times I couldn't count them.

"I'm sorry," he breathed and I could feel how much he meant those words. They spilled through the cracks in my resolve like molten lava, searching for the fissures he'd carved in my heart with every cruel word and action and working to soothe them. They were the words I'd ached to hear from him so many times that it hurt me to even think about it. Because in all the time I'd known him, I'd never gotten the impression he felt an inch of the remorse that was shining in his eyes in that moment. But there it was. Darius was staring at me like he was breaking open and I was the only one who could put him back together.

"Why now?" I demanded. "If we weren't standing here tonight, if we were somewhere else, would you have apologised to me?"

Darius's brow pinched and I knew what his answer was without him having to voice it. Because of course he wouldn't have. He wasn't sorry about what he'd done to the Vega twin he'd vowed to get rid of. He was sorry that he'd unknowingly done those things to the girl who he was destined to love.

"You don't know how many times I wished I could fix what I'd broken between us," he said. "But I had to do those things...I had to make sure you and your sister didn't rise up and claim our throne. It wasn't about you and me, it was about the Council and the Royals. About Solaria and what's best for all of its people. Darius and Roxy weren't a factor in any of it."

"Roxy?" I asked, arching a brow at him. Because he claimed he was sorry, but he wasn't even going to stop calling me that. The name he taunted me with and cut me with. He wasn't really sorry at all because that man who had done all of those things to me wasn't some stranger. He was standing right before me, looking at me like somehow everything had changed between us in the blink of an eye, but how could that be true? How could I just forget about everything he'd put me through?

I clenched my jaw as I forced myself to focus on all of that. On every time he'd made me feel small or weak or humiliated and not on the way I'd felt when he'd held me close or pressed his lips to mine.

Darius seemed to realise where my thoughts had taken me and he shook his head as he stepped closer like he could just make me forget all of it if he wanted me to enough.

"Tory, please," he choked, reaching out for me, his eyes burning with a desperate need.

"You don't get to call me that," I snarled. "You call me Roxy, remember? You do it because that was what my mother called me. And you want to remind me that she's dead every time you talk to me. Because that's who you are. That's what you are. And I don't want anything to do with you."

"No," he growled. "I don't call you Roxy because I'm trying to hurt you. I use that name so that I don't forget who you are or what you are. You're a Vega Princess. You could shatter everything I've worked for my whole life. And if I didn't force myself to remember that fact, then I knew it would be too easy for me to forget about. Forget about challenging you and knocking you down and just...let myself imagine you could be something else. Something that I've wished you could be in the darkest corners of my heart for so long that I can't deny it anymore. I want *you*. And I don't care if you're a Vega or not. I don't care if your name is Roxy or Tory or anything else. I just want *you.*"

My heart was pounding as I looked up into his dark eyes and I felt the truth of those words washing over me. I wanted for them to be enough. I wanted it so badly it hurt. It cut into me and found all of the secret, whispered desires of my heart and spoke them in my ear. Because I ached for this beast before me. I wanted to close the distance between us and pull him close and never let go, but I still didn't trust him. Hell, I didn't even really know him. So how was I supposed to agree to a lifetime in his arms when I didn't even know how tightly he'd hold onto me? What if his love was as fickle as his hatred? Or what if he thought that claiming me for his own meant owning me? I could be walking into a cage by accepting him as mine.

"If I'm right about this, we won't get another chance," Darius begged, raw desperation burning in his eyes as he looked at me, seeing the doubt that warred through me. "Don't you understand? We'll be Star Crossed. Bound to be alone forever. We'll never find love with another. We're meant to be together - it's fate."

My jaw tightened at his words. Because it didn't even sound like he wanted *me* at all. He just didn't want to be Star Crossed. He'd rather have me than no one. But I didn't plan on being anyone's consolation prize.

"Fuck fate," I snapped. "I don't want it. If it's bound me to you then it's a cruel and twisted thing. I don't need destiny to choose my life for me. I'll make my own fate and it won't be with you!"

Panic bled into his eyes at my words and pain seared across my heart.

"Please. Think about what you're saying. If I'm right then this is the moment that our stars have aligned. This is the moment when our souls are due to meet and connect with each other. I know you feel the same pull to me that I feel to you. You're all I think about. All I dream about. You're under my skin and in every thought and I know that I've done a thousand unforgivable things, but I swear I'll never hurt you again. You're meant for me. I'll protect you with my life-"

"It's too late," I said, my voice low and refusing the barest hint of an argument. "This isn't the moment when our fate is decided. This isn't the reason we will never be able to be together. The moment that decision was made was the moment you first laid eyes on me.

The moment I walked into this academy with the chance to find my place in this world for the first time in my life, when I should have been able to make this place my home but you decided to make it my hell instead. So instead of looking at me like I'm the one who is denying fate and stealing your one true chance at happiness from you, then why don't you look at yourself? Look at every vile thing you've said and done to me. Remember burning my clothes off and humiliating me. Remember finding out my fears and bringing them to life. Remember how your magic felt when you used it to trap me beneath the ice in that pool and you left me in there to die." And the more I thought about all of those things, the more I realised they'd been tests. When he'd hesitated before making me climb the ladder to the diving board or when the two of us had held back on speaking the words in our hearts, we'd been failing. And when we'd fought together against the Nymphs, or in those moments that I'd let down my walls with him and we'd been happy together for a brief time, we'd passed. But there were so many more failures, so many more times that we'd hurt each other instead of coming together...

"I know," he said, his voice breaking on that word. "All the awful things I've done to you will haunt me forever. But please, *please* just give me forever to fix them. Let this bond form between us and I'll prove to you how good our lives could be together. I won't force you to do anything or be with me if you don't want to, but at least give us a chance. Kiss me again with the stars overhead and let our story begin anew here."

I couldn't help but stare at him as he drew closer to me, reaching out tentatively and taking my hands into his.

His dark eyes flared with hope when I remained in place, looking up at him as the snow swirled all around us.

His skin was warm against mine, his touch eliciting sparks of electricity which hummed beneath my flesh and set my heart pounding.

His stunning features hovered so close to mine, his eyes open and vulnerable for once as he stood in the snow, offering himself to me. I'd never been able to deny the attraction I felt to him. To this monster who stood before me in the flesh of a man, suggesting that he might just be everything I'd ever dreamed of. Because who didn't want to find their one true love? Who didn't wish for that kind of bond? My whole life, I'd never had someone choose to love me. No one had ever looked at me the way he was now and said that they picked me. The only one who had ever loved me was Darcy and she'd been stuck with me whether she liked it or not. Anyone who had the option had always let me down. Always. And as much as I wouldn't let it show, that had broken something in me until I'd begun to believe that I just wasn't the kind of girl people felt love for. I was too harsh and hard and jaded. No one wanted that long term. Though a secret part of me had always hoped that one day someone *would*. But could I really believe that Darius could be that man? After everything he'd done to me and I'd done to him…

Darius trailed his right hand up my arm slowly like he was worried he might spook me. The fire in my skin was enough to make my knees weak, his touch calling out a desperate lust in me which begged for him to sate it. I craved him, desired him and ached for him in a way I'd never felt for any man before him.

There was truth to his claim about us, I knew it in my heart. This was it. Our one chance to seize a life together. To give my heart to him and let him pull me into his arms like I belonged to him and he belonged to me.

His fingertips brushed up my neck before reaching my jaw.

The desperate beat of my heart was overwhelming, a deep presence seeming to build around us as the magic of this moment grew to its crescendo.

Darius's fingers scored a line along my jaw, his thumb tracing my bottom lip, stroking, caressing. I could feel the memory of the kisses he'd already claimed from me tingling beneath my flesh. But this one would be different. This one would bind us to one another forever.

He moved closer. The stars glimmered in the sky overhead, expectant energy coiling about us.

His breath danced with mine, the scent of him overwhelming me and drawing the darkest desires from my heart.

I'd never wanted anyone like I wanted Darius Acrux, but I'd never hated anyone like I hated him either.

His hand slid to cup my cheek, his gaze locked with mine. For the first time, he wasn't guarded or scowling or pushing me away. He was opening up, inviting me in and offering me everything.

My lips parted for the promise of his kiss.

He leaned closer, his lips drawing nearer, the barest of whispers parting us.

"No," I breathed.

Darius stared at me like he didn't understand, like those two little letters held no meaning to him and they couldn't possibly have spilled from the lips he was destined to kiss.

But they had. And I meant them.

No matter what kind of man he could be for me now, it wouldn't change the kind of man he'd been up until this moment. They were one and the same. Two halves of the same whole. He was my deepest desire and my worst nightmare all wrapped into one.

He shook his head, the tender grip on my cheek tightening as he begged me not to have meant it.

But I had.

"You don't understand," he said desperately. "We're meant for each other. We're destined to be together."

His words cut me open and bled me dry. They were the promise of something I'd always wished to find and something I knew I could never have now.

"So you've realised that all the time you spent torturing me, you should have been falling in love with me?" I asked bitterly. "Well it's too late, you can't undo what you've done-"

"I *was* falling in love with you," Darius replied, his voice cracking. "Everything else wasn't real. That's not who I really am! I-"

"Yes it is," I said fiercely. "It *is* who you are. You can tell me you hated doing it or felt obligated for whatever reason you want, but *you* are still the one who did all of those things to me. You're the one who put us on this path. I never wanted a war with you. But you didn't give me a choice in that. And now I'm not giving you a choice in this." My voice was strong but my heart was breaking. I could feel a great fissure tearing open right through the centre of my chest, but it didn't matter. If the only true love I was ever destined to have was to be built on a foundation of hate then I didn't want it.

"Please," Darius asked again. "I'm giving you my heart. If you give me yours in return I'll spend every moment of our lives proving to you that I can be worthy of it."

"It's too late," I growled, finding some strength somewhere and throwing all of it into my words while the rest of me shattered and died, broken into a thousand pieces I knew would never mend. "If fate is so cruel as to only offer me true love with a man who could hurt me as much as you have, then I'll go without love," I swore. "You want my heart? I'd sooner cut it out than give it to you."

Darius was shaking his head, denying the words I'd thrown at him as he managed to draw me closer. I let him because I had no strength left to fight him off and because the pain of denying the stars was crashing through me like a storm, dashing my soul to pieces while my heart burned away to nothing.

I didn't care if destiny meant for me to be his. I had no intention of letting fate guide my life, especially if it led me to this. To a monster who was built in the image of his father. To a man who would cause me to suffer for his own gain, time and again.

"*Please,* just be mine, Tory," Darius begged.

"I'd rather be alone," I whispered.

I pulled my hand out of his, stepping back as he shook his head again, refusing to believe me, failing to understand that I meant it.

My heart was breaking, something inside me ripping away as I chose this path and sealed our fate. We wouldn't be together. We'd be Star Crossed, destined lovers who missed their chance. But that wasn't on me. It was on him.

And even as I felt the tears spilling down my cheeks, the icy wind chilling them to my face, I didn't relent.

"Tory, I-" Darius followed as I stepped away so I backed up again and again until he fell still.

The clouds drew closed overhead, the stars hidden once more as our constellations fell out of alignment. Something inside me was breaking with a finality I could feel in the depths of my soul. It hurt. It tore at me, ripping at the fabric of who I was and laying me bare for the whole world to see. But I knew in my heart I'd done the right thing. No matter what the stars had to say on the subject, Darius Acrux had made my life a living hell. I wouldn't give him a moment of happiness in payment for that. He didn't deserve it. He didn't deserve me. And that was how it had to be.

My gaze locked with his just as a black ring formed around his pupils. His eyes widened in horror and I guessed the same thing had happened to me too. That was it. We were marked. Star Crossed.

The bubble of peace we'd been standing in shattered suddenly and the blizzard howled in around us to claim this place like it had never existed at all.

I turned and ran from him, leaving him standing in the snow, looking like the sky had caved in on his head and I'd just torn his heart right out of his chest.

Pain like nothing I'd ever felt scored through me, carving a chasm into my heart and blinding me as I raced out into the snow.

My heart was pounding a desperate, panicked rhythm as every fibre of my being ached to turn back. To run to him and wrap my arms around him and kiss him like I'd been fated to. But I didn't. I couldn't. It was too late anyway.

And as a roar filled with pure agony cut through the sky somewhere above me, I knew that Darius knew that too.

We'd never even begun and yet I felt like I'd just lost something so important that I couldn't even breathe.

My pulse pounded, my vision blurred and my heart shattered for the man who had worked so hard to break me for so long.

He'd offered me his heart and I'd turned my back on it despite the agony I'd seen it cause him. I'd left my broken heart there with his too.

And there was no power in the world that could ever fix what I'd done.

Darius Acrux had set out to break me from the first moment he'd ever laid eyes on me. And he'd finally gotten his wish.

DARCY

CHAPTER FORTY SEVEN

Weakness took hold of me and darkness curtained my vision as I knelt beside Orion and his sister. We had to move, had to make some plan to get her somewhere safe. We needed to replenish our magic and find a place she could rest.

"You need to feed," Orion said gently, tilting Clara's chin up. Her fangs were bared and she was breathing heavily, her pupils dilated. "I haven't got any magic left to give you." His brows knitted together like he'd failed her.

"Lance," she said with a ghost of a smile. "You were always so good to me."

"You're my sister," he said as if that was the only answer he needed to give and I understood that entirely.

"Let's get her up," I said gently, moving to my feet and swaying as my limbs weighed heavily at my sides. An emptiness resounded through my body unlike anything I'd ever felt before. I tried to call on my Phoenix, but the power of building that bridge had taken everything from me. It was like the shadows still had a hold of me; chaining my Order form down and keeping it subdued.

Orion cradled Clara in his arms, getting up and blinking heavily as exhaustion took hold of him too.

"Let me down," Clara urged and Orion reluctantly placed her on her feet, steadying her as her toes curled against the icy floor.

She took a couple of steps backwards, tilting her head to gaze up at the high cave roof then dropping her eyes to her hands. She turned them over and over, admiring them, her expression written with disbelief.

"I'm really here," she sighed, a small and hopeful laugh escaping her. It brought a smile to my own lips as relief danced through me and filled me up.

"You'll have to stay hidden," Orion said firmly. "You can stay with me tonight then tomorrow I'll take you somewhere safe." He shook his head in awe. "I can't believe you're actually here. It really worked."

Clara pivoted on her bare heels, her cloak of shadows swirling around her like a sheen of midnight silk. "No, Lance." Her voice echoed off of the roof and for a second her body seemed almost transparent. "I have to complete the spell. The shadows are keeping me here for now, but it won't last."

"How do you know?" Orion questioned and my heart beat harder as I glanced between them.

"They talk to me, tell me things," she said, her eyes glittering with the darkness that had taken root within her.

Orion shot me a look, silently communicating that we needed to get her out of here. He'd have to replenish his magic and try to take hold of the shadows living in her because it was clear they still had a grip.

"It took everything from me when I went into them," Clara whispered, her expression suddenly cold and fearful as she became lost to some memory.

Clara's eyes locked on her brother with accusation and I took a wary step toward him.

"Every drop of blood from my veins was sacrificed to the dark, to transport me across the worlds and leave me in the Shadow Realm to rot," Clara said in an icy tone. Her upper lip peeled back to bare her fangs and my hackles rose on instinct. "I thought you'd come for me but you never did."

"I thought you were dead," Orion said in dismay. "There was nothing left of you."

"Because I wasn't there," she choked out. "I went into the stardust, how could you never have thought to look for me?"

"I didn't know," Orion gasped, looking horrified at the idea of letting her down so deeply.

"All that blood I lost…it's still gone," she whispered, dropping down and scooping the draining dagger from the ground. Fear spiked through me and I raised my hands on instinct despite the fact that my veins were void of magic.

Clara ran the edge of the dagger across her arm and her skin peeled open, but no blood flowed. "I'm nothing but a vessel for the shadows," she rasped as darkness bled into her eyes and took all the light with them.

"Lance," I whispered in warning as the hairs on the back of my neck prickled to attention.

"Your veins are full with our blood and I want it back!" she cried, launching herself at him in a blur of Vampire speed.

"No!" I screamed as her teeth sank into his neck.

"Stop!" He tried to fight, but he was too weak and they fell to the ground in a tangle of limbs. "Clara, stop!" he begged as she dug her nails into his arms and ripped at his flesh like a starving animal.

I screamed in alarm, throwing myself onto her and tugging at her shoulders, begging my magic to aid me. She caught me by the back of the neck then threw me with her Vampire strength, the force she used launching me across the cave. My back impacted with the stone wall and I cried out as I hit the ground, my jeans tearing and my knees splitting open.

"Lance!" I shouted in desperation, scrambling to my feet and racing back towards them as fast as I possibly could.

"Stay back, Darcy!" Orion choked out, but I'd do no such thing.

Clara held him down, her back hunched like a beast as she drank and drank from him. He was horribly pale already, pushing at her shoulders but he was disarmed by her bite as the shadows fuelled her muscles and gave her power.

Panic tore through me as I ran at her, my Phoenix stirring but not nearly enough. I called on the shadows but it was like all of them were under her command, refusing to obey me.

I leapt onto her once more, throwing wild punches and tearing at her hair. She caught my arm, slamming me down onto the hard rocks beside Orion and clutching my throat with sharp nails to hold me there. I thrashed wildly, clawing at her hand as she continued to drain Orion mouthful by mouthful.

"STOP!" I screamed, terror carving a hole through my chest as he fell painfully still beneath her.

She stood suddenly, releasing us both and staring down at me with blood pouring over her chin. The draining dagger was clutched in her hand, soaked in blood which dripped down onto my shoes.

"*No*," I rasped out, rolling over and frantically pawing at Orion. Dread poured over me as my fingers came away hot and sticky and I undid his coat with desperate movements.

Tears blurred my vision as I clasped my hands to the gaping wound on his stomach and pressed down hard. His eyes fell shut and my heart hit a terrifying beat as reality sank deep into my bones. *She stabbed him. She fucking stabbed him!*

Before I could even try and fight her, Clara hissed like a snake and shot out of the cave with her Vampire speed. The darkness seemed to cloud around her as she disappeared into the storm like a wraith.

Panic dashed my heart to pieces as I reared over Orion, cupping his cheek with bloody fingers and shaking him.

"Wake up, we have to get help," I demanded, my voice trembling so violently I could barely get the words out.

His eyes flickered open and I pressed down harder on the wound on his stomach. "Get *up*," I begged, tears coating my cheeks.

He groaned in pain and I released him, shaking from head to foot. "I have to go and find someone," I said, trying to sound brave for him, though I felt anything but that right then as my heart cleaved in two.

"Stay," he grunted, his hand closing around my wrist to keep me there. "Blue…"

"*No*," I stopped him, shaking my head, knowing what he was going to say. "Don't you dare give up. I'm getting you help." I tried to move again but he held on tighter, squeezing my arm with need.

"Please," he rasped. "I need you to be the last thing I see."

"Don't say that," I sobbed as his blood rushed through my fingers. "You're going to walk out of here, Lance Orion. You don't die like this in some dark cave. I need you."

A sob racked through me as he brought his other hand to my face, brushing a lock of blue hair behind my ear. The acceptance in his eyes was heartbreaking and I rejected it with everything I was.

"You've got to face Lionel," he wheezed. "You have to work with the Heirs." He winced as pain racked through him and I dropped my forehead against his, wishing I could pour my strength into him. "I know you can do it, Blue."

"Please stop," I begged. "You're not going to die."

"You made the last few months the happiest of my life, Darcy Vega. I'm sorry for being an asshole when we first met – biggest regret of my life." He coughed heavily and blood slid out of his mouth, making my heart nearly collapse.

Panic juddered through me and I quickly wiped the blood away from his lips, refusing to believe this was it. That I had to give him up, that the stars would really take him from me.

"Shh, don't, please don't," I sobbed, pressing my mouth to his and tasting nothing but blood and cinnamon.

"I needed you so badly, you have no idea," he said, his voice fading as he pressed me back and searched my face like he was committing it to memory. "Now Solaria needs you...as their Queen. Promise you'll claim the throne. Share it with Darius, he's not his father." His hand fell from my face like he wasn't able to hold it there anymore. "Promise," he whispered and the look in his eyes made me give in.

"I promise. But you'll be there too. Darius needs you. *I* need you."

"You don't need me, beautiful. I was always a shitty teacher," he said, taking a rattling breath that chilled me to my core.

I shook my head, wiping my tears away as I clutched onto him, rejecting the possibility that I was really going to lose him.

"I love you," I sobbed and I hated myself for saying it because it sounded like goodbye.

His mouth pulled up at the corner then he fell still, his eyes closing and shaking the foundations of my soul.

I shook him in desperation, my tears washing over him as I pleaded with the stars, tried to bargain with anything and everything I was to bring him back to me. We were supposed to be forever. I'd sworn an oath to fight for him, no matter what it took to be with each other.

I lay a shaky kiss to his forehead, squeezing his hand and vowing not to give up. I'd never, *ever* give up on him. On us. We were meant to be together no matter what anyone said. And death wouldn't get a say in it.

I shed my jacket, pushing it beneath him and tying the arms around his waist as tightly as I could to try and stem the bleeding. Then I ran from the cave, screaming to the sky as his blood dripped from my hands and soaked into my clothes, branding my skin with the scent of metal and death.

"Help!" I screamed until my throat was hoarse. "Help me!"

My Phoenix stirred and I forced her to get up, dragging her power into my veins as the shadows shifted enough to set her free.

I raised my hands toward the sky and cast fire at the heavens, a huge line of crimson and sapphire igniting the entire cliff in the urgent and magnificent light.

"I need help!"

———————————

ALSO BY
CAROLINE PECKHAM
&
SUSANNE VALENTI

Brutal Boys of Everlake Prep

(Complete Reverse Harem Bully Romance Contemporary Series)

Kings of Quarantine

Kings of Lockdown

Kings of Anarchy

Queen of Quarantine

**

Dead Men Walking

(Reverse Harem Dark Romance Contemporary Series)

The Death Club

Society of Psychos

**

The Harlequin Crew

(Reverse Harem Mafia Romance Contemporary Series)

Sinners Playground

Dead Man's Isle

Carnival Hill

Paradise Lagoon

Harlequinn Crew Novellas

Devil's Pass

**

Dark Empire

(Dark Mafia Contemporary Standalones)

Beautiful Carnage

Beautiful Savage

**

The Ruthless Boys of the Zodiac

(Reverse Harem Paranormal Romance Series - Set in the world of Solaria)

Dark Fae

Savage Fae

Vicious Fae

Broken Fae

Warrior Fae

Zodiac Academy

(M/F Bully Romance Series- Set in the world of Solaria, five years after Dark Fae)

The Awakening

Ruthless Fae

The Reckoning

Shadow Princess

Cursed Fates

Fated Thrones

Heartless Sky

The Awakening - As told by the Boys

Zodiac Academy Novellas

Origins of an Academy Bully

The Big A.S.S. Party

Darkmore Penitentiary

(Reverse Harem Paranormal Romance Series - Set in the world of Solaria, ten years after Dark Fae)

Caged Wolf

Alpha Wolf

Feral Wolf

**

The Age of Vampires

(Complete M/F Paranormal Romance/Dystopian Series)

Eternal Reign

The Vampire Games Novellas

A Game of Vampires

**

The Rise of Issac

(Complete YA Fantasy Series)

Creeping Shadow

Bleeding Snow

Turning Tide

Weeping Sky

Failing Light